EMERALD
ARIA
K.C. SPIEGELBERG

EMERALD ARIA

Edited by K.C. Spiegelberg
Maps by K.C. Spiegelberg
Illustrations by Nolan Nasser
Music by Adam Scott

ISBN 979-8-9954967-0-0 (paperback)
ISBN 979-8-9954967-1-7 (hardcover)
ISBN 979-8-9954967-2-4 (special edition)

Published by Glysterverse Media, LLC.

www.glysterverse.com

First Edition: May 2026

Printed in the United States of America

For my beautiful wife,
my partner in song.

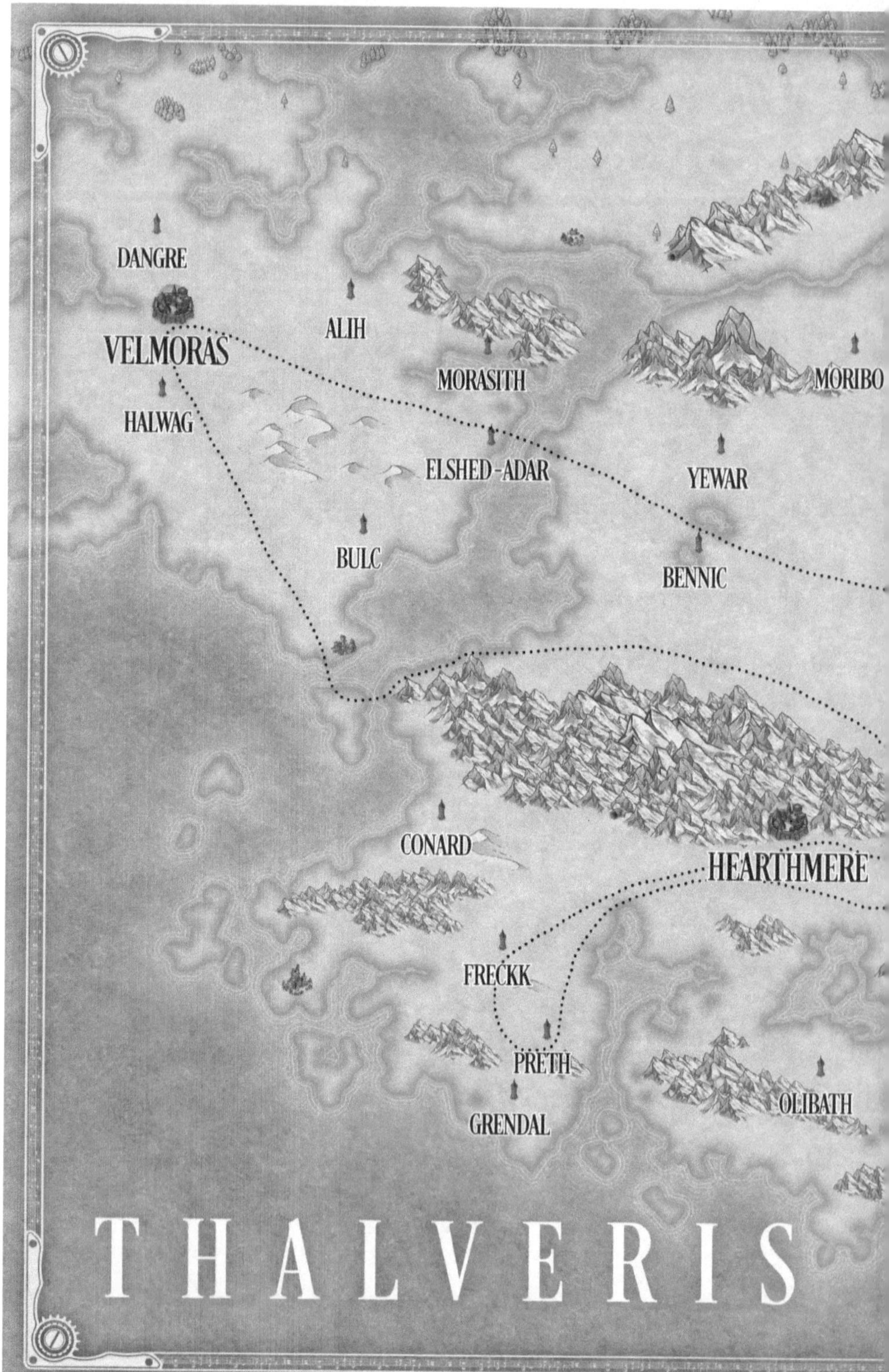

DANGRE
VELMORAS
ALIH
MORASITH
MORIBO
HALWAG
ELSHED-ADAR
YEWAR
BULC
BENNIC
CONARD
HEARTHMERE
FRECKK
PRETH
OLIBATH
GRENDAL
THALVERIS

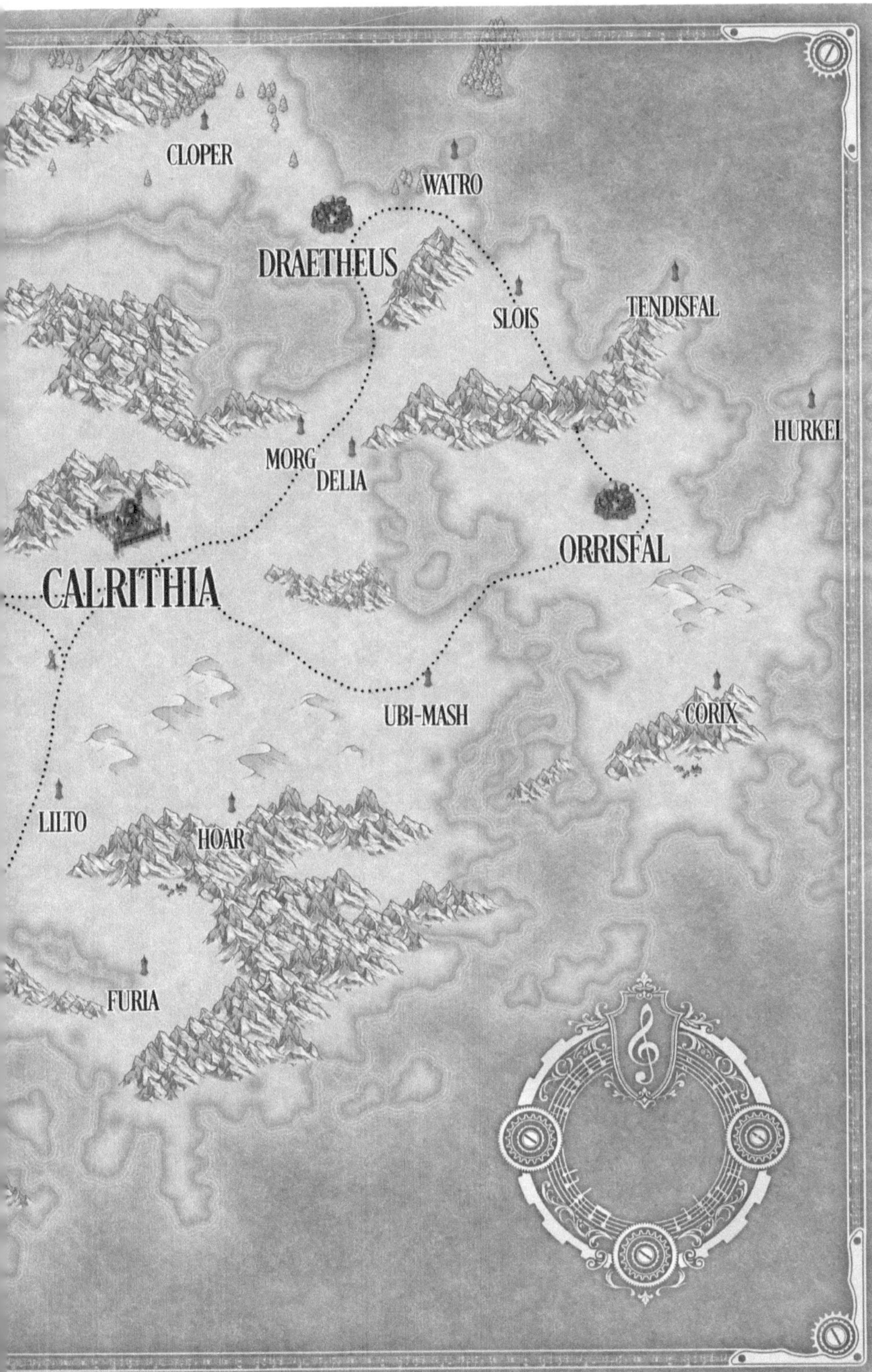

CLOPER
WATRO
DRAETHEUS
SLOIS
TENDISFAL
HURKEI
MORG
DELIA
ORRISFAL
CALRITHIA
UBI-MASH
CORIX
LILTO
HOAR
FURIA

HEARTHMERE
1 - Opera House
2 - The Citadel
3 - Resonance Heights
4 - Cantata Row
5 - GroundSong Commons
6 - Air Dock
7 - Rail Depot
8 - Whisper Ward

May my voice reflect my spirit.

Prelude

Chadden had never seen a man killed with a violin before.

He and a beggar had been sitting against a stone shack, knees drawn to their chests while puffs of precious heat wisped out of their mouths. Inside a city that should have been providing them all with heat, the people in the slums were shivering.

The Empire couldn't care less.

The inky darkness of night covered the agent's approach. A shrill note pierced the symphony of coughs and sniffles of the Whisper Ward, followed by streaking viridian light. Malevolent energy illuminated her pristine white uniform as it screamed through the air.

They had found him again. Faster than before.

Sonic force rippled over frozen mud and sliced through the beggar next to him, slamming into the building and showering the back of Chadden's head with shards. When he opened his eyes after recoiling, she was already towering over him.

She didn't belong in the mud and the muck. Gold buttons glinted in the dim green GlysterLight on a pristine white military coat and dark slacks. The way her eyes sparkled, malevolent and cruel beneath her short silver hair, raised his hackles.

The instrument—an abomination of cogs and wires—was leveled at him like a rifle, pulsing blue-green. She trailed her bow across the strings with sadistic glee, savoring his last moments.

Dirt and grime from months of running caked his coat and dreadlocks, and his throat ached from overuse. His sleep had been haunted by the sound of instruments always behind him. Always emerging from the shadows. Always destructive.

They had made him hate music.

He screamed at himself to run, but his legs were treacherously disobedient. The brass and leather GlysterBoots fastened to his feet were heavy, and the telltale pulsing of power hinted at maybe one more jump. Whoever he had stolen them from hadn't changed the cores out.

She raised a curious eyebrow as he rose, her too-long fingers pausing before her final strike. "No last words?" Her voice dripped with venomous sarcasm.

Chadden was so tired of running.

He brought his shoulders back and puffed out his chest. Her face shifted to mirth, assuming he was taking a final stand. He wasn't a hero, just another failed singer.

He needed the correct posture to sing his last song.

Like a blacksmith at the bellows, he sucked in breath, drawing from a reservoir brimming with the anger and fear of a caged animal. Memories of the last few months welled up in his mind. A singer laughing with him after his audition for the Grand Chorus, slammed against a stone building in the alley they were stumbling down. The friendly woman at the bakery who eased his hunger, lying in a pool of her own blood. It didn't matter how involved they were. If he spoke to them, they were dead. Memories of every person who died helping him crashed down like an avalanche ripping through the mountains. Worst of all, he couldn't even send letters back home to warn his little brother Traven.

He took that sense of loss—that desperation—and allowed it to wash through him.

Skin tingled. Warmth blossomed from his chest, thawing his frozen fingers and bringing the world into focus. He knew now this was exactly what the Arcanum was testing for during his audition. This power was what had gotten him into this mess. It may as well get him out.

A rumble shook from his neck, bursting forth from his lips in a roar of desperation and rage. The air rippled like a heatwave and slammed into the woman with a screaming thud and showering ice. She caught it in the chest, somersaulting backwards into the shack behind her with a crash.

He started running before she could stand, dreadlocks swishing against his forehead as he spun. There was no time to check if it worked, hesitation would kill him. Green vapor drifted from between his clenched teeth.

The glowing boots slipped in the frosty mud and he clawed at the wall for momentum. Whatever strength he had been saving was sapped, but he couldn't die here. He needed to move.

Once clear of the alley, he shifted his ankles and crouched mid-stride. The GlysterBoots whirred and clicked as the clockwork came to life, a burst of green firelight flaring under his soles for a powered jump.

Green slashes exploded through the wooden door next to him, splintering into his face, ripping his cloak, and tossing him off-balance. The gears of his boots locked into position with a whine.

He wasn't ready.

With a dull thunderclap that rattled the metal rooftops, his boots catapulted him into the sky. He arced wildly, careening over the buildings and to the next street. The roof came too fast, and his efforts to roll saved his skull at the expense of his shoulder. He thudded into the metal with a sickening crunch.

His arm went numb, and it was hard to breathe. The coppery taste of blood coated his tongue. Pushing himself up with a shaking arm, his boots scraped against the metal rooftop with an unpleasant screech. A resident banged on the roof from underneath. They would stay quiet if they knew what was good for them. Another violin shriek ripped through the air.

"Slush," he cursed, dropping prone as a chord ripped over his head.

Chadden tried to summon his voice again, but the blossoming pain in his throat slammed his mouth shut. He had done this too many times, and he was so bloody tired.

Again he pushed himself up, hoping his stride would create enough distance between them. Her footsteps rattled the rooftops behind, but he kept his eyes to the uneven rooftops. The boots clicked into position one last time, and an arc of power sliced under his legs as he jumped to the next set of buildings. The boots sputtered and sparked as he landed, the emerald lights fading. The damned things were out of fuel.

A deep boom rattled the rooftops, shaking his feet.

Thunder?

Unseen force slammed into him. Tin roofs and rising steam blurred in the moonlight as he crashed down with a metallic screech. The protective GlysterDome above the city shimmered peacefully and he chuckled at the irony before his view filled with a mass of muscles with a blonde mohawk. "You ain't supposed to kill him, Veyne. She's gonna be pissed."

This was it. He'd never sing for anyone again.

The violinist approached, her chest heaving as blood trickled from her scalp onto her pristine uniform. She pointed the instrument at his face. "He's clearly not dead, but he will be if I see him take another deep breath. You prepare him for extraction. I'll handle the mess on the street."

The hulking man cocked his head, a hint of amusement

building on his square face. The roof creaked under his weight as he knelt down, his hands gently tapping the drums fastened to his waist. Pressure forced Chadden's aching shoulder to the rooftop, waves of resonance beating him down. Each attempt he made to stand was countered with a flash of the Glysterium drums, forcing him back.

"Come, friend, the Empire needs you," the brute sneered.

Chadden's arms quivered in an attempt to rise, but his legs wouldn't move.

Why wouldn't they move?

The assassin brought his face close enough to whisper, his breath reeking of rancid meat. "The Baron has use fer you."

He raised a fist as large as his head, and darkness came crashing down.

Chapter I

Chunks of frozen earth burst skyward as Traven's GlysterHammer slammed down with a thunderous crack. Snow rippled outwards from an emerald flash birthed by the collision and whirled into the frigid air. His fingers went temporarily numb from the vibration. The cold winds of the Ever-Winter swirled, teasing the fur lining of his coat before snaking up his spine. Up the ornate hammer rose, over his wide shoulders, and back down with another thwack. He panted, steam curling off of his clean-shaven dark brown scalp. He could already hear his father's admonition: *You should wear your hat.* It was the same every day; crack the ice, haul the dirt, don't expose yourself to the cold.

Thud. Thud. Thud. The rhythmic heartbeat of mattocks shook the ground beneath his fur-lined boots.

A dozen workers struck the earth in steady cadence, their steamy breath rising through the frigid air. Tenors and baritones sang, instinctively harmonizing to the rhythmic chant while swinging their tools in tempo. Traven added his deep voice while wiping the sweat off his brow. Gathering soil for the crops was hard work. Honest work.

He hated it.

Next to him, his father Asmeri grunted with each laborious swing. The old man was slowing down with every passing year. As a child, Traven would wield a leather mallet and pretend to be Asmeri Caelhardt—vanquishing the frozen terrors of the wastes. Cycles later, he was handed the ornate silver and gold heirloom. His father didn't have the strength to carry it. Every morning he wrapped his fingers around the handle with dread and loathing. Another day in the cold, another day wasted.

The time between his father's swings grew longer. He spent more time resting than swinging these days. He rested now, greying dreadlocks dangling from under his fur hood. How much longer could Asmeri work like this?

"You gonna stare, or keep beating at the earth like yer life depended on it?" his father asked between haggard breaths.

Traven turned away to hide a smirk, and readied himself for another swing when a low, unnatural hum shook the mountains. The swirling wind wrapped Traven's cloak around the dormant warhammer. Shielding his eyes from the onslaught of horizontal snow, he scanned the sky through snowflakes gathering on his lashes.

A smile spread across his face. The hammering around him fell out of rhythm and slowed to a stop.

Their visitors had arrived.

A diminutive black dot appeared from the dreary curtain of grey clouds, growing larger and louder as it descended. His father shook his head and continued hammering, but Traven stood there with a smile spreading across his face.

The airship approached, circling around the massive stone spire that was his home and shaking the snow off of the glass-domed roof. A small surge of panic sliced across his stomach as icicles two stories high plummeted from the tower, disappearing into snow as deep as three men. The dirt pile he had been stacking all morning toppled and slid to the ground as the engines rumbled. Gleaming green and gold sails wrestled with their rigging, snapping in the strong wind. He studied every facet of the technological marvel, noting the capital city's heraldry on the mainsail, a proud winged creature holding two stalks of wheat in its talons. Disk-shaped engines were mounted to the lacquered wood hull, attached by beams thicker than his waist. He didn't even know trees could get that large.

The engines swiveled to retrothrust, flaring in a bright green jet to slow the vessel's descent. Viridian fire pummeled the snow and blasted a curtain of white across the rocky landscape, causing the men to shout in alarm over the crescendo of GlysterEngines. His father cursed and held tight to his hood, clamping it over his ears.

The masthead materialized from the snowy plumes and Traven stumbled backwards while slipping on the snow and ice with a yelp. A tempest of snowflakes swirled around the golden sculpture, and the unmistakably acrid smell of Glysterium burned his nose.

The anchor plummeted from the bow, metallic chains rattling before it slammed into the rock and peppered the landscape with shards. Sailors above tossed mooring lines, and Traven eagerly jumped to action, catching the pin and wedging it between the stones with one powerful hammer strike. His stomach flipped as sailors somersaulted overboard and landed in the snow. With a plume of green vapor they expertly landed, GlysterBoots hissing on impact. One of the men flashed him a smile before rushing to pull at the moorings.

He wanted to be one of them.

The belly of the airship bounced off of the stone with a thunk, then pulled the ropes taut as turbulence jockeyed the flying machine. One of the sailors in the snow blew a whistle, and the force of the engines diminished to a more comfortable drone.

"Did you see their boots?" Traven nudged his father's shoulder.

"Must be nice having all that fancy GlysterTech, while the rest of us scrabble for every ounce of spare heat," Asmeri muttered.

"I wonder if I could get some?"

"Farm folk don't get things like that. Be careful with that hammer while they are here, they might take it, no matter how long it's been in the family," his father said just loud enough for the two of them.

He gripped the handle with his fur gloves and frowned. Why was Asmeri like this every delegation?

A ramp slid out from the starboard side and plunked down. From below deck, the delegates began to step down, gloved hands securely gripping the guide ropes as they gingerly navigated the icy wood. Traven smoothed his coat and brought his shoulders back, smiling at a passing man with wiry hair and brass spectacles. The man pulled his embroidered green coat tight, and Traven could see golden musical notes sewn onto his cuffs and lapel. Looking at his own coat in comparison, he couldn't help but feel a little embarrassed.

A retinue of delegates followed, each stepping on the slippery stone like children just learning to walk in the frozen wastes. While impressively intricate, their coats looked ill-equipped to keep them warm. They wouldn't last more than a half hour in these temperatures.

Traven swung his hammer down as hard as he could, the shockwave causing a few of the visitors to yelp in surprise. Asmeri chuckled and shook his head, turning his head to hide a smirk. He couldn't help but give these outsiders a little Grendal welcome. "I think I'm done, Pa. I better get cleaned up for the competition."

Asmeri set his mattock down and jerked his head to his son's pile. "Need help with that?"

Already lifting the first clod and dropping it on his sled, Traven grunted while hoisting the hammer to his shoulder. "Wouldn't want you pulling your back again."

It earned him a laugh.

A stone ramp twenty feet wide rose to the circular stone tower of Grendal Yodel, their home. The procession shuffled through snow past their knees, and Traven used their path to tug his sled behind them. A man in front of him leaned to his wife and spoke with curious awe, "These walls are as thick as men are tall, built to keep the cold out when the GlysterFurnaces falter."

It's still cold, even with the furnace, he thought.

Thick ice reflected the wavy green streams of light in the sky, glinting beautifully over the black stone. Dangerous icicles hung from the highest levels like teeth. He hated climbing up to the dome and breaking off the ice, but if someone didn't do it, the entire Yodel would collapse.

Wagons from four different Yodels huddled around the base of the tower like children around skirts. An accumulation of snow had already settled on them since the morning, blending their hulking frames into the snowbanks.

The iron doors opened with a deep shudder, ice chipping off in chunks as it swung open. The city-folk pressed against those in front of them, eager to get out of the cold. The air was electric with their nervousness. He wondered what life in the capital was like, if this mild winter affected them so? What he wouldn't give to find out for himself.

Traven shifted from foot to foot, anxious to be inside. His chance to impress them was just around the corner.

The first and thickest of doors groaned shut behind them, and the stabbing chill of the Ever-Winter dulled to an ache. Traven stomped his feet to shed snow from his boots, and the visitors copied him, some looking bemused. Did they not know to shake off their boots? The guard standing inside sang a brief Welcoming Hymn while they shuffled in the puddles of melted snow. Some of them answered the song with their own.

"Ladies and gentlemen," the guard puffed his chest with pride glinting in his eyes. "Welcome to Grendal Yodel. Please give us a moment while the furnaces transition you from the barbaric assault of the frosty wilderness to a warmth only overshadowed by our hospitality!"

Traven groaned. He didn't know the guard knew those words.

He rolled his shoulders while the temperature grew comfortable. Hissing steam pumped in from grates on the ceiling, filling the chamber with life-saving heat. A visitor muttered, "What a brilliant solution. Why haven't the other Yodels done this?"

Pride straightened his back. It was his father's idea, to open the doors in sequence so the precious heat stayed trapped inside where it belonged. The first floor didn't give you frostbite if you were barefoot any more, and they no longer had to gather their coats every time someone ventured outside. The Caelhardts were awarded extra food for a month.

The last door creaked open, and the familiar sounds of home swelled up in a cacophony of laughter, choral practice, and conversation. Traven pulled his sled around the arriving delegates as they raised their gaze to the ceiling ten stories above. Lush hanging plants dangled down the atrium, past ten stories of homes carved into the thick stone walls. Water trickled down from melting ice, warmed by furnaces near the ceiling. They couldn't afford to waste anything. The water fed a circular garden in the center teeming with carrots, potatoes, beets, and spices hearty enough for the cold.

He carefully wove around long, curved tables in the common area, past teams of singers from distant Yodels as they prepared for the upcoming competition. He recognized some of them from cycles past, and gave them a polite nod while pulling his mountain of dirt. A young boy slept with his head on the desk of the Thawing Chamber, and he did his best to offload quietly. Traven used to work here, and he knew staying awake in one of the warmest alcoves was impossible.

An elder intercepted the delegates and guided them around the first floor, a communal area designated for meals, revelry, and performances. A raised platform carved into the thick walls served as their theater, and the aromas from the kitchen next to it set Traven's stomach grumbling. His eyes lingered on the stage; he wanted to sing for a living. Farming until he was too old to lift a hammer was his father's dream.

The Yodel was alive with preparations, streamers of lights hung across the alcove from floor to floor. Workers dashed from the kitchen to plop stone tankards sloshing with rootbier on the longtables, while others spooned mushroom stew into a collection of stone bowls. Orders barked from the head chef caused them all to move a little faster. Someone was already sweeping up the dirt he had dragged in, scowling his way. Tempers were short. Hosting the annual competition was a serious honor.

A quartet on the stage snapped their fingers and practiced under their breath. He strained to hear them, but didn't want to seem too nosy. Others waited off-stage in groups of four all the way up to twenty. Nerves he had forgotten since this morning started to resurface, and a yawn stretched his jaw. Everything had to be perfect today.

Traven shuffled through the crowd, turning sideways to mitigate the width of his broad shoulders. He stood taller than most, so it was easy to see where to weave through the traffic. Stone stairs lined The Commons, spiraling up to the highest apartments. He and his father lived on the fifth floor, their home nothing more than a large alcove carved into the thick stone. A tattered blanket hung as a makeshift door, and behind it were two beds, a washbasin, and a small wooden chest of precious wood. Half-assembled gadgets littered the shelf over Traven's bed, and a single GlysterLamp cast dim green light through the room.

Traven leaned the hammer against the wall and removed his coat and gloves. He rubbed a calloused hand over his bald head, checking to see if he'd need to shave. His mind raced through his songs while gathering the washbasin and cold water. He ran through each phrase, each note, each breath to ensure he had it all perfect. He could hear the applause, even smiling at the imaginary crowd as he shaved.

Asmeri came in as Traven finished, greying black locks of hair shaking as he shivered. He placed his gear down and snatched the razor from Traven's hand with care. "You missed a spot." His voice was gentle.

Traven rolled his eyes, tilting his head as his father's rough and crooked fingers pressed against it. Traven was well past his eighteenth birthday, but he let him do it anyway. "I'm excited for today."

His father's hands paused for just a second, then continued, the razor whispering against his scalp. His fingers were as cold as the silence resting between them. They used to hum harmonies together when he sat like this, but those days were gone.

Traven's brow furrowed and he scratched his beard. "Do you think I'll get a standing ovation?"

Asmeri still said nothing, drying off his son's head with a towel. Cycles of pain hung heavy between the Caelhardt men. Traven's mother had died five cycles ago from exposure, searching the nearby caves. When his brother Chadden left them for the Grand Chorus three cycles later, his father's singing stopped. A single letter told them he had failed his audition, and he'd be finding his way in the city until next season. His father sent letters for months, pleading for him to return. No responses came.

His father knew Traven's dream, and he knew Asmeri wouldn't let him go. "I'm better than he was," his deep voice mumbled.

"Better than he *is*. Don't talk about him like he's dead," Asmeri's tone was as cold as encroaching frost.

Traven fumed as he ran a brush through his close-cropped beard and got dressed in his performance garb, a clean blue coat and fine black trousers tucked into his boots. He loved and respected his father. He knew if he left, Asmeri would have no one. Once, Traven tried to convince him to court another woman. He thought if perhaps his father found love, Traven would be free to chase his dreams. All he got for his trouble was a shrug.

Traven began warming up his voice, filling their home with song as he dove to the lowest extents of his range. He flipped into head voice with barely a perceptible shift, and then up to falsetto with ease. His mother had taught him how to sing in his upper register so he could sing the traditional folk songs without his voice cracking. Everything was always too high, and he hated dropping his voice to a more comfortable octave. He felt like an outsider. *You are fortunate—your voice has power and depth most men would kill for. Embrace your sound,* she had told him.

He was thankful for her lessons. Memories of her were the only thing he had.

It didn't take him long to get his voice ready; he had already spent most of the morning talking and singing with the rest of the farmers outside. Asmeri stood there for a moment as Traven moved to leave, his eyes reflecting a lifetime of pain. He didn't know what to say; neither of them had since his brother had been lost. With a pat on his father's shoulder, Traven nodded and pushed the makeshift door aside. "I hope you come."

Traven went to the railing and leaned on it for a moment. Everyone busied themselves to make a good impression, showing their crafted goods, offering bites to eat from their pantries, or trading spices unique to this Yodel. The rhythm of their home, the shuffle of feet, the beating of rugs, and the ever-present melodies echoed across the stone. His friends gathered on the bottom level with Mrs. Bellamy, their local music director. The other seven singers were already rehearsing.

He pushed himself off of the balcony and made his way down to the common area. Old men sat with smoking pipes around a wooden board of Kings and Queens. One of them had his face so furrowed it looked like his bushy eyebrows would swallow his eyes. The other looked like a cat who had found a mouse, pleased as could be. On the third level a horde of children circled around their mother's aprons, yelping and hooting as they tried to escape each other's touch. He feigned snatching at one of them and they darted away giggling, hiding under the canopy of their mother's skirts.

Mrs. Bellamy was waving him over as soon as he was spotted, her face taciturn. The other singers had already arranged themselves in formation. Men stood in the back with women in the front, deepest voices to highest. Traven took his spot on the end and stood straight and tall, glancing to wherever the ambassadors might be. Every moment was an opportunity to impress. His friend Geshtran tapped a foot with mock impatience. Traven stuck out his tongue.

Their director raised her hands and Traven snapped to attention, pulling his shoulders back and his head high as she had taught him. Goden, one of their tenors, hummed their starting note without a pitch pipe. He could sing any note on command; some people were lucky to be born with perfect pitch.

Mrs. Bellamy focused on the first few notes, then moved on to a trouble section that never seemed to snap into place. The song choice was perfect. A warm, beautiful song with chords that washed over the audience like a wave of sound. Last year they lost by a fraction of a point, the music too technical for the ambassadors. This year would be different.

A few locals and visitors stopped what they were doing as they sang their song, and Traven had to refocus when he noticed their smiles. Their warm-up ended, and Mrs. Bellamy looked over to him while the choir chatted to themselves. "Do you want to run through yer solo?"

Butterflies jumped in his stomach, but he forced a smile. As much as he wanted to prove himself, this was still nerve-wracking. She patted him on the shoulder, producing her pitch pipe. He waved her off with a smile; the pitch had been etched in his mind for weeks.

He let the melody spill from his lips:

Oh men of all ages, please listen to me,
Singing those melodies isn't easy, you see
For my voice grew too low, and now I'm alone
To sing in the depths, the bass clef my home.

His song was about a man's voice growing deeper and deeper as he matured, and could no longer sing the tenor songs popular with the womenfolk. His song lamented that he was sequestered to singing villains and grandfathers, poking fun at the one-dimensional characterization. Near the end, he modified his voice to emulate the lighter tenor sound and the growing crowd chuckled. Then, for the finale he dropped his voice lower and lower until it was almost a growl.

He smiled as a few of them applauded, and he ducked his head in thanks. Mrs. Bellamy patted him on the back. "Good. Make sure you ham up the tenor section. They seem to like that."

The midday bell rang, and Elder Tesius walked with a glacier's pace up the stage. He cleared his throat for everyone's attention. "Ladies and gentlemen, please join me in singing the Hymn of Gathering."

The song began with everyone in the Yodel adding their voices. Children of Thalvaris were taught the various traditional hymns for meetings, meals, and business deals. Aside from learning the plow and mattock, Traven had spent his youth learning sight-reading. He had immediately taken to it in a way that made him one of Mrs. Bellamy's favorites. He auditioned for every solo, and had been floored when she pulled him aside with a serious expression on her face. *You aren't a tenor any more, Traven. I can see the strain in your neck trying to keep reaching those notes. It's time to start singing below the clef.*

It took some time for him to grow comfortable with his voice, but after noticing the older men straighten their backs and clear their throats when he spoke, he embraced it.

The chorus of each Yodel was showing off, and Grendal was no exception. Traven dropped an octave and sang a harmony. One of the tenors loudly pushed the tempo in an attempt to corral the Yodel into a more appropriate pace. Each member of their society sang as well as they could, a symbol of unity and thanks to the Thalverian Empire.

The voices died down, and the elder raised his hands. "Wonderful! The choral section of our annual competition shall begin momentarily. Soloists will perform after our feast this afternoon. May you all sing with clarity, focus, and beauty," he smiled with sparkling eyes.

The Yodel hushed and the lights dimmed. The competitors moved to reserved tables near the stage. Traven joined his friends. He looked over to Schala and Geshtran, their heads together while they whispered. They would no doubt be singing the Union Hymn to each other before the year was over. Traven leaned in. "I think we've got this."

Geshtran chuckled, "Did you see the ambassadors wrinkling their noses as they came in? Like they smelled somethin' awful."

Schala poked him in the ribs. "They smelled you. Would it have killed ya to wash up before this?"

Traven pointed to the ambassador's expensive coats. "They live in the capital; they probably haven't seen a day of hard labor."

"It sounds like you envy them…plan on making the Grand Chorus or somethin'?" Geshtran smirked.

"Damn right," Traven said, more to himself than his friends.

He stole a glance to the ambassadors seated at the edge of the stage. A few of them had a sour twist to their mouths, replaced with fake smiles whenever they met his grey eyes. Grendal Yodel hadn't been this clean in cycles; why did it feel like they didn't want to be here? He hoped this wouldn't affect their scores.

Mrs. Bellamy stood near the end of the third performance, gesturing for them to follow her to the side of the stage. She wiggled her fingers above her head and raised her eyebrows to remind them to battle the insidious tendency they had for singing flat. Once it was their time, she gave them a hug as they made their way up the steps. Traven yawned like he did before every performance and led the back row on stage, his shoulders back and head tall. It was difficult to see everyone in the audience, and he couldn't spot his father. Mrs. Bellamy brought in the rear, bowed to the audience, and then turned to face her ensemble with a serious glint in her eye.

Her hands rose, swaying deliberately to indicate the tempo, and then signaled the sopranos to begin their intro. Their pure tone danced through the air, light and graceful like the wind. The others joined the song, a regional hymn about the Ever-Winter and its brutal and majestic beauty. A baritone entered a fraction late and Traven frowned, his focus disrupted. They had practiced this hundreds of times…why was this mistake being made? The side of Mrs. Bellamy's mouth twitched at the error, but she nodded reassuringly and didn't miss a beat.

Silver drifts crowning earth in white,
With lights of green swirling to great heights.
Sing with the wind, with every voice,
For the Ever-Winter claims us without choice.

She pushed them on, leading the dragging tempo with her hand motions until they neared the end of their song. The Yodel erupted into applause before the last note had finished, eager to sway the ambassadors' opinions with enthusiasm. Traven smiled and scanned the crowd; still no father. He stepped down with a frown, and found himself wrapped in a hug from Mrs. Bellamy.

"Almost perfect," he lamented.

Mrs. Bellamy reached up and tapped him on the nose. "That's the beauty of live performance, nothing is ever the same."

He wasn't sure he agreed. A true professional would be perfect on stage. What was the point of rehearsing something every day if you didn't get it exactly right?

Geshtran looked knowingly at Traven and rolled his eyes with a playful glint. "Not everyone can be as perfect as you."

Traven shook his head and deflected the backhanded compliment. "Just inherited talent, is all."

A chef shouldered by them, hefting a serving tray teeming with steaming food. Exotic spices imported from Orrisfal drew the crowd to sit, erupting in conversation. The cooks had been preparing for days, careful to save the finest of their harvest through the last season. Traven tried to snatch a root in red sauce, but the server ducked under him with fluid grace and a playful wink. He decided to sit with his choir, glancing up one last time to the fifth balcony.

He filled a bowl but barely tasted it, his mind focused on the upcoming solo. His friends laughed and joked while enjoying each other's company, and he tried his best to smile with them. Every note replayed in his mind, every breath and crescendo noted in preparation, until the chatter around him faded. Although hungry, he wouldn't be able to eat until his performance was over. "I'm going to go run through my solo real quick," he said while standing.

Laughter and revelry rose through the Yodel in a symphony of joyful sound. He found his father leaning against the balcony near their home, chewing on a Blisterroot. Traven sang the Greeting Hymn, but nothing came back in return. Instead, his father stretched his back. "You sounded good."

"Thanks." Traven joined him on the balcony. "I wish you still sang."

Asmeri took a deep breath before folding his arms. "That was always yer mother's thing. I don't find much joy in the song any more...not after music took Chadden."

His father's words shattered Traven's planned speech like falling ice. He wanted to bring honor to their family, to make his father proud, but knew it would fall on deaf ears.

"I see you, Traven. I see you fueled by yer mother's praise just like Chadden. She filled your heads with greatness because she loved you, despite everything singing had cost her…and look where that got us." He looked back over the balcony.

Traven had never heard him speak of his mother with such bitterness, such resentment. What had singing cost her? He had never heard Asmeri mention this before. He gripped the balcony with white knuckles.

Asmeri waved to the crowd underneath the lush hanging leaves. "All of this is a distraction. Music doesn't fill our bellies."

Speaking this way went against their culture and tradition. Music was such an intrinsic part of their lives and his father hated it; the one thing Traven was good at. Anger set his shoulders back and rose in his belly. The one person he looked up to the most, his hero, didn't give a slush about what made him special. "Music is everything and everywhere. It's important. I'm not Chadden. I'm better than he was." Traven's voice broke with emotion. The meager lamp in their hovel shimmered and winked out.

"Better than he *is*!" Asmeri's hand slammed the railing, eyes darting to their home. "He's not dead."

Traven shrunk into himself, unsure how to respond.

"You are more like yer brother than you realize…" His father frowned at the lamp until it flared back up. "It doesn't matter, yer nearly twenty now. It's time to put aside these foolish ambitions and settle into yer life here. I can see yer skin crawl every time you pick up a clod of dirt, but you'll have to get over it. I need you here, I need yer help. I'm getting old and weak, and won't be of use for much longer." Asmeri turned and grabbed him by the shoulders, as if to hold him here.

"I'm not a farmer." Traven pulled away, tears of frustration blurring his vision. "I don't want to do this. I want to do more than waste my life making calluses on my hands. I want to be on the stage with people cheering for me. I want people to love me for my voice. I have talent and drive and passion, and I won't let you chain me here forever!" His last words came out in a shout.

The beads in his father's hair clacked as he shook his head. His voice quivered. "I'm just trying to protect you. I don't want to lose you too." A tear rolled down Asmeri's cheek.

Traven crumbled, the walls of resentment and frustration toppling down as he rushed into the older man's arms. He hated that he caused Asmeri pain, hated that he couldn't be what his father wanted him to be. The older man seemed to understand, holding Traven long after he released the embrace. The last time they had hugged like this was when his mother died. Together, they finally let the grief of his mother and brother wash over them. And once enough tears had been shed, Traven stepped back, his breath shuddering.

Asmeri steadied himself and nodded to their alcove. "You need to get hold of that temper."

Traven left his father's side, muttering about inheriting the fire in his belly from him. His resolve always seemed to crumble beneath his father's gaze, no matter how he fought it. More than anything, he wanted to make him proud.

Crying was terrible for singing.

Emotions whisked lyrics to forgotten corners of the mind and eroded breath support. He couldn't let that happen; he needed to be perfect, to prove Asmeri wrong.

Traven splashed freezing water onto his face and took a few steadying breaths. His throat was thick and his head pounded as he hummed the first pitch of his solo. Even as his own voice fought him, he was in tune.

Traven could always sing in the right key if the song was familiar to him. It wasn't quite plucking a note out of the air like perfect pitch, but it worked close to the same. He always knew when he was in tune, and Mrs. Bellamy had warned him to keep his expressions in check when he realized he wasn't. *The audience likely doesn't realize you aren't singing perfectly until they see it on your face. You look like you are at a funeral. Performing is more than just singing, you have to look like you enjoy what you are doing.*

That was always a struggle. He loved to sing, and wanted nothing more than to stand there proudly singing his heart out. He felt like the rest was a distraction from the beauty of music.

Shouldn't his voice be enough?

The cobwebs in his voice took a few measures to clear. There was a heaviness to his sound, a fleeting depth of power he knew would dissolve after a few warm-ups. He embraced it, noting the added depth to his lower range, and hammered the ending an octave lower than usual.

His father whistled and forced an encouraging smile. "Go get 'em."

Down below, the officiants were taking their places for the second leg of competition. The other Yodels broke from their revelry, with ensembles grouped together around The Commons in raucous conversation. He walked downstairs, thoughts chaotic from the argument with Asmeri. A small kernel of guilt sat in his belly that wouldn't go away. Was he being selfish?

Adrenaline kicked in as his feet took the stage. A pre-performance yawn cracked his jaw as he joined Mrs. Bellamy and his friends. "Going to fall asleep mid-song?" Geshtran joked.

"I always yawn before a performance, I don't know why," Traven shrugged.

"So calm and collected. Must be nice." Geshtran nudged him.

If only they could feel the rushing torrent of stage fright. As much as he loved this, as good as he thought he was, there was always an undercurrent of doubt. What if his voice gave out? What if he went flat? A hundred things could go wrong.

He shrugged again. "I've got this."

If he said it enough times, it might start to be true.

The competitors pulled straws to determine who went first, and Traven's heart sank when he drew the first song. With a nervous grin, he raised his straw to his choirmates, who whooped and cheered him on. The coordinator motioned to the stage. "Best of luck, may yer voice be strong and pure."

With shaky legs, he smoothed his coat out and walked up the fat stone stairs. He turned and looked up toward the silhouette of his father leaning against the railing. Nerves threatened to buckle his knees. He took a steadying breath, puffing his cheeks out while people shuffled into seating positions. The ambassadors sat directly in front of him, their score sheets splayed out like a war council on a mock battlefield. Each of them was a master of music, professionals that earned a living through coaching. They would notice every mistake. His left leg trembled and he couldn't stop it.

That was new.

The ambassadors nodded to him, and the gentleman with the fancy coat motioned with his quill. "You may begin."

Traven whispered to himself, "May my voice reflect my spirit."

He lost himself in the performance as his voice filled a silent Yodel. Strength poured into his sound…rich, commanding, charismatic. He wove expertly between vibrato and straight tone. Each choice was deliberate, each note resonant. This song was crafted to showcase his power, and he seized it.

He sang of lamenting his voice change, of the realization that he would never play the hero or the love interest…and was forever relegated to drinking songs and villains. The irony wasn't lost on him, nor on the ambassadors. When he reached the song's climax, his deep timbre lightened, stretching toward the bright, effortless tones of a tenor. Laughter rippled through the panel, nods of appreciation following as he pushed his falsetto to dazzling heights. The green stringed lights dangling above them shimmered and flared, causing some of the ambassadors to gaze upwards in surprise. A few scribbled hastily on their score sheets. He had just replaced those bulbs.

Deep went my voice to the darkest of drones
Oh how I wish I still sang tenor tones

For the finale, he let his voice plunge into its deepest register, a rumbling growl that seemed to shake the very air. The audience inhaled as one, a sharp collective breath. Someone below whispered, "Wow."

He drank in the applause, meeting cheerful faces with a broad, gap-toothed smile. The ambassadors annotated his score, tilting their heads to confer with one another. Traven searched for his father, but he was gone. He took a deep breath and walked off stage to a group of cheering friends.

Mrs. Bellamy hugged him tight. "A wonderful job. You did it."

He chuckled and hugged her back. "Thank you, for everything."

Relieved that it was over, Traven joined his friends in the audience. They listened intently for cracks in the competitor's performances. He couldn't help but raise his eyebrows when someone sang flat, or cock his head when a note was missed. Schala nudged him in the ribs, scowling with disapproval.

Serious talent had arrived in the form of two tenors and a soprano, their voices filling the Yodel with their impressive range. Traven stuffed a pang of jealousy down. He had to give them begrudging nods as each of them stepped off-stage.

The competition ended, and the officiant cleared his throat as he walked on stage. "While the ambassadors tabulate the winning soloist, may we please have all of the ensembles up for the choral awards?"

The stage filled with groups sending each other sideways glances. Traven held his head high, smirking with confidence to his comrades. His expectations were high.

The officiant extracted a scroll from his sleeves and waited for everyone to settle. "In third place, with a score of eighty-five and a half, Rhien Yodel."

The group to his right clapped and hugged each other, their

director taking a small trophy made of Glysterium and bronze.

"Now fer second place, with eighty-six points. Terryan Yodel!" The elder announced.

Traven smiled, and nodded to Mrs. Bellamy. Terryan had been their fiercest competition. With their placement announced, Traven knew they had won. She winked at him. Elder Tesius waited for them to take their trophy with a poorly contained smile. "And in first place, with eighty-seven and a half points, Grendal Yodel!" His voice cracked as he shouted.

The Yodel erupted in cheer. Drinks flew into the air while people fiercely hugged. Traven smiled broadly and stood with pride. They had just won a large share of life-saving Glysterium, and it meant more warmth and comfort for the year ahead. Mrs. Bellamy graciously took the largest trophy and held it aloft, her skin bathed in faint green light. Traven stole a glance at the balcony. *See? I can provide for the family.*

The ensembles filtered off the stage, with the soloists remaining behind. Traven felt the nerves reemerge and tried his best to shove them back down. The singing was over. Now, he needed to see where the scores fell. The elder pulled at a ceremonial wax seal and unfurled the small parchment. "In third place, with ninety points, Endra Falloshorn."

A thin blonde girl with an impressive soprano voice swayed to the elder and curtseyed. She stood beaming as the audience clapped for her, then stepped to the side. "In second place, with ninety-three points, Traven Caelhardt!"

Traven's smile faltered. He bowed at the applause as a wave of heat crawled up his neck. Sweat immediately formed on his shaved head. *How the frost had he lost?* His solo had been perfect. Dreading the sight of his father's disappointment, he looked upwards…but the space was empty. Asmeri hadn't even been there to see it.

He watched with envy as a tenor boy around his age took first place with ninety-three and a half points. The boy's eyes were lit with fiery excitement, and Traven hated him for it.

The soloists took their final bow. Traven stepped off the stage, moving with wooden legs as Geshtran clapped him on the back. His mind raced over each and every facet of his performance. What had he missed? He had been perfect. Chatter buzzed around him, but he was too wrapped in his own thoughts to hear any of it. What if he had added too much humor? Was he not technical enough? It took him a moment to realize the delegate from the capital was standing in front of him, his eyes coming up to Traven's chest. He was startled and took a step backward.

"Pardon me, young man. An excellent job this year, if I say so. Quite humorous," he spoke through a bushy mustache.

"Oh, thank you. Maybe I'll do better next year." Traven felt lost.

"Well, about that." He fished around in his pocket and produced a fist-sized gold coin. "I would like you to have this. It's an invitation to a Grand Chorus audition. While you may have not won the day, I see a tremendous amount of potential in you. It's not every day you see a talented bass."

He slowly picked up the heavy coin with his calloused fingers and flipped it over and over. The medallion bore the same insignia of the airship, with the words GRAND CHORUS engraved on the back. The sting of second place vanished in a rush of elation. He didn't know what to think. "Th...Thank you," he stammered.

"It was my pleasure. I do hope to see you in Hearthmere. I regret to inform you that we won't be headed there directly, as there are months of competitions to judge. If you manage to make your way to the city, you'll have an automatic foot in the proverbial door...if I may." The man's mustache quivered at his euphemism.

Traven scooped him up in his arms. "Thank you so much, sir! I can't believe this is happening. I won't let you down."

The man chortled and wriggled as his feet dangled below him. "Please do let me down!"

Traven laughed in embarrassment and blushed while obliging. "I'm so sorry, I got excited. I have to tell my friends. Thank you, thank you," he repeated as he walked away.

The mustachioed man smoothed his coat out and took a sniff at his clothes with disdain, then laughed at himself and walked off.

For a moment, Traven forgot the room, the crowd, even his father.

Mrs. Bellamy's face lit up when Traven showed her the coin. The rest of the ensemble swirled around him in interest, and Traven felt like his life was finally beginning.

When the rest of the group disbanded, Traven winced at Geshtran while looking to the fifth story. "How do you think my father's gonna take it?"

Chapter IV

Asmeri sat on his bed, the large hammer in his upturned palms. His shoulders were stooped and his head sagged with the weight of the world. Traven slipped inside, gnawing at the inside of his cheek. A thousand ways to start the conversation shuffled through his mind as he shifted his feet. He'd known this conversation would come. He just hadn't expected it tonight.

His father nodded his head at something unseen. A question had been answered, or a decision made. Traven remembered the day his brother left, the fear as he lurked around a corner while their belongings crashed against the walls. Echoes of their shouts pressed in on him now, holding back his words like a dam. There wasn't an easy way to do this.

Traven inhaled to speak, but his father beat him to it. "I think yer making a mistake, son." He set the head of the warhammer on the floor with a metallic thunk.

He opened his mouth, but Asmeri's crooked finger silenced him. The other end of the hammer hit the floor with a clang, and he rose to meet Traven face to face. His jaw quivered, breath rattling through his chest. Was his father about to swing at him?

Traven didn't know what to do, so he stood silently and averted his gaze.

"No," Asmeri moved to meet his eyes. "If you want to be a man, you have to face me. If you want to make a decision like this, you need to see who it hurts."

Traven pulled in a ragged breath and squared his body off. He hadn't been struck by his father since he was a child. Asmeri spoke again, "I can't stop you from going, and after hearing you tonight I understand why you *think* you need to go. But *I* need you to understand that there is a whole group of people out there who will have to work harder because you've left. I will have to work harder because you've left."

Beneath the yearning and ambition, the truth clawed at him. Leaving would weaken Grendal Yodel. And yet, the dream of singing held firmly to his heart. It burned bright, emboldened by the large coin digging into his palm. His mother's reassurance— her belief in him—was enough to bolster his resolve.

"You are a rising star, Traven," his mother had told him. *"Your voice is as strong and pure as your heart. You could sing for Hearthmere someday."*

Asmeri circled him. "I had hoped you would find purpose here, Traven. I thought you were just lazy…you were always buried in music when I needed you pounding at the ice. Can't you just sing for Grendal? Earn us that extra Glysterium?"

If Traven didn't speak up now, he might never build up the nerve again. He didn't want to disobey his father, but it was long past time for him to set out on his own. "No. Mom would have wanted me to try. I wanted to leave with Chadden, but you were so angry."

Traven expected an eruption, but Asmeri stood in silence to consider his son's words. His father cleared his throat and spoke in a weary voice, "You don't know what yer mother would have wanted. She made sacrifices for you and your brother that even I don't understand. The Empire will use you until there is nothing left, and then discard you into their alleys." He paused mid-sentence, glaring at the GlysterLamp. "I want you to promise me that you'll come back if things don't work out. I don't need you disappearing like yer brother."

Was his father letting him go?

Traven's heart jumped into his throat. He tried his best to hide his obvious excitement. The illusion of his invincible father had faded, revealing deep wrinkles and weathered shoulders. His black dreadlocks were threaded with silver, as was his thin beard. His back was slightly curved, and his fingers had deep cracks blackened with grease that persisted no matter how hard he scrubbed. "I will come home if I don't make it. And I'll write to you every week if I do," Traven promised.

The gnarled fingers rose once again. "Don't promise something you can't make good on. Your word is more important than anything else. You'll forget about me soon enough. The city will change you, and you'll grow distant. The letters will start coming once a month, then once a year."

"I won't forget you, and I will make you and Momma proud," Traven's voice quivered.

His father bent down to retrieve the GlysterHammer with a groan. "This belongs to you now. Your grandfather said they called it DirgeMaul in the Unification Wars. Keep yerself safe, and trust nobody. People lie. Everyone is self-interested…and I won't be there to protect you. This will." He thrust the hammer at Traven's chest.

Traven studied DirgeMaul with new respect. For as long as he could remember, the heirloom had been a weight pulling him into the frozen mud. Now it whispered of something greater. A fist-sized Glysterium gem rotated slowly behind a glass port surrounded by musical etching in the silvery steel. Gold scrollwork engraved the edges and mounting rings. The handle had been rewrapped a dozen times, sometimes twice a year depending on the thickness of the permafrost. It was as broad as his hips, yet felt no heavier than a standard sledge.

Asmeri pulled him close with a heavy whisper, "Don't let them destroy you."

Traven choked down a sob as they embraced. His future was about to change, but at what cost? He might never see Grendal Yodel again.

Traven set the hammer down next to his bed with newfound reverence, and plopped onto the straw bed with a thud. His father dimmed the single lamp, plunging their alcove into darkness. Asmeri's voice bounced over the thick walls in the quiet, "I can finally put these two beds together so I'm not dangling off the edge any more."

They laughed together, and Traven exhaled in relief. It was good to finally work through these emotions with his father. It had been a long time coming. Sleep claimed him while he imagined the possibilities of Hearthmere.

☾

Traven jolted from sleep at the sound of rattling stone bowls and cups. His father cursed while catching one slipping off the edge. "Damned airship."

Traven dashed out of their alcove and stared up at the glass dome, hoping for one last look. Sails fluttered by as the wood and steel vessel crept into view, gaining momentum until it pointed its nose to the east and surged forward with a thunderous green pulse. Babies roused from their sleep began to wail at the deep rumbling. What he would give to soar through the clouds.

Someday.

He stepped back inside to see his father shoving provisions into a hefty pack. "I'm packing you a few days' rations, even though you should make it before nightfall.

You know better than to be caught out in the cold."

He was surprised Asmeri was helping him. It was one thing to begrudgingly accept his quest, but another to help him on his way.

"The rail station is to the north? At Preth?" Traven started to dress into his warmest clothes.

"It's almost exactly due north. If the sun starts to set, you've gone too far. Find shelter and reposition in the morning." Asmeri turned to him and poked him in the chest hard enough for him to wince. "Don't be a hero, don't be stupid."

"I know," Traven huffed. He didn't need to be reminded.

Asmeri ignored the tone. "And if you don't make it, turn back and come home. Tracks in the snow will disappear in minutes, so watch the sun if you can."

After all of this time, all of this dreaming, he was finally starting down his own path. Before he had even realized it, he was dressed in almost everything he owned. His fancy coat and boots were packed at the bottom of his bag, and DirgeMaul was firmly strapped between his shoulder blades. A fur hat was plopped over his bald head and he found himself wrapped up in his father's iron arms.

Despite the passage of precious time, neither man wanted to let go. Traven kept quiet, unwilling to provoke another argument from his father. He just needed to savor the moment. At last, Asmeri pulled back and placed three flat-cut gems in his hand. "Glimmer for the GlysterRail, and perhaps a few nights in the city. I wish I could give you more."

"Thank you, for everything." Traven's knuckles groaned as his fist tightened.

His words were waved away. "I think this is a mistake, but I can't let you start off on the wrong foot. It's my job as a father. Remember everything I taught you, and don't forget where you came from. Citizens might give you guff, but you don't have to take it."

Traven couldn't remember if Asmeri had ever been to Hearthmere, but his father made the capital sound like it was as dangerous as being caught out in the cold. He gave a confident smile while imagining a fistfight with a noble, then clapped his father's shoulder. Asmeri held his hand in place. "Tesius was asking for you before you left. I think he wants that clock fixed."

"Couldn't you do it? It probably just needs a new core," Traven groaned.

Asmeri shot him a look that silenced any complaint and Traven nodded. "I'll check in."

Traven pulled the curtain back and the familiar music of his home whispered of morning routine. The joyful spirit of yesterday had faded back into industrious focus. Men were lacing up their boots with low spoken banter and kissing their loved ones before venturing into the cold. Feet shuffled along the stone as a passerby worked up the gumption to seize the day. Schala walked up behind him as he took what might be his final glance of home. "I guess you really are going," she said through a yawn.

He turned and grinned, warmth shining in his eyes. "If I don't leave now, he may try and talk me into staying…more than he already has."

"You always had yer head in the clouds, Traven. Be careful, and please try to be humble." She gently prodded him.

"I'll try," he joked.

She bade him farewell, and his energetic footsteps brought him down to The Commons.

An elder sat on a flattened stone, gnarled wooden cane resting on his lap while he taught a group of attentive youngsters. "And when all was lost, with icy death threatening to take the last of our ancestors, they huddled into a cave fer a sliver of protection. Some of 'em began to sing, unwilling to let the sobs of their family be the last thing they heard. Like a miracle, the caves lit up a brilliant blue-green. Glorious heat leeched from the walls. They had been saved, and the more of them that sang, the warmer it became. The Glysterium was singing back to 'em. That's why we sing now, to stave off the cold."

"But how come the gems don't shine when I sing?" A curious boy asked.

The elder scratched under his woven hat. "That detail has been buried under centuries of snow, sadly. Perhaps only some stones react to our voices, and fate brought our ancestors to the right cave, at the right moment."

Traven recalled spending night after fruitless night singing to his gem collection, praying for just a single light flicker. His stones had all been duds, and Asmeri eventually sent them off to be cut into currency. His father didn't let him have any glimmer, but had handed him the smaller disks of gleam and gloam in recompense. Even with its power spent, Glysterium held some value.

Elder Tesius was casually leaning against the base of the stairs, jaw wobbling as he chewed on a sweet-smelling root. His eyes lit up when Traven passed, and he caught the young man's sleeve with a firm grip while singing the Hymn of Farewell. Traven's eyes sparkled as he returned the song, shaking the older man's hand. "So you've heard," he said while hitching the pack up his shoulder.

The elder pointed to his heavy coat and stuffed pack. "It doesn't take perfect eyesight to notice you carrying everything you own. Does Asmeri know yer leaving with that hammer?"

Traven hefted DirgeMaul onto his shoulder with a nod. "He does. Figured I might need the protection. He also said that you wanted me to take a look at your clock?"

Tesius took his arm and started pulling him toward his alcove. "You've got it right. You Caelhardts seem to have a knack for the mechanical. It's just in here."

The elder pointed to a wooden clock stretching from floor to ceiling, the cogs and springs silent and unmoving. He was always enamored with the carved wooden clock. Pine was almost impossibly expensive, imported from the northern coasts of Thalveris, where you could sometimes go outside with your coat unfastened. He traced his fingers along the wood grain and around the carved inlays. What sort of GlysterTech would he see in Hearthmere?

Opening the door to the innards, he glanced around the room for any spare gems, "Do you have a replacement core?"

Tesius rummaged around as he stuck his fingers into the center chamber, a collection of resonance plates surrounding a singular gem no larger than his eye. He released the spring tension on the housing, and plucked out the spent Glysterium with a satisfied smile. "Speaking of, could you perhaps give my father a position inside as the head mechanic? The cold is starting to bother him."

The Elder plopped a new gem into his hand and chuckled. "Getting your father inside before he dies of old age is like thawing the ice surrounding our Yodel. Your mother had to get three cooks to hold him down for a week when he was dreadfully sick. He couldn't even protest without coughs wracking his body."

Traven shook his head with more than a little pride. Asmeri was the hardest worker he knew.

After he replaced the core and rewound the gears, Traven stepped back and gave the clock a firm knock. The Glysterium flared with a high thrumming sound, and it shuddered to life like a ticking metronome. He wasn't exactly sure how the vibrations from these gems worked, but he knew enough for simple maintenance like this job.

Tesius took his hands into his own and stared up at him through an oversized nose. "We're real proud of you, Traven.

We had hoped you'd marry one of these young gals and sing us to health and happiness…but sometimes the winds of winter take us elsewhere. We'll miss the extra Glysterium from yer victories, but a man has to get out from the shadows of expectation and find his own way."

Traven shifted his feet, gently pulling away. He was anxious to get moving, and wasn't sure how to respond. "I'm sorry for making things harder for Grendal," he said through a tight-lipped wince.

The Elder released his hands, leaving the spent gem in Traven's palm. "We'll be fine. We survived long before you were born."

Traven pocketed the gemstone with a Hymn of Thanks and gathered his gear. Tesius stood and admired his clock while he stepped back into the common area. Men he had been singing with for cycles to the rhythm of chopping ice leaned over steaming bowls of breakfast. Asmeri had already taken his place with them, and a few looked up from their conversation to give a farewell wave. A chorus of men's voices sang goodbye.

Taking one last glance at the home behind him, he set his shoulders and nodded to the guard at the gate.

The ever-present cold cruelly greeted him.

Geshtran stood outside with an arm leaning over his mattock, his hood pulled close to his nose. "You sleeping in today?"

Traven snorted and dropped his pack with open arms. Geshtran did the same, and they slammed into each other with a boisterous hug. "I'm going to miss you, brother. And now I have to find a replacement bass." His friend punched him in the arm.

"Good luck." Traven poked him.

"When I sing for Schala, promise you'll be there," Geshtran demanded.

"I wouldn't miss it. Write me a letter, address it to the Grand Chorus," Traven half-joked.

"You will kill it. Make sure you send some sweets back. I hear they grow sugar in the far southern Yodels and ferry it up there," Geshtran said with childlike glee.

"I promise." Traven took a deep breath. "I better move before it gets too late. I have a long way to go."

His friend punched him on the shoulder and pointed toward the horizon. "I'll walk with you for a beat. I could use an hour of fresh air."

They set out, the cold wind biting at their noses and exposed cheeks. Even a mild day like this was deadly if you were exposed for long. Geshtran spent the hours walking and filling the air with imaginative speculation, excitedly wondering about all the different types of food while Traven guessed at what the audition process would look like. They journeyed together until Grendal's glass dome shimmered at the horizon behind the glaring white landscape. Geshtran stopped and clasped hands with his friend for the last time, then nodded and turned back home.

Traven took a steadying breath and looked up at the sun. *Keep the sun moving from right to left.* Mercifully, the skies were clear.

Don't travel alone. Somehow there are creatures surviving out there; they can feel your body heat from miles away, Chadden had once told him as they huddled near a furnace. He might have been eight or nine cycles old. *Some of them are bigger than an entire Yodel, and can crush you without even realizing it.*

He was pretty sure those stories were meant to keep him inside as a child, but then again, howls occasionally broke through the rhythmic singing of his fellow farmers. Right now the only thing he heard was the wind whipping around his freezing ears. He took one step after another, glancing up to track the sun. His toes and fingers started to ache, and he could barely feel the tip of his nose. The exertion to lift his feet in the blanket of snow had him panting and sweating under his layers, but he knew better than to invite the daggers of chilling air under his coat. He pressed on, one foot after another with a steady rhythm.

Thoughts wandered to his mother, and he wondered what her last minutes must have been like out here. He was little when she died, maybe ten cycles of age. The villagers hadn't even let him see her until she was wrapped in blankets and placed in a stone cairn. It took him months to work up the nerve to go back outside after that. Snow was the enemy, it had killed his mother.

He shook the thought out of his head; the cold had always been here. The Ever-Winter was constant. That truth didn't remove the sting of his mother's death, and time only barely dulled the ache.

Traven's mind was slammed back into the present as the snow gave out.

His vision spun from the grey-blue of the sky to pure white as he tumbled, treacherous snow infiltrating under his clothes and melting on his warm skin. He kicked wildly as he tumbled, desperate to keep his head clear of the jagged rocks. Traven's world was a whirlwind of snow and ice, and ended with his head in a snowbank. He pushed himself up with gloved hands and coughed while cursing his carelessness. Looking up to get his bearings, he met the baleful black glare of a creature twice his size.

FrostClaw.

It was an abomination of stringy white fur walking on all fours. The creature's head hung low and one of its clawed paws was frozen, suspended in the air as it waited for Traven to react. It was so still, Traven couldn't tell if it breathed. Its obsidian eyes stared at him with intensity born of hunger. Two yellow fangs hung from its upper jaw, each longer than his forearm. The beast stank of death and musk.

Ragged breaths curled out of Traven's mouth, and he slowly, carefully, reached for DirgeMaul.

Gone.

Panic seized his body. His heart pounded like timpani, and his mouth went instantly dry. Stories around the furnace about these creatures paled in comparison to the reality coiled a few paces in front of him. He'd thought they were tales meant to keep children inside…now he wished that were true.

Keeping his body still, he stretched his vision to scan for his only hope of defense. There it was, resting just out of reach. With agonizing slowness, he reached out. The creature lowered its belly to the snow, its head and shoulders hovering at eye-level, while it growled a deep guttural warning. Traven froze again, grimacing.

He'd have to do this fast, and prayed the beast was slower than it looked.

Risking what may have been his final breath, he grunted while springing up and snatching his hammer with both hands. His feet flung snow to the sky. A terrifying snarl ripped through the air as he gripped the leather handle and rotated at the hips with a wild, circular swing. The hammer connected with the creature midair.

A shockwave cracked through the stillness as the hammer collided with the creature's maw. The impact sent the beast tumbling, and flung Traven sliding in the opposite direction. DirgeMaul wrenched free from his grip and skidded across the ice.

"Slush," he cursed, scrambling to his feet.

The FrostClaw rolled and dug its six-inch claws into the ice, muscles rippling as it hurled itself toward him with a cloud of snow. Traven dove onto his belly, sliding just barely under the creature with his eyes closed. He reached for the hammer again, and Asmeri's words echoed in his head, *Don't grip it too tight, the shockwave will rattle your bones, your fingers will be numb for days.*

The beast pivoted, anchoring itself with a hooked claw and

spinning to face him. He noticed a fang had been snapped off as it charged fangs-first. Traven shoved himself off the ice with the hammer's butt and swung, this time catching it in the ribs. The impact shuddered through his arms. He felt something grab at his leg, a claw, a tooth, he couldn't tell…and he fell to his stomach, breath punching from his lungs.

His boots slipped on the ice as he tried to stand. The creature made another circle, caution slowing its rampage. It seemed to be limping.

Hefting DirgeMaul in preparation, Traven roared in defiance at the massive creature. Pointy ears pinned back in surprise before it growled. It made a step forward menacingly, head low and prepared to strike. Traven stepped back to keep the distance. He wasn't sure if he had the strength to dodge another attack. Taking another deep breath, he raised the hammer above his head and roared a second time. DirgeMaul keened in harmony and grew warm through his gloves. The creature paused and snarled in challenge.

DirgeMaul came smashing down and chunks of ice flew from the thunderous blow. The creature darted to the side and he smashed the ground again, screaming like a madman. The frozen surface sang in warbling tones, bending between octaves as though the ice itself was tuning a hidden instrument. He'd heard stories of the earth singing before it split open. He never thought he'd be close enough to feel it in his boots. A ripple of vibration shook up his legs like an ancient spirit awakening from its slumber.

The beast instinctively lowered itself with its ears raised, and for the first time it shifted its black eyes away from him. With muscles honed by cycles of hard labor, Traven swung down, his grip just loose enough to keep control. The ice erupted in an ear-shattering crack, rippling in all directions. Traven wondered if he had just traded one ill-fate for another.

The FrostClaw pounced, and ice gave way.

They fell, a blur of fur and fury, hammer and claw, into the black unknown.

Chapter V

Fine particles of snow drifted down to the cavern floor, melting on his face and forcing him to blink. He shivered from the trickle of water leaking down his collar. Light streamed in from the cave-in thirty feet above; there would be no climbing back out. The inch of snow covering his coat told him he had been unconscious for a few hours. He dropped his head and sighed. "Great."

How had he survived the fall?

Underneath him, the bony corpse of the FrostClaw rested, the stench threatening to sour his stomach. His leg thrummed in heat and pain, and he had to work up the courage to assess the damage. Three distinct claw marks had torn open both cloth and skin on his thigh. Blood trickled steadily onto the white matted fur below. He had to do something. Left untreated, and he'd bleed out before he got to Preth.

If he ever got there.

He rolled off the beast with a curse and slid the pack off of his back with a groan. His vision swam, each heartbeat pounding in his skull. It took a few moments of kneeling on the rocky stone floor, waiting for his ears to stop thundering, before his vision returned.

He pulled out an undershirt and ripped off strips to dress his bleeding wound, then tied it as best he could through gritted teeth. His gloves were stained dark with blood; a gift from his mother, now ruined. He didn't have a stick to twist the bandage tight, but the bleeding slowed enough that he could move.

Testing his leg with a wince, he straightened his back. His whole body ached and fought him, and his vision swam as he tried to study his predicament.

The cave gleamed in green and black hues and fangs of stone stretched on into the darkness. A column of whistling wind tousled his tattered pants, blowing deeper into the cavern. Following the flow of fresh air might give him a chance to escape.

Motionless as it was, the FrostClaw still haunted him. Its jagged teeth mirrored the stalactites and stalagmites jutting from the floor and ceiling. Instinct pushed him to create as much distance from the beast as he could. He hefted his pack back onto his shoulders and limped over to DirgeMaul. He didn't like having the beast to his back, not even a dead one, but the direction of the cave presented him with no other choice. With limited supplies and a temporary tourniquet, time was against him.

He needed a way out.

The natural light faded at the first corner, and soon the blackness threatened to envelop him. He whistled and listened to the echoes return with a second-long delay. "One day out and I'm going to die in a stupid cave," he growled while striking the butt of his hammer on the stone.

DirgeMaul pulsed, illuminating the rocks ahead of him in a wash of viridian light. He tapped his lip in thought and struck again, light flaring a second time. The metallic smell of Glysterium made him scrunch up his nose. With a silent thanks to his father, Traven tapped the hammer on the floor to keep the cave lit. He stumbled and tripped as if the rocks grasped at him with treacherous claws, and he cursed more than once when his weight leaned too heavily on his injured leg. Each step threatened more blood loss, and it made the journey arduous. He was impatient to escape this tomb of slippery stone.

He sang, bouncing his voice off of the cavern walls as he tried to shove down the fear of freezing to death, "Might as well be singing if it's the last thing I doooo—"

Something stirred within him, and as the last note escaped his lips, warmth and heat came with it. The cavern walls lit up, laced with veins of Glysterium that shimmered with his song and streaked like lightning into the darkness. Traven froze with a surprised smile on his face and repeated the note, but nothing happened. Was this how his ancestors felt? He tried again, still nothing but darkness and staccato water droplets. No matter how loud, or how forceful he sang, nothing. How had his ancestors conjured heat from stone? He couldn't even get them to flare a second time. Despite his limited knowledge of clockwork and furnaces, the true nature of Glysterium continued to be a mystery.

Traven spent hours trudging across the uneven floor, smacking his hammer down every few steps. DirgeMaul's core would drain faster this way, but that was a small price to pay. Every time the darkness reclaimed the cave, he felt a blossom of panic. He'd gladly spend a core for more precious light. Despair lurked in the back of his mind, but he shoved it down and forced himself to focus on his audition. He recited every song he knew while trudging through stone and shadow. He would make it through. He would not give up.

Over time his bandage had bled through, and he was running out of spare cloth. With fingers trembling from the numbing cold, he paused to sit and redress his leg. All-consuming darkness wrapped around him in a way that conjured imaginary beasts. Visions of monsters stalked him in his mind's eye, ready to snatch him up and rip him to shreds. He knew it wasn't logical, but that didn't stop his heart from pounding. He couldn't see anything, not even his hands as he waved them in front of his face.

He prodded the wound with clumsy fingers, and felt the blood between his fingertips. The ripped flesh felt clammy and tender, and whatever progress he had made with his bandage was ruined with his efforts. He knew he couldn't linger, but he desperately needed a moment to regain his strength.

Pained howling jolted his body back into action. The FrostClaw wasn't dead.

He grimaced while snatching DirgeMaul, shuffling around stalagmites with labored breath. He was in no shape to fight that thing a second time; he could barely stand. Looking behind him, he saw a trail of blood snaking all the way back to the beast.

It was practically an invitation for the FrostClaw.

He dragged his leg as fast as he could over the uneven stone, using his hammer for strength and tearing his clothes on the jagged rock. The cave had begun to shrink, and the top of his hat brushed against the ceiling. He had to tilt DirgeMaul so it wouldn't get wedged between floor and ceiling. Tighter and tighter, the cave grew, forcing him to duck, then crouch. The light shone a thinning path ahead, and the wind blew fiercely to escape its confines. This had to be the way out. He'd be dead if it wasn't. The effort to waddle was too painful, so he started to crawl on all fours, dragging his leg behind him with echoing scrapes. But he realized it wasn't just his body scraping on the stone.

He risked pausing just long enough to listen, and the guttural panting of his pursuer drifted to his ears. It was close, and moving faster than he could.

A whimper escaped his lips, a pitiful sound he had never made before.

His frantic crawl became a slither, the hammer ringing against the stone as it grated. The light flared nonstop, and the acrid smell stung his lungs with each breath. The beast snarled behind him and he screamed. It sounded like it was right on top of him.

His pack kept snagging against the ceiling so he tore it off, dragging it behind him. The smell of Glysterium warred with the beast's musk, choking his lungs as he slithered his way through the narrow crevice. His leg burned, his chest hurt. The wind whipped past him with an impatient howl, causing his eyes to water and forcing them closed. The FrostClaw was here, and the smell of its breath was unbearable. Claws scraped against the floor and ceiling, inching the beast closer and closer. Jaws snapped in anticipation.

The head of his hammer slipped through an opening, and the weight on his wrist caused the stone to dig into his wrist. He let go. A clang sounded across the rocks and a burst of light illuminated a cavernous opening just through the hole. Impossible hope danced in his heart for a split second. The beast roared, shaking the cave and rattling his already pounding skull. Claws raked against his boots and he shrieked. In a panic he released his pack, and could hear it being torn to shreds.

His head poked through the other side, but his chest was firmly stuck. He needed to get through this narrow passage, freedom and safety were just on the other side.

Breath was coming out ragged and staccato, and his vision started to swim as he frantically wriggled. He pushed on with his toes, his wound protesting and opening back up. The more he pushed, the more oppressive the weight on his chest. His fingers found a ledge, but no matter how hard he pulled, he couldn't get through. He was stuck. The cave was too tight. The stone pressed on his shoulders, stomach, and back. The beast's claws pulled at his wounded leg.

He was going to die here.

Traven thought of his father, abandoned and alone. Traven

wouldn't be sending any letters, and Asmeri would be left without answers. He gasped at the nightmarish thought. All of his dreams and hopes of grandeur would end here in this lonely cave. He wouldn't bring honor to his people. He wouldn't matter to anyone. His song would die here in the nameless stone, ripped to shreds by this hateful beast. The realization broke him, and sobs wracked his body. He grunted and thrashed, but it was only making things worse. Now he couldn't take in a full breath.

Another whimper escaped from his throat in his panic, weak and childlike. It seemed to drive the creature behind him into a frenzy. The FrostClaw roared with frustration, claws scraping and tearing at the stone. It was impossible to breathe, and each shudder pressed his chest harder into the stone.

He couldn't die here. He had so much work left to do. This couldn't be his last song.

Mustering all of his willpower, he closed his eyes and thought of his mother. He warred with the chaos in his mind, wrestling each intrusive thought into submission. He knew what he had to do.

Traven exhaled every last ounce of breath in his body and pulled with all of his might through teeth grimy with grit. His body slid with agonizing slowness, inch by inch. He wanted desperately to breathe, but the earth was pressing in on him like a vise. If he stopped now, he'd never draw another breath. His arms rippled and quivered with effort, and his fingers kept losing grip from the sweat. A claw stabbed into the bottom of his foot, piercing through his boot and sending fire up his leg. He howled in fear and anger, pulled one last time, and felt his ribs groan.

He slid through the opening on the other side with a wail. Air tore into his lungs, burning and beautiful.

He would live.

He chuckled uncontrollably, then screamed in defiance through the narrow opening toward that damned beast. His echoing voice dwindled, and the thunder of his heartbeat rushed to his ears.

Traven had pushed too hard, and his body was shutting down.

Chapter VI

Something was wrong with Rolan's cave.

The wind howled and whipped at his chestnut beard, chapping his cracked lips. "What in the hail?" he cursed.

The stale air—perfect for cultivating his precious spores—was blowing out into the snowbank.

Stepping into the cave with his sled, he massaged his meaty shoulders while listening to the wind whip past. Had there been a cave-in? There shouldn't be this much wind.

He tugged a mesh sack from his sled, stained by cycles of foraging. His snow-burned nose twitched as spores tickled his nostrils. Stuffing his gloves into his thick belt, Rolan attached his foraging bag next to the GlysterLamp on his hip.

He ventured inside while flipping the switch on his lamp. It stubbornly shuddered in flares of emerald, earning it a good smack before it gave him steady illumination. "Give me a few hours, you piece of junk," his baritone voice echoed.

Leaving his sled at the entrance, he followed a path he had taken for cycles. Muscle memory guided him around treacherous drop-offs and low-hanging stalagmites. He hardly needed the lamp. Hints of his quarry teased him with mushroom caps tucked into crevices. He passed them by, making a mental note for his next trip. A few more months and they would be ready.

The newfound wind was making his hands ache, and he sneered at the pain while pushing against the cavern walls. He had been looking forward to a little warmth, but something down here had robbed him of it. He grunted at the thought.

His mood improved as he approached his first patch of harvestable caps.

The green and white mottled caps were near to bursting, and some even had begun to split. Six were the size of his palm, just a few days from gone too far. He greedily fished into his pocket and produced his knife. A delicious earthy aroma puffed into the air as he severed the stems and dropped them into his sack, and deeper he ventured.

He was bent down, gently pruning the next batch of mushrooms when a roar shook through the cave. His knife missed and sliced into his thumb.

"Slush," he cursed, sucking at the wound.

He crouched, adjusting the cloth sack on his hip with a few extra shakes as he listened. The spores glinted in the emerald light, scattering like buffeted snowflakes in the gale. His bushy eyebrows furrowed with frustration. The next harvest would be weak.

It was quiet again, and nothing but his shallow breath and forceful wind accompanied his settling heartbeat. Rolan heavily considered turning back and heading home, his sack almost empty. Whatever roared had not sounded friendly.

He waited with his knees bent, knife held in front of him like a sword. In all his cycles, he had never encountered a beast in this cave. In the end, his stomach got the better of him, and he continued to forage.

Then he heard a man scream in fear and fury. Stone trembled and stalactites fell to the floor, shattering into rubble. He sprang into action, battling against his instincts to run home. If someone was in danger, he had to help.

The wet stone was slick, and moving quickly had him studying the floor more than anything ahead of him. He had been this deep a few times, but the air was usually so old and thick that no amount of mushrooms could entice him this far. He strained to listen for a struggle, a roar, anything. All he heard was the scraping of his own boots.

He knew it was foolhardy—rushing forward with nothing but a pocket knife—but he had to try. At least he had the presence of mind not to shout.

Rolan took forks in the path he had never been down before, doubling back when it ended in a treasure trove of mushrooms. He groaned while abandoning more delicacies than he'd ever seen before. They would be ruined by the time he'd be able to return.

Whoever this was, he better be worth it.

Something slithered against the stone further ahead. *This is foolish, I am an idiot,* he told himself. With reluctant footsteps, he followed the sound. The tunnel opened up, and his lantern shuddered valiantly while trying to stay lit. Green light danced around the room, and Rolan sucked in a sharp breath. Blood streaked from a hole barely big enough for a child, pooling beneath a dark-skinned man slumped against the wall. He didn't look to be breathing.

Was the monster smart enough to use this man as bait?

Rolan decided it was too late for that. The moment his little lamp filled the room, he had lost any chance at hiding. Urgency tugged at his core, and it made him rush across the cave with scraping footsteps. The earthy smells of stone warred with the coppery tang of spilled blood. He pinched his nose and prodded at the man's neck with clumsy hands, desperate to find a pulse.

It was there. Barely.

From the bloody hole above, a deep chuff rose the hair on the back of his neck. A single blackened claw poked through the opening, dropping for leverage on the stone lip. He yelped, falling to the floor and dropping his knife. His hands slid over grimy stone until his knuckles brushed against something smooth and curiously warm. He pawed at it, his eyes locked on the claw, before bringing the object in front of him like a shield.

It was a hammer pulsing with power, handle as long as he was tall. Hope blossomed in his chest, and his thick frame mustered the strength to swing. It was far too light for anything but GlysterTech. Where did he get this thing?

Metal slammed into the claw, spraying blood and stone with a brilliant flare of green light. An ear-piercing shriek filled the cave, and the rest of the finger disappeared into the darkness. He could hear the beast recede over the hum of the hammer, eager to escape.

One problem down. One to go.

Rolan knelt down and gave the man a slap on the cheek. "Oy. Don't make me carry you. I've got the day off."

To his dismay, the young man was unresponsive.

"Chords," he cursed. "I'll need to drag you. Your damned hammer probably weighs as much as you do."

He tucked the weapon into the unconscious man's coat, crossing his limp arms and tightening the fasteners to keep everything in place. He shook his head at the mangled leg, then grabbed his coat collar and grumbled, "Nothing to be done about that, can't see slush down here."

He hoped the man would live. While his mushroom expedition had been ruined, he simply couldn't turn a deaf ear to someone so desperately in need. Vittles could wait. The mangled man behind him couldn't.

Returning to his sled was a painfully slow journey. His hands, slick with blood, struggled to keep their grip. By the time he had doubled back for the third time, he was panting. Dragging someone was nothing like carrying crates back home.

He recognized a cluster of mushrooms, then another, and eventually the bright light of the snowy day cast grey shadows through the cavern. Rolan steeled himself and kept his legs churning.

The light was strong enough near his sled that he took the time to pull off the sticky bandages. His compressed lips peeled back in a rictus of disgust. "Chords," he muttered while tossing them out into the snow.

He wrapped the stranger's leg and foot with the rough hands of a dockworker before pulling the body onto the sled and covering him with layered blankets. The warmth made the man mutter something incomprehensible, and Rolan couldn't make out the words as he set the heavy hammer down.

Running through his mental checklist, Rolan fastened his coat, stowed his belongings, and lashed down his sled. As he pulled on his gloves, he took a wistful glance back into the cave. "You better be worth it," he growled before tugging the sled behind him.

The powdery snow groaned under each of his footsteps. He had been pulling for an hour when a shift in the sled made him slow and check on the stranger. The man coughed and tried to sit up, shaking the contents of Rolan's sled. "Easy there, mate," Rolan soothed him like he would a pack animal.

"Why am I tied up?" The ropes creaked as the man strained against them.

"Because I don't fancy yer arse falling off my sled and breaking that leg open again. Sit tight, we're almost home," Rolan explained.

The young man stared up at him with friendly grey eyes,

"Well, thank you. I suppose. I'm Traven."

"Rolan," he replied. "And don't thank me just yet, we gotta get inside before that damned snowstorm catches us. It's been nipping at our arses since we left the cave."

Rolan pulled a skin from inside his coat—kept from freezing by his body heat—and brought it to Traven's chapped lips. He then readjusted Traven's hat and picked up the ropes he had dropped in the snow. "What were ya doing in there, anyways? That's my mushroom cave," he accused.

"I fell through a cave-in while fighting a FrostClaw. I couldn't get back up the way I came, so I followed the wind." Traven sounded haunted, hollow.

Rolan started pulling, speaking through labored breath. "Might have ruined my secret spot, but I reckon that wasn't on purpose. I'll get you home and patched up. Our Caretaker knows her way around battered bodies."

"Where is home? I need to get to Preth before the next rail to Hearthmere arrives." Traven strained to look ahead.

"Then yer in luck, that's where we are headed. Which Yodel are you from? Orba? Grendal? Not too many others this close," Rolan asked.

"Grendal," Traven confirmed.

"You lose your way? Grendal was a straight shot north. You're about a half day east." Rolan sounded confused.

Traven blew out a cloud of steam, looking back at the darkening sky. "I wandered for a while down there in the dark… before the FrostClaw woke back up."

Rolan glanced back, Traven had gone quiet. He tried his best to take the unfriendly edge off of his voice, "Hey, you'll be fine. A few days of rest and you might be able to stand on that leg again."

The sled jerked as Traven turned with a voice dripping with panic. "I don't have a few days. I need to catch the rail."

Rolan cursed as the sled teetered with the jerky movement of the other man, "Chords, mate. What is wrong with you? Hold still."

"My coin," Traven was frantic. "Can you check my pockets, make sure it's still there? I might have lost it in the cave."

Rolan wasn't prepared to stop again, "Can't it wait? Every minute out here increases the chances of us freezing to death."

"If I don't have the coin, my journey has ended before it even began," Traven pleaded.

Despite his better judgement, he dropped the ropes. "Slush, hold on."

Traven twisted his body as he bent down, giving him easier access to his left side. Rolan was careful not to pull the blankets too far, and pulled off a glove once under them to get a better feel for things. He poked around Traven's coat, unfastened a button, and fished around until his fingers came across something round and smooth. "I think I've got it."

Rolan turned the medallion over in his fingers, recognizing the etched heraldry of Hearthmere's Gryphonne and wheat. He knew exactly what it was: a summons to the Grand Chorus.

A smile spread across Traven's face, showing a gap in his center front teeth. "That's it, thank the Chords."

He subconsciously patted the cool metal hanging around his neck, an exact replica. "So yer a singer."

"Aren't we all?" Traven replied.

Some more than others, Rolan thought as he tugged at the sled.

Chapter VII

Traven's eyes fluttered open at the vicious crack of thunder. His forehead had gone numb from the whipping wind, and snowflakes caked his eyelashes. Roiling grey clouds raced overhead, bringing with them a curtain of stinging snow. He burrowed deeper under the blankets, grunting at his throbbing leg.

Rolan muttered a litany of colorful curses as he tugged them through the assault.

Traven spoke with a raspy voice, "Should we find cover until this storm passes?"

Rolan didn't stop moving, his voice a shout over the wind. "We're nearly there. A couple more crests to go. No telling how long the storm will last, and I've no interest in cuddling you under a makeshift drift-hollow."

Traven struggled against his coverings and propped himself up on his elbow. "I can walk if you let me loose."

"Like hoarfrost you can," Rolan argued. "You take a blow to the head while fighting that beast too?"

Traven was about to protest when a wave of nausea knocked him flat. He resigned to tucking himself into the sled. The rhythm of his ally walking through the snow threatened to put him back to sleep, and he wanted to be sure to say something before it claimed him. "Thank you, again. You saved me."

Rolan's shaggy hair swayed from side to side under his wooly cap. "Can't have someone dying in my cave and tracking in all sorts of beasties…although some interesting mushrooms might have grown over yer body by next year."

The memory of that wicked beast clawing at his legs crept into his mind and caused a pressure wave of panic through his chest. He tried to shut it away, shaking his head. He had never felt that hopeless before.

Rolan trudged on, musing to the tall hills on each side of their path. "Food must be plentiful in Grendal. You weigh more than my sled."

"My chorus has won more than a few competitions over the cycles," Traven mumbled, "the extra Glysterium lets us heat more dirt for planting."

"A Hearthmere summons, and a champion to boot. I'm in the presence of royalty." Rolan chuckled.

Traven twisted his mouth while deflecting the perceived compliment. "I only took second this year in the solos."

"You've got a medallion, that should tell you how good you are. You need a parade too?" Rolan bristled.

He noticed the tone, but ignored it. "Do you recognize the emblem?"

Rolan reached to his neck and pulled out an identical medallion with a leather cord running through a hole in the top. "Sure, got one of my own right here."

Traven struggled to sit up again. "You have that around your neck? Why are you hunting for mushrooms when you could be singing in the Opera House?"

The burly man never stopped pulling the sled. "It's a reminder of better times. I like it at Preth, work is honest."

He knew he shouldn't push, but he did anyway. "You can't be serious. Singing with the Grand Chorus is one of the highest honors in our region. You could be competing against Velmoras or Orrisfal right now, for the glory of Hearthmere."

"Yea." Was all Rolan said.

The silhouette of Preth Yodel appeared around the last crest. Whiteout snow made it impossible to see for more than a few seconds before another curtain of white washed away any of the details. Traven stayed quiet while his companion dragged him to the shelter. The Yodel wasn't perched high on a mountainside like his own, but had been built on the flat plains between them. Maybe the hills protected the Rail as it slowed down, or maybe the Empire didn't put that much thought into it. A secondary building had been built to the side, connected by a long tunnel. A dark line in the snow snaked from the building and disappeared into the white distance; they must have been GlysterRail tracks.

Rolan pulled him right to the thick doors of the main entrance without much complaint. He must have legs like iron to trudge through the thick snow for half a day without taking a moment's rest. The sled bumped against the icy doors as he gave it a kick with his fur boots. "Get me out of this damned weather."

The doors groaned and hinges popped, followed by a blast of glorious heat. They wasted no time getting inside, and Rolan helped the doorman seal the doors behind them as Traven studied Preth for the first time. Traven expected the Yodel to resemble his own, but the core stone tower was where the similarities ended. In lieu of a hanging garden, a mountain of metal crates was piled up in the center. The walls were lined all the way to the third floor with supplies and provisions. Preth hummed with life with workers shifting boxes from one pile to another, or offloading the next shipment from hovering GlysterCarts. The smell of rust and hearty stew wafted through the air. In the center, a man with a comically large white mustache straddled the peak of a pile with a long scroll in his hands. The mustache twitched as he scratched down tally marks. A chalkboard ten feet tall was propped up against the stairwell with tickmarks next to the names of the Yodels in the region. Grendal was on the board, with a respectable amount of tallies in the PRODUCE column.

Rolan dragged him down to one of the long tables near the kitchen entrance and started pulling at his restraints. "Stay here. I'll fetch our Caretaker."

He thought to stand, but even sitting up made his head spin. Instead he leaned back, studying the impressive logistics of this trade hub. Everyone seemed to have a task. No one was lazing about…except him. A handsome woman with shiny ebony skin approached and began pulling off his bandages, pursing her lips as Traven grunted.

"I hear you have been fighting FrostClaws in yer spare time?" her voice raised at the end of her sentence.

Traven let out a deep chuckle. "I didn't even feel it hit me. I was so focused on staying alive."

She muttered in return and poked at the wound. "Yer adrenaline was keeping you in the fight. Probably a good thing. I need to stitch these. Bite this." She offered him a coiled leather tube.

He wrinkled his nose and did as she commanded. The pain was uncomfortable as she tugged at his leg, and the leather groaned in protest as he bit down. Rolan returned with a stone cup of water and set it down before curling his lip at the gore. Villagers curiously slowed as they passed by to witness the gruesome procedure. No one paused to chat, or indulge in the gore. A scullery maid carrying plates tsked at the muddy mess Traven was leaving and proceeded to prepare the tables for dinner. Traven looked at the Caretaker, who was working furiously and grunted through her grisly task, "What day is it?"

Without looking up, she spoke, needle clenched in her teeth,

"Second Waltza."

"Waltza? I left home on second Tonica…I lost a day in those caves," he lamented.

"No wonder you look hungry. Didn't you pack enough food for a few extra days? Just in case?" Rolan walked up and offered him a stone cup.

The Caretaker said nothing, and tied off his stitches with deft fingers. She then looked him up and down and curled her lip to Rolan. "Wash him before dinner…and yerself."

"Slush," Rolan muttered as she wiped her slender hands clean.

Traven gave her a nod in thanks as she left. While Rolan moved to do her bidding, he mustered the courage to study his leg. His pants were in tatters, and his puffy leg was exposed to the cool air. Blood had crusted on the frayed edges and stained his dark skin. The wound was angry and red. He cursed at his luck; these were his favorite trousers. He wiggled his bare toes to make sure they all still worked.

"I might have an old pair of boots you can wear." Rolan tossed a damp rag at his chest. "I'll fetch you water, but I'm not washing you."

Traven laughed weakly. "I can manage."

A bell rang, and Traven pushed himself up to sit straight in the sled.

The Hymn of Gratitude started, and Traven smirked to himself while erupting with the first notes. The people around him turned their heads, some of their voices swept up in the confidence of his harmony. Rolan began to sing next to him, mature and precise, his melody dancing with Traven's. Goosebumps raised on his arms. He lived for a good duet.

The song ended, and Rolan clapped him on the shoulder. "You've got some pipes. I can see why you've got a medallion."

"I could say the same." Traven smiled, raising his eyebrows.

The crow's feet near Rolan's eyes deepened as he gave a sad smile. "I've got plenty to do here."

Rolan helped him to sit at the table while sculleries filled it with bowls of steaming stew. Chunks of beef floated in the steaming broth alongside slivers of root and a hint of spice that stung pleasantly at his nose. Traven traced the grain of the wood with his fingers in curiosity, and was startled when Rolan cleared his throat. "Find something interesting there?"

Traven smiled in wonder. "We don't see much wood in our Yodel, or meat, for that matter. Things like these are treasured."

Rolan twirled his spoon in his fingers. "Benefits to being a trade hub. Sometimes we catch a shipment from the North while it loops around the Empire. I guess I take it for granted."

"What sorts of shipments?"

"Pine from Cloper, meat from Dangre or Alih. Sometimes you even see silks from Velmoras, but it's too expensive fer most of us. It depends on which way the Rail is coming. We're lucky the northern regions even trade with us. All we have to offer is Glysterium and some tubers…but I guess the Empire makes sure each capital has enough supplies. We just happened to snatch some scraps."

Something sat wrong with Traven as he ate. The Empire didn't seem terribly concerned about Grendal, unless their shipments weren't made on time. This was the first time he'd had meat in years.

Once finished with their meal, Rolan motioned for him to stay put before dragging his sled away and leaving him alone at the table. Traven made sure to grab DirgeMaul, and used it as a makeshift crutch to test his mended leg. It was far too weak to bear any weight, and he was thankful he could sit for the next part of his journey. Once Rolan returned, he was helped around the controlled chaos of Preth and up the stairs to the alcoves. Above the warehouse area, the noise of industry lessened, and Traven felt his shoulders relax. It was deafening out there.

Rolan's home was meager, but cozy. He hung the lantern from his belt on the hook dangling in the center of the room, where it shuddered and sputtered until it died. Rolan smacked it twice before it winked back on. "You've got a loose connection in there," Traven said as he was lowered onto a feather-stuffed mattress.

Rolan flicked the lantern one last time with a grunt, and it dimmed in response. "Seems so. You know much about GlysterTech?"

"Enough to get myself into trouble. Simple repairs, mostly." He waited patiently as Rolan placed his items back in their particular spots. "Do you have any family here?"

"Dead." Rolan grunted, "Cave-in."

Traven's eyes drifted to a shelf full of carved dolls and rattles before snapping his mouth shut. He remembered the silence after Chadden left.

Rolan's shoulders flinched as he shrugged away a memory. "That's the way of things. The Ever-Winter claims its victims… and we trod on."

"I'm sorry. I didn't mean to remind you." Traven winced.

Rolan stared at him with surprising gentleness in his eyes. "That memory has a tight grip on me, reminders or not." His tone shifted after he cleared his throat. "Fighting a FrostClaw is impressive. That's a monster of a hammer for a farm boy. That have some Glyster infusion?"

"It does, and it's probably the reason I'm still alive." Traven patted the shiny steel head with affection, relieved to move on. "It's been in my family for ages. They called it DirgeMaul back in the wars."

"Messy business, that." Rolan studied him. "Which side were they on?"

"The Rebellion…but we're upstanding citizens of the Empire

now." Traven quickly sang the Dedication Hymn.

Rolan matched his song, then eyed him up and down. "So a farm boy who's had a tussle with a FrostClaw, wielding a supercharged weapon of war, and possesses a voice like a GlysterHorn. Are you running from somethin', or toward somethin'?"

"I'm going to audition for the Grand Chorus. I've been dreaming about it since my brother went to Hearthmere a few cycles ago. I don't know if he made it, but I will. You should come." Traven's jaw shook as he yawned.

Regret showed in the burly man's eyes. "Nah, I just keep it to remind me that I was pretty good once."

"Once? I just heard you sing. I bet you could walk right in and demand a spot."

Rolan chuckled at the thought. "That's yer journey, kid. Not mine."

"Imagine how much better you could make the Grand Chorus. I think you should at least give it a shot."

Rolan looked at him as if he were a silly child. "Have you ever heard them sing? They are amazing—so much better than the Yodels. There are people there who come from generation after generation of Chorus singers, groomed since the day they were born to perform. What hope do I have of competin' against them?" Rolan shook his head. "I think I'll just stay."

"Rolan, if you don't make it you can just come back home. You have to try. What if it works out? You'll never know unless you try."

The alcove was silent as Rolan weighed Traven's words. He had pushed too far. He did that sometimes, talked right over people when he got too excited.

Rolan sighed and pinched the bridge of his nose. "The Rail won't be here for another few days, you can stay with me if you wish.

No use spending up all of yer glimmer renting a room before you even get to Hearthmere."

"Thank you, that means a lot."

"Don't mention it. I'll get yer trousers mended and find that pair of boots, you get some rest. Hearthmere is too damned big for you to be hobbling on a lame leg, but at least a day of rest will help."

Despite sleeping all the way to Preth, Traven's eyes felt like sandpaper. He closed them and drifted to sleep.

Chapter VIII

The crash of dropped crate jolted Traven awake and set his heart racing. Men shouted over each other in words he couldn't make out as the fog of sleep cleared. Simmering discomfort radiated from his leg, exacerbated each time he shifted in the feathered bed. How pitiful was he, one day on his own and he already needed someone's help. A part of him was grateful, but another was utterly ashamed. He should be able to do this on his own.

A pair of well-worn brown workboots had been placed on the floor next to a modest wooden table older than he was. Breakfast, long gone cold, sat in a plain stone bowl. His pants had been mended, laundered, and folded at the foot of the bed. He pulled them on, wincing as he worked the rough cloth around his wound. Rolan had even supplied him with a pair of socks. He'd have to figure out a way to repay the man.

He sat panting at the edge of the bed before attempting to stand. Angry stabs of pain danced up the side of his body, buckling his knees and dropping him back down. Gritting his teeth, he stood on his good leg and hobbled over to the cold meal.

"You aren't 'sposed to be out of bed yet," Rolan grumbled as he entered the alcove.

Traven shoveled oats gone to glue into his mouth; they were bland and in dire need of cinnamon root. "Thank you for looking after me, and allowing me to steal your bed for the night."

"I expect you'd do the same, only way for us to survive in this damned cold." He reached into a cupboard and pulled out a glass jar full of short brown sticks.

Traven took the offered cinnamon and gave him a grin. "Thanks. What do I owe you for the hospitality?"

Rolan dismissed him with a wave. "Didn't save yer ass thinkin' you'd have gloam to spare. Besides, doesn't look like you have much aside from that warhammer."

"I lost my pack in the cave…" Traven quieted.

Rolan cleared his throat at the shift in his demeanor, scratching at his beard. "Rail comes tomorrow morning, think you'll be able to stand by then?" He shifted from foot to foot.

Trying his best to smile, Traven gently patted his leg. "I don't have a choice. I'm not going to let this opportunity go to waste." He gave Rolan a meaningful grin.

"Don't look at me like that, kid. I've got a whole quarter's worth of crates to get loaded and tracked. Hearthmere doesn't stock itself, ya know." Rolan bristled.

Traven quietly stared at him, a faint smile on his lips. His father's tactic. *Let them stew on their words, let their hearts do the talking while you sit in silence.* Rolan furrowed his brow and gave him a firm shake of the head. "Yer young, with a head full of fairytales and dreams. Go on and get yerself chewed up and spat out in the capital."

"You can't be ten cycles past my nineteen. Your life surely isn't over already."

Rolan tugged at the medallion hidden under his tunic with calloused hands. "Chords, farmboy. Who knew pounding the dirt could make you so stubborn? What's your story?"

Traven sat a little straighter in his chair. "My choir has taken first place three of the last five cycles. My mother told my brother and me that greatness coursed through our veins like a birthright. She taught us everything she knew about singing…until the winter took her. I guess when it comes to singing, things tend to work out for me."

A flash of something unreadable passed over Rolan's eyes. He released the cord in his fingers and let it slide back into his shirt. "So what's yer plan? You march into the Opera House, thrust the coin in the receptionist's face and demand an audition?"

Traven shrugged. "More or less. I have the medallion, it's a summons for exactly that. It's why you should be coming with me. You owe it to yourself, and to the glory of Preth." Traven tugged at his lower lip. "Come to think of it, why haven't I ever seen your choir at the competitions?"

"'Cause Preth earns plenty of glimmer from the Rail, don't need to be taking it from the other Yodels. You ever think about letting up from time to time? Let the other Yodels have a win so they don't freeze their asses off?" Rolan raised his eyebrows.

Traven didn't know how to respond. What good was a victory that's given to you? Competing with his voice brought honor to his people; was it selfish of him to help the people he knew weather the winter a little easier? "If I knew someone was holding back so I could win…victory would be hollow."

Rolan shook his head. "You've got talent. Why not use it for the benefit of all?"

"That's why I'm going to Hearthmere. Why don't you?" He hated how defensive he sounded.

Silence filled the room as each of the men measured their next words. Maybe the older man was right, but it went against his competitive nature to let someone else win. Traven didn't mean to lash out, but he certainly didn't appreciate being called selfish. Rolan clenched his jaw and stared at the shelf of carved toys.

Traven was the first to soften. "I'm sorry. It just feels like a waste for you to have that medallion and not use it."

"I've got my life here. Why should I upend that for someone else's dream?" Rolan spoke to the room.

"Because you owe it to yourself. Fear is a better thief of dreams than failure." His mother's words came out of his mouth.

"Yeah. Well, I've got work to do. Rest up," was all Rolan said before stepping out of the room.

⌒

Fear is a better thief of dreams than failure.

Rolan walked down the stairs, far enough away from Traven to get some breathing room. He clutched the medallion in his right hand, running a thumb over the groove worn on the edge. The kid was right, but he wasn't admitting that. At least not to Traven.

"I don't think I can do it, Moira," he whispered to the atrium. "This was yer dream, not mine. I don't deserve this coin."

He could still see her in his dreams. *The hair she had spent hours brushing each morning was tangled and caked with slurry. Her eyes, usually sparkling with mirth, were starting to lose their life. She tried to speak, but the rocks on her chest gave her no room for air. Deadly freezing air poured into their home, whipping at their clothing with vengeful hunger. The walls of the Yodel had kept them safe for too long. He frantically clawed at the stone, tearing his fingernails. Once she could breathe, it came as a rattle. He leaned in close to kiss her forehead, and she whispered, "Go sing, Ro. For me, for us."*

He hadn't been fast enough, and her strength had faded quickly under the rubble. The tears on his cheeks froze before they could fall, and the other men of Preth pulled at him to take

78

shelter. He managed to pull the medallion from her neck while fighting them. "She's still in there! I can save her!" he screamed as they dragged him away from the breach, their breath puffing out in clouds of precious heat.

He wiped the tear from his cheek and shook the memory away with a roll of his neck. He had spent enough time feeling sorry for himself, and he needed to get back to work.

Traven had lost his temper again, at a man who had gone out of his way to save his life…and then fed him. It was an uncomfortable feeling, and one that made him shift in his seat throughout the meal. Sometimes he did this, commandeering the room without consideration for anyone else. Watching someone squander their talent was painful, especially a singer.

He rose on his good leg and leaned against DirgeMaul. It gave him enough support to shuffle outside and lean against the balcony, peering over the edge and down at the mountains of crates.

He spotted Rolan hefting supplies over his shoulders with a jerky motion, worry creasing his forehead. He stalked across The Commons and into a tunnel on the far side, where chilling air blew in steady current. Sculleries scrubbed at the dishes dirtied throughout the day as men ate between shifts, and children huddled near the furnace vents. The familiar melodies of people at work lilted through the space, clipped and utilitarian.

Traven observed them for a long time, studying the community sliding through narrow paths between boxes like running water. Older men, too worn from cycles of labor, leaned with slates in their hands. They catalogued everything with the meticulous care of people used to the watchful eye of the Empire.

The presence of soldiers was perhaps the biggest difference here. Back home, soldiers were a rarity. They would plop down heavily, ice chunks frozen to their clothes, and shivering through requests for shelter. The citizens would smile and happily provide, at least to their faces. Behind closed doors, Traven would overhear grumblings about the exploitations of the Empire.

Here, soldiers patrolled through the warehouse with familiarity and friendly smiles that never quite reached their eyes. They didn't pause to help someone with dropped supplies, or make way for women and children. What would it hurt them to make a little effort to help someone else? Traven supposed their training didn't involve common decency.

But wasn't that what Rolan was trying to tell him?

Chapter IX

After a day of preparing for the rail, Rolan procured bowls of dinner and carried them carefully to his home. Once or twice he grumbled as the brown steaming liquid spilled over his fingers, but dinner survived more or less intact. Traven was snoring, his thick arm draped over his eyes and a leg carelessly dangling to the floor. Steaming broth spilled to the table as Rolan set the bowls down hard enough to wake the man.

Traven stirred, licking his lips and rubbing the sleep from his eyes. "Time to eat?"

Rolan let him hobble to the table. He needed to build some strength if the young man wanted to make the Rail. One day wasn't enough time for a thorough recovery, but it was better than nothing. He studied his guest while they ate, pushing around the soft carrots and potatoes in his own bowl.

He wasn't quite sure what to make of Traven. He was sturdy, built like a fortress from years of smashing at the dirt. There was a mountain of confidence propelling him forward, despite a life of struggle tending crops. Chords, he was naive and headstrong. Despite that, something about the strength of his convictions tugged at Rolan in ways he hadn't been moved in cycles...not since her death. Was Traven truly as talented as he suggested, or was that bravado and self-importance?

Or both?

Traven noticed him staring, and pulled back from shoveling food into his mouth. He wiped his beard and raised his eyebrows. "What?"

Rolan twirled a spoon in his fingers. "I'm just trying to get a read on you. What's yer plan?"

"I'm going to Hearthmere. I intend to make my audition, take my place in the city, and maybe earn enough to pull my father from the oppressive cold." There was that magnetic smile. Despite the relentless optimism, he liked the kid.

And yet, a mountain of setbacks churned in his mind. He couldn't help but push back. "And if you don't make it? You go back home with yer tail between your legs? Tell Daddy you failed?"

"I won't fail." Fire burned in Traven's eyes. His smile was gone, replaced by thin-lipped conviction. "I won't go back to smashing the dirt. I won't fail because I can't go back."

"Nothin wrong with feeding people, honorable work," Rolan suggested.

Traven brushed past the comment. "I owe it to my mother; she told me I was destined for more than farming. She always told my brother and I stories about the Gold Cords and how their voices would inspire entire cities. And...I need to prove my father wrong. After my brother disappeared chasing this dream, he forbade me from leaving. He said my dream was a waste of time. I think he was just scared."

"Sounds like he didn't want to lose the last of his kin." Rolan pointed a spoon at him.

The fire in Traven's eyes disappeared as fast as it came.

He fumbled for words. "Should I go back?" Traven stammered.

"After making it all the way here, fighting a FrostClaw, nearly bleeding to death and freezing at the same time?" Rolan teased him, jabbing Traven in the ribs.

Traven rubbed his side. "It's only a day's travel. I can apologize for abandoning him. Maybe I'll go to Hearthmere next year."

Slush, he had derailed the kid in one sentence. He placed a calloused hand on Traven's shoulder. "Don't let me talk you out of it, I'm just a cranky dockworker. If you don't go now, you probably never will. There will always be a next harvest, then a sweetheart, then little rugrats. Before you know it…you'll be nursing a back bent from cycles of pounding the dirt. If your father has made his peace with the decision, you probably should too."

Traven chewed at his lip while stirring an empty bowl. His head popped back up, and the twinkle in his eyes was reborn. "You should come with me. I think you've held on to that medallion for long enough." He'd never seen doubt burn off so quickly.

Rolan didn't say no, just kept eating with a far away look.

A soft kick to his boot woke him in the early morning. Rolan stood over the bed with bloodshot eyes. Traven stretched and noticed his friend was wearing an overcoat and sturdy boots. "Going somewhere?" He knew Rolan would be convinced.

Rolan spoke in measured tones. "Been awake all night, thinking. I've been hiding here for a while convincing myself that Preth needed me. Yer wounded, and would likely get lost or mugged in the first hour. I think you need me more."

Traven gave him a gap-toothed grin. He knew it was more than paternal concern, but poking the man when he was so obviously conflicted wouldn't serve anyone. "Imagine the two of us singing at the Grand Opera House, two Yodel boys taking on the elites."

Rolan chuckled, "We'll see." He tossed boots over to Traven's feet. "The Rail should be here before breakfast."

It felt good to get back on the road. He was worried the dockworker would have held him down until he was healed. Rolan took a few extra moments to wrap a carved statue in a delicate embroidered cloth and place it in his coat pocket with tender care. He was quiet as they walked down to The Commons and past the mustachioed foreman sitting on a mountain of crates. The old man shouted above the noise, "You look like yer prepared to leave, instead of muscling these crates onto the rail this morning."

Rolan's shoulders hunched and he studied the ground. "Yea, I figured on tossing my hat in the ring for the Grand Chorus."

The man above frowned and scribbled on his parchment. "There's a whole week's worth of work yer leaving me with. The boys will need you for the end of the harvest season. Did this youngster talk ya into this?"

Traven turned his head to Rolan with annoyance. All he did was fan the embers already there. "He's got a voice wasted on hauling boxes. He's good, and he's going to make it."

Rolan placed a calming hand on his shoulder, forcing Traven back with an iron grip. "I've gotta try, Clive. Otherwise it will be a question festering until the day I die. It's been gnawing at me for a while now, this fella just reminded me what it's like to have fire in my belly."

The foreman raised an eyebrow at Traven's outburst, then looked at Rolan with obvious respect. "I'd hate to lose ya. You always pull yer own weight, and then some. Considering ya haven't missed a day of work since I've known ya, I can't give ya a hard time for needing a change." He pointed to a small ornate box near his feet. "I owe ya for the last few shipments, take that and another week's wages. If things don't work out, we'll be happy to take ya back."

Rolan hummed a Hymn of Thanks and pulled a handful of glimmer from the metal lockbox. "Say goodbye to yer missus for me."

"Will do. Yer a good man, Rolan Darrick." The foreman sang a Hymn of Farewell, fondness in his eyes.

Rolan pulled Traven toward the secondary chamber of the Yodel, stuffing the glimmer into his coat pocket. "You don't need to stick up fer me."

He was probably right. "I may have overreacted. I was afraid he would talk you out of it," Traven explained while fastening the neck of his coat.

A cold burst of air reminded him that the chamber through the tunnel was open to the elements. Rolan snapped his collar in place and pulled on his gloves. Traven had to make do with shoving one hand in his pocket while holding DirgeMaul. The cold lurked like a predator in this thoroughfare, and most of the villagers stayed clear of the draft. They had to give way to levitating GlysterCarts pushed by the night crew. Rolan sang his farewells to them as they passed. Some looked at him with confusion, while others patted him on the back and shouted support.

The dock was a domed room with an open archway on two ends. Snow drifted in, swirling in the light and dusting the crates stacked in preparation for the next shipment. Wooden platforms had been set up to flank the steel guide beam stretching to the horizon. Men worked with urgency, shouting orders and shuffling crates to make way for the incoming shipments. Rolan led him to the side, out of the path of crate after crate of goods, while they waited.

A chime rang clear and pure, and the traffic of workers across the rail parted like clockwork. A tremble shook Traven's feet, and a low hum reverberated along the metal beam stretching through the depot. The noise intensified, and he craned his head out of the entrance to catch a glance at the train. The rattling shook their teeth and made snow tumble off the roof in sheets.

It was coming fast.

The GlysterRail roared into view, a black dot followed closely by a plume of snow in its wake. The front of the machine was smooth steel and held together by brass brackets, shaped to slice through snow drifts that grew over the tracks. The deep tone of the rails morphed into a higher keening pitch as the train slowed on approach. Rolan adjusted his pack and shifted on his feet.

Traven looked backwards at him. "No second guessing; you've got this."

Rolan nodded back at him, his smile tight.

The train cleared the entrance and crawled to a stop, green steam curling from a row of exhaust vents on the lead engine. The machine was sleek and smooth, wood and steel polished by the relentless wind. Glass windows lined the top, and an engineer poked her head out with a smile. Each of the segments levitated above the ground, warping the air with powerful energies. Traven had smelled Glysterium every day, but nothing this pungent. It made him pinch his nose and shake his head. The workers began to swarm the train, hauling crates from the platform into the storage cars on board. Preth wasted no time.

"We should get on. These folks will be done in no time and they don't like to wait on people," Rolan gently prodded his shoulder.

Traven nodded and hefted DirgeMaul. Every few minutes, the rail would howl and shudder, green light rippling the air as it inched forward for the next car to be loaded. The passenger cars breached the arch, and Traven could see small children peeking through the glass with big curious eyes. A conductor clad in a heavy emerald uniform stood in the doorway. Rows of brass buttons ran down one side of their chest, and a pocketwatch dangled from a golden chain on their vest. The men approached, their coats flapping from the tumult, before climbing on board. Rolan offered three gloam for passage, and Traven did the same.

The passenger car was more spacious than Traven would have guessed from the outside. Rows of benches with red cushions were occupied by passengers in linen and silk. A man dressed in farm clothes held a small baby, while a couple with the most ridiculous ruffled shirts he had ever seen stared almost too hard out of the window, feigning disinterest at everyone around them. An elderly woman in a shimmering black dress and hair piled on top of her head thumbed through sheet music, scribbling notes with her quill. He had to tilt DirgeMaul and walk sideways to get through, and it earned him more than one dirty glare. Where had they come from? Were they all headed to Hearthmere?

The next car had enough room for them. Rolan chuckled as Traven studied the chairs, the adorned ceiling, the chandeliers, and the wrought iron benches. "You'll have to rein that in a bit once we get to Hearthmere. Folks will try to scam ya the second they realize yer a tourist."

"Am I that obvious?"

"Yep."

Traven sat, shifting in his seat while the thuds and bangs of cargo loading sounded behind him. Rolan took off his coat and set his bag underneath the bench. "You've never seen one of these before?"

"Only at a distance, and that was mostly the plumes of snow it kicked up. This is impressive," Traven mused. "This might be even more impressive than the airships the ambassadors travel on."

The whistle blew as a final warning before departure and Rolan tilted his head to the side while he considered. "I don't think you'll ever catch me on one of those. Flying through the air is…unnatural."

"I think I'll have to go on a ride at least once in my life. Maybe we'll travel to Orrisfal or Calrithia while on tour!" Traven's eyes lit up with childlike glee.

Rolan offered a hesitant smile and ran a hand over his necklace. A tri-tone bell rang throughout the cars and the first hints of motion began. Rolan was right, they didn't waste any time. Traven felt his inside squish as the train rocketed forward with buttery smooth acceleration. The Yodel drifted from his sight and the snow blurred faster and faster until the momentum eased. Rolan folded his arms and leaned his head against the glass with his eyes closed. Fog began to grow around his head like a halo.

Traven was amazed at how nonchalant his traveling companion was. A lifetime of watching these metal behemoths glide by must have dulled his sense of wonder. There were some children staring with their noses pressed against the glass, and he sheepishly wondered if that's what he looked like to the burly man breathing like a pipe organ next to him. He decided he didn't care, and looked out of the glass with them. White shapes blurred by, and the children imagined out loud what sort of devilish creature it might be, playacting how they would bravely vanquish said beasts. He did his best to smile while remembering yellow fangs and coarse white fur. They didn't seem to notice.

His stomach reminded him that there was no time for breakfast this morning, so he reached into his pack and began unwrapping the salted meat his father packed for him. Rolan opened an eye, and leaned over so their shoulders were touching. "That smells good."

Traven offered him a piece. "How long until we get to Hearthmere, do you think?"

"Most of the day, we've at least two stops to make at other Depots." Rolan chewed with an appreciative grunt. "That will give us the evening to find somewhere to sleep fer the night."

Traven groaned inside. His estimation of the hand-drawn

maps of the continent was sorely off. At their rate of travel, Traven figured he could cross the entire continent in that time. Rolan looked back over at him. "So who did you leave behind at Grendal? Surely some sweetheart is weeping over her loss?"

"No sweetheart. It was just me and my Father. My brother disappeared two cycles ago on his way to Hearthmere, I think he might be dead. My mother died a few cycles before that…"

Rolan scratched his head. "I'm sorry to hear that. Something tells me the way you reacted to old Clive back there had a lot more to do with yer past. I'm guessing your father didn't take you leaving easy. How did you manage to convince him?"

"I don't know if I did. We were yelling one minute, then he kind of resigned himself and started packing for me. Said I was making a mistake," Traven murmured. "But my mother… She said I was destined for greatness. She was the best singer I had ever heard." He smiled at the memory. "I think I'd rather believe her."

"No doubt," Rolan agreed.

They traveled in uncomfortable silence to the steady drone of Glysterium, a deep quad-tone that sounded sad to Traven. Every once in a while the train slammed into a snowbank, rattling the glass lanterns and thudding through the cabin. The passengers' bodies swayed with the change in momentum. Mountains and fields of ice blurred by, reflecting the harsh sun in blinding fashion.

"Back at your home," Traven nudged his friend. "Who were those carvings for?"

Rolan thumbed the cord around his neck and stared out of the window, then sighed while shifting a little more toward the wall. "Nobody."

Traven chewed the inside of his cheek, cursing his lack of tact. Rolan had probably lost a child, and here he was just bringing it up like a conversation about the weather patterns. He cleared his throat and tried again. "I'm looking forward to the auditions. I think you are really going to impress them."

His friend tapped his finger against the tempered glass, taking a few heavy breaths. "How do you do that?" Rolan asked.

"Do what?"

"Be so damn positive all of the time. Doesn't it get tiring?" Rolan turned to face him.

"I don't know. Why wouldn't I be positive? Life is great. Everything will work out, you'll see," Traven vowed.

Rolan let out a weary chuckle. "I'm thinking we've led very different lives."

"I've always found that if you want something hard enough, the world falls into place for you. Like now, I have a coin from the Grand Chorus and I'm going to pass the audition. I won't fail because that would mean I have to go home." Traven's voice hardened. "I'm not going back to pounding the ground and living in a carved-out hole in the wall."

The burly man raised his eyebrows. "And things like the FrostClaw? Or falling into a cave?"

"I'm alive. I made it through," Traven stated with certainty.

Rolan turned to him, his head cocked with curiosity. "What a life ya must have had to possess such blisteringly sweet positivity."

He shrugged. "Things have been good. I was the best bass in the region since I was fifteen. I've won so many duels people stopped challenging me. My teacher said I possess an uncanny ability to just…feel music. I know where my part fits into a chord, when something feels off. I'm pretty good at sight-reading too. I think that's why I needed to leave. I was born for this."

"Sure, and that's wonderful for ya…but what about yer mother and brother?" Rolan said with an apologetic tone.

"Yea…I guess that wasn't so great," Traven quieted.

Rolan opened his mouth to speak, then snapped it shut.

Traven took a deep breath and smiled through watery eyes. "But now I sing for them. To honor them. If I stop now, I will let their dreams down."

"That's a worthy cause, I think that's a good way to look at it." Rolan twisted his mouth. "I'm sorry I brought it up."

Traven shrugged at him, then let himself get lost in the sea of white outside for a while.

Traven snorted awake when the momentum of the GlysterRail slowed. They were approaching a gaping wound in the earth. Black and grey stone jutted from a pit ten Yodels wide like teeth. Contraptions of steel beams, chains, and pulleys crawled like slugs across the landscape with plumes of green venting out of their exhaust ports. A steady parade of carts overflowing with shimmering gems, a fortune in each, inched up a pathway that circled the chasm.

The train slowed enough for him to read "RAW GLYSTERIUM" in official Hearthmere stamping as his body shifted forward. Over the hum of the Rail engines, the earth shook with the metallic treads hammering against the raw stone. A sharp clanging rang through the air from a GlysterJack, nearly shaking loose his teeth. A tri-tone sounded in the cabin—marking their arrival—and passengers gathered their belongings to depart.

The workers outside were filthy, their skin covered in black and green dust. Circles of clean skin surrounded their weary eyes, protective goggles hanging around their neck or resting on top of their foreheads. In comparison, soldiers in pristine green uniforms stood at every entrance, casting hawkish glares at the miners. Why did Hearthmere feel the need to protect this depot and not the ones with food or supplies?

A fair-skinned woman entered through the pneumatic front doors, her fiery hair cascading down to the waistline of a white coat flaring over snug black trousers. Her tall black boots clicked as she sauntered past him, as graceful as a FrostClaw. Predatory. Agile. He caught a whiff of crushed razormint and spice he couldn't place. Her green eyes scanned the passengers one by one, quick, precise. When they landed on him, just for a breath, he felt weighed…then dismissed, as if she'd judged his worth and moved on. Heat pricked the back of his neck. He nudged a snoring Rolan in the ribs, who looked up with a snort. "Huh?"

They both watched her walk through the back of the car, and Rolan punched him in the arm. "Falling in love already? We aren't even in the city yet."

He gave Rolan a scowl, betrayed by the smile curling the edges of his mouth. Their chuckles were cut short when she returned and sat across the aisle, facing them. As she sat, her flaring coat revealed a revolver glinting with Glysterium energy on her hip. She pulled her coat close with a snap of cloth and put a finger to her full lips with a wink.

Traven's heart skipped a beat.

Rolan leaned in close and murmured in his ear, "That one has danger written all over her. She's more likely to roast ya over a spit than kiss ya."

Traven shushed him, straightening as casually as he could. He might have let her do both. The woman opened a black notebook and began writing with manicured fingertips. A single strand of hair fell across her cheek.

What was wrong with him?

The Rail thundered forward, and he couldn't help but study her face through quick glances. She tapped her dark red lips with the end of a quill, arching a slim eyebrow as she leaned on the armrest.

Traven tried to summon the courage to engage in small talk, but self-doubt kept him firmly planted next to his snoring companion. He chose to stare out of the window instead.

The bells chimed inside the cabin, and the engineer's voice crackled over the intercom, "My apologies to all travelers. We will be skipping our next stop due to unforeseen complications at Freckk Yodel. If that was your final destination, we will gladly refund your glimmer and hope you enjoy your stay in Hearthmere."

The Red Woman snapped the notebook shut and tucked her quill away. Traven assumed she was meant for the next stop, and quietly thanked the Chords that she would be with him all the way to the capital. Rolan stirred next to him and wiped the drool from his beard. "Complications, eh? Been hearing about that fer a while now."

Traven arched his neck to catch a glimpse outside. "What could it be?"

Rolan glanced up at the woman in the imperial uniform and lowered his voice. "Unrest. Some folk don't tow the line, and the Empire doesn't take too kindly to a disruption in Glysterium flow."

Traven thought back to the soldiers stationed at the last Yodel. Were they there to protect the valuable gems, or monitor production? "It must be pretty bad, if they won't even stop."

Rolan pointed further down the tracks, jerking his head for Traven to take a look.

Smoke, black and roiling, rose into the sky. Green flames licked out from the top of the spire, and the dark dots of people in the snow pushed against each other.

The Red Woman stood and fastened the loose buttons on her uniform. She pointed to DirgeMaul resting in a compartment above Traven's head and then gave him a smile. "Are you going to help keep the Empress's peace with that thing, or sit there and look pretty?"

He didn't know what to say. Her voice was velvety and spirited; a perfect complement to her smirk. Like a fool, he sat there with an open mouth as she adjusted her boots back up her thighs. Her loose hair tumbled to the floor like wildfire. Why did that demand his attention? She sighed, then stalked to the front of the car while he fumbled for words. He wasn't sure why she seemed vexed. What did she want him to do, beat fellow citizens into submission?

The rail approached the burning Yodel. Rolan whistled low as villagers were thrown to the snow by soldiers with longswords and halberds. There must have been fifty or more citizens struggling against the Empire. Some threw rocks, or wielded their mattocks menacingly while inching backwards. These people were simple villagers, and weren't prepared to stand against trained soldiers.

But their sheer numbers threatened to overwhelm the small retinue of guards.

This wasn't right. The Empire was supposed to provide for its citizens, not grind them into the dirt. A flash of red and white dove from the train, rolling through the snow to slow her speed. The rail sped by as she emerged from a plume of fluffy white snow, pistol pointed toward the crowd. The high-pitched screams of conflict blew by, followed by two thunderous cracks that bounced off the surrounding rocks.

"Chords!" Rolan cursed. "Did she just throw herself off the Rail?"

"Did she just kill someone?" Traven pressed his cheek against the window.

The train sped on, and Traven watched the black smoke until it disappeared beyond the horizon. None of it sat right with him. Things were hard enough in the struggle against freezing to death.

He had never seen the Empire like this before.

Chapter XI

The sun had just begun to dip below the mountains when the final tri-tone rang out, clear and resonant as a bell cast in crystal. A thrill surged through Traven's chest as the GlysterRail curved with quicksilver grace around a jagged ridge, and Hearthmere rose before them. After a lifetime surrounded by roughly cut stone and dimly lit Yodels, nothing could have prepared him for such a monumental sight.

The train ascended, gliding along beams of shimmering frost-laden metal above the jagged ice fields and wind-sculpted snowbanks. Alabaster walls as tall as a Yodel and three times as thick, wrapped around Hearthmere in a protective circle, snow climbing the walls as the Ever-Winter pressed against the city's warmth. The city perched on a single mountain, with buildings growing larger and more intricate as they reached a plateau. In the center, a building black as night stood imperiously, glinting with Glysterium. A viridian stream pulsed from the top, crackling upward to a latticework of steel beams and shimmering energy. Buildings of white marble were crowned with gleaming glass hemispheres that caught the last light of the day, refracting it in every direction.

Behind the black tower sat a cathedral, a construction of stone and light, rising with prominent grace above the cityscape. It commanded the skyline, a frozen titan clad in stained-glass armor—the Opera House. His destiny, his dream, adorned in marble and brass.

A section of the GlysterDome shimmered and dissolved to let the waiting airships pour in, eager to escape the frozen air. Once clear of traffic, the green energy shimmered back into place.

As the train thundered on, more and more details came into focus. Rolan pointed out the circular grid, with concentric circles breaking the city into three sections. Steam rose and collected against the dome. Traven had never seen anything man-made this grand. As the rail glided closer, the walls filled the windows until white stone was all he could see. How had anyone built this while assaulted by the weather?

The train followed silvery tracks that converged with a half-dozen others, weaving seamlessly to align with the gaping maw of a rail depot. For an imperceptible moment, as the walls rose up and blocked out the sun, Traven felt uncertainty. Perhaps his father was right—he was used to being the best singer of a few hundred…but thousands? Tens of thousands?

The Rail slowed, and the cabin was plunged into darkness as they passed through the thick exterior walls. Engines roared, and the cabin shuddered as power struggled to slow them. Rolan gripped his armrest to keep steady. Heat warmed his skin like a resonant hymn. Then, as if a curtain on a stage was drawn back, Hearthmere revealed itself.

People walked down cobblestone streets in light coats and shoes with soles impractically thin. One step on ice and they would be flat on their back. Traven marveled at the variety of faces, and could scarcely believe just how many people there were. There were more citizens on a single block than his entire Yodel. He tried to catch every detail as wood and stone buildings whirred by, their windows open to the air. But, most importantly, nothing was covered in snow.

He didn't know it was possible to live like this.

The inside of the cabin darkened under the domed canopy of the depot, and the Rail hissed to a stop at the buffer gate, its engines exhaling clouds of emerald vapor. Inside the station, the train rested on a platform with men pushing floating carts stuffed to the brim with storage containers and supplies. Mechanized suits lifted man-sized crates in arms of forged steel, piloted by men seated in the torso. The cores embedded in the chestplate shone brightly, illuminating the terminal.

Rolan prodded him with a thick finger and handed him DirgeMaul. "Time to go." His voice was tinged with something… concern?

His leg burned as he was led through the cabin and onto the platform, but it was easy to ignore. There was so much to see. The noise was deafening, a symphony of steam, gears, and roaring engines. One GlysterRail had shaken the floor; a dozen coming and going was disorienting. Traven found it hard to think, and for the first time in a long while, the ever-present melody playing in his head was shushed. The passengers behind bumped and jockeyed him without murmuring their apologies. Rolan grabbed him by the arm and led them toward a kiosk planted in the direct center of the building. He managed to limp along.

Large barred windows had people trading glimmer for tickets, and behind them, a queue of a hundred or more had impatient looks on their faces. Rolan kept him moving up a series of stairs and out into the street, where he finally experienced his first true taste of Hearthmere.

The city sang to him.

Traders in their booths chanted at a loud fortissimo about their wares, one often riffing off of another with increasingly complicated note sequences. Street sweepers whistled, carpenters hammered in time with their favorite tune, and mothers hummed to their children. A man with a beautiful baritone voice sang at the terminal entrance, and Traven was reminded somehow of home and his mother's baked bread. Something stirred within him, an ache of longing.

The street leading from the station was wide, GlysterLamps marking every block with signs depicting CANTATA ROW in calligraphic Empire script. Buildings crowded the street, pressing and looming over them like the pushy merchants below. A sign seeking a composer for hire shared space with restaurants where you had to pay glimmer for food, next to another shop that sold fancy hats that clearly wouldn't keep anyone warm in the snow. Traven chuckled at the impracticality.

A trio of children near a corner sang for gloam, a crumpled hat in front of them filled with little dormant Glysterium disks. On a balcony above the street, a conductor with a Glysterium tuning rod gave instructions in sung phrases, his workers answering back in unison as they raised a chandelier into place. The city was alive with a rhythm of vibrancy he instantly was drawn into. But above all of the bustle, he was drawn to the Opera House.

From where they stood near the city walls, Traven could trace his eyes all the way up Cantata Row, higher and higher, straight to the black spire and the impressive Opera House behind it. Building after intricate building lined the cobblestone street, blurring into a sea of white marble and green banners. Rolan tugged at his arm with a wry tone. "Come on, sodbuster. We need to find a place to sleep."

"Hold it," a gruff voice commanded, while a hand grabbed DirgeMaul's handle.

Traven turned to a group of uniformed soldiers. Their pointed steel helmets shining in the waning sunlight. They wore chainmail under an elaborate surcoat of green and gold, and each soldier carried a mace on his belt. The eldest, a man with two quarter notes on his breast, tugged at DirgeMaul. "Where did you get this?"

Rolan beat him to speaking. "It's a family heirloom. We're bringing it to the museum fer the curator to have a look. We've been curious about its history for some time."

The guard looked at Rolan, then to him. "That right?"

Traven panicked. His eyes went wide as he worked through what to say. He had problems with lying, but if he didn't, he might lose DirgeMaul. His father would kill him.

"Of course it is, he's not much of a talker. Simple farm folk and all that." Rolan gave him a big smile while digging into his coinpurse.

The guard glanced down to see Rolan produce two glimmer between his fingers, then looked back at Traven before snatching the coins and tucking them into his pocket. "Move along. Take that thing directly to the museum. If I see you smashing walls or skulls, you'll hang before sunrise."

Rolan pushed him further down the street as Traven glanced behind them, waiting to be out of hearing. "Did you just pay him off?"

"I'll take it out of what ya owe." Rolan walked ahead of him. "It's a good thing they have a museum here."

"You didn't even know?" Traven was incredulous.

Rolan gave him a shrug, his eyes glinting with humor. "I've been here once before, I thought I remembered a museum in passing. Glad I was right."

"Well, thank you for your fast thinking. I wasn't sure what I was going to say." Traven tugged at DirgeMaul's handle.

"I didn't take you for a shy lad, soldiers make ya nervous?"

"I don't like to lie." Traven glanced behind him.

They walked down Cantata Row while looking for an inn with available rooms. Most of the buildings near the terminal were already filled to the brim. Away from the roar of the Rail,

Traven paused at an elaborate building with multiple balconies. A sign decorated in quarter notes was hung near the door reading VACANCY. "How about this one?"

Rolan shook his head. "If ya want to spend all of yer Glimmer tonight. Let's find something less…fancy."

He let his friend lead the way, winding first through the wide central road, then down a smaller, less-crowded alley. Traven pointed to a young woman with a red cord fastened to her lapel and looping under her armpit. "Choral rankings. Grand Chorus will be gold, Regional will be blue, and District Chorus will be red," Rolan explained.

This explanation became even more clear to him as he studied the crowd. Singers with cords held their heads a little higher, and the others gave them space or proffered a melody of deference as they passed. He saw mostly Reds or Blues here and there, but no Golds. Maybe they were too close to the city walls. Rolan stopped at a humble doorway with a sign on it reading "The First Measure."

Inside, an older man bowed his head from behind his desk in the lobby and lazily sang the Welcoming Hymn. Rolan and Traven playfully harmonized a response and the innkeeper raised his eyebrows in surprise. "Fancy a room?"

Traven nearly threw up when the innkeeper told them the price for a night's stay. As he stood with his mouth agape, Rolan plucked the appropriate glimmer from his hand and gave the man thanks. It was more than Traven's father made in a month. The innkeeper led them upstairs to a door with intricate music carved into the wood. "Supper will be right after the bell. Breakfast at sunrise." He left them to get settled.

"How are we going to be able to live here? That nearly cleared me out!" Traven lamented.

Rolan plopped down on one of the two beds in the room and kicked off his boots. "No use arguing, unless you want to sleep in the muck. I forgot how warm it was here."

He was right. There was no sense of ever-present chill, as if the tendrils of frost had been peeled back through the willpower of Hearthmere's engineers. It was a wonderful blessing, to have survival sitting at the back of your mind instead of the forefront. What other marvels of Glysterium would he see here?

He threw his bag down and set DirgeMaul against the wall. "Why did you take your shoes off? Aren't you excited to go to the Opera House?"

Rolan grunted as he closed his eyes. "We have time. Let's have dinner, and then I can take ya there. We might be lucky enough to catch 'em in rehearsal…if they let us in."

That made sense, but it didn't help calm Traven's nerves. He wanted to rush over and thrust his coin at the director. Rolan was right, again. He didn't want to seem overeager.

A deep, sonorous bell rang off in the distance and the city hushed. Traven and Rolan cleared their throats, preparing their voices on instinct. They began the Hymn of Gratitude, but then Traven cocked his head to the side and listened. After a few notes, he darted out of his room and down the stairs, skidding to a halt in the alleyway.

The sound was glorious.

Thousands of people sang in harmony, their voices bouncing down alleyways and across the cobblestone streets like a living entity. Traven felt his breath hitch, and for the first time in cycles…he didn't sing along. He let the music fill him, closing his eyes and leaning against the painted stone walls. It didn't matter how well each voice sang; the chorus of Hearthmere pulled at something deep inside of him. He tightened his mouth and forced himself quiet, listening to the tentative harmonies of less confident singers under the soaring sopranos and tenors, and marveled at the beauty of it all. Rolan met up with him, looking at him with a raised eyebrow while he sang.

The song ended, and Traven felt…changed.

"What was that about?" Rolan asked.

"Have you ever just listened?" Traven asked with reverence. "Not judged, not joined in…just let the sound find that tender spot in your soul? Listening to this city sing was overwhelming, I had to stop and just…listen." Traven exhaled.

Rolan shrugged. "Can't say that I've paid much attention to it." He tapped his lip in thought. "Yer something special, man."

Traven couldn't tell if that was a compliment. It didn't matter. He was finally here.

Dinner beckoned them back inside. The innkeeper had set plates with a cheese wedge, green broth, and a half-loaf of crusty bread. Traven hadn't tasted cheese in cycles, and looked forward to the sharp bite on his tongue. He shoved food into his mouth as fast as he could, stopping only to wash it all down with some wine. Rolan ate slowly, twirling his necklace in between bites. Why wasn't his friend eager to leave? "C'mon! We've got places to be!"

Rolan grunted and gathered his bread while draining his wine cup. "Let a man eat at his own pace!"

They walked through the alleyway and followed it back to the main road. The sun had fully set, and the familiar viridian glow of light flickered as each lantern buzzed to life. A man passed in brass-and-leather boots that flared green with every step. His intricately brocaded robe was embellished with cogs on the hem and vials of glowing green liquid draped around his neck. On his hand was a glove matching his boots, with gears on each joint and lines of green power leading up his sleeve. He stared past Traven with three pairs of spectacles perched on his nose. A single man wore more GlysterTech than the entire collection back home. "The Chorus Arcanum," Rolan said quietly as he tugged on Traven's sleeve.

Traven craned his head as they walked, momentarily

distracted from his mission at hand. Before his voice changed, he had wanted to become an Arcanum priest. He had been sure the stories Elder Tesius used to tell him were embellished. Now, after seeing one in the flesh, he wasn't so sure.

They entered a section of Cantata Row covered in multi-colored tents, and a hundred roaring melodies assaulted their ears. Merchants were selling goods from every corner of Thalvaris. They walked past mushrooms from the caves of Dorda, spices from the northern provinces, and clockwork toys pinging with brass cymbals. Goods were shoved in front of Traven's face, and he wrinkled his nose at them. Rolan glared at them until they shrank away, latching on to the next customer.

The street rose higher and higher, and as they closed in on the Opera House, Traven observed the buildings were more intricate and artistically embellished. His leg still bothered him, but the singular focus on the Opera House tossed the pain to the back of his mind. Red cords in clothes finer than anything he owned wove through the crowd…but then again, most of the people here were better dressed. He looked down at his navy coat, mended trousers, and high winter boots with unease. How would the director respond to his shabby appearance?

A sharp yelp caught his attention, and he whipped his head to see down a nearby alley. Rolan tugged him along, but not before he saw enough of the soldiers roughing up someone scrawling letters on the wall. RESIST.

"Has the unrest come here as well?" Traven paused, trying to get a better look.

"Dunno. Been rumblings about fairness and distribution fer some time. Some folks seem to think it isn't fair that the best government positions and spots in society go to the best singers. They say having an advantage over others is unfair just because of the way they were born," Rolan said without looking back.

"What do you think?" He strained his leg to catch up.

"I think if ya work hard you should be rewarded for it. Being born noble and then having auditions lined up for ya without anyone hearing ya sing is crazy…but then again someone without talent wouldn't make the Grand Chorus…or they *shouldn't*." Rolan continued, "I've heard people with amazing voices in the mines who will never have the chance to be heard outside of the caves they live in."

"But that's what the annual competition is for, so you have a chance to become something greater," Traven retorted.

"Maybe, but the Empress doesn't take too kindly to miners slowing down production even for a few hours. Consider yerself fortunate, friend." Rolan warned him.

They passed a cart bristling with musical scrolls. A young girl sightread from her wares, her lilting melody floating through the air like fresh perfume. Traven was once again impressed with just how integral music was in Hearthmere. He belonged here.

The industrial warehouses, taverns, and guild halls of the terminal depot gave way to music schools, merchant housing, and theatre guilds. As they walked, the buildings became less cramped, with an occasional small garden, choral dorm, or gated multi-storied home. The dormitories grew in size and intricacy, with balconies open to the streets. Rolan pointed toward government buildings made of marble and Traven pulled off his coat while nodding. "It's getting hot."

"Heat rises," his friend grunted. "The closer we get to the top, the less the nobles are reminded of the suffering past the walls."

He felt almost naked taking off his coat. He never could get warm enough in the Yodel, and would often wear his coat to bed. He was warm enough now.

Traven and Rolan seemed to draw the guards attention up here more than most, with their well worn and dark hued clothing. Red and Blue cords dotted the populace, and Traven watched the crowds part to show due respect. More than once a passerby curled their lip at him, as if to say, *What are you doing here?* He found himself flashing a rebellious smile at them, his teeth gleaming in the light. Despite his clothing, he would show them.

The black spire, all sharp angles and shimmering Glysterium, climbed to the sky ahead of them. While everything else in Hearthmere had been artfully crafted to show grace and opulence, it rose with sheer, unyielding dominance. The walls were windowless, designed to keep heat in and eyes out. Each surface was constructed with slabs of functional plating and thick reinforcement. Veins of green pulsed at the base, erupting in a beam of energy that collided with the GlysterDome and rippled over the entire city. A tunnel ran through the center of the foundation, as wide as Cantata Row, and both men shivered with unease as they stepped through. Guards leaned against their spears near the doors at the center of the corridor, nudging each other as they passed. Rolan hurried them through, toward a hanging sign that read: CONCORDIA PLAZA.

Water spilled freely from a three-tiered fountain in the center, bubbling over a pool at the bottom and dropping to the mosaic radiating to the rest of the square. Trees swayed gently in the breeze, protected by thin black fencing around the bases. Rolan prodded him and pointed to the greenery. "What sort of trees do you think those are? Not pine, for sure."

Traven didn't hear him. Despite the sprawling square, the flowing water, and lush trees he had never seen before... something else had grabbed his attention.

The Opera House.

It stood like an Empress overlooking her adoring masses. Great marble columns, carved with twining musical reliefs, supported a triangular pediment draped in green-and-gold banners that swayed in the heated air. Statues of legendary singers with flaming braziers flanked the rising entrance, pointing to the silvery frost-choked sky. At the center, an imperious likeness of the Empress divided the rug-covered staircase, her marble arms folded in judgment. Rows of arched windows lined the façade, each with its own narrow balcony, and above them, a rounded glass roof captured every scrap of natural light. The grounds were unnaturally quiet, and the citizens who walked nearby did so with reverence and awe. Traven completely understood. This place was sacred, the fulcrum of culture in Hearthmere.

With each step toward the staircase, he could feel his throat tightening. He clutched the golden medallion with white knuckles. The pain in his leg was ignored. This was it.

The moment he had lived for.

Chapter XII

Stepping inside the Opera House lobby, the men lifted their eyes to witness an interior bedecked with musical engravings, glittering in light. Life-sized statues of gold and bronze proudly sang to the two-story room, their arms gesturing as if their performances would live for eternity. Two sets of swooping carpeted stairs led upwards to an ornate balcony, and under it rested the box office, closed for the night.

Rolan let out a low whistle as they entered the building, and Traven murmured in agreement, wincing with each step. An older woman in a neat grey bun appeared suddenly at their elbow. "May I help you?"

Traven yelped, his voice echoing off the stone floor. He fumbled into his pocket, heart racing, and produced his coin. "Auditions?"

Her face softened, a release on the wrinkle between her eyebrows. "I'm afraid you have terrible timing. The Grand Chorus is no longer accepting auditions for this season. The music has been learned, and you don't appear to have patrons."

Traven gave her a broad smile. "But we have medallions. We've been summoned."

With a weariness, she bobbed her head impatiently. "Oh, quite impressive." She put a hand to her chest in feigned awe. "And judging by your appearances, you set out immediately without a thought to the proper procedures, or decency, for that matter. You're just like every other hopeful bumpkin tracking mud into my lobby."

Rolan shifted his feet toward the door. "C'mon."

Traven stood firmly and took a deep breath before leaning against a smooth marble column. He gave her a friendly smile despite his frustration. "You are right, we did come straight here. I'm afraid we didn't receive any direction other than a coin placed in our hands and a pat on the back. We would appreciate any help, to prepare us for next season. To do things properly."

Sarcasm washed away from her face. "Yes, well. It's been a long day, apologies. I suggest you start with a fresh change of clothes. You don't need to spend all of your money, but something freshly laundered and mended would be prudent." She waved to his leg.

Traven shifted his bandaged leg out of her sight. She smirked and continued. "The season is nearly over, with only a month left before the performance. If your glimmer is limited, find somewhere to work until auditions reopen. Do attempt to find a patron in that time; it's all but a prerequisite these days."

The rush he had been riding since they rode into the city deflated. He was much further from his dreams than he had realized. He stuffed his frustration down and sang a begrudging Hymn of Thanks. He heard no reply as Rolan pulled him back out of the building. "I might have known," Rolan said dryly.

Traven shoved the medallion back into his pocket. "I can't believe this. We came all this way, have a coin, and get turned away at the door? Doesn't this coin mean anything?" His voice bounced off the marble steps.

Rolan glanced upwards to the twinkling stars. The night had

fully settled. "Don't get to see those very often, too cold after the sun sets."

Traven gave him a punch in the arm. "Who cares about stars? What are we going to do now? I can't go back home with nothing to show; a lecture about running headlong into things is the last thing I need."

Rolan started walking through Concordia Plaza, pausing at the waterfall and running his hand through the clear waters. "We find work, we learn the rules and then play by them. Next season, we'll have our shot. This isn't over, it's just a setback."

Traven sighed and studied his face in the rippling water. "This isn't how I imagined it would be."

"Did you think every card would fall aces up as soon as we arrived? Did you really think it would be that easy?"

"Honestly, yeah." His voice was sharper than he intended.

Rolan gave him the same disbelieving face as before, when he mentioned the Grand Chorus the day they met. The doubt made his skin hot. "That's not how the world works, kid. This city sees bright-eyed prospects every day. How many do you think will get any cord, let alone a gold one?"

"You haven't heard me on stage." Traven mumbled.

"I've heard enough to know you've got talent, but from what I heard today every busker and street sweeper could win the annual Yodel competitions. For now, we need to play the game, learn the city. I saw airships drifting into a dock near the terminal, I can probably slide right into work there. What will you do?" Rolan stood and crossed his arms.

He didn't want to do something else; he wanted to sing. He had been so focused on his audition that doing anything else hadn't been a possibility. "I don't know, maybe I can help someone repair GlysterTech. I did a fair bit of that when my father was busy. I'd rather do that than pound the dirt or work in the mines."

"Then that's settled." Rolan clapped him on the shoulder. "In the morning, that's what we do. Fer now, I hear the roar of a tavern. Fancy a drink?"

Traven hesitated, looking for the source of the noise. "I've never really drank before, and I don't really have glimmer to spare."

Rolan's glare took a mischievous tint. "Then you've got some catching up to do. I'll add it to your tab."

Of the many buildings built at the very edge of Concordia Plaza, one of them cast brilliant light across the stones as patrons filtered through the swinging doorway. Cheerful voices, laughter, and raucous conversation cut through the solemn silence that hung around the Citadel like a fog. Something about that place made Traven's skin crawl.

Concern melted away once they stepped through the entrance, squinting until their eyes adjusted to the light. A sign above the bar read The Crooning Cello, flanked by bottles of every shape, size and color. The main room was full of patrons, the tables teeming with glasses and plates of food. The noise was almost too much to bear.

Traven looked down at his mended trousers and ratty coat, then frowned when he realized his clothing wasn't the only difference between them and the rest of the inhabitants.

All of them wore a gold cord.

Rolan paused, splaying his hand out to push Traven back out of the door, but it was too late.

"What haystack did you two come from?" A tenor voice, melodic and lilting, cut through the clamor

A pale man near Traven's age rose from a table full of singers, red paisley vest shimmering as he approached. His mousey hair was pulled tight against his skull and gathered in a short ponytail.

His lips were curled as if he smelled something disgusting. "This is a reputable establishment, meant for talented singers…

not some…*uncorded*," he spat the last word.

Traven was in no mood to tolerate the disrespect. "I could outsing you any day." He made sure to keep the tone of his voice low for added effect.

The Gold Cord raised an eyebrow, amusement curling into a smile. Men behind him began to chant, "Duel! Duel! Duel!"

"Duel this nobody? I would gain nothing for my trouble." Ponytail flicked his wrist close to Traven's face, his eyes smoldering with hatred.

"Scared a farmboy would embarrass you?" Traven seethed.

Ponytail threw his head back and laughed. His friends laughed with him. "I'd be more scared you would get mud on clothes your entire family couldn't afford."

Traven clenched his fists and tensed his jaw. He had done nothing to deserve this abuse. Something stirred in his gut, something hot and urgent. His nostrils flared as he took a step forward, the hair standing on the back of his neck. Rolan placed a firm hand on his chest while the lights flickered. "Easy friend, you've got a bum leg. Let's go find a place a little more hospitable."

"Shissel Morayne, go sit your pointy nose back with the rest of the tenors and leave these men in peace." A handsome man with a neatly trimmed goatee clapped Ponytail on the shoulder, causing him to wince.

"Leave off, Finn. They don't belong here." Shissel shrugged off his hand.

Finn placed himself between them, handing Traven a glass of unfamiliar brown liquid. "He's my guest, and guests are welcome here regardless of their status." He turned to Traven, studying him with a meaningful stare through a mess of short curly hair. "Do keep your cool, friend. I'd hate for you to ruin my favorite drinking spot."

Shissel stood with his jaw clenching, then spun on his heel

and rejoined his friends. He glared through his drink as he drained the last of the liquid, then elbowed the man next to him and took the glass from his hands. The cacophony of the tavern crescendoed as the patrons lost interest. He reminded himself to be more careful; this building was full of people he needed to impress.

Finn waved for them to follow him further in, to a table at the back corner. Three other Gold Cords looked up at them with varying interest. A plain looking woman with long blonde hair, finely wrought blue dress, and a rod-straight back raised a curious eyebrow. She elbowed a smaller, and somewhat younger brunette with the largest blue eyes Traven had ever seen. She scooted over to give them room, jostling a dark-haired man with a scar running down his right cheek.

"Friends," Finn gestured broadly across the table. "The scowling tenor here is Kael, the blonde is our soprano, Elena, and the brunette alto is Mariss."

Traven stepped forward, setting the drink gently on the table. "Traven Caelhardt."

Kael's eyes flickered up at him dismissively before returning to his meal. Elena gave him a curt nod, and Mariss smiled sweetly.

"Rolan Darrick." Rolan wiped his hands on his coat before offering it for anyone at the table to take. They did not oblige.

"And I'm Finn, baritone extraordinaire. Please have a seat and enjoy a drink with me. It's the least I can do after Shissel behaved so rudely. Some of us have forgotten where we came from, gold cord or not."

Mariss smirked at her friend's remark, giving Rolan an apologetic smile.

Traven and Rolan sat, and Finn stepped over to the barkeep with a waving hand. "So—" Traven trailed his grey eyes across the three of them. "Where do I find a patron?"

Chapter XIII

Rolan wasn't so sure about Kael.

The rest of the singers sitting at the back of the room seemed friendly enough. They were tucked in the corner at a lush round booth and wooden table. Finn appeared to delight in being the center of attention, and comfortably buzzed around the group of friends to refill their drinks, keeping spirits up with a well-timed quip. Elena was polite but restrained, responding with calculated efficiency as she ate with perfect posture. Rolan couldn't help but notice Mariss studying Traven with those big eyes whenever she thought no one was paying attention.

But Rolan was paying attention.

Kael was focused on Traven as he recalled his battle with the FrostClaw, feigning disinterest as he fussed at a splinter on the table.

"So I tumbled down a snowdrift, and landed face to face with it. Chords, did it stink." Traven was waving his hands in excitement. "DirgeMaul had fallen off my back, so I had to scramble..."

Kael looked skeptical, even scoffing when Mariss gasped. That didn't bother Rolan. It was the way Kael studied Traven like a puzzle, focusing on his mouth at specific moments in the story that seemed especially dramatic, then glancing to the lamps overhead in expectation. What was he looking for?

Once Kael noticed Rolan's sour expression, he narrowed his eyes and went back to picking at a plate of sauteed beets.

"And then I woke up, frost biting at my nose as my friend Rolan hauled me back to shelter." Traven clapped him on the shoulder. "I owe him my life."

Rolan blushed as Finn gave him a one-armed hug. "Bravo, my fellow baritone! We can only hope to be as heroic in times of need."

He hadn't really done that much. It simply felt like the right thing to do. He found a part of himself relieved that Traven called him a friend, despite their differences. He'd almost forgotten what it was like to have friends.

"Where did you get DirgeMaul?" Kael asked.

"It's been in my family for generations, all the way back to the Unification Wars." Traven said through sips of ale.

How many of these empty mugs were his?

Kael leaned forward, propping his elbows up on the wooden table. "I'd like to see it sometime. It's not often we see relics of our actual history…untainted."

Rolan cocked his head, and it caused Kael to fold his arms across his chest. "I'm simply curious. We've lost a tremendous amount of history to the trenches of war. The Empire hasn't been…kind to its opposition. I'd like to see something that wasn't destroyed."

Traven scratched his beard, a smirk on his face. "If you can introduce me to a patron, I can bring DirgeMaul."

Maybe Traven wasn't just a starry-eyed kid. Kael smirked back at him. "That's a possibility. But it's not something I can specifically aid you with. Mariss might be of use."

Mariss looked startled, glancing between the two of them.

She gave Traven a pretty smile and nodded. "I can introduce you to Lord Daelthorne. He's always looking for more talent." This one was all smiles.

"Why can't you help him, Kael?" Rolan wanted to prod the man, see where it took things.

Elena cleared her throat. "Kael and I do not have patrons. He has a certain…distaste for the machinations of high society. I belong to a small noble house, and thus my parents act as my own sponsor."

"And Nerise and I have a… special arrangement." Finn chuckled into his mug.

The reddening of Finn's cheeks told Rolan what that arrangement might be. Traven didn't seem to understand, but Rolan sure did.

Kael seemed impatient with the banter, waving his fork as he worked through his next words. His lip curled in a miniature sneer when he spoke. "Patrons bore me. Posturing, positioning, planning, pontificating. It's all so alliteratively dismal."

Finn rolled his eyes, thumbing his mustache. "Ever the charmer. Right, Rolan?"

"But how did you get into the Grand Chorus? Don't they require a patron?" Rolan pointed to his empty mug, Finn scooped it up and headed to the bar with a flourish.

He supposed Finn wasn't all bad.

"That's new," Mariss explained. "It's not an official mandate, but it helps tilt the scales in an applicant's favor. Patrons are where the real power is in the city. Someone may approach, offering additional glimmer, titles, housing, or…other favors. In return you'll sing for their private parties, and they benefit from your choral status."

"Like livestock," Kael muttered.

Traven was leaning forward, locking eyes with Mariss the way Rolan used to with Moira. Did the lad fall in love with every woman who smiled at him? He nodded in thanks when Finn returned with his drink. "It all seems like a convoluted way fer nobles to stay relevant long past their singing days are over."

Elena choked on her drink, and Kael burst out in laughter. Mariss covered her smile with a hand while Traven nudged him in the arm playfully, as if to encourage another joke.

But he wasn't joking.

Traven's smile withered as he studied his friend's face. "Convoluted or not, it appears we could use some help with Lord Daelthorne." He leveled his grey eyes at Mariss.

She pressed her lips together to control her mirth, then spoke with a half chuckle. "It will take some time, but I'll arrange a meeting for you both."

Finn raised a glass. "Enough politics, let's celebrate the meeting of new friends! May you have the best of luck in your auditions, Shissel be damned."

Kael met his gaze with a little more warmth in his brown eyes, dipping his head when they clinked glasses. "Shissel be damned, the Grand Chorus could use another farmboy."

Chapter XIV

Traven would not have drunk so much if he had known what the next day would bring. The morning bells sounded like thunder, and when he opened his eyes, the entire room spun. He groaned, and the sound dragged out of him like a frozen ballast door. He needed water desperately. The sheets on his bed were pink under his leg, he must have irritated the wound at some point last night…but most of the details were fuzzy.

Traven tossed a boot at the man snoring across the room, which made Rolan snort and jump up with a roar. "Chords, let a man sleep through his hangover. Do you have to be so damned chipper in the mornings?"

"I'm not chipper," Traven croaked. "I just need water. Whoever thought drinking was a good idea?"

Rolan half-groaned and chuckled at the same time, then started snoring again.

Traven huffed and sat up, then immediately laid back down when the room turned upside down. His stomach heaved, and cold sweat beaded on his bald head. His head pulsed with every painful heartbeat, and opening his eyes made it worse.

He was never drinking again.

He rolled off of the bed with his eyes closed. Landing on his bad leg made him gasp and fall to the stone, which was blessedly cool. He decided it was a good place to stay for now, and closed his eyes. Even with Rolan snoring, he fell back to sleep.

Traven woke to Rolan tripping over his body.

Rolan crashed down with a curse. "Why are you on the floor?"

"Chords." Traven opened his eyes; the spinning was gone.

Rolan helped him stand up, offering some support for his bad leg. "Ok kid, let's fill that belly with some water and breakfast before you end up making a mess."

"Yeah." His voice sounded like death; it rumbled in his chest.

They slowly worked their way down into an empty dining room. The innkeeper was resting at his desk, standing with an amused smile while watching them ease down the stairs. "Long night, boys? Half the city is already hard at work."

"You could say that," Traven grunted as he plopped down at the nearest table. "Do you have anything to cure a pounding head?"

"Overimbibe, did ya? Tell me you didn't make sick in my room." He called out while walking to the kitchen.

"No. But we might, without something to soothe our bellies," Rolan threatened.

Traven could hear laughter coming from the kitchen, then the innkeeper returned with two bowls of a grey sludge and a carafe of water. Rolan placed a cautionary hand on Traven's forearm. "Slow." He must be practiced at this.

Conversation was light during their breakfast, and when Traven finally leaned back with a full but uneasy belly, he asked in a low rumble, "So what's our plan?"

"Jobs," Rolan replied before drinking the last of his water.

"We've got enough glimmer for maybe a week here. I'm headed to the airdock, the work won't be much different than home."

Traven massaged his temples with closed eyes. "Finn mentioned a tinker who does repairs on the Opera House. I'll see if I can get some work there."

Rolan gave him a funny look. "You sure you know how to do that?"

Traven couldn't muster the energy to be optimistic. "My life wasn't just pounding the dirt and singing songs. Like I said before, I know enough to get into trouble. I should be able to pick it up fast."

He was thankful that Rolan didn't push against him any further, and the two of them sat in silence with their eyes closed. When the innkeeper cleared the table, they mustered the strength to hobble back to their room and finish getting dressed. DirgeMaul had been hidden under the bed, tucked behind a blanket to hide the faint glow. He couldn't very well carry the thing around town, not with soldiers patrolling the streets.

Rolan clapped him on the shoulder and gave him a friendly nod. "Easy on that leg, it looks pretty angry."

"Yea." Traven poked at it with a wince.

"I'll see you tonight, here. I have no interest in going back to that bar any time soon." Rolan ran a hand through his long hair as he stepped out of the room.

That made two of them.

⌒

Traven stopped to rest on a stone bench right as Cantata Row split into two lanes, a carpet of green fur growing between them. In the daylight the color was as vibrant as Glysterium, and he marveled as citizens walked past it without giving a second glance. Further up the hill, trees swayed in the faint breeze with their leaves dancing in the wind. He didn't know plants could

120

grow that large. Above it all, birds flitted from branch to window, chirping their own melodies above the musical commotion of Hearthmere. A sense of peace fell over him, calming his buzzing mind. He sat for a while.

Some people looked him up and down with poorly veiled disgust, but he didn't care. The leaves, the birds, the expertly crafted buildings and sculptures—it all made the sneers fade to a whispering pianissimo. As the city moved around him, he wondered how far Chadden had gotten. Asmeri's insistence that his brother was still alive always felt like denial; there was no other explanation for the lack of communication. Nothing would stop *him* from sending letters. Traven had accepted it, but his father couldn't.

The throbbing in his leg reminded him to keep moving, otherwise he might sit forever waiting to heal.

The looming spire of the Citadel blocked the sun and cast a shadow for blocks, vibrating the stone beneath his feet. The air seemed electric as he passed through the tunnel, and it caused him to shuffle a little faster. What about this place made him so nervous? It felt unnatural and out of place. A black spire in a sea of white marble.

He wondered if the Empire realized the message it was sending.

He wanted to pause at the fountain, but his eyes locked on a building not far from The Crooning Cello. Most of the buildings lining Concordia Plaza looked the same, variations of multi-storied marble estates and shops with orange rooftops. Stairs led from the edge of the plaza: up toward homes, and down to sub-levels for small business. He located The Singing Spanner, and took the steps down, leaning heavily on the railing.

The door opened with a charming melody, and Traven sang the greeting hymn while stepping into a room rich with the aroma of burnt Glysterium and grease. Clocks hung from the ceiling like stalagmites, whirring and clicking with each passing second. The walls were covered in shelves, overloaded with gears, sprockets, coils of brass and glass tubes. He could hear the steady clicking of a ratchet coming from the back and called out, "Hello?"

"Back here," a shaky voice answered.

He pulled his coat close to keep from knocking over a stack of ornate lockboxes encrusted with gems. His father would be delighted with the things here; perhaps he'd pick something up. Once he earned some glimmer.

A man with three pairs of spectacles on his nose hunched over a desk of scattered papers and the inner workings of what looked to be a small furnace. His white hair was slicked back and curling slightly at the collar of his leather vest. He peered up through his glasses, making his eyes look three times the size. "I don't recognize you. Dropping off a repair?" His voice trembled in an odd way.

"Master Perrigew? I'm Traven. Finn told me to stop by and see if you might have an apprentice position available?" He extended his hand for a shake.

"It's just Nawny." He reached out with a hand blackened by grease, then hesitated with a sheepish grin.

Traven took the hand firmly and with a broad smile. He wanted to show he wasn't afraid to get his hands dirty. The smile the tinker returned told him he'd chosen right. Nawny set his ratchet down and stretched his back. "That charmer sent you down here? He always dodged my offers, afraid to do some honest work."

"You won't have to worry about that with me. I come from a farming Yodel; my whole life has been honest work." Traven felt a little silly to say it out loud.

Nawny rolled his shoulders; he must have been hunched over for hours. "Then how did you get tangled up with a Gold Cord?"

Traven fished in his pocket and produced his medallion with

a proud grin. The tinker whistled through his teeth and adjusted one of his lenses to get a better look. "Ah, more meat for the grinder." He went back to the furnace on his desk. "So you'll leave me when the next season starts."

Traven felt himself get warm, unsure what to say. "Well, I can help you until then at least. I'm in sore need of glimmer. I lost most of my things on my travels here."

Nawny nodded impatiently and pointed to a small desk at Traven's hip. "You fix that contraption there, and I'll think about it. I'll give you 'till the end of the day."

⌒

The sky near the docks was full of looming buildings and sluggish floating ships. The air vibrated from the chorus of GlysterEngines keeping things afloat, so much that Rolan's teeth nearly rattled. The air was thick with acrid Glysterium, and yet citizens in passing went about their business hanging clothes to dry and sharing warm conversation. How did they manage to ignore all of this noise?

The streets opened up to a plaza stacked with shipping containers. Warehouses surrounded the square, teeming with a rhythmic activity of pushing and pulling, hauling and storing. It was like home but magnified a hundredfold. Giant constructs lumbered with man-sized containers in their hands. A pilot sat in the open torso, pulling levers and cranking wheels to keep the Cantor-33 suits in motion. Gems the size of his head glowed brightly on the joints and center chestplate. One suit alone probably cost more glimmer than Preth earned in a year.

In the center of the square, small buildings huddled around a repurposed Yodel. Platforms jutted in every direction with airships lashed in place with thick ropes. Containers were lowered by pulleys, powered by glowing contraptions on the ground, and tended to by men too old to lift boxes. The largest ships were

123

docked at the top, behemoths of wood and metal that a hundred sailors would live on for cycles. Smaller, more agile vessels bobbed below them, able to squeeze by ships large enough to topple buildings. Flags of red or white waved at the ends of the docks to help manage the controlled chaos.

In a way, it reminded him of home.

"Here we go, Moira. Back to work," Rolan whispered.

He wasn't sure exactly why he wasn't on the way home right now. He could very easily book a train to Preth, save up some more glimmer, and head back when the next choral season started. Instead, he was swept up in Traven's bright-eyed dream.

And Moira's.

He had made a promise, the last words he had ever spoken to his wife. Traven had the same sense of wonder as Moira, untainted somehow by the harsh realities of the Ever-Winter. Deep down, under his own grumblings, his new friend had reignited a spark long gone dormant.

He approached the largest building of the airdock with conviction, pushing through a door marked ADMINISTRATION and covered in missing posters. Dust kicked up and twinkled in the light of the window, and a man twice as wide as he was tall twirled his red handlebar mustache. He sang a gritty hymn of greeting, and Rolan responded in kind. The wide man smirked. "Voice too pretty to be down here. Where's yer cord?"

"Don't have one yet." Rolan shut the door behind him, dampening the sound of industry behind him. "I'm lookin' for work in the meantime. Been a hauler for a decade at Yodel Preth, just point me in the right direction and I'll start chucking boxes."

The wide man sniffed, nodded as he studied Rolan's thick arms and neck. "Always need more dockworkers. You've got the look. Head over to Warehouse 5 and tell Chauncy you'd like a trial day. If he tells you to come back, be here before sunrise. If yer late, yer done."

Rolan muttered a Hymn of Thanks and ducked back out into the Yard. "That was easy," he muttered.

He paused for a few minutes to study the missing posters outside. Some appeared to have been run through a printing press; others hastily scrawled in ink with misspelled words. There didn't appear to be any rhyme or reason, nothing connecting them…but there were enough to cover the entire side of the building. He tore one off—a hand-written poster of a son from the Whisper Ward. It simply said to contact The Cobbler. He understood the pain lurking beneath those scribbled words.

Maybe he could help.

He tucked it into his coat and slid around the grid of crates being prepared for loading. The warehouses circled the Yard in numerical order, with large painted signs depicting each one. He located warehouse 5 and headed toward it, smoothing out his wrinkled coat.

Chapter XV

Traven was pretty sure he had just spent the day breaking the thing.

It wasn't even clear to him what the contraption was—a combination of gears and tensioners so bound up that he had split a nail trying to pry it open. Nawny left him to it, ignoring the few times Traven cursed and sucked a sore thumb. He had made some progress, working a few pieces loose, but not enough. Once, Nawny called out some sage wisdom: "It's not a good project until you start bleeding."

That had made Traven chuckle. It sounded like something Asmeri would say.

Soreness in his neck and back had replaced his headache, and his fingers were caked in grease. He was thankful for a day of sitting; his leg made everything slower. The ticking of the clockwork dulled his senses, and he had lost all sense of time. At some point, the tinker had left to complete some work at the Opera House and told Traven to watch the shop. It was a show of trust that he found surprising.

Nawny returned whistling and placed a scone dripping with frosting on Traven's desk. He took it with a Hymn of Thanks and devoured it before getting back to work. The tinker peered over his shoulder to see progress, then grunted and walked away.

He was left to work until the sun had set, and the Hymn of Gratitude echoed through the streets. Waddling over, Nawny groaned while stretching his back. "How did we do?"

Traven sighed in exasperation. "Terribly. I think I made it worse." He showed Nawny the pile of loose pieces.

"Well." Nawny plucked a housing from the desk, his voice quivering. "Two potential *apprentices* couldn't manage to get this loose. It's better than I thought you'd do."

He felt a little pride blossom. "It was the hidden latch, tucked under this quarter-note embellishment."

"I thought you were a dirt pounder. Where did you learn your way around a screwdriver?"Nawny asked.

Traven recalled the hours he had spent as a child, holding a lamp for Asmeri while his father worked through a broken furnace, seized door, or spent core. "My father taught me."

Nawny scooped up the pieces and threw them in the desk drawer. "Meet me at the Opera House steps in the morning. I'll have tools for you. We have some repairs that will go faster with two hands."

Traven gave him his signature gap-toothed smile and let out a laugh. "Thank you Nawny, you won't regret it."

"Don't take this the wrong way, but I hope you don't get your cord. I could use the help." Nawny helped him up and out of the door. "Go get that leg checked out, I think it's starting to turn."

⌒·⌒

Dockworkers were honest folk, and Rolan appreciated Chauncy's bluntness.

The warehouse supervisor was hard, but fair. After a few brief questions about his time in Preth and a test to see how well he could read shipping labels, he tossed a pair of leather gloves at his chest and wagged a finger. "You do yer job and we don't have problems. Don't be late, don't be sick. I don't want to hear anything about ghosts or spirits, I have enough of that from the other men."

Rolan was surprised by the last bit. He had never encountered a spirit before.

The warehouse was a long, windowless building, with piles of metal crates stacked to the ceiling. A pall of sweet red dust hung in the air like a fermata, clinging to the workers' clothes and hair. A teamster in a Cantor-33 suit shoved boxes larger than a man, the metal joints clanging in the confined space. It seemed almost effortless, gliding the crates over stone worn smooth from cycles of work. *What would it take to pilot one of those?*

The men treated him with indifference as they worked; he was just another cog in the machine. Rolan stayed out of the way, unloading the floating GlysterCarts as they hovered near the wide entrance and hefting them to their new home. The carts were pulled away, and more arrived with each airship. There was a familiar rhythm here, and Rolan settled into it easily.

The whistle for lunch blew, and the men gathered near the entrance. The air filled with pipe smoke and rough laughter. They didn't say much to him, but by the way they threw insults at each other, he knew it would take some time to earn their trust. These men were forged hard from cycles of hauling boxes. He took an offered scrip of salted meat, and chewed while looking up to the rafters.

"Don't pay too much attention to things up there. Ghost might steal your blood." A dockworker nudged another.

"Never heard of ghosts before. What's that about?" Rolan found himself keeping his eyes low.

"Chauncy will cuss us out for yappin' about it. Says it scares away new blood before their skin toughens." Another worker craned his neck to make sure the supervisor was out of earshot. "Weird things happen around here. Crates move on their own, and I seen the lights twinkling like stars."

"That's just Glysterium flickerin'. Happens all the time," another man interrupted through the smoke.

"Then how do you explain the pretty lady in the rafters?"

"Whiskey, that's how. Ain't no pretty lady flying up there. Shut it before Chauncy docks your pay."

The men quieted, but Rolan's curiosity had been piqued. He looked up at the lights again, and swore for just a second, they flickered.

Chapter XVI

Father,

I have arrived in Hearthmere, battered from a FrostClaw encounter, but with high spirits. Despite that monster's best efforts, I am alive because of a baritone from Preth. He and I are sharing lodging in a room twice as large as our home, with soft beds and no hint of frost on the walls. Don't worry, DirgeMaul is safe with me. I wish I could say the same for my supplies.

I never knew people could live like this, staring through the GlysterDome with only one layer of clothing. They all wear the most impractical clothes, and some even have Glysterium buttons! Can you believe that?

I took a job with a tinker while waiting for audition season to start. It should only be a month or two. I really appreciate the things you've taught me about GlysterTech, even if I grumbled half the time as a kid.

I haven't forgotten Chadden, and once I get settled, my friend Rolan and I can start asking around. I hope you are safe. Please write back.

-Traven

Traven turned to the sunrise after pocketing the folded letter to his father and rising from the steps of the Opera House. He had promised to find Chadden, but he wasn't even sure his brother was still alive. The light crept over the mountain range sheltering Hearthmere and began to paint the city yellow. At first, just the peaks of Resonance Heights caught the light, but then it crept down to the darker buildings of the GroundSong Commons, and finally reflected off of the metal roofs of the Whisper Ward. From up here, he could see all the way to the city walls. The city had been built on a mountain, with Concordia Plaza at its peak.

Nawny shuffled across the plaza with another one of those sweet scones Traven liked, and handed it to him with a sleepy smile. He sang a greeting hymn, and Traven returned it with a voice thick from sleep.

"That might be the deepest voice I've ever heard." Nawny's own voice trembled in that odd way.

Traven took the scone with hungry eyes and took a bite. "I haven't heard deeper," he boasted.

"That doesn't give me much hope then. If you've got a medallion and a voice like that, I'm sure you'll find a gold cord on your shoulder before the year is over." Nawny plopped down next to him, the tools in his satchel clinking together. "And I'll be back to looking for someone who knows the right end of a screwdriver."

Traven didn't want to let the man down, but this arrangement could only be temporary. "I could stop by from time to time, when I have a spare moment."

Nawny chuckled. "Don't make promises you can't keep. You'll be neck deep in music and nobles. There won't be any time in your life for old Nawny."

Traven kept quiet, finishing the scone in one delicious bite. He figured he would be busy, but so busy that he couldn't visit the people that helped him along the way?

He wouldn't let that happen.

Nawny stood back up and helped him to his feet, noticing his wince as he put weight on his leg. "I see you didn't take my advice."

Traven tried to play off the limp. "It's nothing, just tender. It won't slow me down."

"Well I won't make you climb the catwalk today, just in case. We've got plenty to do before the Empress gets here. Come along." Nawny led him inside.

The grey-haired caretaker was polishing the statues when he limped by. She gave him a rueful smile as he waved, and he could feel her eyes on him as they crossed the lobby. Nawny took him through the first set of doors and down a hallway that circled the entire building. Rows of doors to his right were marked as libraries or offices for directors and accompanists. To his left were entrances to the performance hall with letters and numbers marking the rows in decorative lit placards. Everything had been embellished by artisans with musical engravings, from the crown molding to the wainscoting.

Nawny stopped at a door marked MAINTENANCE and produced an ornate silver key with a gem in the center. He hummed an unpleasant note, interrupted by whatever ailed his vocal cords, and the key resonated with him. The door unlocked with the same note, and Nawny led him inside a small room filled with lights, levers, polish, and cleaning solutions. "Our war room."

Traven leaned against the door frame. "So what do you do here?"

"Repairs mostly," Nawny said while handing him a crate of lightbulbs. "There are at least a thousand lights in this building, and they always seem to be popping. Terrible Glysterium fluctuations in this building; the Arcanum says it's our proximity to the Citadel. Risers take a considerable amount of wear, with a hundred singers on them for half the day. We replace parts as needed, and clean when we are idle. No lazing about."

"What is the Citadel? It looks so out of place." Traven followed Nawny back into the hallway.

"An ancient building, maybe the first of Hearthmere. They needed to set the GlysterDome before the rest of construction could be possible. Could you imagine building all of this while freezing your bolt off?" The Tinker explained.

He couldn't. "So it powers the dome? Keeps us warm?"

"More than you know. The Furnace is deep underneath it, a machine as large as my shop, both powering the Dome and heating the city. I got to see it once, an impressive ancient wonder of a machine. Pipes and power lines for days. The Arcanum doesn't allow visitors very often—too risky." Nawny pointed to a dead light fixture, Traven plucked a bulb and handed it to him.

The tinker passed by the light fixtures as if they were nothing, but Traven was in awe. Anything powered back home was a closed system, Glysterium gems inserted into a chamber filled with mirrors and tuning forks. Here, it appeared that there were lines running throughout the building, giving power from a singular source...the black monolith across Concordia Plaza. He wondered how fast it burned through Glysterium, or if they had a better solution. DirgeMaul could eat through a large core in a season if he wasn't careful. It took most of their yearly glimmer to replace it.

What sort of thing could hold the Ever-Winter at bay like this for generations? Was that the reason for the Empire's draconic control of Glysterium? Would they all freeze if shipments stopped? Perhaps survival here teetered on a knife edge, and they all had no idea.

Nawny took him through the first floor as the hall wrapped around the circular building, never turning to enter the auditorium. Traven ached to see it for himself, and vowed to sneak a look at some point. On the end opposite of the grand entrance was a set of doors marked BACKSTAGE. The old Tinker opened them to complete darkness. The hallway had been lit by lamps every few doors, this area utterly black.

His eyes adjusted, at least enough to make out curtains dangling from rigging three stories above them. The floor was painted black, with an X painted in different colors to designate marks on stage. Nawny looked back at him in expectation, then reached up and pulled the curtains back just a few feet…enough for Traven to step through.

Into the auditorium.

The room was a miracle of construction. A testament to his people's willpower. Three stories of balconies hung over row after row of green fabric seats, supported by thick marble columns wrapped in golden fabric. Off to the sides were private balconies, with their own carved railings and thick privacy curtains. Sunlight poured in from a glass dome in the center, the support beams strung with banners of green and gold. He guessed at least five thousand people could listen at the same time.

He limped past the risers and stood at the very edge of the stage, looking down into a pit built to house an orchestra. For just a moment, he imagined performing for all these people, and his stomach lurched with nerves. Could he really do this? Could he rise above the horde of wishful singers, each a champion of their small regions?

He wouldn't quit until he did.

Nawny cleared his throat and motioned for Traven when he turned around. "A beautiful sight, for sure. Let's get to work. You'll likely be in this room often through the next month."

Nawny led him up a flight of black stairs to a broad catwalk overlooking the stage, then pointed to a ladder climbing even higher, to mounted lights hanging from the ceiling. "Eventually these all will need checking. Everything must be perfect for the

Empress's arrival; Director Rivers will have my head if even one light goes out."

Traven very much did not want to climb that ladder. He wasn't afraid of much, but heights made his head swirl.

Nawny led him through the rest of the Opera House, up to the second and third story hallways, each with their own row of offices. Traven counted one-hundred rooms on each floor. After the tour, he was let loose to inspect every bulb on his own. It was easy work, if a little more difficult with his leg beginning to burn. The Tinker was probably right, he should have someone look at it. He just didn't have time.

As the day went on, singers trickled into the building. He paused and gave them a reverent bow, his eyes firmly on the gold cord attached to their shoulders. Most ignored him, or sneered at his clothing. By midday, the halls sounded just like the Crooning Cello. Quartets gathered in any quiet space they could find, filling the space with song, vying for attention against the other groups. He paused to listen while reaching up for a bulb in the ceiling.

Their behavior was familiar; lip trills to warm up the voice, stretches to prepare the body for rehearsal. Some cupped their ears to hear themselves while others tilted their heads back and belted their favorite parts. He found himself humming along with a group of basses warming up, their voices rumbling in the hall. They were good, maybe even better than him.

At the midday bell, the singers funneled into the auditorium with music folders clutched in their hands. A heavy man rushed from a director's office, his dreadlock ponytail swishing along with the tails of his posh red coat. He glanced up at Traven with a blank expression, then pushed the doors open to the auditorium. Traven looked at the nameplate on the door and read MALACHI RIVERS, HEAD DIRECTOR.

That was the man he needed to talk to. Choral season be damned.

Nawny had told him to return to the shop once he was finished, but he couldn't pass up an opportunity to hear the chorus sing. He tucked away the crate of bulbs in the storeroom and locked it with what Nawny had called a Harmonic Key. Traven hummed the note he had heard earlier, and the lock clicked into place.

Warm-ups in the auditorium had already begun, and Traven took a seat in the back corner. It was dark, and he just wanted to listen for a few minutes.

Malachi was sitting at a black lacquered piano, plunking a sequence of notes climbing higher and higher in a warm-up arpeggio. The chorus stood on four-step risers, an amalgam of people from every corner of Hearthmere's province. There was mostly an even mixture of men and women, with ages ranging from his youthful nineteen cycles to folks with greying hair. Some wore clothes traditional to Hearthmere, vests and white shirts, dresses with big skirts and a minimum of three sets of pleats. Others wore loose-fitting clothing that rippled with each breath in shades of vibrant reds and oranges. His cheeks flushed at a woman wearing clothes designed to cover everything, but hide nothing. What region had she come from?

He listened intently to their balance and clarity. A part of him wanted to find fault, a crack in the armor…but he couldn't. Every single singer belonged on those risers…even Shissel. If he was going to do this, he needed to be perfect.

The warm-up changed to a four-part split, and Traven could feel the air vibrate with their resonance. He closed his eyes and smiled. He could stay here for hours…but his time hadn't come.

There was work to do.

Chapter XVII

Working at the docks of Preth was like child's play compared to this.

There was a rhythm to things back home. Trains came every few days, which gave them all plenty of time to unload, catalogue, and prepare for the next shipment. Work was steady, but comfortable.

This was not comfortable.

Airships docked every few hours, dropping cargo down the lifts of the central spire. Each warehouse was designated for specific goods, and GlysterCarts buzzed over the ground to clear the landing area as soon as possible. Keeping Hearthmere fed was a monumental affair, with dozens of Yodels shipping off supplies to support their capital.

He barely had time to dust off his hands from the last load, before another cart floated in and they started all over. He hadn't expected Hearthmere to move this fast.

The men of Warehouse 5 worked together in smooth efficiency. The largest crates were lifted by their Cantor suit, the dockworkers staying well away from the thunderous footsteps. Rolan stepped into their flow, hefting a box of supplies with a grunt, and followed the others inside.

The crate in his arms was marked PIZZO, a red spice that itched the nose and left a sweet lingering scent in the air. Last night, he had to have shaken a pound of red dust from his beard. The crates were sealed, but that hadn't stopped the spice from sneaking into every nook and cranny. A sneeze shook his body as he set his crate down, thundering through the warehouse. He shook his head clear and returned for more.

He thought he heard a giggle from the rafters.

Chauncy was standing at the entrance, a slate cradled in his arm. He didn't dare look up for fear of spreading superstition, but at least one other worker's eyes lifted to the lights. They shared a nod, and continued on their way.

Before long, the midday bell rang. Rolan went to the locker he had been assigned to retrieve a packed lunch…but it was missing.

They were hazing him already?

"Alright, where is it?" Rolan slammed his locker shut.

None of the men answered, some looking genuinely surprised. The teamster in the Cantor suit leaned over his controls with a loaf of bread in his mouth. "Missing somethin?"

"My lunch. Must have grown legs and run off." Rolan studied each of them as they grabbed their food.

"Dunno what you mean, rookie." Another shouldered past him.

Rolan didn't let himself get too angry; he had expected as much. They were pushing him, feeling him out. If he lost his cool now, he'd end up eating lunch by himself for the foreseeable future. He walked by each of the dockworkers, checking to see if they were eating his lunch. He received a mixture of scowls or eyes wide with surprise. None of them had it.

A skinny man named Hennik offered him a slice of meat, but held firm when Rolan grabbed it. Hennik had been the one looking to the rafters earlier, he did it again with exaggerated purpose.

Was he suggesting the spirit ran off with his lunch?

This time, Rolan did cast a glance upwards. Some of the workers chuckled through the pipes in their teeth. "Real funny, boys," he muttered.

Up on one of the highest stacks, just under a GlysterLight, sat his lunch illuminated in green.

He hoped the crates were sturdy enough. "Give me a lift?" He approached the Cantor suit and pointed to the ceiling.

"That's against the rules. I won't be responsible fer a broken leg." The teamster shook his head, leaning back into his leather harness.

"Fair enough." Rolan sighed before approaching the stack and climbing.

His comrades gathered as he scaled the three stories of spice crates. Some of them called up mockingly.

"Look at him go."

"He's like one of them circus performers."

"He's gonna break his neck over lunch?"

"Don't go up there, she's gonna get you."

His forearms and legs burned as he dug his fingers between seams, climbing higher and higher. The haze of red was thicker up here, mixing with the light in a faint brown cloud. It was hard to breathe, but he managed to reach the top after a few minutes. The men below applauded, then laughed when Rolan sat down on the top and opened his lunch. He may as well eat up here. His brow furrowed when he unwrapped the meal; the sandwich had a bite taken out of it.

"Making friends already, Moira." He scoffed.

"Moira," his voice echoed back to him, a wisp of wind tickling the back of his neck.

His skin prickled. The light winked.

With a back straight as the stem of a quarter note, he shoved the sandwich back into his mouth and half-climbed, half-slid down the pile of crates. His heart was pounding out of his chest. The workers below shouted in alarm, some rushing to catch his quick descent. He was careful, despite being scared witless.

Once his feet met the stone, he looked back up to find nothing but a twinkling lamp. He was sure his skin was white as snow. The rest of the men in the warehouse erupted into laughter, and he rubbed the back of his neck in embarrassment. "You lads might be right, after all."

He hoped Nawny wasn't going to be angry with him.

Traven had spent the rest of the day sitting in the last row, studying the Grand Chorus and the way their Director Malachi shaped their sound. Sometimes Malachi would stop them at a spot where Traven would have been perfectly happy, tweak the baritones here, the basses there, and then run it again. The results were always better, impossibly better. He felt his respect for Malachi grow with every measure. Despite his intention to get back to work, he had allowed himself to get distracted.

His back ached from leaning forward with rapt attention, but he didn't care. His stomach angrily growled; he ignored it. Nothing else existed except the Grand Chorus. His chorus.

Asmeri would be ashamed.

Song swelled with the faintest flick of the Director's white baton. When he waved his arms like a calm breeze, the chorus filled the auditorium with buttery smooth legato. If he shifted to choppy beat counts, they would shift to precise staccato. Held notes swelled and retreated, generating energy and interest. Nothing was wasted. Every note was cherished. And still Malachi pushed them, stopping when something wasn't exactly perfect.

Traven was mesmerized, and his very being yearned to be on those risers.

They took a break, and Traven reluctantly pushed himself up to standing. His leg was stiff, and he had to hobble back into the hallway before someone saw him. The rules were unclear about sitting in on rehearsals. He had nearly made it to the lobby when Shissel Morayne stepped in front of him, flanked by three other tenors.

"Again I see you somewhere you don't belong, Uncorded."

Traven drew in a deep breath, setting his shoulders back. "I work here."

The tenor faked brushing dust off of his metallic red vest and leaned in close. "And yet, you don't belong here. You stick out like mud on marble, a stain on this sacred building. Perhaps I'll have Lord Daelthorne give old Nawny a talking-to. You're upsetting the other Gold Cords with your shabbiness."

Traven lowered his head, staring underneath his eyebrows. His voice held the slightest tremble. "I think it's best for you and your friends to move on. I'm just doing my job."

"Is that what you were doing? Sitting on your ass while we rehearsed. Daydreaming about a fancy cord on your shoulder, is what you were doing. Why don't you head down to the District Hall and see if they are handing out red cords? They'll take anyone." The tenors chuckled.

His belly started to burn again. He wasn't sure what to do. He had never met someone who disliked him without provocation. Did Shissel really hate him because of his clothes? He tried to push through the group, but they stopped him. Shissel borrowed one of his friends' canes and tapped it against a lamp mounted on the wall. It popped and shattered, sprinkling the rug-covered hallway with glass. "There, now you have something to do besides ogle us."

Traven clenched his fists, his eyes narrowing. How could

someone be so carelessly obnoxious? Back home Shissel would have been left out in the cold until he came to his senses, but Traven doubted he could carry the man all the way to the FrostLine. His nostrils flared, and something hot and painful blossomed in his throat. As he growled, another light popped down the hallway, and the glass rattled with reverberation.

"I've already told you once, Shissel—stop pestering my friend here before I let him thrash you." Finn's voice called out like a hot knife through butter. The tension in Traven's chest snapped like a taut rope, and he shook his head to clear it. His rage disappeared like heat out of an open window, replaced with an odd sense of calm. The lights flickered playfully, and he remembered them doing the same during his solo back home.

Finn, Elena, Kael, and Mariss put themselves between him and Shissel. Traven was thankful for the interruption, but Shissel was less pleased. "Sticking up for street urchins is beneath a Gold Cord."

"Anyone can be a Gold Cord, no matter their status," Elena interjected with her icy stare.

"Platitudes for the less fortunate," Shissel spat. "A panacea to keep the peasants hopeful. You should know that, Miss Marrenvale. You are one of us."

She placed a slender finger on his chest. "I am nothing like you. Run along, before my father has words with your patron."

As the tenor weighed his next actions, Traven felt a stab of panic. Was Shissel telling the truth? Was he doomed to fail because he was born in a Yodel? Was everyone in Resonance Heights laughing at him behind his back?

Kael took an opportunity to break the silence. "As Section Leader, don't make me report this breach in decorum to Director Rivers. You appear to have destroyed Opera House property. You are expected to behave honorably as a reflection of Hearthmere; you are dismissed."

Whatever fire Shissel had in his belly simmered as Kael spoke. His logic rippled through the other tenors, and some shuffled backwards, pulling at Shissel's sleeve. Kael folded his arms and waited for them to leave.

Once they had left, Traven bent down to clean up the broken glass. Mariss crouched next to him, placing the glass in a handkerchief. "You need to be careful. Shissel is sponsored by Lord Daelthorne just like me. He could ruin things if you push him too far."

"I haven't done anything. He hates me because I'm a farmer, or because my clothes are worn," Traven muttered.

"To that end," Finn leaned against the wall. "We do need to do something about those clothes. I can see your bloody bandages from across the auditorium. Meet me at the fountain tomorrow morning. I'll introduce you to Nerise, and we can at least make you look like you belong here."

Traven was about to protest, but Finn raised a hand and smiled at him in a way that disarmed him. "I'll not hear any argument. You won't get a patron looking like that, and I've plenty of glimmer. Tomorrow. Fountain."

They retreated back to the auditorium for the second half of rehearsal, leaving him to clean up the rest of the glass. Mariss gave him one last glance as they left, a reassuring smile on her face.

He would repay Finn, every last gloam.

⌢

Traven limped up to his room at the Final Measure and settled onto the bed. The innkeeper handed him a wedge of cheese and a carafe of water, and Traven decided to sup in his room. He wasn't in the mood for company, not after Shissel.

The tenor wormed his way under his skin, taunting him with his sharp words and permanent sneer. He knew he should keep calm, but the injustice of it caused his blood to boil. Everything lately had him on edge. Nothing was going the way he had planned. He was scrubbing walls and replacing fuses when he should be singing. He was sleeping in a lumpy bed not much warmer than his old home, with his stores of glimmer rapidly dwindling with every meal. And in the back of his mind, a worry began to eat away at him.

Why was Glysterium misbehaving around him? And why was Finn always there when it did? He ate in silence, reflecting on the Gold Cord's harsh words. *A panacea to keep the peasants hopeful.* Was that all the medallion was? False hope? Hearthmere had already slowed down his ascension to the stage, and now he feared his dream was dead before he had even left home. Was it even possible for someone like him to earn a gold cord? Elena seemed to think so.

Rolan shuffled in, resting his shoulder on the doorframe. "Evening, how was tinkering?"

Traven winced while laying back on his pillow, keeping the knee on his wounded leg bent. "You remember that tenor at the Crooning Cello? I nearly smashed his head in today."

Rolan watched him settle into the bed with narrowed eyes. "Hold that thought. I wanna hear about it, but first I need to see that leg."

"What? It's fine." Traven protested.

"Then a little look won't hurt anything. Off with the trousers." Rolan folded his arms.

"No. I'm not taking off my pants."

"You can do it, or I can do it. You might be broader than a barn, but I reckon that fever has made you weak." Rolan took a menacing step forward, closing the door behind him.

Traven shot him a frustrated look, his eyes bulging. "I said it's fine. I can walk on it."

Rolan knelt down, batting away Traven's hands. "Stop being

bashful. It ain't like that. You can't afford to rip these any further, so stop fighting me."

Traven propped himself up on his elbows. "Fine! Fine. I'll do it."

"So full of yerself, you think I'm trying to accost you," Rolan growled.

He grunted while getting the pants over his bandage, then sat in his undergarments with a frown. Rolan curled his lip at the yellowed bandage. "You got any spare cloth? These bandages look like they haven't been changed since we got here."

"I'm fresh out." Traven huffed. "Aside from DirgeMaul, I'm wearing everything I own, remember?"

"We'll figure something out. Let's take a look." Rolan started to unwrap the bandage, then grunted when he got to the last stubborn layer. The cloth was stuck to his wound, and each tug made Traven grimace.

"Here goes." Rolan placed a hand on his chest, leaning hard while he yanked.

"Chords! What are you doing?" Traven yelped.

"The bandage was stuck, icehead. That's what happens when you don't change 'em every day." Rolan tossed the bandage on the floor and sniffed. "Slush, you gotta take better care of this. It's infected."

Traven wanted to protest some more, but he knew Rolan was right. He had been too afraid to acknowledge it. "I just...I don't have time. We have so much to do."

"We've got a month before we even step foot in the Opera House. You should spend that time resting up, maybe then you'll have both legs when you audition." Rolan shook his head at Traven's stubbornness. "Hold tight, I'll get a washbasin and try to scrounge up some bandages. The innkeeper should have something."

Traven dropped his head onto his pillow and groaned while

his roommate stepped out. He didn't have time to be wounded. He hadn't even begun looking for his brother, and now he needed to find a patron. There might be a month of waiting ahead of him, but he could spend that time setting himself up for success. Rest was not going to get him there.

His eyes had long closed when Rolan returned with a steaming ceramic bowl and a bundle of fresh white cloth. "Bastard charged me two glimmer for these. That's as much as the train ride here."

"I'll pay you back."

"You will," Rolan agreed while wringing a steaming cloth. "Ready? This is hotter than two newlyweds after their Union Hymn."

Traven sucked in a breath and nodded.

The initial contact burned his skin, but the dockworker was far more gentle than he expected. The cleaning was uncomfortable, and once or twice Rolan had to push him back down with two fingers to his chest and a glare that could have mirrored Chadden when he had broken his brother's favorite toy. He resigned himself to gripping the sides of the bed.

"Tell me about that puffed-up brat," Rolan said quietly as he worked.

"I don't get it. He doesn't even know me, and has decided to hate my guts. He kept going on about me not belonging here, that I was inferior to him because of my birthplace. I nearly clobbered him when he smashed a light next to my head, after I spent all day replacing bulbs."

"I think that's more about him than it is about you. I reckon he's got a Gold Cord because of the strings his family pulled, you'll earn it from pure talent. Makes him feel small, so he pushes his power over you while he can." Rolan rinsed the bloody rag and wrung it out.

Traven studied his friend as if he had grown a third eye. "I thought he was just a prick."

Rolan shook the bed with his laughter. "He may be, but usually people who lash out carry a whole shipment of pain on the inside. Better to just ignore him, he'll find someone new to pester when he sees he can't provoke you."

"I'd rather just duel him and be done with it."

"He won't accept a duel. What he said at the tavern was right; he gains nothing from it. If he loses, he loses to a manure-smelling bumpkin…and if he wins, he's bullying someone less fortunate than he. You might be better off just thumping him once or twice."

"I can't risk it. If I assault a Gold Cord, my shot is ruined." Traven took a frustrated breath, then realized what Rolan just said. "I don't smell like manure!"

Rolan raised his eyebrows and gave a little sniff, curling his lips. Traven roared and threw a pillow, hitting him squarely in the face. He was reminded of the way he and Chadden used to poke at each other. Even with his rough edges, it was nice to have someone looking out for him. A smile grew on Rolan's face.

"And," Traven continued. "This is the second time Finn stepped in for me. He seems friendly enough, but I suspect he wants something from me."

"Most people here do. Probably the biggest difference between home and here, nobody is selfless in Hearthmere. Just remember that, and keep an extra eye on Kael. His mind is going a mile a minute." Rolan pulled a folded piece of paper from his coat. "You seen these?"

Traven snatched it, and Rolan started to wrap his leg as he read. "They are all over the lower districts. Groundsong Commons and Whisper Ward. Seems like people are going missing all of the time."

He immediately thought of Chadden. "Do you think that's what happened to my brother?"

Rolan patted his leg, making him squirm in his bed.

"Tomorrow you go to a healer first thing, get a poultice. I cleaned it well enough, but that's as far as I can go. You need to draw out the infection. After work, come stop by Warehouse 5 and we can go talk to the contact on that poster. Maybe you can get some answers."

Traven had no intention of seeing a healer tomorrow; he had too much to do. He nodded until Rolan stopped staring into his eyes to get his point across.

"And," Rolan said as he flopped onto his own bed. "If yer a good boy, you might get to talk to a spirit."

He asked Rolan to elaborate, but the man closed his eyes and started to breathe like a blacksmith bellows. How did he fall asleep so fast?

Adjusting in his bed shot another lance of pain up his leg. Perhaps he would go see a healer.

Chapter XIX

For the second day in a row, Traven watched the sunrise spill over the city.

His walks up Cantata Row as the streetlamps winked out were peaceful. Before the hordes of commerce pushed against the seams of the cobblestone road, he was able to take his time, admire the stonework, and listen to the Glysterium heartbeat of the city. The few people awake at this hour gave him a wide berth as he limped by.

He rested on the lip of the Concordia Plaza's fountain, leg quivering from the hike up Cantata Row. Before falling asleep last night, he realized he had overcommitted. He was supposed to meet Nawny and Finn at the same time. Thankfully, the tinker was punctual.

"He returns for day two!" Nawny called across the empty plaza, his voice quivering in his own way.

Traven grunted and braced against the stonework to stand. Nawny grimaced. "Chords, that was painful to watch. You get that leg checked out?"

"Not yet. I did have it cleaned last night. I was going to ask if perhaps I could use this morning for a few errands, and maybe see about the leg?" He didn't want to lie, but he didn't want to admit he needed to take time off on his second day. Behaving like this back home would have blown gossip through Grendal like wildfire.

Nawny shrugged and handed him a scone. "I'll be backstage working on the overheads. If you don't find me there, I'll be back at the shop. You did a good job, maybe only a few missed bulbs…but you can catch up today. Then we can take a trip down to their furnace; I suspect the Baron will want it replaced before the Empress gets here."

He accepted the scone with an appreciative nod. "I would very much like to see that. The largest furnace we had back home was about chest height."

"This one's a bit larger than that, but still nothing compared to the one underneath the Citadel. If I can get you clearance, we might be able to pay a visit." Nawny gave him a fatherly squeeze on the shoulder. "You get that leg fixed—no need to make life harder than it already is."

He didn't say anything as Nawny ventured to the Opera House, but felt himself growing impatient with people telling him what to do. He would get his leg checked out, but there was too much for him to do today. Maybe tomorrow.

A familiar voice chirped across Concordia Plaza, "Traven! Bass extraordinaire."

He spun around to a grinning Finn and stoic Kael, their arms sporting long loaves of bread. He waited for them to approach him, then sang a Greeting Hymn. Kael's lips curled at the edges just enough for Traven to catch it, and Finn straightened his back with mock seriousness while returning the song in his baritone timbre. He supposed Kael wasn't much of a traditionalist.

Kael repositioned the bread in his arms and led them across Concordia Plaza. "I was hoping to see your GlysterHammer this morning." His tone was measured and controlled.

"The last time I had it out in public, the guards wanted to seize it. We had to pay them off." Traven struggled to keep up with his pace.

Finn noticed his limp and slowed down to walk shoulder-to-shoulder. "There's plenty of time for that, Kael. For now, we need to ensure our bass friend doesn't get mistaken for a beggar. Nerise will transform you. Shissel will eat his feathered hat."

Kael groaned ahead of them. "She won't marry you, no matter how many customers you bring in."

"A boy can try. Perhaps this one will do the trick," Finn retorted.

People had begun to leave their homes for the day and paused with respectful silence, or stepped aside to let them by. A few murmured the Hymn of Greeting as they ventured past the residential district, and Traven stopped singing back when he noticed the Gold Cords weren't doing the same. Sweat was forming on his brow; he still wasn't used to the heat of Hearthmere. Especially this close to the Citadel.

"It's very interesting to me, how much deference is shown to a simple braided cord." Traven mused.

"Being a Gold Cord is certainly commendable, but we're no different than any of them. Well, except Elena maybe. She's practically carved from marble." Kael shrugged.

"And cold as, to boot." Finn punched him in the arm. "Good luck getting her to your apartment."

Traven laughed. Elena was handsome in her own way, but he liked altos…they always seemed more down to earth.

They turned off of the street and onto a pathway lined with box-shaped green bushes. Traven had to pretend not to stare, but he must have failed miserably.

"Oh, just touch one and get it over with. You haven't seen a bush before, have you?" Finn plucked a branch and swirled it between his fingers.

It seemed like sacrilege, to prune something so rare and precious. The leaves were rounded and shiny on one side and smelled fresh when he put them up to his nose. "I had never seen a tree other than pine until a few days ago. Plants back home are just dangling vines or small vegetables. I could almost forget the Ever-Winter was out there."

"It's out there. We'll have to take a trip down to the Whisper Ward one of these days when you start forgetting what it's like outside the walls," Kael muttered.

"Is it just colder out there near the walls?" Traven asked.

"Colder, more desperate. Hearthmere is beautiful in most places, but people go to the Whisper Ward when they have nothing left…and it's still better than being outside. Barely. The heat hardly reaches out there, so freezing is still a danger so close to the wall."

He wondered if Chadden might be shivering in the Whisper Ward right now. Why hadn't he sent a single letter? Hopefully the Cobbler would give him some clues.

Kael led them past building after building carved out of white stone. Storefronts gleaming with GlysterLight illuminated artisanal goods, glimmering golden bolts of thread, or overpriced bottles of wine. He did pause at a window with lacquered canes sitting in a tall bucket, but Finn tugged at his arm with a laugh. "Anything up here will cost you more than a month's stay in GroundSong Commons."

He wondered how much he would end up owing the baritone.

Kael turned into a building with the words "EMPORIUM" chiseled into the storefront. Lush overstuffed lounge chairs dotted the floor, a mountain of fluffy embroidered pillows piled on top of them. Mannequins of men and women showcased intricate patterned vests and billowing dresses in colors Traven had never seen. In the corner were three mirrors from floor to ceiling, with a raised platform for someone to inspect themselves. A sylphlike young woman with hair adorned with glittering Glysterium shot Finn a beaming smile when they walked inside. She had powder and rouge on her face in a way that sharpened her cheekbones and accentuated her delicate features. "Brought in another stray for me to remodel?" Her voice was playful.

"Not just any stray, a friend of special import. He's in dire need of your considerable talents. Meet Traven, soon to be bass of the Grand Chorus." Finn's overly-dramatic bow made his hair touch the floor.

"Nerise." She offered her hand.

Traven shuffled forward to take her hand and cleared a lump in his throat as she bowed. "A pleasure."

"That's a voice, for sure. Perhaps I should have you come read poetry one of these nights for my regulars." She politely removed her hand and circled him with pursed lips. "Let us see what we have here. Tall and dark, with plenty of brawn, though in need of a good shave and a bath. You would do well with creams and golds, perhaps the green of Hearthmere when you are feeling particularly…political."

He rubbed his head while being studied, shooting a wild look to Kael. Kael shrugged as if to say, *You are on your own.*

Nerise traced her fingers across his shoulders and biceps, whipping out a tape measure to wrap around his waist. Finn cleared his throat and leaned against a mannequin. "He'll need a full run of clothes, but let's perhaps start him with something that makes him look a little more…distinguished."

"Quite." She stood in front of him, pinching her lips between two fingers. "I think we will start with green and silver for standard business, with cream and gold on special occasions and solos…You will have solos, correct?"

"I certainly hope so," he rumbled.

Her cheeks flushed when he spoke again, and he could hear some appreciative murmurs from the patrons in the shop. "Poetry night, for sure," she whispered to herself while taking the last of her measurements.

She looked at Finn with a flirtatious smile from behind Traven. "You keep bringing treasures in like this, and perhaps we will have that dinner date."

"Are you sure you want to? I may have outdone myself this time." Finn smiled sweetly.

"Indeed," a husky woman's voice sounded from the doorway.

She stood at the entrance, her luminous brown skin framed by silvery ringlets of hair piled on top of her head. Her silver dress was impossibly tight at the waist, and billowed out to fill the entire doorway. Glysterium buttons dotted her hair, hung from her ears, and covered her neckline. Her dark eyes were focused and calculating. He couldn't be sure, but he thought Kael growled as she and her attendants cleared the space between them.

Finn straightened himself and stepped to the side. "Mistress Thariel Vexlane, this is Traven."

She studied him much like Nerise had, but with something dangerous in her eyes. In a way, it reminded him of the Red Woman on the train. He felt small, despite towering over her. "Traven Caelhardt. How fortuitous we happen to have met here; I had anticipated *catching* you at the Opera House this evening." She emphasized the word catch with clipped consonants.

"Me? How do you know me?" He hated that he stammered.

Thariel whipped open a Glysterium-lined fan and batted at her neckline. "Darling, I know everything in this city."

He thought he was a nobody, but apparently some mention of his passing had been made…but by whom? Should he be proud that his name was already spreading? She reached up and grasped his beard in her gloved fingers, tugging just enough to make him wince. Her face was close to his, and he could smell the powder on her nose. "Do get cleaned up. You could have the strongest voice in the city, but no one will want anything to do with you looking like….this." She released him with a sneer.

Thariel swayed over to Nerise, dropping a purse of glimmer into her hands and discussing something out of earshot. Apparently, she was done speaking with him. His lips twitched as he chewed the inside of his mouth. Kael's words echoed back to him; he felt like livestock. "That was interesting." Traven forced a laugh.

"Dangerous," Kael leaned in to whisper. "Like most of the bureaucrats. She's clever, and powerful. You could use that to your advantage, if you play it smart."

Did he even know how to do that? Singing was becoming more complicated by the minute. Finn shot Kael a firm look before softening. "And she's not terrible to look at, even if she could be my mother. You could do much worse as far as Patrons go."

Traven glanced over their heads to watch the ladies speak. He had a feeling Thariel was building a chord he couldn't hear. The noble's gaze lingered as she drifted past, patting Finn on the chest. The way Finn stiffened made Kael chuckle as she swayed out of the building. A collective sigh escaped them all.

Nerise bounced back over to him and took more measurements while an assistant jotted down the numbers. She worked down his body, and he nervously met Finn's gaze when she neared his waistline. Finn just winked. When she reached his legs, Nerise leaned back and pointed to the wound. "I don't want this bleeding all over my work."

He groaned. Not this again.

He never should have let them get a rise out of him.

The dockworkers snickered every time he passed, elbowing each other over his controlled fall. Hennik, the skinny man who warned him the day before, sidled up next to him at every pass.

"So what did you hear?" He had prodded.

Rolan ignored him. He didn't like making a habit of talking about his dead wife. He kept to himself, stacking crate after crate until the midday bell. Eventually, Hennik gave up, but he never stopped nervously glancing at the ceiling.

He opened his locker, and let out a rueful chuckle. He should have known. "Very funny, slushheads. I think you need to come up with some new material."

Some roared at his luck, while others shook their heads and carried on with their conversations. Whoever was doing this didn't have the nerve to fess up. Hennik appeared at his side and gave a sidelong glance to the supervisor Chauncy, then jerked his head to the rafters.

"If I fall and break my neck, I'll haunt whoever did this in truth," Rolan announced to the warehouse while beginning his climb.

"Rolan!" Chauncy shouted. "What are you doing?"

He was already halfway up the stack. "Getting my lunch sir, I seem to have misplaced it up in the rafters."

Whatever Chauncy said next, he ignored. Traven's leg had him in a foul mood. The man was going to lose it if he didn't choke down his pride and see a healer. Traven was as relentless as a glacier. Rolan understood that idleness meant death out in the Yodels, but he was more than willing to pick up the slack and let Traven rest. He considered saying exactly that.

He wasn't sure if he believed in spirits, but the hair rising on the back of his neck suggested he was more spooked than he wanted to admit. He very much wanted to turn around and climb back to the spice-dusted dirt. Every crate he scaled added another layer of goosebumps. He reached the top and grunted.

There it sat, his lunch neatly placed just under the GlysterLamp. "At least they are predictable."

He considered snatching it and quickly heading down, but

decided that would make the pranks worse. Despite his better judgement, he pulled himself up the rest of the way and sat with his legs dangling over the edge.

Like yesterday, his sandwich had a perfect bite taken out of the edge, too small for anyone down below. "Help yerself, why don't ya," he grumbled while biting over it.

Rolan leaned over and spied Hennik craning his neck between bites. He gave a friendly wave and faked a broad smile. As far as he knew, Hennik was pretending to be timid and meek. He was just as likely to be the trickster as the rest of them. "Can't trust one of 'em. At least they left me most of my meal."

A giggle tickled his ears, so faint he thought it might have been his imagination. He froze, his skin prickling, heart thumping. It reminded him of strange noises he would often hear in his mushroom caves. He took a deep breath and shook it off. "Not today, spirit. Yer just gonna have to enjoy my company. I ain't scaring."

The lights winked in response. His stomach fluttered.

"Just Glysterium fluctuation. You'll have to try harder than that to spook me. Yesterday you caught me off guard. Show me something interesting." Rolan shook his sandwich in the air.

He was a little disappointed in the quiet that settled over the rest of his lunch. The dockworkers were beginning to gather near the warehouse entrance in anticipation of the next shipment, so Rolan wrapped the cheese wedge he had set aside and placed it where he had been sitting.

"For your company," he chuckled to himself.

Chapter XX

Rolan watched Traven limp across the Warehouse square with growing concern. He was obviously in pain, but pushing through it. Rolan was surprised the stitches hadn't ripped.

His back was stiff from a hard day's work, and he spent the time waiting massaging his shoulders. Hennik lingered for a while after their shift, trying to pry small talk out of him. After the fourth time Rolan gave him a one-word answer, he finally got the hint. The man sang a rough Hymn of Farewell and disappeared into the sea of shipping crates.

Rolan started to make a face as Traven neared, but the bass waved his hand. "I don't want to hear it," he puffed.

"I already said my piece this morning. Yer a grown man. If you want a mechanical leg, that's your decision." Rolan shrugged.

Traven opened his mouth, probably to say something smart, then appeared to think better of it. The kid had a sharp tongue when he used it, but his big heart must have intervened this time. Rolan led them over to the central spire and pointed to the dozens of missing posters on the exterior wall. "More of these at the District Chorus house. I checked this morning."

Traven pored over each poster. "What did the District Chorus have to say about your audition?”

“Same thing, wait till next season. Made me feel right stupid about trying to walk into the tail end of concert preparation. They didn’t give a slush about the medallion.”

“Chords, some of these go back ten cycles.” Traven cursed. It always sounded funny to him, as if Traven was trying it out for the first time.

“Only thing I noticed was that it’s all singers. See here? Bass, alto, tenor. Always a voice part.” Rolan tapped a poster.

His friend took a ginger step backwards to take a look at the entire wall. “How many of these are copied on the other buildings?”

“Most, but there are so many it’s hard to keep track.” Rolan answered.

“Let’s take a few of the most recent. The trail will be fresher than these older ones. I don’t know if this is what happened to my brother, but maybe one clue will give us a thread to pull.” Traven looked worn out. “There are far too many for random disappearances. Somebody has to know something.”

“That’s what I was thinking. I wonder if anyone else looked into this?” Rolan looked up to the Dome; the sun was starting to set. “Maybe a Bailiff or guard captain?”

Traven snatched a handful more posters from the wall and splayed them out on a nearby shipping crate. “More than half of these are from the Whisper Ward, only a few in Resonance Heights.”

“Nobles probably don’t wanna advertise one of their own gone missing,” Rolan offered.

“A good chance some of the Whisper Wards are people freezing to death. I haven’t been down there yet, but I hear it’s dangerously cold sometimes.” Traven turned to him. “Should we head down there, talk to your Cobbler?”

“If you can make it. I ain’t carrying you home.” Rolan

punched him in the arm.

Traven scooped up the posters with a friendly scowl and looked to the sky to get his bearings. "Let's go then."

Each step further from the Citadel brought with it an icy chill. Foot traffic was lighter away from the center of the city, and folks that were walking did so with urgency—coats clutched to their chests. The sounds of the airdock dissolved into a silence rare in the city. Cobblestone streets gave way to dirt as buildings halted and the ground sloped precipitously toward the looming walls of the FrostLine. Enormous steel pipes jutted out from the internal heating behind them, bending down to end with a gaping hole somewhere in the maze of shacks. Ramshackle buildings clustered at these openings for what little heat was left. Frost clung to haphazardly constructed shelters facing all directions in a chaotic mess. Any semblance of order the Empire had overseen in the upper districts had been abandoned. Here, people only cared about survival. Rolan felt for the knife tucked into his belt.

Their boots crunched against the dirt and stone as they carefully stepped down the steep decline. The sounds of industry had been replaced with coughs and sniffles, with the occasional shout off in the distance. Traven's breath was coming out in ragged white plumes, but he was keeping up. Haggard people knelt at the base of their homes, a tin cup rattling with precious few gloam. Rolan knelt down and offered a few gloam by placing it directly in a woman's hand, whispering, "I'm looking for the Chilly Cobbler."

The woman looked suspiciously at his leather boots and wobbled her whiskered jaw. "Won't be anything there better 'un what you got. There be a main road circling the whole of it all. Head left when you meet it."

He nodded to her and tossed a slice of bread he had saved for dinner; she likely needed it more. A small animal darted just out of his vision, and Traven jumped.

The old woman cackled mischievously. "First time seeing a rat?"

"I thought they were gone, just like everything else." Traven's voice went up an octave.

"Oh no lad, plenty of beasties surviving out there, just none of them worth eatin'."

What other creatures might be living in the city, hiding in the shadows? Other than monsters in the frozen wasteland, most critters hadn't survived the Ever-Winter. Crates of leather were tracked almost as closely as Glysterium.

They pressed on. A grimy old man bellowed with a gravelly voice, demanding for them to buy his "goods." He pushed a harp string, a broken tuning fork, anything he could salvage. Rolan ducked his head and tried to imitate the villagers' downtrodden demeanor—ignoring him—but it still didn't work. The man cursed at them and spat, but didn't provoke them any further. Traven looked relieved.

They turned left at the only thing they could consider a road, and grimaced when their feet pulled from the mud with a slurp, step after step. "Ugh, this is worse than the thawing pit." Traven pulled up the hood of his coat and tucked his hands into his pockets.

Children with hollow stares and red noses followed them like ghosts. Rolan tried to glare at them while they shoved their hands in his face, but his glower quickly dissolved. By the time they arrived at the Cobbler's, both men had emptied their coinpurses.

The building was a mismatch of metal sheets and loose bricks. A makeshift sign dangled on one chain, reading CHILEY COBLER. The roof was slanted, sagging to one side, and Traven had to duck to get inside. A woman with large bags under her eyes and her hair in a messy bun leaned over a counter piled with dirty and worn shoes. He expected pleasant surprise in her reaction, but instead received suspicion. She looked down at their feet. "What do you want?"

Rolan sang the greeting hymn while pulling out the missing poster—she did not return the song. "Pardon the interruption. I was hoping I could ask some questions and perhaps help you find a….Tanneric?" he read from the poster.

Her eyes darted to the doorway. "I don't know what you are talking about." She folded her arms across her chest.

Traven cocked his head. "Then why is there a poster directing us exactly here?"

She brushed a strand of disobedient hair from across her face and then snatched the poster from Rolan's hands. He caught a glimpse of gold glinting on her finger. It struck him as odd. "Quite a shiny ring you've got there."

She flustered and hid her hand. "You can leave now. I don't need any more help."

Traven leaned an elbow on her counter, smiling as best he could. "This isn't the first time you've been contacted, is it? Who gave you that ring?"

She shrugged and looked up at the ceiling. "This has been in my family for generations. I don't need your help."

Rolan frowned as he mimicked Traven's lean. "People down here are freezing to death and you wear yer ticket to warmth? I don't think so."

Her eyes darted between the two of them, panic creasing her brow. Rolan smiled as best he could and laughed to ease the tension. "Sorry, I'm not doing this very well. I'm not great with words."

Traven cleared his throat. "My brother is missing, too. Been gone for a few cycles now. Have you seen a Chadden Caelhardt? We're not just trying to help you, we're trying to get any clues we can."

She appeared to soften for a heartbeat, then her eyes went hard. "I can't help you. Your brother is probably dead."

Rolan put a gentle hand on Traven's shoulder in preparation for an outburst. His leg was making him more than irritable lately, and they didn't need to scare the lady. "Please, anything. Where were they the day they disappeared? Who were they with? We can pay for information." He patted his empty coin purse.

That seemed to get her attention, but something was keeping her quiet. "I can't."

Traven shook his bald head in frustration. "Look, a ring can't be worth losing your loved ones over. Just tell us and we'll be on our way. Maybe I'll be able to find Tanneric for you and bring him back here."

She leaned in and whispered, "They will burn this to the ground and take everything else I have. Go away."

Traven softened his tone, "Please. I don't know this place, and my brother might still be alive. Let's help each other."

She was quiet for a long time, and Rolan let her think while turning a worn boot over in his hands. Her hands, tucked under her apron, fidgeted as she worked up the courage. "A big man. Largest I have ever seen…with a blonde mohawk and a mechanical arm. I can't say any more. Please go."

Traven gave her a thin smile, then patted Rolan on the shoulder. "Looks like we're wasting our time here." He said loud enough to be heard across the street. "This lady doesn't know anything. Let's go have a drink."

Rolan played along, clearing his throat. "Sorry to have bothered you. We won't do so again."

He quickly thanked her and ducked back outside, looking carefully down the street in both directions. A thin song began to echo through the Whisper Ward, a mournful dirge played through the strings of a violin. Shutters began to slam shut and the children hovering around them had vanished. A glance into the shop revealed an empty room. The cobbler had disappeared to the back.

The skin at the back of his neck prickled.

He grabbed a squawking Traven under the armpit and hurried him off of the muddy street and into a side alley. Once tucked away into a small space between shacks, Rolan tapped his ear and put a finger to his lips.

Who would have enough glimmer for a violin down here?

He might have admired their talent, if his instincts weren't screaming at him to hide. Whoever it was, they had a reputation down here in the Whisper Ward.

Rolan didn't take the time to figure it out. He hurried Traven down side paths and around clusters of shacks, some open to the cold. Families pulled their blankets over the opening as they passed, Traven cursing under his breath. The violin didn't come closer, but hadn't fallen behind, either. "We need to hurry. I said I wouldn't carry you."

Traven grimaced and hopped on one leg back up the muddy slope. Rolan glanced behind them with raised eyebrows. Even if the sun had set, and there was barely a streetlamp down here, they were out in the open. Once the heat started to warm their cheeks, he finally stopped glancing behind them.

"Have you seen anyone matching that description? Big mohawk, mechanical arm?" He slowed enough for Traven to walk comfortably.

"Not really, anyone with a mechanical limb was clearly an Arcanum Priest. I don't think mohawks are part of their uniform," Traven joked.

Rolan noticed his friend's pale face and beading sweat, despite the cold air. "Let's get something to eat and drink. I'm exhausted. You might be able to go on, but I'm about to collapse."

Traven didn't say anything back, and Rolan was thankful. The man was stubborn as stone.

Chapter XXI

For the next two weeks, Traven hobbled up to the Opera House and saw to the repairs under Nawny's tutelage. The tinker praised him as he quickly picked up on things, only needing to be shown something once or twice before running off to do it himself. The work gave him purpose, and distracted him from the growing pain in his leg. Every day Nawny or Rolan would give him that fatherly look, and Traven quickly deflected with a funny anecdote or insisting that he felt fine.

But he didn't feel fine. Walking up Cantata Row was laborious, and he was covered in sweat by the time he arrived at Concordia Plaza. Every morning, he would splash his face in the cool water while waiting for the sun to rise. He couldn't rest. Nawny was counting on him…and he needed every moment inside the Opera House.

His work turned out to be a boon. Every day he would listen to the Grand Chorus rehearse. He had to force himself to keep moving, as Nawny stacked more and more responsibility on him. By the second week he was given full run of the building, with a quick morning check-in to cover any emergencies. Eventually, he started to pick up on the melody, and hummed along with the bass section as he maintained the building. Cantata Row echoed with his voice as he sang on the way back home, and he had even earned a nod from a Red Cord one evening. The music was living in his mind, and he was starting to wake with the concert playing through his head.

A few days after his visit with Nerise, she'd arrived at the Opera House with a large black box tied with a gold ribbon. Finn tapped him on the shoulder, startling him while he was focused on a sparking GlysterLine in the hallway. Hastily opening it while taking care not to get grease on the clothes, he pulled out clothes she said were, "More appropriate for a man of his potential." She had outdone herself, and gave him a reassuring squeeze when he scooped her up in his arms. He changed in the storeroom immediately, tossing the black and brown clothes of his home into a scrap pile and emerging into the hallway in shining cream and silver. This seemed to irritate Shissel even more.

Everything he did irritated the tenor. If he kept his distance, Shissel would mock him for hiding. If he stayed still for too long to bask in the harmonies of the Grand Chorus, Shissel would threaten to report that he was dawdling while important work was to be done. When Mariss pulled him into a corner to sing along with the rest of the quartet, Shissel would sneer and make a sideways comment about wasting her time with peasants. Someone was always there to intervene, be it Finn and his friendly dismissal, Elena and her outright aggression, or Mariss pulling him away from the conflict to sing.

He lived for their little rehearsals, when the five of them worked through the performance set. At first, Finn had invited him as a friendly gesture, but when he started matching resonance with each of them in a way that made the air vibrate, that changed. Their eyes had gone wide in surprise. Even Kael couldn't hide his smile.

Every day at midday, they would wave him over for another

quintet. A few times they sang right in the auditorium, letting their voices bounce off of the balcony above them. He swore he saw Director Rivers look his way more than once, his imperious eyebrow twitching.

Rolan's weeks took on a different tone. The warehouse work was steady, and the first day after he left a wedge of cheese, he opened his locker to find not only his lunch, but a sack of Pizzo spice on top of it. Whoever was picking on him must have grown a conscience.

He started taking his lunches on top of the crates, talking to Moira, or more likely the air. He liked to pretend that someone was listening as he rambled, and it felt good to have someone to vent to. He spoke of the missing people, piecing together what little he had gleaned from his sources. After a few days, he would find something small sitting on the crate. He would leave things too. A few cuts of salami were repaid with a smooth round jade bead. Another wedge of cheese earned him a bundle of quills wrapped in a pink ribbon. It was becoming clearer to him that the warehouse wasn't haunted…but inhabited.

His curiosity got the better of him, and after work on his second week he teetered on hands and knees across the rafters toward a dark corner in the back. The shadows faded away when he neared, and he saw a small blanket next to an empty crate on a row of wooden boards. The lights flickered wildly, and he found himself bouncing to the floor faster than he could say his wife's name.

Investigations into the disappearances were slow. He had convinced Traven to stay home most nights to rest, despite his growling protests. Rolan could cover more ground if he could jog through the streets, which would make the investigations go faster. The prospect of finding clues about his brother kept Traven in his bed, and Rolan was thankful logic had defeated pride.

No one wanted to talk. It was usually the same story—wide

glances to the rooftops while whispering for him to go away. A few of them spat in his face, while others slammed the door on him. He was surprised to see such a visceral reaction from folks outside of the Whisper Ward, but it appeared "Mohawk's" reach extended to the finer points of town as well.

What unnerved Rolan the most were the random instruments playing from the rooftops and around corners. Someone would be playing the flute, or strumming a harp with the same dirge he had heard on the violin. He couldn't put his finger on it, and had no real justification to be wary, but it always made his hair stand on edge. Traven had told him to take DirgeMaul after the third night, and he agreed on the fifth. Whoever it was, they would regret spooking him if they ever met. The guards didn't bother him, as most of them didn't frequent the muddy slopes near the FrostLine anyways.

The contacts Traven had selected were all dried up, and he gathered another set of ten to splay out on the floor of their room. It was there that the two men talked through the clues, but they had more questions than answers at this point. Traven seemed content to theorize with him, and once or twice made comments that hinted at hope that Chadden was still alive. Rolan tried his best not to deflate that hope with sarcasm.

Pay had begun to come in, with Traven offering most of his glimmer to make up for the time he had spent leeching. Rolan had never brought it up, but the young lad had funny notions about honor.

They still practiced their music. Traven insisted on keeping the voice prepared at all times. He was always energetic after working at the Opera House, humming lines of intricate music Rolan had to really focus on to comprehend.

Their friendship was settling into something comforting and brotherly. He appreciated the company, even when Traven was prickly on bad days.

The boy needed to take care of his leg, and soon. The winces were longer, the grunts more prominent. Despite his growing discomfort, Traven wouldn't slow down unless forced to. Luckily, Rolan was stronger than he was.

When Traven barged into their room—his face beaming with excitement—he suspected he had found a clue.

But it was bigger than that.

Chapter XXII

The imminent arrival of the Empress had the entire city working frenetically. Traven's quiet walks up Cantata Row had been invaded by city officials barking orders at men and women hanging banners on every lamp post. Street sweepers sang alongside window washers in a playful call-and-repeat. Every building had been covered in green and gold banners, and every beggar on the edges of the Row had been chased off to the Whisper Ward.

Nawny was already sitting at the fountain when he limped under the Citadel, scone in hand. He jumped up when Traven crossed the threshold and helped him up the stairs to the Opera House. "Big news. The Empress has officially declared her attendance." His voice quivered. "You've done a tremendous job fixing the major things, but we need to transition to cleaning… especially Empress Wiseria's private booth. Start there. Be sure to hit the Baron's booth next, and then work your way from top to bottom."

"Understood," Traven said between delicious bites. He needed to find out where these scones were made.

Nawny paused in the lobby. "She'll be here in two weeks,

but we need to be ready for an inspection in one. The Baron will likely oversee the work, and he's not a man you want to offend. I think you'll do a fine job. I'll be down in the furnace room if you need me."

Traven let his mentor go, and hummed as he gathered the appropriate cleaning supplies. Cleaning was probably his least favorite thing to do, but he needed the glimmer and he didn't want to let Nawny down.

The private booth entrances were on the second floor, and before long he was on his hands and knees, scrubbing at the brass while singing. His voice carried through the auditorium with delicious reverb, even tucked away in the balcony. He sang lightly for a time, then stood to really let his voice loose. He grabbed the gold banister and roared through the first few pages of their concert, his chest shaking with vibrato. This was the only place he could sing at full volume. Every attempt at the inn resulted in angry shouting from the common room.

One of the doors downstairs squeaked as it opened, and Traven instantly lowered from fortissimo to piano while ducking his head. He hadn't expected anyone to be in the building this early. "Hello?" a tenor called out. "Who is that?"

"Slush," Traven cursed to himself. After a few weeks of listening to rehearsals, he could place that voice anywhere.

Director Rivers.

"Hello?" he called again.

Traven popped up from the balcony, waving his cleaning rag with a sheepish grin. "Sorry about that, just enjoying the acoustics."

"Stay there." Malachi commanded.

"Slush," Traven cursed again.

Was this the end of his career as both a tinker and a singer? Were there rules for singing in the Opera House that he wasn't aware of? Nawny hadn't said anything, neither had the headmistress who maintained the lobby. He had been singing while working for weeks. No one had bothered him until now.

The heavy curtains to the hallway peeled back, and Director Rivers popped his head in. He didn't look angry, but he didn't look happy either. It was hard to read him in the dim light. Traven smoothed out his vest and set his rag down, folding his arms behind his back in the traditional choral ready position.

Director Rivers sat down in one of the plush chairs and flicked his frilled wrist. "Do it again."

Traven's mouth went dry. He hadn't prepared for this. What if he missed a note, or forgot a phrase? The music wasn't in a place he would be comfortable performing in front of others.

A flicker of impatience furrowed the Director's brow.

Traven cleared his throat and started the opening phrase. His voice wavered and cracked, and he stopped to clear his throat again. "I'm sorry, I'm not quite warmed up."

"Breathe. Pretend I'm not here," Malachi smiled reassuringly. *As if that were possible.*

He closed his eyes and took a deep calming breath, starting over. His voice came back like an old friend, rich and sonorous. He sang through the first few minutes, adding dynamic rises and falls where Malachi had added them in rehearsals. He didn't have the music, but he had been listening intently for weeks.

His leg twitched, but he placed a firm hand on his thigh and carried on. The auditorium did its part, and the reverberation rang with impossible crispness. Director Rivers raised a finger with a small smile. "Thank you. Are you the one I see Mariss and company singing with in the halls during break?"

Traven returned his hands to his back. "Yes sir. It's just a little fun. I wanted to keep my voice fresh for next season."

"Intend to audition, do you?" He cocked his head.

Traven reached into his pocket and fished out the medallion. He never left it at home. With a shaky hand, he offered it to

Malachi. "Yes, sir."

The Director took it, flipping it over to inspect both sides. Placing it on the arm of the chair, he leaned forward and steepled his fingers. "How much of the set do you know?"

Hope made his stomach flip—this was starting to feel like an audition. "Most of the first half is memorized. I'm still working through the last few movements." He didn't mention that he knew the bass solo perfectly.

Director Rivers sat back, tapping his temple while staring out into the auditorium. "I've been watching you, singing while you work. I see the hunger in your eyes when we stand on those risers. I also hear you from the back row dropping an octave on the final notes."

Traven chuckled at himself. "I'm sorry sir, I don't mean to disrupt your rehearsals."

"Tomorrow, half an hour before rehearsal. I'll see you in my office. I trust you have an audition piece prepared." Malachi stood and offered his hand.

There it was.

Out came Traven's gap-toothed smile as he took Malachi's hand with a vigorous shake. "I do, I will. Thank you for the opportunity."

"I look forward to hearing what you've prepared." The Director released his hand and pulled back the curtain to leave. "A friendly tip…pull back on the vibrato just a little bit. Give those notes some time to linger before you hit people with the warble."

Traven stood there like an oaf as Malachi left. Easing down to the floor with weak arms, he knelt in silence…replaying every note he had just sung. Aside from the shaky start, he sang exactly like he would in rehearsal.

And now he had an audition.

The rest of the morning, he buzzed through the Opera House

without a care in the world. He sang freely, bouncing his low notes throughout the building as he swept, scrubbed, and dusted. Work that would have had him grumbling back home was completed in joyful song.

When the Gold Cords trickled into the building, Traven positioned himself near the entrance with a broad smile. He couldn't wait to tell his new friends. Some of the singers smiled back at him, caught up in his infectious excitement. Nerise's new clothes had gone a long way in improving his standing in the Opera House.

Shissel and his comrades walked up the steps, heads together in conversation. One of them elbowed the tenor and jerked his head to Traven, but he didn't care. Not even Shissel could sour his mood today.

Finn and company were a few paces behind, and Traven waved them down as Shissel sauntered past. The tenor rammed into his shoulder, and all of his weight pressed down on his weak leg. The shove put him off balance, and his leg trembled before crumbling in a searing flash. The wound slammed into a table edge, and he felt something give. Traven yelped while clutching his thigh. His fingers were wet, and blood was starting to pool underneath him.

Shissel and his friends roared while hurrying into the auditorium. Other Gold Cords stopped in shock, some paling at the sight of blood, but Mariss was the first to kneel down at his side. "Are you ok?" She sounded frantic.

"My leg," Traven groaned. "I think the stitches broke."

Elena's eyes narrowed, and Kael put a hand on Finn's chest as he started to pursue Shissel. "Later. For now, we need to get Traven somewhere quiet."

The men lifted him up and put themselves under his arms. He thanked them while hopping on one leg through the hallway. Blood was dripping on the marble all the way to the backstage doors, and they plunged into the darkness inside. Elena stood guard at the doorway, and Finn did the same near the stage after helping Traven to the floor. Did they expect Shissel and his goons to come back?

Mariss took his hand, her big eyes glinting in the low light. "You are going to be ok."

"I'm fine," Traven protested, squeezing her hand. "If the stitches popped, I can get new ones."

Finn produced a small lantern and activated the switch. It was a meager light, but enough for them to see. His face went pale as he shone the dark stain on his pants. "There is a lot of blood."

Mariss shifted down and tried her best to lift the cuff of his pants. After failing that, she gave him a grim smile and tugged at his belt. "Don't get any ideas. I need to see what's going on down there."

In any other circumstance, Traven might have died from embarrassment. The way his friends were behaving had him more concerned about safety than modesty. His pants were pulled down, leaving him in his underclothes. "Chords," Finn cursed, turning his head away.

Mariss covered her nose with her sleeve and coughed, "This is really infected…dangerously so."

Kael returned to his side and knelt down to inspect the wound. "We don't have stitches or a poultice. Mariss…" he left words unsaid.

The rest of them froze. Traven swiveled his head between the four of them as they silently communicated. Mariss looked shocked, while Finn shot Kael an incredulous look. Kael nodded, and then placed a hand on Traven's shoulder. "I can wipe him if need be, I hope it doesn't come to that."

"Wipe me? What does that even mean?" His question was interrupted as Mariss started to sing.

A blanket of warmth fell over his body, and the skin on his thigh began to pull. His heart pounded in his ears as thick pus cascaded over a leg blackened with infection. The muscles in his leg spasmed, bouncing his heel off the wooden floor with a thud. Mariss's velvety voice came out as a lullaby, and he could feel something stir in his heart. He could feel her song, he could feel…her.

For the first time in his life, he saw someone outside of himself. Mariss cared for people in a way that wasn't self-serving. She wasn't trying to prove herself like he was…just connect. Her soul was beautiful, in a way that was unfamiliar to him.

The skin moved on its own, pressing closer and closer, mending on the edges. The darkened skin around the wound shifted to a light brown. Blood stopped flowing onto the wooden floor, and a few uncomfortable moments later, the skin on his thigh was whole again. He was having a hard time catching his breath.

The pain was gone. The connection and warmth faded, ripping away from him in a way that made him ache.

Finn patted him on the head. "I suppose we're a quintet now."

Kael folded his arms. "We need to talk about your temper."

"What do you mean you can wipe me?" Traven exclaimed.

"Quiet," Kael hissed. "You saw nothing, you know nothing. Understood?"

But he didn't understand. He had just watched his leg mend in seconds, a wound that had lasted for weeks—had been bothering him for weeks. The rest of them were far too calm, Elena even looked impatient as she guarded the door. Mariss handed him his trousers and turned around as he got dressed.

"Okay." Traven lowered his voice. "Explain what just happened."

"This is not the place." Kael leaned in close. "Tell no one, not even your baritone friend. You'll have answers."

"He's definitely got the gift, I could feel it." Mariss sounded concerned.

Finn took in a deep breath and blew it back out with closed lips. "He needs to keep it under control. The Citadel might trigger more fluctuations here than normal, but he still shines like a beacon when he gets mad." Was that why Finn was always there when he lost his temper?

He helped Traven stand. "Let's meet tonight, behind the Crooning Cello. Do your best to avoid Shissel until then."

He was exhausted and had to fight to keep his eyes open. Whatever Mariss had done, it had sapped all of his energy. Would he be able to stay awake that long? "What gift? Why is everyone being so secretive?"

"You'll get answers, but not here. Meet us tonight, and try to stay away from the lamps." Kael took a final peek through the doorway.

Chapter XXIII

He could hear Traven long before he burst into their room with his infectious gap-toothed smile. With a whoop, he closed the door and whipped around to face him lying in bed. There were bags under his eyes, but they sparkled like Glysterium despite his apparent fatigue. Rolan hadn't expected Traven to be back so soon; his trips from the Opera House had been taking longer and longer each day.

Rolan propped himself up on his elbows and leaned against the headboard. "You look like a man who just saw his sweetheart naked for the first time."

Traven ignored the comment, cocking his head in consideration. He liked throwing the young man off balance from time to time. Someone had to keep him on his toes. It took Rolan a moment to realize Traven's limp was gone, as well as the grimace he used to make with each step. His pants were dark with blood, which didn't make any sense. "Did you go see a healer?"

"Uh." Traven paused, chewing his lip. "Sort of. But that's not important."

Was he drunk? Even if his leg was mended, he wouldn't be walking around like he was now unless something was clouding his mind. He was practically bouncing. "Not important?" Rolan sat up. "You could barely stand this morning, now you look about ready to do a cartwheel in the middle of the room."

Traven let the words burst out with an impish grin. "I got an audition!"

I'll be damned, Rolan thought to himself.

He gave Traven a warm smile, despite the sinking in his chest. "How did you manage that?"

The dark-skinned man jumped up on his bed and waved his arms. "I was working this morning, cleaning the auditorium when Director Rivers overheard me singing. I thought I was alone, just enjoying the acoustics. He came up and made me sing on the spot. My voice cracked at first, but then my nerves settled enough to power through. I did really well!"

Rolan shoved down his disbelief and kept a smile plastered on his face. Traven had every right to be excited, his dreams were about to come true. He had just hoped they would do it together. Things would be different now. Rolan would be spending the rest of the month stacking crates and stomping through the mud while his friend sat on his behind in the comfortable warmth of the rehearsal room.

That wasn't fair. He knew the Grand Chorus worked themselves to the bone in preparation for the performances, they wouldn't have their reputation otherwise. He shoved the resentment down.

He realized Traven was staring with that stupid grin on his face. "I'll talk to Director Rivers. Maybe I can arrange for you to have an audition too. He'll have to hear you once I tell him how good you are."

"Nah." Rolan waved his hand. "Don't push it. Focus on your audition. You'll only get one shot."

Traven's lip twitched as he battled his sense of honor. He had a good heart and funny notions about the way things should be. It was something Rolan admired. He sat up from the bed and snatched his coat from the bedpost. "This calls for a drink, if you are up for it."

Traven shifted his feet. "Maybe tomorrow, after my audition. Tonight I need to run off with the rest of the quintet."

"Late night rehearsal?" Rolan sat back down.

"No, something else." He looked like he wanted to say more. *It was already starting.*

"Sure, tomorrow. But you pay, Gold Cord." Rolan laid back down with a grunt.

Traven was already opening the door to leave. "Deal."

He could be heard whooping down the hallway and back outside. After his friend left, Rolan pushed himself up off the bed and slipped his boots on. "Doesn't mean I can't have a drink tonight."

Traven yawned as he rounded the Crooning Cello, nodding to the bouncers with newfound life. One of them pointed to his leg with raised eyebrows, and Traven laughed it away. They called after him, but he was already headed to the alleyway in the back.

A cobblestone path in the grass-covered yard led back to a maintenance street laden with shadows, where workers loaded supplies and unloaded trash. His mind was buzzing. It felt wrong to leave Rolan in the dark about his leg, but the way Kael and the rest behaved backstage was enough to stay his tongue. He had agreed to keep their secret, and he took keeping his word very seriously. Even so, he couldn't shake whatever happened between him and Mariss. For a moment he saw into her, and she into him. Afterwards, when the excitement of it all passed and he walked home from Nawny's shop, he felt different. Something rested in his core, something he couldn't quite describe. It reminded him of snow buildup moments before it came crashing down.

The rest of the Quintet were gathered around a tall lightpost. Kael held his hands clasped behind his back, bobbing his head to Elena as he spoke. The scuff of his boot echoed off of the buildings, and they turned to him with mouths snapped shut. Finn didn't greet him with his usual open arms and boisterous proclamation.

Kael jerked his head for them to start walking, and soon the Crooning Cello disappeared around the curved alley. Mariss placed a gentle hand on his arm and offered a reassuring smile. He returned her smile as Finn clapped him on the shoulder. "At least you aren't limping anymore."

Elena shushed him with eyes to the rooftops.

The alley led to another and another. Kael stepped ahead to check each intersection before waving them forward. Were they supposed to be sneaking? He could hear their footsteps echo off of the buildings. Traven figured they were near the edge of the GroundSong Commons, but it was much more difficult to place himself in the city by the backs of buildings. If he remembered correctly, they were close to Nerise's Emporium. Finn stopped them and knocked on one of the doors.

Nerise popped her head into the alleyway and glanced left and right to be sure they were alone. She gave Traven a special smile before letting them in, which earned him an elbow in the ribs from Finn.

They were ushered into the back of her business, where bolts of cloth rested against the walls. Nerise huffed and pointed at his pants when the door closed. "What is this?"

"Sorry." Traven hunched his shoulders.

"We can tend to Traven's wardrobe in a moment, Darling." Finn pinched her on the behind. Nerise swatted his hand with feigned offense.

Elena scoffed and folded her arms, shooting Finn an icy stare.

"So what's with the secrecy? Even Kael is acting more

paranoid than usual." Traven tried to lighten the mood.

"This is serious, Traven," Elena shut him down.

His smile faltered, and he decided to stand quietly until they were ready to speak. As expected, Kael spoke first.

"We had not planned for things to happen this way. There were certain protocols bypassed in order to ensure your safety, and it put us all at risk. You put us all at risk."

"Me?" Traven was incredulous. "How am I at fault here?"

Finn interjected. "What Kael is trying to say is that your injury, paired with Shissel's insistence on bullying you, has forced our hand. While you seem like a great guy, we can't be sure we can trust you yet."

"Trust me with what?" Traven looked at Mariss for answers. She didn't give any.

"Surely, now you have realized that Finn has interceded on your behalf, at very specific moments. Moments where you were very close to bringing ruin on yourself." Elena sounded bored.

Were they talking about whatever was causing the lights to spark?

"With Shissel? I could have handled him if I wanted to. My father always told me to work things out with words. Up until today, things hadn't gotten physical."

"And the tremors? The winking lights?" Finn tapped his nose.

"Fluctuations in Glysterium and all the machinations under our feet. That had nothing to do with me." Traven wanted the explanation to be true. He knew it wasn't.

"It had everything to do with you," Kael interrupted. "Every one of those moments risked a flare-up that could have brought the Empire down on your head."

He quieted, trying to recall the moments Kael was referring to. He had been sure the lights shimmering was a coincidence, the rumblings hadn't been more than what a passing GlysterRail felt like. It couldn't have been him. "A flare-up of what?"

Mariss placed a hand on his chest. Her hand felt warm. "You are a Glysterian...like me."

"In a way." Kael paced the room. "At first we thought like you did. It was a fluke in the Glysterium. But then you did it again, and my suspicions were confirmed."

Traven looked at each one of them. "I haven't heard of this term before, but I'm assuming it has something to do with the way Mariss healed me with her voice."

Elena squirmed while Finn curled his mustache. Mariss was already nodding when Kael began to sing.

A flame, pure and red, danced from his lips and cast light across the scar on his face. It swirled around his head and then around each of them, growing bright enough to illuminate the room. Finn ducked when the flame darted at his hair, scowling at Kael as his face split in a rare smile. His song ended, and the flame winked out with a hiss and a tendril of smoke.

That was nothing like healing.

Before Traven could respond, Elena filled the room with her delicate soprano voice. The air shimmered with creme-colored smoke, settling on Finn's slender shoulders. Finn's body disappeared with a shimmer, and Traven's eyes nearly bulged out of his head. This was impossible. He had never even heard of anything like this.

"You are saying I can do...that?" He pointed to Elena and Kael.

Finn winked back into sight. "Not quite, but you can do something. We just haven't figured it out yet. The last bass Glysterian died before any of us joined the Dischordants."

He caught Mariss staring at him with a pained expression. Since healing him, she had always looked like she wanted to say more. He scratched at his beard while taking a deep breath. "The Dischordants, is their goal as on the nose as it sounds?"

"More or less, but not to simply disrupt." Elena explained. "We are a faction looking to return power back to the people, free from the oppression of the Empress."

He had hitched himself to rebels. What would they do if he ran out of the room? Kael hinted at wiping his mind. He didn't want to disrupt the system. He wanted to climb to the top of it. His legs itched for him to run into the alley, but he needed more answers.

"What about you, Finn? What can you do?"

"Ah." Finn scratched his head. "It's not as flashy as these two. I push and pull emotions, help people feel calm or make them irrationally angry…and other things to do with the mind."

"Like make people forget? Is that what you intend to do with me if I don't agree to join you?"

"Yes." Kael shrugged as Mariss shook her head and said, "No."

Elena groaned. "We hope it doesn't come to that."

He did too.

Mariss pointed a delicate finger into Kael's face. "We aren't wiping anyone. I saw into him, he's honest and loyal. Even if he doesn't join us, he'll keep his vow of silence."

He smiled at the alto as her small frame pushed against Kael.

"We shouldn't have healed him, not before we could be sure." Kael sighed.

"Mariss is right, I take my vows seriously. My word is the only thing I have. You can trust me." His voice rumbled.

Kael ran a finger along the scar across his face. "This is what happens when you trust people."

Don't let them change you. Asmeri's words echoed.

He stepped close to the tenor, tilting his head down to match his gaze. "You saved my leg, and possibly my *life* today. That means something to me. I owe you at least my silence."

Kael clenched his jaw while the rest of them shared worried

glances. The tenor drew in a breath through his nose, and Finn cleared his throat. "Kael."

"Fine."

Traven backed off and folded his arms. "Thank you. Now, why doesn't the Empire take kindly to Glysterians?"

"Imagine a power structure that could be upended by a few upstart singers. What do you know about the Unification Wars? The Tenebral Uprising?" Kael leaned against the door.

"That the Empire went to war against the scattered kingdoms in order to establish a ruler with the vision to keep us all warm in the Ever-Winter. The Tenebral Uprising was just a pocket of resistance by people chafing against the strict rules set to keep us safe." Traven recited the lessons he learned in class.

"Right out of government-sanctioned textbooks," Kael droned. "What they don't mention is that it was the eradication of Glysterians. Our ancestors were wiped out almost entirely. We were a threat to Emperor Thalvaris."

"Our ancestors…as in a bloodline?" Traven's stomach dropped as he thought of his brother.

"Exactly. The gift is transferred through descendants," Elena answered.

"My brother…he disappeared two cycles ago, trying to join the Grand Chorus."

Finn slapped his own forehead. "I thought you looked familiar! Slap some dreadlocks on that bald head and you could be twins."

He had made it to the city. Was Chadden still alive?

Traven grabbed him by the lapels, chest heaving. "Tell me where he is. Where did you see him?"

Finn grimaced, and Traven felt something brush against his mind before it disappeared. "He never made it. Malachi turned him away, and we never saw him again."

"Who could have taken him? Who is doing this?" he demanded.

"Let me tell you about the soldiers in black and white uniforms." Kael whistled another flame to his fingertip.

Rolan was right about the woman on the train.

Chapter XXIV

Everything about the next morning felt fresh and new.
Traven's limp and fever were gone, and even though he struggled through a night of worry and Rolan's snoring, he woke refreshed. Trying his best to be quiet, he gave himself a clean shave and trimmed his beard. Last night, Nerise had thrown a fresh pair of trousers at him, threatening him with an adorable growl if he ruined them. He pulled them on, fastened his white and silver coat, and sat down at the small stone desk near the door to write to Asmeri.

Father,

Your son officially has an audition with the Grand Chorus!

Director Rivers overheard me singing while I was repairing parts of the Opera House...you know how I tend to sing while working. Whatever I did, he must have liked it enough to break protocol. I've already learned so much of the music just by overhearing the rehearsals. They are so talented, and I'm grateful for the chance to be heard.

I'm making friends already, and we've started calling ourselves The Quintet. It's not very original, but at least it's

He tucked the letter into his jacket for later and headed out onto the street, toward his future.

Cantata Row was transforming. Even here, in the GroundSong Commons, the streets were swept clean of trash and debris. Brass railings had been polished, lamps were repaired, and the rickety tents of the marketplace had fresh patches. Guards were marching in twice their normal numbers, stationed at nearly every intersection, and glaring at every passerby. Passing the Regional Chorus hall, he noticed all of the missing posters had been torn down. Worry crept up his spine. He was a Glysterian, he could be next.

He couldn't tell Asmeri; there was no point until he had some more answers. His father would probably drag him by the ear all the way to Grendal if he knew the half of it. He still wasn't clear on all the details, but he knew that he needed to get a rein on his temper...and fast.

Shaking the thought away, and clearing his throat, Traven worked through the cobwebs in his voice. The morning thickness in his voice was missing, a byproduct of his poor sleep. Luckily the solo he had in mind wasn't terribly low, not for him. He would be okay, he had to be.

He sang to the city, walking by morning workers with renewed hope. They nodded as he passed, some pausing to give him a better listen. A Blue Cord stopped their morning walk and gave him a gentle bow. That spoke to him more than applause.

He was early to Concordia Plaza, a product of a healed leg. He should give Mariss a gift; it was the least he could do after she risked her life for him. Traven added it to his list of expenses for this month. Nawny had been generous in his pay, and his coin purse had a healthy collection of glimmer, gleam, and gloam.

As he dipped a hand into the crystal-clear waters of the fountain, he craned his neck to see the top of the Citadel. A surge of power thudded as it escaped the roof and raced toward the center of the GlysterDome. The shield rippled all the way down, across each district before colliding with the FrostLine. Each pulse tugged at something inside of him, warning him to take care. He needed to be careful today—and every day—for the rest of his life.

He wasn't sure what to do about the power resting in his core. It had been quiet through the clandestine conversation with his friends last night, but as he lay in bed, it was all he could think about. It was warmth and passion, connection and flame, begging to be released. When Mariss healed him, it seemed to weaken the meager barriers holding him back. He needed to lean into the cold dispassionate perfectionism he adopted on stage. Every moment from now on had to be seen as a performance.

Nawny seemed surprised when he found Traven in the wide stone plaza, his voice rippling through the morning air. "You look remarkably well this morning." He handed over the scone.

"I am. I finally had my leg looked at." Traven hopped on his bad leg with a grin.

The tinker sat down on the edge of the fountain. "You've been a great help these last few weeks. I know you have an audition today, but remember, if it doesn't work out you have a place at my shop. You don't seem to mind getting your hands dirty, and that's hard to find up here."

Traven chose to savor his scone instead of responding. He couldn't tell Nawny that working as a tinker was honest work, but he wouldn't rest until he could sing for a living. The tinker patted him on the arm and sighed. "Don't worry about working this morning. Make sure your solo is perfect."

He shook his head and licked the frosting off of his fingers. "I can sing while I work. There is a lot left to be done before the Empress arrives...I might even be able to climb up on the catwalk now."

The old man grunted with a smirk. "I'll be fine. Take the time you need, make sure you've given it all you've got. If something is worth doing, it's worth overdoing."

Traven leaned back and considered his wisdom while they finished their breakfast. Nawny eventually stood and shook his hand. "If you do get your cord, come get the last of your pay... and don't forget the little people when you're up on stage."

He took the tinker's hand and pulled him into a hug. The old man cackled and patted him on the back. Nawny would be missed, a surrogate father figure while he was away from home. Traven cleared the emotion from his throat and looked up at the Opera House. "I better get in."

He rose up the steps and all of the excitement and nervousness of his first day rushed back to him. The Statue of the Empress gazed down, and everything Kael had told him last night sank his heart. The weight of the Empire, embodied in her gaze, made his shoulders sink. Was he being foolish? Walking into the most prolific building in the city? He was literally begging for a spotlight when he probably should be hiding. He was torn between the same two forces; self-preservation, and pride.

Pride always won.

At first, his heart pounded as he climbed to the third story balcony to warm up his voice. His throat felt a little hot when he pressed, so he took it easy and drank more water. As his upper range extended and his throat relaxed, he started the music he had prepared.

At any other point in his life he would have sung the piece he performed back home. It was a perfect showcase of his range, flexibility, and humor. But not today.

Today, he would sing the bass solo he had been hearing for weeks.

He wanted to show Director Rivers exactly why he was a perfect fit without any excuse. He wanted to give him something to compare with directly. He wanted to prove he belonged.

And he wanted that solo.

He ran through the song until he was satisfied with where to take every breath, where to swell and where to diminish. His mind critiqued every lazy note, recalled the key to keep him in tune, and envisioned the sheet music in his mind. He was as ready for this as he was going to be.

And only an hour had passed.

Catching an hour of rest was out of the question, his throat would relax too much and leave his voice thick and unresponsive. Instead, he meandered the halls, paced the auditorium, and then finally decided to stand at the door to Malachi's office. Butterflies warred inside his stomach, and he tried to stifle a yawn with his fist.

Traven could hear the director humming—his light countertenor echoing through the lobby. His nerves spiked, the lights fluttered, and he clasped his hands behind his back. Malachi's goatee split into a grin. "Early! Eager! That is what I like to see. Come on in." He pulled out a Harmonic Key and sang in perfect falsetto.

Malachi let him in first. The room smelled of ancient parchment and Gyshweed. Mrs. Bellamy had a private stash of the herb in a lockbox. She would burn a twig or two if one of them needed to recuperate their voice after oversinging. It was a nice reminder of home.

The office was large enough for an impressive wooden desk, shelves stacked full of scrolls up to the ceiling, and a small piano next to the window. A baton encrusted with Glysterium sat on a display stand over the hearth, flanked by candelabras that were utterly out of place in a building wired for Glysterium. There was a warmth in here, a comforting presence he couldn't quite place. The director had clearly curated a sense of home. Malachi set his satchel down and sat on top of his valuable desk, folding his legs. Asmeri would have popped a blood vessel at how casual the man was being with that much wood.

Director Rivers studied him in silence the same way he did yesterday. The stare was intense, as if he were trying to unlock all of his secrets. More butterflies.

Then Malachi smiled and offered a chair. "Sit. Relax. I'd like to get to know you before I hear you sing." He looked slightly apologetic. "I'm afraid I don't even know your name. I don't usually do things this informally, but…"

"Traven Caelhardt, of Grendal Yodel," he answered.

"Farming village." The Director raised his eyebrows. Was there a hint of recognition in his tone?

"I studied with my mother, and our director Mrs. Bellamy. I've been singing since I was thirteen, tenor until my fifteenth year…then bass. We have won the annual competition five times since I joined them." Traven let a fraction of pride slip into his voice.

"Can you sightread?" The Director reached behind him and retrieved a sheet of paper.

He supposed past accolades didn't matter here. Only what he could do now. Traven took the sheet music in his hands and began to study. "Yes sir, my father drilled it into me."

It wasn't a terribly difficult piece of music, likely intended to measure baseline capability. There were a few tricky intervals, and one or two rhythmic changes, but nothing Traven hadn't plowed through before. He hummed through the melody once or twice, and then looked up. "Ready."

Malachi hummed the starting pitch and Traven matched it while adjusting his sitting position. Straight back, edge of the cushion, legs planted.

Traven worked through the notes without error until he missed one of the tricky intervals. He felt his internal temperature skyrocket, but shoved it down and took a deep breath before running the measure again. He finished strong, landing every other trap the music held.

"That's a sneaky jump. At least you knew you were wrong the instant it came out of your mouth." The Director gave him another smile, it helped calm his nerves, but not his anger. He didn't make mistakes like that.

"Yes, sorry about that." Traven clenched his jaw.

The light flickered just enough that Traven snapped his head toward it. Malachi shifted his eyes and tsked. "The dangers of being so close to the Citadel. Power fluctuates all the time."

How much did Malachi know? The butterflies erupted in his belly, and he gripped the arms of his chair until his knuckles turned white.

"You'll get used to it. The closer we are to The Furnace, the more abnormalities occur. It's a shame really, having the lights dim mid-concert. A small price to pay for heat." Malachi hopped off of his desk and sat at the piano, rolling back the fallboard and revealing pristine white and black keys. "What's your starting note?" His hand paused over the piano.

Traven tapped his head as he stood. "I have it here."

"Perfect pitch?" Malachi straightened in his seat, flapping his red coat tails over the bench.

"Not quite, sir. Just memorization."

"Ah, well that's probably for the best. The life of someone with perfect pitch can be a painful one." Malachi's eyes twinkled with knowing. "What will you be singing today?"

"Regulos Mortini: Movement 5." Traven smirked.

Malachi was quiet at first. His eyes sparkled with amusement as he held his mouth shut, a wheeze escaping from the sides. At last, the pressure broke, and he held his belly while he roared in laughter. "Oh I like you. A set of brass balls to match that thunder of a voice. Let's hear it then."

Traven closed his eyes and whispered, "May my voice reflect my spirit."

He slipped into cold, dispassionate perfectionism.

His first note came out with his eyes still closed. When he opened them, Malachi was nodding in time, twitching his hands for each beat. His voice, warm from the morning, bent to his will and lilted through the office with agility and grace. Even fatigued, he rumbled through the lower sections. It wasn't as robust as he would have liked, but there was nothing to be done about that now. On the other hand, he was able to sing in his upper register without blowing the doors off of the study. That was probably for the best. He attacked the diction like a mattock to ice, clearly enunciating each consonant and shadow vowel. He needed to be perfect.

For the last few weeks, he noticed moments where the soloist cut off just a fraction too soon, or breathed when Malachi would sway his arms to keep singing. He honored those moments and more, adding more growth and volume at the song's climax, then dwindling down to a crisp and energetic resolution…almost a whisper.

The Director exhaled sharply through his nose, folding his arms. He cocked his head to the side, dreadlock ponytail dangling over his shoulder. Traven tried to read his face, but Malachi was giving him nothing. The Director sat in thought, and he stood there unsure. Eventually he folded his hands behind his back.

And he thought this morning was an eternity.

"Well." Malachi's eyes focused on the GlysterLamps, his brow creased in thoughtfulness. "I can certainly use that."

The Quintet was standing impatiently, as he opened the door. "Well?" Elena stepped forward.

Traven emerged, a black folder in one hand and a gold cord gripped tight in the other. His smile was as wide as Concordia Plaza.

Finn howled with delight, lifting Traven up at the waist and jogging down the hallway. Kael nodded with begrudging respect while Elena clapped, a rare smile unthawing her angular face. Mariss put her hands to her mouth and jumped up and down. Other Gold Cords, standing idle while waiting for rehearsal to start, cheered for their newest member.

All except Shissel.

He stormed over, face contorted in rage, practically spitting. "This is an abomination. This peasant doesn't deserve to sing with us; he's a nobody."

Finn spun on him, but it was Malachi who stepped into the hallway and put a single chubby finger on Shissel's chest. The chorus froze, and the lobby fell into silence. "He is Traven Caelhardt, bass II of the Grand Chorus. One of Hearthmere's finest, and your *equal*. You will treat him with respect, or you will find yourself without your cord. If you cannot control yourself, I'll make sure you never sing in this city again, Shissel Morayne."

The tenor's eyes went wider and wider with each word. His mouth worked soundlessly as he tried to defend himself, but nothing would come. A hard edge formed in his eyes, and he stormed through the lobby and outside of the Opera House. It was everything Traven wanted.

Turning to him while smoothing out his red coat and white trousers, Malachi took a deep settling breath and winked. "See you tomorrow."

Elena hooked a finger around the cord clutched in his hands and brought it to her chest. She regarded him with a hint of affection in her icy eyes before pulling it up his left arm, looping it over his shoulder, and fastening it to a button on the seam. So that's why that button was there. Nerise was thinking ahead.

A new sense of self-worth settled onto his shoulders like a mantle, and a triad of joy, relief, and vindication swirled together into the sweetest harmony. As his friends congratulated him with genuine excitement, he had to fight down a hitch in his breath. He had done it.

He was a Gold Cord.

The lobby cleared. His friends began their rehearsal, and he stood in the hallway while taking it all in. He looked to the ceiling, as if to search the heavens, and nodded. "We did it, Mother."

He thought back to one of the last things she said to him. *"You were born for more than Yodel life, Traven. Your voice is your ticket to salvation. The question is, what will you do with your destiny? You could rise above the best, and sing in the Empress's Halls of Calrithia. I think you will, someday."*

She always seemed different from anyone else in the Yodel. The way she spoke, the way her eyes lingered on the GlysterFurnaces…she seemed haunted. Yet, when her gaze shifted to her sons, a beaming smile would grow on her slender face. Traven shoved down a sharp, rising pressure in his chest and bit the inside of his cheek. The power fluttered, dwindling like a passing gale as he distracted himself with his next steps.

The city had strict procedures for corded singers, and registration was one of them. He might as well get it out of the way now so he could enjoy the rest of his day.

Malachi's official offer letter in hand, Traven sauntered down the steps of the Opera House and through Concordia Plaza. The Citadel hummed over the burbling waters of the fountain, and Traven growled the pitch in challenge. He would not flinch from its grim aura today.

The air cooled under the thick shadow of the obsidian building, and he tapped the fastener of his collar without thinking. Guards stood at attention inside the tunnel, their halberds crossed over the iron door in the center. A flick of the eyes to his shoulder, a nod of approval, and he was inside. It felt too easy.

Chords, the sound.

The obsidian building acted as a tuning fork, and the room rattled with the forces churning underneath their feet. He could barely think, let alone speak with any comfort. The hair on his arms stood on end; he could taste the energy coursing through the stone. Lamps struggled to illuminate the dark stone of the office he stepped into. Bitter Glysterium struck his nose. A sickly woman with a lace shawl over her head and a plain grey wool dress sat at a stone desk stretching across the entire room, sweat beading down her forehead. The heat was oppressive.

She raised her head, peering through tired eyes while motioning for him to approach. He crossed the room at almost a jog, eager to be out of this building as soon as possible. "I'm here to register as a Gold Cord." He shouted while thrusting his scroll forward.

Checking the calendar next to her ink and quill, she frowned. "Out of season? Auditions aren't for another month." Her voice was shrill over the droning.

Traven shrugged. She unfurled the scroll and pushed round spectacles further up her nose. As she worked through the proclamation, Traven fussed with the cord around his shoulder. It was made of something metallic and shiny, woven into the thick golden thread, and looped a few inches under his armpit. It was pride, belonging, and accomplishment all wrapped into one. How something so simple could invoke so many emotions.

He shifted on his heels, chewing the inside of his mouth. Things seemed to be taking a considerable amount of time. She paused from scribbling her notes to reach over and ring a bell sitting to her left. The interior door whined as it opened, and the roar of the Citadel buffeted the room. Traven instinctively lowered his head. A servant in plain blue robes and a Glysterium necklace shuffled in, grasping his scroll with a mechanical hand before retreating without a word.

She smiled apologetically. "Elevation of citizenship outside of the audition window requires some additional paperwork, I'm sure you understand."

Despite his nod, he did not.

"I didn't see a patron listed in your contract. Do you have someone in mind?"

"I will be meeting with Lord Daelthorne as soon as possible. There is also Mistress Vexlane."

"Ah, yes. Lord Daelthorne does enjoy a large retinue of singers. House Vexlane could certainly use the social currency of a Gold Cord. She may offer you more…attention than the Daelthorne estate."

"Why is that?"

Her face reddened as the interior door opened and the room filled with sound. "You'll see soon enough. If those two don't snatch you up, I'm sure there will be other houses eager to enlist a Gold Cord."

The servant returned, dropped the scroll in her hand, and departed. Traven didn't get so much as a glance. She read through the document one more time before setting it on the edge of her desk, nearest to him.

"Congratulations. May your voice serve the Empire with honor and glory." She went back to writing.

He took the scroll and hurried outside, taking a deep breath as the door closed behind him. Cold air rushed into his lungs, forcing a sigh. The guards chuckled knowingly in the tunnel, as if they saw this reaction every day. A young man walked through the passage and bowed deeply to him as he passed. Traven gave him a warm smile.

That would take getting used to.

Chapter XXVI

Rolan scratched his beard with impatience. What was holding Traven up?

They were supposed to meet at the warehouse for drinks after work, and so he sat on the concrete until his coworkers had gone home and the sun began to dip under the walls of the FrostLine. He stared up at the warehouse rafters and shrugged. The spirit hadn't visited him today, but it didn't every day. He was starting to enjoy the little one-sided conversations, and the solitude above the rest of the warehouse was a nice respite.

A GlysterCart rolled by, and the teamster in the Cantor suit gave him a wave. "Can't get enough of this place, you gotta hang around after your shift?"

Rolan stood and knuckled his back. "'Sposed to meet someone. They forgot about me."

The teamster didn't stop pushing the supplies, and the lumbering mechanical giant thudded to the next warehouse. Rolan exhaled through his nose and headed toward the nearest tavern. "Looks like another night drinking alone," he muttered.

Turning down an alley he hadn't been down before, he eventually found a bar suitable for his mood. The sign dangled by a single chain, ready to clatter onto the cobblestone. Inside it was quiet, damp, and smelled of stagnant water. The barkeep rested his thick hands on a belly protruding from his stained white shirt. He grunted the perfunctory greeting hymn, Rolan barely noticed.

"One ale, and somethin' to eat." Rolan found a table in the back corner. He never liked his back to an entrance.

The barkeep poured him a drink into a stone mug. Food was brought out minutes later, with a meager offering of bread and cheese with some sort of dried meat. Rolan didn't ask where the meat came from, he probably wouldn't like the answer.

Eating in silence, self-pity began to gnaw at his belly. Traven was likely off enjoying his new status. There was no doubt he would succeed in his audition, and he was probably at the Crooning Cello right now. It was fine by Rolan. He had grown used to being alone, since Moira passed.

A violin cried in the alleyway outside, growing steadily louder. He knew that sound, and it gave him worry for the second time. The barkeep perked up in fear? Excitement?

The first patron made him want to bolt out of the inn immediately.

Clad in a white and gold vest and black military trousers, he entered the room with a vibrant blonde mohawk. He was massive, tall enough to duck under the doorway and shoulders nearly as wide. One of his arms had been replaced with military-grade GlysterTech, veins of green power pulsing along the brass and steel. He had to turn sideways to get in the doorway, shifting a glittering pair of drums attached to his hip. His blue eyes were cold as winter.

He matched the Cobbler's description perfectly.

Another entered. A man with rusty chains wrapped around his neck and forearms. Close-cropped hair and a chin made of granite made his head look like a square slab. His fingers, bedecked with golden rings, caressed a curved brass horn pulsing with emerald power. The white and gold uniform he wore was well-fitted, and clean. If the first man was brutality, this one was precision.

Rolan leaned back into his chair and covered his face with his cup of ale. Mohawk cleared his throat to the barkeep and pointed directly at him. The signal was clear. *He needs to leave.*

The barkeep bowed and then walked over, rapping his knuckles on the table. "I think it's best you move along, friend."

He agreed.

Flipping him a gloam for the uneaten meal, Rolan eagerly stepped away from the table without a word.

Another soldier stalked into the inn, a woman with unkempt silver hair and sunken eyes. She carried a violin and bow in one hand, and fidgeted with her necklace with the other. Rolan's instincts were right. Something was insidious about her, and being in the same room made him want to bolt. The man in chains pulled a chair out for her with a devilish grin. She chose another, and the man's smile died on his face.

As Rolan neared the doorway, a rail-thin woman turned sideways to let Rolan pass. She held his gaze with green eyes so bright, they seemed unnatural. She rested her hand comfortably on a large V-shaped pouch slung across her chest, and flipped her straight black hair. He sang a soft hymn of apology while he sidled by.

They just kept coming. Another man forced him to press against the doorframe as he pushed into the room. His back was bent and his shoulders slumped uncomfortably forward, dropping thin black hair over a pale face. Ghastly fingers ran over a silver flute so ornate it looked to belong to the Empress. His aura of malice made Rolan shiver.

And then came The Red Woman.

She sauntered into the tavern, twirling a GlysterPistol. Her tall black boots clicked on the stone floor in a leisurely rhythm. Rolan felt himself shrink as she passed, trying to avoid her gaze.

He could have sworn her eyebrow raised just a fraction. Would she remember him from a few weeks ago? The panic lasted for a moment as she moved on, sitting down in the last chair and motioning with her finger to the barkeep.

The barkeep moved faster than Rolan would have given him credit for, and returned with their drinks without asking any questions. *They must be regulars here.*

Stepping outside, Rolan exhaled and scratched at his beard. He couldn't even drink in peace today. Aside from the Red Woman, he had never seen any of them before. They clearly were in the same unit, but all of the soldiers he encountered wore the livery of Hearthmere. They were something different, specialized. Even their weapons—instruments augmented with Glysterium—told him that much.

He needed to learn more.

Slinking off to the alley a few paces from the doorway, he slid down to the cobblestone and lowered his head. Could he pass as a beggar while listening?

"What is the status of Yodel Farington?" A sultry voice asked from inside. He guessed it was The Red Woman.

"Back in harmony, the errant note has been plucked without much fuss. I did lose a bet with Garrick, he didn't even run. Just whimpered like a baby."

Someone had been plucked? What did that mean?

"Any more ripples from Calrithia?"

"A particularly nosy citizen was flagged by the Baron, it is taken care of," an oily voice droned.

"And the newest Gold Cord, from Grendal?"

"Under surveillance," another voice reported.

They had to be talking about Traven. Had he won his cord? What business would they have with him? Traven was about as honest as they came.

"Keep an eye on him, The Arcanum has grown…demanding lately."

He knew they were being watched, he just couldn't put his finger on why. He needed to tell Traven. As quietly as he could, Rolan pushed himself off of the ground and tiptoed away from the tavern.

All of this talk about plucking, surveillance, and people being "taken care of" confirmed suspicions he'd had for years. The Empire was more than a caretaker. Their message of uniting against the Ever-Winter had always rung hollow to him, when delegates traipsed into his yodel with their fine clothing and noises pointed into the air. The message was always the same; more, faster, more efficient.

"I thought you looked familiar," a voice—smooth as velvet—purred behind his shoulder.

He froze and held his breath. How did she sneak up behind him? Did she know he had been listening? His heart was pounding so hard he thought it was beating through his shirt.

She circled him, picking at his hair. "Tell me more about your friend on the train, the one with the GlysterHammer."

Rolan slammed his mouth shut. She wouldn't get anything from him.

A slight smirk spread on her lips; her blue eyes twinkling. He felt like a mouse being toyed with. "Come now. A few answers now could save you, and your friend, a lifetime of trouble. Short as that may be."

Rolan glowered and stepped to move past her. She placed a green lacquered finger on his breastbone and dragged hard enough it started to sting. "I'm not done with you."

"I don't know what yer talking about. We met on the train," Rolan lied.

The smirk on her slender face grew to a dazzling smile. "Do you frequently let strangers sleep on your shoulder? How magnanimous of you, dockworker."

She already knew too much. He needed time to think. Perhaps if he didn't lie completely, it might be enough. "He was a traveler with dreams to sing in the Grand Chorus. I thought I'd join him."

"And yet." She flicked his shoulder. "No Gold Cord for you." Her red lips pursed in mock pity.

He felt heat flare up under his collar; the reminder stung. She pulled away from him in a swirl of razormint. "Such is the way of things here. The talented soar while the rest of us wallow in the grey slushy aftermath. So now what is your plan? Skulking at doorways for the rest of your life, sticking your nose where it doesn't belong?"

"I'm not the one sticking their pretty nose where it doesn't belong," Rolan retorted. Hasty, too hasty. He needed to be careful.

"My pretty little nose goes wherever it wants." An icy edge formed in her azure eyes.

He wasn't sure what to say, she already knew too much. Anything he said might give away his friend. He chose to say nothing. The severe edges of her expression softened. "Let's make a deal."

"You've got nothing to offer me," he rushed to say.

Her eyes sparkled with mirth. He really needed to keep his mouth shut.

"Let me make this clear. A single word from me and you disappear. No one but Traven would care. Hearthmere would carry on as if you never existed. Or, you could help me from time to time. You've piqued my interest. That means everything you do from this point forward will be known. I leave the choice to you."

She leaned in. "I'd hate for your hijinks to jeopardize your new friend's position. He worked so hard for it."

She stepped away with a wink, and disappeared into the crowd of Cantata Row. "I am not smart enough for this," he muttered.

His ghost giggled in the alley.

Chapter XXVII

“The look on Shissel's face was worth a thousand glimmer!”

Finn shouted over the tumult of the Crooning Cello, drinks in both hands.

Mariss slammed her mug on the table, spilling ale all over her fingers and causing Elena to jump up with a gasp. Her blue dress had been caught in the revelry.

Even Kael smiled at the story, his cheeks red from too much wine.

The Quintet was in high spirits, officially adding him to their roster. No longer would they have to steal time in corners of the Opera House to sing together, they could do it every day on the risers.

It was the best day of his life.

“So tell me about your audition,” Mariss demanded, grabbing his arm.

Her eyes lingered on his, just long enough to put a lump in his throat. “We did sightreading, and that went mostly well. Then I told him what song I had prepared… and he really got a kick out of that!”

“He sang Dietre's solo!” Finn interrupted, having heard the

story already.

Elena snorted, then covered her face with wide eyes and reddened cheeks at the sound. Mariss shook her head and bumped him with her shoulder. Kael arched an eyebrow with newfound respect. "Bold, and a perfect message to send to Malachi. You are here, and you aren't some nobody from a dirt-pounding Yodel. Well done."

Kael's assurance made him smile. Traven had been worried about his upbringing more than he realized. Shissel's insistence that he didn't belong had been getting under his skin—that maybe the stuck-up aristocrat was right. The tenor was sulking in the corner near the door with the rest of his cohorts, trying his best not to look Traven's way. When Shissel finally met his glare, Traven gave him a wink. He would not shrink from the bully again.

Taking another swig of ale, he returned his attention back to his friends. Leaning close enough to Mariss that his lips brushed her ear, he spoke loud enough to be heard. "That reminds me, could you arrange for me to meet Lord Daelthorne?"

She turned her head, bumping his nose with hers. He felt her inhale sharply at his closeness, and then she pulled back. "Of course. He is holding a gathering at his estate this weekend; you should come as my guest."

Finn stood on the table and roared to the inn, forcing his friends to lean back or be spilled on. "My friends! Let us all cheer for Traven Caelhardt. Basso extraordinaire!"

Concordia Plaza shook with the roar.

He had forgotten all about Rolan.

"Slush, I'm so sorry, Rolan," he rushed into their room, leaning a little too hard on the doorway.

Rolan was sitting near the window, chipping away at a small

stone block. He slightly turned his head, his long hair dropping over his shoulder, but didn't say a word.

Traven crossed the room, stumbling over boots and plopping down on the bed. "I mean it, I was about to come to meet you, when Finn asked me to have a celebratory drink with him. I am a Gold Cord now!" He pulled the cord up off his shoulder.

"I figured you would be. Yer a talented man." Rolan scraped against the stone with a small chisel. It looked like he was making a doll.

He dropped the cord and grimaced. "I'll make it up to you, I'm so sorry."

"It's fine, Traven. I'm not your only friend in this city."

Traven winced at the remark. He didn't want to leave Rolan out, things just kept happening to get between them lately. "But you are my friend, and I shouldn't have let you down. I don't usually do things like this."

"I get it. You had an exciting day, probably one of the best in your life."

Traven could feel the discord between them. Rolan's tone and posture spoke to him as loudly as if he had screamed. He had let someone down, and it bore straight into his heart. Another apology formed on his lips, but Rolan set the carving down and turned to him. "You are being watched."

"By the world!" he exclaimed with a smile that immediately disappeared with one look at Rolan.

"Are you drunk?" Rolan pinched his nose.

"Maybe a little, celebrations and all that."

His friend stood and picked up the washbasin near the door. Slowly, deliberately, he carried it across the room without spilling a drop. Traven raised his eyebrows when Rolan stopped at his bed, and promptly poured the cold water on top of his head.

"Chords!" he roared.

"Now we're even. Sober up so you can focus."

Traven sputtered with his arms raised above his shoulders. The floor was covered in water and his clothes were soaked. He would be sleeping in a wet bed tonight. "I'm focused, you flat-brained idiot!"

Rolan stifled a laugh and put the washbasin down. "You remember the woman on the Rail? The one with the pistol?"

"The pretty woman who jumped from a moving train?"

"Yes, the woman you fell in love with at a glance."

"I did not fall in love," he blustered.

Rolan didn't argue. "She's working with Mohawk, the man the Cobbler described."

Traven threw off his sopping wet coat. "Are you sure?"

"There were six of them, all wearing the white, gold, and black uniforms. They were a unit of some sort, although they didn't wear any markings I'm familiar with. I'm sure. I listened to them for a while, and it sounds like they make people disappear for the Empire. You need to be careful, or you'll be next."

"But why?"

"That's what we're going to find out. Tomorrow. When you are sober." Rolan groaned as he settled into bed. "Don't even think about cuddling. You earned that." He gestured to the bed.

Traven fell to his pillow with a wet plop.

For the first time, Traven stepped into the Opera House as one of them.

The risers were filling as Malachi rapped his baton on his music stand. Finn waved at him from the baritone section, and pointed to the edge of the chorus, where the basses stood. A surge of expectant nerves made him smile at the men, black music folder in front of his chest like a shield. The basses, a collection of men from all walks of life, gave him space right in the center. They clapped him on the shoulder and shook his hand as he stepped up to his position, murmuring welcome hymns in rich low notes.

He craned his neck to get a better look at the rest of the chorus, noticing the progression of voices from low to high, left to right. Elena stood frozen in a sea of sopranos, her posture perfect. Mariss gave him a bright smile from the alto section when their eyes met. Kael faced his section, his hands waving as he gave the tenors instruction. Finn stood nearest to him and smirked.

Malachi plunked a rising melody on the piano, and guided them through their first warm-up, and Traven was instantly overcome.

The sound of twenty robust basses wrapped around him like

a warm blanket. Undertones swirled in his ears, warping the sound around him. He fought to keep his voice in check, and not oversing. If he didn't pace himself, he'd be out of a voice before their break.

The chorus split into four harmonies for the next warm-up, and something stirred in his chest. The power lay dormant in his belly, this was something else. This was belonging. The doubts of the last few weeks, the pain and bullying—it was all swept away in a sea of choral exceptionalism.

"Grand Chorus." Malachi ended the warm ups. "We have a new member today. Let's hear it for Traven Caelhardt, from Grendal Yodel."

They did so with enthusiasm, whooping and stomping their feet. The men around him clapped him on the back and shook his hand without a hint of animosity. Their response was a clear message, he was one of them now.

"That being said," Malachi drew an imaginary line across the stage. "The addition of your strong voice changes the texture of the section. I need to see where you fit."

The basses stepped down and stood shoulder to shoulder, clearing their throats and shifting from foot to foot. Malachi pointed to him and the basses around him while plunking a note on the piano. "Hearthmere anthem."

They sang the first few measures before a swipe of the baton silenced them. Without a word, he pointed to Traven and then to a spot further down the line. Traven stepped over instantly.

He sang again with another group of men—just a few measures—before Malachi stopped him again. Down the basses he went, until he stood next to the bass soloist Dietre. This time, they were allowed to sing the entire anthem while Malachi tapped his lip. He twisted his pointed fingers, indicating for them to switch positions, and waved his hand for them to start.

Traven felt his voice lock into place. He and Dietre had

similar tones, rich and velvety, and he felt like a cog finally slipping into position. The air vibrated between the two of them, and the chorus murmured in appreciation. The entire section ran through the anthem one final time before Malachi clapped his hands and told them to take their new places on the risers.

The rest of the chorus had their music memorized, and he felt slightly ashamed as he opened his black folder and brought it up to chest height. The rest of them didn't seem to mind, and Malachi gave him a wink as they began in the middle of their concert set. He vowed to have it memorized in a week. With new placements decided, the difference was earth-shaking. Singing with these men created a wall of sound and resonance, like he had never heard before. His voice was amplified, and he was amplifying. Here, he wasn't the only bass in the Grendal. He was one of the twenty best basses in the province. Caught up in a scaffold of strong voices, Traven marveled at their sound, at how it made him feel.

"Some day," his mother began while mending Asmeri's *coat. "Some day, you'll be one of the best singers, surrounded by people so talented that your heart will ache and you'll be so thankful just to be in the room with them. Some day you'll proudly share your gift with the whole world."*

He wanted it more than anything, to make his parents proud. He saw the way she sang, and even though she never said it…he could tell she had performed somewhere in her youth. There was always a wistful look in her eyes, as if she was remembering a friend lost to time.

A flaring stage light jolted him out of the memory.

Finn had an elbow in his ribs with a baleful side-eye, and heat blossomed under the collar of his new coat. How much could Finn sense with his power? Was that how he managed to always be there whenever his temper flared? The director's eyes rose to meet him, and he slammed the thought out of his mind.

He needed to impress Malachi; losing focus like this wasn't acceptable. That, and there was no telling what might happen if this lingering power in his chest let loose. Control. He needed control.

After taking a deep breath to reset, he buried himself in the music with clinical precision. If he focused hard enough, the power stayed dormant no matter how intoxicating the harmonies dancing around him were.

The rehearsal lasted until dark, and by the end of the day his voice felt raw and spent. It had been impossible not to oversing. He didn't regret it one bit. He knew how to ride that dangerous edge between damage and performance, his voice would be fine tomorrow.

Dietre turned to him when they were finished, and offered his hand. "It is a pleasure to sing next to you. I am Dietre."

"Traven." He took it firmly. "You have a great instrument."

"As do you. We will tear the foundations of this place with all that resonance."

Traven gave him a hesitant smile. What an odd thing to say.

"Cello?" Finn called over the chorus.

He shook his head, there was no way he'd do the same thing to Rolan again. "Not tonight, I have plans with Rolan. I owe him."

"Fair enough. We shall see you next week."

He approached Malachi with his signature gap-toothed grin. The Director cocked his head, with a smirk tugging at his lip. "How was it?"

He could barely contain himself. "Like taking my first breath."

***

He saw the ripple of Traven's arrival, long before his bald head shone in the dwindling sunlight. Cantor Suits, towering above the crates, halted in their tracks, groaning at the sudden shift of weight. Dockworkers paused and dipped their heads, hurrying out of the way. It was disruptive in a way that made his hands twitch. He thought Traven had an ego before—now he would be insufferable.

DirgeMaul bobbed above the grid of crates, and Rolan glanced with concern over to the unit of guards overseeing Warehouse 1. A weapon this close to the temporary Glysterium storage was sure to raise some ire.

But it didn't.

The sergeant took a few steps forward, hefting a mace in his hands as he sauntered closer. His eyes met the golden cord on Traven's shoulder, and his next steps hesitated. Once Traven turned to head to Warehouse 5—away from the Glysterium—he backed away.

Rolan was jealous of that alone.

"At least yer taking this seriously." He pointed to DirgeMaul.

Traven patted the pommel affectionately. "Of course I am." His eyes gained a mischievous glint. "Did you see the guard back there? I could get used to that."

"At least it's one less problem fer us to deal with." Rolan reached into his coat and pulled out the last two of their missing posters.

Traven leaned the hammer against the crates next to him and leaned over as Rolan read. "We have a former Gold Cord named Livingston Tibor, no contact information. I bet someone at the Crooning Cello would have answers. The other is a little girl, family of carpenters by the surname Gollush."

"Might as well see the carpenters first, they are the closest. I haven't heard anything about Livingston Tibor." Traven hefted DirgeMaul back onto his shoulder and jerked his head for him to follow. "It's uncanny how silent the city is about these disappearances, there are so many."

"I reckon those agents I saw in the tavern have something to do with that."

"Our encounter with the cobbler makes me inclined to agree. These white and gold soldiers seem to be paying people off to stay quiet. I think I know why." Traven went quiet, uncertainty dancing in his eyes.

He let the bass work it out in his head, glancing around them to see if anyone was listening. "You know something else."

Traven craned his head over the crates, looking left and right before lowering his voice. "I do, but I need you to swear secrecy."

His curiosity was immediately piqued. "Well, of course. If it helps us figure out what's going on, it might help find your brother."

The hesitation in Traven felt unnatural. The kid was usually so confident and bullheaded. "How do I say this? There are people who can do…unnatural things with their voices."

"I knew someone who could sing two notes at the same time, why would the Empire be hunting them?"

"Not like that. Unnatural was a bad word. Supernatural is more like it. I can't really explain it…but I think these people are something called Glysterians."

"I still don't get it. You are being too cryptic." Rolan dug the toe of his boot into the cobblestone.

He had never seen Traven so squirrely before. The man couldn't stand still, and kept looking around the corner for eavesdroppers. What was he on about?

"Okay." Traven's chest rose as he took a deep breath. "My leg is healed…because someone willed it with their voice."

He chuckled, shaking his head. "I knew you hadn't seen a healer…but that doesn't make sense. You can't just *sing* someone healthy."

"And yet, my leg was mended in a day." he rolled up his pant leg to show a shiny brown scar."

He couldn't deny that. The proof was staring him in the face.

"How?"

"Not important, and I still don't fully understand it. But I think we can assume these disappearances are that. The soldiers you saw hunt these people."

"And they are watching you." Rolan accused more than asked.

Traven went quiet, chewing the inside of his mouth. Was the kid playing some sort of trick on him? "Not a word to anyone, please."

"Of course you are." Rolan ran a hand through his long hair. "Because being one of the best singers in the realm wasn't enough. Have you been drinking tonight?"

A tuft of spice hit him in the back of the head. He spun around to see the rafter lights shimmering. Traven snatched DirgeMaul and stepped forward with a scowl. "What was that?"

He had his suspicions. "My little ghost."

Chapter XXIX

Traven was a Glysterian, whatever that meant.

In all of Rolan's thirty cycles, he had never seen or heard of anything mysterious or magickal. There were plenty of stories about mythical creatures outside the safety of the Yodel. He assumed most of those were to keep children from wandering out and freezing to death. If he didn't know the Red Woman was after Traven, he would have thought his friend was crazy. He wanted to ask more questions, but there were far too many people in the marketplace.

Traven kept turning sideways to avoid knocking people over the head with his hammer. It made him pat the oversized pruning knife on his belt with affection. A dagger was far more prudent in the city. It fit his friend, however. Ornate, powerful, and a little flashy.

They approached a stall with brown sacks of colored spices. Giant ladles rested in open-mouthed sacks of red, blue, deep purple, and black. A swarm of smells assaulted their noses. Anise collided with citrus, and a peppery undercurrent that threatened to force a sneeze. The vendor sang his greeting, and prepared a small cloth sack in anticipation of a sale. "Happy Scherza, Gold

Cord. A pound of Pizzo spice for your missus tonight?"

"No, sorry." Rolan stepped forward. "We're looking for some folk, a Livingston Tibor and the Gollush family."

The vendor spat on the ground and filled up the small sack with a handful of red spice. "Five glimmer," he demanded, pushing the bag toward Traven.

Rolan rolled his eyes and reached into his coin purse. The crates in his warehouse sold for a hundred, and could have filled fifty of these sacks. Five glimmer was highway robbery. He wasn't sure what they'd do with Pizzo spice, but it appeared his answers were hiding behind this transaction. Nothing was free in this world.

The vendor greedily pocketed the coins and cinched the small spice bag. The sack flew through the air and struck him in the chest, puffing a cloud of crimson. The sweet exotic fragrance was a familiar one, as the entire warehouse was covered in red dust. The man leaned back onto his pile of sacks and pocketed his money. "That puffed-up has-been is probably yelling at the foundations of the Grand Chorus. His cord was revoked a few months ago. He'll likely tell you what you want to know for a drink…and maybe more."

Rolan pulled out the other poster. "And the Gollush family?"

"Nope," the vendor said dismissively, and bowed to Traven.

They both muttered a hymn of thanks and walked through the marketplace crowd. "Five glimmer is insane. He didn't even tell us where to find the carpenter." Traven glared daggers at the spice merchant.

"I suspect that was the Gold Cord Special. There can't be that many around here; let's ask someone else."

Off to the side, near one of the tavern entrances, a small woman knelt in tattered clothes. A sign at her feet read: *MUTE, please help.*

Traven saw her first and tucked the hammer behind his back.

His face was twisted in empathy, the center of his eyebrows raised and his lips downturned. Would they have any coin after this?

The woman looked up at them, politely smiling at Traven until her eyes crossed his shoulder. Terror flashed in her eyes, and she threw a hand up to block him. He was oblivious. Traven knelt down and fished in his pocket for a few glimmer. She stood, quick as lightning while pushing his hand away.

"Take it." He offered, confused.

She gathered her sign and ran off, scarf flapping.

Traven knelt there dumbfounded, the handful of glimmer still outstretched. Rolan gave him a nudge with his knee. "I think she feared you would bring her more trouble. Imagine what riches the others might think you gave her…and what they might do to get it."

"I was just trying to help."

"Sometimes the best intentions can have dire consequences."

Rolan had seen it before, when visiting Yodels on their last legs. Any ounce of charity made people pounce on each other like FrostClaws, desperate to fill their bellies. Once a Yodel began to spiral, it was almost impossible to recover from. Less people meant less workers, which meant less singers. Less singers meant less Glysterium, which meant death.

They moved on, asking on occasion for directions as they weaved their way through the busy streets. Most bowed politely to Traven and went on their way, murmuring apologies. If Rolan asked a question, they would answer to the Gold Cord. It was starting to rankle him. A few more blocks, and a dozen more questions later, they finally had enough direction to find their quarry. The carpenter was tucked away on a road adjacent to Cantata Row, three blocks to the West. Rolan hoped it was the right one.

Traven beat him to the door, his longer legs skipping two steps at a time up the rising side-street. He pulled DirgeMaul down to the side and let it rest on the stone. A few seconds after their knock, the door opened to a balding man with round spectacles and a leather apron covered in scratches. "Terribly sorry. We are closed after sunset." His eyes took in Traven's cord, then drifted down to the GlysterHammer.

"The apologies are ours." Rolan tried his best to smile. "We've got a few questions for you, not related to carpentry."

He looked at Rolan, then back to DirgeMaul and up to Traven's shoulder. "I'm really quite busy."

Traven gave him his trademark gap-toothed smile and placed a hand on the door. "We would like to help you locate your missing daughter. We saw your poster."

Rolan unfolded the poster from his coat, handing it to the man behind the door. The carpenter took it with shaking hands. "I'm sorry we missed this poster. You were very clear about their removal, please don't hurt us."

Traven cocked his head. "We aren't here to hurt you. We're looking for clues; We thought you might be able to point us in the right direction."

The man straightened his back and struck his chest with a closed fist, a gold ring glimmering on his finger. "We are loyal servants of the Empire, and are pleased to do our part in keeping Hearthmere safe and warm. You no longer need to keep testing us, we are good citizens."

A flute began to echo in the alleyways.

Rolan placed a hand on Traven's shoulder. "You have done well in keeping your mouth shut. We appreciate your loyalty to the Empire. Have a pleasant night."

Traven was about to protest when Rolan yanked him away from the door and hurried toward Cantata Row. Every time he glanced behind them, Traven would look too. "What are you looking for?"

"Flute. One of them had a flute." He broke into a jog. "We

need to get into a crowd."

"What's so scary about a flute?"

"It wasn't the flute. It was the person carrying it. I could practically taste their malice."

They spilled into the crowd while shouting apologies, Traven nearly falling over from the extra weight of DirgeMaul. A woman muttered a curse any dockworker would be proud of, then covered her face with a gloved hand. Rolan snickered and slowed to a brisk walk. Already, the crowd was parting for them. He wished Traven didn't stick out like a sore thumb. "Maybe leave that cord at home when we do these outings."

"It makes getting around pretty easy."

"It also paints a target on yer head. Did you see how that guy's face turned white as a ghost?"

"That whole interaction was odd. Did you see his ring?"

"Same one as the cobbler, I think. Maybe they were paid to keep quiet?" Rolan couldn't imagine anything that would have stopped him from finding his own child.

Resonance Heights was fast approaching. They focused on slicing through the crowd while Rolan kept checking the rooftops. He couldn't hear the flute any more, but that didn't mean they had lost their tail. Rolan never imagined a flute would invoke that much apprehension.

Ever looming above Concordia Plaza, the Citadel seemed to pulse an even brighter green at night. The golden cog-laden symbol of the Chorus Arcanum gleamed brilliantly in contrast, and Rolan felt something tug at the back of his mind. The thought disappeared as a lone figure stepped onto the balcony, his chest glowing a faint viridian.

The Baron.

He appeared to watch the Row, placing two metallic hands over the railing. Just once, he swore the man's emerald gaze lingered on Traven. Dread sank all the way down to his boots, a single word and they would both be scooped up by the guards. How involved was the Baron?

Traven's shoulders were hunched as they pushed through the tunnel. The guards straightened and gripped their halberds with white knuckles at the sight of DirgeMaul, but said nothing. Rolan kept his head down and shoved his hands into his pockets while they passed. "Like a sore thumb," he grumbled.

As it was every night, the Crooning Cello could be heard across Concordia Plaza. Rolan felt a knot of resentment settle in his belly; they could get sidetracked here. "Remember, we're on a mission."

"I know." Traven seemed unusually stoic.

They approached the revelry, and as Traven took his first steps up the stairs, one of the guards put a hand up in front of him. "Congrats on the Gold Cord. We were placing bets on when you'd get it. I owe Trem some gleam."

Traven straightened his back. "Thank you. It took longer than I would have liked."

"That being said, I can't let you in here with that oversized walking stick."

Traven and Rolan shared a look. Traven adjusted DirgeMaul on his back and gave his best smile. "I promised Kael I would show him, just this once? I have no plans on destroying the bar."

"Bring that sourpuss out here. Shissel is inside and I'm not looking to get my head caved in if I have to stop you two."

Their rivalry was becoming notorious.

Rolan stepped forward, tucking an elbow to keep his knife covered. "I'll go get him. You watch the door for any flashes of white."

He stepped inside with a wince as the lights and noise assaulted him. Shissel immediately rose with a sneer, but his friends tugged him back down. Rolan knew what he was thinking. *Filthy uncorded.*

It stung more than it should have.

Squeezing himself up to the bar, he placed a few glimmer on the table. The barkeep finished serving a glass of dark ale and then leaned his way. "What'll it be?"

Rolan had to speak louder than he'd have preferred. "I had some questions I needed answers to. Do you know what happened to Livingston Tibor?"

The barkeep pushed the glimmer back. "He was banned from this bar long before he lost his cord. He's probably drowning in his own piss in an alley. What do you need him for?"

"He's missing, I'm on a little side project."

"A fool's errand. Nobody finds someone, once they disappear. Your time would be better spent sitting in one of these booths… and your glimmer."

Rolan gave him a curt nod and pulled away from the bar. Kael was sitting in their regular spot at the back of the tavern with the rest of his friends. Rolan tried his best to shove down a blossoming resentment and approached the table.

Elena gave him a surprising grin, and Mariss openly smiled at him with those large hazel eyes of hers. Finn immediately flagged the barkeep for a drink before standing up and giving him a side-arm hug. "Good to see you, friend! Braving Resonance Heights without your comrade tonight? Traven said he would be with you."

"He's outside, bouncers wouldn't let him in with his hammer."

Kael perked up from his mug and stood with sparkling eyes. "Finally!"

The men stood like excited children, and Elena and Mariss waved them off. He followed Kael and Finn back outside, where Traven was having a friendly conversation with the bouncers, pointing to various parts of DirgeMaul.

Kael rushed down the steps. "Chords, it's even larger than I thought."

Traven smirked and tilted the hammer toward the tenor. "Try it out."

He had never seen Kael so animated before. Was he truly this interested in pre-war history? The tenor grasped the handle with both hands and grunted to lift it. "It's heavy, but not nearly as heavy as it should be. What's the size of the core?"

Traven reached over and unfastened the inner housing, swinging the viewport out of the way. A fist-size gem lazily shimmered inside, and when Traven pulled it out Kael dropped the hammer to the ground with a yelp. Finn roared with laughter and bent down to pick up the dormant hammer, his arms trembling with the strain.

Traven inserted the gem back into DirgeMaul and closed the housing back up. Kael bent down and traced his fingers along the gold engravings with rapt attention. He hummed the musical notes etched into the corners, and Rolan thought for sure the gemstone flared. The tenor must have noticed too, silencing himself.

Kael lifted it a second time and spun the handle, finding the center of balance between the massive head and the six-foot handle. "Do you know what this is?"

The bouncers leaned in, eager to be a part of the conversation. "It's a family heirloom, something we use for breaking up frozen dirt." Traven explained. Rolan could hear uncertainty in his voice.

"It is painful that someone so ignorant of this weapon's history has inherited it."

"Easy now…" Traven growled.

Kael ignored him. "I shall cure you of that ignorance. This is VoxFractum—The Shattered Voice." He pointed to the musical notes. "This is the anthem of Tenebral, a hymn of war. You were using one of the most legendary weapons of the Tenebral Uprising as a farm tool."

Rolan whistled between his teeth. They had been storing

a symbol of outright rebellion under their bed, unguarded, for weeks. He wouldn't be telling Kael that.

Finn took DirgeMaul from his friend and took a wide combat stance, a comically serious scowl on his face. Traven shook his head with a groan and snatched it back. He seemed to hold it with a little more reverence than before. "I had no idea."

"I think we should keep this out of sight from anyone who might recognize it." Rolan suggested. "Especially the Arcanum Priests."

"Agreed. I'm assuming you didn't bring this weapon all the way up here just to show me. What are you boys after?" Kael's eyes lingered on DirgeMaul.

"We were looking for Livingston Tibor. He's on one of those missing posters." Traven explained.

"A waste of time. Tibor was a mess, and lost his cord because he couldn't hold his liquor." Kael studied Rolan while choosing his next words. "It's not what you think it is."

"And the others might be?" Rolan interjected. What did these men know?

"We should talk later, in private." Kael said to Traven, his eyebrows raised in warning.

Finn clapped Kael on the back of the head. "So mysterious. Let's get back inside. You two should join us unless you're still playing detective."

Traven looked at him, then back to his other friends. "We're still playing. Besides, I'm not leaving…VoxFractum outside."

Finn and Kael bade them farewell, and as they headed back to the GroundSong Commons Rolan turned with a frown. "Is Kael a Glysterian?"

Traven's face gave him the answer.

Chapter XXX

At the height of Hearthmere, behind the marble pillars and glass dome of the Opera House, sprawled Upper Resonance Heights. Traven had never been here before, but some of the windows in the Opera House had given him a perfect view.

The district was shaped like a fan, spreading from the foundations of Concordia Plaza. The lesser nobles held gated properties of multi-story homes with winding porches, multiple peaks, and more windows than he could count. Each home sat on something called an acre, filled with manicured bushes and emerald fields of trimmed grass, some even sported trees with pink leaves and silvery bark. With the sun directly above, the whole district was a sea of beautiful greenery. Elena's home, the Marrenvale Estate, was among the twelve lesser houses. What artistry people could do when they weren't freezing to death.

Behind those homes, separated by a wide gravel road and a marble wall rising like fortifications, were the eight greater houses.

Iron-wrought gates and brass signs opened to pathways lined with thin trees that looked more like large bushes. Grass sprawled for a quarter mile, before it met courtyards filled with carriages and water fountains. The buildings—second in size only to the Opera House—wrapped around their courtyards with multiple wings three stories high with glass domes of their own. Most interesting of all was the relative quiet.

Instead of tradesmen singing and choruses rehearsing, the pleasant sound of birds chirping over the burble of running water drifted to the sky. Servants worked shears with blades as long as his forearms along the grass with a steady cadence of snip, snip. There were no voices, no song…no harmony. It almost felt wrong. His shoes crunching on the gravel felt intrusive. It wasn't unpleasantly hot, unlike the sometimes suffocating heat of Concordia Plaza. At least he could wear his fancy coat without sweating through it.

There were plenty of guards here, but not the sort that sneered or cast suspicious glares. Their uniforms were shiny and without wrinkles, and most held gleaming swords with intricate scabbards on their hips. At each gate they nodded at him, murmuring some rendition of, "Gold Cord."

Up ahead, near the center of the greater houses, a crowd of patrons with top hats, billowing dresses, and umbrellas filed into the only open gateway. He still didn't understand how women could breathe with their waists cinched as they were. He paused to glance at the Vexlane estate first, and noticed a lack of servants and a slight overgrowth to the greenery. It would have been imperceptible if not for the uniformity of the other estates.

There was one more thing he needed to see.

Beyond the Daelthorne Estate, with the largest and most impressive field of lush greenery, sprawled the Baron's home.

It was difficult to see through the gates, with the topiaries trimmed into a defensive barrier. What he could glimpse was an estate twice as large as the rest, nearly as monumental as the Opera House. Three fountains spilled sparkling clear water in a courtyard as expansive as Concordia Plaza, and the Baron's personal airship bobbed on its tethers. It gleamed in the sunlight, a vessel of gold and black. It looked sleek and nimble, a ship built for speed. Despite the trepidation creeping up his spine, Traven very much wanted to witness it up close.

He doubled back and joined the queue filing through the Daelthorne gate. The guards stationed there stood at attention, arms and weapons tight to their sides and chin held high. The long street to the central building was filled with bristling feathers and flaring tophats. He ran his hand over his smooth scalp, and wondered if he was underdressed. There was nothing he could do about it now, he hadn't started earning his Gold Cord salary yet.

The throng scattered once setting foot in the spacious courtyard, following the direction of servants waving them to the yard behind the home. Laughter and conversation once again filled the air, accompanied by a string quartet. It had been ages since he had heard a cello.

Around the building, a hundred or more nobles gathered under white tents or on the green lawn. Tables with small plates of delicacies had been precisely arranged, and Traven watched the servants expertly replace them as soon as they left the white cloth. Further down the back of the estate, thick bushes had been trimmed into a maze of white archways and yellow flowers. Women huddled together in small circles while covering their faces with decorated fans. A group of men participated in some sport involving wooden balls and mallets, while others set themselves to drinking.

Traven plucked a flute of wine from a servant's tray and stood near the edges of the crowd. He hoped he would find someone he knew.

It wasn't anyone he had hoped for.

Shissel stood next to an elderly man in black coattails and thinning hair. The tenor was already pointing at Traven, his lips curling as he whispered in Lord Daelthorne's ear.

Traven's heart sank.

He had forgotten that Lord Daelthorne was Shissel's patron. His success here was probably already ruined. His friends weren't anywhere to be seen, and Malachi wouldn't be here to defend him. Mariss would be here, but she was too sweet to get tangled in all of this.

Traven pulled in a deep breath, and started his way toward Lord Daelthorne, when Thariel Vexlane stepped in his path. "My, my, what a striking figure you make, when you aren't covered in mud and blood."

Traven bowed, humming the Hymn of Greeting. "Mistress Vexlane, looking beautiful as ever."

She laughed, a familiar husky sound that felt like it was meant just for him. "My boy, flattery will get you everywhere."

He peered over her, trying to keep an eye on Lord Daelthorne. Thariel cleared her throat and rapped him on the forehead with her fan. "Distracted, are we?"

Traven rubbed his head with a friendly scowl. "Apologies, Mistress Vexlane. I was told Lord Daelthorne was looking for more singers to sponsor. Director Rivers advised me to gain some support from one of the noble houses. I suppose I'm a little eager to have that conversation."

Something dangerous sparkled in her eyes. "And in an effort to gain the support of one house, you risk spurning another. Tell me, why would someone of your talents wish to tether yourself to a man who gobbles up singers like a greedy little child? You would be lost in a sea of mediocrity."

Heat immediately crept up his neck. He was so focused on Lord Daelthorne that he hadn't even considered her. "I meant no disrespect. I'm so very new to this. I supposed I hadn't heard you were looking to sponsor anyone, Mistress Vexlane."

Her eyes softened, and a perfect smile spread across her face. "You may call me Thariel, darling. While it is true I have made no proclamation, if a certain singer showcases exceptional talent, I would be a fool not to throw my hat in the ring."

"Are you saying?"

"I said if, my boy. A hundred singers wear that cord. If House Vexlane sponsors someone, they are exceptional."

But wasn't her house in disrepair? Was all of this bluster and posturing? He was completely out of his depth. He was used to hammering ice and singing sonatas, not wading through the machinations of high society. Everyone spoke in riddles and half-answers. It was infuriating.

Thariel gave him a wink. "Your window of opportunity closes as we speak. The Morayne boy has been whispering venom into Old Daelthorne's ear all morning. He may even be pushing for Director Rivers' head. Whatever did you do to ruffle his delicate feathers?"

"Nothing compared to what I'll do if he's ruined my chances." He lowered his voice to a rumble.

Her eyes lit up like Glysterium as she fixed her already perfect black hair. "That's the spirit. Keep that fire in your belly, you'll need it."

She glided away, silver dress swishing as she cleared the path between him and Lord Daelthorne. The old man was resting on his cane, nodding to his guests as they came to pay their respects. Traven closed the distance between them in long strides, clearing his throat and smoothing out his creme and silver coat. Shissel nudged Lord Daelthorne in the side and made a remark he couldn't hear.

"Lord Daelthorne, I am Traven Caelhardt. I have newly joined the ranks of the Grand Chorus, and Mariss Venisse tells me you are looking to bolster your ranks of talented singers."

Lord Daelthorne's jaw wobbled as he turned his head to Shissel with a knowing look. His voice was thin and raspy. "I have heard a great deal about you, Traven Caelhardt. Shissel here was just telling me about your…unorthodox admission to the Grand Chorus. How did a mud-slinger such as yourself skip protocol and propriety? There are noble singers patiently waiting their turn for next season, and you deign to jump the queue."

"It's my understanding that anyone can join the Grand Chorus as long as they have the talent. I have the talent, and an opportunity presented itself to me. Why shouldn't I have taken it?"

Shissel snorted into his glass. Lord Daelthorne shot him a sharp look that erased his mirth. "Because there are ways to do things—feet you don't step on. Surely you aren't so special that you can skirt tradition."

"Tradition would have had me funneling glimmer into this city while I waited for a turn that may never come. Judging by what you are saying, I may not have even gotten it next season. It appears as if I made the right choice. You don't think someone who takes their opportunities would be a valuable addition to your ranks…over someone who was handed it?" He pointed at Shissel.

"Careful now, boy." Daelthorne wagged a finger. "Shissel here is one of the most talented tenors Hearthmere has ever seen."

"He's quick to mention it."

Lord Daelthorne rapped his cane on the grass. "So you strut in here demanding patronage as if I'm some ripe fruit to be plucked from the boughs of the city, having skirted tradition, and insult my most talented singer. And you expect me to take this favorably? I'm afraid not. I have no place for you."

"He put you up to this. Didn't he?" The heat in Traven's chest began to rise, and he stepped toward Shissel.

The crowd around them fell into silence as Traven raised his voice.

Control. He needed control.

"Shissel has my House's best interest at heart. You have nothing to offer us."

The tenor narrowed his eyes and pulled at Lord Daelthorne's arm. "You'll never be anything more than a glorified mud-slinger. Go back home to your mommy."

The vein on Traven's forehead bulged. How dare this sniveling, spoiled child invoke his mother? How dare he threaten the success he worked so hard to achieve? It was time for Shissel to face him without Finn to protect him. He felt the power inside of him jump to his throat, his muscles tense, and he didn't choke it down. His voice came out in a roar, rattling the glasses nearby. "Duel, now!"

Shissel froze. "You can't be serious."

"Lord Daelthorne, I officially challenge Shissel Morayne. If he's your best singer, I'm about to show you how big of a mistake you've made."

The Lord smirked, looking between the two of them. The crowd murmured in the background, and Traven could see Mariss frantically shaking her head behind them.

"Very well." Lord Daelthorne bowed his head. "I accept."

Chapter XXXI

Mariss pushed through the crowd and skidded to a halt in front of him. "You can't do this. Shissel is one of the best duelists in Hearthmere. He lives for this."

Traven rolled his neck and stretched his back. "I've won a large portion of duels myself, Mariss. I can't back down now; there are too many people watching."

She wrung her hands and scanned the crowd. Leaning in close—so her whisper could be heard over the excited chatter—she brushed against his ear. "Keep it under control. One wrong move here, and you won't make it out of the courtyard."

He nodded, leaning his forehead against hers. "I will."

A thin man with a long curled mustache and monocle traced a circle in the grass. The crowd stepped backwards, careful not to spill their wine. Once satisfied with the makeshift arena, he blew a pitch pipe for silence. "Ladies and gentlemen, singers and songstresses, we are gathered to witness a battle of talents in honor of the great Unification Wars. Let every note and breath reflect the sacrifice the Empire had to endure, as brother fought brother in song and steel. May today bring you honor, no matter the outcome, and may the Empress bless your voices."

Traven had never heard this before. Brothers fought in song and steel? What did that mean? When he asked Mariss, she shrugged and simply offered. "I barely pay attention to the ritual any more. I think perhaps our ancestors sang while fighting, probably for rhythm. That was ages ago, who really knows?"

Shissel sauntered into the clearing with a round of applause. Lord Daelthorne thumped the earth with his cane next to Thariel, her eyes as focused on him as the FrostClaw out in the wilderness. Mariss's hand lingered on his arm until she stepped away, the hidden warning still playing in her eyes. Traven paced back and forth, clearing his throat and practicing a few lip trills.

Even if everything else about his life had changed, duels were still the same. He had won most challenges before; he would win this one, and prove them all wrong.

The judge raised a coin above his head, pausing for dramatic effect before flipping it into the air. Shissel called "Heads," before he knew what was happening. As the challenger, he was supposed to go first. Maybe duels weren't the same either.

The coin showed heads, and the look Shissel gave him had Traven wondering how easy the tenor's nose would break. He forced that instinct down and drew in a deep breath. If he wanted to prove he was worthy of his cord, brute force wasn't going to do it. The judge stepped backward and motioned for Shissel to begin. "The floor is yours."

Shissel made a show of it, stretching his neck and back while working through some warm-ups with his silky high voice. Traven followed suit, shaking the cobwebs off and testing his range. Some days his voice was playful and agile; other days he would be gravelly and hit like a GlysterHammer. Today he could split stones with his voice. He whispered, "May my voice reflect my spirit."

The tenor began a song in his upper range, singing about a maiden crossing the boulevard. Traven understood the tactic, the tenor assumed he couldn't sing very high. Shissel wanted him out of his comfort zone right out of the gate. Smart.

His adversary sang one verse, then waved his arms in time to signify Traven's entrance at the same tempo. Humming to himself in falsetto, he deftly began the passage in a lilting, intimate tone. Just like upper society, brute force wouldn't work up in this part of his range. He continued the lyrics and melody well, adding vocal flourishes and rhythmic changes while staying true to the description of the fine maiden. He added details about her luscious red hair and dangerous eyes, pulling inspiration from the woman on the train. A few audience members murmured their surprise. He was a bass. Basses weren't supposed to sing this high.

He neared the end of the verse, and waved the tempo with a smirk to his glaring opponent. Shissel feigned a yawn and rolled his eyes to the crowd before jumping back into the song.

The tenor raised the stakes, shifting into a higher key while he crafted a chorus about sneaking a kiss under the arches of the Citadel. Shissel was pushing his voice. Traven could see his neck muscles strain under the tension and rolled his neck. The crowd smiled at his playful lyrics and clear talent. Shissel was a perfect representation of the Grand Chorus.

But so was he.

As Shissel gave him the floor, Traven met the high notes with the top end of his falsetto, a clear and pure tone that would have fit well nestled within any soprano section. He had his mother to thank for this, after enduring night after night matching her pitch while he begged to sing in his own range. *You need to be able to sing as many notes as possible, as beautifully as possible. You can't be all rumble and resonance all of the time.*

He thanked her memory and allowed his voice to stay in the stratosphere for just a moment longer. Shissel had tested the upper ranges of the male voice, but now it was time to take this song into Traven's territory. His new lyrics introduced a guard catching the young vagabond and hauling him away into the Citadel. As the story took them deeper and deeper, so went his voice. When he was able to sing in his chest voice, he added vibrato and darkened his tone. A few men nodded in appreciation, and Shissel cleared his throat. He didn't know Traven could sing through four octaves.

At the bottom of his range, Traven stared with fiery intensity at his opponent, as he signaled the tenor to begin singing. Shissel shook his head just enough for him to notice…then cleared his throat again, and breathed deep.

His voice croaked in a pathetic growl. It was husky, raw, and an octave too high. He tried again, his voice creeping out like a hoarse whisper. In a fit, Shissel flattened his tophat onto the grass and shook his head. The crowd gasped at the outburst, then erupted into applause. Thariel cackled wildly over the cacophony, her gloved hands clapping with enthusiasm. The judge raised Traven's hand above his head. With anyone else, he might have felt guilty about taking advantage of his range, except Shissel was Shissel. And a duel was a duel.

"Well played, hayhead," Shissel growled next to him.

He didn't respond, already worrying about the next section. The breath support challenge was going to be difficult. "Water please," he raised his hand.

Mariss appeared next to him with a glass and a supportive smile. "That was good. He underestimated you. He'll come at you harder next time."

The Judge raised his hands for the crowd to silence, Traven sipped his water and gave back the glass to Mariss with a Hymn of Thanks. She responded in kind.

"Let us now begin the Longevity Trial. Please begin singing the moment I give the command; an early or late start will be met with penalties." He looked at Traven to be sure he understood.

He nodded, signaling he was ready.

Shissel did the same, hopping from foot to foot.

This time, the memory was his brother coaching him near the highest level of Grendal Yodel, their legs dangling over the balcony. *Breathe deep, your stomach is a giant barrel that needs every inch filled with air. Your breath comes from under your lungs. Imagine as you draw air from your mouth that you fill from your back to the front. Don't let your shoulders rise, that's a shallow breath. Keep the hips forward, and shoulder blades back. Breathe.*

He drew in breath through the entire four-count the Judge prepared, filling his lungs to near-bursting. He would have to sing in the upper range of his chest voice, where notes took little effort to sustain and produce. Anything too low would deplete his reservoir quickly, and anything too high would run the risk of cracking under weak breath.

The two of them began singing a single sustained note, Shissel a fair margin higher than he. Looking directly at each other, they sang for ten seconds, neither man showing any signs of wear. Twenty seconds went by, and he could feel his heart beating in his neck. He wondered if anyone else could hear the pulse in his voice. Thirty seconds, and Traven could feel his reserves depleting. He tightened his abs to wrestle the last bit he had, and furrowed his brow. Shissel showed no signs of wavering, a half-smile forming when he realized victory was in his grasp.

At the forty-second mark, Traven bent over while gasping for air. The crowd murmured as he pulled in a few heavy breaths with his head hanging low. Shissel continued well into the minute mark, then resolved his note with some added vibrato and a flourishing bow.

Traven clapped for his opponent despite himself. That was an impressive feat. At forty seconds that was the longest Traven had ever sung…and it was nowhere close to his competitor.

Thariel gave him a conciliatory half-smile. Mariss approached him and placed a hand on his back. "You could have won against nearly anyone else. Shissel is full of hot air," she said loudly enough for the tenor to hear.

"Leave us, Mariss. Your boyfriend has a duel to lose," Shissel boasted.

He felt heat rise under his collar as Mariss's cheeks reddened. She looked at him and grimaced. "You've got this. Let's go, bass."

The Judge waved the crowd silent. "For our final round I will judge the technical prowess of each combatant. You both shall sing a single passage with as much complexity as you can, keeping the notes within the reasonable range of a middle voice." He gave them both a warning glare.

"Once the passage has been repeated by the other, the sides will switch. Points will be deducted from three for each phrase not exactly repeated, until the loser has run out. The combatants are currently tied one to one. Let us begin with Master Caelhardt."

Clearing his throat, Traven began a thrilling sequence of notes that ripped through accidentals, accented with crisp diction. His voice lilted and shifted from forte to piano. Shissel followed him exactly, smirking at the relative ease as if to say, *Is that the best you can do?*

Shissel then began his section, using an interesting technique where he allowed his voice to do something that Traven would describe as a controlled crack...except it was an exact octave above every time. The chance was passed to him, and thankfully he could replicate the technique well enough for the Judge's satisfaction. The tenor was good, very good. Worry was beginning to make him sweat.

This time, Traven would try something different. During his adventures through the nearby cave systems back home, he found he could curve his tongue slightly enough to create an overtone.

By moving his tongue, he could adjust the overtone pitch. He tried that now.

Thariel clapped with delight when Shissel looked completely panicked. He sang for a few modulations, remembering when he had ww his father this trick—when he felt the power surge. A tremor that shook his body.

Not now. Not in front of everyone.

He felt it crawl up his body like a spider. His tone wavered and the overtone disappeared. Traven tried to force the power back, but it fought him, cracking his voice. Sweat formed on his brow and his leg started to shake with adrenaline. It wanted to be let loose, it *needed* to be let loose. The Glysterium gems fastened to Shissel's coat shimmered and winked like candlelight. He was losing control, he needed to stop…but the magick wouldn't let him. He slammed the memory of his father behind a black void of emotion…and stopped singing.

The crowd collectively gasped, with some smirking at his perceived failure. The embarrassment threatened to summon his power again. Thariel cocked her head curiously while fanning her face.

Had she seen? Did she know?

The urge wouldn't go away. It rested there in his throat, ready to claw its way out if he sang another note. Shissel tried to repeat his technique, but growled as he failed to do so. Another point for him.

For the next round, Shissel poured every ounce of his skill into the Call and Repeat. He sang through sixteenth and thirty-second notes so quickly that even if he wasn't battling for control, he might not have been able to remember the right order. Sweat trickled down his back. When the Judge signaled for Traven to repeat it, he opened his mouth…

And the ground shivered.

It was a subtle shake, as if an icicle had fallen from the top of a Yodel while he was nestled inside, but it made him clamp his mouth shut. He shouldn't continue. He couldn't.

The Judge raised his hand for Traven a second time, but he shook his head and gestured to the tenor. He couldn't continue, there was no telling what would happen. He conceded.

Shissel jumped into the air while pumping his fist, Traven sneered. The crowd applauded politely, some with confused looks on their faces, some clearly disappointed. The duel had been close, no doubt it would be the talk of the District for weeks. He'd never live this loss down.

He stood there shaking his head, afraid to speak, afraid to move.

Mariss and Thariel both met him as the crowd collapsed on them. Traven bowed his head and gave Mariss a sad smile, she returned it with a quick hug. Thariel snapped her fan closed and lifted his chin with two fingers. "Despite the loss, I am impressed. I would like to invite you to a personal soiree of mine—just a few guests—to discuss your potential patronage."

But he had just lost. He stared at the cord on his shoulder, wondering if he truly deserved it.

He wanted to smile, but worry had him chewing the inside of his cheek while looking for an exit. Thariel pressed hard against his jaw, leveling her eyes at him. "Head up, a loss with dignity is better than a win without."

Grimacing, he met her eyes and nodded. His father had always said something very similar.

"I'm going to kill him." Traven growled as he burst through the door and then slammed it shut. The lamps dimmed and fluttered back to full brightness.

"Who?" Rolan took a peek out into the hallway.

"That petty, aristocratic, thin-blooded Shissel. He ruined my chances of picking up Lord Daelthorne as a sponsor. He had already made up his mind before I even went to his party." Traven ripped off his coat and hurled it at his bed.

Steam was practically coming out of the boy's ears. "I think it's high time you challenged him to a duel." Rolan growled.

"I did!" The lights flickered wildly. "And I lost, in front of everyone in Upper Resonance Heights…in front of Mariss and Thariel Vexlane…because of this!" He gestured at the winking lights.

"Okay," Rolan kept his voice level as he grabbed his friend by the shoulders and looked at the lights. "Deep breath. What happened?"

Traven's chest heaved. "I was winning. He couldn't outsing me…and then I felt the power. It was so close to erupting, and I chose to shut my mouth instead of destroying everyone around me."

They needed to get out of here. The whole building was probably a light show right now.

"Which is monumentally better than outing yourself to these Hunters, but anyone who knows anything about Glysterians will surely notice all of Cantata Row flickering, as you stormed down here. We need to go. Grab the hammer, lose the cord."

Traven unlatched the golden braid from his jacket and stuffed it into his pocket. "I'm not leaving it behind."

There probably wasn't time to argue. "Fine, throw on yer old coat. We'll be cold in the Whisper Ward."

Traven pulled DirgeMaul from under the bed and followed Rolan downstairs. The innkeeper called out to them, but neither of them responded. He probably would have paid the man to keep quiet, but judging by the fear he'd witnessed in the carpenter and cobbler, he didn't have enough coin. Instead of the front exit, Rolan took them through the back door and into the service alleyway, skirting most of the GlysterLamps on the main road.

They walked in silence while the temperature dropped, tapping their collars closed to keep their warmth in. He had forgotten to grab something to eat, intending to sup with Traven, and was starting to regret it. Traven must have been thinking the same thing. "I'm starving."

"Stay back here. I'll get something fer us." Rolan pointed to a dark archway.

He stepped into the light of Cantata Row and purchased a few loaves of bread that would have been fresh this morning. Thankfully he was given a steep discount. While the merchant bagged his purchase, he peered up and down the street.

And felt the blood drain from his face.

Leaving the Final Measure, was a thin woman in white and gold. Stringy silver hair fell across half of her face. Rolan quickly slipped through the crowd and back into the alleyway with their bread. "Hunter, at our inn."

Traven's eyes went wide, and he gripped the hammer until the leather creaked. They needed to hide, not fight. Rolan growled at him. "I need you to stay calm. One flicker, and we're dead."

The bass nodded, pulling in a deep breath and closing his eyes. DirgeMaul shimmered for a split second before going dormant. They couldn't afford to stay much longer, but if his friend didn't get his emotions under control, it wouldn't matter how far they ran. Satisfied that Traven was calm enough to move, Rolan peeked around the corner.

A group of shift workers was making their way from the Warehouse District, large enough for them to hide behind. Rolan put his finger up, waited for the men to cross the alley, and then waved Traven behind him. They hurried into Cantata Row, Traven ducking so his head didn't poke over the crowd. Everything about the man stuck out. No wonder he thought so highly of himself.

After passing the Rail terminal and into the Warehouse District, they ducked back into another side street close to the Frostline. Workers leaned against the glittering stone, puffing on cigarettes that filled the air with an unpleasant stench. Traven glared at them as their faces became illuminated with the amber glow. "They'll ruin their voice."

"That's what you are worried about right now?"

The thin, haunting melody of a violin drifted between the buildings, and they both scrambled to run. She was toying with them; otherwise she'd be silent. She wanted them to run.

And so they did.

Traven was keeping pace well, despite the massive hammer in his hands. Their breath puffed white clouds as they wove around the cargo containers of the warehouse square. The front doors—so large they needed to be opened by Cantor suits—were locked shut for the night. Rolan dashed to the employee entrance on the side and shook the door handle. It was locked.

"Slush," he muttered.

Traven pointed to DirgeMaul with hunched shoulders, indicating he could smash the lock. Rolan shook his head vehemently, they needed to be silent. Sprinting back to his friend, Rolan sat down between crates. "Can't get in. We need to get to the Whisper Ward."

A steep, muddy bank fell precipitously behind the last of the warehouses, and they slid down to the huddled metal shacks near the city walls. It was a cold night, colder than he would have thought in the city. He wondered if they could convince anyone to let them huddle inside. Was there any hospitality down here?

They walked through the back paths, stepping on large stones to hide their tracks and keep their boots free of mud. Clothes hung on lines stretching from shack to shack, and there was a sharp smell of ammonia in the air…he didn't see much running water.

A playful cascade of notes whispered over the rooftops, pushing them back into a jog.

Rolan started to push against doors, but none of them opened. A few patrons from inside shouted angrily for them to go away, so he stopped doing it. Traven growled between breaths. He was getting impatient.

Rolan had an idea.

Looking up for the building-sized steam, he steered them through the alleys for the most direct route. People were always huddled near the heat, and it might give them a place to hide. He'd have to do something about the hammer, though.

Traven slipped and bumped against a nearby building with a clang and a flash of emerald light. "Slush," he cursed before pumping his legs into a full sprint.

Steam blotted out the moonlight as they rounded the last corner. A crowd huddled close to an exhaust pipe three meters wide, warming their hands on the vapor. Rolan slowed down and pulled Traven into a space between buildings. "We need to do something about DirgeMaul."

Traven looked pained. Rolan knew it was important to him, but right now it was a beacon. "Here." He tugged at the handle.

His friend resisted for a split second, then sighed and let it go. Rolan nodded and dunked the hammer into a barrel of sitting water, then draped someone's hanging clothes over the pommel. It was a pathetic disguise, but it had to do for now.

They approached the steam vent with their heads down and hoods up. Traven kept looking back at his hammer. Someone made space for them, shuffling through the mud with a slurp. The chill of the night started to leech away, and Rolan sighed in gratitude. How did people live like this?

The silence was sobering. In a world where music was everything, the people down here had forgotten why to sing. He tried to remember the last time he sang more than a Hymn.

Footsteps, followed by a playful melody.

She had been closing the distance on them, even at a sprint. Traven's eyes shone in the dim light, wide as saucers. Rolan pulled his hood down and hunched over, his friend quickly followed.

"Evening, fellow citizens." Her voice held a tinge of mirth. "Have you seen my two friends? Big men, one bald with dark skin, and another with shaggy brown hair. I have been looking for them all night. I'd hate for them to get lost."

The group said nothing. Rolan had been counting on this.

She circled them, playing a tone that reminded him of regret. "Come now, surely the Ever-Winter hasn't stolen your voices. Three glimmer to anyone who tells me where they are."

Mercifully, silence was the only answer she received.

"They are quite remarkable. One carries a hammer worth a year's stay in the GroundSong Commons."

One of the inhabitants shifted their feet and stole a glance at him. Rolan kept his head down and ignored them. What would win out, fear or survival? The more these people had time to think, the worse his chances of escaping.

"Very well." Some of the humor in her voice had dissolved. "Enjoy your steam."

She skulked away, thrumming on her violin until the melody disappeared behind the roiling steam of the furnace. He wondered how long they would have to stay here. Their inn had been compromised.

⌢

Rolan's feet were numb.

Some of the people in their huddle had shuffled away to sleep, disappearing into the mist like wraiths. A few times, the violin could be heard in wisps, but only for the first hour or so. It had been blissfully quiet, and Rolan suspected it was well past midnight. He nodded for Traven to follow, and they went back to retrieve DirgeMaul.

"What do we do now?" Traven shivered.

"We need somewhere to sleep. We can't go back to the inn tonight…or ever."

"I think room and board down here might be hard to acquire."

"We have to try. We'll freeze to death otherwise."

Were there even inns down in the Whisper Ward? He had yet to see a building large enough for more than one family, and he doubted anyone would let them hunker down for a night. "Let's try the main road, the one that runs through it all."

Then they heard the screaming.

Traven was the first to move, his long legs pumping through the mud and toward the sound. Rolan cursed and tried his best to keep up. The man was fast when he needed to be.

Rounding the corner, they stumbled upon a squad of soldiers throwing people into the mud. A woman shrieked as her husband pushed against them and caught a cudgel to the head for his trouble. He fell face first, and didn't move to get up. A young boy scrambled to check on his father, and another soldier backhanded him. The boy fell against a nearby wall with a rattle.

Traven stepped forward, DirgeMaul humming ever so slightly. "Slush," Rolan cursed as he stepped in front of him. "We can't do this. We need to hide."

Traven tightened his grip. "They are hurting innocent people."

"We don't know that they're innocent." He hated the words.

Traven looked down at him like he was crazy. "They are hurting children." DirgeMaul flickered.

"And…" Rolan placed his hand on DirgeMaul's head. "There are ten of them, with the backing of an entire army at the sound of a trumpet. We should go before they see us."

It was too late. A soldier spat on the ground and walked over. "Move along now. Official Empire business."

Traven pushed his chest against Rolan's hand. "Empire business involving pulling children out into the freezing air and murdering their father?"

"These rats are dissidents, members of the Dischordants. They've been hoarding Glysterium. Now move along."

"If they had Glysterium," Traven growled. "They wouldn't be shivering."

The soldier drew his cudgel, whistling for his friends. "Looks like you have an unauthorized weapon. We'll be confiscating that."

Rolan felt the hair on the back of his arms rise. Traven's chest felt so hot that steam should have been coming off of it, and he had to remove the hand holding him back. He stepped to the side as the guard approached, hand on his dagger. He didn't want to fight, but it wouldn't take much for him to defend these people.

The guard approached, his hand reaching out to grab DirgeMaul.

A shockwave threw him back into his friends, a low resonating note bouncing off of the buildings. His chest thrummed with the impact. It sounded like Traven's voice.

A nearby lamp flashed bright enough to illuminate their faces. A soldier screamed, "Dischordant!"

Rolan turned to his friend with wide eyes, then grabbed him by the collar and yanked him away from the FrostLine. He hoped none of the guards saw. Thankfully, Traven didn't fight him. They sprinted through the alley while shouts and whistles followed.

The violin had to be close.

The Whisper Ward was a maze of buildings, and more than once they had to skid to a halt at a dead end. Racing footsteps alerted them seconds before they cut to another alley, toward the steam. Once or twice he thought he saw a flash of white darting over the rooftops.

A lance of green light exploded into the mud, inches from Traven's face. The bass yelped and slammed DirgeMaul to the ground with a resounding thud, throwing his body to the left. Rolan slipped while trying to keep up, sliding a knee into the mud before scrabbling after his friend.

They turned and turned, their path careening toward the center of the city while slipping in the mud and muck. He didn't dare look behind him, but it felt like the soldier's footsteps were on a collision course. The sounds of the violin were ever present, a never-ending sonata of pursuit. More explosions, inches from their heels. Rolan could feel the power singe the ends of his hair.

And then they turned to a dead end.

It was over.

Traven halted just enough to think, then pulled back DirgeMaul into a swing. A little red-headed girl winked into existence right in front of the wall. "You two are making a racket." she giggled.

His ghost.

She sang in a sweet little soprano voice, and creme colored smoke twirled around Traven's body. He disappeared right in front of his eyes, then so did she…and then so did Rolan.

Chapter XXXIII

A little invisible hand grasped Rolan's finger and tugged him back the way they came. He looked down and saw nothing. No feet, no swinging arms, just fresh footsteps in the mud as they ran. How was this possible?

He was pulled down one alley and then another, under clotheslines and around discarded buckets. Groups of soldiers crossed their path, and he felt a tiny hand press his chest until he was flat against a building. Once the alley was clear, he was yanked back into a jog until the next set of soldiers. He thought she was taking random turns until he realized she was guiding him through the maze of shacks with efficient familiarity. On and on they raced, back up the slope to the GroundSong Commons and across the Warehouse Plaza. When his boots struck against the cobblestone, he realized they were silent.

No wonder his coworkers thought their warehouse was haunted.

She guided them up a pile of crates stacked against the wall and onto the roof. Once they were up, Traven and the girl winked back into the moonlight. She put a finger to her lips, panting heavily, and walked toward an open skylight. He and Traven shared a look of awe.

Teetering as she stood with bags under her little eyes, she waved them down into the window before disappearing into the building. Rolan leaned down and squeezed himself through. His shoulders scraped against both sides. Traven dropped DirgeMaul down into the hole, before struggling himself through. She giggled as they grunted in their effort.

They were on the platform he had explored earlier. The darkest corner of the warehouse…where he thought someone might be living.

The little one plopped down on her makeshift bed, a collection of ratty blankets next to a half-destroyed crate. She had been so lively when she first appeared. Hiding them must have drained her something fierce.

"You're a Glysterian." Traven whispered excitedly.

"No, I'm Half-Step." She yawned.

He stopped Traven from correcting her with the wave of a hand. "What Traven meant to say was, thank you. Thank you fer saving us."

"You would have been clobbered, or sliced. Violin lady doesn't like rules." She pulled his half-eaten loaf from her pocket and gnawed on it. She was missing one of her front teeth.

"Hey!" He was about to snatch it back, but decided she could use it more.

Half-Step hesitated, then pulled the bread from her mouth and held it out for him. He shook his head. "No, it's yers."

Traven let loose a light laugh and sat cross-legged on the rough wooden boards. "Are you up here by yourself?"

Half-Step shrugged while continuing to gnaw on the bread.

He scratched his beard. "How long have you been following us?"

She pointed at Rolan and mumbled through chews. "Following him."

"Ok, how long have you been following him?"

Looking at Rolan with a mischievous scrunch to her nose, she shrugged again. "Since he started giving me presents."

It reminded him of something. Rolan's eyes lit up as he dug into one of his coat pockets. He pulled out two stone figures, one from his home and the other he had been working on. "This one is for you." He placed it in her hand. "And this one was my daughter's. I think she'd want you to keep an eye on it."

Traven raised his eyebrows, and Rolan cleared his throat. "Her name was Alleria…she died in an avalanche."

She took both of them with a squeal and placed them with tender care on her blankets. Rolan didn't turn his head at Traven, who was staring at him. He didn't like talking about his daughter.

Half-Step pulled the bread from her mouth and wiggled on her bed. "Was Moira her mommy?"

His inhale was ragged and his voice faltered. "She was."

"She probably can hear you. My mom and dad can hear me when I talk to them." She nodded knowingly.

"Did you lose them?"

"In a blackout. I was shivering so bad, one of my teeth popped out. They covered me like blankets so I could get some sleep…and the cold got 'em." She spoke as if it were the weather.

Traven turned his head between the two of them. "I'm so sorry. I lost my mother to the cold too."

"The embrace of the Ever-Winter is undiscriminating." Rolan sighed.

"I hate that saying." Traven grumbled.

So did he.

They sat in silence, sharing the stale bread, and listening to the building groan and pop under the temperature changes. Rolan's thoughts went to the night he failed to save his family, and his heart grew heavy.

Traven, always one to lighten the mood, stretched his back and grunted. "So, how do you do your invisibility trick?"

"My magick?"

"Yes…your magick. How do you do it?"

She put her head down on her blanket and yawned. "I sing and think about sad things."

Traven's eyes sparkled. "What sort of song? A sonata, an aria? What key and time signature? Is it the same song every time?"

Half-Step's eyes grew wider with each one of his rapid-fire questions. She started shaking her head and sat back up with bewilderment. "You talk. A *lot*. I had to sing *so* much to keep you quiet."

Traven closed his mouth as Rolan cackled. "You do talk a lot."

The bass rubbed the top of his head. "I'm sorry. I'm just very curious." He paused while chewing his lip, clearly troubled. " I think I can do magick too."

"You can." She stated plainly.

"How can you tell?"

"Because you make the lights twinkle. That's how they find you. Can you go invisible too?"

"No…I'm not really sure what I can do. The ground shakes sometimes when I get angry."

She laid back down. "That sounds boring. I like disappearing better."

Traven paused while his forehead creased and he pressed his lips together. The next words came out in a rush. "How do you control it? How do you stop it from just…happening?"

Half-Step shrugged her little shoulders as if someone had asked where her missing toy was. "I dunno, you just gotta practice."

Rolan studied Traven's face as he turned his way. The smile

was gone, replaced by weariness and desperation. He offered his friend an apologetic smile and raised his eyebrows. "Hey, don't look at me. I'm just an innocent bystander, amazed that there is such a thing as magick."

"The Hunters make anyone magick disappear." Her eyes darted to the window.

"But why?" Traven drummed his fingers on DirgeMaul.

She shrugged and closed her eyes. "I'm tired. It's bedtime."

Rolan did not appreciate the thought of sleeping on these boards. "We can find a new place to sleep tonight; I have glimmer. You should come with us. It will be warmer."

"Nope." She replied.

He knelt down to her level and wiggled his bushy eyebrows. "It will be warm…and there's lots of food."

She shook her head, "I have to stay here."

Traven sounded frustrated. "Why?"

"I can't tell you; it's a secret. I can't hear important things all the way up in Resonance Heights, people don't like kids hanging around up there." She pouted.

Rolan doubted he could get her to budge. "Can you at least tell us where these missing people go?"

"To the big black tower. To disappear." She picked at a blanket.

"The Citadel?" Traven's voice rose. "Who takes them?"

"Violin Lady and her friends. The people in the white coats. The meanies who chase me."

Rolan had half a mind to pick her up and haul her back to the street. She wasn't safe here. "You should come with us. We can keep you safe."

"I saved your biscuits back there. You should stay with me." She stuck out her tongue.

"Nope." Traven mimicked her little voice. "I'll clobber them with my hammer next time. You'll see."

All of the humor melted from her sleepy little face. She looked Traven dead in the eye and whispered, "Never fight them. Just run. Always run."

He tried to get more answers out of her, but her eyes fluttered closed and her breathing grew even. Rolan pulled the threadbare blankets over her and then tried to get comfortable on the floor. "We'll convince her tomorrow. Let's try to get some sleep."

He knew Traven wouldn't be sleeping tonight.

Chapter XXXIV

Rolan woke the next morning to find Traven sitting in silence, DirgeMaul resting on his thighs as his long legs dangled below. Half-Step was already gone, off to whatever mischief she got up to. He'd have to convince her to leave this makeshift attic some other time. The bass rolled the gold cord between his fingers.

"Morning." Rolan stretched. His back had a hundred knots.

Traven nodded, tucking the cord away. "She left an hour ago. Tried to be quiet, but I'm a light sleeper."

"How'd ya sleep?"

Traven took a long time to answer, long enough that Rolan thought his question hadn't been heard. When he did turn around, the boy looked ten cycles older. It was more than lack of sleep, last night had changed something.

"I think I should go home," he said with a whisper.

"Go home? After achieving yer dreams?"

"There's something going on in this city. A sickness I don't quite understand." Traven tucked the gold cord into his pocket. "People live without fear of freezing to death, and still they sneer and cajole each other. There's a fear here, like everyone is afraid

to say what they really mean. I think it's because of the Empire…
do you really think those people were dissidents?"

He remembered his words. "I was just trying to save us
from…well…what happened."

Traven's face darkened. "Yeah."

"So, what did happen? Is that what bein' a Glysterian is all
about? Tossing people around with your voice?"

His friend chuckled and rubbed his bald head. "I don't know.
Any time I press Kael on it, he just tells me to wait, to be patient.
I just…It's getting harder to control."

Rolan wasn't quite sure what to say. "The little one said
emotion drives it. Is it the same fer you?"

"Yea." Traven rapped a fist on the wooden slats below him.
"Mostly when I lose my temper."

"So keep it in check. Didn't yer parents teach you how to do
that?"

Fire shimmered in Traven's eyes, and Rolan felt himself
recoil. He didn't want to be on the business end of his friend's
voice. Traven caught the reaction, and his face contorted with
conflict. The fire dissolved, and he cleared his throat. "My father
always had a little edge to him, and it got much worse after my
mother passed. I don't usually get this angry, but there's this
pressure I can feel building behind my eyes. I just want to be
respected here. I thought my voice would be enough to make me
belong."

Rolan took a deep breath and softly smiled. "Well, let me
start by saying that yer a good fella, and it has nothing to do with
yer voice. Sure, ya might be a little bullish…and stubborn…and
infuriatingly optimistic, but ya got an honorable heart. Just try to
keep your head, don't let people like Shissel get under your skin.
He's afraid of you."

Traven looked wounded.

"Not like that. You threaten the way he sees the world. There's no chance someone who grew up digging dirt could ever stand as an equal to his pampered ass. Then you came in and didn't take no for an answer. You got that cord with just yer voice. He probably pulled every lace-edged strings he could."

Rolan stood and stepped over to the window in the ceiling. "Work starts soon fer me. You just keep your head down. I think maybe DirgeMaul stays up here until we get a new place to live. I saw an apartment at the edge of the warehouse square. It ain't pretty, but maybe that will help us lay low."

Traven rose with him, his gaze lingering on the hammer. "Do you think she'll try to sell it?"

"If she can lift it far enough to a pawn shop, she earned it."

It was good to hear Traven laugh.

Rolan procured the apartment after work. The paint on the walls was chipped, and the heating duct barely worked, but it had enough space that the men didn't have to share a room. The main room served as both a kitchen and common area, and for the week they had lived there, it had been used maybe once. Traven stashed DirgeMaul in a tall armoire and hadn't taken it out since. Even if the soldiers hadn't seen their faces, the hammer was a dead giveaway.

Rolan spent every lunch up in the rafters, bringing a spare lunch and talking to the shadows. Half-Step would whisper to him, sharing funny stories or telling him about how things were changing in preparation for the Empress's arrival. Talking with her reminded him of Alleria in the best and worst way, and he found a pang of loss every time his lunch was over. A small part of him had wanted Moira's spirit to be with him, but the little rascal's toothy smile and scrunched nose smoothed over that emotional ripple. He wanted to scoop her up and protect her from the whole world.

Their journeys to the Whisper Ward had been halted, with both men unwilling to revisit the depressing state of the lost and forgotten. He could see the war behind Traven's eyes as he put on his fancy creme and silver coat, and wondered if being a Gold Cord was everything his friend wanted it to be. From time to time, he would catch Traven staring out of the window, jaw clenched as he chewed the inside of his cheek. He could tell when the bass particularly bothered—the lights would dance. The singing was gone, and Rolan found himself missing the way he could hear Traven coming long before he entered their old room at the inn.

Sleep came easy for him, the drone of airship engines acting as a lullaby. On occasion, a falling crate would pull him out of his dreams, and he could hear Traven sighing deeply at the intrusion from the other room. He would hate to be such a light sleeper.

Near the end of the week, Traven returned from rehearsal with an embroidered envelope in his hand. He handed it over to Rolan with a mixture of excitement and worry, hopping from foot to foot as he waited for Rolan's response.

Dearest Traven,

You are hereby invited to the Vexlane Estate on the fourth Scherza of Dulcember, 3 p.m. Attire is formal.

I look forward to your attendance. Prepare two songs of your choosing, and choose well. This may be the opportunity you are looking for.

-Thariel

Rolan whistled through his teeth. "Perhaps the duel fiasco didn't backfire like you thought it did."

"I can't shake the feeling that this is all connected. Should I go?"

"You've been cooped up in here all week, staring at the crumbling walls after rehearsals. You need a patron, and you don't have Lord Daelthorne to lean back on. Do you have any other suitors in mind?"

Traven fussed with his coat and wrinkled his nose. "No. What would I even wear? I don't have anything formal."

"Best visit that cute little seamstress, then."

Chapter XXXV

Nerise fussed at the buttons of Traven's new long-tailed white and gold coat. Pin clenched in her teeth, she pulled and tugged at hems and seams he didn't even know existed. Finn had stretched himself across one of the lounge chairs, buckled shoes propped up into the air.

Traven was in a valiant battle, keeping his eyes from her plunging neckline as she knelt in front of him. Why did she have to wear such low-cut dresses? The way she batted her eyelashes and smirked at the most innocent remarks, made him jumble his words, which made her giggle and scrunch up her nose, which then made it worse. He decided to focus on the curls piled on top of her head, expertly arranged to mimic a flower arrangement. Hair was safe.

With a heavy exhale, Nerise stood and gave him a coquettish smile. "You will slay them tonight."

Traven hoped so. He had already run through his songs three times this morning, but nerves were beginning to worm their way into his stomach as the day wore on. He was as prepared as he was going to be.

"Relax, they will fawn over you. You'll barely get a word in, and whatever you do say will come out like rich honey," Finn spoke while chewing a cluster of round purple fruits he called graypes.

Nerise murmured something that sounded like approval, and Traven chuckled when Finn jolted up to stick his nose an inch from her face. His goatee quivered as he chewed. She startled back and laughed at herself. "Your voice is lovely too, my pigeon."

What an odd pet name, he thought.

Finn seemed satisfied, dropping a graype down her bodice before plopping back on the couch. Nerise reddened and darted into the back room of the shop. Finn called out, already halfway after her, "Care for some assistance, dear?" Traven cackled.

Alone in the shop, he stepped up to admire himself in the mirror. He had spent some time at the barbershop after picking up one of his favorite scones. The barber had done a remarkable job; his beard had been expertly trimmed, and his head was smooth and shiny. His white coat rested over a golden vest and black shirt, with white pants and golden shoes. He thought it was ridiculous, but Nerise swore anything less would be insulting to Mistress Vexlane. He needed to impress, and Nerise swore she would make him unforgettable. He raised his hands to his hips and struck a formidable pose, raising one eyebrow the way Finn did when he was especially pompous.

"Well, don't you think highly of yourself." Mariss rested her hip against the doorway.

Traven nearly fell off of his stool. "I'm not. I just...Mariss! What are you doing here?"

She walked in with a package under her arm. "I had some repairs to drop off for Master Daelthorne." She set it down on the counter. "Are you ready for your debut?"

"I guess so."

Mariss looked at him from head to toe. "Nerise really does a good job. She complemented your dark complexion quite well. The gold really screams, 'I'm a Gold Cord now, hear me belt.'"

"Is it too much?" He looked back at the mirror.

"No," she said hastily, then cleared her throat and stepped a little closer. "There's something else."

Traven felt his stomach flip as the pink in her cheeks faded. What could it be? One moment she was all self-assuredness, and the next she was blushing and burying her face in her hands. He gestured for her to continue.

"I think you should tell Malachi you aren't feeling well, and miss rehearsal. Just for Modera." She met his eyes, and he could almost feel her concern.

Traven couldn't believe what she was saying. "Why would I miss rehearsal? We are only a few weeks away from the concert. Every rehearsal is important."

"Because of what we talked about…about the soldiers in white. You've been nailing it in catch-up sessions. Just one day, can you promise me?"

"Promise you what?" Finn returned, his face unusually serious.

Mariss's face reddened, and she took a step backward while glancing at the door, "I was just…telling Traven it might be best if he didn't come to rehearsal on Modera."

"Traven will be fine, Mariss." Finn gave her a loaded stare as Nerise entered the room. "I'll take care of anything that pops up."

Mariss stammered and took another step back. She clearly wanted to say more, but Nerise being present seemed to catch her tongue. "Of course. I was being silly and thought maybe… we could have lunch together while we toured the city. Forget it, sorry to bother." She darted out of the shop. The clicking of her shoes against the cobblestone quickly faded.

"Typical Mariss." Finn smiled and clapped his back. "Although I am surprised she was so bold as to ask you directly for a date. You must have made quite an impression."

"You know she wasn't asking me for a date." Traven frowned.

Finn punched him in the arm and jerked his eyes toward Nerise. "You have nothing to worry about. I'll be there if anything in rehearsal goes sideways. Let's go grab a pint so I can teach you how to woo our alto friend." Finn gave Nerise a wink as they left.

Nerise snickered behind them.

"I'll join you, but I don't want the alcohol to affect my voice," Traven insisted.

"Ever the professional. I'll have to drink for the both of us, then."

He was early to Vexlane Manor despite Finn's best attempts at keeping him in the Crooning Cello. After leaving Asmeri out in the cold while Traven slept in, he had always vowed to be early. He would never forget the man shivering uncontrollably, expecting a short stint outside, but let down by his own son. He had never been late to another thing.

Despite the slightly overgrown lawn and wild topiaries, The Vexlane Estate evoked the same sense of wonder that he had when stepping onto the Daelthorne Estate. Water fountains bubbled in defiance of the icy winter past the FrostLine; three total in front of a double staircase leading to heavy wooden doors. The intricately carved wood was enough to sing the wealth of House Vexlane in fortissimo.

A servant bowed as he approached, eyes lingering on the gold cord on his shoulder. The doors opened in a way he would imagine evoked Thariel; slow enough to set the nerves on edge, but purposeful. The creaking of the wood echoed into the home, and he reached out to slide his fingers across the grain.

The foyer was bigger than his entire apartment, with a multi-level chandelier of shimmering green light. The floor was checkered black-and-white tiles, and the walls were all paneled wood with brass edging. Painted portraits of serious-looking men filled the walls, generation after generation of Vexlanes. A yawn escaped his mouth, and he reflected how this was exactly like preparing for a performance.

Every inch of the Vexlane Manor was covered in ornate musical scrolling and multi-tiered molding. Vases sat on pedestals with flowers in colors Traven had never seen. He reached out to touch them, and one of the servants cleared his throat with an apologetic smile. "Please refrain from touching her roses."

"They can be quite temperamental," Thariel's husky voice echoed through the foyer.

She descended from the double staircase, her silvery dress crisscrossed with slashes of red—similar to the roses he was admiring. She glided down the stairs as he bowed to her. She gave him a special smile while her gaze lingered. "You look remarkable, Traven."

He liked the way she said his name, with disarming familiarity. He gestured in her direction and cleared his throat. "As do you, Mistress Vexlane."

"Thariel, my dear. At least when we are alone." She winked at him.

He turned his head to see a number of servants quietly standing at the corners of the room, their faces a few inches from the walls. He didn't consider them to be alone. How many times had they seen her play this game? He shoved that thought down and smiled. "How do you manage to grow these flowers?"

She waved a dismissive hand and spoke with a voice saturated with boredom. "My servants keep them pollinated; they cannot grow without it. I'm glad you like them." She plucked the rose nearest to him and placed it in his lapel. "You see, you have to know exactly when to *prune* them." Her eyes lingered just long enough to make him clear his throat. The nearest servant, the one who warned him before, fidgeted ever so slightly. She stood so close that he could smell the powder on her nose.

Traven stammered, glancing back to the servants. Thariel laughed at his wild-eyed expression. "Pay them no mind. They are not here to judge, my pet."

It was an odd thing, to feel like you were stepping headlong into a trap while feeling like it's everything you wanted.

He stepped back. "Thank you…Thariel. Has anyone else arrived?"

"Not yet." She played with the curls on her head while taking his arm. "It is customary to come fashionably late, so others can witness your arrival."

Everything seemed so backwards compared to home. Being late would be rude.

She led him into a waiting parlor that rivaled Director Malachi's study. Wooden bookshelves—so tall that you had to use a rolling ladder—were filled with leatherbound books. Pillowy lounge chairs had been placed in the center of the room, so that people could sit and converse with ease. A table to the side was covered in glass bottles and short drinking glasses. A contraption sat next to it, looking like a large brass flower with a square wooden base. "Is that…?"

She glided over to it, obviously proud. "A phonograph. My father commissioned it from the Arcanum as a parting gift while he wasted away. Let me show you."

Thariel flipped a switch and a metallic voice groaned to life with a crackle. The song projected from inside a flower-shaped brass horn. He had seen something like this in Nawny's shop, but it hadn't worked. Traven instinctively hummed a harmony, and she cocked her head while pouring a drink. "Do you know this song?"

"I don't. I just do that sometimes; harmonize." Traven explained.

"But how do you know what to sing?" She offered him a glass of dark liquid.

He took the glass but didn't drink. "Music has patterns. I seem to be able to pick up on those patterns and know where my voice is supposed to fit. I don't know why."

She took a deep drink. "Because you are special, and talented." She stood with one arm folded under the other, wine glass resting near her face. "I think you have what it takes to earn a Purple Cord."

Back home, people whispered about singers even better than the Grand Chorus. His mother used to laugh at the stories, telling people they were getting carried away. The Grand Chorus was as far as he had ever dared imagine, something he knew he could aspire to…but the Empress's personal choir? Only legends sang for her. While the city of Hearthmere was beautiful, it was said that Calrithia dwarfed any other in splendor. It had always seemed so far away, impossible. Thariel noted the hunger in his eyes, and tapped him on the nose. "There's that ambition. I hear you. I can help."

He was nodding without realizing it. Imagine how proud his father would be…if he sang for the most powerful person in the world. He hoped she wasn't giving empty praise. Even if she was, he might gain just enough exposure to manifest it himself… if the right person heard him.

He sat down to contemplate his next course of action as Thariel walked to the doorway. "You are welcome to warm up here. You'll be singing two songs for me tonight?"

"Yes," he rushed to say. *Too eager.*

He knew what she was doing—promising him the world, dangling the carrot, but didn't care.

Placing his drink on the table, he ran through some warm-ups to get limber. His voice felt good, if not a little worn from speaking all day. A morning performance would have been preferable, when his voice was strongest. He worried his lowest notes would falter when heat started to build in his throat…and then began to worry about his magick.

He couldn't get emotional, not tonight. If he faltered here, it would very well be the end of him. There were too many lamps, and too many witnesses. He was terrified and curious at the same time. What would his power be? Even without answers, he pieced together that powers were voice-specific after seeing Elena and Half-Step do the same thing.

So what could a bass Glysterian do?

A faint rustling came from behind one of the many doors, but no one pushed through to see who was singing. Was someone trying to get an early peek at his performance? He pretended not to notice and began his solo, focusing on the tricky sections. He didn't want any surprises. Tonight was his first official debut, his first public expression of talent, and he couldn't mess this up.

Not after losing to Shissel.

Chapter XXXVI

Left to himself, Traven paced the parlor and let his fingers run across the books on the shelves. He hummed through a low arpeggio, letting the base of his neck vibrate while he circled the tall room. The phonograph was still running and was interfering with the song in his head. He stepped over and flipped the switch, letting the voice melt away in a way that made him chuckle. There was still nothing like a live performance.

A small mirror on the wall gave him the opportunity to adjust his vest and straighten the cord on his shoulder. He stood there studying himself, noting the bags under his eyes. He wasn't sure how much longer he'd be able to sleep near the airdocks. Straightening his back and rolling his shoulders, he muttered. "You can do this. No screw-ups today."

Pulling away from his reflection, he noticed a map of Thalveris stretching across one of the tables pushed against the wall. Someone had taken great care with the scroll, with fanciful calligraphy noting the capitals of Hearthmere, Velmoras, Orrisfal, Dratheus, and Calrithia—the seat of the Empress.

With this one piece of parchment, the reality of how sheltered he was became apparent. Grendal was tucked away on the southern end of the continent, a speck on the southern edge of the map, barely noticeable. No wonder he was dismissed so quickly. He was a nobody from nowhere. If Preth was a day's travel, the entire Empire would have taken weeks.

Would he ever see it all? Could he? When every step brought him closer to danger?

A soft knock on the door pulled him away from the map.

The servant girl motioned for him to follow, her stare lingering on him while she tucked a strand of hair behind an ear. She took him through a hallway and into the dining room where laughter and conversation trickled through the estate. Taking a few more moments to collect himself, ensuring his coat was perfect, he gave the servant a smile. She blushed and averted her eyes, while pushing the door open.

Thariel stood with her back to him, swiveling with pride etched across her smiling face. Gesturing for the room to quiet, she wrapped her arm around his and started inside. At least two dozen couples in coats and gowns hovered around the flagons of wine, drinking and gossiping with each other over light laughter. A murmur followed him like a growing fog. How many of them had heard of his loss to Shissel?

Thariel must have a different definition of "small gathering."

She guided him around the room like a prized animal. The table stretched across the entire dining hall, piled with enough steaming food to feed his entire Yodel. Silver utensils twinkled from lamps at every place setting, flanked by crystalline drinking glasses. A chandelier hung from a ceiling painted like the sky, light blue with gentle clouds and twisting vines framing the scene. Servants buzzed around the room in black and white uniforms with trays of wine and light snacks. Even as a dwindling House, Thariel had more wealth than he had ever seen before.

And nobody else seemed to notice.

"Ladies and gentlemen, House Vexlane would like to

introduce to you their newest protege, Traven Caelhardt. I am delighted to be his sponsor, and look forward to many cycles of solos and banquets to laud his accomplishments." Thariel smirked at him with a raised glass in her gloved hand.

Her protege?

Heat flushed his neck, and his magick bubbled. Traven waved with a nervous smile; he had never agreed to be her protege…not yet. This might be what he wanted, but he didn't know her terms. What were her expectations? Did it even matter? Could he say no if he wanted to?

If he pulled back now, embarrassed her in front of her closest and obviously powerful allies, he'd end his career before it started. She had snared him in one sentence, and smiled sweetly while doing so. His breathing became rapid and short. His eyes grew dark.

He needed her, and she knew it.

She led him through a procession of dignitaries as his mind reeled. He barely remembered shaking their hands, and he couldn't recall a single one of their names; he was terrible at that in the best of circumstances. Half of the room had smiled and curtsied before something shook him back into reality.

Red hair.

She leaned in the corner with her white uniform and barely concealed pistol. A thin smile crept onto her darkened lips, and she winked at him through her bangs. He stiffened visibly enough that her eyes sparkled. Thariel tugged him past as if she was invisible. Why was she here?

Chords, why was someone so dangerous and so beautiful at the same time?

That wasn't important right now; he needed to get out of here.

He was reluctantly brought back to the head of the dining table where Thariel stepped back and waved her hands. "And now, for his debut. Traven, bass of the Grand Chorus." His heart thudded against his embroidered vest, and he looked to the nearest door.

Traven took a shaky breath, and tried to calm himself. The Red Woman arched an eyebrow from across the room, forcing another wave of panic. All of the clarity he had worked on, all of the control he mustered—destroyed. One moment he was reeling from Thariel's proclamation, and now he was at very tangible risk of outing himself.

The nobles shuffled their feet as he stood there stunned. At possibly one of the most important moments of his life…he couldn't remember the first words of his song. Why were the words gone from his mind? He had done this hundreds of times. Thariel cleared her throat, and gave a sheepish smile. Some of the dignitaries smiled back in empathy; some did not.

He needed to calm down. Cold, dispassionate perfectionism.

"May my voice reflect my spirit," he whispered.

Instinct saved him, and as he hummed the first notes the words started to rush back. The first few notes were harsh and aggressive as he wrestled himself under control. The longer the song went, the clearer his mind became. That was the way with him—music reached down into his core.

The crowd's icy impatience melted away as he relaxed and allowed his voice to reach them. They chuckled as he mimicked the vocal qualities of a tenor—lilting and bright—and murmured with approval as he showcased his impressive range. His self-confidence grew, and he found himself holding the Red Woman's gaze as he carried through his song. Her cheek twitched, but she didn't break the connection. Let her see he wasn't intimidated.

Thariel beamed, clapping enthusiastically as he hit his lowest notes, but he barely noticed. He smiled, pressing the depth of his voice until the glass on the table jingled. Worry creased his brow until it wasn't his power…it was just him.

His second song was stronger than the first, a raucous battle chant that he could sing at forte and pump his fists. The crowd joined him, and some of the men even broke decorum by banging their fists on the table.

Across the snow through wind and hail,
We brothers march into the vale.
Our hearts are pure, our voices strong,
We brothers march with glorious song.
If life is lost through winters might,
We brothers fight with GlysterLight.

Thariel stood from her seat and clapped along, urging the others. They joined her, rushing his pace just enough for a tinge of annoyance, but he simply nodded and tried his best to keep his timing. Once the song ended, Thariel dove in under his arm to hug him from the side. "Bravo! Bravo!"

As he soaked in the crowd's admiration, the Red Woman stepped out of the room.

Had he betrayed himself? Would he leave the building alive? The lights hadn't flickered even for a moment.

Traven leaned down and growled while the applause dwindled, "We never agreed to this."

She craned her neck up to his ear, lips just grazing him. Her perfume was suffocating. "Darling, you were mine the moment I set eyes on you. Fear not, everything I do will be to your benefit from here on out. Trust me."

"How can I?" He pulled back angrily, then quickly softened as patrons lifted their eyebrows in surprise, "when our first interaction began with deception?"

"I'll make it up to you. Name your price." Her eyes took on a dangerous glint as the gems set in her hair winked at him. He was grateful for their warning.

"We'll talk about it later, my Patroness," he growled, stuffing his anger down.

Thariel paled at his tone, but recovered quickly as three men in top hats and lacy shirts clapped him on the back, wine glasses sloshing, and commented to Thariel on the power of his voice, roaring into the air as they mimicked his battle cry. Some of the other men in the room joined them. He summoned the best smile he could, and sang along. Why weren't they talking directly to him?

When those men walked away to refill their drinks, an elderly couple shook his hand and congratulated Thariel on her new acquisition.

Was this what patronage was all about? He'd do all of the work while she basked in the glory? Why did it feel like Thariel was taking all of the compliments for his performance?

She had robbed him of agency, and the more he dwelled on it, the more resistant he felt. His father had warned him many times, *"The world doesn't work the way you want it to, son. You've got to learn to roll with the punches."*

He wasn't sure this was what Asmeri had in mind.

Thariel adjusted his coat with a snap of her wrists. "Relax, enjoy tonight. Tomorrow we begin building your empire."

Chapter XXXVII

Selice slipped out of the dining room. Like a wraith, she tucked her white coat close and slid into the shadows. It wasn't very often that she took the time to enjoy a performance. She had nearly forgotten why she was here. Traven was talented; his voice rich and attractive in a way she hadn't heard since the Baron. That particular voice was gone now, replaced by Glysterium and servos.

A pity.

Sticking to the shadows of the dimly lit manor, she reflected on Traven's mannerisms. He commanded the room, even though he was clearly out of his depth. People reacted to his presence, averting their gaze or flipping their hair as he smiled at them. The way he stared into her soul with those grey eyes had made her uncomfortable, like he was challenging her. And yet, those eyes were gentle—kind even. At the announcement of his patronage, delicious fire flashed in those stormy eyes. She hadn't been expecting that. Was he surprised at the announcement, or had a decision been made for him? It wouldn't be the first time Thariel had made this move.

And yet, no Glysterium response. Not even when he spotted

her in the corner. She liked to do that sometimes—play with her prey, linger just close enough to knock them off-balance. It gave her power.

She knelt down behind a bookshelf and pressed the wood with her lacquered fingernails, revealing the dining room just enough to give her a clear view of the soiree. The wood of the shelves vibrated with his performance. He liked to use his voice like a hammer. She took that as a reflection of his character, blunt and honest. Direct.

She could use that.

He was more composed with her gone, and the realization made her smirk. The dockworker friend was too jaded, too suspicious. Traven would be fun to play with. He still had no idea what world he was stepping into.

She watched him whisper to Thariel with a dangerous glint in his eye, who gave away such an imperceptible moment of panic that anyone not trained would miss entirely. She was afraid of him.

Who wouldn't be? He was taller than most men, lean and strong, and with a voice like thunder. There was an energy in the room, swirling around him like the sycophants gobbling up the Vexlane estate's finest wine. Men like him could shape nations if given the right stage. Perhaps that's why the Baron had requested that *she* shadow him, and not Veyne or Lysara. She could handle strong men without destroying them.

As he was led around the room he kept craning his head, scanning the crowd. He was looking for something.

For her.

Selice shoved down the flutter in her stomach and growled. He was a target. She belonged to the Empire, there was no room for anything else.

Sliding backward into the hallway, she took a deep breath and pivoted on her heels toward the door. A servant jumped at the scowl on her face, but she paid them no mind as she left the manor. Despite initial reports, Traven didn't appear to be a Glysterian. No fluctuations, no signals. There needed to be more testing; she had to be sure. The Baron would be displeased.

There was other business to attend to, other places to be. She was weary, and her impending report would take the last of her energy. Walking down the lawn and across the main road would be a waste of time, so she darted through the bushes and over the fence to the next estate. She made no sound, sprinting through the shadows.

The Baron's estate had armed guards around every corner. She slipped by them with relative ease in the moonlight, even in her bright white coat. It was a game for her, and she liked to surprise him whenever she could. It kept her dangerous in his eyes, useful.

She scaled the granite molding like an acrobat, whipping her body in ways that allowed her momentum to carry her to the second story, then the third as she gripped a railing or circled a column. Silent as a FrostClaw, she perched on top of the balcony railing, looking inside.

There he sat. Brooding.

The Baron slumped in his chair, facing a roaring fireplace while nursing a glass of bourbon she had procured from Velmoras. His Glysterium-desecrated body pulsed with its own heartbeat, casting eerie shadows across a room full of pictures of a woman and child. His family, long dead. The fireplace crackled and spit embers, giving off heat so precious she would have once killed for it.

"Sire," she said with a slight tinge of playfulness. She couldn't help herself.

"Selice." He didn't adjust to see her, staring into the fire.

"Unfortunately I have nothing to report from tonight's performance. He appears to be a normal, if talented singer." She stopped at the double doorway, ready to escape at any rise in temperament.

"Interesting, even with Thariel's little surprise? I imagined the shock would have woken him up." He said evenly. He was more robot than man now.

She hesitated with her next thought. "Perhaps…he's nothing more."

"Take him, nevertheless. We have ways of being sure."

"Now? After no showing of power? We haven't done that before; it's not right," her voice took an icy edge.

His glass shattered into the fireplace as he hurled it into the hearth. The servos on his legs whirred menacingly as he stood. "You forget your place, street urchin,"

She was already poised to leap, her legs bent as she reached for Aria's End. It was unsettling how quickly he shifted from calm to spitting rage, even after all these cycles. His Glysterium eye zeroed in on the weapon at her hip, and he raised a warning finger.

She fought the quiver in her voice. "There was a request to wait until after the Unification Concert. As I said, he's talented and it would be a waste for them to lose him. It would give me, us, time to be sure he's to be extracted."

His lips curved at the slip of her tongue. "No doubt Malachi made the request. He cares more about spectacle than the survival of our people. A Purple Cord will arrive soon to evaluate him. The interruption will remind the director where he stands. If your hesitation proves unwarranted, perhaps we can discuss relocating your services to Calrithia."

She nodded in deference, cursing him under her breath. After all these cycles, he would send her away? She couldn't let that happen.

He dismissed her with a pompous wave of his mechanical hand, pouring himself another drink before settling back down into his chair with groaning servos. She took a quick glance around the room, and noticed a dozen new paintings of his wife. He was spiraling.

She left the Baron to his demons.

Chapter XXXVIII

Throughout the night, as Traven drifted from couple to couple, Thariel's laughter sliced through the crowd like quicksilver. If she wasn't directly at his side, directing the conversation to his future prospects, she was always in sight. He quickly realized what her looks meant. A direct stare from across the room meant he was on track, and when she pursed her lips, he knew it was time to move on. Whatever her plans were, he wasn't aware of them.

The conversations danced between where he got his voice and what it was like growing up on a farming Yodel. How had he managed to learn such talent while shoveling dirt? What was it like taking a bath for the first time? Was it true that people ate each other when times got hard? His shoulders were starting to sag. They smiled in a way that never reached their eyes, and managed to mention their estates, their standing, or their pedigree whenever possible. To them he wasn't a good singer; he was just a novelty draped in a gold cord.

Traven wished his voice was enough, but apparently his past would always cling like a bad smell.

"Now the mountains of Draetheus are a sight to behold, if you manage to catch them when they aren't blocked by those dreadful plumes of smoke, constantly churning from their factories…they do make a glorious sunset. I daresay you've never seen that many colors before…" For the last ten minutes, an elderly man with slicked silver hair had him cornered. Every time he shifted his feet to leave, the man would step over and continue his rambling.

Traven's drink had been empty the last three times he checked.

Despite his lingering anger with Thariel, he was grateful when she glided over with her glittering Glysterium jewelry and pulled him away from the pontificating man. "Lord Grandene, I must introduce your conversation partner to Lady Onell. She has been quite patient."

Lord Grandene continued talking long after they stepped away, and Traven gave her an appreciative pat on the arm. She returned his look with a wink. He grinned despite himself. If only she hadn't trapped him the way she had. "Lord Grandene is tremendously loose with his wealth, especially as it concerns travel. We may use him to procure an airship to the other capitals."

And so the night went on for him. Introductions, refilled wine glasses, impromptu solo sessions upon request, and no less than three invitations for a private performance. When the time came for the Hymn of Gratitude, all eyes went to him for the starting pitch. At least in this, they deferred to him. It felt right.

The night wasn't all for Traven, however. Thariel positively beamed as she told jokes, batted her eyelashes, and pulled the strings necessary to rebuild her family's name. Judging by the way the nobles responded to her, her maneuverings were working according to plan.

The guests trickled out of Vexlane Manor until Traven and Thariel were alone. She flopped on a plush couch, her arms draped over the sides with strands of hair dangling over her face. She avoided his glare while sipping some water. He wanted answers.

Traven had spent the night being her plaything, weathering

questions draped in condescension and judgement for things he had no control over. He had played nice, kept things civil, held up his end of this ambiguous bargain. He needed to regain control of the situation.

Back and forth, he paced, heels bunching the rug into ripples. The lights dimmed each time he spun, and by his third pass, the chandelier flickered wildly. He stopped in front of her, anger blazing in his eyes. "You deceived me." The room darkened.

She looked at him with feigned innocence, then saw the set of his jaw and exhaled. Her eyes could have matched the Ever-Winter for icy death. "I am tired. It was a good night, and you were as charming as I could have asked for. Let us leave it at that for now."

He stepped toward her. "I never agreed to be your protege, and yet you lied…to people who would avoid me like the *plague* if I turned on you."

She had to crane her neck upward to meet his gaze, the leather in her chair groaned as she adjusted. "Tell me, Traven. What do your friends in the Grand Chorus say about me?"

He frowned. "That I should be careful. That you are far too clever for your own good. They also said you have lost favor recently, and will do anything to get it back."

"All true." She stood and stepped close. Her perfume, dulled through the hours, clung as she approached. "I *am* clever, and while my house has lost some of its influence over the last few cycles, I saw *you* as the perfect opportunity to regain some of it."

She jabbed him in the chest. "But you seem to have missed a very important point, and I'm happy to remind you. You are extraordinary, and I saw it the moment we met. Would you rather have waited for months after your arrival for some scraping of a lord to dangle promises in front of you in hopes of making you one of their minions? How long before they recognized the pure potential you have?"

Traven pursed his lips in consideration. It was hard to ignore the compliment. "But you still deceived me. You lied."

"Darling," she purred. "Everyone lies."

His back stiffened. "I don't."

She studied him for a moment, her eyes darting across his face. "Not to others, perhaps. But you lie to *yourself* every day."

He bristled with indignation, pulling back from her. "I do not."

"No? I see you in rehearsal, craning your head, desperate for attention. I see you lingering after a performance to ensure anyone with compliments has the time to find you. You paint a pretty picture of confidence and bravado, but in the quiet moments, between songs, the real Traven emerges. I *hear* you."

Her words clawed at his insides. He opened his mouth to protest, but she placed a lacquered finger on his lips. "But you need not worry, Master Caelhardt. You are already as good as you pretend to be, just believe it. Be the shining, handsome, charismatic man with the voice of thunder. You already *are* to me."

He stumbled back into a bookshelf as he stammered, "I...I think I need to go."

She placed a gentle hand on his forearm. He wanted to pull away, but didn't. "I recognize that you feel owed something for how tonight transpired. I believe I can ease that discomfort."

She extracted a Harmonic Key from her bosom and handed it to him. "An apartment in Resonance Heights. It is yours, the first of many advantages of being a Vexlane protege."

Traven took the key. As gilded with strings as this was, he would be grateful for a night's sleep without the droning of the airdocks. "Thank you. Now please don't lie to me ever again."

Thariel looked at him the way his mother used to when he was throwing a tantrum. "Darling, you would have me swear to the truth with something we both know to be a lie."

He stepped into the cool air of Upper Resonance Heights, taking his time to step down the stairs and down the path of the Vexlane Estate. The moon was directly overhead, and he guessed it close to midnight. He was conflicted. He saw the merit of tying himself to House Vexlane, but he rankled at the method she took to make it happen.

She was right. She had the ability to open doors for him in ways that might have taken months or cycles with someone lesser. The mountain of invitations tonight was a prime example of that…but at what cost? Would he become a liar? Would he traipse around in Resonance Heights with a fake smile and golden chains around his neck for the honor of singing on that gilded stage? He couldn't do that. He wouldn't be a liar, whatever the cost.

Traven was so caught up in thought that he didn't notice Mariss standing at the gate, until he nearly ran into her.

"Hey." She smiled sheepishly.

"Hey, Mariss. Have you been waiting for me?"

She met his pace as they continued home, her cheeks reddening. "I wanted to see how it went."

"It went as well as it probably could have…despite Thariel pulling a fast one on me and announcing I was her protege without consulting me," he tried to sound cheerful and failed.

She turned to him with wider eyes than normal. "She did not!"

"I stood there like an oaf; I was so taken aback."

"That was underhanded, but I wouldn't say it was completely out of character for her. She plays the game better than most, I hope she treats you well." She gave him a comforting smile and bumped him with her hip. She always seemed to do that. A playful touch here, a lingering gaze there. He wondered what had changed when she healed him?

"Thanks, Mariss."

They walked through Upper Resonance Heights and through Concordia Plaza without saying much, simply enjoying each other's company. Once in a while, she would pause as if she was going to speak, then she'd shake her head and continue on. He didn't press her on it, lost in his own thoughts. It wasn't until Cantata Row narrowed at the GroundSong Commons that she finally spoke. "I need you to promise me you won't come to rehearsal on Modera."

This again.

Traven turned, pinching his nose. "What's going to happen that has you all worried?"

She stepped close, lowering her voice. "Someone will be evaluating our rehearsal. They are from the Empire, and that doesn't happen unless something is wrong."

Did this have to do with the incident in Whisper Ward? Had the soldiers seen his face? He cursed his temper and took a deep breath. "I can't just miss rehearsal. We have a performance in a few weeks. Malachi was very clear about attendance during crunch week."

"Just tell him you don't feel well…or I can. Just promise me."

Now he was even more confused. "Why are you so worried? Finn says he can handle whatever it is. If things went sideways, Elena could make us disappear, or Kael could set someone's hair on fire."

She scoffed. "Kael wouldn't risk revealing us. His mission always takes priority."

Us. It stung a little knowing he wasn't a part of them, not fully.

She stole a glance at the rooftops. "An emissary from Calrithia has arrived at the Baron's behest, a Purple Cord."

Traven frowned. "But that's a good thing. Our chorus sounds great, we've been polishing for weeks."

"It's not a good thing, Traven. Purple Cords are like us… They are Glysterians." Her voice trailed off to a whisper.

No wonder the Purple Cords were legends…but what part did they play?

Traven grabbed her by the hand and stepped into an alley. "If a Glysterian works for the Empire, maybe things aren't as bad as you think. Maybe we are taken to be trained, to be honored."

She tapped him on the forehead. "Then why the secrecy? Why hold the truth about us with such an iron fist? Why are we hunted and not celebrated?"

Those were good points. He wanted to throw a positive spin on this, but nothing added up. "There is a lot I don't know. None of you will tell me. You drop this bomb about miraculous power and some special bloodline, and then refuse to elaborate." He tried his best to keep his voice down.

"So please, stay home until we can give you more answers. Miss a rehearsal. It happens all of the time."

He couldn't. The concert was important to him. Even if what she said was true, he still wasn't sure he wanted to be wrapped up in their little rebellion. Tonight had given him a taste of what his life could be like. He would find a way to control his power, to stay hidden. "I'm not missing a rehearsal. I can't lose the momentum I'm building here."

Her eyes hardened. "That's what you care about? You stupid stubborn man. Not everything is a chance for you to show how brave you are. Just once use your head instead of pushing your way through."

"Mariss, I'm sorry. Whatever it is, Finn will handle it."

She tore away from him and punched him in the chest. "You flatbrained idiot."

The strike hurt beyond physical pain. He wanted to chase

after her as she took off down the street, footsteps echoing off of the buildings. She would understand if he explained to her how long he'd had this dream…how much it meant to him. He needed to make Asmeri proud, and he would stop at nothing.

He had hoped their conversation could have been about anything else, rather than whatever the Empire was conspiring. Instead, he stood in the center of a dark street, feeling more alone than he ever had back home.

Chapter XXXIX

Traven walked into the warehouse apartment looking more out of place than ever before.

He was impressive, admittedly, bedecked in gold and white as he stepped into Rolan's room. The busty seamstress had outdone herself. There was something different about him tonight, but it wasn't his shiny shoes and golden coattails. He looked…weary, as if some of his exuberant sheen had been worn off.

From his bed, Rolan watched him pace around the room. He was chewing his cheek again. Had the soiree gone poorly? He wasn't going to ask…Traven would open up eventually.

He didn't have to wait long. "Well, I have a patron." Traven stopped at the window and pulled the curtain aside. He sounded like someone describing a bad shift in the weather.

"Isn't that what you wanted?"

Traven let the curtains drop. "Yes…but not like this. Thariel didn't ask me, she blindsided me with an announcement in front of all of her noble friends. I had to accept, or risk ostracizing myself."

Rolan grunted. She sounded like a clever one, for sure. "You don't get to lead a noble house by being polite."

"I felt like a piece of property. She paraded me around, showing me off to all of her stuck-up friends." Traven tossed his shoes into the hallway with a clatter. "This isn't happening the way I thought it would."

"At least it's happening." Rolan fought back the resentment in his voice.

"And then the Red Woman was there, so I'm probably five minutes from being detained. I probably shouldn't have even come here."

He wasn't even listening. The kid was falling into his dream and throwing a tantrum about how it happened.

Rolan had heard enough.

"Traven," he interrupted. "Yer getting what you wanted. You've got a Gold Cord, you have a patron. Some of us aren't so lucky. Take this fer what it is, and do what they do; use it to yer advantage."

The bass opened his mouth to speak again, but Rolan shook his head. "This is the reality of things. People use people to get ahead. Life here is no different than beyond the FrostLine; the enemy is just more sophisticated than freezing to death. Now use that big brain of yers, and capitalize on your new status."

He was taking a risk talking to Traven this way, his friend was getting more dangerous by the day. Thankfully, the lights didn't shimmer.

Traven rubbed his face with both hands and groaned. "You're right, I'm being petulant."

"I don't know what that means, but if it means whiny…you are correct." Rolan folded his arms.

The corners of his friend's mouth lifted, and a bit of the sparkle returned to his eyes. "At least I have some good news." He reached into his pocket and revealed a crystal key. "I have an apartment in Resonance Heights. We don't have to live down here with all of this noise any more."

"That's great news." Rolan scratched his beard. "Are you going there tonight?"

"We are going there tonight. Grab your stuff."

"I don't think I'll be joining you."

"What?" Traven blinked slowly.

He hated to do this, when the kid was already down. "I'm not going to live in Resonance Heights. It's too far from work, and I'd stick out like a sore thumb." His shoulder hitched as he pointed to a coat covered in red dust.

"I can get you some new clothes."

"No, it's ok. I'm fine right here."

"But this is temporary. You'll be a Gold Cord before you know it. It's the least I can do. You've taken care of me for the last few weeks, let me take some of the load."

Traven wasn't listening again. "It's ok Traven, I don't even know if I'll make it." Heat was starting to build behind Rolan's voice.

His protests were ignored. "You will. All of this is just survival. This new apartment is the next step in our real lives."

"No, Traven. I need to go home, away from magical death instruments and degenerates in white uniforms."

"We can stop them, I just need to work on figuring out this magick."

"I said no!" Rolan shouted with balled fists. "I'm not your charity case. I don't need your help. I've been taking care of myself fer cycles."

Traven's voice softened defensively. "I'm not saying that, I just figured I owed you after all you've done for me. I'm returning the favor."

"You don't think sometimes! You just plow through the world like a damned GlysterRail through snow. This wasn't even my dream. This was yours. I don't even know if I want to be here." Rolan gripped his bedpost. "I was fine back home. I didn't need more!"

"But you owe it to yourself to try! You earned your medallion for a reason."

"Yer bulldozing me again." Rolan snatched the medallion from around his neck and threw it to the ground. "This isn't even mine! It was Moira's. She made me promise to make my life better, and I'm sitting here doing the same damned thing I was at Preth, except I'm lost in a sea of strangers. Worse than that, there are people out there actively trying to kill me."

His chest grew tight as memories of the past gripped him. He was so tired of it all—the never-ending deluge of ice and pain and disappointment. Traven reached out to grab his shoulder, but he pushed it away. "I'm going home. I don't belong here."

"But I need you here."

"You have yer *Quintet*," he snapped.

Traven looked wounded. "Look, I'm sorry. I didn't mean to make you feel like a charity case. I wanted to help you like you've been helping me.."

"Save it, Traven. I'm done with this city…this *dream*."

Traven looked down at the floor, his chest heaving as he worked through his thoughts. "Then take DirgeMaul. I owe you my life, and it's the only thing I've got worth anything."

"I'm not taking the hammer."

"Then…take it back to my father, please. It's useless here. I can't walk around with it, and they could use it back home."

Rolan could agree to that. "Fine."

The Gold Cord rubbed the top of his head, jaw clenched. Rolan kept his focus on the lamp on the wall. He needed to be ready to run if it came to that. An airship flared its engines outside, and Traven winced.

"Yer a good man, Traven. Try to hold on to that for as long as you can." He stared firmly into his friend's eyes.

Traven rested a hand on his shoulder, gave him a silent nod, and then walked out of the room.

⌢

Traven climbed the steps to his new apartment, his mood matching the dark obsidian of the Citadel looming overhead. Everything was bittersweet. Each step forward extracted a cost. He had a patron, at the expense of freedom. He had gained his prestige, and lost a brother.

He put the key to his lips and hummed a single pure note. The key responded like a tuning fork, resonating with his voice and then producing its own pitch. It slid into the lock with a satisfying clunk and the door chimed a faint melodic tune. The door opened, and Traven paused to take it all in.

It smelled of gyshweed and linseed oil, and was every bit as elaborate as Thariel's mansion…just smaller. The long entryway had polished wooden floors and vaulted ceilings. A Glysterium chandelier cast twinkling green light over sculptures, vases, and a bowl overflowing with glimmer by the door. An elaborate red and gold rug led into the main room, and he passed a portrait of Empress Wiseria that hung from floor to ceiling. Her eyes seemed to follow him no matter where he stood. "I could sell this chandelier and buy an entire Yodel," he murmured.

Moonlight streamed in from windows stretching from floor to ceiling, and he was treated to his own personal view of the Opera House. The apartment was a single large room—something called a studio—with a staircase leading up to a loft. He climbed up to find a bed that could have accommodated three of him, with more pillows than he had ever seen in his entire life.

Below, a round table with musical engraving along the edges anchored the room around a kitchen, a writing desk, and a couch similar to the ones in Nerise's boutique…if a little less embellished.

He wished he had someone to share it with.

The writing desk reminded him that he hadn't written to Asmeri this week, so he climbed back down and took a seat.

Father,

I wish you were here. Everything is moving so quickly, and it's hard to keep my bearings. I have a sponsor now, but she's crafty in ways I can't understand. I miss the honest, straightforward way people talk back home. Everything here is nuance and maneuvering. It's exhausting. The rules are different here, and I think I need to stop trusting people.

Singing is going well. I have new friends that are helping me learn the music. The concert is only a week off, and I would really love it if you came. I'll have your ticket paid for, and I'm including GlysterRail fare in this letter.

My friend Rolan is going home, and he promised to return DirgeMaul to you. It's too unwieldy in Hearthmere, and I think you could use it more. Rolan saved my life, please treat him like family. Give him all the hospitality you can, even when he refuses.

I miss you. Please come listen to me sing.

-Tre

He paused before sealing the envelope. Was it selfish of him to expect Asmeri to make the trip? He had barely made it to Preth, and likely wouldn't have survived if not for DirgeMaul. Tapping his lip in consideration, he finally decided to let his father make that decision. Asmeri likely would decide for himself anyways.

D id he really want to leave?

Rolan sat on the edge of his bed as the morning light drifted in through the window. Dark shadows of airships had already begun funneling through the Dome, and he could hear men shouting as they went about moving the daily supplies that kept Hearthmere alive. DirgeMaul rested against an overstuffed pack by his feet—everything he owned was ready to depart. The kid was right, the hammer was going to cause more trouble than it was worth. In Hearthmere, people waged wars with voices, not weapons.

"I think it's time to go home, Moira. I'm just not cut out for this."

Despite the words coming out of his mouth, his legs refused to move. Something big was unfolding around Traven, a world neither of them knew existed. The kid was talented and strong, but wisdom only came from cycles of life wearing you down. There was a lot of wisdom coming Traven's way.

And then there was the girl.

Half-Step was all alone, orphaned like so many other children, and hunted by imperial agents. Was he really going to leave her?

What kind of a man was he?

Maybe she would come with him, away from the dangers of the city, and settle into the simpler rhythm of a Yodel. Living above a warehouse was no life for a child. She needed time to experience life without worrying about her next meal, or who was lurking around the corner. The alcove back home could use the chatter of little voices again. He just needed to find her.

Hoisting the pack onto his shoulders and hefting DirgeMaul, he dropped his apartment key on the table—along with this month's rent. He couldn't leave the landlord out to dry. The man had mouths to feed. It wasn't the nicest place in the city, but he would miss the heat and relative privacy.

Rolan stepped down the crooked steps and ventured down the alley leading to the warehouse plaza. He never quite got used to the torrent of acrid air tousling his hair, or the spikes of cold air as the GlysterDome shimmered out for each airship. Rolan ducked into the maze of crates littering the plaza, and emerged at Warehouse 5.

Chauncy was eating an apple, while Hennik waved his arms mid-sentence—no doubt he was raving about Half-Step's antics. She took every opportunity to cause mischief, especially if Hennik was nearby. Twice she had stuffed his hat into his ale, and his pockets always seemed to be stuffed with pizzo spice. "Darrick, yer late."

"I'm headed home, Chauncy. I've had enough of the city."

The supervisor spat on the ground. "That's a damn shame. You were just starting to get useful."

Rolan chuckled, he had been moving faster than the others for weeks. "I apologize fer the short notice, but there's a Rail this evening, and I have matters to attend to back home."

A crate slammed into the floor from atop a pile in the back of the warehouse, scattering a mountain of spice and filling the air with red dust. Hennik sneezed with wide eyes. "You've angered the spirit. She's taken a liking to you."

If only he knew the truth.

"I spose I'll go have a chat with her. Be ready to catch me if I get tossed from the rafters." Rolan dropped his pack and strapped DirgeMaul between his shoulder blades—it would be easier to climb this way. The other dockworkers had gotten used to his daily climbing regiment, and kept shoving crates as he started up. It was harder work with the hammer, but cycles of work had built him some spare muscle.

The lights flickered before he managed to pull himself to the top, and completely winked out as he sat. "Don't go," her voice danced around him.

"I think I have to. Things are getting dangerous around here, and I miss home something fierce."

"Nope, you stay here and keep me company. I like our lunches."

"Well, you can come with me. You can use Alleria's bed, and there might be a crate or two of pizzo spice you can filch from. I only snore a little."

"You snore a *lot*." She appeared next to him, feet dangling off of the edge.

"Well…my alcove is better than a dusty old warehouse. I can even have Mistress Korda bake you some sweet potato cookies every week." He nudged her with his shoulder.

She leaned against him. "I have to stay here."

His throat tightened while looking down at her messy red hair. He should have brought her a brush one of these last few weeks. "What's so important here? Do you have friends?"

"I would miss playing hide and seek with them, but they always accused me of cheating. They're prolly right." She looked up at him in the darkness. "No, I gotta stay for other reasons. It's a secret."

"Is it something you have to do? I could help you, and then

we can get out of here.”

What was he doing? He barely knew this little girl, and he was ready to scoop her up and take her in as his own. She didn't deserve the pressure of filling an Alleria-sized hole in his heart. She drummed her feet against the crate, her little lips pressed tight.

“Ok, well I sure will miss our little lunches.”

“Stay here. Traven needs you.”

“Traven has new friends who are far more important than I am.” Rolan ruffled her hair. “I'm just gettin' in the way of his rise to fame.”

“But he's your friend.”

“Yea…he is. But every time I look at him, I'm reminded of what I'm not. I'm not as talented, or driven. It's hard to be around him sometimes.”

She grabbed his hand with her little fingers and squeezed them. “But…I'm your friend.”

His chest bucked at those innocent words. Breathing all of a sudden became impossible. He squeezed her hand back, and inhaled a shuddering breath. “I am. But I'm scared of the Violin Lady. That's why you should come with me.”

“I can protect you. We can just disappear whenever we need to. I'm getting better at doing more people.”

“Oh, little one. I think a life of living in the shadows sounds pretty miserable. Are you sure you don't want to come with me?”

“I told you I can't. I have a secret mission.”

“Then tell me what it is, and we can leave once I've helped you.”

“Nope. It wouldn't be a secret.”

Rolan sighed and gave her a pretend scowl. “Then maybe I'll just stuff you in my bag and take you home anyways.”

Half-Step stood and disappeared as her magick swirled through the air. “Can't catch me.”

And just like that, she was gone. He called out to her a few more times, but got his answer when the lights winked back on.

⌢

Rolan twirled the rail ticket in his fingers as he sat at the terminal. He stared up at the curved steel ceiling, trying to divine the correct path forward from the rivets in the extruded steel. The argument with Traven replayed through his mind. He didn't want to be someone's pet, and he certainly didn't want to depend on someone else.

Was that how Half-Step felt?

A GlysterRail glided in, crackling with emerald energy and filling the air with its unpleasant aroma. His train, his ride home. Was he a coward?

A few cars down the platform from the engine, Kael stepped onto the platform. He had his collar pulled close to his face, but the scar running from eyebrow to jowl and spiky black hair gave him away. He looked to be in a hurry, and didn't notice Rolan, despite the hammer leaning next to him.

He was about to call out when a flash of red hair appeared behind the tenor.

She was clearing the crowd with confident strides, her razor-sharp gaze focused onto Kael. One hand stayed close to her hip, where Rolan knew her pistol was. The people instinctively gave her white uniform space, and Kael was losing ground. Rolan barely knew the tenor, but he was Traven's friend. "Slush, she's going to kill him," he muttered.

He crumpled the ticket and stood to reach for DirgeMaul without realizing it. Kael and his pursuer were quickly out of the terminal, and Rolan paused just long enough to consider his actions. Would a hammer be enough to stop her? Probably not.

He was feeling a little bit like Traven today, and hurried to pursue her.

301

The Red Woman turned down a small road that Rolan recognized led toward the west side of Hearthmere, where he had questioned the Cobbler. Rolan mirrored her walk on the next street over, knowing it curved just enough to make up some distance. He probably should turn around and head back, mind his own business. Kael could handle himself.

He walked with one hand nervously holding the handle of DirgeMaul. Ahead of him, he could hear soft footsteps. He slowed and paused to use an alcove for cover, watching where the streets intersected.

Kael walked into the clearing before pausing to check his tail. Rolan wanted to call out, but he wanted to get the jump on the Red Woman. If she saw him approach with DirgeMaul, she'd kill him before he crossed the street.

Hearing the telltale staccato steps of high heels, Kael spun around and picked up the pace. Rolan waited until she crossed, then a few more moments before taking pursuit.

Kael took them through a fairly straightforward path toward the outskirts of town. It was easy to follow her flowing red hair and pristine white uniform. She walked with a dramatic sway to her hips that even a wary Rolan had to appreciate. She didn't appear to be concerned about stealth, as if she dared her prey to run.

The temperature dropped as they descended into the Whisper Ward. He grunted while buttoning his collar. Why was Kael headed this way? Bad things seemed to happen down here.

The Red Woman paused at an intersection, dropping to one knee and tracing a black gloved hand through Kael's tracks when a burst of orange flame struck her in the back, knocking her to the ground.

Rolan froze. *What was that?*

The Red Woman spun in the air as she fell, landing on her smoking back and whipping out her pistol. Two thunderous cracks split the silence as green energy rippled through the Whisper Ward. Rolan pulled DirgeMaul off of his back, and cut through a narrow alley between shacks, toward the direction Kael was headed. He plowed through bedsheets hanging out to dry and kicked up dirt as he ran, panting already from carrying the hammer.

Another crack of thunder placed the Red Woman ahead of him. Through the space between buildings Rolan saw another burst of flame, followed by a heroic tenor melody lilting through the air. Shutters slammed shut and doors locked as he passed; they wanted nothing to do with this kind of trouble.

The slums went eerily quiet as he pressed through the homes. Kael was seen dashing ahead of him in the next large street, and he was about to call out when a blur of red hair and razormint perfume slammed into him from the side.

Rolan crashed into a nearby shack, rattling the roof with a grunt. The Red Woman was already picking herself up off of the ground, her uniform half-caked with mud and muck. She looked wild, already pointing the pistol in his direction.

He whipped DirgeMaul in front of him, and caught the pistol at the end of his swing with a loud *clang*. The woman shrieked in pain, weapon flying through the air and sinking into the mud. She nursed her hand with death in her green eyes and hissed at him, "You!"

This was a terrible time for a conversation.

Rolan ran, his side screaming at him from his impact with the shack. Kael raced far ahead. He wanted to yell, but he needed to save his breath. If the maniac behind him got an open shot, he doubted she would miss. Rolan didn't have a fireball to send her way…just this massive hammer weighing him down.

He was an idiot, and way out of his depth. She hadn't been after him, not until he struck her. Kael was long gone, thanks to his distraction, but now he was in the hot seat. He should have gone home. He should have minded his own business. Another blind turn had him doubling back. He cursed and chose another direction. Why didn't the Whisper Ward have street signs?

He didn't glance backward, just kept running until he bounced into something midstride that he couldn't see. His legs tangled with the Glysterhammer, and sent him sprawling into the mud. "Oof." A little voice sounded next to him. "Watch it, Big Fella. My sister's gonna kill ya."

Half-Step shimmered into view, then grabbed his hand and made them both disappear.

Chapter XLI

Despite himself, he snatched Half-Step up and hugged her tight. Her little body went rigid at the sudden affection. "You had me panicked," he chastised.

She stuck her tongue out as he set her down and closed the door to the shack they had ducked into. "We gotta go."

Rolan resisted. "I have a…friend back there, that needs help."

She turned around and kicked him in the shin. "You will both die if you go back. That hammer can't beat her. Why are you down here? I thought you were going home."

He couldn't believe this little urchin was staring him down. She looked hilariously disheveled, hair askew, and caked in mud. He cleared his throat to calm down and set DirgeMaul against the wall. "I was…and then I decided to stay. Kael needed my help."

"Your friend is a goner. She doesn't let anyone escape her hunt." She plopped down on the floor, cross-legged.

"Your sister?"

"That's a secret. Don't tell Traven."

So she did have someone looking after her. "Do you think he's already dead?"

Half-Step looked confused. "She doesn't kill people unless

she has to, she takes them. She's not like the others."

Somewhere under all that flirtatious danger, the Huntress had a heart. Rolan tried to peek around the door. "Do you know where?"

"Sure, but I'm not allowed down there."

"Can you show me?"

She pursed her little lips and then snapped her fingers toward a toe wiggling through her shoe. "If you get me new shoes. You ruined these with your big old boots."

The little schemer.

"I know just the place." He smiled.

Half-Step released her magic, and his skin started to prickle as the creme mist circled them. DirgeMaul pulsed in response, illuminating the abandoned shack before it vanished and plunged the room into darkness. She grabbed his hand before they disappeared, and then ventured back outside.

Turning down the main mud road, he stopped in front of the Cobblers and hesitated.

The shop was dark, and the door hung off of its bottom hinge. His boots scuffed on the filthy stone stairs, and he peeked inside with DirgeMaul protectively in front of him. "Hello?"

Nothing but steam and airships pricked his ears.

Half-Step shushed him, her little body pressed against the side of the building. She needed to stop scowling at him.

Right. Subtle.

Rolan swiveled his head down both sides of the road. No one was paying attention to him. With a deep breath, he stepped into the store and found what he had been dreading.

Feet stuck out from behind the counter—lifeless and still— with blood pooling around them. The boots and tools, once on the countertop, had been swept to the floor in whatever conflict had taken place. The air smelled coppery and foul—she had been dead for a few hours. He heard what happened to people when they died, but he wasn't prepared for the stench. It was unlike anything he had smelled before.

He retched into the corner, leaning against the hammer with an angry grunt. "Slush."

This was his fault. He had pushed her to talk, despite her hesitation. She had been right to be afraid, and paid the price for talking. That burden rested solely on him.

Stubborn tears formed in his eyes, and his breathing became ragged. Who had done this? What was so important that a nobody like the Cobbler would be silenced so ruthlessly?

Half-Step entered the room with a quiet mewl, she was careful not to let her shoes touch anything unwanted…there wasn't much room to step.

He should tell her to disappear, this was no place for a child.

Setting the hammer into the corner, he delicately tiptoed through the mess and knelt down to the body. Her clothing had torn, and a gaping hole had exploded in her chest. Blood was everywhere. He heaved again and choked it down with a grimace and a shaking head. He needed answers, and he hated himself for how he was going to get them.

Chords, the smell.

His hand froze over her body. Did he really want to do this? Someone could be watching him right now, waiting for him to come back. The hair on the back of his neck rose at the thought. He needed to get out of here.

With trembling hands, he gently lifted her arm. Her ring was still there, caked with blood. That intricate symbol mocked him with its familiarity, but he still couldn't place it. Her bloated fingers made the gruesome task more difficult, but he persisted, despite everything in him screaming. The ring gave way, and he sighed as her hand dropped to the floor, pushing himself away from her with a whispered prayer.

The tin roof groaned. Rolan froze. Half-Step's eyes went wide.

He hadn't checked the roof.

Tucking the ring away, he slipped on the blood-covered floor and banged his knee with a curse. A rhythmic thumping began to resonate with the rooftop, getting louder, more insistent. Scrabbling to DirgeMaul, Rolan's skin tingled with adrenaline. He needed to get the girl out of here.

Half-Step shrieked a discordant melody, and disappeared right in front of his eyes. Papers and shoes flew aside as she quickly escaped the store like vapor.

With a white-knuckle grip on the leathery handle, Rolan pressed himself to the wall next to the doorway and waited to swing on whoever came in next.

But they didn't come through the doorway.

The rooftop sheared off with a keening screech, raining metal shards that tore holes through his coat. Rolan cursed and ducked his head, allowing a massive man in a white uniform to roll into the room and onto his feet.

The assassin's hands rapidly struck the GlysterDrums at his waist. The room warped with power, and he could feel the pressure change in his ears. It made him queasy. Boots and paper tumbled away from the mohawked man as his eyes sparkled. The thrumming became more insistent, and Rolan knew he was running out of time.

He scrambled out of the building, while the man laughed, and hid around the doorway. He'd smash the agent's face as soon as he cleared the doorway.

Rolan was surprised again.

The storefront exploded in shards of stone and glass and thunder. Debris peppered his body as he slid across the street. A brick struck him in the temple, and he felt his vision waver and lose color. He needed to stand, to fight, but everything was suddenly heavy. Rolan couldn't focus on anything except the pain blossoming in his side.

The laughter kept coming.

He focused on that, letting anger rise in his chest as he grit his teeth. What kind of monster reveled in destruction like this? Who would treat life so carelessly? How many people had this monstrous man destroyed…and for what?

The assassin sauntered through the loose stone and rubble of the ruined storefront. Rolan pulled the last of his strength, and stood with DirgeMaul at the ready. What was left of the roof sagged and teetered behind him.

Mohawk paused, uncertainty in his face at the glowing GlysterHammer.

Rolan didn't think. He charged with the hammer swinging behind him.

Mud and ice splattered the nearby shacks as Rolan missed his first strike, the hammer slamming into the ground. The large man had slipped to the side, but teetered as the Glyster-powered shockwave rippled toward him. Rolan struggled to keep his footing as well. A metallic fist ripped through the air, and Rolan ducked barely in time.

The drums began to hum while Mohawk persisted. Power rippled through the air in miniature shockwaves, growing more and more intense with each beat. The force beat against his ribs and buckled his knees. He needed to get out of here.

Rolan slid backwards in the mud as the pressure forced itself upon him. His head pounded with the rhythm, almost as if his entire body was resonating. His chest pulsed in the pain of seismic undertones. Gritting his teeth, he turned to run, and was slammed in the back by a blast of sound.

Ears ringing, he staggered to his feet a few paces from where he'd landed. Mud caked his face and hair, and the laughter started again behind him. "This is hopeless, man. You come with me now."

"Never," Rolan spat, clutching the handle of DirgeMaul with white knuckles as he rose on quivering legs.

He felt the pressure building again, and shook his head with defiance. The drumming increased, louder and louder, but Rolan was through being toyed with. He slammed the ground in front of him, and a conical shockwave rippled toward his enemy. His arms screamed with fatigue, as he slammed down a second time, stepping closer. The assassin flinched back as the force knocked him off-balance. The drumming faltered as Rolan kept hammering, stepping closer and closer. He needed to connect with the large man, and he needed to do it before he couldn't lift this massive weapon any more.

Mohawk grunted through the shockwaves and twisted his body backwards, then slammed his hands on his drums with a thrust of his hips. The blast caught Rolan between swings, and he rocked backwards with the hammer above his head. The weight toppled him over, and his eyes went wide.

As quickly as he could, Rolan twisted his groaning body so the hammer came down behind him. The impact threw him toward the man in white in a glorious wave of green and blue shimmering mist. DirgeMaul came back around, and cracked against muscle and bone with a sickening crunch. The big man slid down the street with a high pitched yelp, panic in his eyes.

Rolan collapsed to one knee, chest heaving. The assassin's devilish smile and unhinged laughter were gone, replaced with a snarl. The man rose while wincing, wiping blood from his mouth. "Playtime is over."

Rolan paled. How was he still standing? These hammers were supposed to crack through icebergs in a single swing.

Once again, he was out of his depth.

"You've played with your food long enough, Garrick. Let's

find him a new home," a jovial voice behind him said.

Rolan swung DirgeMaul around blindly, and the screech of a brass horn tore into his arm with green slashes of searing fire. Ribbons of his blood flew through the air, and he lost all feeling in his right arm. The hammer sank into the mud, and the man in chains from the tavern bent down to pick it up.

"I want him dead," Garrick said with a wheezing rasp.

"No senseless killing. We have orders," the other man argued.

"Slush the orders! He broke my ribs," Garrick coughed angrily.

"She'll kill you for disobeying her. Have you gone so soft that one little upstart can get the best of you? You'll live."

He bent down in front of Rolan, who was clutching an arm torn to shreds, "I'm Dain, and you'll be coming with us now."

Rolan wasn't listening. He could see bone through the torn skin and muscle of his forearm. It burned like hoarfrost, and he felt the heat escaping through his wound. His ears pounded with every heartbeat. Where was Half-Step? Had she escaped?

His eyes flitted to the intricate brass horn hanging from Dain's neck. The agent noticed and wagged his fingers, the chains around his wrist clinking together. "I wouldn't do that. You'll end up hurting yourself. You still have your fingers, let's keep it that way."

Dain took his ruined hand with a grip of iron, sending a shockwave down his arm that threw a grey curtain over his vision. Rolan fought against him and another wave of pain rippled through him, nausea turning his stomach. "Hold still. I need to tourniquet this before you bleed out," Dain commanded.

Mohawk limped closer. "Is this him?"

"Soldiers saw a GlysterHammer last week, there's a GlysterHammer." Dain pointed.

Rolan's breathing was short and rapid. He needed to move, but the monster's knee was on his stomach.

"Garrick, can you stop his squirming?"

"My favorite part." Mohawks boots crunched in the mud as he approached. "Nighty night."

He was knocked into blackness.

Chapter XLII

It was the most comfortable bed in the world, and Traven still couldn't sleep.

As the sun began to stream in through the circular window, Traven punched a pillow and threw it against the wall. Rolan was headed back home, going back to isolation and hard labor while he drank sweet wine and paraded around in fancy clothes. There was a power lurking inside of him that very well might get him killed, and the Quintet had given him no guidance for weeks.

His patron had played him like a fiddle, utterly trapping him in a golden cage while calling him sweetheart and patting his cheek. On top of all that, he still had no answers about his brother. His investigations stopped as abruptly as they had started, with some maniac wielding a violin sniffing at his heels. If he was captured, his father would be utterly alone.

He couldn't let that happen.

He buttressed his mind with pride, and he remembered how far he had come. He was a Gold Cord, the first in his family, and now the most important people in the entire city were happy to enjoy his company. Because of his voice, because of his talent. He would keep this power stuffed away so that it wouldn't interfere with his aspirations. Whatever the reason people were disappearing, he would not be one of them.

With steeled resolve, he hopped out of bed and cleaned himself up in the washbasin. The water was fresh, with a hint of goraroot—spicy and masculine. At least Rolan was safe now, away from whoever these white-clad soldiers were.

He shook the pressures from his mind, and shifted to his task for the day. Thariel wanted him to visit after breakfast, expressing her *"desire to strategize his rise to fame and take advantage of the momentum he had already built."* He wasn't sure what that meant, but he was certain he'd be listening to washed-up nobles before the day was over.

Taking long strides out of the apartment, Traven hummed the last movement of the concert set. There was always a song in his head, and today it was The March of the Defiant Five, a song of the five cities standing against unity under the Empire. It felt... appropriate. He smiled as a few Gold Cords passed him by, but that smile quickly evaporated as the Citadel's looming presence leeched into his bones.

The place might as well scream oppression and intimidation.

A quick stop to the baker lifted his spirits, and he stopped at Nawny's shop to deliver his favorite breakfast. The old tinker gave him a friendly hug, and tried to convince him to spend a few hours as his assistant. "You are worth at least three of these louts," his shaky voice grumbled over the sounds of two men tinkering in the back.

He politely declined, making a joke about keeping his fancy clothes clean. Nawny nodded, thanking him for the scone before setting out for final preparations at the Opera House. The Empress was due any day now.

Pastry in hand, Traven bit into the delicately flaked roll and rotated his hand to keep the jelly from spilling onto his clothes. A few drops hit the stone, and were quickly gobbled up by tiny yellow birds flitting around him. He probably looked silly, hunched over himself like this. He didn't care; he was starving.

He walked down the lush acreage of Upper Resonance Heights, licking the last bit of sweet frosting from his fingertips. A carriage sat in front of the Vexlane Estate, a contraption of gears and levers, brass gleaming in the sunlight. A servant was polishing the metal and lacquered wood as if it weren't already spotless, sweat rolling down their nose. Oddly enough, he itched to step onto the machine and poke around. Where did that come from? Traven wiped his hands on his pants, and rushed inside, vowing to study the carriage when there was time.

Traven found himself once more surrounded by wood and smoke, shimmering lamps, and overindulgence. He was beckoned by a servant, and tried his best not to watch her hips sway as she led him up the staircase. She glanced back more than once with a smirk, and he pretended to study the paintings lining the walls.

Through a set of ornate doors, the servant girl gave him a private smile and motioned for him to continue. He almost bumped into the door frame as he watched her walk away. Thariel stood on the far side of another library, staring out of her balcony with binoculars. "Come, my Traven. I have something exciting for you today."

He walked obediently to her side with his arms clasped behind his back. "Another meeting with the nobles?" He tried to sound excited, and failed.

She pulled her binoculars away from her face. "Not today. Today, we strategize."

He wasn't sure what to say, so he stood in silence. He was a dirt-pounder, after all.

Thariel waited for a response, then nodded at the lack of pushback. She must think him cowed. "I've arranged a visit to each of the minor noble houses this week. You'll be singing for them during dinner, to get your name out there."

She was doing it again. "I need you to confide in me before I've been volunteered for things. What if I had said no? What if I had other arrangements?"

She turned back to the window. "Darling, I know you don't have other arrangements. We must strike while the iron is hot, as they say. And you, my charming young bass, are as hot as they come. For now, I need you available to me first and foremost… after the Grand Chorus of course. We may need to move fast to get you into position before the Empress arrives."

He paled. "Into a position…to catch the Empress's attention?"

She slowly turned her head. "Oh yes, if we can position ourselves to bend her ear with a talented, rising star such as yourself, House Vexlane may see itself on top once more."

This might be the best of worst news for him. On one hand, this could be an opportunity to cement him as the newest premier singer. On the other, he could have a flareup and ruin it all. Thariel let him stew on that for a moment before she hissed at whatever she was looking at through her spyglass. "This cannot persist."

Traven was about to ask, when Thariel thrust the binoculars to his chest and pulled him down by the collar. *Did she have iron for arms?* "Look there. At the mines just beyond the wall."

He tried his best to look through the glass, but found nothing but the frosted black walls of the FrostRim. It took him a moment to figure out how to nearly cross his eyes to bring things into focus, then he spotted the building-sized drilling crane teetering outside the city walls. "What am I looking at?"

"The bloody Dischordants have my workers in a frenzy. That crane could topple over any moment. The miners are too stupid to know how good they have it. The Baron needs to do something." She spat his name.

The crane bobbled back and forth, and Traven wondered how many people would be needed to shake something so large…and which of his friends had instigated it.

"What are you going to do?"

Behind the veneer of honey and smoke he had grown accustomed to, Traven saw his first glimpse of the real Thariel. The depth of her vexation was revealed in how quickly she fanned herself, how her eyes never left the mining site. A vein pulsed at her temple. She wrinkled her normally untroubled brow, and rapped a fan against the stone balcony with a sharp snap. "They need to be reminded who holds the power here. I'll handle it. I need you focused on building your reputation. We lost countenance when you fumbled that duel, let's be sure to challenge people we know we can defeat, in the future."

He scoffed and clenched his teeth. If only she knew what could have happened if he had persisted. He tried to change the subject, shift the energy in the room. "So tell me about your plans."

She looked at him in annoyance, then inhaled and smiled at him. "Yes. *Our* plans." She walked toward one of her plush lounges and settled into it. "Perhaps it's best I let you know your part when it becomes necessary."

She wouldn't dismiss him this time. "Humor me, I might offer something you haven't thought of."

She turned her head to him appreciatively and smirked. Did she think him a simpleton? "Very well. Other houses will wish to challenge you for honor in the Court. When you visit these lesser houses, I want you to embarrass their singers. Show them what real power is. Remind them that my house is not to be trifled with. If done correctly, they will challenge you, and you will win. Over time, your prestige will grow. Vendors will clamor over themselves for you to wear their goods. You'll use Nerise, of course…it's in my best interest for her to drive court fashion"

He frowned. Court fashion was going to be his rise to the top? That wasn't quite what he had in mind. Thariel didn't wait for him to respond. "The better you perform, the more solos and private concerts you hold. The more concerts you hold, the more opportunities I have to exert my own influence. Your voice opens doors that glimmer cannot. Eventually, I'll hold the Baron's attention, and perhaps the Empress…because of you."

It was a reminder. He was just a tool, a means to her ends. He may as well be the binoculars draped over the chair. Still, he needed to play this game. The prospect of having the undivided attention of the Empress was too tantalizing. He imagined standing center stage in Calrithia, purple cord draped across his shoulder with thousands of people cheering. Was that even possible? A lowly ice-smasher?

He shook himself out of his daydream. He really needed to get his head out of the clouds. "To what end?"

She snapped the fan in her hands, her sharp gaze directed his way. "To influence trade routes, to rise above the Baron and House Thale, and to ensure my house never falls this far again."

Traven had nothing to measure the success of House Vexlane against, but he certainly had never seen such opulence in one place. What more did she want? He decided it was time to lean on her. "I'll help you."

She nodded as if he said the snow was white. "Well of course…"

"But, I need something from you," he added.

The way she bristled gave him a small measure of satisfaction. People didn't make demands of Thariel Vexlane. He wanted her to squirm, and waited for her to acquiesce. She nodded and smoothed her dress in front of her. "What is it you need?" her tone was guarded.

Maybe now he could finally get some answers about Chadden.

"Access into the Citadel, alone." If the Empire was involved in the disappearances, perhaps they would keep records of their misdeeds. He could use that.

An amused look cascaded across her face, and she giggled.

"I don't have that kind of power. Why do you want to throw yourself into that den of wolves?"

"I'm very interested in Glysterium technology. I've always loved to tinker with the newest contraptions and wish to see more." *Everybody lies.*

She must have seen right through it. "And you think the Arcanum would give you free access to any number of things that might level the entire plaza without supervision? Tell me the real reason."

He sighed, and contemplated how much of a risk he needed to take. He was a terrible liar, and even worse at subtlety. "I need to find out what happened to my brother. I need access to the records."

Her face took on an odd expression that he couldn't read. Curiosity? Fear? She took a sip from a nearby wine glass, and tapped the rim with her finger while in thought. "I'll have my men investigate for you. What is your brother's name?"

"Chadden Caelhardt."

Her reaction was subtle, but Traven caught it. A twitch of her lips, a singular raised eyebrow. The wine in her glass rippled as a tremble shook her hand. She wouldn't meet his eyes as she fussed with the hem of her silver dress. "I'll see what I can do Traven; you have my word."

But why wouldn't she look at him?

It was Modera, and rehearsal was fast approaching.

Dread tugged at Traven's feet as he climbed the steps of the Opera House. The streaming green and gold banners lazily swayed in front of the marble support columns, matched by dancing trees dotted throughout the grounds. He was a few minutes early, an act of stubborn defiance to whatever threat had kept him awake all night. A swirling mess of nausea still clouded his mind from fatigue.

He was caught between honoring his friends' wishes, and honoring his word, his professionalism. He couldn't miss rehearsal; Malachi was very clear on that.

Finn, Mariss, and Elena were standing just inside. It looked like none of them had slept much either. Dark circles showed under their eyes. Elena saw him and tightened her lips. Mariss shook her head. He had hoped she would appreciate his dedication; it was clear she did not.

Clearing the foyer to meet them, Traven smiled as best he could, shrugging. "Let's make the best of this we can. I'm sure everything will be fine."

Neither of the ladies responded to him. His mother used to do that from time to time whenever his father had angered her. *So that's what Asmeri felt.*

Finn took a deep breath, and did his best to muster a friendly face. "Right, everything will be fine. Nothing to worry about, ladies."

"Why is he here?" Kael called from behind him.

Traven spun around. Kael looked like he had been through an ordeal. An ugly bruise covered the side of his face, and his clothing was tattered and unkempt. Traven noted two large holes in his cloak. "What happened to you?"

Kael pushed past him and pointed to Finn. "Stick to the plan. The additional variable doesn't affect things in a meaningful way," he looked at each of them until they nodded.

He didn't need to say it out loud. Traven was the variable.

"What plan? Can you tell me what's going on?" Traven pulled at Kael's shoulder.

"No." Kael turned his head toward him, then shrugged his shoulder away. "Keep your head down and try not to attract too much attention to yourself."

His tone stung. *"If you can,"* was left unsaid. Is that what Kael thought of him? Was he some prancing fool shouting for everyone to look at him? Maybe he was.

The unrest between him and the Quintet bothered him like an unbalanced ledger. He wanted to make it right, to say the right thing. But he also wanted to impress Malachi and the rest of the singers. He was stuck, and no amount of smiling was going to fix it.

The risers were filling with people engaged in conversation. Traven waved to his fellow basses and took his position. Finn sat down close enough that Traven moved over and joined him. "I'm sorry if I'm causing you all more trouble."

"It's not that." Finn had his eyes to the floor; he was uncharacteristically serious. "There are things going on that I can't explain to you."

Traven felt a little hurt. "You can trust me. I love singing with you guys."

Finn shook his head. "It's not about trust. You are new to all of this. Just sing like normal today. You'll be ok."

He wanted to believe him, but Finn's normally high spirits were absent.

More Gold Cords trickled into the auditorium until it rang with conversation and laughter. Traven began to run through some warm-ups, and noticed the normal richness of his voice was gone. He wouldn't be nearly as powerful as he usually was. Maybe that was a good thing.

Mariss glanced at him more than once as the risers filled, and scowled whenever they made eye contact. What was about to happen?

Malachi walked in, his broad smile beaming, and his coattail flapping as he approached the stage. "Let's go, let's go. Do some warm-ups on your own. I see some of you have already." He winked at Traven.

At least someone appreciated his dedication.

He glanced at Kael, who teetered where he stood in the tenor section. Shissel, standing next to him, had been insufferable since his victory. The bullying had stopped, but the snickers of his social circle were nearly as bad. Thankfully, there was no interaction between the two of them today. He wasn't sure he'd have the patience.

Malachi stepped in after finishing some musical notations, and began unified warm-ups. The lack of sleep made Traven's voice thinner, and he found it easier to sing with the higher voice parts as they climbed the scales. Unfortunately, he also noticed a warmth building up in his throat that warned him about oversinging. That shouldn't be happening this early in the day.

With a week left before their concert, Malachi had ceased the incessant starting and stopping every few measures and allowed them to run through entire movements. Traven enjoyed the way the director relentlessly smoothed over every detail, but judging by the shifting feet and heavy sighs over the last few weeks, he might be alone in that regard. Between movements, Traven studied the back of the auditorium. The anticipation was killing him. As Malachi signaled for them to take their halfway break, Traven nudged a nearby singer. "I should have slept more. My voice isn't behaving."

The bass responded reassuringly, complimenting his tone before stepping down for a drink. Maybe he didn't sound as bad as he thought.

The usual chatter of a mid-rehearsal break broke out. Traven avoided conversation in order to rest his voice, instead taking a seat next to a silent Finn. The baritone was humming to himself, his knees wrapped against his chest. His friend's demeanor had him rattled more than Elena's sharp glares, or Kael's bruised body. Maybe the Purple Cord wouldn't come today. Maybe Mariss had been mistaken.

A hush spread through the auditorium like a snowdrift, and Gold Cords who parted the streets with a glance split the center aisle with reverence. Even Shissel, with his snide and cocky smile, stepped aside with a hint of a bow. A willow-thin man—draped in a dramatic silver cloak and black suit—walked gingerly through them. His face had an ageless quality, framed under dark hair swept to the side.

Malachi glanced at the visitor, and then whipped his head toward Traven. It was just for a split second, but the expression cemented itself in his mind. Panic. Why would Malachi be worried about him?

The Director hopped down from the stage, and grasped the stranger's hand with an enthusiastic handshake, gushing about how much of an honor it was for them to visit, and how well prepared his chorus was. "You'll be quite pleased, I'm sure. The Empress will not be let down by Hearthmere."

The Purple Cord said nothing, smiling politely as they shook hands. His gaze swept over Traven as he studied the chorus, and he couldn't tell if his eyes lingered for just a second longer than the others. His stomach sank on instinct.

Finn cleared his throat next to him, and then nodded up to the balcony.

Two blue-robed figures shuffled into their seats, their mechanical arms and legs glinting green from their glowing medallions. What was the Arcanum doing here? Traven felt his chest tighten.

Malachi hurried everyone back into position when the break ended. Finn moved one position closer to Traven as they found their spots, to the confusion of the displaced baritone. Thankfully, they shrugged and clasped hands with the singer next to them. Finn just nodded his way, tension building in his flexed jaw.

The Purple Cord sat at the piano, crossing his legs with dramatic flair, and resting a limp hand on his knee. He smiled a perfect smile at them, eyes twinkling with familiarity. Malachi rapped his baton on the music stand, and pantomimed a deep silent breath for them to start. "Intro to Movement Four, right before the solo. Deitre, you just step in front of the basses when your time comes."

Singing began, the chorus enthusiastically springing into life. The auditorium rang with the power of a hundred eager voices. They wanted to impress this delegate, and Traven was struggling to hear himself. They were all loud, far too loud. Malachi scowled and brought their voices into control with a sharp gesture, only for the tempo to start jumping ahead of his motions. He brought his hands down intentionally and overemphasized to wrestle them back down. "Stay with me," his voice sounded strained.

This wasn't like them. They hadn't rushed in weeks. Traven's eyes darted to the piano.

The Purple Cord was moving his lips along with the song. He must be familiar with the piece. The priests above set a whirling contraption on the balcony edge that began to pulse faint light. Worry ate at him. They were looking for something.

For him.

He shook his head, and snapped back into focus as they approached Traven's favorite section. It was a passage about two brothers clinging in the cold, basses weaving beautifully under a series of triplets while the rest of the singers held a clashing dissonant chord. He thought of his brother, and nearly lost his voice with a knot of emotion. Even pulling back for a moment, the purity of his tone shook. He remembered Mrs. Bellamy, repeating the same instructions she gave each year. *Sing with emotion, but don't let that emotion take it too far. You have to find that sweet spot between vulnerability and detachment.*

The Purple Cord sang more openly with them, a smirk coiling on his lips.

He missed her, more than he realized. It had been over a month since he had left them, and this was the first time he had thought about them since. He felt it bittersweet that he might not ever see them again, and vowed to visit once their performance was over.

Heat blossomed in his chest. Lights dimmed.

The power resting inside of him sprang into life, climbing up to his throat. He quieted out of panic, and Finn slightly cocked his head. A vein pulsed at his temple and sweat beads had formed on his forehead. Even if the stage was always hot, he had never seen Finn sweating.

Finn's voice punched through the chorus; a sharp rise in dynamics that Traven knew wasn't there. The Purple Cord raised his head and listened as if he had heard something interesting, and Traven felt the surge of power in him subside.

The men on the balcony scribbled into their books with nodding heads, while Malachi struggled to keep the Chorus under control. His brow was wrinkled in frustration. Singers shifted from foot to foot in discomfort, and Traven felt a pressure building right behind his eyes. Deitre placed a hand on his back while passing by, his solo was about to begin.

The rest of the chorus quieted while Dietre proudly stepped in front of his peers. Finn's shoulders bounced as he struggled to regain his breath. This was out of the ordinary, Finn had excellent breath support. He was second only to Shissel.

Mariss was already looking his way. She mouthed, *are you ok?* Why wasn't she watching the Director?

Traven nodded, and shifted his attention to Elena, whose lips were moving when sopranos had a four measure rest. It was all wrong. Everyone was out of character.

As Dietre reached the height of his solo and his voice began to soar, Traven felt the pull in his chest return. Finn visibly shuddered and took another deep breath. The lamps overhead shimmered and blinked, and Traven could swear swirls of purple smoke began to stream from Dietre's mouth. The Chorus murmured, earning a baleful stare from Malachi, whose back was turned. The Arcanum priests leaned their heads together.

Dietre recoiled at the smoke and missed an entrance. His voice shook with uncertainty and he glanced back at the chorus with obvious distress. How many Gold Cords had magick?

The solo ended when Malachi silenced them. The Purple Cord stood and leaned into the Director's ear to whisper. Malachi nodded with a gulp, scanned the chorus until he landed on Traven, then flitted to Dietre. "That needs some work. Let's run that after rehearsal wraps up. Return to your spot, please." He almost looked relieved.

The priests and Purple Cord left as abruptly as they arrived, and Finn exhaled. There was no time to question him, for Malachi quickly dove into the rest of the rehearsal. He revisited the section they rushed, making each part repeat their phrase for an hour until they lined up perfectly. With the visitors gone, they all returned to nearly impeccable precision.

Rehearsal ended early, and Traven looked back at a shaken Dietre. Traven put his hand on Dietre's shoulder to ask him what happened, but Finn poked him in the ribs and jerked his head for Traven to follow. "What was that?" Traven hissed in Kael's ear.

Kael shot him a dangerous look. "Not here."

He had so many questions, and he needed to know what exactly just happened with the Purple Cord. They breached the exterior doors when Kael swiveled on his feet and cursed while hiding his face. "Slush."

The Red-Haired woman sauntered through the lobby and down the hallway. Her eyes met his for just a moment, flashing in recognition before she flipped her hair with a smile and walked away. She really was pleasant to look at.

Elena nudged him in the ribs with a sharp elbow. "Dangerous."

He nursed his ribs as they left the Opera House. "That's what I keep hearing."

"I think…" Finn gasped between breaths. "That Traven deserves some answers."

Chapter XLIV

Everything hurt.

Rolan's feet dragged through an inch of grime and dirty water. The air was suffocatingly hot and smelled of burnt Glysterium. He could taste blood in his mouth. Everything was muffled; the scraping of his boots, the deep voices ahead of him, and a deep rumble that shook his body.

As his vision was restored, he witnessed two mountains of men pulling him by his coat. White coats, Glysterium weapons. His arm was on fire, and pain lanced through his shoulder with every step.

The big men mumbled something that sounded like concern.

"Let her worry about that. He shouldn't have been sticking his nose where it didn't belong. Did you see that Glysterian with him? The Half-Pint?"

"Half-Step," Rolan mumbled under his breath, confused and foggy.

Dain glanced behind him with an arched eyebrow, DirgeMaul propped up on his shoulder. Anger rose in Rolan's belly. That was Traven's, he needed to get it back. He jerked his head to the man called Garrick and grunted. Garrick sneered back at him, his eyes cold with anger. "Go back to sleep."

Rolan was afraid he'd be struck again, but Dain shoved Mohawk. "Easy, mate. Why don't you go on ahead and start the paperwork."

"Paperwork," Garrick spat. "You just don't want to do it."

"Damn right," Dain chuckled. "And because you lost your head back there, I get to call the shots today."

Rolan could practically see the gears grinding in Garricks mind, grasping for a comeback. He gave up and glared at Rolan before storming off with heavy sloshing footsteps.

"Where are we?" Rolan groaned through lidded eyes.

Dain chuckled. "On our way to your new home. You'll love it there. Heated quarters, a full meal at least once a week, and plenty of invigorating conversation."

Rolan doubted it very much. He tried pushing himself up out of the water as Dain dragged him, but it just caused the larger man to shake him until his teeth rattled. Everything went fuzzy again.

For a time, he drifted in and out of consciousness. When he woke it was a little hotter, a little louder. Were they in access tunnels to the Citadel? Dain whistled an unfamiliar tune. How could the man be so unbothered, when he was dragging a dying man to his doom?

Heat and sound rose in a sustained crescendo, droning out Dain's whistles and causing sweat to drip into his eyes. Each step was pain, growing worse, until he couldn't bear it any longer.

He should have gone home.

⌢

"Wakey wakey," Garrick kicked him in the boots.

More pain.

He was in a small, windowless room. Garrick and Dain stood side by side, shoulders brushing the wall. Rolan gritted his teeth at the sight of DirgeMaul, wrapped in chains around Dain's back. The large men found humor in his defiance, and smirked at each other.

"Where am I?" He repeated to them, his voice hoarse.

"No more questions." Dain demanded, stepping to the side.

A meek brown-haired woman shuffled in, wearing the blue robes of the Chorus Arcanum. She nodded in deference to the two men before kneeling down next to him, prodding at his broken body. He hissed when she pulled his tattered sleeve back, and she grimaced. "This will not heal well."

Garrick spat into the corner. "As long as he lives, I don't give a slush." He moved to walk out of the room.

Dain called after him. "I thought you wanted to be here for this."

"I got paperwork."

"Then go find another alto and get those ribs fixed, you pansy."

Did the Empire have Glysterians too?

The woman began to sing in her low and velvety voice. It was an earthy song, laden with wisdom and sorrow. A rush of cool air blew his hair back, and he felt the unnatural breath work its way through the cuts and bruises on his face. Everywhere the breath touched him, it stung as his skin began to knit back together.

"You don't need to fix him up all the way, just keep him alive," Dain ordered.

The cool breeze stopped as she turned to look at him with a hint of disgust. "You know that's now how this works. It heals where it wants, I just keep going until it's done."

She continued, her song racing across his body until it met his shredded arm. He wondered why she couldn't see her magick, like he could Half-Step's…until the pain struck him like a thunderbolt.

He howled like a wounded animal.

The pain he felt when his arm was shredded might as well have been a lover's kiss. Everything in his body throbbed. His vision narrowed, and little spots of light danced in his eyes. The woman grimaced again but kept singing. The pain of mending pulsed like a heartbeat, matching his quick and panicked breath. His heels scraped against the stone floor as he writhed and shuddered. His voice went immediately hoarse as he cried out.

Time lost all meaning for him, and he felt like he had been shaking for hours. Dain at some point had stepped out. The pain lessened to a dull ache, and his senses began to return. The alto murmured something of an apology before standing, leaving him to lay in a puddle of his own sweat. Was his arm fixed?

He didn't want to look.

Behind the threads that remained from his tattered shirt was a frail forearm laced with streaks of purple and red. It looked like all of the muscle had been sloughed off and the skin had grown over the bone. He couldn't move his fingers, even though it felt like he was. He instantly felt the loss clamp over his heart like a steel trap.

He would never be strong again.

She left the room and Dain closed the door behind them, his steel blue eyes darting over his body with a tsk. "Shame."

The door locked shut with the familiar tone of a Harmonic key. Rolan grunted while dragging himself against the far wall. His feet nearly reached to the door. He probably could touch both walls with his arms outstretched. Trying, he whimpered when his useless limb throbbed with the effort. He'd rather have lost it than this.

His life as a dockworker was over. He studied his deformed arm with reeling eyes, noting how the skin sagged in odd places, and clung to bone in others. It was hideous. He was hideous.

"They gone?" A voice called from the hallway.

"Who is that?" Rolan groaned.

"I'm Bricky. I'm in the cell next door." His voice was hoarse and weak.

"Rolan."

Bricky tried to sing The Greeting Hymn, but his voice kept cutting out. He quit and chuckled sadly. "Not enough to drink; ruins the cords."

"Where are we?" Rolan demanded, hitting his head against the wall in frustration.

"Under the Citadel, friend. Can't you hear the furnace blaring underneath us?"

"I wondered what that was."

"You ok? It sounded like they were ripping you into pieces."

"It felt like it. Someone came in and healed me. I'm still unclear how." He was so tired.

"One of them Glysterians working for the Empire, I reckon. Is that why they snagged you? Get caught singing a little more than the city prefers?"

Rolan perked up, leaning forward with a grunt. "Is that why yer here?"

The man in the other cell went quiet for a long moment. Rolan wondered if he had fallen asleep, but then an answer came through the hallway. "Yep."

"What can you do? Can you disappear into the shadows?" Rolan had no idea how magick worked.

Bricky chuckled. "Nothing like that. I made the GlysterLamps shimmer one night while arguing with some friends. One of them white-coated devils roughed me up and brought me here. Said I was a Glysterian. I'm not really sure how long I've been here. A few meals, at least."

Rolan had to get out of here. He couldn't die next to this stranger. Half-Step was out there alone, and Traven was skipping alongside cave vipers poised to strike at any moment. Bricky asked him a question, but he was focused on what he should do next. Dain had mentioned conversation in a tone that suggested he wouldn't be doing much of the talking. He would have to make a break for it whenever his door opened.

If it ever opened.

Chapter XLV

Kael insisted they go back to Traven's apartment, shushing anyone who spoke about the rehearsal. "Ears everywhere," was all he dared to mutter.

Mariss stayed close to him, her apparent anger dissolved into concern. Finn shuffled his feet and fell behind, as if he hadn't slept in months. Elena wrapped an arm around his waist and helped him along. They all glanced behind them at every corner, scanning the rooftops. The air, normally balmy, held an ominous chill.

Traven led them inside, and Kael muttered under his breath at the portrait of the Empress while walking through. Finn plopped down on the couch and draped an arm over his eyes. Elena helped him take his boots off and dropped down next to him.

Traven pulled a seat out for Mariss, offering an apologetic smile. Leaning on the table with his knuckles against the wood, he asked. "What the hail happened?"

They were quiet for a long time. He began to tap his finger on the wood. None of them wanted to look at him. Mariss traced her fingers along the wood grain of the table. Finn might have begun snoring, and Elena looked to join him soon. Kael stood looking out of the window at the Opera House with his arms clasped behind his back.

Traven slammed a fist on the table, making Mariss yelp. "I deserve answers!" He shouted.

Kael's voice was placid. "As far as you know, nothing happened other than a standard visit from the Empress's delegate."

Traven stormed over to him. "Then why is Finn passed out on the bed when he would be dancing on the bartop any other night? Why did the Chorus seem so uncharacteristically disorganized? And what the hell was that purple mist coming out of Dietre's mouth?"

Kael sucked in a deep breath. "You stand at the precipice of information that will change everything." He turned to him and leveled his steel blue eyes. "It may very well jeopardize the reason you came to Hearthmere in the first place. I can give you answers, or you can continue your ascent into society. Once we start, I cannot let you go until we wipe you…and maybe your power manifests next month without our assistance. That is what you want, isn't it?"

It had been what he wanted. It was the only thing he had ever wanted, but there was an undercurrent he could no longer ignore. His flareups were getting stronger, his control more tenuous.

He took a deep breath and nodded. "That was what I wanted, but none of it is going the way I had planned. I'm doing more damage while rushing headlong into every trap. I need information, I need to know how to control this. I need to know what happened to my brother."

"People disappear all of the time. They don't return. Your brother is probably dead." Kael said it like he was reading a stock report.

At some point during his stay in Hearthmere, he had stopped believing that. His eyes grew dark, and he leaned toward Kael while sneering. "Could you talk to us like we are your friends instead of a piece on the Sleckboard?" Power flared within his chest. The lamps flashed wildly and the entire building shook as if it had thundered. Elena shot up with a shout and Finn popped his eyes open. "What the hail?"

"You need to control your temper. Anyone watching us just had confirmation of a Glysterium disturbance." Kael frowned while glancing out of the window.

Elena practically screeched, "Anyone watching? Are you out of your slush-blasted mind? The whole room just shook. I felt it in my teeth."

Fear scrambled his dinner and put his lungs into a chokehold. Did he just make the entire building shake with his voice? It was like the Whisper Ward, but stronger. He paced around the table while trying to regain his composure.

Finn rose from the bed with shaky arms and a bewildered look on his face. "Did Elena just curse?"

Mariss let out a small chuckle, which she quickly stifled with a fist to her mouth. Normally, Traven would be grateful for the baritone's levity. But he needed answers. He was tired of walking around with blinders. His hands wouldn't stop shaking. "Someone please tell me what's happening to me."

Finn rose on wobbly legs and leaned a little too heavily on his shoulder. "The power is growing, maturing. If you don't learn to control it, the Empire will catch you, or you'll burn out your voice."

"What does that mean? Why is it just starting now?" He looked helplessly at Mariss, who smiled knowingly.

"We don't know what caused your awakening, maybe it was Mariss's healing. Perhaps our friend Aveline can better explain it. She knows far more than we do." Elena yawned, laying back down.

"Aveline would make his head spin," Kael said, taking a seat. "Traven, the most important thing is you need to ensure that no one outside of this room knows your capabilities."

He wasn't even sure what he was capable of. Two days ago, the possibility of a little girl materializing out of thin air was beyond his imagination. Everything was turning on its head. He put a hand on the top of his chair to hold steady as the room spun.

Kael steepled his fingers. "Right now we need you to understand that your temper can betray you. Emotion seems to be the easiest way to call your power. You wondered what was happening today? The Purple Cord is a Glysterian in the employ of the Empress. They were looking for you."

Traven couldn't believe what he was hearing. "Me? Not all of us?"

They each hesitantly nodded. Kael continued. "We've had training, experience in stifling our magic. Elena can even mask the Glysterium response if she's prepared. You are untrained… and I take the blame for that."

"So train me."

"We need to know where you stand first. For all we know, you'll be wearing a purple cord next week and all of our secrets will be in the hands of the Empire." Elena put a pillow over her head.

Traven slumped into his chair, looking at Kael. "This is about the Dischordants."

"Too right." Kael stared back at him, his dark eyes cold and discerning. "And this is where you decide if you are with The Empire, or us."

"But I don't know what that means. What is your purpose?"

"Safety." Mariss rubbed her arm.

"Purpose." Elena grunted.

Kael spoke last, hobbling over to serve them all some wine. "Truth."

Traven took a cup and swirled it while working through those answers. "Honorable enough, but that tells me nothing."

Finn emptied his drink and plopped on the bed with a groan.

Kael ignored him. "The Unification Wars were more than just…uniting the different regions. It was an eradication of Glysterians and their history. They have erased us from the collective memory of Thalverians."

"But couldn't we just…fight back? I just shook a building with a little outburst...you can make people see things." Traven pointed to Elena.

Kael took his time with his wine. "The Empire has gotten very good at combating magick. You remember the redhead in the white uniform passing us in the Opera House? She's one of the Hunters, she nearly killed me last night."

That was unfortunate. Traven had hoped Rolan was wrong about that one. Mariss made a noise he couldn't quite place. Had he made a face? There had to be a way to fight this. "So get the word out on the street. Get people talking about it again. They can't kill everyone."

"They have before," Elena chimed in. "It didn't matter if they were Glysterians or not. Anyone caught speaking about it disappears before nightfall. They are everywhere."

"So what are you Dischordants up to? What's the purpose?" Traven twirled his empty cup.

Kael sipped. "I need to know if you're comfortable with turning a blind eye to the abuses of the Empire…or if you want to do something about it. I can't divulge any more until then."

Traven could feel the weight of this decision on his shoulders. "Would I still be able to sing?"

Mariss put a hand on his arm. "We still sing."

"It's the best way for us to keep tabs on things. As Gold Cords, we have access to people and places that would otherwise be barred to us. The better we perform, the higher we can go. We will sing until the noose gets too tight. Tonight was close to that." Kael braced his hand on the lip of his cup.

"What exactly happened tonight?"

Finn brandished a pillow like a sword. "I was locked in a heroic battle with that Purple Corded fool. He was pushing our emotions, it's something baritones can do. He wanted us to have an outburst, and I was doing the opposite…dampening things for us. Bloody exhausting work."

Traven turned to Elena. "And you?"

She sat up slowly, glancing at Kael. Kael shrugged at her, "It's up to you."

Swallowing hard, she folded her arms and looked out of the window. "I made an illusion…to take the Empire off of your scent."

Traven's heart sank. "Wait…are you saying to make the purple mist come out of Deitre's mouth?"

She nodded with her eyes to the floor. He couldn't believe it. Someone was about to be taken on his behalf. "But he was innocent," Traven whispered.

The rest of the singers in the room fell silent. Kael looked annoyed, but Traven didn't care. "I wouldn't have agreed to that, if I had known. I wouldn't have sacrificed Deitre for myself. What if he dies?"

"It doesn't matter. You are more important than Dietre," Kael interrupted him.

Traven's face twisted with disbelief. "It does matter. Otherwise what makes the Dischordants any more virtuous than the Empire? Why? What makes me special?"

"Glysterians are rare, bass Glysterians even more so. We… need you." Mariss finally spoke up.

"For what?"

"You are the last voice part Aveline needs," Elena flopped back on the bed. Finn shoved her to the edge."The last bass died cycles ago."

Just this once, he wished he wasn't special.

Traven poured the only bottle of wine he had left into the goblets on the dining table. "So who is Aveline? Why does she need me?"

Finn's voice sounded froggy. "Oh, she's a brilliant composer. Dabbles in GlysterTech in her spare time, and happens to be the brains behind our little…operation."

"And the goal of this operation is…?"

Kael's mouth twitched as he silenced Finn with a glare. "Not so fast. We need your allegiance, or Finn wipes your mind."

Traven whipped his head to the baritone. "You can do that?"

Finn shrugged.

A lifetime of dreams, slipping through his fingers like powdery snow.

He wanted to believe he could do this on his own, but he knew better. The guile it would take for him to stay hidden without their help—he just didn't have it. Admitting that hurt a little. Even if they wiped his mind and he arrived at rehearsal tomorrow oblivious to what was going on, how long would it take before Shissel caused a spike in his power? Kael was too logical, too protective. He wouldn't jeopardize the Dischordants to save him, bass or not.

Every turn he took in Hearthmere had him face to face with a dead-end. He just wanted to be the best singer in Hearthmere.

But he could be more.

"Ok." Traven stood and started to pace around the table. "On one condition, you help me find my brother."

"Like I said…" Kael began.

Traven silenced him. "You help me or I walk. Finn can wipe me."

Kael glowered at the interruption, but took his hand anyway. "Let's arrange a meeting with Aveline."

He wouldn't be like Kael. He wouldn't trade lives.

Rolan had no frame of reference to measure the passing hours. He slept whenever he was tired, which was all of the time. Healing had taken every ounce of strength he had and left him shaky and starving. Bricky would occasionally engage in small talk, and Rolan learned he was a traffic controller for the airdocks, with a bad habit of drinking away all of his glimmer. It wasn't uncommon for him to end the night shouting at the moon, except this time, the lights twinkled in response.

"How did you make that happen? The twinkling?" Rolan asked while scratching the wall with his dirty fingernail.

"I can't really say. I got quite angry because someone questioned the efficacy of my double-shoe method. You really should try it, keeps the feet warm even when stepping outside into that damned abyss. You'd be surprised how quickly frostbite can take the toes, even when the sun is shining."

This was the worst part about Bricky. Rolan appreciated the company, but trying to keep his new friend on the same conversation topic was like herding rats. That conversation led into the details of frostbite on every extremity, which segued into some girl he had fallen in love with cycles ago. Apparently this was somehow related to how bread was made in a shop close to Cantata Row, and Rolan had to step in when that conversation led to where Pizzo spice really came from…and not where everyone said it did. "Bricky, you said you got angry and started shouting? You weren't singin'?"

"No, sir, I haven't sung anything more than the greeting hymns and the Hymn of Gratitude. Hey, did you know the Hymn of Gratitude was a tradition of one of the rebellious tribes and the Empire incorporated it to keep the civilians pliable for integration?"

"Bricky!" Rolan shouted. "I need to know how you made the lights flicker."

The rhythmic clicking of steel on stone silenced them both. Green light shone through the slit in his door, and for a moment he thought he heard the gears of a clock. The Harmonic Key rang its simple melody, and the door opened to a man taller than Dain or Garrick. He recognized him from the balcony of the Citadel.

Rolan didn't hesitate.

His legs—shaking like wet noodles—slid across the damp stone. As fast as he could, he scrambled to get past the man in the doorway. He was slow, far too slow. His body was malnourished and beaten. A metallic hand closed around the top of his head and lit his skin on fire as his hair was nearly yanked out. "No," was all he heard, before being thrown against the wall with a crunch.

The man ducked through the doorway, glowing green eye intensely focused on Rolan's shuddering body. The man stood to his full height with arms clasped calmly behind him, his trenchcoat framed a glowing Glysterium chest, brushing to the floor. Rolan tried to get his legs underneath him, but the man twitched in a way that made him freeze like a cornered animal.

He could die, right now.

Behind him, the Red Woman slipped into the room and tossed a metal chair between them with a bang. She then pulled out her pistol with a flourish and leaned against the doorframe. The rage he had seen in the Whisper Ward was gone. She was all razormint now.

The Baron sat, and his coat flared enough for Rolan to see two mechanical lower legs. *What kind of man would do this to himself?*

The grey-haired man watched the question forming in his mind, and spoke with clipped, precise words. "Frostbite is brutally thorough."

Rolan didn't know what to say, he kept eying the open door while his mind whirled through an escape plan. He hadn't been ready, he would be next time.

The Baron leaned forward ever so slightly, and Rolan jutted his chin out. The Red Woman let out a pretty little laugh. "He's got spirit. I admire that."

The man didn't take his emerald stare off of Rolan. "Your hammer, where did you get it?"

Rolan shook his head and clamped his mouth shut. The older man sat there patiently, leaning back into his chair. The whirring in his arms and legs filled the silence. His eye and chest pulsed in unison.

The man sneered in annoyance, taking a slow breath. "Loyalty is commendable in my subjects. Unfortunately, yours is misplaced."

Rolan shook his head in defiance. He wouldn't betray Traven. If he was going to die here, he would do it with a clear conscience.

The way the Baron's eye bore into his soul was unsettling. It made him grit his teeth. "Perhaps another one of your comrades is worth your secrets. The little girl with red hair. Would you like her to stay safe?"

The Red Woman stiffened. Her pistol dangled on her extended finger while her eyes took a dangerous glint. The muscles in her forearms flexed as she clenched her fists. She wasn't looking at him, she was looking at the Baron. So there was some loyalty between the sisters.

The Baron looked back at her with a faint expression of surprise. "She won't hurt you, not unless I tell her to."

Rolan tried to stay calm, but hissed through his teeth. "You leave that little girl alone."

A smirk appeared on the Baron's face, his good eye twinkling with amusement. "This isn't a transactional relationship. You will tell me what I need, and what happens to you will be up to my discretion. If your strength fails before I get what I want, I'll pluck that urchin from the Whisper Ward and see what secrets I can glean from her."

There was something chilling about how frozen the Baron's face was. Emotion flickered for just a fraction of a second, before cold detachment replaced it. It was as if the man inside the machine had breached containment before the GlysterTech regained control. The Red Woman cleared her throat, glancing out of the doorway.

Rolan's options were running out. If he stayed quiet, Half-Step would be found and dragged into one of these cells. She could only go invisible for so long before there was a slip-up. She was only seven cycles old, at best. He scrambled for a scrap of information that might save her. "I am a Glysterian."

The Baron inhaled through his nose and straightened his back. "That wasn't so difficult, we didn't even have to remove your fingernails."

He said such things with eerie detachment, like a man convicted that his actions were righteous. Those kinds of men were dangerous.

Leaning in with a whir of his servos, he whispered, "Show me."

The Red Woman tightened her grip on the pistol at her side as she took a step in front of the Baron.

What could he do? Rolan's heart sank. He knew he didn't have the gift. He had tried it a dozen times while walking back and forth between the apartment and the Whisper Ward. Whatever it was that created the spark within a singer, he didn't have it.

Half-Step was doomed, again.

It was his fault. Again.

"Sir," The Red Woman broke the silence. "You will be late for your next appointment."

The Baron stared at him for an eternity, measuring him to the last miserable inch. He then sniffed in disdain and stood painfully slow, servos reeling. Rolan could see the clockwork machinations of his knees spin and shift. The Red Woman stood at the ready as his back was turned, shaking her head in warning. The Baron left the room, and she bent down to snatch the metal chair.

"Help me," Rolan whispered to her.

She paused. Long enough that hope blossomed in his chest before giving him a sickly sweet smile. "Little Mouse, you play games without knowing the rules." She held up a bandaged hand. "I owe you for this. Rest up, you'll need it."

"Selice," the Baron called from the hallway.

And she was gone, the Harmonic Key clicking the locks.

Chapter XLVII

"Let's go, folks. We have one week left," Malachi commanded, stomping his cane on the stage for emphasis. His eyes looked dull and sleepy.

The risers groaned as the Grand Chorus jockeyed into their assigned marks. Traven rolled his shoulders and cleared his throat while the rest of the basses filtered into their position. The spot next to him was empty.

Dietre's spot.

It didn't sit well with him.

Traven expected the halls to be filled with speculation and chatter. Instead, he entered an Opera House full of scared singers. Gold Cords huddled together, whispering in corners and behind curtains. The sparkling energy of a performance week was more like a low hum. Warmups were a struggle. Each entrance was slow and under pitch. Malachi plunked a note on the piano after each pass. "Flat. Again."

Traven was no better than the rest of them. He was distracted by all of the people pulling him in different directions. Asmeri never wanted him to be here, Rolan resented him for his Gold Cord, Thariel played him like a puppet, Malachi demanded perfection from him, and the Quintet expected him to be some sort of freedom fighter.

He was exhausted.

Malachi gave up trying to tune the chorus and jumped right into the beginning of their set. Thanks to his time working, and his friends drilling him every break they took, Traven had the entire two-hour performance memorized. The chorus performed adequately, but everyone cleared their throats a little more and sang with less gumption. At each pause, their eyes scanned each other—wondering who might be next to disappear.

Traven was no better. He was unfocused, distracted.

"You are all singing technically correct, but that won't get you far enough. Technically correct has the Empress on her airship before the intermission." Malachi slammed his cane on the floor with a resounding thud.

His jaw flexed as he stared down each singer, row by row. "I'll just say it. We lost a singer yesterday, I don't know exactly what happened, but the Arcanum is looking into it. Right now, that doesn't matter. We have five days before we sing in front of the most important people in Thalvaris, and thousands of your fellow citizens."

The chorus murmured. It was rare for Malachi to speak off topic. "To that point, we are missing a bass soloist."

Back to business.

Malachi waved in front of him. "I need anyone interested in the solo to stand here."

Finn leaned over and gave him a broad smile, but Traven was having a hard time getting his legs to move. Three men from his section stepped down to the floor, and a few other basses looked directly at him. They wanted him to go. He wanted to go.

It took a tremendous amount of effort for him to take the first step. The men parted ways for his descent. As he stepped down, Malachi closed his eyes, turning his head.

Finn started clapping, elbowing his fellow baritones to join in. His enthusiasm rippled through the chorus, and soon most of them were cheering. Even Elena clapped politely.

Traven was the third in line. He held his wrist behind his back while each bass ran through the solo. Some did quite well, earning a surprised half-smirk from the Director. The second bass didn't quite have the depth needed to hit the lower notes, and growled his way through—ending with an embarrassed shrug.

Malachi gestured for Traven to begin, a sad smile between his mutton chops.

He sang well. Malachi had already heard this performance once, and now he had worked through the nerves of unfamiliarity. Shissel snickered to his right, and Kael nudged him in the ribs so hard he let out a small yelp. Traven ignored him. He forgot all of his troubles for the few short minutes he sang in front of his peers, and thundered through the low parts well enough that Malachi closed his eyes and nodded his head. The chorus murmured behind him appreciatively. He couldn't have done better, and Malachi looked miserable for it.

The fourth bass, an older gentleman with pure white hair, chuckled and gestured to Traven with his shoulders up to his ears. He looked at Malachi with chagrin, who nodded enthusiastically and motioned for him to start.

The older man was talented, and sang well enough to earn him a spot in any chorus in Thalveris. Some choristers nodded their heads as he finished with a kind smile.

"Section leaders, consult me please." Malachi moved to the far end of the stage.

Kael stepped down with the other section leaders, singers who knew their voice and music as well as the back of their hand. In addition to the standard gold cord, each one of them sported a silver bead dangling at the end, signifying their honorable position. Malachi spoke in hushed tones, while the others nodded.

Then each of them took turns speaking.

It took ages. Traven's palms started to sweat.

The huddle ended, and Malachi motioned for everyone to take the risers. "It appears we have a consensus. The solo goes to Traven."

The Grand Chorus applauded, and he bowed his head. He wanted this, but still felt bashful at their attention. These were the best, and despite knowing he deserved this chance—he felt privileged.

Malachi didn't smile, instead taking a deep breath before rapping his cane on the floor. "Traven, please meet with me during break. There are a few things to discuss."

Had he done something wrong?

Malachi said nothing to him until the door to his office was fully closed and locked.

Traven sat down with butterflies in his stomach. Why did it feel like this wasn't a congratulatory pep-talk?

"You knew that solo was yours." Malachi stated, more than asked.

"Well, I had hoped. I've been practicing it for fun."

Malachi limped over to his desk and sat down with a grunt. "It was a good showing. You'll impress the Empress, if you sing it the way you did today. Hail, you probably would have impressed her with what you gave at the audition."

There was something more Malachi wasn't saying. Traven kept his mouth shut and waited for the other note to land.

"And, that's the point of bringing you in here. You are rising fast, earning the respect of your section. I see the way they turn to you after a rehearsal. I didn't regret bringing you into the chorus for a second…until yesterday."

His stomach lurched. What did Malachi know?

"That sharp breath of panic, the widening of your eyes. You know what I'm talking about."

"I don't have any idea..." he began to protest.

"Traven. I know what you are. I've been doing this for decades. Judging by your reaction, you know what you are, too." Malachi stood and walked to his door, unlocking it and peering outside before shutting it again.

"And I don't care. You are extremely talented. As far as I'm concerned, that's all that matters. I want you in this chorus, because it brings glory to our city, to me. The Arcanum does not show up to my rehearsals unless they have suspicions. They were looking for you, and found Dietre."

Traven tried to protest again, but was silenced with a single finger. "Your audition took place in secret for a reason. An Arcanum priest must be present for all auditions. They test for... certain things that you would have failed."

"But how did you know? There were no flickers while I was working here."

"Because you are the spitting image of your brother."

When Traven entered The Crooning Cello after rehearsal, the bar erupted into a roar that shook its foundations. Gold Cords clapped him on the back, offered him drinks, and invited him to sit with them. He was more than one of them, he was a soloist. A week ago, it would have been everything he dreamed of. Today it was just background noise. He tried his best to politely decline, carving through the chorus and toward his friends in the back. Malachi had given him information, and he needed to do something with it before his head exploded.

The barkeep cocked his head as he approached the bar, it was usually Finn who ordered for them. "Is the private room available?"

"A little celebration party?"

"Something like that." Traven half-lied.

Darling, everybody lies. Thariel's voice replayed in his head.

"It's free, don't trash the place."

Traven waved to his friends in the back corner and then pointed to the door behind them. "We need to talk."

Mariss and Elena shuffled out of the booth as Finn feigned seriousness. Kael shook his head and followed them all inside. Traven shut the door behind them, dulling the cacophony of the Cello.

"The floor is yours." Kael pulled out a chair.

Elena folded her arms and tried to read his face. She wasn't going to like this, his plan was suicide.

"I need your help getting into the Citadel." He said carefully.

Finn burst out laughing. "Are you insane? You want to step into the viper's nest on purpose? For what?"

"He knows something." Kael answered for him.

Traven didn't care if he seemed reckless or headstrong. Not when it concerned his brother.

Traven put a firm hand on Finn's shoulder, forcing him to sit. "Chadden auditioned two cycles ago, and failed. Not because he was a bad singer, but because he was marked by the Arcanum. When Malachi pulled me aside during break, he said Chadden was taken to the Citadel after his audition. I need answers."

Unsurprisingly, Elena's back stiffened. "If it's been two cycles, there is no way your brother is still in there."

"Traven, how do you know you can trust Malachi?" Mariss rested her hand on his. "He could be setting you up for the same thing."

Traven shook his head. "He didn't even want me to audition for the solo. He wants me to lay low, so I can be a Gold Cord for as long as possible. He was trying to tell me to be careful."

"While giving you information that would obviously propel

you straight into enemy hands." Kael traced a finger down the scar on his face without realizing it. "From anyone else, I would be skeptical…but Malachi can be trusted."

Elena's eyes widened for a flash, then her face quickly returned to icy stillness. "Regardless, it's been two cycles. Whatever happened to him, it's very unlikely he's still there."

Finn leaned back in his chair. "What about the log books? Those priests are always jotting down secrets in those little blue books."

"I would certainly like some answers of my own." Kael tapped his finger on the table.

Traven finally sat down with his friends. "So when do we go? How do we do it?"

"We don't," Kael said with a sigh. "It's too risky, and too close to the Empress's arrival. Security is already three times what it usually is. We need to wait."

"I'm not waiting," Traven said through a clenched jaw.

Elena flipped her straight blonde hair, smacking Kael in the face. "I don't even know if I can make five people invisible, especially not making us silent at the same time. Three is already very taxing."

Mariss folded her arms, rubbing her shoulders. "I can't go in there." Whatever her story was, she obviously had history with the Arcanum.

"Then we take three. Me, Kael, and Elena." Traven turned to Finn. "No offense."

Finn laughed while shaking his head. "None taken, as much as I want to honor our pledge to you, I do not want to go in there." I can go with you, to help ease your entrance…but once inside, you are on your own."

"Mariss, can you be nearby? In case we need healing?" Traven asked.

"We aren't going." Kael interrupted. "I need to confer with

Aveline, and the timing is all wrong."

A burble of anger danced in Traven's stomach. "I will go alone if you don't help me. My father needs to know what happened to his son. I need to know what happened."

"Can't you wait just a week or two?" Finn's eyes sparkled as the lights dimmed.

Traven felt his anger subside, his thoughts solidifying as the anger whisked away. "Finn, I don't need you to calm me down." He said plainly.

A nervous chuckle confirmed Traven's suspicions. Finn had no reservations against using magick on his friends. The anger returned, but the interruption had dulled the edge on his voice. Traven stood and put a hand on the door. "I will be going on my own. There is an access tunnel underneath the Opera House, in the furnace room."

"Give me two days. I need to run some scenarios with Aveline." Kael stood with him.

"I'll give you one."

Chapter XLVIII

Rolan woke once again to the chime of a Harmonic Key. It wasn't pleasant any more.

A wave of relief washed over him when Dain slipped sideways into the room, but then plunged into cold despair when Garrick followed. Sweat began to bead on his brow.

Garrick watched him scramble on the floor and push himself up against the slimy wall. Rolan couldn't get far enough away. He clutched his ruined arm and flared his nostrils. The man with the mohawk looked down at him with a menacing smile.

The door slammed behind them as Dain stretched his neck. "Today we'll be having one of those lovely conversations I mentioned. Garrick here has license to do whatever it is in his power, and I'll be asking some very simple and innocent questions. If you answer satisfactorily…you might just see the moon tonight."

Rolan watched the two mountains of flesh share a glance. He wouldn't be leaving this cell alive. Garrick's foul breath assaulted him as he leaned close. "Oh, please be difficult. I would very much like that." *Had he been rutting around in the sewers?*

He only had enough strength to groan. He barely knew

anything. Bucking his head at Dain, his lips curled. "Save your energy. I'm useless to you."

Dain feigned a hurt look, placing a dramatic hand on Garrick's shoulder. "You hear that? He's not quite ready to talk yet. Should we give him a few more days without food? Or should we accelerate the process?"

The hunger flaring in Garrick's eyes was unnerving. He looked like a wild animal clawing at its cage, pacing with predatory eagerness. "The second one."

Garrick swung a fist to his belly. Rolan could swear his spine cracked as the breath whooshed out of him. Doubling over, his body spasmed while fighting for another breath. It wouldn't come. Dain studied him with disinterest as he lay there, praying a breath would come. Garrick licked his lips. The bastard was getting off on this.

Before he could recover, Garrick hefted him up by the shoulders and pressed him against the cold stone wall. His metallic fingers dug into his skin, tearing his flesh. A breath mercifully came and Rolan sucked air through cracked lips.

Dain stepped behind his friend and cocked his head.

"Not yet," Dain decided.

Garrick threw him to the floor, and he tried to catch himself with his weak arm. It crumbled under his weight, and his shoulder crashed to the stone. Did he feel a bone snap? It was hard to tell under the lightning storm in his body. He let out a small cry, then clamped his mouth shut.

"Oh, look, the words want to come out on their own." Garrick stood over top of him, bending down at the knees.

Dain raised a single meaty finger. "Let's start easy. Where did you get the GlysterHammer?"

Should he answer? How could that implicate Traven? It was from a time nearly forgotten. Garrick raised a fist when he hesitated, and he blurted out despite himself. "It's an heirloom from the Unification Wars! Traven gave it to me to protect myself."

"Interesting, and why did he think you needed to protect yourself? Up to no good, were you?" Dain lightly tapped his fingers on the brass horn attached to his hip.

Rolan grimaced. "After our little dance, it would appear that was a logical concern."

Dain laughed heartily, slapping his hand against the stone wall. Garrick looked back to his friend with a stupid grin, then joined him in laughing. The idiot didn't even know what was so funny.

"Ok, funny man, what were you doing at the Cobbler's last week?"

It had already been that long? Time was slipping away from him. Garrick flipped him over onto his back and knelt onto his chest with knees made of anvils. His ribs groaned under the weight. "You take too long," he grunted while lifting Rolan's bad arm.

The brute shook it like a rattle, and waves upon waves of fiery electricity jolted through his body. He couldn't move under the weight of this monster, and he couldn't escape the onslaught of pain coursing through him. His vision went white and a dull buzz dampened his hearing. *Death might be better than this,* he thought.

Rolan panted when the torture stopped, noticing his arm was still held at the wrist as the fog cleared. Garrick made no motion to get up.

"The Cobblers, why were you there?" Dain repeated.

"I'm looking fer missing people," he said between ragged breaths.

"Why? Who sent you?" Garrick interrupted.

Dain frowned and tapped his friend on the forehead. "Remember your role, my meatheaded friend. The question remains, however. Who sent you?"

Rolan shook his head. "No one. I saw the posters on the walls and decided to investigate. I'm alone."

Dain narrowed his eyes. A shift in his face nearly turned Rolan's bowels to jelly. He tapped Garrick's shoulder and nodded. Garrick slammed his ruined arm on the stone.

The world went dark. He should just sleep. Sleep was good.

Dain lifted a hand to Garrick and bent down a little closer to his face. His golden ring glinted on his thick finger. "I don't believe you. The friend you came into Hearthmere with, the rising star, he's got some interesting friends. Are you one of those interesting friends?"

A squeeze of his ruined forearm brought the world back in fiery clarity. He drew in a fast, ragged breath. Why couldn't he just pass out already?

He was talking about the Quintet. If only Traven would have listened to his warnings. They were going to get him killed. Wading through the sea of throbbing pain, he shook his head. "Traven is just a silly boy. Drunk on his own talent and big-headed enough to fill the room. He's nobody."

Dain straightened back up and raised his voice to a near roar, "That lie stinks more than the last one, Garrick."

Garrick dropped his dead arm and backhanded him across the face. Blood splattered in an arc across the wall behind them. His ears hadn't stopped ringing from that blow when another came, and another.

And another.

His head spun, a symphony of pain wracking his brain. His arm throbbed like a tremolo violin, his dislocated shoulder roared like a brass section, the pain in his split lip was sharp like a flute solo, and his head pounded like timpani. Garrick as the Director was nightmarish. Was he going to die?

It took him a moment to realize Dain had asked another

question, he tried to shake away the fuzziness. "What?"

Another smack to the head. He couldn't focus, and he blinked hard to clear his sight. "For Chord's sake, I can't hear you." His fattened lips made every word a mumbled mess.

"The ring you stole, what do you know about it?"

Rolan didn't understand what the ring had to do with anything. He still hadn't pieced it together. "I don't know. It looked familiar, and out of place in the slums. I figured she didn't need it anymore," he lied.

Garrick's chest rumbled with a chuckle. "So he's a sneak and a thief, but doesn't even know the Arcanum sigil."

Dain narrowed his eyes and hissed at his partner. Garrick scowled and clamped his mouth shut while the other man rolled his shoulders. "Where do your friends meet?"

Rolan tried to gather his thoughts, but the pieces kept slipping through the cracks. The Arcanum was involved in disappearances…and with these Imperial agents? What did GlysterTech have to do with Glysterians? He lost the thought again when Garrick impatiently squeezed his shoulder with an iron grip.

He couldn't give up Traven. If they found out…he'd disappear too. He needed to come up with something to distract them, but he couldn't wipe the cobwebs from his mind.

He would have to give up Kael. It would give him time to think as they investigated his tip. It would give him time to escape. He hated doing it, but he couldn't give up Traven. "One of them was in the Whisper Ward, Selice was following him. I was following him too." He recoiled when Garrick raised his arm for another strike.

"More details," Dain commanded.

"He was coming from the GlysterRail. I lost him when I collided with your commander."

"Who was he meeting with? Where was he going?"

"I don't know. I didn't have time to ask him about his day." Rolan coughed up blood.

Dain placed a hand on his friend's shoulder with a warning look. Garrick scowled, spitting in Rolan's face while getting to his feet. The chains around Dain's wrists jingled as he knelt down and cupped his chin, twisting his head to the left. It almost felt gentle in comparison. "See how much nicer we can be if you are cooperative? Lying for your friends won't get you anywhere, it just increases the pain you receive. We've roughed you up enough, and I think it's time we give you some positive reinforcement. If you answer this next question, I'll make sure you get a hot meal even the Baron would be happy to eat."

Garrick made a surprised sound and stiffened, Dain waved him away without taking his eyes off of Rolan. "But lie, and we question the little girl. You see, we found her earlier today."

It couldn't be true.

Half-Step was too smart, too tricky. Dain could see the skepticism in his eyes and nodded. "Oh yes. We have her. The little bugger gave us a good chase, but she can only go invisible for so long. In fact, I can bring you a memento the next time we chat. Maybe some of her hair…or maybe one of her fingers?"

Rolan sneered and spat blood in Dain's face. "To hail with you brutes. You deserve to rot."

Dain looked almost hurt. He sniffed with disdain and slowly stood. His knuckles popped as he flexed his fists. "You and Garrick are going to continue this conversation." He clapped his friend on the shoulder. "I'll bring the Soothsinger. Have fun."

Garrick gave him the most unnerving smile he had ever seen.

And then they were alone.

F*ather,*

I could use your guidance right now. So many things are happening so fast. I think I have a lead on what happened with Chadden, but can't discuss it here. I don't know who might read this before it gets to you. I think it would be best to talk to you in person, which leads to my next news:

I've been chosen as a soloist for the Empress's Concert in a week. I know it's a hard journey, and I don't expect it...but I've enclosed a ticket just in case you wanted to come. We can talk about Chadden afterwards and share some of the best imported sweets you'll ever taste. Maybe you can stay for a few weeks and attend a soiree with me? My patron is a handsome woman, but be careful... she might have you wrapped around her finger before you know it.

How is Rolan? He should have gotten to you by now. Send him my thanks.

I love you Father. I hope you can be proud of me.

P.S. Tell my friends I said hi, and thank Mrs. Bellamy for me. I wouldn't be here without her.

-Tre

Traven melted a dab of wax and stamped it with a custom signet he had paid Nawny to make. When he pulled away the stamp, a perfect bass clef had imprinted onto the golden wax. He sat at his desk, staring at the letter and wondering if he should even send it. Asmeri had been right, the city was eating him alive. Would he even recognize his own son?

He hoped so. Underneath his fancy clothes and big apartment, he was still a hopeful farm boy, looking to be the best singer in the world. Things were just…more complicated.

Opening the door to his apartment, he lifted the cover to his letterbox to place it inside, and noticed a letter already there. The Vexlane crest had been stamped into a silver seal. He swapped the letters and broke the missive open.

My Darling,

What a wondrous job you have done. Congratulations on the solo. Because of your talent, the Baron would like us to attend the pre-concert Gala this weekend.

Please see Nerise for fresh attire, I have already taken care of her compensation.

-T

He shouldn't be surprised that Thariel knew. No doubt she had informants listening to every rehearsal, reporting on every note he missed. More concerning, however, was the invitation. Could he come face to face with the literal face of a system working toward his demise and not destroy everyone around him?

Something Kael said rattled in his mind. *The higher we get in society, the closer we get to answers.* The tenor was right, as usual. If he wanted the truth about Chadden, he needed to stop being afraid. It was time to embrace the cord on his shoulder.

The day passed in typical pre-concert chaos. Concordia Plaza had been transformed with colorful gold and green tents. Vendors sang with increased fervor, some voices cracking as they pushed too hard. Guards drove beggars to the shadows, clubs threateningly raised. Tension hung in the air like a dissonant sustain, and Traven wasn't sure how it would all resolve.

Rehearsal sped by with the chorus running rapid-fire sections that had been troubling them for weeks. Malachi was hard as steel, refusing to let a single missed note pass. The chorus was exhausted, but he still drove forward. Everyone could feel the Empress's imperial presence descending upon them.

Traven glanced over at Kael between breaks with expectation. Would they help him, or would he have to brave the obsidian citadel on his own? He was usually pretty good at reading faces, but Kael's was a fortress of concentration.

When the sun began to set and rehearsal skidded to a halt, the Quintet stepped behind the stage after rehearsal. Kael brought them close. "Aveline doesn't support this, but she recognizes the oath we took to bring you into the Dischordants. We will honor your demand."

Traven let out a sigh of relief. He really didn't want to do this alone. "Thank you. I probably couldn't do this without you…I don't even know how to use basic magick."

Kael snorted. "Magick is for fairytales. But that does remind me of something. Do you have the Harmonic Key to access the sublevel?"

He didn't. He was hoping they would find a way to get through it without having to steal from Nawny. "No."

"Then lesson one starts now." Kael directed Elena to the stage to provide cover.

Finally.

"Are you sure?" Mariss hissed.

Kael ignored her. "Emotion is the easiest way to trigger your power. The trick is to keep it in check enough that it doesn't explode, or shake the entire building when you get upset. It doesn't have to be anger or fear, any strong emotion will do. In fact, you might want to tap into something sad or bittersweet. This won't take much power."

"What do you think I can do?"

"Aveline and I have been theorizing about your flares. Your voice affects things on a subharmonic level, it's why you create miniature earthquakes. If you can channel that power into a single source…a Harmonic Lock, for example..and sing the proper note, you might be able to break the lock. Can you recall the note? I remember you mentioning pitch memorization."

"I can remember the note, I just don't know about trying this out tonight…for the first time."

Mariss stepped between them. "Traven is right, this is the worst way to start his training."

"We have to start somewhere. Traven wanted to do this tonight, we don't have the luxury of waiting." Kael's tone was accusatory. Traven clenched his jaw.

Finn cleared his throat. "I can help him regulate while he practices."

"Here? But what about the Arcanum sensing us?" Traven swiveled his head.

"There is nothing backstage for you to break. We are in a dead zone." Kael pulled a Harmonic Lock from his pocket.

"Ever prepared." Mariss droned.

The tenor hummed a single note, and the Harmonic Key chimed. "Sing that note, while pulling from your power. Remember, nothing traumatic."

This was worse than singing in front of thousands. More vulnerable.

He thought of his father's last embrace. A hug filled with fear and uncertainty, of mountains of unspoken words between them, and of heartache at constant loss. Finn grunted and began to sing, swaying with the pressure building inside of Traven's chest.

He hummed the Harmonic Key's signature, and felt the emotional spike in his stomach lurch and jump. It didn't want to be controlled, it wanted loose. Finn's breathing increased between each note, and the nails rattled under Traven's feet.

"Easy." Kael warned.

His voice cracked as he considered the heartache Asmeri must be feeling right now, alone in his lukewarm home. The curtains around them rattled and the stage groaned. Finn wiped the sweat from his brow and pressed harder, Traven could feel the baritone's presence in his mind, softening the edges of his memory.

Mariss shook her head, reaching out to touch Traven's shoulder. She let out a yelp when Kael pinched her wrist.

Traven focused on the sadness in a way he hadn't done before. With Finn's help, he could see the emotions from outside of himself. He could logically catalog how his body reacted, how his heart raced. It gave him control. He focused that emotion into the Harmonic Lock, directing his voice into the contraption. The magick fought him, the memory sharpening to something mournful and catastrophic.

No, that's not how it was.

He closed his eyes and wrestled with the heat in his throat, he tightened the music into a gentle pianissimo, barely a whisper. The floorboards calmed with his temper, the curtains silenced, and the Harmonic Lock popped open.

Finn fell backwards panting, a nervous laughter bubbling from his lips. "Chords, your voice is like a GlysterRail."

He had done it.

"I didn't kill us all." Traven's voice sounded hollow.
The Quintet shared a moment of laughter.

Chapter L

❝The plan," Kael explained. "Is to use the sublevel pipes to gain access to the lower levels. The first three floors contain The Furnace, so it will be impossible to hear each other. We need to move through quickly. Above that is administration, where we might be able to find something. Just above that are the Quarters for both Arcanum priests and Hunter cadre, we cannot engage them directly. Elena, you cover us as best you can. Traven, you stay calm and open this one door. That's all I need from you. Finn will be there to help you focus. I'll be there to protect us if things go sideways. We don't engage, we misdirect, and we run at any resistance."

As much as he wanted this, it was happening so fast. Mariss gave Traven a hug as they prepared to leave. "Don't lose your head."

He squeezed her with one arm, letting the butterflies pass before he gave her his gap-toothed smile. "I'll be careful." He'd take a worried Mariss over an angry one, any day.

Elena sang, and her magic drifted around them as she waved her hands. Her fingers danced in a circular motion and Finn disappeared, then Kael, then Traven. Her teeth bared as the magic fought her, shuddering around her body as she tried to cover herself. Her eyes went cold, and the magic snapped into place.

"Remember, we aren't silent. She can only make us invisible." Kael whispered. "Let's go."

Walking while invisible was complicated, without Half-Step holding his hand. Traven stepped on someone's shoes as he moved into the hallway and heard a sharp inhale. A moment later, he bumped shoulders with someone else. Finn cursed, and Kael shushed him. If he took short shuffling steps he was sure not to step on anyone else's toes, but he risked rumpling the carpet. There had to be a better way to do this, even if they tied strings to each other. His outstretched hand grasped someone's shoulder and he gave it a comforting squeeze. It felt small, slender, and he assumed it belonged to Elena. She didn't shrug him off.

The door leading into the basement swung open, and they jockeyed themselves trying to get through. He bumped someone again, and grunted when it sent him into the doorframe. Kael didn't shush anyone this time; they were too exposed. Stairs led them down to the sub-level, with a riveted steel door at the end. It was his turn.

He thought of his father again, and the emotion was less sharp—almost manufactured. The magick didn't want to come. The reservoir of power resting inside of him wasn't pushing against his mind like it had been these last few weeks. It was as if the small exercise he had done was enough to sate it. Finn was singing behind him, and he could feel the buffer on his mind. Would he be able to do this without the baritone? Watching his memory from outside of himself, he wrestled with the power. Why was it harder this time? He sang the note quietly, directing his power to come…but it wouldn't. The buffer in his mind relaxed, and Traven could almost feel Finn's reluctance. He needed more emotion, but they were still working through how much.

The walls shook and his chest tightened. Traven shook his

head and closed his eyes. He didn't need to see. He needed to focus.

The power came, rippling through his voice. A part of him wanted to study the feeling, so maybe he could control it. Another part of him wanted it gone as soon as possible. If only there was a way for him to practice without the Hunters knocking at his door. A worry for another time, as usual.

He pursed his lips and blew the note toward the hole in the door. His voice resonated with the steel—with the Glysterium inside the lock—and the mechanism chimed for him.

The rumbling thunder of the GlysterFurnace trickled into the hall when the door opened, and a wave of heat peppered their skin. Stepping inside, metal coated his tongue and burned his nostrils. Motes of green danced in the stale air, and Traven could swear he heard a faint song. The room was dark, but Traven saw a four-chambered Glysterium resonator. The four barrels—as tall as he was—connected to a central burner and cast steady light and heat into the room. A series of smaller pipes grew from the top and into ports at the ceiling—off to the rest of the Opera House. How many buildings in Hearthmere had dedicated furnaces?

Kael led them around the furnace and through another doorway. Traven envisioned the city in his mind's eye, and nodded when the hallway turned toward the Citadel. They crossed under Concordia Plaza, following pipes lining the walls with faint lamps fastened to the stone ceiling, and ended at wall black as night. A steel door blocked their way.

"Slush. Now what do we do?" Finn cursed.

Elena shushed him, and Kael pulled a key out of his pocket. "We have a way in."

Traven put a hand on the key as Kael inserted it. "It's Aveline, isn't it? She's part of the Arcanum. That's how you know so much about the Citadel."

Kael turned the key. "Not important. Elena?"

Finn stepped backwards and let Elena shroud the other three. This was where he would wait, ready to Soothe anyone who started snooping. Her magick settled quickly, and Kael took their hands. "Quietly. Let's tax her as little as possible."

Elena scoffed. Traven could imagine her eye roll.

Sweat trickled from his scalp and down his collar. He popped the first two buttons at his neck while entering the bowels of the Citadel. A guard sat with his head tucked to his chin on the other side, his short sword resting across his lap as he snored. It reminded Traven of the sleeping child in the thawing room back home. A smile crossed his face as they tiptoed past and ventured down the passage. Pipes as round as his shoulders lined the walls, and steam burst occasionally through pressure valves. One caught him in the face, and it took everything in him to endure the pain in silence. It might not have mattered, considering the roar of The Furnace.

Kael guided them with caution, squeezing their hands when he wanted them to stop. At times Traven had to press himself against the searing pipes, grimacing while priests shuffled by at an excruciating pace. Some had their heads buried in scrolls, muttering as they read. Others poked and prodded at clockwork inventions with brass manipulators attached to their hands. This was taking too long, and they hadn't even made it to the administration level. How long could Elena keep her illusions up? He hoped she would last long enough for him to get answers.

Their maintenance corridor finally intersected with the main hallway, and Kael took them to the right, away from The Furnace. Traven might have wanted to see it, in another life. Mechanical voices shouted over the roar, and he could feel the blistering air buffet his open shirt. He could barely stand the minutes they had already spent down here, how did these priests survive working all day? Behind them, Traven could see two priests on metallic stilts and brass claws for hands. The robes over their shoulders jutted at odd angles, hinting at further modifications underneath. Perhaps it was best they were more metal than flesh.

Kael led them up a flight of stairs, where the noise and heat thankfully relented. They breathed easier after stepping through an open blast door and into a green and white tiled room with wooden desks and shuddering lamps. Kael muttered. "Are you ok?"

The lights brightened. Elena whispered, "I'm fine. Sorry."

She was dampening the lights too?

Of course she was. Constant use of her power would be flickering the lights this entire time. Not only was she keeping them invisible, but she was hiding her Glysterian signature at the same time. Would he ever have this much control over his power? His success with the locks was turning his dread into curiosity. Maybe he could learn to live with it.

Each desk was uniform, with lamps precisely positioned in the upper left corner. A single black notebook sat closed in the exact center. No deviation, no customization. The Baron must keep a tight rein on his workers. Despite knowing his friends were there, he jumped when drawers started opening on their own. Kael must have started searching already.

Traven followed suit, rifling through their belongings and thumbing through notes about trade routes and Glysterium influx. He moved on to the next desk and found nothing, then another with nothing. "This isn't what we're looking for."

The drawers stopped opening, and he could hear someone shuffling close. "Next floor. This room is full of shipping and trade routes." Kael whispered.

"Hello?" a voice called out.

Traven held his breath. The lights flickered.

A middle-aged man with a round belly over a white vest twirled his mustache while stepping into the office. He waddled to the center of the room, a few feet in front of Traven, and then turned around shaking his head. "The oddest slush happens down here."

An exhausted Elena shimmered into view as the portly man left, waving toward the exit before disappearing again. They followed him out of the office and into the main hallway. Traven understood the layout of each floor by the H-shape of the outside walls. A cluster of offices led to a long hallway, then back to another cluster of rooms on the other side. A spiral stone staircase sat in the center of each room, and the next was full of scrolls and desks littered with paperwork. *This was going to take all night.* Elena wouldn't last that long.

Traven wasn't looking for paperwork, he was looking for his brother. He reached blindly for his friends and pulled them up the stairwell. Kael's bony body stiffened and pulled away, Elena did so with less resistance.

The next floor was the same thing, but with a focus on maintenance and repair records. Traven moved quickly on, his patience growing thin. The lights were flickering more often. They were running out of time.

Floor after floor they climbed. Three rooms circling the staircase, a hallway to the other side. Some rooms held people, but not the sort Traven was looking for. His impatience caused drawers to be left open, scrolls littered on the floor. Kael muttered something about Aveline being pissed, but Traven didn't care. After the fifth floor, Elena warned them her power was failing in a weak voice. She needed a break.

They ducked into a closet, shoulder to shoulder, while Elena caught her breath. It was hot, and Traven's shirt stuck to his broad chest. "How much longer can you do this?" Traven whispered.

"I don't know. I had no idea this place was so expansive." Her eyes were full of worry.

Kael sounded frustrated. "This can't be what we are looking for. We need to go higher, into the head priests's study."

"Lead the way." Elena settled her breathing before enveloping them in her magic.

Kael took their hands and brought them out of the office and through the hallway. Another flight higher, and the sounds of conversation flowed through the staircase. Lesser priests sat in conversation with each other in a long hallway of cots and footlockers. Some of them sported augmentation, but most did not. The rooms flanking the staircase belonged to higher ranked priests, but none so high that piqued Kael's interest. He went higher and higher, Traven was having a hard time keeping his breath. How was Elena still singing?

Kael finally stopped them at a door marked *Brother Graddot, Head Priest of GlysterTech*. Traven listened at the door, then whispered. "I can hear a quill."

"Hide." Elena commanded.

Traven snuck around the corner, hiding in a hallway full of reflector panels and housing materials. Kael must have had the same idea, as he winked into view across the room. Elena knocked on the door, calling out in the same voice as the portly man downstairs. "Brother Graddot?"

She could imitate others?

The door creaked open, and Traven's eyes went wide as Shissel darted from Elena's position and down the hall. An older man with goggles over his eyes, mechanical hands, and a glowing Glysterian necklace peeked out of the doorway. "Who is that?" he scowled down the hallway.

Brother Graddot shuffled past them, his back bent from cycles behind a desk. Once he rounded the corner, both of them hurried back to Elena. She was holding the door open to a room not dissimilar from Nawny's shop.

"How did Shissel get down here?" Traven began to ask.

Elena covered her smile with a slender hand. "I can do more than just make people disappear."

Kael hurried into the room and headed straight to the desk on the far end. Elena stood near the doorway and hurried Traven along. "I'll watch for his return. Go."

The room was full of prototypes so intricate that he barely recognized the pieces. He wanted to spend some time studying them, but forced himself to help Kael read through a stack of journals he had pulled from the desk.

"Furnace Fluctuations, Glysterium Anomalies, Yodel Incidents…." Kael read through each title, tossing the book to Traven as he did so.

"Hurry," Elena whispered.

"Here, Glysterians." Kael started flipping through the pages, working through the dates.

"Hurry!" Elena whispered more frantically.

Traven tossed the unused books back into the desk as Kael thumbed through the pages. He stopped flipping and dragged his finger down a row, then mumbled. "Son of a bitch."

"What? Where is Chadden?" Traven tried not to shout.

"I knew it, they took my father. These bastards will pay." Kael spat.

"Your father? What about my brother?"

"Kael!" Elena shot him a deathly glare.

Kael flipped through more pages toward the back of the book. "One moment…ok Chadden Caelhardt, baritone. Sequestered to the Thule estate for…research?"

Traven snatched the book to read for himself. Kael massaged his wrist with a scowl. His brother might still be alive…but for research? Would Chadden ever work for the Empire? "Where is the Thule estate?"

The door creaked open, and Elena made them vanish.

"Little birds." An oily voice rasped through the doorway. "Come to play?"

Traven didn't hesitate. As soon as he saw the man's thin body and greasy black hair he threw his invisible body against him, shoulder first. A silvery flute, glimmering in the light, clattered to the floor as the Hunter slid down the black stone. He could hear Elena and Kael running behind him, and a glance behind him showed the two forms shifting like a mirage. She was losing it. "Drop it and run!" Traven shouted.

A piercing note ripped through the room. The closeness of the blow caused Traven to feel his torso for an injury, but didn't feel anything. Elena, fully visible, opened her mouth to sing again before shaking her head. "I can't, it's gone."

"Nullification." Kael hissed. "Run."

They practically slid down the spiral staircase, using their hands against the stone to slow their descent. They passed the barracks, the industrial-piped underbelly, and finally arrived at a dank, dark corridor with two guards sitting at a rotting wooden table. They shot up with surprise on their faces, and caught two blasts of fire in their chests. Kael rushed to their smoldering bodies and scrambled through their keyring. He ripped one off and fumbled with the door while the sound of a flute echoed above them. Traven had slowed him down, but he was still coming.

The door opened just as a lance of viridian light bounced across the room, hitting Elena in the arm. She grunted and spun to the floor, but Traven was close enough to catch her. Blood trickled onto his nice coat. Finn shot another fireball at the Hunter as their feet became visible, they hopped out of the way and called down mockingly. "No way out from there, little birds."

They rushed through the doorway and past row after row of cell doors. At the end of the room was a metal barricade, long rusted shut. "Slush, we're dead," Traven cursed.

Kael shot three blasts at the door with his voice, watching the fire splash harmlessly against the steel. "Hey, what's going on out there?" A thin voice called through one of the cells.

"Traven, do something." Kael pointed to the door.

What was he supposed to do? Finn wasn't here to help him control his power. He could open a lock with his voice, and maybe shake the hail out of something…but this door was rusted shut.

The Hunter peeked his head through the doorway, and Finn shot three more fireballs down the hall. A piercing note filled the room, and the fire disappeared. "Mine's gone too!" Kael cried.

"Slush." Elena dropped to one knee.

He needed to do something.

Traven stepped in front of his friends and tensed his body. He pulled from a different memory this time, one of anger and humiliation. He recalled the way Shissel had tripped him into the table, ripping his leg open. He pulled from that without fear, without hesitation, and bellowed at the top of his lungs at the Hunter. He didn't need to be safe right now, he didn't need to be controlled. He needed to save his friends.

Power, angry and raw thundered through him.

The stone groaned as Traven's power rippled through the hallway, dust and rubble slicing the Hunter's face. The Hunter raised his flute with a smirk, and caught a tidal wave of sound in the chest. The thin man flew backwards and crunched against the far wall, his head dropping to the floor. Blood trailed down the stone.

He didn't get back up.

Traven didn't pause to look. He moved Kael into the hallway and faced the rusted door. They couldn't go back the way they came. Elena's magick was gone, and there would be more trouble if anyone else saw them. He needed to make a way out.

He sucked in more air, remembering the day his mother died. He felt the freezing cold, the iron arms holding him back from the certain death of the Ever-Winter. He watched Chadden scream, his father become stone. A tear rolled down his cheek as he tensed his body. The air crackled with little sparks of green, and the power erupted from him once again. His voice thundered, slamming into the rusted door with sonorous intensity.

The door groaned as the hinges fought against his power. He growled at the resistance, as if the metal could stand against him, and tightened his stomach as if he was singing fortissimo. With a painful shriek, the door sheared off of its foundation and slammed into a monstrous metal heat duct behind it. Sparks flew as the metals collided, and the earth trembled as it slammed to the ground.

Kael clapped him on the back, Elena leaning against him. "Well done."

Traven led them into the darkness, his throat hotter than after a day of oversinging.

*T*aven, *do something.* Rolan heard through the fog of sleep. And then all hail broke loose.

He screamed and clapped an ear with his good hand as the horrific screech of shearing metal filled his cell. He thought he heard a deep voice booming in the undercurrent, but he must have been delirious. His last session with Garrick had left his mind slow.

Footsteps filled the hallway outside of his cell, with people shouting orders to give chase. What on earth had just happened? "Bricky?" he called out.

"Did you hear that?"

"Of course I heard it—are you nuts? What was it?"

"I dunno, I heard some fella playing a flute and then my ears started bleeding. You ok?"

"I haven't been ok since I got here."

Someone opened the slider on the door to check on him, and his eyes fluttered closed.

⌒

"You ok over there, mate?"

Bricky's voice jolted him back awake. He picked his blood-crusted forehead off of the stone and tried to brush the hair matted to his face…forgetting that his arm didn't work the way it was supposed to.

He had never felt this kind of exhaustion. His entire body felt a thousand times heavier, and he struggled to open his eyes…so he decided not to. After Garrick had railed into him, the SoothSinger stepped in to yank him away from death's door. She washed her magick over him like a hammer, and he felt every bone reset, every muscle reattach. He even felt the healing wrap around his throat, destroyed from screaming for hours. Garrick hadn't asked him any questions, just inflicted pain. It was senseless, gratuitous.

"It was mighty brave of you, protecting your friends the way you did. I don't know if I would have been able to do that. You're a good man, Rolan."

He didn't care what Bricky had to say, the man had been meandering through his own mental maze long before they had ever met. Something in him had broken last night, he couldn't remember things clearly, just the screaming.

"They are monsters," he croaked.

"Especially the one with the mohawk. I don't mind the other one, sometimes he comes to talk without the brute. He's even brought me food a few times."

Bricky wasn't clever enough to realize Dain had been pulling information out of him. It didn't take much to get Bricky going, so Dain didn't have to force him. A reassuring word, a hot meal, and Bricky was happy to have an audience. Rolan felt sorry for him—in a way—but not as sorry as he felt for himself.

Resentment had blossomed inside of him at some point during his torture. He didn't deserve this. He was stuck down here, probably headed to his death, for what? Traven was enjoying the finest Hearthmere had to offer, while he was caked in mud and blood and grime.

He grasped that feeling firmly and clutched it close. They would pay.

Panic shot through him like a bolt of lightning when the Harmonic Key chimed.

Dain wasn't alone, but thankfully, it wasn't Garrick. Behind him, a willowy thin man with side-swept black hair entered the room. He looked disgusted, carefully placing his feet in the cleanest spots and keeping his clothes tight against his body. He cast wary eyes at the walls, as if they would start slinging filth. The most interesting thing, however, was the purple cord on his shoulder. Dain pointed a commanding finger at his chest. "Behave yourself."

He wanted to laugh, but it came out as a rattle in his lungs. It appeared the SoothSinger hadn't completely healed him.

The Purple Cord nodded to Dain and motioned for him to leave. A priest in Arcanum robes slipped in behind him and placed a GlysterLamp on the floor. The priest cocked their head at Rolan's bloody body and pulled out a sheaf of paper while signaling to the Purple Cord. The agent looked unsure, then sighed and locked the door behind him. Rolan struggled into a seating position against the far wall and stared at him with a challenging glare. The hum of The Furnace vibrated through his body.

"I am Vesh, may I have your name?" He didn't look menacing, or combative. He just looked…bored.

Rolan said nothing, spitting into the corner with disdain. He would give nothing today, they deserved nothing.

Vesh's forehead creased in consternation. He appeared used to his words being heeded the first time. Rolan didn't give a rat's ass if a purple cord was on his shoulder. The man pinched his nose with two fingers and took a deep, frustrated breath. "Alright, it appears I'll actually have to work today."

Rolan wasn't sure what to expect, but it surely wasn't singing.

Vesh hummed a gentle note, his nasal tone drifting through a simple melody. Rolan turned his head to stare at the corner, he wouldn't give him the satisfaction of an audience. The lights pulsed brighter, almost dancing with the song. He wished he was back home, lifting boxes was surely better than getting your body broken over and over again. Pleasant memories of drinking with comrades drifted through his mind, and he formed an image of his dead parents laughing with him at the common table. Why did that memory surface? He shook it away.

The singing stopped, and that melancholy feeling stopped with it. The room went dim. "Alright, nostalgia won't do it. How about anger?"

Vesh sang again, a militaristic tone with abrupt staccato notes and glottal attacks. Traven would be a better audience for this craft. Rolan inhaled swiftly, his nostrils flaring. Traven was the reason he was down here, suffering. The injustice he felt at his capture grew from an ember of frustration, to a furnace of wrath. He daydreamed of the things he would do to Garrick, to Dain. He dreamed of slamming DirgeMaul into the Baron's chest, or slapping Traven in the face and telling him to grow up. He was angry, and he wanted to burn the world down.

Vesh nodded and sang louder, more aggressively. He smiled with pride—like a craftsman at one of their projects—as Rolan's chest began to heave. His eyes grew wild. Rolan was losing control. He struggled against his weak arm, wanting to grab the singer by the throat and make the song stop. The purple cord pushed harder and harder, waves of emotion building bricks of wrath into a cathedral of destruction in Rolans mind. Emerald light flashed with each note, and the priest scribbled in the corner with a bored yawn.

He felt every slight against him, every unkind word and point of aggression he had ever felt in his life. Something pressed against his psyche, urging him to lash out. He remembered being mocked, being pushed, being ignored. That last little piece of resistance shattered inside of him. He wanted to punish them all, and snarled at the man singing in front of him. What was wrong with him?

Bricky howled in the other room.

He wobbled to his feet and took a step forward, another blossom of anger as his ruined arm dangled, uselessly. The Empire was to blame for his loss, and this man was a part of it. He wanted to watch the Purple Cords life dwindle in his bare hands. Someone needed to pay for all of this injustice, this helplessness he felt. He would choke the life out of this man, and smile while doing it.

The singer stopped his song and smiled politely while looking back at the priest. The robed man shook his head and tucked away his papers, and Vesh sighed. "Thank you for your cooperation."

Rolan's ire started to fade, like embers of a dying fire.

The door unlocked, and the two interrogators left him, turning their backs. Rolan was already standing—this was his chance. He lurched forward, crossed the small room, and nearly reached the door when Dain placed an impossibly firm hand on his chest. "Not today, little warrior."

He slid backwards from the push, slipping on his own blood. Anger simmered down into frustration, and he dropped to his knees. What was he thinking? He was too weak to stand, why did he expect to get past Dain and survive a chase? What had that purple cord done to him?

After a few moments of reflection, Bricky chimed in, "I need a drink."

"Me too, friend. I need to get out of here." Rolan sat back down.

"Then you might have to start talking. You won't get very far if you don't have enough strength to stand on your own two feet."

He assumed someone was still listening. "I don't have anything to tell them, I'm not involved in whatever it is they are so worked up about. I was just trying to help people…to have a purpose."

"Oh these white-uniformed devils are surely behind it. I remember one time, a dark-skinned fella was being chased through the Whisper Ward. I saw them split my friend in half trying to get after him. Hell of a thing. That boy gave them a fight before he was hauled off. I saw him throw a woman into a building with his voice…or maybe she tripped. I had been drinking a little bit, the memory gets a little fuzzy these days."

"Did you feel whatever it was that Purple Cord was doing to me? It felt like he was pulling strings in my mind. I wanted to do things I never thought I could do." Rolan sounded devastated.

"Aye, I think he was another one of those Glysterians. You said he had a purple cord? That's the Empress's Chorus," Bricky's voice was filled with wonder. "I thought those were only myths. I wonder why he's in town?"

Rolan was afraid he already knew that answer.

Chapter LII

The Purple Cord approached Selice as she inspected the shattered doorway. "Captain, I have concluded my investigation. The prisoner shows no signs of the Glysterian bloodline, even at breaking point."

She studied three separate tracks in the muck, one female and two males. The soles were flat, indicating high society. No one wore flat-soled shoes in the mud.

Vesh cleared his throat. "It is clear to me that the person you are looking for may be down that tunnel, rather than locked in that cell."

She walked back into the prison, stepping over rubble with her high-heeled boots. Her gloved finger bounced across the soot on the walls. Fire had been used here. A tenor. How did they get down here unimpeded? Was the female a soprano?

The Purple Cord took a deep breath. "Wouldn't it be prudent to clean up the remnants of whatever battle took place here?"

Selice noticed the floors were stripped clean from the rubble—the debris was deposited at the guard table—where Orlan lay lifeless against the stone. His head was crushed at the back, matting his greasy hair with blood. Pity. She'll need another flutist.

Who had enough power to clear a room of rubble and throw someone against the wall hard enough to kill them? Veyne would know.

"Captain!" Vesh stomped his foot.

"You may go," she said waving with one hand, picking at the bloody rubble embedded in the wall with the other. She didn't need his report, things were moving faster than his intel.

The Purple Cord left in a huff, and she felt her shoulders relax. Someone so close to the Empress sniffing around her home made her itch between the shoulders.

"Hate those purple cords." Dain stepped into the room, wrinkling his nose at the dead flutist.

"They have their uses, even if their motives aren't clear to me." She arched her back in a stretch.

His eyes followed the curve of her body, setting her hair on edge. Even after all these cycles, he still made her wary. Of the two brutes, Dain was the more dangerous. Garrick was simple— easily manipulated. Dain was sharp. Ambitious. What he did in his spare time would make hardened criminals blush.

"Have Veyne accompany you to the slums. She can follow those tracks." Selice commanded.

"I'll take Garrick."

"Garrick has orders. Follow yours." She met his cruel eyes with a dead stare.

Dain grunted, clapped a hand to his chest, and swiveled on his heel. His challenge for command would be coming soon. She could feel it.

An Arcanum priest pressed himself against the stone as Dain thundered past. He peered down his nose through green-glassed spectacles at the scarring on the walls with a tight grimace. Selice stretched her neck and tried to remember his name. These priests were all so forgettable.

"Commander." He gave her a slight nod, perfunctory and dismissive.

His tone straightened her back. She would almost prefer leering, over the Arcanum's clinical appraisal of the world. She pointed to the shattered doorway. "What do you make of it?"

The priest bent down and plucked a pebble between two brass fingers, crushing it into dust. His glacier, plodding pace reminded her where she stood. He would not be rushed. Deliberately, he positioned himself between the dead Hunter and the gaping hole in the wall. "He stood here and threw your friend thirty feet into the wall, hard enough to crack their skull. Then," the priest turned around. "He destroyed the door with a singular vocal blast. Our fluctuators detected only two flares large enough to do this. Two blasts, and then typical Glysterium anomalies afterward. Likely cloaked by a soprano."

"He?" Selice asked. "How do you know it was a he?"

"The other voice parts typically do not manifest seismic resonance at this scale, not alone. Whoever did this was a bass Glysterian." His eyebrows rose up while tracing his hand along the wall. "And a powerful one. He would be valuable."

She felt a flutter in her stomach and growled. Something didn't add up. If it were Traven, why was the prisoner still locked behind the door to her left? Surely he was here to rescue his friend. Was he here for something else?

She spun on the priest. "Has anything been stolen?"

He had just killed someone, with his voice.

The way the hunter flew into the wall replayed in his mind over and over again as they ran to the Whisper Ward. The way his eyes flared in surprise as Traven's voice barreled through the flute's magick. The way his head smacked against the stone—he would never forget it.

He focused on putting one foot in front of the other, splashing through an inch of dirty water as his friends sped ahead. His voice was hot and scratchy, and there was an emptiness inside of him. A fatigue deeper than muscle dragged at his steps.

Kael slowed down to trot at his pace. His breath was labored, but even. "Don't dwell on it. We need to hide. You are slowing down."

Traven sneered and picked up the pace, leaving Kael behind as he joined Elena. "How is your arm?"

"Fine, I'm more tired than anything." She kept her eyes straight ahead.

When they approached the end of the tunnel, and the muck and mud of the Whisper Ward came into view, she wrapped them in creme colored smoke. Kael sighed in relief as the magic blanketed him. "Not gone forever."

She held their hands, pulling him deeper into the underbelly of the city than Traven had ever been. He could still see their footsteps and hear the mud spurting with each step, but at least they were invisible. Elena stopped them in an alley, where his hand was pulled down to the mud and toward a thin window near the ground. He crawled in—lamenting his white coat—and dropped into a small room with dirt walls.

He flickered into sight, and soon, so did Kael. Elena was the last to appear, sliding through the window with a hiss. "Mud in my hair."

"We can rest here for an hour or two." Kael sat on the ground catching his breath. "Tomorrow morning we can reconvene and debrief the others."

"I just killed someone." Traven whispered.

Kael opened his mouth to respond, but Elena placed a hand on his shoulder. He closed his mouth and nodded.

"I just hurt someone, with my voice."

Elena knelt down and cupped his face with her hands. "And

I thank you for it."

How could she? Traven tried to pull away with a look of disgust, but she held firm. How could she say such a thing? Elena pulled his head until it was resting on her shoulder. He resisted, but she didn't let go. "What you did was protect your friends in a life or death situation." She whispered in his ear, "you saved us."

He crumbled, falling against her as they knelt. His breath came out ragged and hoarse, and his shoulders shook as he burst into tears. Elena held him quietly as he worked through the pain. Her straw-colored hair fell over him like a shroud. He had lost something, and tainted himself in the process. His voice was a weapon, capable of destruction, when all he wanted to do was bring joy. Was that all he was destined to be? A weapon? Did he dare sing ever again?

She let him go as he leaned away, his grey eyes locked onto her blue. Whatever icy armor she typically wore, it had been doffed for this moment. It was what he needed, and she saw that.

Kael awkwardly put a hand on his shoulder. "What you did was noble."

His temper was quick to flare. "Were you after the truth of my brother, or whatever you were looking for?"

The tenor cleared his throat, glancing at Elena with uncertainty. "Both. It was an opportunity to finally learn what happened to my father. My mother told me he was a drunk, that he left our family in a stupor because he couldn't provide for us. She let me believe he froze to death." There was something new in his eyes, underneath that cold logic. "Now I know the truth, and you know where to find your brother."

"Not really, where is the Thule estate?"

"That would be the Baron. Auren Thule," Elena said carefully.

The Baron. The Citadel. The Hunters. Strand upon strand had been connecting them to the disappearances. He couldn't piece it together yet.

If only Rolan was still here. He had a way of seeing things nobody else did.

"Then it appears we have a Gala to crash."

Chapter LIII

The next morning, Traven lay in bed with a sour stomach and pounding headache. He remembered feeling like this when he and Chadden used to stay up all night to watch the auroras through the glass dome of their Yodel. His father would drag both of them out of bed by the ears before the sun had risen.

Traven's sleep had been laced with recurring visions of violence and death. His joy was gone, replaced with ash and bile. He had hurt people before, but nothing more than a fistfight as a child. This was different. This had made him different. *Don't let them change you.*

He had failed at that in every way.

The realization settled heavy on his chest as he lay, surrounded by a cloud of pillows. He was angry in ways he never had been before, his temper short. It reminded him of Asmeri after his mother died. Death had a knack for washing away joy.

He needed to move. Chadden wouldn't be safe unless he stopped feeling sorry for himself. Traven could mourn the man he thought he was another time.

Thariel had left a note on his dining room table while he was gone. It didn't sit well with him; that she had unrestricted access to his quarters—even if she had given it to him. The letter reminded him to acquire clothes for the Gala, "befitting a Gold Cord Soloist." She didn't want to be embarrassed. He struggled to conjure enough interest to care, but set out to visit Nerise anyway.

Nerise was all smiles when he entered her shop. "Traven! It's so wonderful to see you again." She whirled around him, black patterned dress swirling around her bare legs.

"Hey," he sounded like death.

Her eyes nearly reached the ceiling at his tone. "Darling, you look like you barely got any sleep. Finn came in far past the hour he usually does after a raucous night of drinking. Did you two get into some kind of trouble?" She winked at him.

He tried to summon a smile, and failed. "Yea, you could say that."

She pursed her plump lips while leading him to her mirrored dais. After circling him again, she snapped her fingers. "Whatever has you in a slump, I'm sure it will all work out in the end. You've surrounded yourself with good friends. Finny is a rare man."

He did smile a little at the idea of calling him Finny at rehearsal this afternoon. Her eyes sparkled at him with mischief, and he noticed the makeup she wore made her hazel eyes pop. "You've got the weight of a sixteen-part chord on your shoulders today, love. Don't forget to let yourself be human, like the rest of us."

Why did she say that? Was he that easy to read?

She left for supplies, and Traven studied himself in the mirror. He needed to shave his head, and the bags under his eyes made his skin a deep purple. He wore a simple black shirt and emerald vest—another gift from Nerise—that she hadn't seen on him yet. He figured he would honor her during his visit. She came back quickly, with a shining gold bolt of cloth and matte paisley patterns, and raised it up to his head to get the right color. Nerise scribbled down on the notepad resting on a small table, then patted the chair next to her. "Sit."

He obeyed, exhaling loudly.

"You are a rare soul in Hearthmere, so don't let the machinations of the rest of us wear you down, or change you. Finn talks about you like you're a breath of fresh air, about how you're even more optimistic than he is…which is impossible. The group needs you for balance, and maybe, a moral compass." How much did she know?

He squirmed under her long-lashed stare and nodded. "Thank you."

"You don't need to be perfect for them to love you, Traven. You just need to keep showing up. Otherwise, you'll burn out and leave nothing for the ladies to swoon over. And they are swooning."

He finally let out a laugh. "If they are, I haven't seen it."

"Oh, that would be improper. Imagine how many fathers would be demanding your head if they heard what I hear in the powder room. Now you run along and sing. I've got something remarkable to sew up for you; you'll knock them dead."

Did she have to say it like that?

Before their rehearsal, the Quintet reconvened backstage. It was starting to become their little base of operations, when the revelry of the Crooning Cello made quiet conversation impossible. Kael briefed the others on the information obtained, and winced while telling his friends that Traven had managed to kill a Hunter—it was a surprising show of emotion. Mariss had gasped, tears welling up in her eyes. He knew she would understand. Finn didn't say anything, but gave Traven a sidearm hug and a firm nod. Their empathy didn't erase the black tar in his belly, but it did take off the edge.

They had enough time for Kael to run through a barebones

plan concerning the Gala. Traven would be there, with all attention on him as a featured soloist. Finn and Nerise had an invitation, which gave them the perfect excuse to be there. Lord Daelthorne frequently brought Mariss to these types of occasions, which left Elena and Kael. The plan was simple; Traven would sneak off to warm up before his performance, and open up an exterior window. Kael and Elena would climb in to search the lower levels for Chadden. It was up to Finn and Traven to conjure up an acceptable excuse to meet them. Finn was not concerned in the slightest, but Traven wasn't so sure. If Thariel intended for him to stay in the spotlight all night, how was he going to find a moment to breathe? At the soiree, he was barely given a moment to use the restroom. And then, there was the ominous question: how would he handle being face to face with the man responsible for his brother's capture?

He couldn't lose control again. Chadden was counting on him.

It was a marvel how every rehearsal could invigorate and drain him at the same time. The basses leaned on him harder every day, swelling into a crescendo a little harder when he did, nailing consonants when Malachi pointed in their direction with praise. The section leader—a soft-spoken man with clinical precision as it came to music—asked his opinion on the best technique for nailing notes below the staff. Traven was glad to oblige, and found himself smiling after their encounter. He was earning their trust, not because of his birthright or status, but because he was consistently producing quality music. This was all he wanted; a chance to prove himself.

Afterwards, Kael had pulled him aside. The tenor was giving him one last chance to back out, to simply enjoy the Gala. Traven waved him off with a scowl. Nothing would stop him from finding his brother. Kael didn't push him, nodding as they went their separate ways. As much as he hated being alone right now—with the memory of a dead man etched in his mind—he needed to focus before tonight. Traven entered his apartment and found a pleasant surprise.

Nerise had dropped off his clothes during the day. A

mannequin stood in the center of his apartment, draped in black, white and gold. It was the finest display of artistry she had created yet. Traven circled a pristine white coat, and traced his fingers along the gold scrollwork on the collar. A note was pinned on the lapel.

Humility is for the weak.
-Thariel

Glysterium buttons—more ornamental than practical—lined the right side of his chest. He considered popping them out of their housings and selling them, but remembered the bowl of glimmer sitting at his front door. He didn't need to do that any more.

The coattails reached past golden trousers made of an exotic material that shimmered in the GlysterLight. Golden epaulets sat on top of the shoulders with a fastener for his cord; he had seen the jewelsmiths shaping these with miniature hammers on the first few days in Hearthmere. This must have cost Thariel a fortune.

Humming to himself, he tried the clothes on. First came a white undershirt with more frills at the cuffs than the fancy tablecloth on Thariel's table. He buttoned a black-on-black vest across his chest, pulled on the coat, and then struggled mightily with a pair of golden bracers that covered his wrists.

Looking in the mirror, he realized that Thariel was sending a message. He looked like a general, his attire a reminder of the hunter he killed. This was armor, draped in gold musical lace. The neck was a tad tight, but only enough to press against his throat as he swallowed. The epaulets made his shoulders stiff, and his wrists were impossible to bend. The gleaming black shoes hadn't been broken in yet, and his feet were already tired from standing on risers. It was a small price to pay for how imperious he looked.

Nerise really had outdone herself.

He arched an eyebrow as he pretended to woo the Empress. There would be plenty of time for him to be serious. Here, away from prying eyes, he was free to be as goofy as he wished.

He needed to be goofy; everything lately was pressure and pain.

Resonance Heights was abuzz with the rush of fancy shoes echoing across the cobblestone. The socialites pressed against military checkpoints at every entrance to Concordia Plaza, eager to separate themselves from the increased security. Was it because of the Empress, or what they had done in the Citadel? He had seen her airship lazily crawling across the sky during rehearsal, through the glass dome of the Opera House. Malachi had scowled when half the chorus lost focus.

The guards bowed at the cord on his shoulder and looked confused as he passed. One of them half-saluted before an officer stopped him. That alone earned Nerise a hug. The nobles behind him scoffed as he skipped the line, and he could hear their protests. It was a nice reminder of what his life could be. His back straightened as he adjusted his collar; they weren't singers, after all.

The murmuring continued as he took long strides past a queue of well-dressed nobles standing on the road between the largest noble houses. He could feel their eyes on him—their curiosity. Would one of them stop him? Would they dare?

Nerves bubbled in his stomach. A pair of guards in the purple and gold livery of Calrithia had been stationed at the entrance of each houses's gate. How did they manage to look aloof and impatient at the same time?

Wedging his way through the crowd, he crossed the Vexlane gateway, clapped a fist to his chest at the guards, and ventured into her property. Thariel must have hired a few more hands to clean up her grounds. The topiaries were manicured, and the lawn was soft and even. Whatever her plans to revitalize her estate, they were working.

The sounds of the crowd diminished, blocked by the barrier of topiaries, and he took a deep breath. He missed the quietness of home. The walk up the long pathway to his patron's home gave him time to reflect. Tonight was his official proclamation of talent. He would be presented to the highest officials of the Empire as a soloist for the Grand Chorus. And all he could think of was his brother. The conflict between his ambition and loyalty clashed like a diminished seventh.

Things were happening so fast. If only he had Rolan to give him some perspective.

The rest of the Quintet had their merits. Finn was charming and charismatic in a way that made him feel like he had two left feet. Mariss's compassion reminded him that the world didn't revolve around him. Elena had strength in her core that refused to bend, no matter the storm. And Kael, despite his cold practicality, held them in focus when things grew dire.

But none of them grounded him like Rolan.

He should have fought harder for Rolan to stay. Traven had been so wrapped up in his new status, that he let his shadow eclipse the dockworker. When this was over, he would go back to Preth and make it right; he owed Rolan that much.

His new boot clicked on the first steps of Vexlane manor, and doubt wiggled back through the cracks in his confidence. Was he actually ready for this? Or was he pretending? Thariel's reaction as he stepped into the lobby slammed those doubts shut. Her eyes lit up in surprise. A smile split her face from ear to ear. "That girl is a magician."

Traven chuckled and posed for her. "Not bad?"

"My dear, this is positively murderous. If there was any question about where you were from, it will be eradicated entirely tonight. Come in, you dashing young force of nature." She waved him inside.

He was a sucker for compliments.

Traven could smell the food on her long table as soon as they went inside. Cinnamon and garlic danced to his nostrils alongside thyme and rosemary. It was borderline overwhelming to the senses. She had prepared a roasted animal, with a short snout and curly horns. Juices cascaded down its crisp red skin. Fruits were piled high, and he marveled at the payres and apples. He looked around the room for more people. "Is all of this for us?"

"For you, my dear Traven. For all of the hard work and success you've had. I knew you were special, and now Malachi sees it too." She sat down at the far end of the table. "And soon you will win the Empress's heart."

He ignored the seat on the far side of the room and chose a chair next to her. He didn't care if it wasn't proper. "I don't want to wear my voice out shouting across the room."

"Ever the professional. I appreciate your dedication." She smiled knowingly while pouring red wine into his glass.

He chose the water instead—aware of the effects wine had on his vocal cords. Wine could happen later, when his mission was complete and he was free to continue this charade. He wanted to be absolutely clear-headed tonight. If Thariel noticed, she made no fuss.

She did not wait for him to eat. "I've arranged a single slot for you to sing, and I have no doubts you will do well. I must warn you that the Baron can be…intimidating to some, do not let him distract you from our mission tonight."

"And that is?" Traven's stomach jumped. She had an odd way of wording things

"Tonight, we have an opportunity to gain the attention of the Empress. She'll be busy negotiating whatever trade deal she and the Baron are currently feuding over. It's why she is here a day early. It will be up to you to be so impressive, that you make it impossible for her to ignore you. If you do it right, we will have her ear before the night is over."

He faked a smile. "Imagine that."

The bravado he felt outside crumbled in his head. It was all lies. The Empire, the dream. The cord on his shoulder, the manipulation. He was already sick of it. He was nothing but leverage.

Thariel didn't seem to notice his face darkening. "Do this well, and you will be financially secure for the rest of your life. Warmth and wonder will be all you and your family know."

His family. "My brother, Chadden. Have you had any luck?"

She hesitated. He could see it in her eyes. The fork headed to her mouth froze in the air. "I have not, my sweet. I'm terribly sorry. I had my two best men scouring the records for days."

He straightened his back and exhaled, letting the hum of the lamps fill the empty space. Thariel dabbed her lips with a cloth and cleared her throat. "Have you decided on a possible maiden? Perhaps the Marrenvale girl?"

He caught the change in topic for what it was, but smiled politely. "Elena is just a friend."

Thariel blushed. "And far too lowly for a man of your talent. She belongs to a small house, we can do better than that."

He wasn't interested in having a relationship arranged for him. By anyone. "I think it's best if I focus on solidifying my position in Resonance Heights."

"A pragmatic point of view, but might I offer another? By linking yourself to a powerful house, you could do exactly that, without singing a note."

What was she getting at? The way she pulled him close, pressed against him, and called him pet names suddenly took on a new light. He scowled. "What are you saying?"

This time Thariel appeared to notice the edge in his voice.

Her eyes fluttered, and her face froze like it always did when she was scheming. "I'm saying…that not all marriages need to be… romantic." Her voice was tight. Her words, careful.

Traven's eyes narrowed. Was this another thing he would lose? Could he not have love, either?

A servant stepped in from the hallway. "Madame, the Empress's retinue is circling Resonance Heights. The GlysterBuggy is ready."

Thariel looked relieved at the interruption. She smiled sheepishly and stood, plopping her napkin over her plate. Traven looked down the table at all of the wasted vittles. "We've barely had time to eat."

"We must ensure our announcement order is precisely perfect. We cannot be so early that we'll be forgotten, but not too late so as to find the Empress bored. If you must eat, please take care of that coat. It's far too pretty to be stained, and I'm certain Nerise would slit your silver throat."

He harrumphed and snagged a few morsels to eat on the way. Thariel was already moving quickly, covering the silver on silver dress she had chosen with a shiny emerald shawl. She never moved this fast; it reminded him just how serious tonight was.

And she only knew half of the song.

The wood and brass body of Thariel's GlysterBuggy shook as it idled on the cobblestone. Puffs of green exhaust tainted the sweet air, belched from exhaust ports on the undercarriage below the velvet seats. Traven hummed along with the engine as it droned, playing with variations in pitch and enjoying the dissonance. A self-conscious glance at Thariel showed her hiding a smirk behind white gloves.

The buggy tilted as he rested his hands on the side to get a better look. Bright emerald light beamed through a glass port on the floor, and a rotating gem shot light at refractor panels. Random tones chimed as energy shot out from the Glysterium. It was arrhythmic, yet pleasant. A series of leaf-springs intended to keep their ride smooth had been attached to the bottom. He was careful not to sully his trousers while inspecting the underside. His patron cleared her throat, and he felt himself grow hot under the collar. "Sorry."

"You can play mechanic some other time, dear. Help me up."

Thariel stepped past him, taking his outstretched arm with an appreciative pat on the hand. Traven thought they could simply walk to the Gala, but wasn't going to complain. This was almost as exciting as riding an airship.

Once they had settled into the carriage, the driver pushed a lever on his right and the buggy lurched into motion. The food in Traven's hands tumbled, and he snatched it out of the air before the sauce sullied his coat or the seats of the GlysterBuggy. Thariel shot him a warning look. He apologized with a full mouth and quickly shoved down the rest. He hoped there would be food at the Gala.

The driver blared a horn as they thundered across her estate, and the guards scrambled to part the crowd. They didn't appear to be slowing. Couples jumped out of the way with a glare as they sped along, blanketing them in a cloud of dust and fumes.

They barrelled past the queue, teeth chattering and brass pinging, and turned into the Baron's estate in spite of the throng of people standing there. The nobles scattered, and Thariel pretended not to notice while fanning her face. Traven tried to wave in apology, but another bump had him grasping the side of the buggy. They sped past rows and rows of tall narrow trees, and Traven had to look away when his head began to spin.

Ahead of them, patrons were shuffling into the Baron's mansion. Golden statues of the Thule family proudly stood in front of precisely cut marble. They looked noble, benevolent. Bushes were trimmed into perfect squares, lining the entire facade of the mansion. Why was every tree in this city manicured to look man-made? Everything was precise, from the spacing between trees, the taut snap of the banners in the wind, and the exact angle of shutters on the second floor.

The black and gold airship—magnificent from this distance— had turned the grass near the landing pad a sickly yellow. It felt symbolic, how something that provided his people with life could destroy nature.

Standing near the front doors were two Cantor suits gleaming in the moonlight. Miniature GlysterDomes shimmered on their right forearms, pulsing in time with the power core in the chestplate. Barrel-sized fists of interlinked lacquered steel plates gripped swords as wide as his chest. Those hands could crush a man like a wineskin. Traven couldn't see the soldiers piloting these mechanical behemoths, but he could sense them watching through layers of thick steel.

Behind the Thule estate bobbed The Fortissimo, the personal conveyance of the Empress. While the Baron's airship was black and menacing, The Fortissimo managed to look twice as agile despite being three times its size. Streamers of purple gently swayed over the bone-white wooden planks. Golden accents circled three rows of gun ports stretching from bow to stern. It was one of the most beautiful things he had ever seen, and it still sent chills up his spine.

Thariel stepped down from the brass contraption, commanding the attention of every person waiting to be seen. He wasn't sure they were pleased at their arrival, but he figured attention was attention in Thariel's mind.

She held her head high, waiting for Traven to offer his arm. Together, they proudly sauntered through the crowd and through the open front doors.

A servant hurried to greet them, feet tripping over the guest list dangling to the floor. Half of the city must have been invited, and they had just cut in front of them. Traven tugged at his stiff collar.

The foyer was a much larger version of Thariel's opulence. One of the world's most precious resources, used for decor. Brown lacquered bookshelves, tables and chairs lined the hall. Chandeliers hung from the high vaulted ceilings covered in fresco paintings of the Unification War. He could see the Empire in its infancy, proudly defeating a disheveled and barbaric rebellion. There were GlysterHammers, GlysterBlades, and Thunder Cannons being used to wage their righteous war. The painter had done a wonderful job depicting the Empire as heroes. The whole manor reeked of cigar smoke and incense, and he worried for a moment about the health of his voice. It ultimately didn't matter, he couldn't leave if he wanted to. It all felt wrong, wasteful.

Thariel slid her arm back around his and pulled him through the doorway. String instruments played a concerto in a corner, and Traven wondered if the cello was made of real wood. The sound was rich and resonant, something impossible to achieve with the stacked leather instruments he had grown up with. Thariel leaned in. "We follow Lord and Lady Chambeau, the third largest estate in Hearthmere. The Empress has already arrived. We are poised to strike."

He found it oddly charming, the way Thariel viewed these political maneuverings. She moved them like units on a battlefield, poking here, retreating there, until the perfect moment had arrived. She would sometimes whisk him away from a conversation with a hurried apology before presenting him to the next lord and lady, none of which names he could remember. He was never good with names, but could remember faces forever. She danced through these social events like a ballerina, or a bladesmith.

The doorman gave Thariel a nod, which she returned politely. His voice cut through the Gala. "Lady Vexlane and her soloist, Traven Caelhardt."

His chest tightened the way it did before stage curtains parted. Thariel held him back for a few breaths, adjusting her hair and letting him settle before flagging the doorman. Stepping inside, the music rushed to his ears. The ballroom was pure indulgence. Five-tier chandeliers twinkled with more Glysterium than he had ever seen—and there were three of them. Servants whisked around the room with silver trays, keeping the crowd's wine glasses full. An artist had painted the dance floor with a silver sprawling tree with vibrant red leaves. The ceiling was open to a second floor, with guests lingering on the balcony to watch the dancing below. Several Gold Cords circled the room, patrons at their side, and gave Traven a friendly smile.

Tables had been pushed to the corners of the room, where rivers of graypes ran through thinly sliced hills of meat. A pile of nuts and berries had been carefully arranged to resemble a mountain range, with wine running from the top and into a basin. Half-Step was scrounging every day, and food was being used here as decoration.

The room hushed when they entered. Thariel let him step ahead of her, and he stood alone, to officially be on display as the Grand Chorus soloist. It was nothing like his childhood daydreams. He had always pictured his mother by his side, his brother singing with him, his father proudly beaming. Now he was alone, walking into a viper's nest.

A woman, slender and ageless, sat silently across the room. Empress Wiseria—livelier and more imposing than the portrait hanging in his apartment—commanded the room. Every eye tracked a raised eyebrow or flick of the wrist. Nobles bowed and scraped, desperation clear on their faces. Her dress, a purple and blue storm of Glysterium layered fabric, settled around her frame. She looked bored, petulant even, regarding her sycophants with a slight sneer. Attendants in sheer silky clothing flitted around like embers—endlessly fussing with her dress, her hair, or her drink. He felt himself blushing as his eyes skimmed across the shape of their bodies. Were they not cold...or ashamed?

A man rose from among the nobles in a deep green suit, his chest pulsing with light. A mechanical eye focused on him, and Traven felt pressure build in his chest. A deep breath didn't help to clear it. He knew this man from the balcony. His brother's captor, wading through the dance floor, his legs clicking and whirring.

Thariel nudged him and whispered into his ear, "careful."

"Mistress Vexlane." The Baron's voice was deep and warm.

Traven fought the urge to clear his throat the way other men did around him. "Baron Thale." She curtseyed. "I would like to introduce Traven, your brightest star."

He didn't belong to this man.

The Glysterium eye snapped to meet his gaze, and the room appeared to darken. Thariel studied her dress as tension filled the space. Dread followed this man like a shadow, and Traven was reminded of the bile-inducing aura of the Citadel. Fire blossomed in Traven's stomach, and he shoved it with a growl. He could let himself loose right now, tear this man's artificial heart out with a shout.

It was a foolish fantasy. There were almost as many guards here as guests, and the two battle-suits outside would tear this place apart if he attacked. He would bring the entire Empire down on his head, before he ever saw Chadden.

The Baron smiled through a well-groomed salt and pepper beard, and offered a hand of brass, sprockets, and springs. Traven took it and squeezed just enough to recognize strength for strength. A gap-tooth smile split his face. "An honor, Baron."

The metallic hand was painfully strong, and miniature jolts of pain pricked his palm. As hard as he squeezed, the Baron met his might. Traven kept his face still, but could feel his jaw flex.

The man's stoic facade cracked into a surprised smile that never reached his eyes. "A fellow bass! It is good to see one of us getting the spotlight instead of those pesky tenors, isn't it?" He pointed to Shissel, loitering near the fringe.

Traven chuckled as the Baron continued. "You have made quite a splash in my city. A month ago I had never heard of you. Now you appear to represent my finest singers. A shame about your duel with the Morayne boy."

"You heard about that?" Traven frowned.

The Baron finally let his hand go. "I've heard a great deal about you."

Traven's hair stood on end, and his countenance faltered. Bowing to Thariel, the Baron leaned in close to Traven's ear. "It appears," he growled. "That subtlety is not your forte." He flicked the epaulets on his shoulder, and walked away.

Traven hated that he flinched.

Thariel slid close to his side and grabbed his arm as the Baron left them to the party. "Come, there are a few people we need to placate."

The tension left his body as if his strings had been cut. Traven had been poised to run, or maybe to fight; he wasn't sure. Everything about the Baron had set him on edge, from the whirring servos to the glinting eye. Even as he smiled, the air crackled with coiled violence.

Thariel pulled him toward familiar faces, nobles she had introduced him to at the soiree, but he couldn't focus. He had just shaken hands with the man responsible for his brother's capture. The man was confidence and charm; it made him feel like a child. His patron elbowed him in the ribs, and it snapped him back into the conversation in front of him.

It was the same stale talking points, and his patience with underhanded comments was wearing thin. He was already on edge, and the smiles he forced ended up looking more like a grimace. To his dismay, Shissel approached, no doubt to remind him of his loss. A look from Thariel stopped him mid-stride. She wouldn't tolerate her charge being distracted tonight.

It was too late for that.

The Baron was busy wading through the crowd, his cold stare parting the dancers as their faces paled. He gripped the mechanical arm behind his back, the fingers flexing the way men did when fighting frostbite. Traven wondered if the augmentations were painful.

Thariel fanned herself as their latest conversation partner stepped away. "I need to excuse myself. Mingle, charm, win their hearts."

She disappeared into the growing mass of tophats and extravagant dresses. The food he devoured earlier, and the growing nerves of a pending performance made his mouth dry, so he cleared the dance floor and filled a glass.

The table had an ice sculpture of a winged beast arching its back. Meats and cheeses had been arranged around it to look like blossoming flowers. He didn't recognize most of the food, but that didn't stop him from placing one of each on his plate.

"Keep your eyes forward, don't acknowledge me," a soft woman's voice commanded from behind.

He stiffened, but pretended to continue fixing a plate. From the corner of his eye, he could catch a shimmering blue dress and white gloves grasping a champagne flute. She didn't look at him. He could barely see her round spectacles and hair pinned into tall ringlets on top of her head.

"When you are dismissed to prepare for your solo, Kael will be waiting for you. Ensure you aren't followed. The Huntress is watching you even now," she said under her breath.

"Aveline?" he guessed.

"After the concert tomorrow, Mariss will bring you to me. We need to teach you control; you are a liability until then. Steal their hearts tonight, Traven. We need as much influence as we can get." She stepped away, sipping her glass.

"I wouldn't be a liability, if your friends would teach me instead of brushing me aside," he growled, but she was already gone.

A liability. Not an asset. Not talent. A liability.

He waited long enough to not arouse suspicions, then turned to the room and studied the crowd. His food might have been delicious, but he barely noticed. A few people danced with their partners on the marble floor. Most chatted in small circles, or eyed possible suitors from across the room. Aveline was gone, a ghost in a sea of dignitaries. There were games upon games being played here, and he didn't know the rules.

Then *she* appeared.

Red hair pinned to the side with a Glysterium brooch, a few strands dangling over her cheek. A sleek black dress had replaced her snug uniform, hugging her athletic body. Blue eyes stared at him like a bird of prey, and her footsteps carried her across the dance floor while time stopped.

He put his drink down and met her half way, offering his hand without realizing he had done it. "A dance?"

Her red lips curved ever so slightly, and her eyes sparkled. He could have melted. "It would be my pleasure."

He gently put a hand at the small of her back, and held the other up above his shoulder. She leaned in close enough to be pressed against him, and his breath hitched. She smelled of razormint, and was possibly the softest thing he'd ever touched. He cleared his throat. "I'm Traven."

She didn't look up at him, studying the crowd. "Selice."

Why did learning her name give him butterflies? He knew he shouldn't be doing this. This woman was a figurehead for everything going wrong in Hearthmere. She was dangerous, lethal. And she was pressed firmly against him. One quick motion, and she could have a knife between his ribs. As if she could hide anything in that dress.

His heart was pounding out of his chest. Should he run? She was scrambling his brain in the most intoxicating way. Reaching up and placing a hand on his chest, she purred, "Careful now. We don't need to do this tonight. Let us just be two beautiful people making everyone in the room envious."

He looked up and saw that she spoke in truth. Most of the room had shifted their attention to them as they swayed. The string instruments had adjusted their song to something slower and more dramatic, accentuating the perceived romance. How did she know what he was thinking?

They danced for a few measures before he leaned down and put his lips next to her ear. "I know what you are," his voice trembled.

Her chuckle sent shivers up his spine as she pressed her cheek against his. "I know what *you* are."

"You took my brother." He hissed, holding her firm.

"You killed my flutist." She batted her eyes.

She pulled away just a fraction and he immediately felt the loss, but she wasn't leaving him yet. Instead, she whirled around his arm, twisting a leg around his as she spun. He caught her on the other side and cupped her back as she arched to the floor, her hands and hair brushing the marble. He lifted her back to his face, and he could feel her breath on his lips as they locked eyes.

He couldn't breathe. Her icy blue stare swept away the room like a frosty gale. She let out a throaty laugh and wrapped her arms around his neck, pressing firmly against him. He inhaled, and felt a yearning inside that had him prepared to throw it all away.

She winked and whirled away, and he couldn't take his eyes off of her as she swayed into the crowd. It felt like she had taken a piece of him with her.

He stepped toward her without realizing it.

Her name was Selice.

Traven knew she was playing with him, but he wished she wasn't. Despite everything she was, what she represented… he *needed* more time with her.

"Ahem." Thariel impatiently bumped him with her hip.

He apologized, then raised his hand to offer her a dance. She slapped his hand away with a playful smile. "We can dance another time, young man."

He could feel the heat coming off of his bald head. What was wrong with him? He should be focused, not daydreaming about the redhead. Thariel laughed off his embarrassment and tugged him toward the mass of people near the Empress. "It's nearly time for your performance. Why don't you take one of these side rooms and prepare?" She gave him a lingering look.

Was it that time already? A yawn forced its way through.

He gave her a nod and straightened out his coat. The Baron studied him with an unreadable face, hand stroking his beard. Selice knew what he was. Had she told the Baron? *I've heard a great deal about you.* She must have.

He forced himself to walk slowly, to appear casual.

They needed to believe he was a professional, that he wasn't intimidated by their golden statues and painted frescos. Traven took the opportunity to get a better look at the Empress.

It was impossible to place her age. Her almond-shaped eyes spoke of decades, while her porcelain skin was as smooth as fresh ice. Jet black ringlets of hair fell perfectly in place over her temples, bedecked with Glysterium gems. Her dress was more ornate than his clothing, with at least three shades of deep purple and diaphanous white silk sleeves cascading to the floor. Her attendants had to carefully step to miss them. If her agelessness wasn't enough to intimidate him, the very air felt thick in her presence.

Behind her, in the shadows, leaned a tall man with straight straw-colored hair down to a strong square jaw. In his folded arms, a curious-looking baton flicked with the music. The tip lazily flared a brilliant red with each beat, and Traven couldn't take his eyes from it.

He bumped into someone with his head turned, and scrambled to catch them as they fell. Finn caught his arm at the same time with a bewildered expression on his face. "Careful, friend! A lesser man would have been trampled, thrice over."

Traven made an apologetic face, but it was quickly dismissed. "No worries, big guy. Just try to watch out for us simple folk." The baritone patted his bicep.

Nerise was standing next to him, wearing an impressive assortment of analogous colors in reds and purples. Her neckline was dangerously low, and accentuated by a gemstone tucked perfectly between her breasts. "You look amazing, who is your stylist?" She winked at him.

Traven was thankful for their presence. He squeezed both of their shoulders at the same time. "Thank you for being here."

Finn leaned in close and pulled on his sleeve. "That redhead might be the death of you."

Traven didn't even argue. "I know."

Traven winked and left the two of them to dance. He trusted Finn to be in his position when the time came. Now it was his turn.

A guard whose eyes darted between the Empress and the rest of the Gala jumped when Traven stepped toward the doorway in the corner of the ballroom and smiled. "Find any trouble?"

"Just you." The guard joked while placing a halberd in his path. "The rest of the estate is restricted, my lord."

Traven patted his shoulder. "I'm going to be singing for the Gala very shortly. I need somewhere private to warm up." He pointed to his gold cord.

The guard looked around nervously, his face twisting while his mind worked. Traven wondered if he needed to call Finn over for a little nudge, but the baritone couldn't take his eyes off Nerise. "Please," Traven asked. "I can't warm up here. I can't even hear myself think."

He nodded and opened the door with a concerned scowl. "Follow me. And no funny business."

They ventured down the hallway, past suits of armor and artistic carvings. Traven pointed to the exterior rooms. "Could I get somewhere with an outside window? My voice could use some clean air, without all this smoke."

With a roll of his eyes, the guard crossed the hallway and opened the door. "This is the reading room. Please remember to close the window when you are finished."

The door closed behind him in a room lined with books from floor to ceiling. The air was mercifully clear of smoke, and he took a moment to take a deep breath with his eyes closed. There was so much going on, so many moving pieces. Thariel was doing her maneuvering, Aveline had her mysterious plans. The Baron clearly had his eye on him, and he was about to sing in front of the Empress. By himself.

And then there was Selice.

He couldn't shake the dance from his mind. He had danced with girls before, but no one had ever tied his wits into a ball like this. The smell of razormint still lingered on his vest, and he could still feel her pressed against him. He wished she was still there, inches from his face.

What was wrong with him? He needed to focus.

A few more deep breaths, and he pressed his ear to the door. If the guard was still there, he was as silent as the wind. Traven crossed the room and released the latch to the window. Fresh air rushed into the room. Kael's head popped up from the ledge. "Took you long enough. Do you need another moment to meditate, or can we come in?"

Traven shushed them and waved them into the room. "Stay here until I leave the hallway. There are guards at every entrance in the ballroom. I can't say if there are more."

Elena slid through the doorway in a brown leather tunic and snug breeches. He had never seen her in plainclothes before. True to fashion, she arched an eyebrow as he stared. "It's likely. I'll keep the two of us quiet."

"Finn and Aveline are in the ballroom," Traven added.

"You go distract the aristocrats, we'll take care of the rest." Kael motioned to Elena.

She sang them into nothingness, and Traven ran through some vocal warm-ups. As he did so, he closed the window and stretched his neck. He was stiff, and the coat on his shoulders was giving him some tension. The pieces were in motion, now it was time for him to sing.

He opened the door, turned down the hallway, and bumped into the flickering chestplate of the Baron.

Whatever facade of warmth the Baron wore in the ballroom was completely gone, replaced by mechanical observation. "What have we here?" He rumbled.

Traven stammered and stepped backward as the Baron's body clicked and whirred. He wasn't sure what to say, and instead, his mouth opened and closed a few times.

"Who were you talking to in there?" He peered into the room.

"Vocal exercise, I was warming up at different registers. It's something we do back home," Traven lied.

"Grendal Yodel, if I remember. Mother died from exposure." The Baron cocked his head.

Traven felt the heat rise in his belly. Even if it were true, he couldn't stand the reminder. The way he spoke of death felt cold, callous. He seemed more machine than man, as if he had tried to craft humanity out of himself.

The Baron took a deep breath through his nostrils and offered a compassionate smile. "I lost someone to frost once. Two someones…actually. My condolences."

Traven swallowed hard, impatient to be away from this man. "Thank you. If you'll excuse me, I have a performance."

The Baron gave a single nod. "That's precisely why I'm here. We are ready for you."

He hoped Kael and Elena were already on their way. He couldn't hold the door open any longer. The Baron walked with him, matching his stride. "Take care not to let Selice keep you up all night, you have a *big* day tomorrow."

Traven nearly choked. "It's not like that. We've only just met."

His laugh was clinical and short, just a few chuckles. Opening the door to the ballroom, he paused for enough time to say, "Enjoy your solo."

The words dripped with malice.

The stringed instruments decrescendoed into silence, and Thariel raised her hands while standing in the center of the ballroom. The rest of the visitors had been ushered to the sides. She beamed at the Empress. "Your majesty, House Vexlane is proud to present their brightest rising star, Traven Caelhardt."

Applause swept him to the dance floor, with the help of an impossibly strong shove from the Baron. Another spike of anger. A rumble of thunder. *Someday soon*, Traven vowed.

The room hushed expectantly. Traven's shoes squeaked on the glossy floor as he pivoted and bowed in one smooth motion. He couldn't be sure, but it looked as if the Empress had raised an eyebrow. His leg shook, and he gripped his knee to keep it steady. There was no time to be nervous, not with his brother in the building. Under his breath, he whispered, "May my voice reflect my spirit."

And then he began, the room in rapt attention.
I walk the fields where the frost takes men,
and I breathe from the ice with a vow.
Let my voice be the power they fear again,
I carry the storm in me now.
The blade in my hand may fail and fall,
the shield at my arm may break,
but the note in my chest will answer the call
and the earth itself will wake.
Let winter bite deep through skin and bone,
let the night come black and wide;
I am the flame that stands alone,
I am the voice that will not hide.

The Baron nodded in satisfaction, impressed at his choice of song…or his performance. There was no way to be sure. Selice had reappeared next to him, looking distractingly gorgeous. Traven made sure not to look her way again. He couldn't have a flare up. Finn was off in the corner, his mouth clamped shut while Nerise kept an elbow in his ribs. Thariel positively beamed.

He had known this song for cycles, but never really knew the truth behind the lyrics. Tonight he chose it in defiance. Once or twice his power threatened to manifest, and he choked it down while the chandeliers winked. He couldn't have an incident, not tonight. His voice rang through the room like it had never before.

If my brothers fall, I rise for them;
if my breath runs short, I roar.
For the song we bear is our battle hymn,
it is blood, it is bond, it is war.
So mark me well, you who stand opposed:
I do not bow, bend, or flee.
For the power I hold is the oath I chose
and the frost only bows to me.
Let winter bite deep through skin and bone,
let the night come black and wide;
I am the flame that stands alone,
I am the voice that will not hide.

At the end of the song, he could hear the burble of the wine waterfall on the other side of the room. Not even the servants shuffled about to tend to their masters. He was in his element, this was what he was made to do. With a satisfied smirk, he ended with a resonant hum to portray the eerie silence of a forgotten battlefield…and the rest of the room finally breathed.

He had sung in front of the Empress, in front of the most important people in Hearthmere.

I've done it, Mother.

Malachi began to lead the applause, and then went white as the room plunged into eerie silence. The Empress stood and raised two fingers into the sky. The man with the strong chin pushed off of the column and cleared his throat. "Traven Caelhardt, the Empress hears you."

Someone gasped off to the side. What did that mean?

The room exploded into deafening chaos. Traven turned his head to Thariel, whose face had gone white. The Baron's shoulders tensed, and his eye flared brighter than the chandeliers above him. His head whipped to the Empress, and for just one moment Traven thought he might attack her. The mechanical hand splayed out like claws, then grabbed a nearby chair and slammed it into the wall. Before the pieces could clatter to the floor, he was already thundering out of the ballroom. The man in red stepped in front of the Empress, baton flaring in the air. Was he a bodyguard?

An attendant handed something to a stunned Malachi, who walked out to Traven as the room filled with thunderous applause.

The Director knelt before him, his mouth pressed to a thin line. "I told you to lay low. I can't protect you now."

Malachi reached up and unsnapped the cord from his shoulders. Traven moved to stop him, but froze. The golden braid fell to the floor, and the director snapped a purple one in its place.

Chapter LVII

The monstrosity was finally gone.

Kael ran the calculations through his mind. The performance would last three minutes, with an additional five added for the inevitable fawning and praise. Afterwards, Traven would fumble about while Finn orchestrated their departure. Padding for an additional five minutes of interruptions, Kael estimated the two of them had roughly twenty minutes before someone came looking for the dashing new bass. Elena would last half that, based on her longevity in the Citadel heist.

This was an exercise in foolishness. Traven was rushing headlong toward an inevitable confrontation that logically ended with them dead or imprisoned. Nevertheless, they had made a pledge. Traven's voice was that important.

In his mind's eye, he could envision the entire floorplan. This morning, he had rifled through the architectural drawings—acquired by one of their agents—and committed it to memory. It only took a glance. That was just how his mind worked.

Most days it was a curse.

Elena squeezed his hand as the door closed, and he pulled her down the hallway. Two lefts and one right, down the main hall, and into the kitchen. The pantry would be locked, and behind it would be a passage into the sub-levels, where the architecture had been mysteriously absent. Now they just had to make the journey.

Calculations ran through his mind at each door. If there was someone inside, they would have to create a diversion. Elena could make an illusion to distract them, but each additional use of her magick would sap her reserves. Four rooms—with four distractions—would cut into her time by three minutes exactly.

They could offset her fatigue by short rests, thirty seconds at most, before continuing. Reintegrating invisibility cost more than maintaining it, the loss rate made stopping inefficient.

Nineteen minutes.

The main hallway held one patrolling guard, halberd resting against his shoulder. His back was to them, and he seemed to miss the door opening wide enough for them to slip through. Elena was keeping them quiet, with only two people she could muffle their sound with ease.

They tiptoed past the guard and waited until he stepped toward the end of the hall. Thirty seconds passed. No shimmers of Glysterium, no disturbance in the air. She was getting better.

Eighteen minutes.

Another hallway, a mirror image of the first. No guards. Their steps brought them to the third doorway on the left, and he paused to listen on the other side. There should be servants here preparing for the next wave of refreshments.

He pressed them against the wall, waiting for the inevitable opening. With approximately five hundred guests, at an estimated rate of fifty servants, the door should be opening…now.

Seventeen minutes.

The servant crossed the doorway back-first, her hands full of an overloaded silver tray. Kael reached over and held the door open for just a fraction longer, sliding into a room of controlled chaos.

The kitchen was impressive, almost industrial. An assembly line of chefs hunched over preparation tables, while others briskly tended to the ovens. Pots and pans hung in the center of the room, low enough to easily retrieve. Herbs and spice hung over a roaring fire, filling the room with a pleasant amalgamation of smoke and spice. How much better would fire-cooked food taste? There was no time to test it.

Sixteen.

The pantry was on the far side, open to the room for ease of traffic. This was unexpected, but a welcome change. He wouldn't have to burn a lock yet.

There were too many people in the room, eleven of them. The probability of bumping into someone was in the high eighty percent. He gave Elena a squeeze, and she returned it in understanding. Elena was always decisive, it was why he preferred her.

The fireplace roared, flames licking the ceiling and illuminating the room. A chef cried out, falling backwards against a table with tongs in his hands. The rest of the room pivoted and hurried to assist like clockwork. Their preparedness was logical; in a building full of wood, a wild fire could be catastrophic.

Anyone paying attention would have realized the flames cast no additional heat, or that the hanging spices weren't catching fire. It wasn't relevant. It worked, and they could move.

Aveline's information had been critical about the hidden passage here. Despite the years they had spent working together, he had not deciphered how exactly her connections worked. Even a world-renowned composer would not have the information she did. Again, irrelevant. She knew the location of the hidden doorway, they would use it.

Fifteen.

The pantry was just as large as the kitchen. They shouldered past rows of salted meats and bundles of greens. *Behind three caskets of wine, to the left of the broomstick.* Aveline's instructions flit to the front of his mind.

It was nearly imperceptible. A gap in the mortar; impossible to see in the dim light. He felt at the smooth stone and pushed with two fingers where the mortar split. The wall gave way with a click, and he heard the hinges clatter over the clamor in the kitchen. He felt Elena brush by him, and he slid sideways to follow her into the hidden chamber.

The door closed and latched on a set of springs, and Elena released her magick while puffing her cheeks. She had done well. Acrid, stale air grew more potent as they descended a stairwell and arrived at a thick steel door. Gone were the ludicrous embellishments of the upper rooms, this door was industrial. Utilitarian. Fortified.

It was his turn.

Fourteen.

Elena began to sing once more. Not to cast illusions over them, but to mask the song churning in his chest. They didn't have a harmonic key; his intel ended here. The variables grew exponentially past this door.

He hummed, the power coming to him easily, like taking a breath. Emotion was the initial catalyst. His father teaching him mathematics in their alcove, the day before he disappeared. It worked well for Glysterian initiates, or someone like Mariss, who wore her emotions on her sleeve. He was not that. For this he needed just a kernel of the memory. The rest, he kept catalogued under *unnecessary attachment.* A tightening of the abdominal muscles, slight restriction of his throat. All second nature.

Flames poured from his mouth, oranges and reds licking at the key hole as he precisely held an F4#.

Thirteen.

His lips puckered, focusing the fire until it burned blue and began to whistle as it seared the door. Blackened steel shifted to a dark brown, then red, then yellow. Smoke curled from the key hole.

Twelve.

Metal groaned, louder than he would have preferred, but it was too late to stop. Elena shifted on her feet behind him, her song masking his pitch. She was always impatient. Molten metal crept from the key hole, and he pulled the warm handle until the lock gave way.

Elena's magick swirled around them as the pungent aroma of burnt Glysterium wafted past. He hated the smell. "Who's there?" a voice called from the other side.

Kael did it without thinking, sliding through the doorway and thrusting his magic at the man with one motion. Fire sped into the man's open mouth, cauterizing his vocal cords and fusing his throat shut. The man's eye bulged in surprise, pain, and realization. Casualties were not preferred, but expected.

As the man slumped to the floor while clawing at his throat, Kael took stock of the room they had entered. A long hallway with ten doors—five on each side—opened up to a central chamber with an operating table illuminated in the center. Pipes jutted from the floors and funneled Glysterium energy into pressure chambers and contracting bellows.

Eleven.

The doors had slits built into the middle, and Kael peeked through to find the first room empty. It was a cell, the white padded walls stained with blood and low green lighting. Surprisingly, the door was unlocked. Likely to expedite transport of subjects. He opened the door and knelt beside the scrabbling guard. A slip of the blade between his ribs, right into his heart, and the man's struggle ended. A lackey of the Empire, complicit in the oppression of his people.

Elena helped him drag the man into the cell, letting her

magick fade. They were alone in here.

"Who the frost opened this door?" A deep voice bellowed into the laboratory, shaking with rage.

Ten minutes early. Something had happened upstairs.

They muscled the corpse into the corner—out of the viewport—and pressed themselves against the white padding. Elena couldn't hide them right now, information was unclear on how sensitive Auren Thale's augmentations were at detecting Glysterians. Kael just knew he could.

Metallic footsteps stopped at the door, mere feet away. "Where is the guard. Fire him, and have him flogged for his incompetence."

Kael snuck a look into the viewport. The fiery red hair of the Huntress blocked his view. A spike of nerves bundled in his stomach. She was more capable of discovering him than the Baron, especially in his current state. Elena raised her eyebrows at him, and he shook his head. There was nothing they could do right now but wait.

Logically every corner of the laboratory would be searched

"Sir, the cord changes things." The Huntress's voice was wary, hesitant.

"We've moved well past stating the obvious by now, Selice." The Baron snapped.

The scraping of heels on the stone was followed by an impatient sigh. "What is the move?"

Heavy silence followed the question and tempted Kael to peer through the viewport. Surely they weren't talking about Traven's acceptance into the Grand Chorus. This was different, new information.

"Take him," the Baron commanded.

"Sir—" she began to protest.

"Take him, Selice! His bloodline has been verified."

"Sir." Her voice was shaken. "Malachi has requested a

temporary stay, just for the performance tomorrow. We owe him."

How was Malachi tied into this? Aveline would need this information.

"To hail with the director. I cannot allow the Empress to take him, we need his voice."

The cord. The Empress had claimed Traven as one of her pets. That's why the timetable had been disrupted. Scenarios rattled through his mind at the possibilities. They could have an inside agent to the seat of the Empire, he just needed to think through how to best position Traven mentally. The bass was volatile, irrational, demanding.

"Sir." Selice had reset her tone, a mask drawn over her emotions. "If we take one of her chosen the night before the cities greatest performance, a performance meant to honor the Empress…it will be suicide. She'll take the city."

The walls rang with the thunder of metal on metal. Elena instinctively covered her ears, and Kael ducked without realizing it. "Something must be done!" the Baron roared. "Do your job, figure out what happened down here. I'll return shortly."

"Where are you—" Selice called out, silencing herself as the pinging of his footsteps disappeared.

Elena shifted to peek through the slit in the door, then thrust her magick over them like an icy blanket. The door groaned open, and red hair cascaded down Selice's face. Kael froze, holding his breath while the Huntress studied the room with half-interest. "What a waste of time." She growled. "He'll tear everything down for a single singer? I'll hold this damned city together myself."

Her eyes passed over them, and he considered for a moment the knife on his belt. Her neck was close, and he had a grudge to settle. The opportunity passed, and she slammed the door behind her. Another voice—sharp and gravelly—mused from outside. "How do you intend to do that, Commander?"

Kael was grateful that he had hesitated.

"Send Lysara. She is not to do anything but shadow the Glysterian unless he's in danger of capture."

"Growing fond of him? I saw the dance."

"I'm just trying to keep the city warm." Selice's voice was tight. Controlled. "To hail with this. Have a priest investigate the chamber tomorrow."

Her heels diminished out of his hearing. He waited two minutes, ear to the door, before opening it. Time was running short, and he no longer had enough information to analyze the operation. Elena reappeared, gasping, her knees on the floor. "I need to rest."

"You did well. Let's find Chadden and get out of here. I will likely need you for extraction, so rest," Kael said while inspecting the next cell.

"What happened up there?" Elena took the other side of the hallway.

"Traven is a purple cord now. We can talk about it later. Let's be quick."

"Kael?" a deep voice called from the next cell.

He knew who it was before peeking through the viewport.

Dietre sat on a stone platform, clothes torn and eyes sunken. The man looked to have aged a decade since his capture. Should he respond? Should he confirm? Elena would want to free him.

No. Freeing the bass would only complicate things, raise too many questions. Dietre had seen and heard too much. He didn't need more variables.

Elena turned to him, her mouth opening to speak, but he waved his hand. "No."

He watched her back straighten, her jaw clenched. Unexpectedly, water welled up in her eyes. "No. We can't," he reasserted.

A tear fell down her porcelain cheek and her lips quivered. What was wrong with her? She wasn't usually like this. Orders were orders, the mission took priority. She reminded him of that more often than he did. What was different? Traven.

The man's black and white morality had embedded itself into their group in a surprising way. Elena was clearly having trouble with the consequences of their actions. Perhaps bringing her was a mistake.

No. She was integral to the mission…and important to him in a way he hadn't acknowledged. The tear down her cheek cast an overtone over his calculations, and doubt flickered for just a moment. No time for emotion. They had to keep moving.

Shaking his head, he moved to the next door. Elena shuddered and closed her eyes, lips compressed. He would help her come to terms with this later, help her see the logic. Right now that didn't matter, because as he opened the last slit, his face paled. "Get Finn. Tell him he will need to control Traven. We've found his brother."

Chapter LVIII

The telltale pinging of the Baron's footsteps jolted Rolan awake. He sat up and cleared the fog in his mind. Every damn time he started to get some good sleep, someone was barging in or making a ruckus. He was exhausted.

Something was different this time. The pinging was rapid and uneven. He could hear the Baron's agitated tone long before his words came into focus. "How dare she?!"

Rolan stood on quivering legs. If he was going to die today, it would be on his feet. The Baron stopped short of his cell, presumably at Bricky's door. "She thinks she can just fly in and steal one of our most valuable resources? How does she expect us to survive?" His voice echoed through the halls.

The hallway shook with a loud bang. He had to cover his ears as the sound of screeching metal and stone assaulted him. With curiosity, he dragged himself to the door and peered through the small slot. The Baron wrestled with the steel, tearing it apart with his mechanical arm. Bricky yelled incoherently from the other side.

The door gave way with a deafening bang and slammed to the floor with a cloud of dust.

Rolan clawed at his door when the Baron stalked into Bricky's cell. "Talent is limited as it is, she knows this. She means to ruin me, to ruin Hearthmere! Traven is mine!" the Baron roared.

Bricky's shouts were replaced by the sounds of wet gagging, and he could see the Baron holding his comrade by the neck, feet dangling a foot from the ground. Rolan banged against the wall with fury. "Stop it! Let him go!"

The glowing emerald eye whirred to his cell, and Rolan clamped his mouth shut. He couldn't save Bricky, he couldn't even save himself.

The mechanical man jerked his head in his direction, sneering as Selice rounded the corner. Her eyes were wide as saucers. "Get rid of him. He's useless."

Rolan backpedaled, his feet clumsily tripping him to the hard floor. Even though he had heard it a dozen times before, the Harmonic Key sounded more menacing than ever. This was the end. No one would be able to warn Traven. Selice strode into the room with a grim face, curiously leaving the door open. Despite the dust and grime, her white uniform was still impossibly clean. His eyes went wild, and he shook his head while fixating on the pistol in her hand. Could he escape? Did he have the strength to bowl her over and run?

She didn't look at him, but watched the Baron exit the dungeon with her pistol pointed at Rolan's head. Bricky's whimpers faded with the metal footsteps, and finally Selice turned to him. She lowered the pistol. "Get up."

He was confused. "What?" he croaked.

"If you can't stand, then I may as well shoot you right here. Get up," she commanded.

He tried, but could tell he wasn't moving fast enough. He expected her to strike him, but she didn't. There was a hardness to her eyes, and a bit of terror. He understood the feeling. Once she was satisfied he could stay standing, she stepped into the hallway and pointed down the hole blasted in the prison a few days prior. "Run."

A sneeze made his ribcage rattle, why did he smell Pizzo spice? She shoved him, and it gave him enough momentum to disappear into the darkness.

⌒
·

Traven squeezed Thariel's shoulder as she stood as if frozen. The Baron and Empress had departed as soon as she made her announcement, and the court nearly exploded in excited whispers. He needed answers.

"Thariel, are you ok?" he repeated.

She nodded and took a steadying breath, painting a smile over her furrowed brow. A crowd of people had surrounded her, eager to be involved in whatever gossip tonight would produce. The veneer faltered as she scowled at their crowing, then put an arm around him. "We're done, I'm going home."

He nodded, picking up her shawl and grimacing to the guests' performative concern. She should be pleased at this outcome. He had done exactly as she had wished, she had the Empress' ear. Finn stood near the doorway with Nerise, a grim look on his face. He whispered as they passed, "Not good."

Finn too?

"What does it mean?" He whispered back.

Thariel spoke up instead, dread in her voice, "It means you have been chosen. It means you belong to her now."

"Never mind that," Finn tugged at his shoulder. "We found him."

Traven spun around, releasing Thariel's arm. "Show me."

⌒
·

Rolan leaned heavily against the rounded passage with his good arm, his breathing was labored and hot. Selice was ahead

429

of him, constantly turning around to see if he was keeping up. He wasn't sure where they were going, but he knew it was away from The Furnace. He was surprised enough that she let him go, but now she was helping him?

It didn't make sense. He had been hit in the head too many times.

Should he go back? The Baron had Bricky. He slowed down to rest against the curved wall. "Keep moving." Selice grabbed him by the collar.

"Just leave me. I can't move any more. I've got nothing left." He closed his eyes.

She bent close to him, sweet spice lingering with his overbearing sweat. "I'm not leaving you down here. Move those tree trunks you call legs, you big lug."

He groaned. It was too hot; he couldn't remember his last meal, and his legs shook with every agonizing step. "I can't carry you." She growled. "You need to move before someone finds us."

"Oh it's too late for that." Dain's voice echoed from the darkness.

"Bad man." Selice whispered before she shimmered, her severe features shrinking and softening until Half-Step stood in her place. Creme-colored smoke drifted out of her open mouth, and they both disappeared.

It wasn't Selice, after all.

Traven jogged down the stairs as the rest of the Thule estate emptied. The guard had taken one glance at the purple cord on his shoulder and lowered his eyes to the ground. He went wherever he pleased now.

The decor of the building shifted from lacquered wood to brass fittings and steel panels. Acrid air stung his nostrils while they descended through the hidden doorway, and his eyes began to water. Finn covered his nose with his sleeve and ventured deeper. Thankfully, the sub-level was empty.

The Baron preferred isolation.

Elena came from around the corner, dread pulling the sides of her mouth down before she even saw them. She took a look at Traven and frowned. "It's not good."

"Is he alive?" His voice echoed off of the steel.

"Come," she ordered, her gaze flicking to his shoulder.

They followed her through the dark hallway, past steel doors with little slits at the waist level. At the end of the corridor, past eight cells, was an open door. Traven felt his heart pounding in his skull as he stepped through. Something was very wrong, he could feel it in the acrid air.

Kael held an impossibly thin black man in his arms, kneeling on the floor. The tenor's face was taut, expression grim. Traven pushed past him. "Chadden?"

He barely recognized his brother.

He was unshaven, his greying beard scraggly and unkempt. The dreadlocks on his head were frayed and torn in places, and his skin was taut around protruding bones. Green light pulsed through his veins, illuminating his grey skin. It looked like they had been pumping Glysterium into his body. His arms and legs had been removed, replaced with brass caps and tubing. Why would they do this? Was this what happened to everyone the Empire took? This wasn't his brother, it couldn't be. Chadden was so strong, so confident. This man was about to die any minute. Traven took his brother in his arms, breath ragged, and pulled him close.

He wasn't conscious, and was barely breathing.

But he was alive.

He expected a torrent of emotions, fearing he would collapse the building down on them with anguish…but instead he felt… nothing.

Finn was already singing, sweat beading on his forehead.

He glared at the baritone. He was being soothed, his emotions suppressed. That should have made him angry, too. This wasn't the first time Finn had used his power without permission. He wanted to feel this. Kael stepped between them, his eyes lingering on his purple cord. "We need to get him to Mariss."

Kael was right. Mariss might be Chadden's only hope.

Finn wavered, leaning against Elena's supportive arms. "We need to go, I won't last long."

⌒

Rolan's ears felt like they were bleeding.

Dain was still behind them as he scrabbled to escape. The GlysterHorn in his hands screamed down the tunnel in arcs of viridian energy, bouncing in random directions before fizzling into the mud. Little hands dragged him through the water, closer to the end of the tunnel.

She had found him. She had saved him. His little ghost.

Half-Step had done things he didn't know were possible. A cloud of darkness enveloped everything as soon as they had gone invisible, with banging cymbals crashing all around them. She was trying to distract Dain with frantic desperation.

Still the large man came, slowly, deliberately. He knew Rolan was broken, and he wanted to toy with his prey.

Half-Step snuck him into a corner and sent a vision of herself sprinting down another pathway. It worked for a few minutes, until her visage disappeared and Dain returned down the main line. Over and over again he returned, and each time her magick was a little weaker.

This wasn't right. He should be protecting this little girl, not the other way around.

She sent the Hunter off on another tangent, but this time he didn't follow it. Instead, Dain rushed ahead, clipping Rolan in the

432

leg and sending him sprawling to the slippery floor. His bad arm screamed in agony as it took his full weight. Half-Step fell in the other direction, and her magick fizzled away.

"There you are, you little slush." Dain raised the horn to his lips and aimed at her little chest.

She screamed.

A shockwave erupted from her, shattering the horn and sending shards into Dain's face. He fell to the ground with a roar, and Rolan dragged himself back up to standing. They raced on as their pursuer writhed behind them, cursing their names.

Blessed heat gave way to oppressive cold, and she pulled Rolan through to muck to find a better place to hide.

⌒

"I don't know if I can heal this." Mariss leaned over Chadden.

They were in the GroundSong Commons, hiding in a nondescript building Kael used as a safehouse. It was spartan by Gold Cord standards, but he didn't care about that now. Traven had placed his brother on the dining room table before collapsing, Finn buckled next to him, resting his head on Traven's shoulder. His anger had receded into despair. Finn was too tired to keep him sedated.

"Please try. He's barely breathing." Traven pleaded.

He needed Mariss to save Chadden; he couldn't lose his brother a second time. Rage simmered in his belly at the entire world, but fear overpowered him. Fear and agony.

Kael lit a candle with a quick chirp of his voice and carried it around the room. There were no GlysterLamps here, by design. Elena kept to the door as usual, listening for any surprise visitors. She looked as if a strong wind could blow her over, and she kept narrowing her eyes at Kael.

Finn had already begun snoring; he had exhausted himself.

Chadden hadn't stirred since they had carried him out of

the Baron's estate. Elena was able to shroud all of them long enough to escape through the back of the property, and they stuck to the shadows while making their way to the safehouse. He kept looking down at his brother's aged face the entire time, accelerated by whatever cruel things they had done to him. There were sharp words between the soprano and tenor, but whatever transgressed was quickly squashed. He didn't care, he needed to get Chadden safe.

He heard a soft knock on the door.

Everyone froze.

Elena opened the door and was heard mumbling. After a few moments, the woman in the sparkling blue dress and elbow-high gloves walked into the room.

"Aveline." Kael sounded relieved.

She looked down at Traven and Finn with sadness. "We need a new plan."

They couldn't relent for even a minute. Traven sneered.

Chapter LIX

Mariss sang until her voice was hoarse and she could barely stand. Aveline stopped her with a warning about burnout, and sent her to bed. Finn slept in the corner, and Elena had fallen asleep against the front door.

Chadden had improved, but only enough that his breathing was steady. He didn't move, despite Traven shaking him over and over again. Kael and Aveline left him alone to be with his brother, murmuring in the other room. He fell asleep studying Chadden's frail face, barely able to recognize his big brother.

Kael cleared his throat when the sun rose, leaning against the wall. "We need to talk."

Traven sat up from the stone floor and stifled a yawn. "I'm done with this city."

"Fair. But I'm afraid that wouldn't be possible anymore, not with that." The tenor pointed to the purple cord around his shoulder.

"I don't even know what this is. I thought I was being honored, and everyone is treating me like a leper."

"It still is an honor…it's just…more than that. You belong to the Empress now. She's made her claim."

Traven didn't give a slush about that. He placed a hand on Chadden's chest, to see if it still rose. "What does that mean?"

Aveline stepped in through the doorway. "It means you'll be perfect for our plans. You will have access to places even I cannot go, no questions asked. Purple Cords do whatever they wish, so long as they serve her."

More plans, more scheming.

"What if I don't want that? What if I want to take my brother home and never sing again?"

"They will hunt you to the ends of Thalvaris. There is no Yodel where you can hide. Chadden will be brought back for more experimentation, your father will beg for death as they question him. For answers he doesn't have."

"To what end? What does she want from me?" Traven slammed his fist on the table.

Aveline took his hands in her own, her round spectacles reflecting the candlelight. The sudden tenderness caught him off guard. "I haven't the slightest inclination. She gobbles up her pets without rhyme or reason. Maybe you'll simply sing in her chorus, or maybe you'll serve her in her quarters. I am not privy to her whims."

Life as he knew it, as he imagined it, was over.

"But as I said before, we can use this to our advantage."

"How?"

"Purple Cords outrank everyone except the Empress herself. You will have power, power we can use to end the mindless abuses of this system."

"I just wanted to sing!" Traven shouted. The table rattled with his temper.

She squeezed his hands tighter. "And sing you shall, in a way that shakes the very foundations of this Empire and puts the power back in the hands of the regular people. If you leave now, if you stop singing…we will be stuck in this abusive cycle."

He was trapped. He should have stayed home, with Asmeri. His father was right all along.

"Why do you need me?" Traven's eyes softened with doubt.

She wouldn't let his hands go. "Because you are the last piece of a puzzle I'm trying to solve…to change the world."

The first thing Traven did in his apartment was rip the Empress's painting from the wall. He couldn't bear seeing those almond eyes following him during his concert preparations. Aveline had convinced him to stay, so he might have a chance to stop what happened to his brother from happening to anyone else.

Traven didn't know what that meant, but it struck a chord in him. He had been used by this system, it was time he used it to his advantage.

He felt foolish, preparing for the concert when all of this was happening. But this was part of the plan. He would play the part, smile sweetly, and tear it all down from the inside. The rage he had felt simmered below the surface. He kept it there, let it linger.

He headed to the cleaners and joined the line of Gold Cords waiting their turn. The Greeting Hymn he sang to them was returned by a full 16-part harmonic response, and then a chorus of laughter. Spirits were high, it was their time to show the city the fruits of a year of rehearsals. A few chorus members congratulated him on a job well done last night, and some asked what it felt like to be hand-picked by the Empress, fawning over his cord. He shrugged, saying he had nothing to compare it to. That answer seemed to disappoint them, but he struggled to care.

The women running the shop operated like lightning, understanding The Grand Chorus had important preparations to complete.

He emerged with his gold and green robes, with the colors swapped from the rest of the chorus, to designate him as a soloist.

Robe in hand, he walked through Concordia Plaza and noticed attendants adding more decoration to an already elaborate Opera House. Ropes were being tied off in a serpentine pattern, in preparation for the throng of people purchasing tickets. Workers froze completely when they saw his shoulder. He didn't understand, yesterday they had joked with each other. He was the same person.

But was he?

Inside the Opera House, in the green room behind the stage, he found the Quintet hanging up their robes while whispering to each other. They all had bags under their eyes, and Mariss kept covering her mouth as she yawned. Elena clenched her fist while continuing her debate with Kael. Finn gave him a sad smile, but didn't stand. Things between them hadn't been the same. Could he ever trust the baritone again?

Traven stood there, regarding his new family with a sad smile. "I'm going to miss you all."

Kael placed a reassuring hand on his shoulder. "It's a good thing. You did well last night."

He knew Kael's words weren't said lightly, the tenor rarely gave reassurance. Elena nodded at him with a small smile of her own, and Finn clapped him on the shoulder. "You really outdid yourself last night. Seeing Thariel drop to the floor was worth getting all dressed up."

"Like you don't get dressed up to go to the washroom." Elena poked, but her heart wasn't in it.

The weight of last night made their banter hollow. They were wary of him, of what he might do. So was he.

"Is Chadden ok?" Traven looked at Mariss.

"As well as he can be." Mariss chewed her lip. "Aveline is watching over him. You should visit him before we go on stage.

I can't be sure, but color seemed to be returning to his cheeks."

He looked at the floor, picking at his robes. "I don't know if I can do this."

Finn came close for a hug. Mariss joined him, followed by Elena, and eventually Kael. Traven's breath shuddered. "Thank you all, for everything you've done."

"We aren't done yet, my friend. Sing tonight for *yourself.* Sing for Chadden." Kael squeezed a little tighter.

Chapter LX

"You had a nightmare." Half-Step picked at her toes, sitting on his chest.

Rolan groaned. Garrick's sadistic glee tortured him even in his sleep. Would he ever forget those nights? Would he ever be the same?

Probably not.

Something inside of him was broken.

Half-Step hopped off of his chest and went back to stirring a small pot of soup. She must have used an entire bag of Pizzo spice, the scent clung to the walls. "Did Bad Man do that to your arm?"

Rolan sat up, his ribs on fire. "He did."

"He should die for that." She kept stirring.

"He will."

Rolan watched her wrinkle her nose while working through the emotions. Children shouldn't have to deal with these sorts of things. How callously she spoke of killing. His heart broke for her again. The little rascal brought the ladle to her lips and slurped it loudly, humming at the taste. "So spicy."

"I need to get to Traven. He's in danger."

"Nope. You stay here."

"Kiddo, I can't just sit here and do nothing. He's walking right into a trap, ready to snap from a thousand angles."

She scowled at him and pushed him down with her scrawny arms. "You can't even fight me. You rest today, we can find Baldy tomorrow."

He tried to rise on one arm, but she pushed him back down again. "Do it again and no soup for you. You look like you haven't eaten in a month."

She was probably right.

⌢

Malachi pulled the piano bench and placed it in front of the chorus. He sat down gingerly—with the help of his cane—and smiled at all of them one by one. "This is it," he said, his voice thick.

"This is the culmination of all of the hard work we've done. The testament to everything I've asked of you, and what you gave back to me. We are making beautiful art, worthy enough to honor the Empress, and Hearthmere. I thank you for that, because I'm just up here waving my arms and barking orders. You showed up every day, sometimes twice a day, and gave me everything I demanded.

By my estimation, you are the best chorus in Thalvaris. Tonight, we prove that to our Empress. We're going to do a full run-through of the movement, perhaps hit a few entrances I want to nail down…then I'm going to let you free for the rest of the day, to bask in your own glory.

Let the city see you in your robes, let them revere you for what you bring to our culture. I thank each and every one of you. Now let's make some art."

He returned the stool and pretended to bow at the audience. The chorus chuckled as he spun around and raised his baton.

They took their collective breath, and began to perform as if the auditorium were full.

The chorus was focused, and Traven could feel the electricity in the air. There was a slight rush to their tempo, but Malachi easily brought them back, and nodded when they obeyed. More than a few times, Traven reflected on how thankful he was to be a part of something so beautiful. Despite all of the machinations, the stress, the disappearances. Here he could let that all wash away, and try to just sing. This was the one place he felt safe.

His solo came, and he stepped down while envisioning a full auditorium. Five thousand imaginary people directed their adoration at him. He smiled broadly, raising his arms before beginning a tremendous rendition of his music. His voice rang true as the night before, and when he finished, Shissel was the only one sending him looks of disgust. When Traven scowled, the tenor averted his gaze.

He was a Purple Cord now.

As he returned to his position, he felt a pang of sadness. If he was to become whatever the Empress demanded of him, this was the only performance he'd have with these people. It was a bittersweet sensation. He looked around at the people he had grown to appreciate, respect. A few smiled back as if to share his sentiment.

They roared into the final act with building key changes and ever-climbing dynamics. His voice was tired, hot from overuse and exhaustion. Malachi's gestures evolved into wider and faster motions, indicating a tempo change, an increase in sound. They sang into the last few measures of a grand finale, and when they finished, Malachi stood there panting. Gratitude shown freely in his eyes, matching the broad smile spread across his face. "Yes! That. Do that tonight!"

The chorus whooped in excitement. Finn did a little dance on the risers, and Traven tilted his head back and closed his eyes. He needed to savor this moment.

"I need all of you dressed and in place backstage half an hour early. You are free to go until then, but don't overtalk. Save your voices, hydrate, and I'll see you tonight."

Finn turned to him as the risers cleared and cleared his throat. "Well done. You truly have an amazing voice, my friend."

Traven offered him a diplomatic smile. Even if he understood Finn's actions, it still felt like betrayal. "I'm going to miss you."

Finn laughed and clapped him on the back. "You said that already. But don't fret, our plans will have us back together again before you know it. Then you can show me around Calrithia… on an airship."

He let himself laugh. He wanted their friendship to last. "Deal."

Elena and Mariss met up with them and wrapped him in a hug. He squeezed them tight, and Mariss squealed a little bit. "Not so tight, you'll crack my back."

Elena smiled at him. "Drinks before the concert?"

Traven shook his head. "I'm going to Chadden."

No one argued. If tonight was his last night as a free man, he wanted to spend it with his brother—asleep or not.

Mariss poked him in the ribs, her shoulders hunched. "I'll go with you."

Chadden had been laid in the only bed of the safehouse, and Aveline was sitting bedside when they walked in. Traven gave her a solemn nod, and she ducked out of the room.

He sat down, the springs in the bed creaking under his weight. How could someone once so brave, so lively, look like death itself? His brother, his best friend, was reduced to a skeleton of a man.

Mariss rubbed his back as he sank down to touch foreheads

with his brother. Tears streamed down his face, and the bed shook with his sobs. "I'm so sorry big brother, I should have come with you. Maybe then you wouldn't be like this." His fists balled up the sheets.

The power inside of him lurched, and the floor rattled. He tried to wrestle it down. Was this his life now? Was he going to have to fear every strong emotion for the rest of his life? Would he destroy the room every time he became upset? He was so tired.

"Little brother," Chadden whispered.

Traven's throat seized, and his eyes snapped open. Chadden pushed against his forehead affectionately. More tears.

"Chadden, I'm here."

"Tre?"

Traven whispered in his brother's ear. "I'm so sorry. Look at what they've done to you."

Chadden tried to sit up, but he lacked the strength. "You need to hide. You can't let them find you."

Even now, his brother was trying to protect him. "Chadden, I can't hide now. I need to protect you."

Chadden's laughter sounded like a death rattle. "I'm a goner." His eyes, grey as Traven's, took in his chorus robes and purple cord. "You look just like momma."

Traven didn't understand. "Who did this to you? How did they find you?"

"Th…" He was starting to fade.

"Please Chadden, I need to know. Who did this?"

"A woman. Promised me everything."

Tomorrow we start building your empire.

He knew before his brother said the words. The half-promises. The coy redirection. She was at the heart of it.

"Thariel Vexlane."

The room spun as Chadden faded back into unconsciousness. His ears buzzed, and the walls of the room squeezed in on him. It was her, it had been the entire time. That's why she was upset last night, the traps she had been laying had been demolished with one simple phrase. *The Empress hears you.*

Mariss froze with her hand on his back. "What did he say?"

She had wanted nothing to do with him until his power manifested at the duel. She had recognized it, and sank her claws into him just like the FrostClaw. He wasn't special, he was leverage. The social events, the scheming, the performances… all priming him to be locked in a cell, arms and legs removed. Traven swallowed heavily, his voice trembling. "I think Thariel is involved. I think she did this."

"But why would she? She needs singers for social clout?"

He would destroy her. He would rend the foundations of her home until it was all rubble. Power surged in his stomach, and he held it with a grip of desperation.

"I intend to find out."

Chapter LXI

Cold, dispassionate perfectionism.

Eyes to the ground, Traven stepped outside and turned toward the center of the city. Mariss stumbled after him, her face pale. "Traven, wait. Please don't do anything irrational."

The lights of Cantata Row shuddered as he passed, as if the city itself was recoiling from the burbling energies clawing to escape. Civilians stepped backward with a gasp; he couldn't tell if it was because of his cord or his mood.

A patrol marched ahead of them, and a soldier put a hand up to halt traffic for ease of passage. Traven ignored him, jaw clenched. He wished they would stop him.

One glance at his cord saved them.

The column of soldiers halted as he trudged by. The Cantor mech in the back shuddered and spasmed, man-sized sword clattering to the ground as servos failed and gemstones flared.

Mariss jogged to keep up, her short legs struggling to keep pace. "Traven, please calm down. Stick to the plan. We can deal with her later."

He spun in front of the Citadel, his grey eyes cold as the Ever-Winter. "I am as calm as the situation allows me to be."

Mariss couldn't understand. She hadn't held her brother's broken body, a victim of sadistic experimentation and greed. She hadn't been mocked, bullied, and manipulated every step through Hearthmere. Everyone loved her. She was sweet, empathetic, talented. How could she understand?

Electricity sparked under the Citadel, arcing through the tunnel as he stalked through. The pulsing black heartbeat of the city skipped.

He turned past the Opera House and waded through the crowd. Once his cord was noticed, a ripple through the bowing populace cleared his way. He didn't care, the novelty was gone. Mariss grasped at the sleeve of his chorus robes and pulled him to a stop. "Where are you going?"

He didn't turn to look at her, his eyes focused on Upper Resonance Heights. "To the Vexlane Manor."

She whirled around to meet his face, her eyebrows raised in compassion. "There is no time. If you go now, you'll miss the performance."

Did that even matter now? "To hail with the performance. Why should I play their game?"

"I know you are angry, you have every right to be. But please, just think. You could destroy her right now, and throw away everything we've worked for. You are so close to changing things for the better. Imagine a scared little child right now, terrified because their voice is doing things they don't understand." She stood firmly in front of him.

He growled and thought of the little red-headed urchin.

"Think of someone else worried about their disappearing brother or sister. If you kill Thariel right now, they will find you. They will take you, and you might end up just like your brother."

Green vapor escaped from his mouth at the mention of Chadden. "I'll kill them too. I'll tear it all down."

Her eyes welled up. "You are just one man, Traven. Powerful

as you might be, you stand no chance alone. We do this together. Methodically. As a Quintet. This isn't a solo act."

Dissonance warred with the rage burning inside of him. He hated that he might not be enough, that she might be right. He needed to be right. He needed this wrath.

No. He could do this. Another step forward, but she put a hand against his chest. He felt their connection then, subtle. She was manipulating him. It should have sent him into a rage.

Traven stood there, vapor streaming from his mouth, lights crackling all around him. The people cowered in fear. It wasn't his cord, it was the way the air rippled with painful energy. He was something they didn't understand, couldn't understand. How could they love him when he looked like this?

His anger fought back. It was addictive and insidious. His chest bucked, and a tear fell down to his beard. It all hurt. He just wanted it to stop. He could do this, for Chadden. He wanted to do this.

But Mariss stood in front of him, accepting, loving. She saw the anger and understood it. His assumptions clashed against their connection. He had never asked what she had endured, what she escaped in the Whisper Ward. He could feel it now, shredding his understanding like paper. A little Mariss, scared and alone. Freezing. Her parents had shunned her, terrified of the Empire.

He didn't have to be the best singer. He could be something else, something more meaningful—for that little girl.

The rage settled. Not gone, but begrudgingly obedient in a way that it never had been before. He wasn't sure what the shift was, but he could feel it deep in his bones.

She took him by hand and led him toward the Opera House, through a crowd electric with anticipation. His footsteps felt leaden, but grew easier as his mind managed to piece together a rickety scaffolding of identity. Asmeri had been partially right. Life wasn't just about singing, it should be something more. It would be something more.

Shissel was standing with his friends in the lobby, preening while the audience filtered into the auditorium. Seeing Traven, he stepped in the way, face contorted with a sneer. Traven turned his head, and the lobby rattled. Someone in the room shrieked, and the glass of the chandelier rang crystalline tones. His eyes bore into the tenor, and Shissel hesitated. It was enough for Traven to pass.

They walked in silence through the building and into the green room. The room flickered as he wrestled with a whirlwind of emotions. Finn approached and put a hand on his chest, his anger flared in resistance, then cooled enough for his friend to grab his attention. "Traven, please hold it together."

"I'm trying." He gritted his teeth.

Mariss pulled Finn's hand away. "He needs some time."

"What happened? Is Chadden—"

Mariss yanked his arm as the GlysterLamps brightened, a threat evident on her face. They stepped away, Mariss waggling a finger in the baritone's face. It was almost enough to lighten Traven's mood.

Malachi gathered the Chorus for some last-minute warm-ups. They stepped into position in the cramped room, shoulder-to-shoulder. His voice was shaky at first, but music began to do what it always did for him. The cloud over his mind cleared, and he could focus on the music. After the Director was satisfied, he nodded to them and clapped his hands. "I'm proud of you all. Let's get into position backstage and get ready to make Hearthmere proud."

Traven walked to a secluded area, between the folds of the curtains. It was dark back here, and most of the singers were gathering in the opening behind the main curtain. Finn approached, probably to apologize, then paused when Traven knelt down and closed his eyes. "May my voice reflect my spirit," he whispered.

He sat there in silence, crouching on the balls of his feet while letting the solo repeat in his head. He had a job to do, even if he wasn't sure what that entailed yet. A yawn stretched his jaw. He had to get this perfect. He had to be perfect. Everyone was watching.

Thariel would be watching.

His anger flared, eager. One of the lamps popped, raining emerald sparks down on his head. Mariss wasn't there to keep him calm, and he wasn't sure he wanted her to.

Finn dashed over to his side, humming while grasping his shoulders. He was doing it again, using his magick without permission. How many times would this happen? How many times had it already happened? Traven met his stare with fury. "Don't you dare soothe me!" He spat.

The baritone backed away, smiling nervously. "Traven, whatever it is, please calm down. If you erupt tonight this all goes to waste. Everything you've done, everything we've done… it will be for nothing."

"She betrayed my brother, why should I care what we've built?"

Kael and Elena rushed up, and the three of them drew close to block the conversation from the rest of the chorus. Traven growled. "Thariel was the one who betrayed Chadden."

Kael grimaced. "Slush."

Elena looked panicked. "What do we do?"

Kael rubbed his temples, impatience curling his lip. "We continue, we press on as planned. This changes nothing."

"This changes everything!" Traven shouted, and another lamp popped.

They were staring at him like a caged animal, one of those beasts captured and put on display in traveling carts. He could feel the questions heavy in their eyes. Had they made a mistake?

Malachi calmly stepped up to them, his arms behind his back.

"Friends. Could Master Caelhardt and I have a moment?"

Finn stood protectively over him, looking at Kael for direction. Elena pulled them both away and began to confer with Mariss. The Quintet left him. Alone. Traven panted, waiting for the Director to speak. Malachi looked up at the lamps and then back down to him. "I'm sorry it all happened this way."

Traven lowered his eyes dangerously. "How involved are you?"

Malachi gave him the slightest of nods. "I'm the reason you are still here, and not buried under the Citadel…at least until last night. I can only do so much to protect you, and the Baron agreed to wait until after our performance. Now that you've been flagged by the Empress…even the Baron can't touch you. You belong to her."

"I belong to no one," he hissed.

The Director gave him a sad smile. "I'm sorry things are turning out this way. The only advice I can give you is to give the performance of your life. You are an amazing singer, one of the best basses I have ever heard. Perhaps the Empress will place you in her chorus, you happen to possess the exact qualities she looks for."

He meant Glysterians. He would never wear a purple cord, not after tonight.

"How can you expect me to sing now?" Traven slumped to his knees.

Malachi kneeled down. "Sing like your life depends on it. Not everyone gets this chance. You owe it to yourself."

You owe it to yourself.

He wanted to do this for himself, for his father, for his friends. He wanted their love and approval, he needed it. It was all he had ever wanted. But everything was a mess, nothing was like he envisioned.

Could it work? Could he infiltrate the highest circles of the

Empire and have the guile to deceive them? He realized he didn't really have a choice. It was either that, or exile.

Traven took a calming breath and muttered through clenched teeth, "You're right. If I'm going to go out…I might as well do it singing."

Malachi stood and offered him a hand up. "And you will be magnificent. I'm sorry I couldn't do more, but we all play with the music given to us."

The curtains began to part, and Malachi nodded for him to get into position. The Quintet each watched him with nervous eyes. He didn't dare look at them as he joined the basses.

The crowd roared as Malachi walked on stage, his limp barely noticeable. He bowed once, then motioned for the chorus to begin filing onto the risers like they had rehearsed. Sharp turns, up the risers, and then another sharp turn across the stage.

"Ladies and Gentlemen, Hearthmere is proud to present this year's Unification Concert in honor of our Empress Wiseria. We will be performing a series of movements created by the brilliant Aveline Pursain. Please enjoy." Malachi bowed one more time, then turned to his chorus as the last few singers moved into position. They shuffled back and forth, getting into their "windows" as Malachi liked to call it. Some cleared their throats, others rolled their shoulders.

Traven closed his eyes and drew in a deep breath. Emotion robbed breath support. Anger threw your voice out of tune. He needed to be calm. Focused. The Director's hands went up, and as one, the Grand Chorus began to sing.

One hundred singers, unified in their goal, despite the myriad of backgrounds and desires. The room filled with their soaring voices, and Traven let himself get lost, let himself forget everything except the music. Music was magick in its own way. Music was everything.

In comparison to everything going on around him, this was

simple. Pure. Remember the breath here, watch Malachi for the cut off. He was one piece of an instrument, wielded by the Director.

One cog in the machine.

The thought threw him off. Was this all a part of a greater pattern? Was their culture, their Empire, part of a greater system? His tone slipped just enough that Malachi's eyes flitted over. Traven wrestled his voice back, focused on the music.

The performance was speeding by, as he tried to grasp the fleeting thoughts dancing around the music in his mind's eye. The annual competitions, the drive to call singers to the capital to test their mettle. The way singers were revered, their cords a status symbol. Was it all orchestrated? Was his whole life a fabrication of an Empire looking for people just like him?

His solo was fast approaching, and he steeled himself. There was no time for these doubts. He needed to do this well, or the sacrifices of the Dischordants would mean nothing.

Malachi gave him a confident smile and nodded purposefully. Traven stepped down with lead in his belly. The chorus reduced their sound to an accompanying drone as he took his position. He took a deep breath to begin. Too long. He needed more time. As he sang, his eyes crossed the crowd. Would Asmeri have come? He knew exactly where he should be, and when his eyes hit the correct seat, his heart fluttered. Asmeri was there, smiling, eyes full of pride. His tone wavered, and he shoved down his relief with a flicker of GlysterLight.

He couldn't linger on his father for long. It was distracting him, and his power threatened to distract. On the balcony, the glowing eye of the Baron studied him like a predator. The subtle threats and intimidation of last night replayed in his mind. The truth of his brother, locked underneath him as he danced and sang, tortured him. Another surge of power, rising to his throat. He shoved that down with a brighter surge of stage lights. The audience looked up, distracted by the flare. He didn't want that, he wanted them looking at him.

Seated next to the Baron was the Empress, her attendants fanning her in an illuminated box of greens and purples. From here, he couldn't see her cold, expressionless face. What would he be to her? A singer? A concubine? A slave?

The power escaped. His voice split into three separate notes at the same time, an eerie harmony, unnaturally resonant. He had to shield his eyes as the lights at the front of the stage flashed wildly. He shoved the power down deep, growling a few of his notes to keep things under control. It flared up again, insistent to be freed. His control was thin, his anguish too forceful. The front lights fizzled—plunging the stage into darkness—and he could see who was sitting in the front row.

Thariel.

Whatever control he had gained, whatever barriers he had erected, dissolved in an instant. Power flared from deep within his soul, and burned through his body from head to toe. His chest bucked, and his throat clenched. It was taking over. The lights through the auditorium flickered and pulsed, flashing and popping. A murmur grew in the audience like roiling thunder, and the chorus behind him quieted as the stage shook. The risers rattled and groaned. White-uniformed agents appeared on the balconies and near the exits.

Magick flowed through him like a raging maelstrom. His mother dying, his father's disapproval, his brother's torture. The way the nobles mocked him, the way they played games and moved him as if he were a piece on a game board. The Baron's intimidation, the Empress's mandate.

And Thariel's *betrayal*.

The power lurched out of him with a catastrophic boom. A shockwave threw the chorus behind him to their feet and over the risers. His body twitched as resonant magick released with a thunderclap, pulsing toward the ceiling in a way that shattered the glass dome. He roared a primal scream, and his power ripped into the balcony, the ceiling. Stone and steel fractured, buckling under its own weight.

The Opera House groaned and the auditorium filled with screams. Guests ducked under the seats, shielding themselves from the raining glass, while others scrambled over each other to escape. His power ceased, smoke curling from his mouth and nose as goosebumps covered his body.

Chandeliers crashed into people below, slicing their faces or crushing their bodies. The building trembled like a caged animal, rumbling under his feet as marble pillars split into pieces and threw fist-sized chunks into the air. The supports under the main balcony exploded, and with a crack it fell to the first floor, crashing down onto the people below. Everything slowed to a crawl as he locked eyes with his father.

Asmeri had been gripping the chair in front of him, terror widening his eyes as the audience died. A boulder thudded into the chest of a man next to him, and while trying to help the lifeless man up, a rafter crashed onto his back. Traven screamed. His power exploded the wooden stage in front of him as his legs gave way, and he fell to his knees. Splinters of wood ripped through bodies, embedding in the seats and painting the rubble in red mist. Asmeri was gone, crushed under the weight of his son's failure. Blood leaked down the marble auditorium floor like water.

He had nothing left. He was everything the Empire feared he would be. Finn tackled him to the ground, screaming for him to stop, but it was too late. The Opera House was falling down around them. People were dead, too many to count. His throat burned like he had swallowed razorblades.

Arcs of green energy struck the stage around them as the Hunters leaped over the rubble. Finn dragged him by the chest, yelling at him to run. It didn't matter any more.

"Let them take me. I have nothing left."

Rolan was limping through the tunnel of the Citadel when he heard an unmistakably deep voice roar from the Opera House. The glass dome erupted in a shower of deadly glittering shards, and a crack raced from the steps all the way to the base of the water fountain. A woman froze as a shard lanced through her body and splattered the cobblestone with red. The Citadel rang like a bell, matching the sung note, and the steady stream of viridian light powering the dome twisted and sputtered.

As the first snowflakes fell on his shoulders, he heard the screams.

What had Traven done?

Soldiers knocked him to the ground, racing toward the crumbling building. Cantor Battle Suits thudded through the plaza, crushing the intricate marble tiles under their tonnage. Everyone was being pointed to the Citadel, with soldiers yelling over the sickening groans of failing steel beams. "To the tunnel, seek refuge under the Citadel!"

Rolan rose on shaky legs, gripping his cane in disbelief. He could see his breath as the green energy field overhead fizzled, and retreated along the structural supports. The Ever-Winter was clawing back as fast as it could. Everyone needed to get inside.

A flash of white darted across the rooftops, followed by another, and another. Red hair danced in the frigid air like a battle standard as she studied the alleys from the third story of a nearby building. A moment later, she soared along the roofline and across the street, skidding across the tiles before disappearing deeper into the city.

23/15/1877

Official record of Glysterian anomaly.

Subject: Traven Caelhardt - Bass II

Incident: Glysterian surge beyond any known recorded capabilities. Opera House severely damaged. Death toll estimated at 2,000 civilians and climbing.

Pruning was postponed due to influence from Director Rivers, slated to occur immediately after the Unification Concert. Director Rivers to receive punitive measures.

Empress Wiseria - unharmed.

Baron Thule's condition - unknown.

Hunter Cadre activated upon explosion. Subject fled with the assistance of four other suspected Glysterians.

Response: Potential for additional Glysterium Matrix disruption. Subject placed at the head of the Empire's most wanted. Hearthmere guard increased and Hunter Cadre powers temporarily expanded to neutralize the threat.

Additional information: The subject's power surge resulted in the destruction of three out of four backup cores powering The Choir. The Chorus Arcanum has requested the

INSTALLATION OF ADDITIONAL FAIL-SAFES. GLYSTERIUM MATRIX CURRENTLY OPERATING AT 56%. EMERGENCY TEMPERATURES REPORTED IN MULTIPLE HEARTHMERE SECTORS.

HUNTER ASSESSMENT: WHILE THE SUBJECT HOUSES POTENTIAL FOR EXTREME DESTRUCTION, I BELIEVE HE CAN BE DETAINED AND PLACED WITHIN THE CITADEL FOR STUDY AND POSSIBLE WEAPONIZATION. I STRONGLY RECOMMEND LESS THAN DEADLY FORCE UNTIL EFFORTS TO DO SO CREATE LESS THAN OPTIMAL CASUALTIES.

CAPTAIN SELICE VIRELL, HUNTER CADRE

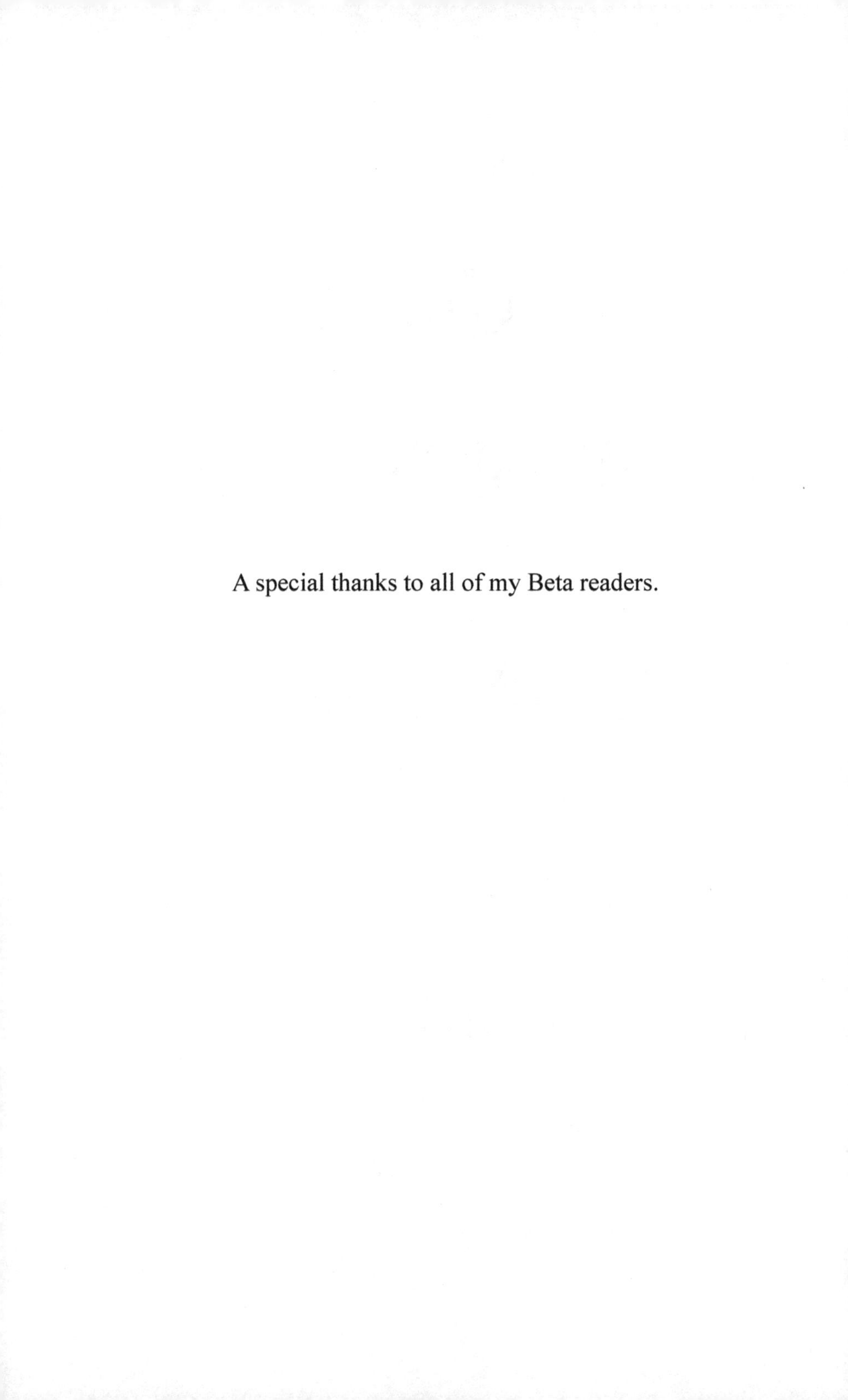

A special thanks to all of my Beta readers.

BACKERS OF THE REALM

CITIZEN

Meshia

Prolo Team

DISTRICT CHORUS

Sophia Anderson
Steve Foerster
Charles Mason

Chase McGlinchey
TJ Muir
Florentina Nitschke

REGIONAL CHORUS

Anthony Degennaro
David Heskett
Jonah Houtz
Christopher Jobin
Loraine Lewis
Craig Lynch
Erin Mannon

John Queen
Clayton Reed
Diego Riley
Cody Terrance
Erin Wolfe
Jai

GRAND CHORUS

Tim Carter
Johnathan Costello
David Ellis
Josh Glantzman
Josh Grant
Pete Holmes
Stephen Jackson
Chris Kordella

Jessica Lambright
Heather Lewis
Benjamin Port
Aaron Schroen
Steve Skrzycki
Tatyana Webb
Jennifer Williams
Jim Windak

BACKERS OF THE REALM

EMPRESS'S CHORUS

Juli Eckman
Paul Johnson
Charles Packard

Nick Ruimveld
Robert Ruimveld

PATRON OF THE VOICE

Jack Baer
Justin Fiebeger
David Green
Noah Gustafson
Paul Krause
Andy Lewis
Kaylea

Jason Lynch
Kate Malloy
Sonnet Rumora
Brandon Smith
Tyler Wells
Christopher Goetting

GLYSTERIAN

Josh Houle
Julieanna Nalett
Joe Perotti
Kellie and Stephen Rochholz

Without all of you, EMERALD ARIA could not
have happened.

Stories grow when they're shared.

If Emerald Aria resonated with you, a short review helps bring the next song to life.

BOOK 2 OF THE GLYSTERIUM SAGA

EMERALD REQUIEM

COMING 2027

Mr. Milner Gets Divorced

Jane Hadley

To the evening crowd at Bin.

Chapter 1

Thursday, January 7, 1954
Minneapolis, MN

Stephen Vincelli had a weakness for tall men. He also had a weakness for the bathhouse when he was feeling especially sorry for himself. His greatest weakness, however, was falling for married men.

He was at the Hennepin bathhouse because he was currently indulging his weakness for feeling sorry for himself. He liked to go to the bathhouse and catch the eyes of strangers on him and feel like he was real. Their hands and mouths didn't hurt either. It was, all in all, a strong counterargument to the intrusive notion that he was entirely invisible, a ghost wandering a world that had no use or care for him. Visiting Kreuger's bar also helped assuage this feeling, but it had been particularly bad the past few weeks, what with Christmas and New Year's Eve with no one to kiss. So he'd left his scruples behind and taken the streetcar all the way to Minneapolis.

The Hennepin bathhouse, with its sprawling steam rooms and communal bathing pools, fortified Stephen's humanity like nothing else could. Made his hands solid and his blood thrum with life. All his mundane qualifications, his pertinent details, his almosts and not quites, didn't matter. His underwhelming resumé, his dead-end job, even his dismal high school GPA was null. At the bathhouse, he was a warm, virile body. He could be anyone he wanted to be.

Today, he was Shorty, christened by the fellow who'd whispered in his ear. It wasn't an inaccurate nickname, and nicknames were best for this sort of situation, so Stephen accepted it with a good-natured nod and followed the guy to the locker room. When it became evident the fellow had something more than the dark room in mind, Stephen got excited in spite of himself. It was a gamble to go to a second location with someone new, but Stephen couldn't resist the siren call of unspooling potential.

The January air was biting cold, a shock after the heat and steam of the baths. Stephen followed the guy across Hennepin Avenue. There were a number of hotels surrounding the crumbling Lumber Exchange Building that housed the Hennepin Baths. The guy suggested the Milner Hotel, which Stephen tried to casually dissuade him from. He certainly wasn't in a position to pay for a hotel room, so he was at this fellow's discretion, but turning tricks at the Milner Hotel felt a little too raw. Which was completely stupid, because it had been the better part of a decade since Stephen had talked to Joe Milner. He'd just rather not see his childhood friend's surname emblazoned on the pillowcase while he was getting cornholed.

They ended up at the Hotel Vendome next door, which had the virtue of being slightly closer than the Milner, and the guy didn't seem too bothered by it anyhow. It was his money. Stephen couldn't be too picky. Things proceeded quite nicely as clothes were re-shed, which was actually frustrating because ideally, Stephen would like the baths to stop providing so much positive reinforcement. It wasn't the kind that lasted, the kind he really needed.

Stephen felt like an apparition returned to his tangible body as the trick ran his hands over his skin, his eyes sharpening and his mind clearing, like seeing in focus for the first time in weeks. He was real. He was alive. He was desired. The guy was really eager, desperate almost, but not in a pitiful way. He was generically good-looking, tall like Stephen liked, with a charming smile that suggested he did a good deal of glad-handing in his real life. He sucked Stephen's cock like it was a sacred relic.

Afterwards, Stephen laid out on the shabby bedspread next to the guy. He'd come to think of him as Stew, since he sort of sounded like Jimmy Stewart when he talked. Stephen turned towards him and caught Stew looking at him consideringly.

"Can I see you again?" Stew asked. His voice had a persistent nasal tone, and his smile was fully confident in Stephen's anticipated reply. As well he might, with a mouth that greedy. Stephen bit his lip. So much about this was surprisingly encouraging. Usually, Stephen ended up in bathroom stalls or the bathhouse dark room for a furtive hook up that was always more about release than any sort of connection. The hotel room was a splurge, one that made him think Stew might be looking for something more, like Stephen was. Being able to see Stew laid out on a bed in the waning afternoon light had been liberating. Made him feel less like a dirty secret.

"That could be arranged," Stephen shrugged with a smile. He leaned in and put his palm to Stew's cheek. He glanced at Stew's lips then moved to close the remaining space.

"Uh," Stew said, flinching back. "What're you doing?"

Stephen felt his stomach drop like a rock. He flinched

back too. "What?" Like he didn't know.

Stew gave an uncomfortable frown and sat up. "I, uh, I'm sorry if I gave you the wrong idea…"

"So you *don't* want to see me again?" Stephen clarified. It sounded pathetic in the stark brightness of the room. Stephen felt himself flicker insubstantially.

"I'm married," Stew scoffed, like that explained everything.

"Sorry if I didn't see your ring," Stephen sneered, glancing toward Stew's conspicuously bare ring finger. Perhaps all of Stephen's weaknesses were interrelated, because the tall men he met at bathhouses were almost always married.

"I don't see how my being married has anything to do with meeting up again," Stew said with an exasperated expression. "There's already enough pressure in every other part of life. You seemed to enjoy yourself well enough. Why couldn't we help each other blow off a little steam from time to time?"

Stephen got up and retrieved his underwear and worn wool trousers, dismissing several retorts. What he really wanted to ask this guy was whether he'd ever considered the possibility that homosexuals could find companionship, or domesticity, or—heaven forbid—love. Whether they could exist outside of bathhouses and basement toilets, the dingiest of forgotten shadows. Whether their desires could ever be anything more than "blowing off steam."

"How many kids you got?" Stephen asked, because he was a glutton for punishment.

"I don't see how that's any of your business."

Definitely at least one, then. Stephen shrugged his shirt back on and buttoned it up. His undershirt was in need of a wash now, so he stuffed that in his pocket. "It's nothing personal. I just don't step out with married guys."

Stew snorted. Stephen's hands faltered as he fastened his belt. He braced.

"Who said anything about stepping out?" Stew laughed then. "God, next thing I know, you'll be asking for my pin."

Stephen sucked on his lip for a moment to stop himself from saying something bitchy, but it didn't work. "You were already begging for my dick, so I don't see how it's that big a reach."

Suffice to say, Stephen wasn't too broken up about it when they left the hotel and went their separate ways. After riding the streetcar back to St. Paul, he went straight to Kreuger's. He ambled up to the shabby building on Wabasha between 5th and 6th Streets with his hands in his pockets and shouldered through the door with his chin tucked below the collar of his jacket. The warm galley bar was welcome after the biting January chill. It only had one small, oval window at the front, filled with a neon "Liquor" sign. The bar didn't have any other signage to distinguish it, nor did it need any. That one sign told you everything you needed to know. Mr. Kreuger was a silent sentinel behind the bar, and Stephen dutifully stopped there first, ordering a beer. There were no free rides at Kreuger's.

The place couldn't be more non-descript, an honest, simple, dingy blue-collar bar—a perfect sanctuary for queers. The Kreugers put up with them too, as long as they kept it discreet and always bought something. Stephen craned his neck to inspect the occupants of the back corner booth while he waited for his beer. Mae West was holding court with Frank Atlas, Walter, and Dickie. Marge was there too, he presumed, because the smoke was coming up from the near side of the booth like a chimney.

When Kreuger sloshed his beer on the bar, Stephen seized it and sidled down the long, narrow dive toward his friends. Oh god, Carol and Jack were in the adjacent booth again. Stephen quickly averted his gaze and hustled into the back booth.

"Vinny, there you are," Frank Atlas said. "Tell them—"

"—I'm not helping you try to get Dickie to lift weights with you," Stephen cut him off. "We all know you're just trying to corner him in the locker room, and the only reason you keep trying is because Walter can't kick your ass without help. Did you see the Two Blind Mice are here?"

"Bless their sweet, simple souls," Mae West crooned. He was a sweet sort of sissy with bottle-blonde hair and hands that flopped off his wrists like noisemakers at a New Year's party.

"You'd think they'd give up after striking out so many times," Walter sighed.

"Oh, now he has an interest in sports," Frank groused. "You know, when you all waste away with porcelain bones in your old age, don't say I didn't try to help you. I'm heading out."

"Not on my account, I hope," Stephen deadpanned.

"No, I'll take that honor," Walter said, glowering at Frank over crossed arms. "Tell all the gymnasium boys we said 'hello'."

Frank snorted and stood. He was a hulking fellow, tall with big shoulders. Stephen had been interested when he first met Frank, but things had fizzled out pretty quickly when he realized Frank was less well-endowed in other areas. Chiefly intelligence, of course. Chiefly.

Frank charged past the Two Blind Mice and gave a manful nod to Kreuger as he headed out the door.

"Where have you been?" Dickie turned to Stephen with a curl of his upper lip. Dickie was an elegant bitch who would never be caught dead somewhere as smelly and sweaty as a gymnasium. His tastes ran more to expensive silk scarves, finely tailored wool trousers, and shiny polished shoes. Walter was the only fellow in their set who could afford to be his boyfriend. Dickie had creamy skin and delicately carved features in perfect symmetry—objectively, a beautiful man. He and Frank would make a fine-looking couple if Frank didn't waste all his money on subscription Charles Atlas guides. And if Dickie wasn't so awful at covering up how head over heels he was for Walter.

Stephen squirmed in the booth and busied himself with a long draught of his beer.

"Stephen," Walter intoned. "How's that New Year's resolution going?"

"Fine. Just a teeny tiny, minor setback," Stephen confessed around the rim of his glass.

"I thought you weren't cruising anymore," Marge said with a tobacco smoke sigh. She was a glowering bull dyke dead-set on compensating for her delicate bone structure by letting her eyebrows grow together. She and Stephen had hit it off immediately a few years ago by virtue of the fact that they were both Italian.

"I'm not," Stephen said, but his voice curdled like it was a question.

Dickie scoffed. "What happened to true love?"

"I'm still looking for it. I just … didn't find it at the bathhouse." Stephen winced into his beer.

"What *did* you find at the bathhouse?"

Stephen grimaced. "Another tall, dark, married man."

"Wow, you sure can pick 'em," Mae West sang. "Maybe you should pick up the Two Blind Mice? At least then the wife knows she's getting cuckolded."

"Dear god, I'm a poof, not a pervert," was Stephen's requisite reply.

"You're quite right," Dickie said. "Frank let them pick him up once. He said he couldn't walk straight for a week and it weren't on the fellow's account."

"I'm sorry, what?" Marge exclaimed. Any suggestion of penetration made the bridge of her nose wrinkle.

"I'm not one to air someone else's *private* business," Dickie replied with relish. "Only that I understand the husband isn't the only one with queer tastes."

Two Blind Mice indeed. Fact was, though, it was slim pickings this time of year. Everyone was hard up after Christmas and it was cold as a witch's tit. Things wouldn't pick up at all until Winter Carnival at the end of the month, and Stephen was loathe to wait that long to meet someone he could be serious about.

The bell above the door that was chipped with enough layers of oil paint to prevent nuclear fallout chimed as a burst of frigid air barreled down the galley. Stephen, seated in the best spot for casing the door, leaned out the booth a-ways, then made his report to the table. "It's just Red."

The rest of the group sagged. Red, a bespectacled man in his forties, perched on his usual stool at the bar and took to chatting with Mr. Kreuger. He was a notorious cruiser, often flitting in and out of the bar to "check his traplines." The old fairy held no interest to the back booth crowd at any rate—beyond being a perfectly decent middle-aged man, he was plain as could be, and had a long-term partner at home besides. It made Stephen spitting mad, to be entirely honest. Red got the best of both worlds, and he didn't even have any looks to make it make sense.

"Well, true love eludes the hopeless romantic once

more," Mae West declared sorrowfully with a sweep of his hand.

"I think that's giving him a little too much credit," Walter commented. "It wasn't all that long ago that he was waltzing in here bragging about his latest conquests."

"You know, I'm right here," Stephen said churlishly. "You don't have to talk about me like I'm not."

Dickie ignored him and replied to Walter, "You're right, darling." Then, he turned to regard Stephen. "What inspired your noble change of heart?"

Stephen glowered at him. "You all make me sound like a chippy-chaser."

"I'm sorry, are you not?" Dickie again, his naturally sarcastic voice positively dripping.

"I'm not! I was seeing Dale for six months, I don't know why you're slandering me like this." Stephen crossed his arms and pouted. The bell for the bar chimed again and he glanced over at the door. "King Crab."

"Oh bless his heart for coming back here," Mae West cooed. "Surely he must know by now his reputation precedes him?"

"I mean, it's preceded him for years," Walter said. "How does anyone know he still even has crabs?"

Glances ranging from offended to bewildered to exhausted (that was Dickie) ricocheted across the booth. Apparently, no one had a ready answer to that question.

"Listen," Stephen said, trying to steer the conversation back to his own miserable love life. "I admit, there was a time when I enjoyed playing the field. I didn't know any other gay fellows growing up and I'll admit, I've been enjoying sowing my wild oats."

"'A time,'" snorted Dickie. "Try the better part of a decade."

"Shut up," Stephen gave him a shove with his shoulder, eliciting a yelp from Dickie. "This place has lots of potential tricks, but how's a guy supposed to come in here day in and day out, see idiots like you setting up house together, and not want something like that for himself?"

"Awe, hear that Walter?" Dickie crooned. "Vinny's jealous of our quaint domesticity."

Walter grinned at Dickie like he was the only person in the room, and it made Stephen want to crawl under the table, although he wasn't sure if it was the envy or of the fact that everyone could probably see it on his face.

"Fine," Stephen said before Walter could start reciting poetry or something. "Maybe I am a little jealous. But most guys out there don't think there's anything more for men like us than anonymous encounters in men's bathrooms. It's pretty evil of you all to make me hope."

Now even Dickie looked moony. What a nightmare.

"I want to invest my time and energy into someone who cares to know my real name," Stephen barreled on. "Someone on my side, through thick and thin—"

"Oh, darling, you want a *husband!*" Mae West declared.

A husband, a companion, someone whose touch could reinforce that Stephen was still flesh and blood and hadn't winked out in a blink of loneliness like a dying star. Not to be melodramatic about it or anything.

"Well, maybe," Stephen hedged, "not in so many words, but yeah. And why shouldn't I want someone like that? Companionship isn't a purely female occupation. Plenty of men have found lifelong partnership together, whether or not they were having sex."

"Absolutely," Marge agreed with a jab of her cigarette. "We all ain't any different from anyone else. In fact, we're doing the world a favor by not contributing to overpopulation."

"Cheers to that," Mae West said, raising his glass.

"Love is too expansive to be limited by these piddly man-made ideas like marriage," Stephen continued. "I want something bigger. I want to have a great passion before I die. Is that so much to ask?"

The bell at the door chimed again. Stephen trailed off as he leaned over to see who'd come in. Like the previous new arrivals, he recognized this man, but unlike the others, it was the last possible person he'd expected to see.

"Holy shit," Stephen said.

"And lo, his prayers are answered," Dickie quipped, but his smile faltered as Stephen's jaw continued to wag. He leaned forward, almost pushing Stephen out of the booth as he craned for his own look.

"I don't know what he's all worked up about," Dickie reported to the group. "It's just some run-of-the-mill 9-to-5er."

To anyone else's eye, Dickie would be correct. The man was tall, with sandy blonde hair and a smart hat. He had a camel wool overcoat with a suit underneath it. Shiny patent leather shoes. But Stephen knew his face like the past eight years had never happened, like they were still sitting on the last row of bleachers with their thighs pressed together, laughing as Stephen talked shit about the football players on the Central High School field. Joe Milner, his face still as round and shiny and sweet as ever, was in Stephen's bar. He was *in Stephen's bar.*

"For cripe's sake, Vinny," Marge said, "put your tongue back in your mouth and tell us what's wrong with you."

Stephen looked back at the table of his friends. His real friends, the ones who knew him and still stuck around. He wrinkled his nose.

"It's no one."

"Bullshit," Mae West leveled in a timbre much lower than he usually used. "Give it up."

"Well, it's…" Stephen's face twisted into a full grimace. "…my soulmate."

Dickie looked like he wanted to bash his face through the table, but also like he might strangle Stephen if he didn't keep talking.

Stephen couldn't even hold a straight face through that. "It's a guy I knew growing up. We were real good friends, and we told each other we were soulmates. But he was never interested in me and got married straight out of high school. So yeah, it's my soulmate, but also, not at all." He laughed, to give them permission. They didn't.

Pity dawned one by one on the face of all the boys. One had to live under some sort of rock or look like Dickie to not have one of those unrequited coming-of-age stories.

"He must have a hefty pair to be showing up around here like that," Walter said, craning over the back of the booth to get a look. It was nice to be defended, even if Joe Milner was about as threatening as a wet noodle.

"Are you going to go talk to him, Stephen?" Marge asked. "Go on, go offer him a smoke and catch up."

"Are you insane?" Dickie admonished. "Stephen can't take that kind of risk. What if the guy's a snitch?"

"He probably has no idea where he is," Marge dismissed. "He looks like one of those city government guys. Probably just wants a beer on his way home."

Everyone in the booth was now on their knees on the cushions, craning up to get a good look at the newcomer. Stephen buried his face in his hands, mortified. But he couldn't quite manage to stop looking at Joe through his fingers.

"City government guy? All the more reason to treat him like *persona non grata*," Dickie said. "Besides, he threw Stephen over. What kind of friend calls you a soulmate and never talks to you after getting married?"

"The kind who harbored a little more than friendly affection," Mae West surmised, a lifted brow directed at Stephen.

"Stop it, you're torturing me," Stephen said miserably. "He didn't leave me in the lurch. I stopped talking to him. I just couldn't do it anymore."

Walter leveled Stephen with a serious expression. "That's damn hard to do. Good for you, Stephen."

"Thank you, Walter," Stephen said, straightening a bit at the acknowledgement. "It *was* hard. He kept calling my mom, asking for me. Wanting me to come to his wife's dinner parties."

"Two Blind Mice?" Marge snorted.

Stephen cast her an impatient look. "*No*. The calls stopped after I got my own place. As far as I know, he still calls my mom now and then. She loves it." Except he never managed to get his own place and he was so embarrassed, he was still lying to his friends about it. So every time Joe called, he got to listen to his mother chat him up. He only had enough strength to refuse the call; he still sat on the steps eavesdropping on every ounce of information he could glean from one side of the conversation. That hadn't happened in years. Not since Marion had their second baby. Fuck.

"Oh, he's looking this way!" Walter hissed, and they all ducked down at once in the most glaringly obvious display of Not Looking at Someone in the history of the world.

Stephen had nowhere to hide, seated at the end of the booth as he was. From where Joe Milner stood at the bar, Stephen was clearly visible. And he was looking this way, a sort of puzzled expression on his face, which made sense considering that he'd just caught a whole booth's worth of slack-jawed yokels staring at him. His eyes met Stephen's, and Stephen was very sorry to report that the effect those green eyes had on him had not waned one bit in the past eight years. Stephen looked sharply away at his own hands, unable to hold the connection. When he got the guts to look up again, Milner was no longer looking their way.

"Did he see you?" Mae West hissed.

"Yeah, he definitely saw him," Walter reported, peering round the edge of the booth like a film noir villain.

"Is he coming over?" Dickie asked.

Marge rolled her eyes. "Just go offer him a smoke and say 'hello.' The longer you hide over here like a ninny, the more awkward it's going to be. Just get it over with."

Stephen looked at her and then back at Joe Milner. He was half sitting, half leaning on a barstool and sipping his beer awkwardly, like he'd never drank at a bar by himself before. Like he was an approximation of a normal man, dressed in the costume and lurking in all the usual places. Except this wasn't one of the usual places. What was he *doing* here?

Stephen entertained the possibility of getting up and saying hello. He scarcely managed to imagine walking up to Joe Milner, heart in his throat, before he had to shut the whole operation down.

"Nope," Stephen said as he scrubbed his face in his hands. "I'm not going over there. He didn't recognize me."

"Well, I'm sure he will once you say, 'Hi, remember me? I'm Stephen Vincelli, your soulmate, from high school,'" Dickie pointed out.

Stephen groaned and buried his face all the way in his arms. If Joe glanced over, Stephen certainly wasn't going to appear to be nonchalant, well-adjusted, or better off without him. He pushed himself upright and inhaled deeply.

"I'm going to the toilet."

✦

Chapter 2

Joe Milner was beginning to like Thursdays. Before, they'd been unremarkable. Just another day in the long ticker tape of days where Joe did the same thing. Get up, go to work, have lunch, do more work, head home, eat dinner with his family, go to sleep. It was a routine that had a sort of comfort in its regularity. But this New Year's, Joe had resolved to shake up his life a little bit. Try something new. That was getting a drink on Thursdays.

It had actually been Marion's idea. She'd been nudging him more than usual recently, looking for his attention, trying to get him to do things with the children, pushing him to tell her all about his day.

He didn't understand why. It shouldn't be any surprise he didn't have anything to talk about. He did the same thing day in and day out, like clockwork. He was a clockwork man. It wasn't as though it had bothered Marion before. Their conversations were always carried mostly by her and her charming chatter.

And yet, for whatever reason, she'd decided Joe wasn't good enough as he was and could benefit from some improvement. Maybe she was right. Joe had everything he needed: a steady job, his own home, a family. He supposed he'd expected it to make him happier, but happiness wasn't the point of life, was it? If it was, he'd have been content to stay in high school for the rest of this life. But as his father had reminded him often, teaching had no potential for upward mobility.

Despite being pressed into it, Joe was enjoying his Thursday drink after work. It was a perfect little chunk of variation, an easily accommodated addition to his daily routine. The little hole-in-the-wall bar he'd found near City Hall was simple, too. It was run by austere Germans with no patience for nonsense and certainly no interest in chatting him up. Joe was able to sit at the bar and drink his beer in peace.

He liked the peace. Despite its proximity to work, he never saw anyone he knew. Well, except for the first time he went there. He'd seen his best buddy from high school, but Stephen hadn't recognized Joe—or if he had, he'd made it pretty clear he had no interest in catching up.

It was a nice place. Joe could depend on the little bar's patrons to leave him alone.

This was his third visit, and Joe felt at ease enough to not survey the booths for signs of Stephen Vincelli. He'd admittedly been a bit apprehensive about running into him again on his second visit, but Stephen hadn't been there, so Joe figured it must have been an aberration. Stephen had dropped him like a bag of bricks after high school, so it might have been awkward to keep running into him. Or perhaps not. Marion said it was normal for childhood friends to grow apart. Joe took a stool in the middle of the bar, ordered a Hamms, and focused on enjoying the way the bubbles tickled his throat as he swallowed.

If Stephen came into the bar, Joe didn't notice, because he was focused on enjoying his newfound indulgence. Not that Joe would have minded if Stephen wanted to catch up. It had been eight years since they were in school together. There would be so much to talk about. He wondered what Stephen did now. Joe imagined he'd have become a lawyer, perhaps—he'd had the affinity for arguing anyway, though his family lived down on the Levee and didn't have much in the way of tuition. If they'd been a little older, old enough to enlist before the end of the war, that wouldn't have been a problem because of the GI Bill. Maybe Stephen had enlisted to fight in Korea. Joe knew a lot of classmates who had done that. Maybe he'd done a tour and gone to school. If he'd done that, he'd still be in law school.

Joe noticed a drop of beer on the bar and shifted his paper coaster to soak it up. The bar had two long shelves of liquor bottles behind it, backed with a big mirror that was desilvering around the edges. The reflected fellow seated in his overcoat looking back in that mirror was him, but looked strangely unfamiliar. Maybe Joe wasn't used to seeing himself from that angle.

He could see the booths reflected in the mirror too. They were mostly empty. There were a few older guys drinking together in the front, laughing loudly. Toward the back, the last booth in the field of the mirror, held another group of fellows with two girls. It was a group of five or six, Stephen Vincelli was among them. Darn it. He must have shown up after Joe got there. He would have had to walk right past him.

Joe tore his eyes from the group and focused on his own reflection. His mouth set into a thin line in the mirror. So what? So Stephen wanted to pretend they didn't know each other. That wasn't anything different than what had been happening since graduation. Or the wedding, he supposed. Regardless, it was foolish that Joe would feel disappointed by it now.

Joe glanced back. Stephen was sitting next to the two

girls on the one side of the booth. There was another fellow on the other side, telling a loud story and waving his hands around enthusiastically. Joe perked his ears. He could hear the voice, but over the general din in the narrow galley bar, he couldn't make out what the fellow was saying. That was okay. He didn't want to know anyway. It was none of his business, and Joe Milner was not a snoop.

Joe wondered if Stephen was dating one of the girls. It was odd that he was squeezed in with both of them. If they'd been on a double date, surely the girls would sit with their dates. Joe considered the profiles and thought the blonde girl complimented Stephen's Sicilian coloring nicely. They'd make a nice family. The other girl was sort of surly. She laughed loudly at the other fellow's story and smoked incessantly. Stephen wasn't much for that kind of girl, as far as Joe could remember.

Stephen looked happy. The other fellow—the loud one—hadn't been at the table with Stephen the first time Joe had come to the bar. He was tall, muscular, and good-looking, with a firm jaw and droopy eyes that made him seem woeful and steadfast. Maybe he was dating the other girl.

Stephen had a lot of friends. Joe was happy for him.

Joe glanced at himself in the mirror again. His face was tight and wrong. He frowned down into his beer.

He should go.

It was too bad too. He'd liked this little bar, but he didn't want to keep running into Stephen, especially if he didn't want to acknowledge that they knew each other. Stephen had friends here. Joe would find another bar.

✦

The three-story tall Indian Statue of Peace that presided over the towering atrium of St. Paul City Hall frowned down at Joe a week later as he walked across the slab-tiled floors toward the elevators. Joe glanced up at it and returned its frown before passing through. Ralph Nelson was standing at the opulent art deco elevators already, so Joe didn't need to press the button.

"Thank god it's Friday, eh Milner?" Ralph was pushing forty, balding and of middling height. He had that jolly sort of nature that ended up dominating conversation at the coffee machine.

"Yeah, thanks Nelson."

"You got any special plans for the weekend?"

Joe shrugged. "Some house projects. Dinner at my mother-in-law's. Nothing too special."

"Ah yeah? I'm going to the Grande Day Parade for the Winter Carnival. It's great fun for the whole family."

"Oh, really? I've never been."

"You've never been?!" Nelson looked genuinely affronted. "I thought you grew up in St. Paul."

"I did. I guess, maybe I went as a kid? My mother brought us up at the Sokol Hall. We didn't do a lot of Winter Carnival stuff."

"That's a damn shame, if you don't mind my saying," Nelson said, shaking his head as the elevator chimed its imminent arrival.

"What's your favorite part of the carnival?" Joe asked. Joe was partial to asking folks about their opinion. It got them talking and took the pressure off him for a bit. It was an especially useful tack with his children. The elevator opened its shining brass doors, and he and Nelson boarded. "You're headed to nine, right?"

"Oh yeah, thanks," Nelson said. "The Grande Day Parade is great and all—my girls love the Queens of the

Snows and all the Princesses, but my favorite is Vulcan Victory night."

Joe frowned as he pressed the button for floors nine and eleven. "Vulcan—are those the fellows with the masks and the capes that drive around in that old firetruck?"

"Yeah! They hop off and kiss girls and leave them streaked with greasepaint. The mark of the Vulc!"

Joe blinked then belatedly smiled, realizing he was meant to think this was amusing. "The Vulcans. Is that a reference to the Greek god of fire?"

"Probably. I don't know, they've been around for decades. They're the harbingers of spring, at least according to Winter Carnival legend. Every year, they fight King Boreas and his four winds to take the land back from winter and bring spring."

Joe tried to figure out if Nelson was serious. "Fight?"

"Well, just figuratively. It's a load of fun, Milner. You should go."

"Maybe I will," Joe said as the elevator stopped on level three and let in a bespectacled young woman carrying a stack of files. "Say, Nelson, do you have a favorite bar around here? I'm looking for a new watering hole."

"Oh, yeah! You gotta check out the bar at the Ryan Hotel. It's crawling with Winter Carnival royalty this time of year. It's a gas."

Joe tried not to frown. "Oh? Sounds fun."

"It is. I'm going after work if you want to join me."

Joe thought about the ambient din of Kreuger's little bar. Of Stephen and his friends laughing in the booth. The sticky floors and the way the barkeeper polished glasses with his bar towel. It really was too bad. "Sure, that'd be fun."

"Great. I'll meet you at the Peace Statue at five." Nelson grinned as the elevator doors opened and he strode off to his office.

"Could you please get fifteen for me?" the girl with the folders asked. Joe glanced over at her and felt terrible he hadn't asked her when she'd first boarded. He was standing right in front of the bay of buttons and it would have been awkward for her to reach around him to press her floor.

"Oh, my apologies. Of course," Joe said shamefacedly.

The streets were packed with people as the Vulcan Victory Parade pushed down 6th Street. It was the first weekend in February, and Joe stood in the crowd flanking the street to observe the countless torches parading by. He smiled as the Golden Rule float drifted through, illuminated by hundreds of lightbulbs and a giant papier-mache valentine heart.

"Mother, look at the heart!" Charlie called. Joe's six-year-old son pointed his finger at the float with a grin and tugged on Marion's arm.

"Wow, would you look at that!" Marion exclaimed and wrapped her arms around Charlie. Joe held little Linda on his shoulders and smiled. The family was loving the spectacle.

"My stars, is that Joe Milner?"

Joe looked up and saw Ralph Nelson making his way toward him through the crowd, flanked by his twin daughters. Mrs. Nelson followed.

"Oh, hi Ralph," Joe greeted in return, shaking his colleague's hand. He'd gone to the Ryan Hotel with Ralph again this past Thursday. By that point, he'd drank deep from the Winter Carnival chalice. He had a Winter

Carnival button pinned to his overcoat, and he'd even gone with Ralph to look for the treasure chest over their lunch break, following the clues in the Pioneer Press. Ralph was right. It was fun.

"I'm so glad to see you and the family out here! Hail the Vulc!" Ralph exclaimed, pumping his fist in the air. Mrs. Nelson reached around Ralph and offered her hand to Marion.

"Hello! I'm Eunice. I've heard so much about you," Mrs. Nelson greeted. Marion grinned and shook her hand. They proceeded to delightedly chatter together. Joe enjoyed how sociable Marion was. He suspected they'd be hosting the Nelsons for dinner sometime soon.

"We saw the Vulcans earlier before the parade," Ralph said, leaning into Joe conspiratorially. "We had to hustle the girls out of there before they got smooched." He laughed with his belly.

"Have you ever thought about becoming a Vulcan yourself?" Joe asked.

"Oh, no! The missus would kill me." Ralph said. "They were at City Hall last week. They managed to mark the whole education department. The next day, the girls launched a counterattack against the superintendent. I guess he was the one who let them all in."

"In the office?" Joe asked. "That's a little unsporting, isn't it?"

"I assume that's why they launched the counterattack," Ralph chuckled. "What are you doing after this?"

Joe shrugged. "Going home with the family, I suppose. It's already way past Linda's bedtime." He bobbed his chin at the punchy four-year-old draped over his head.

"Ah, come on! The party afterward is the best part!" Ralph chided. "The missus is taking the girls home, and I'm heading out with some of my pals. You should join us!"

Joe blinked. "Oh, wow, that's real nice but—"

"—Yes!"

Joe glanced over at his wife. Marion was grinning at Ralph. "Yes, Joe, you have to go! You should have some fun." She pushed him encouragingly by the shoulder.

Joe felt his cheeks heat a bit. He wasn't sure he really wanted to wander around town with a bunch of drunks all night.

"Alright!" Ralph boomed, pulled Joe into his side with a friendly embrace. "It'll be a boy's night!"

Joe tried to smile, but his heart wasn't in it.

Chapter 3

Stephen was tipsy. It made sense, it was Vulcan Victory Night, and Kreuger's was packed to the gills with raucous Carnival-goers. Stephen was standing near the jukebox with Dickie, Walter, and Frank Atlas, who was cruising so blatantly Stephen was concerned Mrs. Kreuger was going to kick him out. He'd already goosed three fellows on their way to the bathroom and followed the third, who'd nodded his invitation. If it had been anyone else, it would have been a tasteful trick (though risky given there was only one stall in the men's room). But it was Frank, so Stephen already heard a full flavor and texture profile of the man's semen.

Suffice to say, Stephen had finished his last beer more quickly than he otherwise would have.

The Kreugers didn't hire any extra help for Winter Carnival. They were doing good business considering they were running a sweaty rotation of service at the head of the bar. It was unseasonably warm outside—just under freezing even though it was 10 o'clock at night—which meant that it was sweltering like the Amazon rainforest inside the bar even though the door was almost perpetually open.

"Hey, look, Vinny, it's your soulmate," Dickie snickered.

Stephen looked up sharply. He hated how his chest clenched as he saw Joe Milner's head floating above the crowd near the head of the bar. He was so tall. Christ.

"Shut up, Dickie," Stephen said and pretended he didn't care, even though he was definitely sizing up Joe's situation. He was with some other guys, because he was buying a round at the bar. Mrs. Kreuger served him four beers. Stephen craned, trying to see if he'd brought his wife.

"You're so far gone," Walter teased.

"I've only had three beers," Stephen argued.

"I mean you're hopeless for that guy."

"He's married!" Stephen was so exasperated with this perpetual twist of fate. "And he's not interested. Believe me, I checked."

"What? When?" Dickie's eyes widened with interest.

"In high school," Stephen muttered. "We drank cheap malt liquor together, and then I jerked him off."

"That doesn't sound like 'not interested' to me," Dickie observed.

"Yes, thank you Dickie," Stephen drawled. "Afterward, he wouldn't look me in the eye for a week. And then he introduced me to his future wife. So not only was he not interested, but he was so horrified, he made a point to marry the first woman willing rather than talk to me again."

"Beard," Walter said.

"Who're we talking about?" Frank Atlas leaned in.

"Vinny's soulmate from high school is here," Walter said, pointing the neck of his beer bottle toward the man in question.

"Soulmate?"

"Vinny jerked him off, and he was so affronted, he got married." Dickie was enjoying this too much.

Stephen tried to melt into the jukebox pumping out "Rags to Riches" by Tony Bennett. Maybe he could become a record by the Platters or something.

"So what's the question? Are we trying to find out if he's one of the boys?" Frank asked.

"I think I've pretty conclusively determined he's not," Stephen said testily.

"I dunno, a decade's a long time—"

" —Eight years."

"Huh?"

"Not a decade."

"I rounded up."

"Well, don't. I'm only 26."

"That's almost 30."

"*You take that back!*"

"What I'm *saying* is—it's been a long time. Maybe he's come around."

"Or *maybe* he's still *married,*" Stephen groused, his arms crossed.

"Go on, go say hi," Frank chided.

"I will not."

"Oh for cripes' sake, Vinny," Dickie sighed. "It's just some guy. He's not actually your soulmate. I'm beginning to think you don't understand that."

Stephen sighed and pushed himself off the jukebox. He turned around and looked each of them dead in the eye. "You are all terrible, and I hate you," Stephen said, then turned on his heel and pushed his way toward the bar.

He was just going to get a drink. That was all. He'd drank his last beer too fast because Frank Atlas was disgusting, and now he needed another one.

"Hey! I know that guy!"

Stephen looked up as he bellied up to the bar. There was Joe Milner, looking loose and sweaty, smiling with a beer in his hands. He was drunk. His grin was lopsided, and his eyes were glassy. Stephen had seen him like that before. (He'd jerked him off like that before. *Shit.*)

Milner pressed his way through the people that separated them and wedged himself next to Stephen along the bar.

"Hi, Stephen," Joe Milner said. There was an echo to his words. The hundreds of times he'd said Stephen's name over the years, ricocheting back to him across time.

Stephen set his jaw. "Hi Joe. Long time, no see."

Joe's smile settled into a little quarter moon affair. He looked more like himself than when he was grinning. More like the boy Stephen had known. "You're looking well."

"Thank you. You also." Stephen couldn't help but be curt. He hadn't dwelled on it, but apparently he was still angry.

Joe's green eyes were placid. "I saw you here a few weeks ago. I thought you didn't recognize me."

Stephen shrugged. *I did, but I just didn't want to talk to you.*

"Seems like you have a good group of pals here," Joe went on, glancing up toward the jukebox and Stephen's useless friends. Joe's smile widened. Stephen looked back over his shoulder to see what the hell those idiots were doing.

Oh, jeez. Walter had one arm around Dickie, and Frank Atlas was waving with waggling eyebrows. Stephen grimaced.

"They're okay," Stephen said. He turned back to Joe. "What are you drinking?"

"Just Hamms," Joe replied. "I had some sort of Vulcan Victory cocktail at the last place."

"How was it?"

"Terrible," Joe laughed. "But I'm flying pretty high now, so it's not all bad."

"You enjoying the carnival?" Stephen asked as his beer arrived, and he lifted it to his lips. Joe watched him sip it with that same little quarter-smile.

"Yeah, it's been great. My pal Ralph over there has been showing me the ropes." Joe nodded toward a middle-aged man laughing raucously with several other fellows his own age behind them. "I haven't ever done the whole Winter Carnival before. We even tried to find the treasure chest on Thursday."

"Yeah, you've got the button and everything," Stephen said, nodding toward Joe's chest. "Did you find any clues? Obviously you didn't find the chest."

"No, we just rambled around the riverbank for an hour or so over our lunch break." Joe smiled down at his hands, then glanced up. It was uncanny the way he could look up at Stephen like that when he was so much taller. Goddammit. If Joe had been a regular trick, in a bathhouse or something like that, Stephen would have tried a casual touch after a look like that. But this was Joe Milner. His wedding ring was glinting on his left hand like a warning beacon. Even if, in some miraculous turn of events, he was up for some hanky panky, he was *not* what Stephen was looking for.

"Well," Stephen said, pushing off the bar. "Hope you have a fun night."

He made himself turn around and push back through the crowd toward the jukebox. He hoped Joe didn't follow him. Actually, he hoped he did. No. He didn't. He really didn't. He couldn't handle a heartbreak like that ever again.

"How'd it go?" Dickie asked.

Stephen winced. "I'm beginning to wonder if my

problem isn't that I haven't found someone I could fall in love with, but that I'm too terrified of getting hurt to try."

"What was that?" Dickie leaned in.

Stephen sank into his inevitable insubstantiation. "Ah, nothing."

Dickie shrugged and gave him a tentative pat on the shoulder. Dickie was never much for comfort.

Later, Stephen was drunk and miserable. The bar was too loud, too close. Frank Atlas was sloppy, and Walter and Dickie took off to go be sickeningly adorable or something. Stephen didn't care. Red had arrived to check traplines inside Kreuger's, and Stephen was sloshy from too many beers, so he pushed his way to the front and out onto the street.

The air was cool and clear and felt good against his sweaty face. People thronged over the streets. 6th Street was still shut down from the parade, and folks staggered across the sidewalks and into the street. Stephen leaned up against the cracking paint under the neon "Liquor" sign and pulled out a cigarette from the pack in his coat pocket. A few fellows banged into Kreuger's, and the din from inside blasted out onto the street until the door swung shut again. Stephen dragged on his cigarette.

The mailroom manager at his job at Dayton's department store gave him shit for smoking Chesterfields. "That's a woman's cigarette," he'd say. "Now, Camels. That's a man's smoke."

Big deal. That guy could sit on it and spin. Chesterfields tasted better. Camels tasted like licking an ashtray off of a toilet seat.

The door to Kreuger's swung open, and the noise blared for a moment. Stephen glanced over, and his heart dropped into his shoes.

"Hey," Joe Milner said, leaning against the wall next to Stephen. "Can I bum one?"

Stephen took a long drag to fortify himself. Eventually, he nodded, the cigarette hanging from the corner of his mouth as he dug the pack out of his pocket. He handed it to Joe, who pulled a cigarette out with his long fingers and put it in between his narrow lips.

Joe patted his pockets and sighed. "Got a light?"

Stephen grimaced. He pulled a matchbook from his pocket and handed it over. Hell if he was lighting it for him.

Joe struck the match after a couple tries and dragged on the cigarette.

"Didn't know you took up smoking," Stephen said.

Joe shrugged. "I didn't."

God, if Stephen didn't know better, he'd think Joe was using it as an excuse to talk to him. Yuck. That was definitely how Stephen felt about it.

Joe leaned against the wall next to Stephen. If it had been senior year at Central, they'd have been close enough that their arms would touch. Of course, that was not the case presently. Stephen was relieved for it. Really. He was. Sure, he was also ashamed that he was so nostalgic for that touch he was marking its lack now, but it was still worlds better than pining after how it had once been between them.

"You much for the Winter Carnival?" Joe asked, smoke on his lips. Stephen looked away.

"It's fun. Can't really avoid it living in this town."

"No, I s'pose you can't." Joe cleared his throat. "Do you

root for King Boreas or the Vulcans?"

Stephen snorted. "I can't say I have a soft spot in my heart for either, but the Vulcans have the promise of spring, which is hard to compete with. Despite the fact that they're complete perverts."

Joe laughed. It was a rare thing that Stephen had turned flips for in high school. Now he was earning it without even trying. He couldn't help but feel a little puffed up about it.

"The girls in the education department at City Hall launched a counterattack on them," Joe reported. He did it in the same self-satisfied way Stephen remembered him conveying gossip in school. Not particularly relishing in the drama, but rather keen to offer something he knew would spark Stephen's interest. It was unfair how little he'd changed.

"It's the least those old codgers deserve," Stephen said, interest duly sparked in spite of himself. "I mean, don't get me wrong, I don't blame the Vulcans for taking what they can get. Those costumes aren't terribly flattering from any stretch of the imagination—" Joe laughed again, and it bolstered him. "—I'm certain I wouldn't be caught dead in one."

Stephen paused to modulate his voice. He'd gotten a bit too free just there, between the alcohol and standing next to drawling Dickie all night.

"I'm beginning to think my coworker would give his left arm to be one," Joe shared in a more conspiring tone. He'd leaned in, shoulder brushing Stephen's. Stephen was drunk enough that it took him a moment to shift subtly away.

"What, is he interested in philandering and terrorizing the city streets in a run-down old firetruck?"

Another chuckle from Joe. It was like gold. "I'm not

one to gossip."

"Oh stop it, we're old friends. Yes, you are."

Shoulders were touching again. To hell with it.

"Well, his eye's been on the wander tonight. To tell you the truth, it makes me a little uncomfortable, the way he was here with his wife and daughters earlier, and now he's trying to flirt with girls half his age at the Ryan Hotel."

"Some fellas just like to have a little fun. They don't mean nothin' by it," Stephen said, and he had no idea why he said it, except that it seemed like the thing fellows said in these situations.

"Maybe. I would never," Joe said, straightening and nodding at the cigarette he had awkwardly pincered between his fingers.

"Things still happily ever after for you and…" For the life of him, Stephen could not remember her name.

"Marion." Joe's eyes were fixed on his hand now. "I can't imagine ever betraying her like that. Even if it was part of the fun of the Winter Carnival."

"Of course," Stephen said. He thought hearing about her would hurt, but it didn't. Not at all, in fact. Perhaps time did heal all wounds, because what he felt was sort of free and generous. A rightness, a sense of clarity. Was this … forgiveness? He smirked to himself. Whatever it was, it felt like a wall crashing down and behind it was some sort of peace. A simple, innocent desire to catch up with an old friend, without the anxiety of that time he'd made Joe come. That was in the past, now. It really didn't matter at all.

"You ever settle down? Get married?" Joe asked, all innocent.

Stephen glanced at him then took a drag off his stub of a cigarette before flicking it to the pavement and stubbing it out with his shoe. "Nah. I think I must be a serial bachelor." It was the closest he could get to telling Joe the truth.

"I thought that might be the case," Joe replied obtusely and dragged off his own cigarette. "You're too adventurous to be tied down."

This warranted full side-eye from Stephen. "Oh?"

The door to Kreuger's crashed open, loud voices spilling onto the street along with Frank Atlas.

"Jeez, there you are," Frank said to Stephen, lurching forward before doubling back with a second glance at Joe. "Oh, who's your friend?"

Stephen, taking advantage of the attention Frank commanded from Joe, gave the bitchiest glower he could muster. "Just a friend from school."

"Well, he must have a name," Frank wheedled. He was the king of wheedling.

"Joe. Joe Milner," Joe said magnanimously, juggling his cigarette to offer a handshake. Frank took it, and it was evident he'd given a hard squeeze to show off. Joe grimaced and pulled his hand back as soon as he was able.

"Nice to meet you, Joe," Frank purred in the voice he liked to use with Dickie. Stephen doubled down on his glower.

"Don't you have somewhere you need to be, Frank?" Stephen said, not even caring that it was a blatant line to get rid of someone.

"Yeah, that's why I came to find you, idiot," Frank replied. "I thought we were going to the Coney."

Stephen gave a long-winded sigh. The Coney Island bar was prime for tricks during the Winter Carnival. It was all blue-collar beers in the front, but near the bathroom, there were drunk, hungry dogs looking for someone to show their belly to. In essence, Frank Atlas' playground.

The door to the bar burst open again, this time spilling out Joe's embarrassing friends. Three red-faced, blundering forty-somethings stumbled out laughing and hanging off each other. At least now they were even.

"Milner!" one of them blared like a foghorn. "There you are! I told yer wife I'd keep track of ya'. Whatcha doin' wanderin' off li-that?"

Joe gave that wide, wooden smile. "Just getting some fresh air."

"Who's yer pal?"

"Oh, this is Stephen, a friend of mine from high school. We just ran into each other."

"Ah, tha's why they call it Saint *Small*, amIright, Ralph?"

"Oh yah, that's what they say. Winter Carnival's a prime night for it too. I ran into a fella I knew from grade school in Lakeville last year. I tell yah, it was a trip!"

Joe's friend, Ralph, was a real charmer. All vein-popping cheeks and wet, cloying mouth. Stephen glanced at Frank and saw him doing his shit-eating grin.

"Hi there, fellas," Frank said, leaning down to crush the hands of Joe's coworkers. "Great night for it, ain't it?"

"Ah, who's this now? A friend of yours, Milner?"

"No, this is Stephen's friend. Frank, right?"

"That's right. Pleasure to meet you guys, really." They were falling over themselves for Frank's good-ol'-boy routine. God, what a nightmare. "Where you heading next?"

Stephen frowned, and Joe's friends all chimed in with dissenting ideas.

"We're just crawlin' our way down 6th."

"Nah, I thought we were gonna hit up the theater where they beat King Boreas."

"That happened hours ago, ding-a-ling. 'S past eleven."

"Well," Frank said with his big man voice that made Stephen's knees go a little wobbly entirely against his will. "I have it on good authority the Vulcans will be dropping by the Coney Island Tavern before the night is out. That's where Steve and I are headed. You guys should join us."

The flock of middle-aged men let out an array of affirmative bleats. Frank grinned and started off toward Wabasha, then tossed a charming look over his shoulder. "Come on, Steve, aren't you coming?"

If only looks could kill. Frank knew he hated that nickname.

"Yeah, come on Stephen," Joe said with that endearing hint of a smile. He also knew Stephen hated that nickname. "Let's go check it out."

Stephen scrunched his nose up at the stark contrast between his old friend and new. "Fine. But know I'm joining under duress."

The Coney Island Tavern was packed to the gills. There were throngs of people outside, smoking and laughing. Inside, it was another galley of a dive centering around a long wooden bar from back in the early days, before Prohibition, with a brass rail and gleaming mahogany under beer-smeared lacquer. The tiny place was wall-to-wall with people, beers slinging down the bar like an assembly line. Their group of six pressed into the crush.

"Oh," Joe huffed as he squeezed inside the door. Stephen was right behind him. It wasn't even weird that they were being jostled together in the crowd of bodies inside this place. "You don't think there's any chance of getting a drink under these conditions?"

"I highly doubt it," Stephen replied, his eyes swiveling

toward the booths opposite the bar. Even if they had to share, it was better than standing room. "Aha, look! Those guys are leaving. Come on!"

He grabbed Joe's hand and dragged him away from the bar. The fellows clearing out one of the booths toward the front scarcely stood from the table before Stephen slipped in. He was short and wiry; it was easier for him to move through the crowds than someone like, say, Frank.

Joe held his own well and levered himself onto the opposite bench. "Wow, we sure got lucky! If I didn't know better, I'd think it was St. Paddy's."

"Nah, neither of us are Irish," Stephen replied. Joe's middle-aged coworkers were still at the bar, but Frank was making his way toward the booth.

"Nice job, fellas!" Frank boomed when he approached them. He stepped up on Stephen's side and managed to take up three-quarters of the booth by himself. "Jeez, what a crowd!" He leaned in close to Stephen and said for only Stephen to hear, "It's a real ten-course meal, eh?"

Stephen refused to dignify this with an answer.

"The only thing that would make this better would be if we could manage to get a drink," Joe said. His voice was a little too loud, his smile a little too wide, his eyes a little too unresponsive to the grin he was attempting.

"Did we lose the others?" Frank blared half-over Joe's comment. He leaned into Stephen again and whispered, "Because I'm telling you, that Stan guy was looking tight, and he reminds me of my neighbor's dad growing up. I'm just saying, I could get behind that."

Stephen fully winced, because he was drunk and mortified and not good at hiding it. He grabbed Frank's inflated bicep, yanked him close, and hissed, "Don't. You. Dare. Go to the back, find yourself a mournful sissy to bend over your couch like you normally do, and *don't embarrass me.*"

Frank gave him a look and said, "Fine, don't get your panties in a twist."

With a roll of his eyes, he hopped down to the floor and wrestled his way toward the men's bathroom.

Stephen was only just relaxing his jaw when Joe said, "He seems nice."

Stephen's eyes snapped over to Joe.

"Oh, Frank?" Stephen managed something distantly related to airy. "He's fine, I guess."

"He's really…" Joe shrugged his shoulders and biceps in a half-hearted gesture referencing the Charles Atlas ads in the backs of comic books.

"Yeah," Stephen confirmed slowly. Was he spouting a platitude or did he mean something? "Frank's vainer than Narcissus. He'd drown himself in a mirror in an instant if it'd let him."

"Oh, well, I just mean…" Joe met Stephen's eyes. "I'm just very glad you have a friend like him."

Jiminy cricket. Stephen had seen about a hundred different significant looks in his life. He knew one when he saw one. "No, no." He glanced over his shoulder to make sure he was out of earshot, then leaned over the table toward Joe. "I wouldn't call him a *friend*." God, how could he say this politely so Joe would understand? "Barely acquaintances."

Joe's eyes widened a bit. Cripes almighty, did he think that meant Stephen and Frank were just fucking? *No.*

"To be blunt, I don't like him very much," Stephen said. "Frank's superficial and shallow. When I, uh, make a new friend, I want to be able to, you know, have a conversation with him. About things that matter." God, his cheeks were bright red. If Joe didn't already think he was up to funny business, he sure must now.

"I can definitely understand that," Joe nodded serious-ly.

Stephen nodded too until he felt like a chicken, because now if he tried to engage Joe in anything resembling meaningful conversation, it would appear as though he were hitting on him.

"My, uh," Joe started into the silence awkwardly, "my wife can get conversation going with anybody. Friend, stranger, she's got a way with everyone."

Stephen smiled, relieved at the break in the awkward silence and relieved that he wasn't experiencing bru-tal heartbreak hearing about Joe's wife, even when it was being presented in a clear, intentional contrast to Stephen's implied queerness. Golly gee damn, forgiveness was incredible! "She sounds like a peach."

"She is," Joe insisted, even though Stephen was sure he hadn't been sarcastic. "She's a wonderful wife and mother. A wonderful woman. She deserves everything and more."

It was weird how Joe said this, like he was despondent about it. Stephen did not—absolutely *did not*—ask.

"So you got kids?" he asked instead.

"Yeah. Two of 'em," Joe rubbed the back of his neck like he was embarrassed.

"How old?"

"Six and four. Boy and girl, one of each flavor."

Stephen knew what he was supposed to say under these circumstances. "Wow! Well, congratulations! I had no idea the guy who puked in a water fountain would end up raising the future generation. Well done, well done."

Joe laughed, seemingly in spite of himself. His green eyes were strained.

"And I'm sure they're both perfect little angels, too," Stephen guessed. "Not a toe out of line."

Stephen was rewarded with another laugh, a little less tight this time. "Yeah, of course. I'm the quintessential hard-ass."

It was a little painful to watch him try and pretend this was hilarious and all in good fun, because it was pretty obvious it wasn't.

"Well, I could never do it," Stephen said, leaning back and radiating casualness into the conversation. "You're good, you know that? Just a damn good man. I suppose you take them out back and play catch?"

"Of course."

"And you give the little one horsey rides?"

"Naturally."

"Wow, all the classic Dad stuff! Damn, I wish my dad had done stuff like that."

"I know, me too. I feel like growing up in the Depression, we got cheated."

"We sure did." There was a bowl of half-eaten peanuts on the table so Stephen reached out and cracked one open. "So what are you up to these days? You got a job, I assume?"

"Yeah, I work up at City Hall."

"Doing what?"

"I uh, do bookkeeping mostly."

"Just mostly?"

"Well, I'm, uh, I guess I'm up for a promotion soon."

"Oh yeah, what kind?"

"City comptroller."

"What!?" Stephen slammed his hands on the table. "You're *what?*"

"I'm not the comptroller," Joe scrambled to clarify. "Not yet. The current comptroller is sort of, you know, grooming me."

"That's a big damn deal, Joe!"

"I know."

"Your wife must be thrilled. She making plans to re-decorate?"

"She's been looking pretty closely at the G-E appliance catalog."

"Damn, what are you gonna do when you get your hands on the city purse strings?"

"What? I dunno. Whatever the mayor tells me to do, I guess."

"Well, I want more Winter Carnival events. Not the family-friendly kind, either. The kind that appeals to drunks and barflies. How about an ice hockey game, but it's a drinking contest?"

Joe spluttered a laugh and they were back, back to the easiness they'd had leaning against the wall smoking, an echo of what they'd had so long ago. It was sweet and wonderful and, goddammit, it felt so *right*. Maybe Stephen had been wrong about Joe. He'd been all mixed up back then. He'd barely known he was a queer. He'd loved Joe and doted on him and called it best friendship. Soulmates, but between two friends. It wasn't unnatural—it was honorable. Who said romantic love was the only love? Stephen had even gotten into the whole Biblical *agape* love for a while, just looking for a way to explain what he was feeling, before he quit going to church entirely. But then Joe had got married, and Stephen decided that there could be no way he could stay friends with Joe and survive the heartbreak. Maybe he'd been too preoccupied with himself and his own feelings. Because there had been something very magical there. Not sexual, but intimate nonetheless. Sex wasn't everything. Stephen knew that well enough. Maybe this kind of easiness was worth it.

So he let himself enjoy Joe's company. They laughed

and ate all the peanuts and eventually, the middle-aged city workers got a round of drinks and brought them up to the booth. Ralph and his buddies were straighter than a can of beans, but they could have been more boorish, Stephen supposed. It didn't matter, because he and Joe were carrying on their own conversation the far side of the booth.

"Did you ever go to law school?" Joe asked.

Stephen rolled his eyes and flicked a peanut shell. "No. Of course not."

"It's not that far out of the realm of possibility! Lots of guys who grew up on the Levee get on the GI Bill and end up with degrees."

Stephen gave him a flat look. "Really. I sure ain't met 'em and I'm still living on the Levee."

Joe's mouth worked for a moment before he said anything. "Not that it matters, or anything. There's all sorts of good, honest work these days for fellas willing to look for it."

"Yeah, that's what they say," Stephen said. "It's been hard for a lot of guys, after the war, but I think it's better than I can ever remember it being."

"I just consider myself lucky I never had to go," Joe confessed, pushing all the peanut shells scattered across the table into a neat little pile.

"You're telling me," Stephen said. "I'm not hurting or anything, don't get me wrong. I'm working odd jobs and making ends meet."

Joe's brow crinkled, possibly with worry, and Stephen hastened to smooth it away by saying, "I mean, I have a couple gigs I do. I sell men's shoes at Dayton's, and then I pick up some extra hours processing books at the Central Library. It's enough to live on, which is more than some guys can say."

Chapter 4

It was early the next Wednesday when Joe sneaked a glance at the alarm clock on his bedside table. It was 3:47. Still too early to get up. He let his breath out in one big sigh and stared up at the ceiling. There was a crack up there. He wasn't sure if it was just a shadow or if there was a trace of water damage there too. If it was the latter, he'd need to go check the asphalt roof after work. Which would require a snow shovel and a ladder. He could probably get it secured over the weekend though.

He glanced at Marion, curled up with her back to him, snoring. She'd be disappointed if he took on another house project this weekend. She kept telling him she wanted them all to go tobogganing. Which would be fun. He knew it would be. He just … he needed to make sure the house was going to make it through the thaw in a few months. It would help him sleep better.

He wished he could say this was a rare occurrence, waking up at this ungodly hour, but it wasn't. He'd made a bit of a habit of it lately. It was damned annoying too, once it got started. He'd be so tired by the end of the day, he'd fall asleep in his armchair, and then stay up too late, then wake up too early because he'd slept, and it would all just repeat itself day in and day out.

Joe resolved to lock it all out. He closed his eyes resolutely. This time it would be different. He began counting backward from 100. That helped him keep off his spiraling thoughts long enough to fall asleep. Sometimes.

He reached 86 when he thought about Stephen Vincelli. It had been so good to run into him at the Winter Carnival and catch up. He looked like he was doing so well. Well, he looked well at any rate. His news about his job—jobs, rather—had been a little disappointing. Not that Joe was disappointed in Stephen or anything. It wasn't the easiest job market, with so many more women looking to work too. Jobs like bank tellers and clerks were increasingly being filled by girls with typing certificates who would work for a fraction of the pay a man would. It was demoralizing for the fellows out there trying to support a family.

Not that Stephen was supporting a family. Although, Joe wondered if he was supporting his mother. They'd always been close, and Joe was confident she was still living on the Levee too. The Levee was the little Italian neighborhood on the riverbank under the High Bridge that flooded nearly every spring. It was a cheap place to live, but one also had to get used to managing water damage more regularly than Joe would ever be willing to.

If the crack in the ceiling was water damage, Joe would need to take quick action. If you left stuff like that, it always got worse. And you never knew if a little water stain was just a spillover from a bad storm or insidious evidence of a much bigger, hidden problem. Marion just had to accept that tobogganing would have to happen another weekend.

Joe wondered if Stephen lived on the ground floor. If he did, he probably didn't have any carpets. Why bother, if they were just going to get ruined every year? He wondered if Stephen would be interested in a job at City Hall. He knew a few departments that were looking. He didn't remember Stephen being particularly good at figures, but he was a smart fellow. He'd been a natural at most things in school. English, debate, football. All the things that got an outgoing high school boy friends and accolades. It was a wonder he'd spent so much time with Joe, considering.

Certainly, Stephen wasn't a natural at *everything*. He'd been great at setting up double dates for them with girls, to movies and bowling and the usual things, but he'd never managed to pin one down. Joe understood why that had always been so hard for him. Stephen preferred … the company of other fellows. That was fine. Frank seemed like a great friend for Stephen. Joe wanted someone like that for him. Strong, capable, good-looking, at ease with people. If Stephen couldn't settle down with a wife or a family, he deserved to have a companion who complimented him.

Actually, when it came down to it, it didn't surprise Joe that Stephen was juggling multiple jobs. He'd never had an affinity to apply himself to one thing. He was a jack-of-all-trades, master of none. Too distractible to buckle down and build his skill at one vocation. Maybe that was the trouble with Frank? Stephen was too busy chasing novelty to notice this good thing in front of him?

Joe resolved to stop by Kreuger's again that Thursday. It had been so fun to spend time with Stephen again, and perhaps he could nudge him a bit, enough to see that Frank was a good, solid sort of fellow.

Joe wrinkled his nose. He was being nosy, wasn't he? Besides, settling down wasn't what men like Stephen did. Did they? They couldn't very well pick out curtains and host dinner parties for the Ladies Auxiliary. He wasn't particularly sure what men like Stephen *did* do. Men like him— jeez, it was also entirely possible Stephen might still find a girl to settle down with. Joe shouldn't make such sweeping assumptions. But when Joe had clumsily broached the subject because too much beer made his inside thoughts his outside words, Stephen had said he wanted a friend he could talk to about things that mattered. He'd made no denial. And it wasn't like he was some deviant trying to entrap unsuspecting men in public restrooms. He was … he was like Joe's great uncle Francis. Yes. Men like him could have a partnership, share a home, live out a discreet life of mutual companionship.

He wondered what kind of job Frank had. Maybe with a combined income, Stephen could afford to move out of the Levee?

Joe was ruminating again. He tried to remember what number he'd left off at and refused to open his eyes and see how much time had passed. It would be fine. He'd nod off soon. He started counting down from 100 all over again.

✶

That evening, Joe thought he was going to nod off into his chicken and rice hotdish.

"Ew!" Charlie cringed as Marion glopped a serving onto his plate.

"Charlie!" Marion admonished, rounding the table to place a smaller helping onto Linda's plate. "How rude."

Joe dragged his attention to the table. He should probably say something.

"I don't like peas," Linda joined in.

"I didn't ask if you liked peas," Marion sighed. "You

like chicken and you like rice. You've eaten this before. Remember before Christmas? You argued for fifteen minutes and then you tried it and you liked it."

"But I don't like peas," Linda repeated with perfect four-year-old logic.

"Look," Marion said with a sigh as she sat at her place across from Joe. "Daddy likes them. Don't you?"

Joe blinked. He fumbled his fork and took a hasty bite. "Yes! Mmm, that's delicious, Marion. Thank you."

Charlie watched him chew with a disgusted expression. "Gross."

"Charlie!" Marion threw her hands up and shook her head in exasperation. It was understandable. This happened a lot. "That is so rude! You cannot tell people that you think their food is 'gross.' Imagine what your friends' parents would think, if you said something like that their family dinner! You don't talk like that to your grandmother, do you?"

"No," Charlie said. "We get dessert at Grandmother's house."

Marion glared mutinously at him. "You shouldn't need a reward to eat your dinner! You don't get rewarded for doing the basic things you're expected to do. Now eat."

Charlie crossed his arms and glowered back at Marion.

Joe had disliked peas when he was a child, too. Of course, when he'd been a child, there'd been soup-kitchen lines and shanty towns on the river flats. His mother had ensured he ate everything he was served and been grateful for it. The belt had been the alternative. Joe was loathe to threaten that. Marion agreed. But Dr. Spock said that it created anxiety for a child if his father declined to discipline him.

Joe cleared his throat. "Chuck. Your mother worked hard to make this meal. Now you'll eat it and be grateful."

Charlie gave him an incredulous sideways look. He didn't say anything. Joe watched him with what he hoped was a stern expression and waited. After a few moments, Charlie looked away and sighed. "Sorry, Mother."

Charlie pushed the food around with his fork. Then, he took a sullen bite, glancing up at Joe as he did so. Joe gave him an encouraging nod. Charlie looked away, but he swallowed and forked another bite.

"Well, I'm not eating peas," Linda declared, then shoveled a big bite into her mouth. Their second child ate almost anything. She just liked imitating her older brother.

If Joe was honest, he hated that it worked. It wasn't that he wanted to get into an argument with his children, or not have Marion's back. He just wished that fathering wasn't so … punitive. When Marion first told him they were expecting Charlie seven years ago, he'd imagined playing catch and teaching him how to ride a bike and building snowmen in the wintertime. But he was always too tired for any of that. Charlie didn't even bother asking anymore. All Joe did was do chores and tell his children 'No.'

After dinner, the kids were arguing about whose turn it was to pick what they watched on the television that evening. Joe had bought the television with the hope that it would keep them occupied for a bit so he and Marion could get things done around the house. If he had known it was going to be such a source of conflict between them, he'd never have bought one in the first place.

Marion, of course, in her eternal wisdom, managed to convince them they both wanted to watch *Disneyland*, which of course they did. She was a wonder.

"Joe, are you alright?"

Joe looked sharply at the hand on his forearm, then up at his wife who regarded him with concern.

"What?"

"I was just saying I can't believe it's already Wednesday."

"Yes," Joe said. "The days do fly by."

"I know, but I mean Valentine's Day is already on Sunday. And we've got tickets to the opera tomorrow, remember? I can't wait. Can you?"

"Uh." Joe had forgotten about that. His mother had given them tickets to the St. Paul Opera. He couldn't remember the show. Something Italian. Darn, he'd been hoping to stop by Kreuger's before coming home, but if they were going to a show, he'd need to go home direct to get ready and bring the kids to Marion's mother's house before the dinner reservation. Oh *darn it*, the dinner reservation. "No, I can't wait, either, honey. Say, did you make the dinner reservations?"

Marion looked at him for a long moment. He knew full well he was supposed to have done that and had utterly forgotten.

"No, I thought you were going to do that," she said.

"Oh, right, yes," Joe said, snapping his fingers as if he'd only just remembered. "I'm sorry, darling, I've had so much on my mind at work. I'll go call right now."

He pushed out his seat and started for the kitchen.

"Can't you wait until after dinner?"

Right. He hadn't eaten anything yet.

"Of course. Sorry," he muttered and sat back down. Now the children were giving him a strange look too.

* * *

Marion made him two martinis after the children went to bed, which meant she was in the mood. Joe had managed to get reservations at the Lexington supper club so he'd endeared her to him. If he'd known it would make her look at him like that, he would have let himself be a bit more disappointing.

It wasn't that he didn't want to make love to his wife. It wasn't that. He was just so *tired*, and he hadn't had the chance to catch a nap in his armchair before dinner.

"Come on," Marion said, standing over his chair and taking his hand. "Time for bed."

She said it with the same relish Ralph had for the Vulcan Victory Parade. Joe pressed his lips together and pushed them into a smile.

In the bedroom, he sat on the edge of the bed and unbuttoned his shirt as his lovely wife zipped down her house dress. She was more full-figured than she'd been when they'd married. Two babies had filled her out. She was beautiful, rosy-cheeked and eager, and Joe felt guilty for not being more excited to please her. All he ever wanted was to do right by her.

She crossed to him and pressed her palm on his cheek. "I love you so much, Joe."

She leaned down to kiss him. Her lips were wet. Why did kissing have to be so wet? Joe's heart was racing now, but it wasn't doing anything for the problem that, of course, he was again having downstairs. He put his hands on her hips and tried to concentrate.

"Mm," she murmured and slid down onto his lap, one leg on either side of him. He hadn't meant to direct her to straddle him, but she didn't seem reticent. She still had her girdle and brassiere on. Her stockings too. He pushed his hands up and down her back and hoped she didn't notice how dormant he was underneath her.

Marion caught one of his hands and led it meaningfully to her bosom. Joe held back a flinch. He didn't understand what was wrong with him. Marion had a lovely bosom. Any fellow would be panting to touch her.

"Mm, Joe, that's wonderful," she moaned. She was rolling her hips on his lap now too. She'd noticed he was still soft. She had to have. She was trying to get him aroused. Why else would she behave so wantonly?

It sort of embarrassed him to hear her, but then he felt a stirring in his lap. He chased it in his mind. Yes, that was it. It felt good. He closed his eyes tight. He wished she'd stop kissing him and let him concentrate. He often thought it would be easier if he could do it from behind, but the indignity and disrespect of such a position was enough to make him dismiss it out of hand. Sometimes thoughts of it alone improved the situation. But he shouldn't have to think about things like that to make love to his beautiful wife.

No. The stirring he'd felt disappeared. Come on, please, *no*.

"Everything okay?" Marion said quietly as she stilled and sat back. Joe reached down surreptitiously to adjust himself.

"Yup, everything's fine."

"Joe, I can do that."

Joe's face went hot with shame. "No, it's okay."

"Really. I want to."

He looked up at her and sighed. "It doesn't matter. I'm just really tired. I couldn't sleep again last night."

"Oh, I'm sorry." She reached out and took his hand. Well, there's that good and gone. He couldn't get aroused when she looked at him with such pity. "We can just go to sleep, if you want. Try again later. I'm sure after a night of good food and fine culture, we'll be raring to go."

God, she meant tomorrow. "Yup."

He gingerly helped her off his lap, then rolled into

the bed, yanking the covers up to his chin. She puttered around the room for a minute, removing her underthings and putting on her nightgown. Joe carefully averted his eyes until she climbed into bed beside him.

"That was really nice, Joe."

"Yup."

It was a terrible reply. He knew that, but he was too embarrassed to think of anything else to say. The silence stretched out between them. She was only inches away from him, but it felt like miles.

"I love you."

He pretended to be asleep.

Chapter 5

Joe ducked out of work early the next day to make sure he had time to stop by Kreuger's before he had to get home and get ready for the opera. He was feeling a bit better after actually managing to sleep through the night. Despondence and humiliation were unpleasant, but they were also exhausting, which in this case was useful. Joe had a spring in his step as his shoes tapped out a rhythm on the cold, stone floors of City Hall. They spun him through the revolving door and onto the street.

Kreuger's was only two blocks away. As he neared, he began to worry whether Stephen would even be there. He didn't know what hours he worked, or when he did overtime at the library. Joe reminded himself that it wouldn't hurt to try—if he had a beer in silence, it was certainly not the worst thing to happen before he reentered the chaos of his loving household.

When he pushed open the cracked black-lacquer door, a cloud of stale cigarette smoke greeted him like a familiar friend. Joe felt his shoulders relax an inch or so. Mr. Kreuger gave him a brusque greeting, and Joe ordered a Hamms. As he waited for Mr. Kreuger to fill his pint, he leaned on the bar and took a cursory look around.

"Hello there."

He looked over toward the female voice that had greeted him. In the booth just across from where he stood at the bar sat a woman and a man, each nursing a beer.

"Good afternoon," Joe said.

"I've seen you here a couple of times," the woman said genially. "I'm Carol, and this is my husband, Jack. Why don't you join us?"

"Oh," Joe said with a smile. It was novel to be noticed by strangers. They were a handsome couple and seemed friendly. "Thank you, but I'm waiting for a friend."

"Oh, too bad. Maybe next time?" Carol replied with a tilt of her chin.

"Sure," Joe said. "I'm Joe, by the way. Joe Milner."

"Pleasure to meet you, Joe," Carol said, shaking his hand.

"Very nice to meet you," Jack added, taking his turn to shake Joe's hand. His voice was low, surprisingly low, given he was more on the tall, wiry side like Joe was.

"Oh, hi Joe."

He turned around and was startled to see Stephen at his shoulder. "Oh, Stephen, there you are."

"What's got your goat?"

"Nothing, you just startled me."

"Hi, Stephen." This was Carol. She was grinning up at Stephen in a way that made Joe think they were already acquainted.

"Hey Carol." Stephen's voice was tighter.

"You remember Jack, I'm sure."

"Sure do. How you been?" Stephen reached out and shook Jack's hand.

"Can't complain," Jack said, that rumbling bass continuing to draw Joe's ear.

"Well, I hate to beg off, but Joe and I have some business to attend to," Stephen said with his own genial smile, replete with dimples. "It was nice to run into you."

Joe was reminded of how Stephen had departed last weekend at the Coney Island Tavern as he resolutely steered Joe to the booth at the back of the bar.

"What was that about?" Joe asked when he'd been deposited into the booth.

"Nothing," Stephen said. "But maybe steer clear of Carol and Jack in the future."

How rude. "Why?" Joe asked, a little annoyed and embarrassed.

"Oh, they just . . . They like to pawn guys for drinks and stuff."

"Oh." Joe thought about that for a moment. "I dunno, I don't mind buying a round of drinks for friendly people."

Stephen leaned back in the booth. He had one arm draped over the top of the upholstered cushion. "That's where you and I differ. But I suppose if you're offering . . ."

Joe frowned at him. "Fine. I didn't get a chance to grab my beer anyways after you so rudely manhandled me back here."

Stephen pursed his lips in a very familiar way, like he was trying too hard to be annoyed to laugh, then waved Mrs. Kreuger over.

"What'll it be?" she asked, hands on her hips.

"Two Hamms please," Stephen said sweetly.

"Sorry, just one, I left mine on the bar," Joe amended.

Mrs. Kreuger looked up at the bar and nodded. "Two beers, one already poured. Very well."

She shuffled back behind the bar and fetched the beer Joe had abandoned.

"Oh, now I feel like a nincompoop, making her go get it for me."

"She knows it's my fault, don't worry."

"What 'business' did you drag me over here for anyway?"

Stephen stilled and pulled his arm down from the cushion to sit up more straight. "To be totally honest, none. I was just trying to save you from getting, uh, cleaned out by those two. We call them the Two Blind Mice."

"I thought there were Three Blind Mice," Joe said, pushing a coaster around the table. "Isn't that how the nursery rhyme goes?"

"Yeah, that's the guy who, uh, pays the price." Stephen scratched the back of his neck and peered out to look at the bar. "I wonder what's taking so long with those beers."

"It's been less than a minute. Keep your shirt on."

"I'm sorry, did I appear to be losing my shirt?" Stephen said archly.

Joe couldn't help but laugh.

"So what are you doing here, Joe?" Stephen asked.

"Just stopping in after work."

"A little early, isn't it, for City Hall?"

"Yeah. I have to take Marion to the opera later, so I wasn't going to have time if I left at five."

"Have to? Do you not like the opera?"

Joe blanched. "Uh, no, to be honest. I don't know why I'd want to watch a bunch of people sing in a language I don't understand for three hours."

"What opera is it?"

"I can't remember. Something in Italian, I think."

"The Barber of Seville?"

"No."

"La Boheme?"

"What?"

"How about Rigoletto?"

"How do you know all of these operas?"

"I'm Italian. It's my business to know about operas."

Joe grinned. "Well, maybe I'll bring *you* next time my mother gives me opera tickets. Then you can at least tell me what they're saying."

"Oh, hold on a minute. I'm not *that* kind of Italian. All I can say is *cheprecca* and *prosciutto* and *capish*."

"And Rigoletto, apparently."

Stephen was grinning. It felt so good to see him smile like that again, with his dimples indenting his cheeks. It evoked such nostalgia in Joe that he had to look away. Which was fine, because their beers had arrived anyway.

"Where's all your friends?" Joe asked, looking around the bar.

Stephen shrugged. "Most of 'em work until five. The rest don't usually bother showing up here until then anyway, since they know that's the witching hour."

"Oh." Joe wasn't too upset about having Stephen all to himself, but he'd been hoping Frank would be around. He thought he could get them talking about something meaningful, like Stephen wanted, to show him that Frank could handle it. Politics or literature or something like that. He hadn't thought too much about it. "So what are you doing here, then?"

Stephen nodded in this rolling way, like he should have seen that coming. "I only worked till two at Dayton's today, and I didn't feel like going home then coming back downtown."

"Two was a few hours ago. What have you been doing between then and now?"

Stephen's mouth twitched. "Just tooling around."

"Oh," Joe pushed condensation from his beer around on the table, then remembered to put it on the coaster. "That kind of sounds nice."

"It's boring. Trust me. I'd rather be working and getting paid."

"Of course. I just mean that these days, I'm always at someone's beck and call. My boss, my kids, my wife. Not that I mind, you know, it's just sometimes it would be nice to have absolutely nothing to do and no one to disappoint."

Stephen looked at him a long moment. "I'm sure you're not disappointing."

Joe felt his face heat. "Of course not, I don't mean that. I don't know why I said that." He laughed and tried very hard not to swipe his hand over his face.

"Looky who's here!" A slender man with peroxide blonde hair came sauntering down the bar, looking at Joe and waving.

"Oh no," Stephen muttered.

"Have I met this person?" Joe asked through his teeth as he smiled and waved at the approaching man.

"Not yet," Stephen muttered. Then he turned and grimaced at the newcomer. "Hi Mae."

Joe tried not to frown disapprovingly at him, but for heaven's sake, Mae was a woman's name. Perhaps it was one of those strange fraternity names, like what rich fellows at Harvard called each other in novels.

"Joe, this is Mae," Stephen said painfully. "Mae, this is Joe."

"The so—"

"—My friend from high school."

"Oh, a pleasure to meet you, Joe." Mae offered his hand like royalty, like he expected Joe to kiss his ring. Joe twisted his own hand and managed to shake it.

"Pleasure's all mine," Joe said. "Is Mae . . . short for something?"

"Mae West. Because I'm her spitting image, can't you tell?" Mae laughed outrageously and patted his hair. Stephen had his head in his hand and looked like he was trying to hide under the table. Joe pursed his lips. Well, this Mae was certainly a character, but surely Stephen didn't need to be embarrassed to know him. He seemed like a hilarious fellow, full of slapstick humor and theatrics. Perhaps a little eccentric, but Joe liked interesting people. It was much better than talking about carburetors for four hours.

"Why don't you join us, Mae?" Joe said and stood. "Sorry, I have to leave in a bit, so do you mind scooting in?"

"Not at all, darling," Mae replied and winked at him as he slid into the booth. "I'm so delighted to finally meet you. I've heard *so* much about you."

"You have?" Stephen asked guardedly.

"All good things, all good things," Mae assured. "From Frank, you know. He said you were charming company last weekend at the Coney."

Joe perked up. "Oh. That's very nice of him to say."

"I'm sure it was. And Frank Atlas doesn't say nice things as a matter of course, so take it to heart as the compliment it is."

"Atlas? Is that his real name?"

"No," Stephen grumbled. "Everyone around here gets ridiculous nicknames."

"Oh." Joe tried not to look too eager. He had such a mundane name. He wouldn't turn his nose up at a nickname that made no sense to anyone else but his friends. Perhaps if he made his Thursday drinks a long-term habit, he might get one someday. "What's yours, Stephen?"

"Vinny," he replied. "It's just short for my last name."

"No, it's not!" Mae crowed. "It's short for Vincent Price on account of that *horrible* mustache you tried to grow last year."

Joe almost spit beer he laughed so hard. "You had a

mustache?"

"I thought it would help me make more sales at work," Stephen sniffed.

"Did it?" Mae asked.

"Inconclusive," Stephen bristled.

"It makes a comeback from time to time," Mae said to Joe conspiratorially.

"It does not!" Stephen argued.

"Well, the way you grow body hair, darling, one need only to sneeze, and you've got a beard like Rip Van Wrinkle."

Mae wasn't wrong. Stephen had a 5 o'clock shadow and it was only 4:30. He ran his hand over his dimpled chin like he was checking for unwanted growth. Joe laughed again and was pleased to note that one corner of Stephen's mouth twitched up too. His left cheek was just scarcely beginning to dimple.

By the time 5 o'clock came around, Joe had met the two girls he'd seen Stephen and Frank with before. Their names were Marge (the surly one) and Violet (the pretty blonde). He stuck around just long enough to be polite, but then had to beg off if he was going to get home in time to change. Everyone wished him a lovely time listening to Italian, and he left the bar with a smile on his lips that he couldn't shake all the way back to his parking spot.

✦

It was very difficult to be carried away by a story when all the words were in a different language. Throughout the opera, which turned out to be La Traviata, Joe watched people in colorful costumes flit around the stage, singing loudly and incomprehensibly, while he wondered what Stephen and his friends were doing.

Joe wasn't sure how long they usually stayed at Kreuger's. After all, the Winter Carnival was sort of a special occasion. But none of them seemed to have children or families to go home to, so it wasn't outside the realm of possibility that they might spend all evening visiting in that cozy back booth.

Marge and Violet seemed nice. Joe wondered whether they were dating any of the fellows. Marge was awfully crass and sort of mannish, but Violet seemed like a perfectly adequate date, if perhaps a little vapid. He couldn't help but notice how eccentric Stephen's set was, but he was determined not to be boring about it. He liked interesting people. Even if they were a little queer, it didn't mean that they should be outcast or avoided. Joe was married, he didn't need to worry that anyone would get the wrong idea. Besides, even if Mae did tell horrifically dirty jokes, he still made Joe laugh. (Perhaps more out of shock than humor, but did it really matter when just the act of laughing felt like such a relief?)

The opera really felt like a waste of a babysitter. Marion was so affable, it might have been nice to bring her to Kreuger's and introduce her to everyone. She got on famously with pretty much anyone she met, and perhaps she would improve Joe's own reputation, given he was terrible at conversing with most people. It took so much effort to think of what to say; he admired Marion's skill with it.

But when the opera ended, he didn't say anything about getting a drink after. He just listened as Marion railed against the ending (the heroine died; it had been wholly unnecessary, from what Joe could glean) and drove them back home to their corner lot in Little

Bohemia.

When they arrived, Marion made a beeline to the liquor cabinet and mixed martinis. Oh damn, that was right. And the children were gone overnight at Marion's mother's house. There was no getting out of it. Joe's shoulders tightened under the pressure to make a better showing than he had last night. He sipped his martini and let his head press back against the antimacassar while she talked.

"I don't really understand what they were trying to do with Violetta," Marion was saying, waving a hand in emphasis.

I didn't really understand anything they were trying to do because it was all in Italian, Joe thought but didn't say.

"She's a courtesan with a heart of gold. Okay, yes, we get it. She has to have a heart of gold otherwise she'd be a bad example. But then why make her a courtesan to begin with? It's like they want her character to be everything and nothing, all at once. Be alluring, but be pure. Be available, but be steadfast. If I didn't know better, I'd think the fellow who wrote the thing was indulging in a fantasy of how he'd capture the heart of a woman who, in reality, was very much not interested in him. The entire plot hinges on Violetta being a courtesan, like her having sex out of wedlock was an irreparable blot on her character. And no one, not even Alfredo, seems to question that."

Joe tried to nod encouragingly, but she must have noticed the way he locked up when she mentioned sex, because she continued, "We waited until we were married to have sex, but I'm wondering now why. Why did we have to do that? I don't think anything would have changed. Before our wedding, I'd convinced myself it was some sort of wild, irredeemable thing we could never take back. But it's just fun. Well, fun that sometimes results in babies, but that isn't a fate worse than death or anything."

Joe was bright red now. He couldn't help it.

"Oh, don't be so bashful, Joe. If you can do it, you can talk about it, can't you?"

No, he certainly could not. He wasn't even sure he could do it anymore, so talking about it was right out.

"Joe, come on." Marion smiled and sat on the arm of his chair, very nearly on his knee. He looked up at her, and she reached out to caress his cheek. It did feel nice when she did that. "Maybe we just need to try something new?"

He thought about turning her over on her knees, grabbing fistfuls of her rear-end while he pushed into her. He couldn't even begin to articulate why he thought this might help. It made the act feel more animalistic, maybe, which was both shameful and perhaps freeing. She couldn't look at him with expectation or tenderness that way. Joe couldn't say any of this. He could scarcely bear thinking it. So he just shrugged and gave a slight nod.

Marion bit her lip and grinned. "Oh Joe, you're like a tomato. Does that mean you have an idea?"

Joe shook his head furiously. Which was ridiculous because he did have an idea, and what if it did help? What if it was the key they needed? What if she liked it? He would never know if he didn't try.

Marion leaned down, cupped his cheek, and gave him a long, tender kiss that tasted like gin and olive juice. "Why don't I just go get out of this getup and you can join me when you're ready?"

Joe blinked at her. His throat felt tight but he managed, "Sure."

Marion smiled, that sweet, sort of pitying but also

hopeful smile that Joe had learned to hate. That smile either portended or confirmed his woeful inadequacy. Then, she stood and did a little sashay as she walked to the back bedroom.

Once she was gone, Joe slid down in the chair and pushed his hand over his face. He was so flushed he was a little sweaty. Dear god, he absolutely could not screw this up two days in a row. Actually, it had been a long time since it had worked out. She hadn't had an interest at all when Linda was a baby and refused to sleep through the night. He was sure they'd done it since then, but now that he was thinking about it, he couldn't be sure. He looked down at the martini glass in his hand and drank it down in one gulp. Then, he went to the liquor cabinet and swilled another shot of gin. Just for safety. He was not going to mess this up again.

He could hear Marion humming in the back bedroom. She'd tried playing music once. Joe had just felt more humiliated, like Frank Sinatra was witnessing his shame.

Joe went into the bathroom and pushed the door closed behind him. He looked up into the medicine cabinet mirror and grimaced. *You're a goddamn lucky sonofabitch to have a woman like her. Get it together, man.*

He begrudgingly unbuttoned his trousers and made use of the facilities quickly and efficiently. Then he closed his eyes tight and pulled on himself a bit. It wouldn't hurt to get a little head start on things. She would like it if he was ready for her.

He'd been ready for her when they got married. More than. This didn't used to be so difficult. She enjoyed it so much, Joe'd been relieved. He'd worried he wouldn't know what he was doing. He'd never so much as kissed a girl before her, at least not more than a brief kiss good-night. He and Stephen had taken out plenty of girls, but none of them been particularly interested in him. It made sense. Stephen was charming, handsome, and easy to get along with. Joe was gangly and awkward and couldn't string more than a sentence or two together. The fact that Marion wanted him still surprised him, even a wedding and two kids later. And if he couldn't get this problem under control, she'd realize she'd settled far below herself and resent him for the rest of their lives.

God, it wasn't working. He had to think about things that were arousing. Kissing and naked bodies and touching forbidden places. He thought about breasts. Marion of course had a great pair. Some football player had told him so at a party his senior year of high school. *That girl has a great rack, but she don't put out*, he'd said. And Joe had ended up with her. He'd felt proud when he'd married her that fall. She was gorgeous, and she was all his.

Stephen had been at that party too. And all of a sudden, Joe remembered what had happened at that party and dropped his hands to his sides. No. He didn't think about that party. Especially not while doing what he was doing.

"Everything okay in there?" Marion's voice was artificially light.

"Yup," Joe replied. "Just wanted to wash up a little."

"Okay," she called.

Try something new, she'd said. Well, he was in such a pickle, he was willing to try just about anything.

Joe squeezed his eyes shut and let the memory come. He'd hated that party. It was so loud, and everyone was drinking. He'd drank some malt liquor, and it hadn't sat well with him, so he'd gone upstairs to sit in one of the bedrooms. Stephen had found him there, wondering if he was okay. He'd sat next to him on the bed, and they'd talked for a long time, about graduation and college and what they'd do with their lives now that they were grown, passing a bottle back and forth. Joe had been maudlin, and Stephen had held him close to comfort him, like always. But Joe had been drunk, and Stephen had been so close, rubbing his shoulder, his fingers sort of just playing at the edge of his collar. So it sort of just happened, entirely without his thinking about it. And Stephen had noticed and, well. Helped him out.

They hadn't kissed or anything. It had been quiet and brief, and Joe had probably made a goddamn fool of himself, because it had felt so good, so incredibly good. The first touch was the best touch, Joe was certain, better than anything he could have imagined and certainly better than anything he'd known since. Stephen had tough hands and a firm grip. It had barely taken any time at all.

Joe shivered at the memory he had suppressed for so long, and his body snatched its indulgence from him before he realized what was happening, and then it was too late. It felt too good to stop, the image of his hand working up and down his length overlaid with the memory of Stephen doing it. He shuddered over the open toilet, snatching breath in short bursts.

Joe opened his eyes.

Well, it had worked. Too well.

✦

Chapter 6

Stephen was beginning to look forward to Thursdays. He'd worked an early shift today, and he had a stocking gig later, so he got to Kreuger's early. What he really should have done was go home and sleep, but he couldn't make himself be responsible. Not when it was Thursday. Turned out Red was the only one there, so he ended up talking to him at the bar for a while to kill time.

"Are you waiting for someone?" Red asked around five. He had a slight accent, Russian or something. He was old enough to have come over on a boat after the Russian Revolution, after all.

"What? No."

"Because you keep looking over my shoulder at the door. Like you're waiting for someone."

Stephen had the self-awareness to be embarrassed. "No. I just have a temp job for third shift, so I'm hoping to run into a few more people before I have to go."

Red nodded and tossed a dollar on the bar. "Hope he's worth waiting for."

And like an absolute asshole, he just sauntered out of the bar, leaving that little jab poking out of Stephen's chest. And fate was an asshole, too, because Joe Milner slipped through the door right as Red left. Red held the damn thing open for him.

Joe saw Stephen immediately and smiled. It was the small smile, not the big grin that sometimes flew around when he'd been drinking, and Stephen had to admit that he really enjoyed how his green eyes stayed round and reeling. There was something so comforting about Joe being uncomfortable.

"Hey, good to see you," Stephen said as Joe walked up to the bar beside him.

"Yeah, you're a sight for sore eyes," Joe replied and the smile cracked a bit.

Stephen tried not to preen as Joe shook his hand, solid and firm. "How was the opera?"

"Oh, you know. Loud and confusing. There was a courtesan? She had some lovers, they fought over her, she died of heartbreak or TB, I'm not quite sure which."

"I truly could not tell you which opera that is."

"It's not all of them?"

Stephen laughed and pulled out a cigarette while Joe ordered himself a Hamms. "So what's new?"

Joe sighed. "I found a crack in our ceiling that's turned out to be from a minor leak in the roof. It's not a big issue now, since the snow's all frozen, but I have to get to the bottom of it before the thaw, or it'll be a much bigger issue. But I'm exhausted thinking about that. What have you been up to?"

"Oh, nothing much," Stephen said on an exhale of tobacco smoke. "I did a stint as a waiter on Saturday for the big Valentine's Day event at the Ryan Hotel. Got to wear a monkey suit and everything."

"I bet that was something to see," Joe smiled.

Stephen caught himself leaning in and stopped, turning back toward the bar. "Yeah, it was pretty glamorous. Lots of sparkling rhinestones and sweeping silk gowns. Money and alcohol, an elegant combination until about midnight, when the wives started getting sloppy and the fellows' eyes started wandering."

Joe gave a huff of a laugh and thanked Mrs. Kreuger as she handed him his beer. "Any exciting revelations I need to know about the city elite? Strictly in my capacity as future comptroller, of course."

"Yes, I'm surprised you weren't invited, now that you're heir apparent," Stephen said. "I thought I'd see you with your pretty wife on your arm, all spruced up."

Joe's eyes flicked up then, and Stephen got the sense that those kinds of reminders were unwelcome. Perhaps his wife was among the things he didn't want to be exasperated by. Well. Stephen flicked his cigarette against a nearby ashtray. If Joe was indeed lurking at Kreuger's to avoid going home, Stephen had no compunction about being the alternative he chose. Even though that smacked of a slippery slope that would leave Stephen crumpled at the bottom with a broken heart.

"I don't think the comptroller does a lot of the hob-nobbing, which I'll admit is a relief. I would be terrible at that."

"Hobnobbing?"

"Yeah. I can't talk to people."

"Really? You're talking to one now."

"You're different. I know you."

Stephen felt his heart lurch, and he dragged hard on his cigarette. "I suppose, but you talked with Mae West last week with very little trouble. And she's a celebrity."

Joe laughed, and Stephen swelled.

"So, is the city election in April going to change your position?" Stephen asked. He'd made the connection reading the newspaper that morning, and he wondered if a measure of the tension Joe carried into the bar every Thursday was connected to city politics.

Joe tipped his head consideringly. "It could, but unless there's a big upset, my boss is clear to win reelection."

"That bodes well for your future. Wait, how are you being groomed to be the next city comptroller if it's an elected position? Does that mean you plan to run for office?" Stephen could hardly imagine Joe door-knocking to convince people to vote for him.

Joe shrugged and pushed his beer around in small circles, spreading the ring of moisture underneath it. It wasn't exactly the response of an eager candidate that Stephen might expect. "Yeah. My boss doesn't plan to move on for another term, obviously, since he's running for reelection, but I think he has his eyes on a city council seat in '56. He'll want me to backfill and keep the comptroller office stable."

"Is that what you want?"

"Of course—city finances suffer a lot from administrative changes, just from loss of institutional knowledge alone. It's important to maintain financial stability if the mayor wants to get his agenda through quickly. I don't really understand why the office of comptroller is elected anyway. Seems to me it would benefit from the stability of a long-term civil servant."

Stephen put this through his Joe Milner translator. It was rusty from disuse, but he still had higher fluency than most. "So you do want to become the comptroller, but you don't want to run for it?"

Joe gave a sigh. "Yeah. That would be ideal. But I don't make the rules, of course, so I'll grit my teeth through it. My boss said he'd help make sure it all goes smooth. Besides, it's not like I have any skeletons in my closet or anything."

Stephen frowned. Just Joe's presence at Kreuger's would count as a skeleton in some voters' book.

"Vinny and... hey, it's Joe!"

Oh great, Frank Atlas had arrived. Objectively, Stephen should be grateful because Frank could play straight better than almost anyone else from their set, except for maybe Walter, but Stephen was still having nightmares about the possibility that Joe might be trick-fodder for him, and he couldn't help but want to keep Joe as far away from Frank as he could. Strictly for his protection from Frank's high likelihood of venereal disease, of course. Oh, and more generally to keep Joe safe from himself. He wasn't like some of these married guys—he was honorable and shy and seemingly devoted to his wife. Not to mention his reluctant ambition for political office. Shit. Stephen needed to get his head on straight.

"Oh, hi Frank," Joe said with a half smile and turned on his barstool to shake Frank's hand. "You care to join us? Or should we head to the usual booth?"

The usual booth? Stephen did not know how he felt about Joe assuming he was one of the boys now, especially considering that he was, for all practical intents and purposes, *not* one of the boys. That kind of ignorance could get a fellow into trouble with this crew. Stephen took a drag and glared at Frank as soon as Joe looked away from him. Frank didn't appear to notice.

"Let's get the booth, why not?" Frank said jovially and slapped Joe's shoulder. Guess they were going to the booth, then. Stephen picked up his beer and followed. Frank got there first, and Joe sat down across from him. Stephen was left with the devil's choice of either sitting next to Frank and risking Joe thinking that they were more than begrudging rivals, or sitting next to Joe and having Frank tease him for the rest of his life. Stephen chose the latter. Frank already teased him anyway, so what did it really matter?

It was a mistake, though. As soon as he sat down, Stephen was forced to acknowledge the unholy awareness of Joe just six inches away from him. Maybe his forgiveness had worn off. Or maybe he'd spent too many years shamelessly cruising married men and now it was a habit he couldn't shake. Stephen and Joe would be thigh to thigh when the others arrived, just like they had in high school. The echo of that long-ago intimacy would be special sort of bespoke torture made just for Stephen. He hurriedly reassured himself that he could leave at any time. He didn't have to endure this. Of course, he didn't make any move to leave.

"So what did you do for Valentine's Day, Frank?" Joe said so conversationally, Stephen almost ribbed him again for saying he wasn't good at talking to people.

Frank's eyes went positively devilish. Stephen gave him a warning glare. "Nothing much," he said with a smirk. "I didn't have a date so I just went to the bathhouse."

Stephen tried to murder him with a glance. It didn't work.

"Bathhouse?" Joe said, puzzled. "Don't you have a bathtub where you live?"

Frank made a doleful expression. "No. It's not so bad, though. It's actually pretty fun—"

"Thanks Frank, but I could do without the play by play of you washing your toes," Stephen cut in, just in time. Frank was good at playing it straight, but he was also a shameless cruiser. This wasn't the first time Stephen had noticed him looking at Joe like Wile E. Coyote eyeing the road runner. It didn't help that Stephen still couldn't tell whether Frank wasn't what Joe was looking for, either, a thought that he hadn't managed to dislodge from his craw since the Winter Carnival. "What did you do for Valentine's, Joe? Take your wife anywhere nice?"

Joe shrank slightly again, like any mention of his wife made him instantly feel guilty. Frank noticed too, and a sly grin crept across his stupid mouth. Cripes, maybe Stephen should just leave and let Frank try his luck. Either Joe would go along, get his rocks off, and disappear, or he'd be horrified and disappear. Or Joe and Frank would fall in love and Joe would leave his wife and they'd get an apartment together and Stephen would have to watch the whole thing and pretend like he was happy for them. Again.

Nope. Definitely not, under any circumstances, letting Frank try his luck.

"Well, like I told Stephen, I took her to the opera last Thursday, so we—"

" —Oh, you were here last Thursday? Sorry I missed you," Frank simpered. Stephen tried to grind his heel into that great lummox's foot, but he missed.

"Yeah, I could only stop by for one quick drink, and then I had to skedaddle," Joe explained. "We saw La Travail or something—"

"La Traviata," Stephen corrected.

"Yeah, that's the one. Anyway, since we made a big night of it on Thursday, we didn't really do anything on Sunday for Valentine's."

"Sure, but you got her chocolates or something, didn't you?" Frank said, crossing his arms to the benefit of his large biceps.

"Oh, jeez. I probably should have, shouldn't I?" Joe looked down into his beer forlornly.

"Yeah, you probably should," Frank winced. "It's not too late to do it today!"

"Yeah," Stephen piled on, because watching Joe realize a mistake in real time was like watching a dog through the bars at the pound. "Actually, it probably would mean more, because it's not some socially-mandated holiday. If you brought them today, they'd be for no reason at all, other than because you were thinking about her."

Joe studied his beer, his face scrunched tight. He sighed. "I suppose you're right..." he conceded at length.

"Hey, what are you doing? Making the new guy cry?" It was Marge, and she was flanked by Dickie and Walter.

Stephen glowered at them. "No one's crying."

"We're just teaching Joe how to woo his wife," Frank winked.

Stephen gave him a sidelong glance. It was an imposition in the extreme, bringing a married fellow into their group. Kreuger's was one of the only places he and his friends could socialize openly. But he selfishly wondered if perhaps it would have a moderating effect on his friends. If nothing else, talk of Joe's wife would remind everyone that Joe was off limits, and not just because he was Stephen's high school soulmate (dear god, he should *never* have told them that). Marge and Walter and Dickie weren't any sort of threat, happily coupled as they were, but Frank and Mae both cast wide nets, and then there were the other fellows who fell in with them from time to time. As much as he wanted Joe to keep coming around, but he didn't want to shock him too badly.

Damn Frank, inviting him to the booth. If Stephen could have it his own way, he'd have stayed at the bar with Joe on his own. Then he wouldn't have to run interception on bathhouse comments. But he also didn't want to miss out on visiting with his friends. He was selfish, dammit, and wanted to spend time with Joe and his friends both. In fact, if he could guarantee Joe wouldn't balk at crass talk, he wouldn't mind letting Joe into the circle, as long as he also didn't end up being a notch in anyone's bed post. And if he could ensure it didn't blow up Joe's political career, and then, therefore, the lives of everyone else. All of this was a massive red flag, but Stephen couldn't manage to care when Joe's green eyes were peering over his beer not six inches away from him.

Those inches shrank pretty quickly as Marge, Dickie, and Walter scooted in, and then Mae and Violet showed up not five minutes later. Stephen was on the end next to Joe, thigh to thigh—thing of wonders, thing of nightmares. Frank was on the other side of Joe, a perfect little sandwich, and he engaged Joe with ready conversation about sports and other manly watercooler chatter. Stephen smoked another cigarette, finished his beer, and chimed in to the multiple conversations ricocheting around the booth, swallowing any panic that threatened to bubble up by insisting to himself that he felt nothing at all and everything was completely normal.

"Are you all going to be able to make it on Saturday?" Walter asked when there was a lull in the conversations. Frank and Mae nodded, and Violet said, "Of course."

"Yeah, I might be a little late, because I work until five," Stephen said.

"Late to what?" asked Joe.

"Walter and I are having a little dinner party on Saturday," Dickie said, leaning his shoulder against Walter's in a way that could not be mistaken for anything else. "Would you like to come?"

Stephen tried to catch Dickie's eye and shake his head in a stilted, subtle way that Joe wouldn't notice. He was already worried enough that Joe would be scared off by his friends at Kreuger's. If he was invited to one of Dickie's parties, where the cocktails flowed and everyone knew there was no Mrs. Kreuger to patrol for obscenities, he would get much more than an earful.

Joe's eyes brightened considerably. "Uh, yeah, that would be great. Where is it?"

Dickie's generous mouth crept into a smile, and he gave Stephen a slight lift of his brows before he said, "We have a little bachelor pad in Capitol Heights. We like to entertain. I'll write down the address for you." Dickie pulled a pen out of Walter's breast pocket and started writing primly on a coaster. As an afterthought, he added, "You're welcome to invite your wife." It wasn't the most enthusiastic endorsement, but it was more generous than Stephen expected from Dickie.

Joe was grinning, accepting the address. "Thanks. I sincerely doubt we can get a babysitter at such short notice, but it's nice of you to ask. More often than not, we have to divide and conquer. She spends a lot of time with her Ladies' Auxiliary, so I'm sure she won't mind if I make plans for myself for once."

Dickie gave Stephen a hard stare, mouth firm and eyebrows expectant. Stephen pretended not to notice.

Joe was late getting home. He'd had two beers at Kreuger's instead of one and also stopped at the drugstore for some chocolates for Marion, like Frank and Stephen had suggested. Silver lining, he had a peace offering in hand.

As he drove through Seven Corners, he rubbed his hand absently down his right thigh. Once everyone had arrived, he'd been pressed up against Stephen, and he was having a hard time not remembering every other time Stephen had ever done that. It was awful. Joe had been so good at not thinking about that graduation party, but after last week, it seemed like he'd forgotten how. He wasn't sleeping any better than normal, but now he was revisiting that memory like a security blanket, staring at the crack in the ceiling and thinking about how Stephen's hair smelled and whether or not he'd actually felt Stephen's lips on his neck or if that was an embellishment he'd added later.

Marion had been gracious as usual after he'd completely blown it in the bathroom the other night. She'd kissed on him and tried all her usual tricks, because he couldn't bear to admit to her that he'd already finished by himself. If he did, he'd run the risk of her asking why and there was no possible way he could explain. The memory was off limits. At least, it was supposed to be.

The trouble was, the persistent memory was getting all mixed up with the Stephen he was re-befriending now, and it was sort of embarrassing. At the bar today, when Stephen had lit his cigarette and took a drag, Joe had the intrusive thought about whether his memory of those lips on his neck was real or imagined. How if he felt them again, he'd be able to conclusively test the theory. He'd unlocked the memory as an efficient means to an end, but it'd been too efficient and now it was entirely inconvenient; the way it was intruding into his actual interactions with Stephen was a problem.

It wasn't a problem Joe couldn't solve, though. He just had to focus harder on the present, remember that Stephen deserved better, and he would be fine. He was good at hiding his feelings; he was pretty sure Stephen wouldn't notice. And if Joe's life so far was any indication, nothing ever came of thoughts like that anyway, so what did it matter?

When Joe got home, he apologized for being so late

and handed Marion the chocolates. She was a little puzzled, but mostly tickled, and the children convinced her to give them each a piece before bedtime.

Later, as he was getting undressed, he was reminded of the address in his pocket and the invitation to Dickie's dinner party. When he joined Marion in bed, he interrupted her reading to say, "I've been invited to a dinner party."

Marion put her book down. "Really? That's wonderful. When is it?"

"Saturday," Joe said with a wince.

"Oh, that's soon," Marion said. "But maybe we can find a neighborhood kid to babysit? I don't want you to have to say no."

"No, I don't either," Joe said, pushing his brows together like he was puzzled. "Actually, you know what? What if I just went on my own this time? Then we wouldn't have to bother with a babysitter."

"You mean I stay behind?"

"Well, yeah. They're just a bunch of fellows from the bar. I don't think anyone else is bringing their wives." This was one hundred percent true, since none of the Kreuger's crowd were married. That he knew of, he supposed. "You'd probably be bored anyway."

"Oh," Marion said thoughtfully. "I'm sure that'll be fine. You'll have to tell me all about it on Sunday."

"Yup."

✳

Chapter 7

Joe headed out at five o'clock on the dot on Saturday evening, pecking Marion on the cheek and patting the children's heads, telling them not to wait up. He was fizzing with excitement at the night that lay ahead. It had been so long since he'd socialized with other fellows, independently from Marion. Nearly everything they did, they did together. Marion was right—he needed his own friends, his own social life.

He arrived at the address Dickie had written down at 5:23 and parked, waiting in his Ford Anglia outside the apartment building until the clock hands ticked to 5:30. He was about to get out of his car when there was a knock on his window. It was so unexpected, Joe nearly jumped out of his skin before he rolled down the window.

"Hey, Four-Eyes, what are you doing? Waiting in your car?" Frank asked, stooping down to look at him through the window like a cop.

Joe scrambled his glasses off and tried not to look sheepish. "I didn't want to be early. My wife hates it when people show up early and rush her."

Frank gave him a bemused smile. "That's very thoughtful of you. Here, we can walk up together."

He gestured for Joe to roll the window back up, which he did, and then pulled the door open for Joe like a valet.

Joe climbed out of the driver's seat a little self-consciously. "Thanks."

"Think nothing of it," Frank said with a grin. He was a huge man, taller than even Joe by an inch or two, and broadly proportional. His neck looked like it could snap his tie.

"You're looking very well turned out," Joe commented. He cleared his throat, finding his voice a little hoarse.

Frank preened. "Thank you. Dickie likes these things to be very civilized. He likes most things like that. Probably why he prefers Walter to me."

Joe's heart lurched in his chest. He hadn't expected Frank to be so…blunt. He blinked hard and tried to train his expression, then looked up at Frank. "Oh?"

Frank just shrugged affably, like he'd said nothing out of the ordinary. "That's alright. He's not the only boy with a pretty mouth in the world." Then he looked down at Joe and winked.

Joe looked away quickly, blood rushing in his ears. He'd seen Frank leave the Coney with a man. He'd seen how Dickie and Walter were with each other. They shared an apartment and hosted dinner parties together. He'd met Mae West, for heaven's sake. He understood, intellectually, that they were queer, both in the interesting and exceptional way, and in the more double-entendre way. He just hadn't been quite this confronted with it before. He glanced at Frank sidelong.

"Stephen is," Joe started, then realized he could not bear to make himself comment on the qualities of Stephen's mouth, regardless of whether or not he'd been harboring a preoccupation with it as of late. "Stephen is very nice."

Frank scoffed. "He is nothing of the sort. A viper disguised as a man, really. But he's a solid friend, if that's what you mean."

"I do mean that," Joe said. He was twisting his gloves in his hands. He wasn't sure what he was allowed to say. "I've known him for a long time, and behind his sarcasm is real, genuine humor and care. I just don't think you should write him off so easily."

Frank raised an eyebrow at him as he held the gate of the brick apartment building's courtyard open for him. "Hm. Maybe I won't." He led Joe to the door of the building and pressed one of the buzzers. "Maybe you shouldn't either."

Joe furrowed his brows and shook his head. What was that supposed to mean?

The door buzzed open, and Frank showed Joe upstairs to the appointed apartment. At the sound of their knock, Dickie opened the door, wearing a sumptuous velvet smoking jacket with a carefully matching silk tie.

"There you are! Welcome. Now we're just waiting for Vinny. Come in, come in."

Joe followed Frank in through the door and noticed Dickie giving him the once-over, like he was deciding whether or not Joe was civilized enough to attend his dinner party. Joe desperately hoped he would not be found wanting by someone who made Gene Kelly look gauche.

"The bar's over there," Dickie directed. "Mae's making martinis, and they're deadly, so make sure to drink a few. Otherwise we won't have any fun!"

Mae had hip checked the bar cart and was shaking a martini shaker with a feral grin on his face. For a split second, Joe entertained the concern that perhaps he had not fallen in with the sympathetic sort of queers, but a more predatory brand, but then he saw Marge and her blonde friend, Violet, chatting on the sofa, and he shook that thought right out of his head.

"Do you like to dance, Mr. Milner?" Violet asked with a pretty smile. She was a stocky sort of girl, built for farm labor and childbearing, with her soft, golden hair done up in a fashionable bob. She had on a nice purple evening dress with little wrist-length gloves.

"I'm afraid I have two left feet," Joe said apologetically.

Violet frowned, and Marge nudged her with her shoulder. She was wearing trousers, as usual, with a button-up blouse and sweater that made her look like a short, fine-boned college letterman. "Don't sulk, Vi. Vinny will dance with you when he gets here."

"Oh yeah," Violet perked up.

"Besides, all of Dickie's records are classical dreck," Marge continued.

"I heard that!"

"Can't dance a step to any of it. If he had a polka record, that would be one thing—"

"Don't make me come over there!" Dickie shouted. He was in the doorway to the little galley kitchen where Walter's shadow labored over the stove. Joe couldn't help but grin at the familial discord.

Frank was at the bar cart holding a glass while Mae poured hazy liquid from the martini shaker.

"Would you ladies like a drink?" Joe asked.

"I already have one," Violet said, displaying her glass.

"I'll take another one if you don't mind," Marge put in, holding up her empty martini glass. "Thanks for playing go-fer, Milner."

"My pleasure," Joe replied and took her glass over to the bar cart. Mae was keen, like how Joe's son was about frogs and rocks, only Mae's object of fascination was the chemistry of alcohol.

"Come, try this, Sleeping Beauty," Mae directed, waving him in with his hands. "It's my signature martini. I call it the Gay Nineties."

Joe scarcely processed what he said. Did he just receive a charming nickname?

Frank took a sip. "Cripes, that's stiff!"

"It's 90 proof," Mae grinned.

"I sincerely doubt that," Frank said skeptically. "What makes it gay?"

"You, darling. When you finish it," Mae winked at Joe. "It's a nod to Mae West's oeuvre. You ever see a Mae West movie?"

"Uh, I think so?" Joe hedged politely.

"She and Cary Grant did a whole slew of them back in the thirties. I grew up going to those movies."

"Oh, I'm sorry, I don't really recall seeing any of them in particular."

"*Klondike Annie*, maybe? Or *She Done Him Wrong*?"

Joe shrugged helplessly. Just then, the buzzer sounded again, and Dickie bustled across the living room. "That must be Vinny!" He pressed the button on the wall and hovered near the door. Joe took the martini back to Marge on the sofa.

"One Gay Nineties cocktail for you," he said. Marge and Violet collapsed into giggles. Well actually, they both brayed like donkeys, so nothing was particularly giggly about it. It was a pretty funny cocktail name, given the company. Joe wasn't sure if it was polite to laugh too.

A knock sounded at the door, and Dickie swung it open.

"Vinny, you're here!" Dickie leaned in and gave Stephen a kiss on the cheek, but Stephen's eyes were already on Joe. And Joe was of course looking at Stephen, who was the new arrival and everything. He was definitely not thinking about that sleepover at Joe's grandma's they'd had in high school. They'd stayed up into the small hours of the morning talking about everything under the sun, and agreed that they'd been born to be friends. Soulmates, Joe had said. Good god, how embarrassing. He hoped Stephen didn't remember that.

Joe felt a heavy arm over his shoulder and looked up at Frank, who had a cigarette in his mouth.

"Hey Dickie, you don't mind if I smoke, do you?"

"No, there's an ashtray on the coffee table. Vinny, Mae's making cocktails so go help yourself."

Frank looked down at Joe with a crooked smile, holding out his cigarette pack. "You want one?"

Joe looked at the cigarettes, then back at Stephen, who was sauntering over to Mae with his hands in his pockets, apparently unhurried to say hello. "Sure."

Joe plucked a cigarette out of the pack and Frank flicked his lighter for Joe.

"Yes!" declared Violet from the sofa. She had a case of records at her feet and was holding one aloft. "Duke Ellington!"

She stood and brought the record to the player that sat in one corner. It was an old Victrola, a taller, narrow speaker cabinet covered in tweed and a lid that opened on the top.

Joe plucked the cigarette from his lips as he turned out from under Frank's arm. "Thanks," he said absently, then crossed over to Violet as she called out, "Vinny, you'll dance with me, won't you?"

Stephen was a few feet away at the bar cart, getting Mae's run down of the ingredients to his Gay Nineties martini. "Sure, I'll be right there."

"What's on this?" Joe asked, coming to Violet's side and peering over at the album sleeve.

"'Vagabonds,'" Violet said, pointing with a finger. "Let's see, ooh, 'Mood Indigo'."

"'Mood Indigo?'" Marge had perked up.

Violet looked over her shoulder at her and grinned. She was pretty when she smiled like that. "You thinking about dancing, Margie?"

Marge raised a brow at her, then glanced around at the other fellows. "Maybe. Let me smoke first."

Joe looked at Marge for a moment, then back at Violet's fond expression, the way she tucked a lock of hair behind her ear and smiled this private little smile. And then Joe realized Marge and Violet weren't going on dates with any of these fellows, or any fellows at all for that matter.

"Hey, Joe, how you been?" Stephen said. Joe turned and accepted the genial handshake.

"Great. You?"

"Ducky. You drinking this swill?"

"Hey, I resemble that remark!" Mae called from where he was sashaying with the bar cart to the jazz trumpet opening the album.

"Mae, I swear to god, if you spill that industrial waste on my rug, I will end you," Dickie called, even as he took a glug of his own drink.

"Dinner's on in five minutes, ladies and gents!" This call came from Walter in the kitchen. "Dickie, get me one of those glasses of industrial waste."

"Fine. But you'll regret it," Dickie said. He begrudgingly crossed to the bar cart and glared at Mae while pouring the drink himself.

"Honestly," Joe said in a low voice to Stephen, eyes flicking down to his drink. "I haven't had the courage to try it yet."

Stephen dimpled. "It's deadly. Not because it tastes bad, but because it tastes like it's barely got any hooch in it at all."

Joe hunched his shoulders a bit to sip at his very full

glass. The drink tasted citrusy, with a strawberry flavor and that searing intensity that came with a drink that was mostly alcohol. "Oh no."

"Exactly."

Violet was dancing with Mae now, leading him around the room in a serviceable foxtrot. It was queer, a stout lady like her leading an effeminate man like him, but in a comforting way. A way that made the world feel much kinder and less brutal. For all the grief the Kreuger's crowd gave each other, they gave each other something no one else could—a place at the table, as a matter of course.

Mae West's drink was absolutely deadly. Within a half hour, everyone except Walter was nice and tight, just in time for dinner to be served. It was a full dinner, with a soup and salad course, then rice with mushroom sauce and lamb in some sort of mint sauce. It was a meal worthy of a supper club.

"Wow, this is delicious," Joe said as he sopped up mushroom sauce with his roll.

"Walter is an excellent cook," Dickie said in the proud, warm way a husband might praise his wife.

"You should have seen what he came up with for Thanksgiving," Stephen said. He'd been seated next to Joe with a carefully printed little name card at each place.

"Oh, yeah, he made these amazing cheese-stuffed pickles!" Frank exclaimed. "I still think about those little things."

"You could make them yourself, you know," Walter pointed out. "I shared the recipe with you."

Frank laughed like he'd dropped a punchline.

"But really," Joe said, "you could open a restaurant with food like this."

Walter glowed at the compliment as Dickie smiled a

little more weakly.

"That would be a dream," Walter said, "but I've got the golden handcuffs at the bank. I make too much now. I could never hope to make that much running a restaurant."

Dickie rubbed Walter's shoulder. "Someday, though."

"Someday," Walter agreed.

"That reminds me," Stephen said, "did you get that wine job at the Lexington, Dickie?"

Dickie curled his lip. "*Sommelier*, Vincent. And no," he sniffed, "their wine collection was miserable. There was nothing at all to work with, it would have required me to sacrifice my principles."

"Ah, well. To better pastures, then," Stephen raised his glass and the whole group toasted to the future.

"Speaking of futures, I was meaning to ask you, Joe," Walter said, "do you know this fellow who's running for mayor?"

Joe blinked away the urge to wince at the mention of work. "The incumbent or the challenger?"

"Can't tell, they're all named Joe," Stephen laughed. "Is that a problem at City Hall?"

"Or does it make life more convenient?" Mae West countered. "Imagine, no need to learn anyone's name. Everywhere you turn, all you need to do is call 'Joe!' and your every need will be fulfilled."

Joe smiled. "There are a lot of us. Some of us go by Joseph, but there are also plenty of Franks and Ralphs and Johns as well."

"Reasons more women need to be on city council," Marge said. "Although, I wouldn't be surprised if one of the lady candidates were named Josephine."

"It might help her campaign!" Mae declared. "She can shorten it to Jo. It'll help people at the polls feel more easier voting for a woman."

"There's not any ladies running for city council," Frank scoffed. "That's ridiculous."

"There are," Joe said. "Two, actually."

Frank made a perplexed face and pushed a forkful of lamb into his mouth. Joe was beginning to understand why Stephen didn't see Frank as a good conversation partner.

"I meant to ask about the challenger," Walter said, lassoing the conversation back to his purpose. "Joseph … Deacon? Dietmer?"

"Dillon," Joe corrected absently as he cut into his lamb. "I think he's got a good chance. He's got the labor endorsement."

"Oh, damn," Walter said. "Mr. Mayor better look out. Is everything chaos at City Hall in anticipation of the election?"

"Not in my office. But there's a lot of speculation flying around."

"Joe's boss has his own reelection clinched," Stephen added for the benefit of the rest.

"Yeah, he's pro-union, so he doesn't have too much trouble." Joe enjoyed how Stephen wove in his interjection, making it conversational. It made him feel a little less self-conscious talking about himself, even when he'd been asked.

"Ugh, enough politics," Dickie said with a roll of his eyes.

"Agreed," Joe said.

"I propose we spend the interim between dinner and dessert playing a party game," Dickie declared. "Charades, perhaps?"

Mae clapped his hands together as a few others lent their approval. Marge gave a loud groan. "Aw, come on.

Charades?"

"But you're so good at it!" Violet exclaimed.

"No, *you're* so good at it," Marge replied. "I just ride your coattails the whole way through."

Stephen leaned over toward Joe, who automatically moved in kind, like there was a magnetic pull between their heads. "Those two have the same brain," Stephen said under his breath. "There's no other possible explanation for the way they destroy everyone in charades."

"We'd better try to get on their team," Joe whispered back.

Stephen chuckled. "That's right. You like to win."

"Hard work pays off," Joe replied. "But I'll admit, I'm not any good at charades."

Chapter 8

Ten minutes saw the party move back to the living room, where Dickie passed around scraps of paper and pencils to everyone and collected prompts in a bowl. Stephen did his best to put in some easy ones because he knew his friends, and knew that if he didn't lob some softballs, Joe would be up shit creek without a paddle.

Stephen failed to get them on Marge and Violet's team. Dickie masterfully declared the teams in a matter-of-fact tone that brooked no argument while Walter lurked at Violet's side like a vulture. So Stephen and Joe ended up squeezed onto the spindly-legged sofa with Frank while Mae hovered near the bar cart, shaking the cocktail shaker and declaring that the real winner of charades was the one who wrought the most chaos. Suffice to say, Stephen didn't have a lot of hope for their success.

Mae refilled everyone's drinks as the game began. Violet went first as Marge set the kitchen timer to a minute.

"Okay," she said, drawing a scrap of paper from the bowl and studying it with her lip between her teeth. "Oh I think I know who wrote this."

"No talking!" Stephen accused. He was going in with a multitude of handicaps; he wasn't going to be soft on the rules.

Violet rolled her eyes, then shifted her shoulders and

hips, tipping her head to the side.

"Mae West!" Marge blurted.

Violet grinned and pointed at her. "You got it!"

"Who wrote it?" Joe asked their team as the others carried on furiously guessing the next prompts before the timer ran out.

"Me, of course," Mae tittered with a dramatic wrist flip.

Stephen rolled his eyes. Maybe he shouldn't have tossed in a bunch of softballs after all. "I hope somebody put some tough ones in there."

"I don't," Joe muttered. His hands were in fists on his thighs.

Stephen leaned into him. "Don't worry. I'm sure Walter put in something like 'fixed-rate annuity'. It won't all be inside jokes."

He wished he'd been more right about that than he turned out to be. Marge and Violet were prime evil. Marge had actually put in "that time we got ice cream after almost hitting a tractor outside of St. Michael." And Marge had acted it well enough that Violet got it within ten seconds.

"Hey, it's not really fair if Marge is stacking the deck for Vi," Stephen groused. "Maybe we should have two bowls, filled by the opposing team."

"But then all the prompts will be impossibly hard, and we won't be able to score," Dickie condescended.

"That's what he said," Frank muttered with a crooked grin.

Stephen tried to glower at Dickie and Frank at the same time, but they were both shameless hooligans seated at opposing sides of him, and the effort was wasted. He glanced surreptitiously at Joe. He was certainly not as at ease as he could be, but Stephen couldn't be sure if that was due to the queer jokes or Joe's nervous competitive streak. In high school, he'd always been keen to win, which often led him to refuse to play. He had a savvy for odds and they were usually not in his favor. Even social games set him on edge. Perhaps he was so focused on making a successful guess, he hadn't noticed Frank's crass joke.

Unfortunately, Frank was undeterred as the game proceeded. If Stephen didn't know better, he'd think he was purposefully trying to provoke Joe. To what purpose, who could say, but Stephen wasn't about to put up with it.

When Stephen got up and, after a nice run of correct guesses, drew the "pitcher" prompt, he did his best to square himself up and execute the gesture clearly the first time, in spite of the fact that the timer was about to buzz. Joe looked like he was trying hard not to stand as he blurted, "Throw! Ca—Pitch! Pitcher!"

Stephen grinned and pointed at him as the timer rang out. "Bingo!"

Frank gave his curly smile, leaned back and draped his arm over the back of the couch, behind Joe's head. "I dunno, I always thought you were more of a catcher."

Stephen tried very hard not to react, because maybe Joe wouldn't get it if no one reacted. But it was pretty challenging when Stephen had, in truth of fact, cornholed Frank on more than one occasion. Shameless sonofabitch.

It didn't matter. Mae West nearly fell off his chair laughing, and Dickie howled. Joe glanced askance at the group with a clueless half-smile, then looked at Stephen as if for guidance on how to respond. He should have been able to enjoy an efficient point, but no. Of course not. Not with this band of hooligans. Now Stephen had to field his filthy friends trying to traumatize his childhood buddy, who for some absolutely inexplicable reason kept coming back for more, as though this gang of misfits was his ticket to the country club.

Stephen met Joe's eyes and shook his head. "Ignore them. They're worse than frat boys."

He relinquished the turn to the opposing team and squeezed back onto the couch. It was more of a loveseat, really, and three adult men didn't particularly fit even if one of them wasn't a behemoth. Stephen was thigh to thigh with Joe, once again, and he was even doing a good job pretending like he wasn't hyperaware of it, because Frank was about to make him scream he was behaving so badly. His arm was across the back of the couch, and he was tickling Stephen's neck with his finger. Dear god in heaven, was this absolutely exasperating meathead trying to come on to him literally across the shoulders of his naive straight friend? After they'd had multiple very clear discussions about how every time they hooked up, it was always a frustrating disappointment? Either that, or Frank was trying to drive Stephen to actual homicide. Regardless, it was beyond the pale.

Stephen leaned back and glared at Frank. He was already looking, the prick, and smiled when he succeeded in getting Stephen's attention, running his finger up Stephen's neck to his earlobe. Stephen severely mouthed the words, *Quit it.*

Frank looked up at him from under his brows and tossed his hand as he mouthed, *Catch.* Stephen used his eyes to promise murder. *Fuck off.*

Frank's smile only got wider as he lifted his hand away, thank god, then pointed his fingers toward Joe's neck. He waggled his eyebrows.

Stephen wouldn't be surprised if steam was blowing

out his ears. *Don't. You. Dare.* he mouthed. Frank put on a little theatrical moue and looked at Joe the way someone might look at the dessert tray at a restaurant after they'd ordered a salad.

So it didn't surprise Stephen, a few turns later, when Joe got up to be the actor and the score was so woefully behind they had no hope of catching up, that Frank scooted in and hissed in Stephen's ear, "You're passing up some prime rib, Vinny."

"Shut up," Stephen hissed back, crossing his arms over his chest.

"I'm just saying, he's not flinched once tonight. He's game," Frank nudged his shoulder in emphasis.

Joe was fishing for a slip of paper in the bowl as Marge turned the timer.

"Stop thinking with your prick, Frank, and play the goddamn game."

"With you thinking so hard your overactive paranoid little peabrain's short-circuiting, someone's gotta keep their eyes on the prize."

"I told you—"

"Yeah, yeah, I know. No married guys."

"He's *straight*."

Frank snorted. "Okay, if you say so."

The timer started ticking, and Joe peered at his paper nearsightedly. He opened his mouth a bit, then swallowed, his eyebrows slanting at a distressing angle. He looked up at Stephen for help.

"Just do it," Frank brayed.

Stephen tried to nod encouragingly. Joe gave a sigh and put his hand out palm up, like he was cradling something in his hand. Then he brought the hand toward his mouth.

Oh no.

"Blow job!" Mae shrieked.

"Give head!" Frank piled on.

Stephen felt a roaring in his ears, on top of the roaring of his friends cycling through slang terms for oral sex and the roar of laughter coming from Dickie and the other team. Joe's face turned bright red, and he snapped his mouth shut. He flailed for a moment to keep from talking.

"Cocksucker," Frank guessed.

"Blow job!" Mae tried again, like he was sure it had to be that. Which made Stephen suspicious about what sort of havoc he'd tried to wreak when he wrote his prompts.

Stephen couldn't worry about that right now. He had to save Joe with a normal guess. A not-oral-sex guess.

"Try it a different way?" Stephen suggested, trying to be heard over the din.

This got more laughs from the other team.

Joe winced. His flush was going all the way down his neck now. It would be endearing if Stephen wasn't so horrified. Joe wrinkled his nose and tried to sort of hand whatever it was he was trying to portray in his palm back and forth between two cupped hands.

"Cock! Penis! Prick! Rod! Throbbing member!" Frank concluded with a flourishing gesture that was *not* helping.

Stephen couldn't think with all of this going on. His face was hot too, probably twisted in a horrified expression, probably making Joe feel even worse.

Joe put his hand on his face in exasperation.

"Cumshot!" Frank cried.

"Blow job, blow job, blow job!" Mae squealed.

Joe shook his head and winced as the timer buzzed. "It was hot dog."

Dickie fell on top of Walter laughing, holding his belly and kicking his foot out.

Stephen turned to his worthless teammates and said, "What the hell is wrong with you?"

Frank took umbrage. "I didn't hear you guessing anything different."

Mae ignored him and stood, digging in the bowl. "I could have *sworn* I put 'blow job' in there!"

Stephen turned to Dickie. "Some party," he snapped and stood, grabbing Joe's arm and hauling him toward the narrow glass door that led to a balcony overlooking the courtyard. "Piss elegant. Just a whole lotta class."

Joe let him drag him outside as Stephen shook his head and seethed. As soon as they were out on the balcony, which was scarcely big enough for the two of them, Stephen dug in his pocket and lit a cigarette.

"I'm sorry. Those guys are absolute bastards."

"It's fine. It's just a game." Joe shrugged. His face was shiny. It'd been hot in there, and it certainly didn't help being humiliated by a bunch of ragged queens.

"No, you have every right to be upset. You were earnest, and they were trying to bait you. I'm ashamed to have brought you here."

"No, I invited myself," Joe said resignedly as he leaned over the railing, looking resolutely out into the snow-sodden courtyard. "Your friends shouldn't have to censor themselves just to include me. I'm sure I made it worse by acting so embarrassed."

"You are the last possible responsible person. I assure you." Stephen blew an angry cloud of smoke over the balcony. "Dickie should be horrified."

Joe shrugged again, this time in a sort of sideways way that turned him away from Stephen. It made Stephen rub his fingers at his temples, leaning forward over the railing too.

"It feels nice out here," Joe said at length. It was unseasonably warm again, the temperature hovering around freezing and the light rain that had been drizzling earlier in the day now turned to snow.

"Yeah," Stephen agreed, because he didn't know what else to say. He was almost one hundred percent certain this was going to be the last time he saw Joe. "I really am sorry, Joe," he muttered as he pulled hard on the cigarette.

Joe shrugged and leaned forward on the railing beside him. "It's okay."

"No, it's not. I should never have let you come to this. They're always sloppy and drunk and obscene—"

"—Stephen. I know. I have two eyes, I can see. I know your friends are all…" He gestured vaguely.

"Queer," Stephen finished for him, rather severely.

"You say it like it's a bad thing."

"You don't think so?" Stephen wanted to grab Joe by the shoulders and shake him. *You don't think so?* he wished he could say. *Then why did you run away? Why did you say nothing to me after we were together, like it never happened? Go off and marry your fucking wife and have your little family and leave me to assume that I'd done something so horribly wrong that it required sacrificing our friendship?*

But he couldn't say any of that.

And Joe shook his head. "I don't know. They're interesting."

Stephen just blinked. He didn't know what the hell to do with that, whether it meant they were fascinating or disgusting.

"I've been stuck in a rut," Joe added. "Just doing all the things I'm supposed to do and never taking any joy in it. I've tried too. It feels like I'm watching a movie of someone else's life, sometimes. So I just … I like it here. Even if it's embarrassing. Because at least, you know,

I'm just me here. I'm not the assistant comptroller, or Marion's husband, or Chuck's father. I'm just me."

Stephen stilled. "Oh."

Snow swirled in the silence.

Joe took a deep breath. "I mean, if Mae West can be himself, then I sure as hell can be whoever I am."

Stephen couldn't do anything but stare at him. "And, uh…" He licked his lips; his mouth was suddenly dry. "Who are you?"

Joe threw his hands up uselessly. "Hell if I know." He finally—*finally*—looked at Stephen. Looked at him with those green eyes and that round, hound dog face, like maybe Stephen knew something he didn't. It was a look that, on an ordinary trick, Stephen would have bet on as an invitation. Goddammit. Frank was probably right. But this was Joe Milner. He couldn't gamble something as precious as the scrap of friendship they'd managed to wrestle back. Especially not when he *knew* that Joe would end up going back to his easy life, with his job and his wife and his family, just like every other married man Stephen had ever been with. He wasn't so stupid that he'd break his own heart like that.

Besides, Joe just looked at him. He didn't lift a hand, didn't move any closer, didn't do any of the other things that might turn a welcoming look into an invitation. Stephen turned and looked out over the courtyard, taking a drag on his cigarette. "Hell if any of us know. Some days I'm just happy I take up space."

"That space is lucky to have you in it," Joe replied. "Can I have one of those?"

Stephen handed him a cigarette and even lit it for him. Paper crackled and embers lit Joe's careworn face as he inhaled. Stephen's stupid friends were probably watching them through the window with their noses pushed up against the glass, like there was a chance that there'd be some sort of climactic kiss in the snow, with swelling orchestral music and soft lens lighting. And maybe they were right, maybe there was a chance for that. But Stephen wasn't going to take it. Stephen wouldn't do it because he had no interest in destroying himself.

✦

Chapter 9

Stephen went to the bathhouse again that week. He went twice, actually. He figured if he was going to get bent out of shape over a married man, he might as well get a good fuck out of it. One of them actually made him forget entirely about Joe, even if it was just for an hour, because he'd railed the guy so good he was pretty sure he'd gone cross-eyed. It was the kind of sex that made you want to quit your job and do nothing but fuck for the rest of your life. It was why he'd turned up at the bathhouse a second time.

The second time, he'd ended up on his knees in a toilet stall, which was fine but certainly not what he'd been chasing. A good reminder why he was supposed to be giving up cruising.

Thursday rolled around, and Stephen had to work until six. It was a good thing, because if he'd worked an earlier shift, he probably would have ended up at Kreuger's again, drinking and waiting for Joe. This way, he was unlikely to even run into him. Joe could spend his weekly watering-hole session with some of the other regulars, listening to Frank's crude jokes or laughing at the Two Blind Mice with Dickie. Feel like himself without dragging Stephen's stupid heart into anything.

Speaking of dragging, Stephen dragged himself round

to Kreuger's at about 6:30, eager for a drink and some time sitting down after a long day of running up and down the stairs at Dayton's trying to cover shoes and beauty at the same time. Ruth had called in sick, and it'd been busier than usual. As he pushed open the door, he was taken aback by a body in his path.

"Oh, sorry—"

"—There you are!" Joe exclaimed. "I was just about to give up on you."

Stephen stood in the doorway with his heart hammering in his chest and couldn't come up with anything other than the extremely obvious. "Here I am."

"I have an idea I wanted to talk to you about," Joe said. "Here, come in and I'll tell you about it before I go."

"That's okay, I wasn't really planning to stay long," Stephen said, glancing over Joe's shoulder to see if the gang had spotted him. "We can just talk out here."

Joe nodded and stepped outside, letting the door thump closed behind him. He pulled his coat up around his collar and then checked his watch. "Actually, do you want to go someplace else with me? I have a little bit of time."

"Don't you have to get home for dinner?"

Joe shrugged uncomfortably. "Marion left me something, but they're all at her sister's for the evening. Maybe we could get a bite?"

Stephen valiantly resisted the urge to smile. A smile would mean delight, which would mean affection, which would mean he was already sliding down that slippery slope to perdition. He did not succeed in resisting Joe, however, and said, "Okay."

They ended up at Mickey's Diner, a streetcar turned greasy spoon on the corner of St. Peter and 7th Streets. They bellied up together at the counter and picked up two menus.

"Damn, I forgot there's no booze here," Stephen said.

"Oh, sorry. Of course, you'll want a drink after a long day—we can go somewhere with a bar." Joe actually started to stand up. "The Coney's across the street—"

"Don't be ridiculous, the waitress already saw us," Stephen hissed and yanked Joe's elbow till he was seated again. "I'll just get a milkshake. Maybe I'll even share it with you like old times." Stephen winced at himself. So much for self-preservation.

The waitress, with a sixth sense for patrons on the fence about staying, descended upon them and took their orders before they had a chance to think anymore about it.

"So what was it you wanted to talk to me about?" Stephen asked, refusing to enjoy what felt like, for all intents and purposes, a date.

"Right! I was walking down to lunch today when I overheard some women in the elevator talking. Apparently their supervisor in the court office quit, so I asked them if the position would be refilled. They said the notice should go up any day now."

Stephen blinked at him. "What's this got to do with me?"

Joe's eyebrows furrowed. "Well, I thought you could apply."

"Me?" Stephen asked. "I—well, wait, what's the job?"

"It's an office manager position. You'd manage all the schedulers—that's the girls I met in the elevator—as well as make sure the office has everything they need, answer phones, and assist with court scheduling too."

"You mean, set people's court dates?"

"Yeah."

Stephen frowned. "I mean, thanks for thinking of me and all, but I'm not qualified to do that job."

Joe's eyebrows flew up. "Of course you are. You do stocking jobs already, and customer service at Dayton's. That covers the office management and the phones. And in high school, you were the football team manager senior year. You scheduled practices, made sure everyone showed up, and somehow you made them all feel good about it."

"It's football, of course they felt good about it. Being on the football team is the greatest social capital there is in high school."

Joe had the audacity of waving his protest away with his hand. "Besides, I know the hiring manager, and I can put in a good word for you."

Stephen stared at Joe for a long moment, pushing against the weak thread of hope that threatened to bubble up. "You don't have to do that."

"Don't you get it, Stephen? I want to," Joe said, his puppy-dog brows all confused and knotted between his green eyes. His mouth worked for a few moments. "Unless, you'd rather I not interfere." He sat back. "I'm sorry, I just assumed you'd want to get a new job. That was really rude of me."

"No, you're right, I hate my job," Stephen sighed, slouching down on the red plastic barstool. "I just ... well, it's still tough out there."

"I suppose," Joe said, brows still furrowed. "Jobs leveled off since Eisenhower was elected. But—"

Stephen let out a frustrated sigh and looked over his shoulder. There wasn't anyone else sitting next to him, so he leaned forward and said, under his breath, "Not for people like me."

"What's that supposed to mean?" Joe asked, not bothering to be quiet.

Stephen gripped Joe's wrist and pulled him closer so

he didn't raise his voice. "I mean, there's a reason Dickie didn't get that job at the Lexington, and it wasn't because he couldn't be bothered to work with their limited wine selection."

Joe blinked. "Oh." He looked down at Stephen's hand around his wrist, and Stephen abruptly let go. "I ... but you aren't like that."

"Like what? A sissy?"

"I mean, you don't seem like you're ... you know." Joe whispered. He was looking over Stephen's shoulder, his voice finally properly hushed, absently rubbing his hand around the wrist Stephen had held.

"Well, that didn't help me in the end, anyway," Stephen bristled. He didn't know why he'd expected Joe to understand that passing as straight or not, the same threats lurked around every corner for them all. He turned to face the counter but continued talking in a low voice. "A few years ago, someone called the office for the company I used to work at and told them I was a queer, and that was all it took. I lost it all: the job, the reference, everything. So now I work at Dayton's." The caller had actually called him a cocksucker, but he didn't need to be that specific.

"Jeez," Joe said, turning to face forward too. Then, "So ... you've worked in an office before?"

Stephen looked at him, affronted. Joe had that little private smile playing on his lips. "That is not what you're meant to get out of the story!"

Joe laughed, the sound clanging against the walls of Stephen's heart in warning. *Look out, you dumb-dumb,* it seemed to chime. *Before it's too late.*

"Listen, though," Joe said when he'd recovered. "If you have a reference from me, you won't have to have that place as a reference."

Stephen grumbled but didn't protest.

Joe pressed his advantage. "Come on, it's worth a try, right? Worst thing that can happen is that things stay the same."

Why was it that the status quo did feel like the worst possible outcome just now? Stephen didn't hate his life. He grew up during the Depression; he knew how important a job was. Even something like his job at Dayton's. Once a fellow found a job, he stuck with it till he died if he wasn't stupid. It was just … he'd been floating around like a ghost with nowhere to haunt. It wasn't the job, or where he lived, or even his income. It was his loneliness that made him thin and insubstantial.

Stephen watched silently as the server brought their food and set it on the counter before them. The milkshake glasses glistened with condensation in the warm interior of the railcar. He glanced up at Joe, who was preoccupied with picking up his hamburger and taking a big bite out of it. What if he *could* be an office manager? What if he could get a more stable income, get an apartment like Dickie and Walter had? What if he could work at the same place as Joe, day in and day out, meeting up for drinks after work and laughing together like they used to? What if soulmates didn't have to be romantic? What if they were companions, bosom friends, through thick and thin? What if they just never were more?

Stephen sucked on the straw in his milkshake and struggled to get anything to come out. Just like life, wasn't it? Even the littlest things were impossible. "I'll think about it."

Joe didn't seem to like that answer, but his mouth was too full of hamburger to say so. Over his shoulder, a gust of cold air blew in as a man and woman entered the diner. Stephen peered at the man for a moment before the fellow looked up and made eye contact. Recognition passed between them at the same time.

Joe looked over his shoulder. "Who's that?"

"No one, no one, don't stare," Stephen hissed and turned them both around urgently enough that it probably looked more conspicuous than it had when he was just staring.

"Do you know that fellow?"

"Sort of."

Joe raised an eyebrow at him. "What's that supposed to mean?"

"Nothing, just let it go."

Joe looked very curiously over Stephen's shoulder. Stephen stole a glance too. The man and woman sat down at one of the small booths that flanked the opposite side of the railcar from the counter, the woman facing away. The man met Stephen's gaze again and his eyes were heated. He couldn't tell whether it was in a good way or a bad way. It made a shiver run down his spine regardless.

Joe went back to his hamburger, and Stephen did his best to tuck into his own, even though he felt like the man's eyes were on him the whole time.

"Stephen, you have to tell me," Joe said when he'd set down his burger and started in on his fries. "He keeps looking at you."

"Does he?" Stephen said, resisting the temptation to look over his shoulder again. Joe's eyebrows went up with speculation. "I mean, I don't care either way."

"Yeah, you really look like you don't care," Joe frowned. "Come on, you're making me nervous. He's not going to wait for us to leave and hold us up in a back alley, is he?"

Stephen snorted. "God, no." If he did, it might be fun, though.

"Come on, I can handle it," Joe said, pitching his voice low as he snuck another glance at the guy. "Your friends made me act out a hot dog. I'm not a wilting flower."

"Fine," Stephen said, not knowing why he said it because he had no idea how Joe would react. "I met him earlier this week. We had … an encounter. Just for one night."

Joe's face expanded with understanding, then contracted again. "Just for one night?" Joe hissed in his ear. Stephen flinched. "Isn't that dangerous? Seems to me it would be safer to find one friend to, you know, have an arrangement with."

"It would be, but wouldn't you know it, I can't find anyone interested in that," Stephen said sourly.

"But surely Frank—"

"—*No*. Not Frank. Never again."

"*Again?*"

Oh jeez. Stephen winced. "Listen, I'm not going to pretend like I've been making a whole lot of great decisions since high school, okay?"

"Was it bad?"

"No, it was amazing," Stephen admitted, looking over his shoulder at the guy again. He glanced away when Stephen caught him looking. Very nice.

"Then why never again?"

"What? Oh, you mean Frank. No, Frank was terrible, for a multitude of reasons."

"Oh, so that guy was the amazing one?"

"Um. Yes."

"Oh." Joe considered this for a minute. "What's his name?"

Stephen shook his head. This had gone too far. "I don't know. It doesn't matter anyway. I'm not going to see him again."

Joe furrowed his brow exasperatedly. "But you're seeing him again right now."

Stephen tried not to give a frustrated sigh. "Yes, but this wasn't intentional. See that lady with him?"

Joe's eyes followed and his expression stilled. "Oh."

"Yeah," Stephen steeled himself and drank from his milkshake with as much dignity as he could muster. "He was just getting his rocks off. She's what he's actually looking for."

Joe blinked. "Is that … common?"

Stephen shrugged. "Yeah. Either that or I have extraordinarily bad luck."

Joe hunkered over the counter and stirred his ketchup with a French fry. "How do you meet people? Apart from Kreuger's, that is."

"Why do you want to know?"

Joe shrugged. "I just want to understand. You can't help solve a problem you don't understand."

Stephen peered at him for a long moment. "Bars that have a reputation like Kreuger's are the best place. Sometimes you run into people in everyday life," *like friends at a graduation party*, he didn't add, "but mostly, it's in all-male places, like bathhouses and public toilets."

"Public toilets?" Joe repeated, perturbed. "How is anyone supposed to fall in love in a public toilet?"

Stephen hadn't braced for that. He hadn't considered that Joe would see homosexuals as anything other than men with a queer taste for sex. To have him introduce the idea of love, something Stephen longed for so much he could barely acknowledge it, hurt more than he could have predicted. He swallowed hard. "Now you see the problem."

"That's certainly part of it," Joe replied feelingly. "I suppose it's not safe to find one another more openly."

"No," Stephen said in clipped tones. "No, it's not. Even with the fellows at Kreuger's, we're all one anonymous tip away from getting fired."

"Do you think it was one of them that called your office?"

"No," Stephen said. "Not any of the regular crowd, anyway. I could have been more discreet back then."

"It's not your fault," Joe murmured. The words sort of dropped into Stephen's ears like anvils. Goddammit, he had to get out of here before Joe ripped him to a bloody pulp with earnest sentiments. "Cripes, Stephen, he's coming over."

Stephen started. "What?" He looked over his shoulder just in time to see the man approach the counter on the seat just next to him. He was tall and proportional, with wide shoulders and a hard jaw. His brow was so severe it shadowed his eyes. Stephen couldn't believe he was seeing him again. It made him think crazy things that smacked of hope, which was ridiculous because Stephen knew what was most likely coming and was already bracing for it.

"What's it gonna take?" the guy muttered after ordering a coffee from the server behind the counter. "What, do you want money?"

"No," Stephen replied, voice just as low, acutely aware that Joe could hear everything. "It's just a coincidence."

"Like hell it is—"

"—I came in here first," Stephen cut him off. God, this was exasperating, not to mention embarrassing in front of Joe. None of this would have happened if they'd just had one more drink at Kreuger's. "Are you saying I predicted you would come in here? How could I possibly know that?"

The man frowned.

Stephen felt affronted enough to add, "Maybe it's you who's following me."

The man twitched his nose and grimaced. "Keep dreaming, fairy."

He moved down the counter to collect his coffee, then rejoined his wife. Or whoever she was. Stephen hadn't bothered to even look for a ring.

There was a clatter of coins on the counter.

"Come on, Stephen, let's get out of here," Joe said. "I'll drive you home."

✳

Chapter 10

Joe's heart was thrumming and his skin felt like it was buzzing as he climbed into the driver's seat of his Ford Anglia. Stephen slumped into the passenger seat, his dark features flat and glowering. If Joe didn't know that look, he'd fear Stephen was angry because with his thick eyebrows and deep-set eyes, he looked positively thunderous. But Joe was pretty confident that the person Stephen was most upset with was himself.

"Sorry," Joe murmured as he leaned over and fetched his glasses out of the glovebox. Stephen's eyes followed his hands.

"You wear glasses now?"

"Just when I drive." Joe glanced over at Stephen as he turned the engine. His brow was curiously twitched up now, in sharp focus through Joe's egg-head glasses. He could see the trace of a dimple teasing one cheek. "Don't laugh."

"I'm not laughing."

Joe's fingers twitched on the steering wheel as he pulled out of the parking spot and turned onto Kellogg Boulevard. He felt the same way he did when he was figuring out a problem, whether it was at work balancing the books or figuring out a repair on the house. He could see Stephen a bit more clearly in this moment—and it wasn't just the glasses.

He'd been spinning in circles around Stephen and his mouth and that time so long ago when maybe Stephen had wanted him. But seeing Stephen interested in that fellow, learning about what he wanted and how different it was for him to meet somebody—it reminded Joe to remove his own selfish nonsense from the equation. Stephen had a life. He had a heart and desires and a community of people who could meet those desires. Joe wasn't part of that, nor should he be. It was a good reminder, and he felt more clearheaded than he had in two weeks. He was keen to stay in this feeling of control, one he often didn't get to claim. He had confidence that for once, he could be of use to Stephen instead of the other way around, and it wasn't just the job he'd heard about this afternoon making him feel that way.

"How are you doing?" Joe asked, signaling his turn and waiting for traffic to clear.

Stephen shifted on the bench seat. "Fine."

"Try that again," Joe said. It was a gentle tone, but direct.

"Shaken," Stephen admitted. "Sorry. You ended up paying the bill and everything. What do I owe you?"

"Nothing," Joe said. "Tell me how to get to your place."

Stephen's face twisted for a moment. "I don't really want to go back there yet."

"Oh," Joe said. He headed toward 7th Street instead of turning down toward the Levee. "Where to, then?"

Stephen sucked in a breath and then pushed his hands over his face and into his hair, tipping his head back. "God, I don't know. Maybe I should just go back to Kreuger's."

"I can bring you there if that's what you want," Joe said,

jogging to the right lane of the road as he slowed to a stop at Seven Corners.

"I don't know what I want," Stephen said. "You should know that by now." He pushed his knees up against the dashboard and slumped down in the seat.

Joe nodded. He couldn't really disagree. Luckily, he was feeling decisive—a rarity, but lucky nonetheless. When the light turned green, Joe headed straight, following Kellogg Boulevard up the hill toward the cathedral and the hospital.

"Is that why you didn't say hello the first time I saw you at Kreuger's?" Stephen asked at length.

"What?"

"The glasses."

Joe glanced over at him. "No."

"I just thought maybe you didn't recognize me because I was too far away."

"I recognized you."

They parked on Selby Avenue, and Joe left the stupid glasses in the car. They headed into Boyd Park and Joe picked up hot sugared nuts from a fellow selling from a stand. Paper cones of nuts warming their hands, they crossed traffic and strolled side by side in companionable silence down Western Avenue toward the mansions of Summit.

Even with the heightened efficacy of his mood, it still took Joe six blocks to ask, "So is this all why you stopped talking to me?"

Stephen looked up at him, but he didn't reply.

"I wouldn't blame you if it was," Joe said. "It's not something a lot of guys would take in stride."

"My mother doesn't even know," Stephen said hoarsely. "She might suspect, but we've never talked about it. Not like this."

Joe nodded and waited. He was satisfied when Stephen filled the silence.

"In a lot of ways, I'm lucky," Stephen said. "A few years ago, I knew a guy who got caught in a car with a trick he'd picked up during Winter Carnival. He ended up in the slammer for maybe a year, year and a half. I ran into him a few months ago. He was like a shell of a person. All the joy in his eyes was gone."

"Just because it could be worse doesn't mean it's not hard," Joe said. It was something he told himself, sometimes, when he was awake at three in the morning feeling sorry for himself. It had worked once, to bring him down off the spiraling thoughts. Only once though.

"I guess. I felt awful. Like I was betraying him by getting away with something he'd been caught at."

"Everyone deserves to be happy," Joe said, aware he was spouting platitudes now but not able to think of anything better to say. "It shouldn't matter who you love. It's still love, regardless."

"I don't think I've ever been in love," Stephen said. It was such an innocuous thing to say, entirely unsurprising from a man in his late-20s. It still struck Joe deep, somewhere between his chest and his throat. It was probably for the best; it meant Stephen likely didn't remember that whole soulmate confessional. "I've met people I liked who left me behind, and I've met people who liked me but weren't what I was looking for. Those are both sort of non-starters for love."

"Yeah, they tend to be." Joe didn't really know what he was saying anymore. His tongue was still sticking to the roof of his mouth over the never-been-in-love thing.

Stephen sighed as they both leaned against the retaining wall at the Summit overlook. They'd arrived at the top of the Smith Avenue hill, where Summit curved around the bluff and gave off a fantastic view of the river valley and the West 7th neighborhood below. The sun was setting, reflecting pink and purple and orange off the snow-covered city.

"I can almost see my house from here," Joe said absently.

"Oh yeah? Whereabouts?"

Joe pointed west. There were frostbitten tree branches and a sea of fluffy white roofs and smoking chimneys.

"Nice."

"It's my grandma's old place," Joe said. Stephen would remember. They'd had a few sleepovers there. Joe's mother never let him have friends sleep over (the noise, her nerves, etc.). When his grandmother heard that, she'd provided Joe with a loophole.

"Oh yeah," Stephen smiled. It wasn't a grin by any means, but it made his cheeks dimple, and Joe was ready to call that a win. "She was hilarious. I suppose she's passed, if you're living there now. Did she ever learn any English?"

"Not a word, as far as I can tell," Joe replied. "Czech only until the day she died."

"Nice," Stephen said. He was reaching deep for the nuts in the bottom of his paper cone. His fingers glittered with sugar as he brought the handful to his lips. Joe really needed to stop thinking about his mouth. Every time the man lit a cigarette now, Joe stared like a dog. "How did you know, Joe?"

"Know what?"

"That you were in love?"

Joe's shoulders seized. *Because she made me feel like you did.* Absolutely under no circumstances could he say that. "I dunno. I just knew." Platitudes. He rubbed his face with his wrist, since his fingers were sticky.

"It's okay," Stephen said. "Things change."

Joe gulped in a breath. He couldn't help it. How was it that Stephen Vincelli could look at him and with just four words, reach down and pluck out his heart for them both to see?

Stephen didn't say anything. He just put his hand on Joe's arm and squeezed. Joe closed his eyes and fought against the prickling behind them.

"I don't know what's wrong with me," he whispered. As though it wouldn't count as a confession if he didn't put his voice to it. "She's perfect. She's friendly and kind and a loving mother. She's everything I ever thought I wanted."

He'd never said those words out loud before. He'd thought they might feel vindicating, like relief, but they felt more like an indictment.

Stephen's hand snaked round his shoulders and pulled him tight against his side. "I know."

The cold air stung as Joe wiped his cheeks with his wrist. He sniffled with as much dignity as he could scrape together. Dammit. He'd had himself together, but now he was falling apart again, nothing more than a collection of crumpled up pieces sacked up in his suit.

He pulled away when he started to become aware of Stephen's warmth pressed alongside him. All of this was getting worse. The awareness of Stephen, the memories that chased along with the sensation of his firm hand on Joe's bicep, the preoccupation with his friends and his love life and his mouth.

"I gotta get home," Joe said. "I'm late. Marion'll be back soon, wondering where I am."

Stephen's hand dropped. He nodded as he crumpled his paper cone in his hand. "Of course. I can walk home from here. It's basically a straight shot down Smith."

"No, I said I'd drive you."

"But you're late, and I got nothing better to do and nowhere to be." Stephen gave him just one dimple. "Don't worry about me. Just get yourself home."

Joe was in such pieces he let Stephen push him back off down Western toward his car. By the time he got in the Ford Anglia, he was devastated by the begrudging realization that he needed to find someplace else to drink. His heart, not to mention his marriage and his political career, couldn't afford the indulgence of Kreuger's. Of Stephen.

Even so, when he drove back down the hill on Smith Avenue, he slowed down and waved to Stephen on foot as he passed. It was a sorry farewell.

✦

"Where have you been?" Marion demanded in a hushed whisper when he got home. "It was your turn to do bedtime stories."

"I know, I'm sorry," Joe said equally low. "My friend from the bar was having a hard time so I offered to give him a ride." *Lies. Lying to your wife now. Men doing honest stuff don't have to lie to their wives.*

"Oh," Marion frowned. "Ralph?"

"No," Joe admitted and compelled himself to be honest. Just because he was harboring dishonest thoughts didn't mean his actions hadn't been above board. "You do know him, though. Stephen Vincelli, from high school?"

"Oh! Stephen?" Marion grinned. "I didn't know you were friends again. Where did he go off to?"

"Nowhere. He's still right here in St. Paul," Joe said with a grim smile.

"That's nice. You should invite him and his wife over for dinner on Saturday. Do they have any kids?" Marion was always after couples who had children who could form a feral pack with theirs and leave the adults alone to socialize.

"Uh, I don't know." Why did saying Stephen was single feel like an incriminating admission?

"So what was the hard time all about?" Marion asked after she'd checked on the kids in their room to confirm they were asleep.

Joe scrambled. "He's looking for a new job," he said. Not a total lie, more wish fulfillment if anything. "He's been stuck living down by the Levee."

"Oh my gosh, really? I didn't realize people still lived down there. Doesn't it flood every spring?"

Joe shrugged.

"Well, you've got to get him a new job, Joe. I'm sure you know someone over at City Hall who needs some help. Especially with this election going on. Did you know I saw a yard sign across the street from my sister's for a Republican? I couldn't tell you what he was running for, but I thought that was just the strangest thing. Isn't St. Paul supposed to be the City on a Hill?"

"Seven hills," Joe agreed. He just hoped she'd go on talking about her dinner with her sister and forget to ask him any more questions. She did, because she and her sister didn't get along very well. She often ended up coming home with a lot of bunk parenting advice she needed Joe to agree was bunk so she could proceed to ignore it without feeling guilty.

As she launched in, Joe wondered whether Stephen had been avoiding letting Joe see where he lived. He'd redirected them in the car and again on the overlook. It made Joe curious. But that didn't matter. He was going to stop following Stephen around like a lost puppy. Take control of his life. He'd felt the capacity for it earlier. He knew it was in him. He would go to bed early, get a good night's sleep, and in the morning, it would be better. He would be better.

*

Chapter 11

Joe got a good night's sleep that night. He even got to City Hall with some energy to get things done. He'd accomplished double the amount of work he normally did before lunch. What he hadn't counted on was a message from Stephen when he got back to his desk.

"You got a message from a Stephen Vincelli," the secretary, Judy, said, handing him the slip of paper. She was an older woman who'd been widowed in the war and now took it upon herself to manage the comptroller's office instead of a household. "It says he wants to go for the job? I figured you'd know what he meant."

Joe nodded as he looked at the paper, script looping around the S and V of the name. It was pretty evident without even having to think about it that his desire to get Stephen on his feet was much, much greater than any guilt he felt about his own ulterior interests. None of which he was ever going to act on anyway. Besides, even Marion agreed it was important to help a friend.

After work, Joe went round the block to Kreuger's and was relieved to find Stephen at the booth with Walter and Dickie without any waiting. Stephen did a double take when he saw him.

"Joe, what are you doing here?" he said when Joe approached the booth. "I thought you were strictly Thursdays only."

"I got your message," Joe said, cutting straight to the point. It was strange to feel so uncommonly nervous when this place had been such a refuge for him the past month. "So I brought you the job application."

He handed the paper to Stephen rather than set it on the table and run the risk of a ring stain ruining the neatly typed form. Stephen looked down at the paper and nodded. "Right." He looked up and smiled. "Thanks."

Joe squeezed his own heart, somehow. Better than feeling Stephen squeeze it for him.

"What job is this?" Walter asked.

"It's an office manager thing, at the court office," Stephen replied, his eyes back on the application.

Dickie's lip curled. "Are you sure you're qualified for that?"

Joe informed him of Stephen's time as football team manager before he could remember that he wasn't supposed to be here in the first place. He turned to Stephen. "Let me know if you have any questions. I gotta get home."

"Sure thing." Stephen's dimples, mercy. "Have a good weekend."

"Thanks," Joe managed and turned on his heel to walk out before he could convince himself that it'd be okay to have one quick drink with the boys.

"Hey Joe! Wait." It was Walter's voice.

Joe swallowed hard and paused to get his smile on right before he turned. "Yeah?"

"How will he reach you if he has questions?" Walter asked, a little more paternal than was necessary.

"What do you mean?" Joe gritted his teeth slightly against the interference.

"If he has questions."

"He can just call my office—"

"Yeah, Walter, I'm a big boy. I can use a phone," Stephen said with a roll of his eyes.

"Could have fooled me," Dickie put in. "Since you don't even have one."

"I told you—"

Joe waved his hands to make everyone stop talking and seized a napkin. "Here," he said, writing his home phone number down with the pencil from his pocket before he could think better of it. "This is my home number. Just call if you need anything."

"Okay," Stephen said as Joe stuffed the napkin into his hand. "Thanks."

"Yup," Joe said by rote and then hurried out of the bar before anything else could breach his defenses.

✦

Stephen stared after Joe.

"'Just call if you need anything,'" Dickie repeated, flicking ash off the end of his cigarette with a significant glance at Stephen. "You need anything, big boy?"

"Shut up, Dickie," Stephen said, stuffing the napkin in his pocket where it proceeded to existentially smolder against his thigh.

"What's got into him?" Walter asked, looking over his shoulder at the door thumping closed behind Joe. "He's usually more, I dunno, filled with doe-eyed wonderment."

"Perhaps we've just been treated to his straight-man persona," Dickie drawled. "Everyone's got one. Even Marge. Did I tell you about the time I saw her at Dayton's?"

"That was the time *I* saw her at Dayton's," Stephen said. "I just told you about it, and I shouldn't have apparently, because you're the biggest gossip in St. Paul,"

"What's the big deal about Marge at Dayton's?" Walter asked.

Stephen shook his head as Dickie whispered, "She was wearing a *dress*."

Walter's eyebrows jumped toward his burnished brown hair, but instead of commenting, he said, "Well, tell us what this job is all about, Vinny."

Stephen looked down at the application again. "Joe heard about it in the elevator at work yesterday and told me he thought I should apply and that he'd be a reference for me."

"Oh my god," Dickie said seriously. "It's government corruption. Only, it's corrupt in your favor."

"Cronyism, I think is what you're thinking of," Walter corrected.

"No, I meant what I said. Corruption. Corruption like the cops in the thirties helping out all the liquor-toting hooligans."

"Is it corruption for a guy to put his friend up for a job?" Stephen bristled.

"If they find out you're a fairy, yeah, probably," Dickie drawled.

That sat very ill with Stephen. If it hadn't happened before, he wouldn't be so concerned. But it had, and he didn't want to be the cause of Joe's political ambitions (as mildly ambitious as they were) crumbling in the face of a scandal.

"You don't look so sure, Vin," Walter commented.

"I'm not," Stephen said. "I was this morning. I do want to try. But working for the city makes me uneasy."

"I can't imagine," Dickie said, crossing his arms. "Those

big marble halls, filled with cops. Scheduling other people's court dates, you said? If one of us were arrested, would you be the one to decide when we go to court?"

Stephen had not thought of that. He balked.

"Maybe that would be useful," Walter pointed out. "If he saw one of us was indicted, maybe he could accidentally lose the charges?"

"Paperwork does get complicated," Dickie agreed.

Stephen frowned. "Now who's corrupt? I haven't even applied for the job yet and you're already figuring out ways to cheat the system."

Walter ignored him. "He probably wouldn't have any of that stuff cross his desk anyway."

"Won't find out until he *applies*," Dickie replied, giving Stephen a significant look.

✦

Stephen had absolutely no intention of calling Joe for help. However, there were several items on the application that, once he got started, he realized he needed advice on. There was a line to add a licensure, which of course Stephen did not have. There was also a space for additional information that felt like it could potentially be helpful, perhaps to explain away the lack of a license (in what?), if only he knew what to write in it. So on Saturday afternoon, Stephen slumped down the stairs to the parlor of the boardinghouse, application in hand, and called Joe.

As soon as the call connected and the child's voice answered, Stephen realized calling had been a mistake.

"Hello, Milner residence. Who may I ask is calling?" The trebley attempt at diction, the boyish scrape, the lightly fuzzed s-sounds that all belied childhood served as stark reminders that Joe was a father, and a husband, and didn't owe Stephen anything at all.

"Uh," Stephen said. He wasn't going to hang up on a six-year-old. Not when he'd done such a polite job of answering. "This is Mr. Vincelli, calling for Mr. Milner. Is your father at home?"

"Yup," the child said and god, he said it just like Joe did. Like a knife to the heart. "Hold on just a minute."

Stephen took that minute to get a goddamn hold of himself. Joe had been odd, after they'd gone to Mickey's and run into that trick. Since he'd admitted to Stephen he was struggling. Everything just felt big and emotional because that's how they'd felt when they left the Summit overlook. It wasn't the actual measure of their friendship, or the weight of this conversation now. It was okay to get down to business, get a little help, and lean on a friend to make a step up in life. He didn't need to make anything else of it.

"Hello?" Joe's voice over the line was flat.

"Hi, Joe, it's Stephen."

"Oh, hi." Joe's voice took on some color, and Stephen tried to ignore the way that puffed up his chest. "Run into some trouble with that application, then?"

"Sort of," Stephen replied, unwilling to admit it. "There were a couple of questions that felt like a specific answer was wanted, and I figured I'd ask your advice on how to answer it."

"Sure thing. Shoot."

Stephen launched into the list of questions he had, ticking down the application with his pencil and cradling the phone between his shoulder and his chin as he carefully noted Joe's advice.

"Okay, I think that's it," Stephen said, sitting up and

forward in his chair, preparing to end the call.

"Great," Joe replied. His voice was easy now, friendly and more confident than Stephen was used to hearing at Kreuger's. He supposed this was what Joe was like in his element at work. Perhaps he was better suited to comptroller and elected office than he assumed. "When are you turning in the application?"

"Oh, I suppose Monday," Stephen said. He hadn't thought about it. "You think I should wear a suit?"

"Yeah, definitely," Joe said. "You'll want to turn yourself out nice, if you can. Flash those dimples."

Stephen squinted and laughed. What an odd thing to say. "Okay, I'll be sure to shave real good then."

"It'll be easy," Joe said. "Once they meet you, you'll sweep them off their feet."

"I'm not sure whether I'm supposed to be applying for a job or romancing the hiring manager."

Joe laughed, sudden and loud, and Stephen preened, leaning back in his chair and stretching the coiled phone cord with his fingers. "I suppose there's a fine line between charm and flirtation."

There certainly was. Stephen closed his eyes for a moment, then cleared his throat. "I'll make sure to press my suit, then. What floor's this court office on, anyway? City Hall is huge."

"Oh sure, and there's several. There's a criminal court office, but you're applying for the civil one."

"Right."

"That's on the fifth floor. Why don't I just meet you and walk you up there. Then I can introduce you."

Stephen pulled his legs up into the chair. "Will that be odd? I mean, I'd appreciate the support, but I don't want to seem like I can't do things on my own."

"Not at all," Joe said. "You're good at hobnobbing with

folks. Just smile and say all the usual pleasantries. Peltier, the city clerk, likes guys who can make him laugh."

"That why he likes you?"

Joe snorted. "Not at all. He likes me because I keep us in the black, and I know how much money he can spend on new employees like you."

"Wow, Mr. Fancy Pants," Stephen drawled. "What time should I meet you?"

"Monday you said? How about one, just after lunch?"

"Shoot, I work until two. Do you think it's okay if I show up at three?"

"Yeah, I usually take a coffee break around that time. It shouldn't make too much of a difference."

"Okay. Great." Stephen could feel the call coming to a natural conclusion, but he didn't want it to end. Which was selfish. "I'll see you then."

"See you Monday." Joe lingered for a moment. "Say, before you go, you've dealt with water damage down on the Levee, right?"

"Boy, have I," Stephen snorted. "You got a water problem?"

"I still got that leak in the bedroom ceiling," Joe said and proceeded to explain, in detail, what he'd figured out so far. Flat asphalt roof, crack in the ceiling, paint swelling a bit around the crack. Joe had moved the rocks off the area of the roof and assessed the layer of tar. Stephen spent fifteen more minutes on the phone listening and asking questions and offering absolutely zero practical advice because people on the Levee dealt with water damage; they didn't prevent it. But it was nice anyway. Nice to talk, to exchange jokes, to hear Joe laugh and feel the satisfaction of causing it. It felt normal, just entirely natural. Platonic soulmates, but for fixing roofs.

Stephen didn't bother thinking much about it. He let

himself enjoy talking and to take comfort in the way their conversation soothed the vulnerable spaces they'd cracked open up on the overlook. They talked the afternoon away, until Joe finally begged off when his wife came in to cook dinner. Stephen realized he'd probably been sitting in the kitchen this whole time, in the same kitchen where his grandma had made them Linzer cookies when they were juniors in high school. God, he could see Joe sitting there on the stool, his long legs tucked up underneath him like a spider. He smiled to himself as he said his goodbyes and confirmed their meeting on Monday.

As he set the phone in the cradle, his mother came in and said, "What's got you smiling like that?"

Stephen shook his head and climbed out of the chair. "Nothin'."

"Some girl, huh?" Mrs. Vincelli nodded knowingly. "Well, keep her well out of here, at any rate. You know there's no girls allowed at this boardinghouse."

"Yeah, I know. Just you, Ma."

"That's right."

✦

Chapter 12

"Are you alright?"

Joe looked up from his desk and through the door at Judy, the secretary for the comptroller's office.

"Yeah, I'm fine. Why?"

"You keep tapping your pencil," Judy said, her eyes flicking significantly at the pencil thrumming between his fingers.

"Oh." Joe stopped immediately. He hadn't noticed he was doing that. "I'm sorry, I'll stop."

Judy gave a curt nod, the kind of perfunctory gratitude afforded to someone who was certainly not deserving of it. Joe turned back to his ledger and tried valiantly to concentrate.

His eyes flicked to the clock on his wall. It was ticking slow, he was certain of it. Ever since lunch. He wasn't sure why, exactly, but he was worried he'd get too absorbed in a task and miss the time he was supposed to head down and meet Stephen.

"Judy," Joe said before he could second-guess himself. "Can you let me know when it's ten to three, please?"

"Sure," Judy said, peering at him. "Sorry, do you have an appointment I didn't know about?"

"Sort of. Not really," Joe fumbled. "It's more a favor for a friend."

"Alright. I'll remind you."

"Thanks."

He looked back down at the ledger, the numbers all lined up neatly in columns. He checked his adding machine. He didn't really need it—he could do the figures in his head—but he liked it neatly confirming all of his conclusions in a thumping rhythm.

God, he'd had a hell of a time concentrating today. He hadn't slept well all weekend. After consulting with Stephen, he'd gone back up on the roof and found the elusive tear in the tar layer. He'd repaired it. He'd scraped and painted the crack in the ceiling, but he was still lying sleepless at three in the morning, staring up at the flawless expanse of shadowy eggshell paint and thinking about things he shouldn't.

Things like Stephen Vincelli and that man from Mickey's Diner. He'd been a tall man, with shoulders like a football player. Angry eyes. Joe couldn't imagine that man looking gentle or tender. Which made him wonder about the nature of his encounter with Stephen.

He wondered a lot about that encounter. He'd spent three nights now wondering. He'd wondered about the nature of that encounter six ways from Sunday, to the point that last night, he'd finally thrown the blankets off and stalked to the bathroom, where he'd stood over the toilet and pulled himself off because he was so sick and tired of thinking about this, he didn't even care anymore what it took to make it stop. The images and scenarios he'd considered scared him, but not enough to make them go away. His imagination was running rampant with that errant memory he'd let through, and now it was a damned deluge, leaving him in a tangle of jealousy and arousal and frustration. He laid next to his wife night after night and thought about Stephen naked, with this other man. Touching each other and … kissing each other and … other things he didn't dare name. Things he could see, in his mind's eye, but not say. Things that were definitely *not* 'hot dog.'

After not sleeping and thinking all these intrusive things, Joe felt like a crazy person. He couldn't talk to anyone about it, he couldn't do anything about it, so it just sat there in his brain, running reels behind his eyes and taunting him. He was terrified that when he saw Stephen, all he'd be able to think about was this and then he'd flush or act strangely, and Stephen would *know*, he'd just know. And he'd botch up the entire introduction to the city clerk and the only person who'd really suffer was Stephen, who hadn't done anything at all, other than try to privately live his life.

Joe pushed a hand through his hair, then twitched his hand away and smoothed his hair back down. It was important he get this right. For Stephen. Besides, if he could charm the city clerk, maybe he'd have what it took to get elected comptroller in '56.

The lines of numbers ticked together in meaningless sums. Joe had other wonderings too. Wonderings about that man, who the woman had been, and whether Stephen would ever see him again. If Joe had thought Frank was a good-looking option, this man was Gregory Peck. What would it take for a fellow like him to choose a discreet life with someone like Stephen? Joe didn't think it was such a tall order. Stephen was himself, after all, funny and charming and gregarious, with that chin and those dimples and that dashing, boyish smile that stretched across his dark-featured face like a welcome mat. He had a fantastically large nose, straight and sharp, very commanding if the fellow liked things like that. Joe evidently did.

God, that was the absolute worst part. It wouldn't be so bad if Joe could think about Stephen and wish him happiness. But he wanted him in a way he shouldn't. He thought about what Stephen deserved, and what it meant for fellows like him, and all the other things Joe had learned since he started visiting Kreuger's. Frank Atlas alone was an education, and he'd only spent an hour or two with him last Thursday without Stephen's moderating presence. Frank had told Joe all about public restroom etiquette, and ways to signal fellows subtly. Joe had internalized none of it. Except he now had a clearer context with which to imagine how Stephen and this tall, dark, handsome fellow had met. They were filthy thoughts, things he shouldn't be thinking about at work certainly, and they were causing him enough discomfort that Joe was beginning to mildly panic about whether his desk was large enough to hide his lap from Judy's view. Dear Lord, that would be an absolute disaster. It didn't bear thinking of.

Joe was in a state by the time he watched the clock tick to ten minutes until three and Judy gave her timely reminder. He had managed to get himself under control by counting along with the second hand for the last five minutes. One-one hundred, two-one hundred, three-one hundred… Now that the time had arrived, Joe stood up and brushed his trouser legs.

"I'm off to see the city clerk," he told Judy. "I'll be back in thirty minutes at the latest."

"Okay," Judy replied, scarcely looking up at him.

Joe strode out the door and made his way to the elevators. He spilled out of the elevator doors on the ground floor and spun toward the vaulted atrium and the towering peace statue. Joe checked his watch, saw he still had five minutes to wait and folded himself into a stance that minimized his jiggling knee.

When Stephen appeared through the revolving doors in his black overcoat, his sharp suit and tie just visible between the lapels, with his hair pomaded, Joe tipped back slightly against the wall for support. It was like he was seeing him for the first time at Kreuger's in January all over again, except that didn't make any sense, because he'd just seen him two days ago, for heaven's sake. It was probably because he was all spiffed up. But why should a suit and a little pomade make his heart beat double time? Stephen deserved better than a despondent friend who used him as fantasy-fodder to escape his perfectly adequate, stable marriage to a dynamite woman. Joe owed it to him to get his life together and help lift Stephen up into this job he was eminently qualified for.

"Hey," Joe greeted with a stiff smile. "You clean up alright." And as Stephen approached, he flinched away the involuntary urge to kiss him on the cheek. Just a peck, like Mae West sometimes did to greet people at the bar. Like Joe might greet Marion in public. It was such a jarring instinct that Joe flung his hand out in front of him instead for a handshake.

Stephen regarded the hand with a bemused smile and took it gently in his own hand. "I do work at a department store. Please compliment my shoes."

Joe looked down at his feet and gave an admiring nod to the shiny patent leather while he felt Stephen's grip slip away. "Very nice. Ready?"

"As I'll ever be," Stephen replied with a winning smile, dimples gleaming.

Joe tried to relax. Stephen would carry perhaps ninety percent of this interaction. There was very little he could do to mess it up.

They went up the elevators and Stephen asked a

few questions about the city clerk that Joe answered at length, eager for the normal, appropriate topic even as he couldn't quite make himself meet Stephen's eyes. He was so on edge, he was certain Stephen had noticed. It made no sense for Joe to be more nervous than Stephen right now. It was Stephen who needed to put out a good showing to get a job and a significant salary increase.

They got out on the fifth floor, and Joe led the way down the hall, paneled with some rare Amazonian hardwood that had come cheap when they built this tower during the Great Depression. He pushed into the city clerk's office and the secretary looked up at him. She was a Black woman around Joe's age, with cat-eye glasses and her relaxed hair in a ponytail.

"Hello, is Mr. Peltier in?" Joe asked. "I'm Joe, from the comptroller's office."

She blinked. "Which one?"

"Oh, the assistant. Not the comptroller," Joe replied sheepishly. Stephen snickered.

She shrugged. "Mr. Peltier is in his office. You can go right on in."

Joe gave his gratitude and led Stephen across the antechamber to the door of the city clerk, Lawrence Peltier. He gave a courtesy knock, then opened the door.

✶

Chapter 13

Joe was nervous. Which made Stephen nervous. Maybe he didn't think Stephen was such a shoo-in for the job after all. Maybe Stephen's suit looked too cheap, and Joe was embarrassed. God, it didn't matter. It was too late for any of that. All Stephen could do now was smile and say all the expected things while Joe introduced him to the city clerk.

Lawrence Peltier was a slab of a man pushing fifty with a big, mobile grin. He shook hands with a vice grip and Stephen squeezed back as hard as he could, distantly grateful to Frank Atlas of all people for training him into this manful ritual.

"So, you're looking for work, huh?" Mr. Peltier asked as he rounded his desk again and sat down. "You on the GI Bill or anything?"

"No, sir," Stephen admitted. "I didn't have the honor of serving."

"He's done a great deal else, though," Joe put in and waved for Stephen to hand over his application. "You'll be hard-pressed to find a fellow with this breadth of experience."

Mr. Peltier looked down at the application and reviewed it with a rumble.

"You married, Mr. Vincelli?" Apparently, he was one

of those fellows who had no compunction for polite pleasantries. A strange animal to encounter in the Midwest, and unsettling at that.

Stephen blanched. "Uh, no sir."

Mr. Peltier frowned. "Hm. The staff in our scheduling office is mostly women. I'm sure I don't have to tell you, Mr. Vincelli, that I have no interest in some chippy-chaser leading the girls round by the nose down there. I'm partial to a married man, on that account, for this position."

Stephen blinked. "Oh." He bit his lip and glanced at Joe. Seemed like that was that.

"Oh, Mr. Peltier, I assure you, I've known Mr. Vincelli since high school," Joe said. Stephen was impressed at how good-ol'-boy he managed to sound. "He's the most honorable fellow I know, and I work for the city. I know a fair number of honorable fellows."

Mr. Peltier gave a bark of a laugh, though Stephen wasn't sure whether it was because Joe was honest or joking. And in that moment, Stephen made a decision. It might have been a careless one, but it looked like he was screwed anyway, so it was worth one last shot.

"I daresay I don't know as many honorable fellows as you do," Stephen drawled, switching his weight from both feet to just one and letting his hand dangle from his wrist. "But I do work with a fair number of ladies down at Dayton's, and I can assure you, sir, I haven't met one who didn't trust her honor entirely with me."

Joe turned to Stephen with alarm in his eyes, but Stephen ignored him, watching instead as Mr. Peltier's eyes narrowed, studying Stephen carefully. Stephen held his gaze and waited, pursing his lips like Dickie. This was either brilliant or suicide. But he felt like it was worth the gamble, somehow. It certainly addressed Mr. Peltier's concerns about having a casanova in the cuckoo's nest. He could only hope if it went sideways, it wouldn't blow back on Joe.

"I see," Mr. Peltier said slowly, his eyes drifting back to Stephen's application. "Well, if Mr. Milner says you're the honorable sort… You can head back to your desk, Milner. Take a seat, Mr. Vincelli. Tell me more about your responsibilities at Dayton's."

An hour later, Stephen found himself walking out of the city clerk's office laughing genially at some joke Mr. Peltier had cracked, a job offer letter burning a hole in the breast pocket of his suit coat.

"I'd say we'd better have a drink to celebrate your newfound luck, Mr. Vincelli," Mr. Peltier said as he led Stephen into the hallway toward the elevators. "How 'bout we stop by the comptroller's office and bring your friend along? Make it a party."

"That sounds great, sir," Stephen gushed. He felt a million miles tall—a rarity for someone of his stature. They rode the elevator up and Stephen followed as Mr. Peltier burst into Joe's office, startling the secretary.

"Milner!" Peltier boomed. "We're going to the St. Paul Hotel to celebrate."

Joe looked up from his desk, the chug of the adding machine silenced. "Really?" He looked at Stephen and a grin seized across his face—a real one, one that reached his eyes. "Stephen—that's fantastic!"

Stephen couldn't stop grinning himself.

"Drinks are on me!" Mr. Peltier declared.

Joe sprang to his feet and crossed to the door where Stephen was. He clasped Stephen's hand and pulled him in for a bracing hug, one that lasted only a brief second. Joe almost immediately shrank away, like he'd forgotten hugs were not a part of their catalog of exchanges anymore. Stephen didn't even care. Joe could be as uncomfortable as he wanted. Stephen owed him the world for putting him up for this job. He could do whatever he wanted as far as Stephen was concerned.

The St. Paul Hotel was trimmed out in a fresh dusting of snow and looked like an opulent gingerbread house as the three of them burst in from the cold. Inside, the hotel was decorated in the style of the palace hotels of the Gilded Age. It had the reputation for being a hotbed of organized crime, and as far as Stephen knew, it was still under the thumb of the Goldberg family, notorious gangsters turned city leaders upon the repeal of the Volstead Act.

"You ever been here, Mr. Vincelli?" Mr. Peltier asked as they sat down at the bar.

"Can't say I have," Stephen said with a grin.

"Best cocktails in the city," Mr. Peltier declared as the bartender handed him an old fashioned he didn't have to order. He turned to the bartender. "They'll have the same, Sam."

"Sure thing, Mr. Peltier," the fellow agreed, turning to mix two more and sliding them in front of Joe and Stephen.

"Well," Mr. Peltier said, raising his glass. "A toast, to old friends and lucky connections."

Stephen grinned and repeated the toast. He glanced up at Joe as he sipped from his glass, bourbon and orange attacking his nostrils.

Mr. Peltier turned out to be in his element at the bar. He knew everyone who bellied up, and bought another round not just for Stephen and Joe, but for the whole lineup of fellows at the bar. It made Stephen wonder whether the reputation of the hotel had any bearing on Mr. Peltier's seemingly deep pockets. Damn, what did it matter? Mr. Peltier could be Al Capone for all Stephen cared. As long as he was signing paychecks for Stephen's new 9-to-5. It wasn't like he was innocent of breaking inconvenient laws himself.

Mr. Peltier was ordering a third round when Joe cleared his throat awkwardly.

"Sorry, sir," Joe said. "I have to be getting home to the missus."

"Nonsense," Mr. Peltier said. "We're celebrating, and the simple fact is that we wouldn't be if it weren't for you, Milner. Sam!" The bartender practically jumped to attention. "Bring the phone round. Milner's gotta call the missus."

"What? No, thanks sir, but I need to get home—"

"—Or what? She'll leave you? I sincerely doubt that. There's an election coming on. Just call her and tell her you have to work late." Mr. Peltier was as Stephen had pegged him. Direct, unconcerned about what others thought, and a complete steamroller.

Joe sort of dithered and Stephen felt bad for him as the bartender set a phone on the bar top for him.

"Everyone!" Mr. Peltier bellowed to the bar patrons. Stephen was drinking deep from his cup as the entire bar silenced and looked to his new boss. "Shuddup, Milner here's gotta tell the missus he's working late." He made big eyebrows when he said working and several of the other fellows at the bar snickered. It was a testament to Mr. Peltier's personality and status as a regular that everyone stayed quiet.

Joe glanced around uncertainly.

Mr. Peltier frowned. "Milner. Level with me. Are you having a good time?"

"Yes."

"If there weren't an obligation at home, would you

want to stay?"

"Yes." Joe glanced at Stephen. "I suppose I would."

"Then call and tell her what's what. You're the one bringing home the bacon. If you want to stay out, stay out."

Joe's woeful eyebrows knitted together as he lifted the phone from the cradle. Stephen wanted to be a good friend, he really did, but he also wanted Joe to stay. Surely, just this once, he could be selfish. Joe was his friend, and he couldn't have gotten the job without him. Was it so bad to want to celebrate together?

"Hey, Marion," Joe said into the receiver and the whole place felt like it was hanging off his every word. "Sorry, I'm not going to make it home for dinner. There's a report the mayor wants before we leave. I'm not going to be back till late."

It was as easy as that. Stephen probably should have felt bad about it, but he was sipping on a third old fashioned, and Joe was finally—finally—warming up now that he'd hung up the phone. He was leaning against the bar, smiling as Mr. Peltier carried on a rant about how the mayor hadn't made sure the printing company making his campaign signs were union and now he was under fire in the papers. His elbow was nudged up against Stephen's, and Stephen couldn't remember the last time he'd felt so solid, so real.

✳

Drinks turned into dinner at the hotel restaurant. Peltier ordered filets mignons for all three of them and introduced them to several people passing by, including the proprietress of the hotel. After dinner, they ended up back on the bar, each nursing yet another old fashioned and feeling real tight while Peltier glad-handed a collection of old gangster types he apparently knew.

"I can't believe you!" Joe laughed, nudging Stephen with his elbow. "I thought you'd screwed the pooch back there, when he asked if you were married."

"Me too," Stephen wailed. "I saw my life flash before my eyes, I swear to you. A life of pretending I'm extremely invested in whether a fellow buys Oxfords or wing tips, working odd jobs to pay rent on a room on the Levee, and you know what? I said fuck it."

Joe sputtered in his drink. Stephen probably shouldn't swear so bad, but this bar was full of high-class bastards, and Stephen was *drunk*.

"Well, you certainly shocked me," Joe managed between laughs. "I never woulda thought you could be so blatant, yet tasteful."

"That's me, Joey. Audaciously discreet." Stephen gave his winningest smile, the one he saved for the boys at the bathhouse.

Joe snorted and his cheeks went a satisfying shade of pink. "Well, it paid off anyway. Jeez. I guess managing a staff of all girls, it makes a kind of sense."

"I never thought it'd *get* me a job, that's for damn certain." Stephen pushed his orange wedge around the rim of his glass. He glanced up and caught Joe watching his progress. "Where'd Peltier get off to?"

Joe looked up and over Stephen's shoulder to survey the bar. "Not sure. Don't see him anymore."

"Well, if you're out late," Stephen hedged, "maybe we can stop by Kreuger's and tell them the good news before you head home."

He really expected Joe to say no. But when Joe looked back at him, green eyes glassy and earnest with a quarter smile caught the corner of his mouth, he said, "Sure. I gotta sober up anyway before I drive. These things are deadly."

Stephen laughed. They tipped some coins on the bar, then headed two blocks east to the hole-in-the-wall dive with the blinking neon "Liquor" sign in the window.

Joe was drunk, alright. He was sort of listing on his feet, like he was a sailor who hadn't got his land legs back yet. Stephen ended up taking him by the elbow and pouring him through the door into the bar. Inside, there were only a few people. Right. It was a Monday night. Rolling in drunk at 9:30 didn't quite have the same wild potential on a Monday as it did on a Friday or Saturday.

It was looking like the only person to celebrate with was Red, until Mae West wandered out of the restroom.

"Vinny?" Mae called, his voice sliding up into a squeal as he scurried up to them. "What are you doing here this late?"

"It's only 9:30," Stephen sniffed as Joe stumbled into his shoulder.

"Are you both *drunk*?" Mae was fully screeching now. "What's happening???"

Red turned around on his barstool with a frown. Joe snorted and Mae's eyes swiveled between the two of them like one of those old cat clocks.

"I got the job!" Stephen burst out. "I'm gonna manage the civil court scheduling office. And you'll never believe what got me the job."

Mae's eyes went wide like saucers, and he looked Joe up and down. "Do tell."

"The city clerk said he wanted a married fella for the job 'cause the scheduling office is all girls, and he didn't want some bachelor running rampant all over the place," Stephen took a deep breath. He was just lucid enough to hear how drunk he sounded. "And so I flipped my wrist and told him I worked with all sorts of girls at Dayton's who trusted me to walk them to their cars—"

"—I don't 'member you sayin' that—"

"—Joe, shuddup and let me tell the story. *Anyway*, the clerk picked up on it and decided to hire me—"

"—He also looked at your application. He didn't *just* hire you 'cause you're not gonna hit on the ladies."

"But can you believe that, Mae? Who ever heard of a fella getting *hired* for bein' a fairy?"

Mae's eyes were still wide, flicking between the two of them. "Were you … drunk then too?"

"No, we got drunk *afterward*," Joe clarified. "At the St. Paul Hotel."

Red turned around. "The city clerk? Lawrence Peltier?"

Stephen did a double take hard enough that Joe sort of fell off his shoulder. "You know him? Wait—how do *you* know him?"

"I know Augie Goldberg, which means I know her brother-in-law, yeah." Red had a brow quirked, like he was amused by drunks on a Monday. "Well, ex-brother-in-law now."

Stephen leaned into Red, hand catching himself on the bar behind him. "What's his deal, Red? He was wining and dining us like we were something important, flashing more money than a city clerk has any right to."

Red smirked and shrugged. "I'm not at liberty to say."

"Well, I just want to know whether I'm gonna get arrested for colluding with some corrupt city government shit."

Red snorted. "Yeah, Lawrence Peltier getting arrested. That's rich. I'd like to see the cop with balls big enough to arrest Lawrence Peltier."

"Oh my gosh, he's a crooked clerk?" Joe leaned over Stephen's shoulder to stare at Red.

"You really are oblivious." Red looked up at the both of them. As amusing as Monday drunks were, Stephen realized belatedly that he'd probably rather not be trapped between them. "Just see how far that information gets you at City Hall."

"I mean, I wouldn't ever say anything," Joe said in a poor imitation of a more sober man.

"You better not," Stephen said, turning on him and finding himself much closer than he'd expected. "That guy's got dirt on me now."

"Oh, yeah, and he'll use it too," Red said, slipping out from the barstool and slapping some coins next to his empty pint glass. "Watch yourself, Stephen. He's a decent sort of guy, but stay on his good side."

"I'm sure Stephen can handle that just fine," Mae said with an impish purse to his lips, bouncing one hip suggestively like his namesake.

"Oh, come on, he's my boss, I'm not gonna do anything with my boss," Stephen exclaimed. "Besides, I told you, I'm sworn off married guys."

Joe listed to one side. Stephen wrinkled his nose as he tried to prop him up again.

"Just because he hired a queer doesn't mean he's one of the boys," Stephen added, absently fixing Joe's askew jacket collar.

"Stephen, don't say that word," Mae said.

"He's not married anymore," Red said. "But he's definitely not one of the boys either."

"I'm still trying to figure out how you know all this, Red." Mae put his hand on his hip.

"I'm Augie Goldberg's cousin, that's how." Red grinned.

"Augie who?" Stephen asked. God, he sounded like he had marbles in his mouth.

"The St. Paul hotel owner," Joe whispered back loudly. "We met her, 'member?"

"Coulda been the city clerk myself," Red sniffed, "but there's too many girls up there. Besides, I've got bigger fish to fry."

"Like shameless tricks in the Arcade basement restrooms?" Mae said acidly.

"Takes one to know one," Red replied and winked at him. Then he pulled on his coat and left.

Stephen felt a little deflated as he leaned against the bar.

"You gonna order something?"

He yelped as Mrs. Kreuger poked him in the back.

"Gah, sorry, uh. You got any pop?" Stephen was grasping, but neither he nor Joe could drink anymore. Joe had to sober up to drive home, and Stephen had to work early at Dayton's in the morning. Had to get a meeting to put in his two weeks' notice. He couldn't help but grin as Mrs. Kreuger glowered at him.

"No."

"Oh. Uh…"

"Bar's for paying customers *only*."

Joe pulled on Stephen's shoulder. "We can just go."

Stephen looked back at him and let his alcohol-soaked brain run away with what they could do to kill time instead. Wander around the city. Throw snowballs in Rice Park. Get cozy behind a bush. You know, just friend stuff.

"Yeah," Mae added, "I was just heading out anyway."

"Are you drunk?" Joe asked, turning on Mae.

Mae snorted. "Darling, it's *Monday*."

"Then could you drive us home?"

"What?"

"I mean, do you drive? I have my car here, but I'd be a hazard behind the wheel."

"Joe, it's only a mile or two," Stephen said, hearing his sloppy voice in that weird, third person sort of way again. He didn't know why he was arguing. He was drunk and stupid. Keeping Mae with them was the absolute best idea from a self-preservation perspective. Except, he didn't really want to preserve himself.

"I only got the one car. I'm not gonna risk it," Joe shrugged him off. "Come on, Mae, please?"

"How am I gonna get home after I drop you idiots off?" Mae crossed his arms.

"You can just take the car for the night, and I'll meet you here tomorrow and get it from you."

Mae's eyes went big. "Oh *really?* And what's your wife going to say about that?"

Joe shrugged. "Nothing. She never goes in the garage unless I'm driving her somewhere anyway."

"Well, in that case, alright. I'll give you boys a lift."

Mae West was a terrible driver. Actually, Stephen was quite sure he'd never driven a car before in his life. He killed the engine four times before they were able to pull out from Joe's usual parking space on 4th Street.

"Where to, fellas?" Mae asked as he skidded onto Kellogg Boulevard. "I'm at your service."

"Down the Levee, first, I think," Joe slurred.

Joe and Stephen were both in the back seat. Stephen was stuck behind the driver and Joe was strewn out, his legs leaving very little in the way of legroom for Stephen. This annoyed Stephen, so he spread his knees out too, battling Joe by shoving his knee against his thigh.

"Come on, you two, no fighting," Mae chided as he turned down Eagle Street. "Oh, wow, this is a big hill."

The car began to trundle down the road, descending to the river flats below the bluff. Joe's hand gripped Stephen's knee.

"Oh, here we go, boys!" Mae squealed. His tone was as cheery as ever, but with a thread of tension that wasn't normally there. "Which one's the brake again?"

"Ha ha, very funny," Stephen groused, trying to ignore Joe's fingers pressing into his trousers. He glanced down, saw the long fingers pulling the wool of his suit pants. Saw the thin gold band around his ring finger. Stephen took a fortifying breath and looked out the window.

"Of course, I'm just joking, ha ha ha!" Mae tittered as the car barreled faster, toward the stop sign at the train track. He ground the gears and killed the engine again. "Ope, there they are!"

The car screeched to a halt halfway on the train tracks. Joe's grip on Stephen's thigh seized tight enough that Stephen could very solidly assume that he was only holding on for dear life. Stephen himself was gripping the window crank with one hand while the other braced against the back of Mae's seat.

"Who put that train track here?" Mae giggled and restarted the engine. He shifted into gear and turned right on Spring Street, heading into the Upper Levee neighborhood. Then, Mae let out a screech and slammed on the brakes.

"What the *hell*, Mae?" Stephen shouted as his chin bounced off the back of the driver's seat.

"I just saw something!"

"Have you even driven before?"

"I think it was a cat. Oh my god, what if I hit someone's

cat?!"

"I don't think you hit a cat, Mae. We would've felt it."

"I'll just check."

"Jesus Christ, Mae."

It didn't matter. Mae had swung the driver's door open.

"Mae! Put the damn parking brake on!" Stephen bellowed.

"Oh!" Mae kicked down the parking brake with a ratchet, then scurried out and around the front of the car.

Stephen collapsed back on the seat. "Dear god, Joe, he's a worse driver sober than you would be drunk."

Joe hiccupped. Stephen looked at him sideways. Joe had his chin tucked down like his neck had just given up, and he looked up at Stephen. His hand was still on Stephen's leg. There was nothing to explain it away now.

"You turned out real nice today," Joe said, the corner of his mouth tugging up a bit wistfully. Stephen reached down and squeezed his fingers around Joe's hand, pulling it up and holding it between them. He didn't know what he was doing. Mae would be back any second.

"Thanks," he murmured. Joe's eyes were drifting down to Stephen's mouth before flicking back up. Stephen's forefinger and thumb closed around Joe's ring, wiggling it back and forth, reminding himself and Joe what hung in the balance between them.

"We're drunk," Stephen said with a weak laugh.

Joe cleared his throat and nodded. Stephen looked up at him, risked looking into those earnest green eyes.

"And you're married," Stephen whispered.

Joe's face crumpled a bit. "And you've sworn off married guys."

"I have," Stephen choked out. It wasn't his imagination. Joe was thinking about it too. It was vindicating, even if it was simultaneously brutal.

"And I wouldn't do that anyway." Joe's voice was reedy and thin. He curled his hand out of Stephen's and pulled it into his chest. "I've, um … I've got a family to think of."

Stephen was unprepared for how devastating that was to hear. He'd been trying to keep himself safe, but there was no such thing, was there? Not when it came to Joe Milner.

"You're a good dad," Stephen found himself saying. "And a good husband too."

"I lied to her to stay out with you."

"To celebrate!" Stephen really didn't know what the hell he was trying to do. Put Joe off easy? Comfort him? For Chrissake. "You got me a job I never would have thought to dream of, Joe. You changed my goddamn life. Nothing about that is wrong."

Joe winced. He didn't say anything in reply. Stephen looked out the front of the car, shifting his knees together to keep to himself. Mae was moving in and out of the glare of the headlights like a diva soprano who couldn't find her spotlight. God, wouldn't it be a poetical tragedy if Joe did all this to help Stephen get a job at City Hall only for them to go back to not talking again? Stephen would still at least have the job, so that was something. He'd done the math. It would take him three months to save up enough to move into his own place. If he could find one.

Mae whipped the car door open with a thunk. "Coast's clear! No cats were harmed. False alarm!"

Stephen rolled his eyes and said under his breath, "I could've told you that."

Joe snorted. Stephen glanced over at him and gave him a friendly nudge. Joe's hound-dog eyes regarded him sadly, but his mouth quirked at the corners.

Chapter 14

Joe was glad he'd helped Stephen get the job when the Ford Anglia pulled up to Stephen's place and Joe recognized it. It was a boardinghouse, but it was the one Stephen's mother ran. Joe had visited once or twice in high school (against Stephen's will, he might add). Joe didn't say anything, of course, but he was relieved he'd been stupid enough to keep throwing himself in Stephen's way. His nerves were shot, but with the exception of lying to stay out late, he was fully certain he'd done all the right things. Well, maybe fondling Stephen's knee was another exception. And reminding Stephen that he'd sworn off married men, like if he hadn't, things would be different. God, was the dating pool that awful for guys like Stephen? That one had to specifically swear off married men, like if you didn't, you'd end up with some philandering bastard as a matter of course?

None of it bore thinking about as Stephen disappeared inside and Mae released the parking brake.

"Where to now?"

Joe sighed and lolled his head back to look at Mae without lifting it from the back seat. "Get back to Venice Street and up to Smith."

"You got it, Captain!" Mae chirped. He then proceeded to kill the engine twice before managing to get into second gear. God, knowing Joe's luck, Mae would end up flooding the engine and they'd be stranded. They'd have to trudge a block back to Stephen's, and he'd have to see Stephen's mother. She'd put them up, of course, and then he'd have to call Marion to tell her what had happened. But with enough embellishment to keep in line with all the other lies he'd told. Then maybe Stephen's mother would be full up, so he'd have to stay in Stephen's room… Goddammit. Shut up.

Mae managed to get them up the bluff without killing the engine again, which earned him ample, genuine praise from Joe as they headed back to West 7th Street.

"You alright, Sleeping Beauty?" Mae asked as he pulled up in front of Joe's four-square, perched on a dark corner in a neighborhood already asleep.

Joe shook his head. He'd been dozing. "Sure I am. Why wouldn't I be?"

Mae shrugged. "You tell me. Or not."

Joe frowned.

"It just seems to me," Mae mused, "that you're finding a whole lot of excuses to spend time with our Vinny."

"We're old friends," Joe argued. Though he wasn't sure who he was arguing with, Mae or himself.

"Of course. Vinny's got his little tough guy routine, but he's a real softie when you get down to it. He's been jerked around a lot."

"Oh."

"We're all rooting for him to find a fellow who can give him all that he deserves," Mae added, a bit primly, like he was sorry to take Joe down a peg but he'd been left with no other choice.

"Me too," Joe scrambled to put in. "I want that for him too."

"Good," Mae replied. "Then don't get in his way."

Joe swallowed hard. "Right. Yup." He took a deep breath in through his nose. "Well, thanks a lot for the ride, Mae. I owe you one."

Mae smirked. "My pleasure. I thought I'd *never* learn how to drive."

"I'm not sure you have."

Mae let out a hoot of laughter.

Joe pushed the door open and managed to clamber to his feet. He leaned down before he shut the door again.

"I'll see you after work at Kreuger's tomorrow," Joe reminded Mae.

"If I'm not halfway to New York City by then!" Mae singsonged in reply.

"Ha ha, very funny," Joe said. "Seriously, don't steal my car."

"How could you possibly accuse me of that!" Mae said, affronted.

"Because you just said you were going to."

"I was *joking.* You got the joke. Come on. We both know I couldn't even get it on the highway without stalling out."

Joe chuckled. "I'll see you tomorrow."

"See you tomorrow." Mae gave him an impish grin. "Say, you know—"

"Yeah?"

"*I* don't mind a married man." Mae gave a saucy wink worthy of his namesake.

"Ha ha." Joe shut the door and shook his head before he could follow that suggestion to its logical conclusion. Then he turned around. The house loomed above him. He pressed down that crawling feeling in his throat and forced himself to walk inside.

Joe made it all the way into bed before Marion rolled over and glowered at him.

"Where have you been?" she hissed.

Joe jumped about halfway to the ceiling. "Jeez, Marion."

"Don't 'jeez' me!"

"Sorry, you just startled me."

"Why don't you explain where you've been, and don't bother telling me you worked late, because it's 10:30 and you smell like a liquor barrel."

Joe swallowed hard. "I went to the bar after we finished with work. It was a long night. Everyone else was going." God, it sounded so weak.

"You know, Joe, in all the years we've been together, you've never lied to me. I would believe you, wouldn't ask you anything more, if it weren't for the fact that I called your office at 4:45 and your secretary said you'd *already left.*" Marion sat up. She'd been terse on the phone at the bar, but Joe had been so desperate to finish the call after being observed by pretty much everyone in it, he hadn't noticed anything else. Shit. Her hair was in rollers, and the shadowy room did little to disguise how spitting mad she was.

Joe swallowed hard. He could scramble to double down. But she was right. He wasn't a liar. Panic was already rising up in his throat. "I … I …" He winced and buried his face in his hands. "I don't know what's wrong with me."

"What are you talking about?"

"That's the problem, I don't know."

"Well, where were you?"

"At the bar at the St. Paul Hotel," Joe admitted. He could only look at his hands. "Stephen got the job I put him up for and we went there with the city clerk to celebrate."

"Why didn't you just tell me that?" Marion was exasperated. Joe could see the path forward, the path out. It would be so easy to apologize, to dissemble and let her tell herself that simple story. But that felt like a lie too. It was a lie too. Because Joe wasn't innocent. He'd been running his thoughts around Stephen for weeks. There was no corner of his mind he could hide from the fact that he was helplessly infatuated. He'd touched Stephen's knee, and he didn't regret it one bit. He had no confidence in his own honor if Stephen were less honorable.

"I've been encouraging you to make friends for over a month, Joe. Why would you feel like you have to lie to me? Is it because you got drunk?"

"No," Joe replied. His throat was all tight and close. He couldn't look at her. He didn't want to be here. He'd rather be anywhere than in this house.

Marion sighed and shook her head. She rubbed her hands over her face and Joe didn't deserve her. He didn't deserve her forbearance. He couldn't love her, he couldn't please her, he couldn't even lie to her properly to give her peace of mind. He'd been trying, for years at this point, to play the part of the man she deserved, but he was terrible at that too. No matter what he did, he would hurt her.

"I can't do this."

The words had hissed out of his lips, like he was a creaky bellows. His stomach dropped and his heart clenched and he watched her shadowy face look up at him.

"What?"

Joe was a coward. He wished he could take it back. But he couldn't, he'd said it, and he'd meant it. He still meant it. He said it again, with his own voice this time. "I can't do this."

Her shoulders seized up near her ears and she took a shuddering breath. "Joe, I don't understand—"

"—I don't either," he said. He wished he could sound in control, firm or certain, but his throat was clenched tight and his eyes were surging with tears and his voice betrayed him. "I don't understand what's wrong with me. But you deserve someone who loves you well, who can't wait to come home to you, who c-can make love to you, and I've tried and tried, Marion, to be that man, but I'm not. I'm not."

"Joe," Marion's voice wasn't any steadier. She snatched his hand and squeezed it tight. "Joe, we can figure this out. Whatever it is. Please."

Joe took a deep, shuddering breath. "I can't."

He stood up, got out of the bed, his body carrying him away before he hurt either of them any more. He stumbled out into the hall, into the kitchen, and stared at the old hob. The one his grandmother had used. The murky darkness layered with the bright warmth of memory, of his grandmother monologuing in Czech while he and Stephen ate Linzer cookies hot off the tray. Stephen's easy grin, dimpling his cheeks. Joe hadn't known what love felt like back then. He'd thought it would be different, something big and loud and more. With swelling music and fireworks. But it had really always been that simple.

Dear god, it had always been him.

Joe threw on his coat and boots over his pajamas and walked out the front door. He took his time to open and shut the hulking thing. He didn't want to wake anyone up. The houses were all dark. The streetlamp on the corner was a weak weapon against the shroud of night. It scarcely lit a circle five feet around it. The sidewalks were clear, even though there was still plenty of snow on the ground. The clouds were clearing and a few stars were twinkling, like nothing had changed. Joe's house was on a corner that was more of a bend in the road than a cross section of two streets. Mae had his car, so there were only two ways to go. He started walking in the direction of the river.

Joe couldn't just go to Stephen, declare his feelings, and expect anything to change. Stephen had made himself very clear. He wasn't interested in messing around with anyone who wasn't serious. And Joe, as much as he loved him, couldn't be certain of anything. What if it wasn't just an unsuitable match with Marion? What if he was defective? What if he wasn't able to make love to anyone? Joe refused to hurt anyone else.

Besides, he was still married. He had two children that he desperately wanted to shield from all of this. He wasn't sure what he'd actually done, or what Marion would do next, or what he even wanted. Well, he did know what he wanted. He wanted to turn back time, back to that graduation party. He wanted to kiss Stephen on the mouth instead of quietly pant with his eyes closed as Stephen acknowledged the thing he'd never had the courage to admit. He wanted to wake up that next day, head pounding, and go to Stephen instead of hiding and pretending he didn't remember it. He would give anything to go back and prevent this entire mess from ever happening.

The temperature wasn't too bad, but it was below freezing and the cold bit at his legs through his pajama pants. He'd gotten about three blocks before realizing he'd turned left on the quickest route toward the Levee. He absolutely could not walk to Stephen's house. It was the middle of the night. It was over a mile away. It was freezing cold. What would Stephen's mother think?

Joe had no excuses. It took him the better part of an hour to walk all the way down to the Levee. His head was pounding. It was almost midnight. He'd barely seen any cars the entire journey. His breath was huffing clouds of condensation in the cold air, his ears and nose half froze, as he looked up at the second half-story of Stephen's house.

The windows were dark. Of course they were. It was the middle of the goddamn night and Joe was a goddamn fool. Maybe Stephen was sleepless, though. Like Joe was. Maybe he also laid awake, wishing to go back in time, to make different choices. Although Joe couldn't imagine what Stephen would need to go back and change. Maybe to box Joe's ears and tell him to wake the hell up.

Joe shifted foot to foot, hands shoved in his pockets. It was cold. He looked up at the window on the gable. That was Stephen's room. He knew because he had been here, that one time, when Stephen had forgotten something for school—he couldn't remember what it had been, but it'd been important enough that Stephen had to go back for it, even if it meant Joe seeing his house. Stephen had run himself in circles trying to keep anyone from seeing his flood-bedraggled house. The fact that Joe had visited, had been invited (albeit begrudgingly) inside, made him stand taller, prouder. Made him determined to be worthy of it. He'd been so certain that destiny had made him to be lifelong friends with Stephen. Oh, how he'd taken that for granted.

Perhaps he could take a snowball and gently lob it at the window. Even if Stephen was awake, he had no way of knowing Joe was there, standing in the front walk in the middle of the night like an absolute loon, remembering and regretting and longing. A brave man would do it. A man who knew his own heart would do it.

Joe stood there for fifteen minutes. He even made the snowball. He played a hundred possible scenarios inside his mind of how Stephen might react. And he concluded, after careful calculation of odds, that the best course after all was to go home.

✳

Joe slept on the couch. Well, if you could call it sleeping. He wasn't sure whether he'd slept at all, or if he had slept but he just didn't remember it. At one point, the dog came out and snuffled his face. He was pretty sure he'd been sleeping when that happened. He thought maybe the dog was concerned for his welfare, might provide comfort as animals do in times of crisis, but the old mutt had just waddled back to Marion and the bedroom as soon as she'd confirmed that he was indeed still alive. Millie had always been Marion's dog anyway.

Joe took care to make sure he got up and tidied away his makeshift bed before the children awoke and got ready for school. In spite of his aching guilt and a pounding headache, Joe went through the motions like nothing had happened. He was good at that.

Marion did too, though he thought his coffee was a bit weaker and her stare was a bit harder than usual. Marion was good at going through the motions too. Though, she usually only did it for her mother or her sister. It was foreign to see her do it for him. It made his chest ache for her, but not in longing or regret. Mostly in sympathy.

As soon as she returned from putting the kids on the bus, she hung up her coat, marched to the dining table, sat down, and faced him. He admired how formidable she was, even when it was turned on him.

"Is there someone else?" she asked. Point-blank. Joe fumbled his coffee cup but miraculously didn't spill any on his clean, white shirt that looked infinitely more turned out than he felt. "Because if there is, I need to know."

There was. But there wasn't. Because 'someone else' implied that the other person reciprocated, that there was at least the risk of an affair going on. And there wasn't. Stephen wasn't interested in anyone who would do that. He'd made himself clear.

"What do you mean?" Joe asked. Marion rolled her eyes so hard it looked like it hurt.

"Look here, Joe," she said. "No more of this avoidant, monosyllabic bullshit. You can't drop a bomb on me like you did last night and refuse to talk about it. You can't sit there and drink your coffee and pretend like everything is okay. *You* told *me* that you can't do this anymore. That I don't deserve you. Which is nonsense, because you're a perfectly nice man, at least you were before you pulled this. I'm not going to pretend like I haven't noticed you've been distant, but I thought it was just pressure. You know, pressure after Linda was born, and pressure at work. You put yourself under so much *pressure*."

He did. He did do that. He nodded.

"So much, you can't sleep at night because you're up worrying about a goddamn crack in the ceiling. I've got news for you, Joe. Lathe and plaster ceilings crack. It's what they do." Marion's mouth tightened. "And now you've got me talking for you again. Goddammit, Joe. Tell me what you're thinking!"

Joe opened his mouth. He wanted to. But his mind went blank. Maybe it *was* pressure. "I … I don't know."

"You don't know, or you don't want to say?" God, she was so annoyed with him. He was just making this worse.

"I don't want to say." He could at least tell that truth. She'd been so gracious to offer him multiple choice.

"Okay, well whatever it is you're not saying to protect

me, here's the story I'm telling myself instead. I'm imagining you've fallen in love with some woman at work and she's occupying your every thought and that the distance I've been noticing has actually not been about pressure, but about how you're regretting me and wishing you could be with her instead. And then I'm wondering how long this has been going on, and whether you've been two-timing me for years, not months. And then I'm thinking about how my great-aunt Phyllis opened up the door to this strange lady and found out her husband had a second family he wasn't supporting and what if that was what you're doing too and—"

"—Okay, stop, stop," Joe said. He had to put his coffee cup down because his hand was shaking. "I don't have a second family."

"Good!" Marion exclaimed, throwing her hands up. "That's really good. But you know, you haven't said anything about the rest of it."

How could he tell her? How could he tell her that it was true, that he was thinking about someone else, without telling her that it was a man? He had no idea what Marion thought about homosexuals. No idea whether she'd be tolerant or angry or scared, whether she'd think he was sick, whether she'd try to protect their children from him. He couldn't take that risk, not when he wasn't even sure that he was one. He just wanted Stephen.

"There's someone else," Marion said for him.

Joe nodded despondently. He shoved his hands over his face because he couldn't look at her.

"There's someone else, and you can't even say it."

"I'm too ashamed!" Joe blurted into his hands. "I'm sorry."

"You should be," Marion replied. He forced himself to look up at her hard face. "Both sorry and ashamed."

She looked at her hands and Joe put his face back in his. The silence was booming. The tick of the clock felt like a time bomb, except in reverse because the bomb had already gone off.

When Joe managed to look up from his hands again, Marion's face wasn't hard anymore. It was cracked and broken, with tears crawling down.

"I don't know what to do," she sniffed. "I don't know what to do, and you're not any help at all. You won't even talk to me. How can we fix this if you won't even talk to me? Am I so awful?"

"No! No, you're not awful. It's me. It's all me. I'm … I'm …" God, this was so hard. "You were wrong. I *am* a liar. I've been lying my whole life. To you, to Stephen, to myself. When you said I wasn't a liar, last night, I realized … I try so hard not to be, but I am."

"I don't get it, Joe. If you didn't want me, why lie about it?"

"I just wanted to be good."

"Well, if you want to be good, and you lie to try and be good, doesn't that make you bad?"

Joe's elbows sort of collapsed and he buried his head into his arms on the table. "Yes," he moaned miserably.

He could feel her gaze on the top of his head like his hair was on fire.

"I don't want to be married to a liar," she said at length. "But I also don't want to hurt our family. So where does that leave us?"

"I don't know."

"I don't know either."

Chapter 15

Stephen didn't even care that he was hungover. He'd had a spring in his step since he woke up. His manager at Dayton's had been frustrated by how cheerfully Stephen resigned. Now, his two weeks' notice duly filed and his shift finished, he was partaking in a tipple of the hair of the dog that bit him at Kreuger's and regaling anyone who would listen with his triumph at City Hall.

Mae was there too, spinning Joe's car keys around his finger and embellishing Stephen's tale with embarrassing details, to the delight of Marge and Violet and, to perhaps a lesser degree, Dickie, who was clearly envious and resentful that Stephen had managed to *land* a job with his limp wrist. Stephen felt bad for him, distantly, but he also had been jealous of Dickie and Walter for years, so he figured turnabout was fair play.

"So you've landed the coveted 9 to 5, have you?" Dickie drawled. "I suppose a toast is in order."

"Don't sound so excited."

"Oh, I'm sorry, did I sound excited? I was going for passive aggressive and bored." Dickie's name sure did suit him. The bell at the front door rang. "Oh look, there's your patron now. Perhaps he'll buy us all champagne, allow the rest of us to soak up a splash of your cup that doth spilleth over."

"Christ, Dickie, layin' it on thick?" Marge said.

"Joe, look!" Mae cried as Stephen turned around in the booth. "I didn't steal your car!"

Stephen expected to see Joe with that sheepish grin on his face, happy and laughing like last night. Like so many nights before, when they'd sat in this booth all together and it felt so familiar, like his high school self and his present self had somehow integrated into a shiny new man who could get a job at City Hall. But one look at Joe and Stephen could tell something was seriously wrong.

Stephen scrambled out of the booth and headed Joe off, before the boys started sniping at him too.

"Hey," he said when they approached one another midway down the bar. "You don't look so good."

Stephen didn't really notice that he'd reached out to touch Joe's arm until he flinched away from it. Joe had dark circles under his eyes, making him look more like a hound dog than ever.

"I'm okay."

"Did something happen at the office?" Stephen asked. *Did hiring a queer blow up in your face?*

"No, everything's fine at work." Joe leaned to the side a bit and intersected with the bar. "I'm just hungover."

"Why you here then?" Stephen leveled a skeptical brow.

"Mae's still got my car keys." Joe flicked his chin toward the booth, where Mae was crawling over positively everyone to get out from the corner.

"Don't worry Joe," Mae singsonged. "It hasn't got so much as a scratch on her."

"That's lucky, because you live in a slum," Dickie drawled, cigarette smoke pouring from his mouth like condemnation.

Mae ignored him and bounded up to Joe and Stephen.

"Awe, you're looking worse for wear, Joe. What did you do to him, Stephen, make him drink battery acid?"

Joe's expression hollowed somehow. Stephen tried not to let his worry show on his face.

"Just give him his keys," Stephen said, snatching them out of Mae's hand and dropping them into Joe's. "You gonna stay for a drink?"

"No, I gotta get back," Joe said, glancing up at the bar. "Besides, if I ever see whiskey again, it'll be too soon."

Mae scoffed. "You'll be back, Milner."

"Certainly not on a Monday again," Stephen murmured. His eyes were stuck on the line between Joe's eyebrows. "Here, I'll walk you out."

Joe was resigned as they walked out of the bar and onto the street. The wind was picking up between the buildings and Stephen had left his coat inside.

"What's going on?" Stephen asked, crossing his arms against the frigid air biting through his sweater.

"Nothing," Joe said. "Everything. Shit."

Stephen blinked. This was too public a place. "Let's walk to your car. Mae said he parked it on this block."

They walked down Wabasha about half a block, where the Ford Anglia was parked on the hill sloping down to Lowertown.

"Christ, I hope he put the parking break on," Stephen muttered as Joe got in the driver's seat, then reached across to unlock the passenger door. The wheel was turned toward the curb, so that was something. He pulled the car door open and climbed in. It was a bit warmer, out of the wind.

Joe had both hands on the steering wheel. After a long moment, he let his forehead clunk down on it as well.

"Joe?"

"I told Marion."

Oh Christ. "Told her what?"

Joe took a long breath in. "I told her I can't be the husband she deserves."

Stephen's mouth was hanging open.

"What?" That sounded bad. "Are you—?" Couldn't ask that question. That would be too pointed. "I didn't realize things were that bad."

Joe nodded against the steering wheel. "I don't know what to do. She's furious."

Stephen cycled through several replies before he landed on, "I can't imagine." He felt guilty, which was ridiculous, because holding hands in the back of the car for two minutes did not break up families. Wiggling a man's wedding ring when he was looking at you like you were the only other person on planet earth wasn't a goddamn ultimatum. Dear god, Joe had even outright said he'd never do that to Marion. This wasn't what Stephen wanted-ed. He squirmed in his seat and said nothing.

"I don't know what to do," Joe repeated, "but I don't want to take it back."

"Do you want," Stephen took a careful breath, "to leave her?"

"I don't know!" Joe cried into the steering wheel. "No. Yes? If we didn't have the children, I think yes. But we do, and I don't know what that would mean for them, and I don't want to ruin their lives!"

"Ruin their lives?" Stephen frowned. "Joe, my dad left when I was ten. It was the best thing that happened to our family."

Joe looked up at him, and Stephen could tell immediately that it had been the exact wrong thing to say.

"Not that you are bad for your family, Joe, no, that's not what I meant," Stephen fumbled. "I mean that sometimes staying together *isn't* the best thing for the kids. Sometimes—oftentimes, really—parents who stay together for their kids make for an awful childhood, full of anger and resentment and disdain."

"But I don't want to leave them," Joe said. His chin shook. "I don't even want to leave *her*. But I don't want to be her husband. Does that make any sense?"

Stephen paused. It made no sense, actually, but now was not the time for brutal honesty. "If you weren't her husband… What would that mean?"

Joe sighed. "It'd mean … it'd mean she'd be free."

"And you?" *You'd be free? What would* that *mean?*

"I wouldn't have to keep pretending."

Stephen's hands were fisted in the fabric of his slacks. It was insanity to imagine that that moment last night could have led to this. He couldn't think of a way to ask that didn't sound selfish and presumptuous. But the timing was *poignant*. He couldn't ask about himself, though. This was too serious, and Joe needed support quite desperately. He wouldn't get it from anyone else, knowing his family and having met his work friends, so Stephen had no choice but to try. He knew Joe well, and he knew the man needed an eternity to put his thoughts together, so he just waited. But god, this was torture.

Joe's voice was a crack and a squeak when he did finally speak. "I think I have to leave her, Stephen. I don't think I have a choice."

Stephen reached out and put his hand on Joe's shoulder. The way Joe was acting made him scared. It was all very well and good to smoke cigarettes and bemoan the moral hypocrisy of the institution of marriage, but in reality, in the everyday lives of people, *especially* people with children, divorce simply was not done. In fact, barring proof of abandonment, adultery, or some other grievous abuse, it was impossible. Stephen felt strongly that regardless of

Joe's specific reasons, he was at least partially responsible for leading Joe down the primrose path to perdition. He owed it to everyone involved to help in any way he could, and keep his own damn selfish feelings out of it.

"You always have a choice, Joe," Stephen said. He squeezed his hand over the shoulder of Joe's camel coat. If he believed it hard enough, it would be true, right? "Nothing is set in stone. Maybe there's a million people who have an opinion on what's best, but when it comes down to it, you can only do what feels right for you." Stephen wasn't sure where he was going with this. "Only you and Marion can decide what your marriage is, or isn't."

Joe stilled. He nodded slowly, staring at the steering wheel. "God, Stephen, this is hell. Every time I think about going back to that house, I feel sick to my stomach."

"That's … not good, Joe."

"It's really not. My kids must think I hate them."

"You don't."

"But I act like I do." Joe let out a frustrated sound. "And now I'm ruining your evening with my hysterics. I'm sorry."

"Not at all," Stephen replied. "This is what friends are for."

Joe's mouth twisted as he nodded. He glanced up at Stephen, made a half attempt at the ghost of a smile. It was the kind of smile that could break Stephen's heart. And after trying to keep his distance, trying to keep his feelings in check, Stephen realized with a thumping sort of finality that he would do anything to help this man, regardless of how much it hurt himself to do it. Wanting him, loving him—none of that was an option. It never had been. These were errant feelings, hopeless dreams declared dead so long ago they scarcely mattered anyway. Joe faced something bigger—much bigger—if he truly needed to end his marriage, and Stephen would see him through it, not because it benefitted him, but because it benefitted Joe. That was the only way Stephen could love him.

Joe resigned himself to going home and Stephen kept a strong, can-do attitude up all the way until he drove away, leaving Stephen nothing more than a shadow on the sidewalk. All he wanted to do was melt into the nearest wall and cry, but he couldn't do that. He wasn't so invisible that he couldn't be seen or heard at all. He couldn't even go home, because the boys would make his life a living hell with insinuations if he left with Joe and didn't come back. So he steeled himself and went back into Kreuger's.

"Vinny! I hear you're celebrating!" Frank Atlas had arrived while he was gone.

Stephen nodded and made a quick, resigned calculation. "That's right! Next round's on me!"

Chapter 16

"So," Mae West said as Stephen slid into the booth on Friday evening. It was just the two of them so far. "You wanna talk about it?"

"What?" Stephen deflected.

Mae raised a carefully curated brow. "You went home with the Frank on Tuesday. Something must have happened."

Stephen's lip curled. He'd needed to feel corporeal again, and he didn't have it in him to try. Frank was easy, and he could also smell desperation a mile away, like a shark. It hadn't even been worth it. He'd just wanted to feel his skin solid and real against someone else's for a while. Instead, he got cold feet and an embarrassingly consolatory can of Hamm's beer.

"I don't want to talk about it," Stephen said.

"Something to do with Sleeping Beauty? He didn't show up yesterday like he usually does."

Stephen scowled. "Don't call him that."

"Why? He's a sweet little darling just waiting for you to kiss him and wake him up."

"Mae!" Stephen swatted at him. "Nothing's happened with Joe, at least nothing that's any of your business, or mine for that matter. I just got too wrapped up in celebrating, and I didn't want to go home, and Frank was there."

"Good ol' reliable Frank." Mae snorted. He sat back, head tilted, and regarded Stephen for a long moment. "Vincelli, you're a mess."

Stephen rubbed his hands over his face and took a deep breath. "I know."

"You're all wrapped up in that man," Mae observed. "I know we teased you about calling him your soulmate—"

"—I should *never* have told you bitches that—"

"—but is he? Actually?"

"That's not the right question," Stephen sighed. "Maybe some people don't get soulmates. Maybe it's a stupid lie society tells us to force us into traditional marriages, so we have children, get jobs, and work until we die."

"It *is* a stupid lie," Mae sniffed. "I certainly haven't got any use for a soulmate. Where's the fun in that?"

"Right," Stephen attempted. "Who wants to sleep with the same man for the rest of his life anyway?"

"Some people do," Mae said. "Not me, certainly, but … maybe you?"

Stephen scrunched his nose up like that idea smelled foul. "Well, if I am that sort of man, I've been doing a pretty terrible job of it so far."

"Sleeping with Frank certainly didn't help," Mae observed.

"I didn't sleep with Frank," Stephen sighed miserably. "I couldn't go through with it."

"You put up with the smell of Frank Atlas' apartment and you didn't even go through with it?" Mae frowned. "Darling, do you think perhaps you were trying to fit a square peg into a round, Sleeping-Beauty-shaped hole?"

"Why is everything pegs and holes with you?" Stephen sneered helplessly. "Is that the sort of thing that passes as advice?"

"Not at all," Mae replied. If he'd been wearing pearls, he would have clutched them. "I'm just asking questions."

"I already got a mother to ask me annoying questions, Mae," Stephen said. "I don't need you piling on."

"Poor Stephen," Mae simpered and patted his shoulder, just like his mother might. Stephen was petulant about shrugging him off.

Dickie and Walter arrived then, resplendent in sunset-tinged tender glances and affectionate little touches. It was the insignificant stuff of solid, reliable love and Stephen couldn't even console himself with excitement about his new job. Marge and Violet weren't any better when they arrived. Stephen ended up leaving the booth to go talk to Red at the bar, but he didn't have much of a chance as the door opened with a ding and Frank Atlas entered. He was rosy-cheeked from the cold, handsome as ever, and ruined it immediately.

"Hey, there, Vinny-baby," he said and slung an arm manfully over Stephen's shoulders.

"Nope." Stephen ducked right out of his reach. "None of that."

"Aw, come on." Frank waggled his eyebrows. "I gave you a shoulder to cry on. We're bosom buddies now."

"I didn't cry!"

Red was looking over his shoulder at them with one eyebrow reaching for his hairline as he stood and pulled on his jacket. For once, Stephen wished he actually was invisible.

The door rang again with a puff of frigid air as Red slipped out, and a woman walked in. The patrons by and large didn't give her a second glance. But Stephen did, because he knew her. And she was *Joe's fucking wife*.

Marion Milner was short, plumper than Stephen remembered, with dark hair fashionably brushed-out. She was wearing a matching set—her dress, coat, and hat were all made from the same green wool. She looked very well turned out, except for her wide, skittering eyes and her hands that twisted her gloved fingers.

Stephen was just entertaining the idea of hiding when her eyes alighted on him.

"Stephen?" she said. "Stephen Vincelli? Goodness, it's been so long." She walked up to him with the ghost of a polite smile. "I wish I could catch up, but I'm trying to track Joe down. Have you seen him?"

"Joe?" Stephen said stupidly. She knew that Joe had been spending time with Stephen. Playing dumb wasn't going to help.

"Yeah, I know he usually comes here for a drink on Thursdays. I figured since he wasn't at his office, he might be here."

"Oh." Stephen was just churning out zingers here. "Um, sorry, I haven't seen him. Today." Christ, it sounded suspicious to say it like that. Didn't it?

"Oh," Marion frowned. "Do you have any idea where I might find him? His secretary didn't have any useful suggestions, but then again, she wouldn't."

"I'm sorry?"

Marion looked up at him and her eyes welled quite suddenly with tears. "Sorry, I shouldn't have said that."

"Vinny, you coming?" Frank. Fucking. Atlas. "I'm sorry, ma'am, is my best friend bothering you?"

"No, not at all, I'm sorry." Marion sniffed in a horrified way and pulled a handkerchief from her purse, holding it over her nose and mouth like it might prevent her from being perceived.

"Frank, go away," Stephen said through gritted teeth. He had no idea what to do, but he knew for damn certain

Frank wouldn't make anything better. He went up on his toes and craned over Frank's bulk to make urgent eyes at Walter, who was watching from the booth. He skidded to his feet and came right over.

"Frank, Dickie wants to tell you something," Walter said.

"Sorry, ma'am, I didn't catch your name," Frank said over him. He put his hand out and when Marion automatically grasped it, he lifted her hand to his lips. Stephen wanted to scream.

"Milner," she said, then cleared her throat. "Sorry, Mrs. Joe Milner."

Frank and Walter both looked like they'd been electrocuted.

"*Really?*" Frank said, his wide eyes turning significantly to Stephen.

Walter hustled. "Come on, Frank, Dickie's waiting." He steered him by his behemoth shoulders back to the booth.

Stephen watched them frozen. Fuck. What a disaster. He scrambled. "I'm sorry," he managed. He thought to say her name but he had no idea what to call her. 'Marion' was too familiar, but 'Mrs. Milner' would catch nastily in his throat. "Those are my pals." Make it seem normal. "Joe's too. Sorry, they're neanderthals'."

He forced himself to look back at Marion. She wasn't actively crying anymore, so that was good news. "I'm sorry," Stephen said again. "Gah, I keep saying that—I mean, I haven't seen Joe today. I don't know where he is, if he's not at work…"

"I kept telling him to invite you and your wife to dinner," Marion murmured. "I … this is so awkward. I just … I need to talk to him. Urgently."

"Okay," Stephen said. His lungs were too tight to

breathe properly.

"Did he tell you what's going on?" Marion whispered.

Stephen winced. "Yes. Some."

Marion's face scrunched up, and she started to cry again. She reached up and grabbed Stephen by the lapels of his jacket. "Do you know who she is?"

"What?"

"The woman he's seeing?"

Stephen experienced an awful sensation in his stomach, like he was free-falling. He opened his mouth, but his tongue was stuck to the roof of it. He closed it again. It was taking him too long to respond. He should have been surprised by now. Maybe he should be. Maybe she knew something he didn't know, and Joe had been two-timing her with his secretary all the time, under all of their noses. But he really didn't think that was the case. Regardless, it was too late to deny it. Marion's brows were crumpling, and she was shaking her head.

"Joe said there was someone else," Marion whispered. She still had Stephen by the jacket. "Just put me out of my misery."

"Are you sure you want to know?" Stephen heard himself say, and wanted to kick himself. Someone sidled by him and almost did. "Would it change anything?"

Marion's chin worked. "Yes, it would. Then I'd know who to blame."

Oh *fuck*.

"Marion!"

Stephen looked up and saw Joe walking down the length of the bar. Red was behind him, resuming his perch at the front of the bar and watching carefully. There was this small, childlike voice in Stephen's head that cut through the general horror of the whole situation. It said, *This is it.*

"Marion, what are you doing here?" Joe said, taking his wife's arm.

"Looking for you," she hiccupped, dropping Stephen's lapels and turning to face Joe.

"Well, here I am."

"Why weren't you at your office?" Marion's voice was quiet. She knew she was making a scene. It looked like that knowledge was making it harder for her to hold it together. Stephen looked over at the booth helplessly.

"I took a walk," Joe said.

Marion pursed her lips. "In this weather?"

Joe looked sheepish. "Yes. It was bracing." His cheeks were pink. It was probably true. Stephen wondered if Red had seen him and brought him back here. He didn't think Joe would have come in today, if he hadn't yesterday. "Come on, let's go."

Marion glanced back at Stephen. Her eyes were fierce. "No."

Joe looked at Stephen too. He was guarded, his eyes intent, like he was saying *What did you tell her?* Stephen shook his head minutely. *Nothing.* There was nothing to tell. Wasn't there?

"Come on, Marion, let's go to the car," Joe tried again, gently tugging her arm.

Marion grimaced, then let Joe pull her away. The two of them slipped as covertly as they could out the door of the bar, the bell ringing with finality.

Stephen sagged against the bar. The boys flowed out of the booth like water and surrounded him.

"What was *that* all about?" Dickie asked.

"That's Joe's wife?" Marge added, looking at the door. "*Damn!*"

"Stephen, are you okay?" Walter asked. "What was she saying?"

Mae put a hand on Stephen's forehead. "My god, remind me to call you in an emergency. You're sweating bullets, but you didn't break!"

"I…" Stephen slowly came back to life. "What? What's there to break?"

"Well, you know," Walter said with a shrug of his shoulders.

Dickie rolled his eyes. "You've been fucking her husband, of course."

Walter and Mae both hit Dickie.

"Shut *up*!"

"Don't get us kicked out, come on, Dickie," Walter hissed.

"What? I'm being quiet."

"I'm not!" Stephen cried, then modulated his voice. "I'm not doing—that."

"Yeah right," Frank rolled his eyes. "How'd you get that job, then?"

"Are you kidding me?" Stephen hissed. He was furious and he was going to take it out on someone. "If I'm *fucking whoring myself,* why would I go home with *you*?"

Frank's expression flattened. "Low blow, Vin."

"Hate to hurt your enormous ego, Frank, but if I was—"

"Come on, get back in the booth," Marge whispered urgently, trying to herd the whole group back into the corner. "Kreuger's coming this way."

They all shut up and wedged themselves back into the booth, suddenly very cool and casual and not at all vulgar.

Mrs. Kreuger followed them. She peered at them through narrow eyes as she approached the booth. "Looks like you need a second round." It wasn't a question.

"Yes, please, beers all around, on me," Walter fumbled with a sloppy, nervous grin.

Mrs. Kreuger nodded and sidled back behind the bar.

"Holy shit, that was close," Mae gasped.

"Come on, she can't not know—" Frank said.

"Not after all the tricks you've pulled in her men's restroom." Dickie said primly.

"No, I'm sure she knows. She doesn't care, as long as we're *discreet*." Walter hissed the last word accusingly at all of them. The group paused to reflect upon this.

Stephen was the first to break the silence. He was still stuck on the previous revelation. "I can't believe you assholes thought I was cuckolding that woman!"

"Well, what are we supposed to think, Vinny?" Mae groaned. "The two of you have been mooning after each other for weeks. Given your track record, we made the most obvious assumption."

"Occam's razor," Marge added.

Stephen was incensed. "Well, *nothing's* going on between us." Except she'd said Joe said there was someone else. Why would he say that if there was nothing between them? This was way deeper than Stephen had ever thought it would go, especially without any hanky panky whatsoever. He'd thought he'd teeter on the edge of temptation a little longer until he broke and made a move, and Joe would either take him up on it or laugh in his face. Well, he knew Joe well enough by now to know Joe wouldn't laugh at him per se. Probably worse; he'd let him down gently.

"I know we were spending a lot of time together, but we're old friends," Stephen said. "It's no secret his marriage is on the rocks, but I didn't think he'd actually do anything about it."

Marge's eyes went round like saucers. "Is *that* what's happening? Holy moly, Vin, is he leaving her?"

Stephen winced. Was it his business to even say?

"Vin, oh my *god!*" Marge was so beside herself, she fumbled for a cigarette.

"What?" Stephen looked at the others, who were all staring at him similarly shocked.

"Is he leaving her for you?" Mae squealed. He was having a hard time staying discreet. "Oh, Vinny, that's so *romantic!*"

"No, it's not!" Stephen exclaimed. "It's horrible. And it's goddamn news to me! He's apparently telling her there's someone else, and I don't even know if he's talking about me, or someone different, or just making excuses."

"He told her there's someone *else?*" Marge took a puff on her cigarette like it was the last thing that made sense.

"Oh, he's definitely talking about you," Dickie drawled.

"I'm a homewrecker!" Stephen wailed as he buried his head in his arms on the table.

"Does it even count as cheating if it's another guy?" Frank speculated.

"I'm a homewrecker, and I didn't even get anything out of it!" Stephen pushed himself up. "Just a boatload of guilt and a broken heart." He collapsed back on the booth cushions just as everyone silenced and Mrs. Kreuger slid a pitcher of beer onto their table. Walter picked it up and started filling everyone's glasses.

"Oh, Vinny…"

"Shut up, Marge, and give me a cig."

She handed him one. He struck a match in their pity-filled silence. His fingers were shaking. He wasn't quite solid enough to get the damn thing lit.

"I retract my previous statement," Mae declared. "This is not romantic. This is some bona fide bullshit."

Stephen finally got a flame and inhaled deeply as he lit the cigarette.

"He didn't even tell you?" Walter repeated, like he was stuck on that point. "You've had no conversation about it at all?"

"He told me wanted to leave her," Stephen said. "On Tuesday."

"You idiot," Frank said, arms crossed. "He told you that on Tuesday, and you went home with *me?* What did you want, a written invitation?"

"And he didn't tell you *why* he wanted to leave her?" Walter asked.

"No. I didn't ask," Stephen admitted.

"I tried to give them a chance to kiss on Monday night, but they didn't even try," Mae pouted.

"What are you talking about?"

"The cat, Vincent!" Mae threw his hands up. "I didn't actually think I hit a cat. For Pete's sake."

"What cat?" Frank asked.

"Wait a minute—" Stephen leaned around Frank to square Mae in his sights. "You fabricated hitting a cat with the car just to get us to kiss?"

"Well, you certainly weren't going to do it on your own," Mae huffed.

"Is 'cat' supposed to be some sort of code? How was I supposed to know that, Mae?"

"Listen, if two drunk idiots panting for each other can't make the best of a few minutes alone in the back seat of a car, then I don't know what more I can do for you." Mae threw his hands in the air.

"Did it ever occur to you that I didn't *want* to kiss him? I don't want to get in the middle of his marriage, or his family! I told you all—and I *meant* it—no more married men!" He stabbed his cigarette into the air in emphasis.

Silence permeated the booth as his friends made sideways glances and raised eyebrows at each other.

"Damn, Joe's gonna have a rude awakening after doing all this to leave his wife only to find out you don't even want him," Frank said. His arms were still crossed. Stephen wanted to kick him.

"Shut up, Frank."

"He wants him," Marge said. "Of course you do. Right, Vin?"

Stephen had his head in his hands. He squeezed his fingers tight around his hair and pulled in frustration. "Yes, but not like *this!*"

Pity filled the silence until Stephen wanted to just crawl under the table in shame.

Dickie started to laugh. "Oh no, and now you're going to be coworkers!"

Stephen rubbed his hands over his face. What a disaster.

✳

Chapter 17

It was mid-March, and Stephen's first day working for the court scheduling office. Joe knew this, but he hadn't talked to Stephen since he'd extracted Marion from Kreuger's two weeks ago, so he wasn't sure whether he should go down and say congratulations, or leave well enough alone.

He stood from his desk and stretched stiffly. He'd been sleeping in the spare bedroom for the past two weeks and his back was deeply unhappy about it. It was an old, saggy mattress on a creaky brass frame from the last century. The children still didn't know about that—he was careful to get up before they did and make the bed tight—but they could tell something was very wrong. Marion had hardly talked to him since that night she'd tried to follow him. When they'd got home, she'd interrogated him about whether he was canoodling with his secretary, briefly suggesting Stephen had already confirmed it, then finally gave up, exhausted. She hadn't said two words to him since. She was furious, and she deserved to be. Joe had deceived her. And Stephen too.

God, what must he have thought when Marion asked him who the other woman was? How pathetic he must have thought Joe was, to say there was someone else. At no point had he imagined that that admission would get back to Stephen. Joe was so horrified he hadn't sought Stephen out since then. Stephen hadn't tried to seek him out, either, so by this point, Joe was resigned to the fact that Stephen wanted nothing to do with him.

Fair. Joe didn't want anything to do with himself, either.

"Milner, come see me in my office."

That was the other complication.

Joe picked up his ledger and carried it to his boss' office. Mr. Joseph Leonard, the city comptroller, sat behind a heavy, wooden desk, a little jowly over what must have at some point been a strong jaw.

"Shut the door," Mr. Leonard said.

Joe complied, and braced himself as he sat down in the leather-seated metal chair, his ledger on his lap.

"Your wife called last evening," Mr. Leonard said, "and I have to ask: Is there anything going on between you and Mrs. Marshall?"

"Judy?" Joe said incredulously. Christ, she had to be pushing fifty. Not that that made her undesirable, but it had never actually occurred to him to think about it before. "No, sir."

"Well, your wife seems to think otherwise," Mr. Leonard said. "I thought you took care of things after that episode she made two weeks ago."

"I'm very sorry about that, sir," Joe repeated automatically. Marion had been at the office before she showed up at Kreuger's that night, and she'd been more angry than desolate, with Judy taking the brunt of her questioning. "I did talk to her about it. She assured me it wouldn't happen again."

"Well, she seems to have called instead. Mrs. Marshall was very disconcerted," Mr. Leonard said flatly. "Look, Milner, it's none of my business what you do, but if you intend to succeed me as city comptroller, you need to make peace with the fact that there is no room at all for scandal. The comptroller must be reliable, steady, and efficient. If you're two-timing your wife, you are not going to be able to fulfill the role properly, and if the news breaks, you'll sully the entire mayor's office and city council along with you. Not to mention, you'll have to resign the position and that would put the city budget in the precarious hands of someone without the requisite institutional knowledge to get the job done."

Joe swallowed hard. "I'm not two-timing my wife, sir." It was true, but it felt hollow even as he said it.

"I'm grateful to hear it, but I do not think your wife knows that." Mr. Leonard sighed. "It would behoove you to make her aware of that fact, and go home when you leave the office instead of wherever it is you've been disappearing to."

"I just go to the riverside," Joe said. That was true. He'd been walking the bluff across Kellogg Boulevard to avoid going home. "To walk. To think."

Mr. Leonard narrowed his eyes. "Think about what?"

Joe grimaced.

"Listen, Milner," Mr. Leonard leaned forward. "I'll be frank with you. Marriage is challenging. It has its twists and turns. I don't know what you're in the middle of just now, but it will take work. You can't avoid the problem, you can't turn away from it. The only way is through."

Joe nodded.

"The best thing you can do, for yourself and your career, is to go home, maybe pick up some flowers on the way, and patch things up with the missus. Whatever's drawing you away, dispense with it immediately. Whatever it is, I can guarantee you it's not worth sacrificing your family and career."

Joe swallowed hard. He looked down at his hands, folded over his ledger. "Sir."

"You're dismissed," Mr. Leonard said. "Go, have lunch, pull yourself together. I expect to hear nothing from your wife but pleasantries at the Christmas party."

Joe stood. "Yes sir." He couldn't look at him. He just turned and went out the door, his heart pounding and his chest tight.

"Where are you going?" Judy said as Joe's feet carried him right past his office and out the door.

"Lunch," Joe grunted.

"With your ledger?"

Joe shook his head and blinked. Then, he handed the ledger to Judy wordlessly, and walked out the door of their office suite.

He didn't take a full breath until he got outside. The sun was shining in a clear, blue sky and the temperature was hovering around 45 degrees, but in the sun it felt like proper spring. Joe threw himself down on a bench and tilted his head toward the sky.

Mr. Leonard was right, of course. Completely right, on all counts. Except for that Joe didn't particularly want to be city comptroller, as much as he didn't want to be married to Marion. With the exception of his children, he regretted the trajectory of everything in his life. Most men would follow Mr. Leonard's advice. Most men would wish for advancement, for greater responsibility, for success in their work. Most men would be proud to have a wife like Marion on their arms to celebrate their election to public office. Right now, Joe only wanted to curl up into a ball and disappear.

"I was wondering when I'd run into you."

Joe's eyes opened automatically at the sound of his voice. Stephen was silhouetted by the sun, but Joe could hear his wry smile. The vice around his chest loosened some, because his instincts had no idea what was good for him.

"Congratulations on your first day," Joe said. His voice was hoarse with tension, but hopefully Stephen didn't notice. "I meant to come down and say so—"

"It's alright," Stephen replied and sat down next to Joe on the bench. "It is alright if I sit?"

"Of course," Joe said. "Be my guest."

"Where's your lunch?" Stephen bit into what looked like a ham sandwich on white bread.

Joe looked down at his hands. He'd forgotten it. "I … uh, I'll eat it later."

"Oh."

"How's your first day?"

Stephen's face split into a wide, dimpled grin. Joe's chest loosened more. It was heartening to think he'd done something to help make Stephen so happy. "It's been wonderful. You were right—of course you were right—the job is right up my alley. I've been shadowing the head scheduler all morning, but I think I'll get the hang of it pretty quickly. They're really well-organized down there, and the girls are all real friendly."

"Of course they are," Joe said. "Look at you."

"Hm?"

Joe flushed. "I mean, you clean up nice in that suit."

"Oh, this? Dickie lent me this. It's sort of too tight, but it'll do until I can buy a few of my own." Stephen rolled the shoulders of his suit jacket, which now that Joe looked, did look a little tight. "The girls picked up pretty quick that I'm not particularly inclined to any of them. They're a gossipy bunch, and it seems like word travelled fast before I even showed up today that I have, um, other interests. Anyway, they remind me a lot of the boys at

Kreuger's."

"How?"

"Oh, you know, they talk a lot of trash and joke around. They've all got a bunch of stupid little nicknames for each other."

Joe was relaxed enough to smile now. "That's great."

"Do you want my apple?"

"Hm? No, that's okay. I have my lunch in my office."

"My mother would kill me if she saw me eating in front of you and not offering anything."

Joe smiled and took the apple, for the sake of Stephen's mother. His heart stuttered when his fingers brushed Stephen's. "I've got a stupid nickname now," he said mindlessly as he rubbed the apple on his shirt.

Stephen looked at him sideways. "Oh?"

"Yeah. Mae's called me Sleeping Beauty a few times now."

"Hm."

"Too bad I can't go there anymore." Joe sighed. Stephen didn't say anything. The sun was so bright, Joe had to squint to see.

"Why not?" Stephen finally asked when Joe didn't offer anything else up. His voice was gentle, almost careful. Joe hated it, hated that he'd made things so awkward and tentative between them, hated how embarrassed and miserable he always was, what a damn joke he'd made of his whole life, how much he was screwing up the lives of everyone around him too. He wanted to just blurt out the real reason, tell Stephen he wanted him and throw propriety in the rubbish bin, but as much as it hurt to sit next to Stephen and not be able to touch him, it'd be worse if he forced the issue and alienated Stephen forever.

So Joe let out a long sigh and sank back into the bench.

"I don't know. Things with Marion have only gotten worse since I started going there. I thought if I stopped, it'd get better."

"And did it?"

Joe looked down at his hands. "No. My boss has my number now, too, and he's pressuring me to patch things up and get on with it."

"Is that what you want?"

"What I want hardly matters anymore," Joe said with a hollow laugh. "Everything's about what's best for the family or for Marion or for my boss' plan to make me the next comptroller."

"Whatever eases everyone else's way?" Stephen asked.

"Yes."

"What do you want?"

Joe's face crumpled, and he quickly covered it with his hands before anyone around them could see. There, behind his tightly closed eyes, the only honest answer blazed neon. The word came out from his lips like a whisper, like a dying man's last words, but he said it. "You."

Stephen didn't reply. Joe wasn't sure he'd heard him. Maybe it was best if that was the case. If he'd heard him, they'd have to contend with it. Joe lifted his head from his hands and looked up at Stephen. It was a reckless thing to do. When he looked up, Stephen was staring straight ahead gripping his knees, his chin firm and his eyes glistening.

Stephen took a big breath in. "That's … I … we need to talk about that." He glanced down at his watch twice before he seemed to register what it said. "I have to get back. But we need to talk about that." He looked at Joe firmly. "After work? Meet me in the lobby?"

It wasn't a no. Stephen was stirred. It wasn't a no.

Joe didn't trust himself to speak through his heart in his throat, so he nodded.

Stephen stood. "Okay."

He didn't move.

He looked down at Joe again. "At five, okay?"

"Okay. I'll be there."

"Okay."

Stephen still didn't go. He bit his lip. "You're not going to disappear on me like the last time, right?"

"The last time?"

"The graduation party? Never mind."

Joe's cheeks went hot. "No," he said firmly. "I'll be there. I swear."

"Okay." Stephen nodded to himself. He looked at Joe and his hand twitched. "Okay." He squeezed his hand into a fist. Then, he turned and walked back into the building.

Joe's heart was slamming in his chest. His hands were shaking. He wasn't sure he could go back up to his office, face his boss, when he'd just done the exact opposite thing he'd been instructed to do.

He could not care. A smile was creeping onto his mouth and there was nothing he could do to stop it.

It wasn't a no.

Chapter 18

Stephen was pacing a path around the Peacemaker statue in the lobby of City Hall. The atrium was so lofty, he felt like five floors of civil servants were watching him slowly lose his ever-loving mind. He checked his watch for the seventeenth time. It was 5:02 now. Goddammit, he was such an idiot. He shouldn't even be here to begin with—he was breaking all his own rules. But he was here, which was almost a guarantee that Joe wasn't going to show. Joe had the upper hand, in the end. He always had. Stephen was just begging for scraps.

Footsteps echoed expansively. Stephen snapped his head up and saw Joe walking toward him, briefcase in hand. Dear god, how could he still make Stephen feel like this? He was just walking, in a wrinkled suit with his eyes sagging like a sad, sleep-deprived hound. But it felt just like when Stephen had first seen him walk into Krueger's. The same intense rightness, a swooping inevitability. *Yes. There he is.* And the same sinking uncertainty. *How will he hurt me this time?*

Luckily, Stephen was well-practiced at pretending he wasn't attracted to men in public. "There you are," he said, and was relieved he'd managed it in a solid timbre, instead of in the helpless relief it had started as in his mind.

Joe gave this strange impression of a smile, his mouth determined and his eyes sticking to Stephen in a way he feared others could perceive. "Come on," Joe said, "my car's just a block away."

Car. Right. Stephen fell into step beside him and tried not to think too hard about where they were going or what Joe planned to do. His car was a perfectly reasonable place to have a private conversation. A conversation Stephen had rehearsed in his head all afternoon instead of focusing on impressing the schedulers on his first day. Betty had caught him not listening to her twice.

Stephen was resolved, though. He was prepared. He was going to get to the bottom of this. He wasn't going to let up until Joe told him the truth. And no matter what that truth was, Stephen was going to leave with his dignity intact. He wasn't going to do anything stupid or become an experiment or an excuse. There would be no regrets.

He tried to make casual conversation as they pushed through the revolving doors onto 4th Street. "You get around to eating your lunch?"

Joe looked up at Stephen with a start. "Oh. No, I forgot."

Stephen tried not to roll his eyes too hard. "Glad I gave you that apple."

"Yeah. Me too."

They stopped on the corner of 4th and St. Peter. Joe glanced up the block as they waited for the walk signal. Stephen followed his gaze and saw the flags waving on the St. Paul Hotel. He swallowed hard and pushed his resolve all the way through his stride, into the soles of his shoes as he stepped after Joe toward his car.

Joe unlocked his car door and climbed inside, his long legs compacting like a spider around the wheel. He leaned over and unlocked the passenger door. Stephen took a deep breath as he slid onto the bench seat. Christ, he'd rehearsed this. What was it that he'd planned to say?

Joe started the car and put on those godforsaken glasses. There was something so human about needing glasses. So vulnerable. Stephen shoved the thought away as Joe released the parking break and shifted into first gear, pulling out into traffic. They drove two blocks before Stephen finally got his act together.

"So," Stephen said. "About what you said earlier."

What had been the point of all that endless handwringing if he was just going to flub it anyway? Stephen wished he could let his forehead drop upon the dash.

Joe sort of grunted in a vaguely affirmative direction.

Apparently, he wasn't going to give Stephen anything more. When, oh when was Stephen going to finally recognize a red flag?

"When you said that what you wanted was, well…" Stephen swallowed, then continued, "…me. Um. What exactly did you mean by that?"

Joe's knuckles were white around the steering wheel. His chin wobbled.

"It means just what it sounds like," Joe said. "I, um, I told Marion there was someone else. Because there is. It's you."

Stephen's breath left him all at once. He sort of deflated against the back of the passenger seat. "Wha—why didn't you tell *me?*"

Joe's listless eyes were glued to the road. He was heading north on Cedar Street toward the State Capitol. "What difference would it have made, Stephen? You were very clear you had no interest in someone like me—"

"—I said I have no interest in married men—"

"Right. Exactly. And I have no interest in being a

scoundrel, so I thought it was a nonstarter. But…" His voice tightened, but he doggedly continued, "but apparently none of that actually matters to me, deep down, because I can't stop thinking about you."

Stephen had entertained many scenarios that afternoon. None of them had included quite so blunt a confession. Part of him was furious. How much time and grief would it have saved if Joe could have just figured this out eight years ago the morning after that graduation party? Why did he have to say it now, when he was hog-tied by so many other commitments that he'd made it impossible for Stephen to say anything without compromising his own self-respect? Another part of him, though, was so relieved that he felt a sob choke him without any warning at all. Dear god, it wasn't his wishful thinking. It was real. It was *real*.

And now he was really crying. Hell.

As they passed the shining white granite of the State Capitol, Joe gave a sniff. Stephen rubbed his eyes and laughed. "Look at the two of us. Just crying like babies."

Joe laughed too as he stopped at the intersection with University. He pushed the glasses up and wiped his eyes with his cuffs, then cast a glance up at Stephen. It was good, this levity. Stephen gave him a wistful smile.

"What a goddamn disaster," he laughed wetly.

Joe's smile waned. He lowered his glasses and looked back to the road, turning the car east on University. "Are you just going to leave me hanging?" he said after a moment. His eyes were still on the road. Stephen wondered if he'd brought them to his car so he wouldn't have to look at him while they had this conversation. "I mean, if you do, I wouldn't blame you. I'd deserve it."

"What?"

"Well, I just poured my heart out to you. And I don't

even know if this… well, if these feelings are returned or…" Joe wouldn't look at him. Stephen's heart clenched in his chest.

"Are you kidding me? Of course they are," Stephen blurted. This was *not* what he'd rehearsed, but Joe was driving. It wasn't as though anything could happen while the vehicle was in motion.

"But you haven't called or anything—"

"Because you're married, Joe!" Stephen laughed, but not because it was funny. "I was trying to be respectful. God, Joe, of course I have feelings for you. It's always been easy when it's us. I thought it was just because of the rose-tinted lenses looking back on when we were in school, but now that we've been spending time together again, it still feels the same. In spite of everything, there's nowhere I'd rather be than with you. It's so easy. It's like breathing."

"It is." Joe was smiling. The sun low in the sky set his features aglow in red and pink and orange. "It really is."

"I thought it was just me. I mean, I've confused friendship with love before, but you were the first."

Whoops. Stephen hadn't meant to say that.

"Love," Joe repeated. "It is, isn't it?"

Joe turned left on Robert Street. They were up on the Mount Airy bluff now. He was turning into Cass Gilbert Park, pulling up to the deserted overlook. Oh no. This was not the time to stop in a secluded area. Stephen's heart was in his goddamn throat and he was about to make a huge mistake.

"It is," he confirmed recklessly.

Joe ratcheted the parking brake and killed the engine. The city was glittering in the waning sunlight, snow-capped towers all golden and gleaming. The silence was so complete, every sound felt like a canon blast.

The sound of Joe's palm over the steering wheel. The shift of fabric as he turned to face Stephen. The gust of his breath through his nose as Stephen met his soulful eyes. The booming finality of his hand on Stephen's shoulder.

Stephen had resolved he wouldn't give into temptation. But he had three weaknesses, and they were all Joe Milner. His fists clutched the lapels of Joe's jacket as their mouths crashed together.

Oh no.

Oh no oh no oh no.

Kissing Joe Milner felt like the rightest thing in the entire world. It felt like the bubbly giddiness of getting drunk. It felt like the first free fall on a roller coaster. It felt like a homecoming. All the fragments of their friendship fit together in a complete picture, the same way Stephen's hands felt like they were made to cup both sides of Joe's face. This was so easy. Too easy.

It wasn't a chaste kiss either. Joe's lips were open, his breath in Stephen's mouth. His chin was rough against Stephen's, but it only served to highlight how soft and pliant his lips were. Sirens were going off in Stephen's head, replaying memories of that grad party and the way other parts of Joe had felt under Stephen's hands. The rush of power was heady. Stephen could have him, right now, just about any way he wanted.

"Joe," Stephen gasped as he forced himself to pull away. Joe closed the distance he made, delivering another blinding kiss. His hand came down on the seat right in between Stephen's legs as he lurched forward.

"*Joe.*"

"Shh, please, don't."

God, this was impossible. Joe's chest was up against Stephen's now, warm and solid. All he wanted to do was close his legs around Joe's hand. He grabbed Joe by the back of the neck with both hands and dragged himself away. "Joe, please—"

"Don't make me think about it."

"We have to think about it. We have to *talk* about it."

"But do you feel it?"

"Yes, I feel it."

Joe was crying again. Sinking back into himself, tears falling down his cheeks, his chin tight, glasses entirely askew.

"Joe, look at me."

"I can't!" Joe sniffed hard, like he could shove his tears back with a big enough inhale. "I can't look at you. I can't talk about this. I don't want to do any of that. I haven't felt right in weeks. Months. *Years*, probably." Joe grimaced. "But *that*. *That* felt *right*."

Stephen balled his fists. "Well, *that's* not all I want."

Joe's eyes snapped to him, startled. "That's not all I want either. When I say I want you, I mean I want to be with you."

"You can't," Stephen scoffed.

"I can. I will. If you want me, I'll find a way."

Stephen's throat and chest felt tight all of a sudden. "I don't want you to blow up your whole life for me! What kind of basis is that to build a relationship on?"

It was apparently Joe's turn to scoff. "I don't want to blow up my life for you! It wasn't the one I wanted anyway. None of this is—not the job, not the wife, not the goddamn picket fence and the leaky roof—I'm not throwing it away for you! I'm throwing it away for *me*. If I have to live one more day pretending I'm this person I'm not, I'll—" He jerked in a breath. "I don't know, do something rash."

"Like kiss your best friend?"

"Exactly. Shit." Joe tossed the glasses on the dash and

buried his face in his hands. His voice was muffled a bit when he miserably said, "I'm sorry. God. I'm so sorry I've dragged you into the middle of all this."

Stephen swallowed hard. "It's not the kind of thing I want to be dragged into. But I've been known to do stupider shit for a guy. Well, for you. Specifically."

Joe pushed his hands back through his hair. His hat had fallen off at some point during the proceedings. Stephen wanted to reach over and rub his thumb over that crease between his brows until it went smooth. He wanted to do all sorts of stupid, tender things like that. Joe took a deep breath and smoothed his hands over his trousers.

"I'm going to do it."

"What?"

"That's what I brought you here to tell you. I'm going to get divorced."

God, that word just dropped like an anvil. Stephen didn't want any implication in it. "You should do what's best for you and your family."

"It is. It's gotta be. It can't possibly get worse."

"Them's famous last words."

Joe shrugged. The silence stretched so long, Stephen shifted back into the passenger seat properly.

"I'm gonna set it all straight," Joe said. "I'll set her up well. I'll get a new job, or at least get Mr. Leonard to find a new heir to his comptroller throne."

"What?" Stephen was hoarse.

Joe barely glanced at him sideways. "I don't want to run for office. Have you met me? Can you imagine me knocking on doors and greasing palms and kissing babies? I'd be terrible at it. Probably lose the election anyway, even if there wasn't a risk that the wrong sort of attention would end up on your doorstep. If I get a divorce, Mr. Leonard will give up on me."

"And … that's what you want?"

"Yes." Joe straightened, facing the wheel and gripping it with both hands. "Yes, that's what I want."

Stephen nodded slowly. "Okay. Good." His chin was still tingling from the scrape of stubble. "I would offer to help, but I think it's probably best I steer clear of it all."

"Yes. That makes sense."

Dear god, Stephen was the other woman. He was the Wallis Simpson of the city government. Was there any possible way to get to the other end of this without Joe resenting him for life?

"Stephen?"

When he looked up, he saw Joe rubbing his thumb anxiously over the steering wheel. Joe caught his eye. He'd never looked more like a doleful dog. "Will you wait for me?"

Stephen stared at him. The time he'd already waited swept over him, a decade and more of memories rioting in his mind all at once. He was the same person he'd been in high school, in the same body that had endured the same endless yearning as he was experiencing now. God, who was he kidding? He'd waited this long. What was a few more months?

"Yeah, Joe. I'll wait for you."

✦

Chapter 19

Joe slept. Perhaps it was because he was absolutely exhausted, but after dropping Stephen off at his mother's house and parading through the charade of a family dinner, he dropped into the guest bed and slept dreamlessly the entire night through. When he woke, he felt clear-minded for the first time in months.

He was going to tell Marion the truth.

He'd been lying for months—years really—and none of it had done him any good at all. Even if she hated him for it, even if she refused to let him see the children ever again (it was a possibility, even though he didn't think she'd do something that rash), Mr. Leonard was right. The only way was through.

Since Joe had actually slept, he hadn't managed to get up before the kids, so when Linda poked her head into the guest room, he scrambled to pretend he was just in there changing the sheets.

Linda wrinkled her nose. "What're you doin'?"

Joe tried not to look suspicious. "Making up the guest bed."

"Why? Is someone coming over?"

"Well, no," Joe hedged, desperately scrambling for an excuse. "What're *you* doing?"

Linda blinked. "Nothin'."

"Shouldn't you be getting ready to go to Aunty Eve-
lyn's house?"

Linda blinked some more. "Oh. Yeah." She turned and
scampered back into the living room. Joe exhaled and
hurriedly finished straightening the counterpane.

After breakfast, while Marion took Charlie to the bus
stop and Linda to her sister's house, he called work and
told his secretary he was coming in late. By the time Marion got back, he was sitting at the dining table waiting
for her with two cups of coffee.

"What's all this," Marion asked, hanging her coat on
the hall tree with a wary eye.

Joe steeled himself. "I want to talk to you."

"What about work?" Marion was approaching the dining room like there was a tiger in there waiting for her.

"I told them I'm coming in late."

Marion pulled out the chair opposite from him and sat
down. "Are you going to tell me who she is, then?"

Joe nodded.

Marion's eyes went wide, like she hadn't expected him
to agree. "Oh. Okay." She blinked, her hard expression
wavering as she braced herself. "Go on then."

Joe swallowed all of his nerves. It was difficult. "It's
Stephen."

"What?"

"I'm in love with Stephen."

She didn't say anything. Just kept staring at him like
he'd spoken French.

"Stephen Vincelli," Joe clarified at length. "My friend,
from high school?"

"What the hell are you talking about, Joe? Are you
teasing me? Because if you are, I've had it about up to
here—"

"I'm not!" Joe exclaimed. He looked down. He'd

slammed his hand against the table and coffee had spilled. He gathered himself. "I'm not. I—I'm entirely serious."

Marion blinked some more. "You are aware that Stephen is a man, right?"

Joe rolled his eyes. "Yes. I'm aware. That's why I can't do this anymore. I'm… I'm…"

"Are you trying to tell me you're a homosexual?" Marion's mouth was hanging open.

"I … um … yes."

Marion was staring at him in utter shock again. It felt heavier, this time. Joe wasn't sure whether to interject, to try and explain—he wasn't sure what exactly he would even explain. Not the graduation party incident, or the kiss in the car last evening. What did he have to prove to her anyway? He knew it was true, in the deepest canyons of his heart because he knew what it felt like to be with her and he knew what it felt like to be with Stephen and there wasn't any overlap between the two. So he waited for her to start thinking out loud.

"I … I can't believe … wha—*really?*"

"Yes."

"You're sure?"

"Completely sure."

She blinked again. Her eyes were welling up this time.

"How long have you been seeing him behind my back?" she whispered.

Joe grimaced. "That depends… What you mean by 'seeing'?"

"Have you … have you been *sleeping with him* all this time?"

"What, since high school?"

"Since high school?!"

"No, no, that's not what I meant. No, I haven't slept with him at all."

Marion frowned. "Well then how can you be sure—"

"—I don't have to prove anything, Marion. I know. Come on, you know."

"What do I know?"

"That I have … problems. In bed." His face heated.

"Well, yes, but that's normal, isn't it, when you have small kids? We used to do alright for ourselves."

"Wow, a ringing endorsement."

Marion winced, but she didn't backstep.

"Marion, it's not just that I'm in love with someone else. Even before I ran into Stephen again, you and I had been having trouble—"

"—We had, but it's not anything other couples don't deal with—"

"Marion, we haven't had sex since Linda was conceived," Joe said sharply. They'd never talked about it in so many words. Marion's face crumpled when he said it out loud. "And it's entirely my fault. You've done everything and more. I'm just … I'm not built to appreciate you." His throat was tightening like a fist around his words.

"But you did before. It was good. We were good together." Marion was crying now too. "I don't understand. Why didn't you tell me before?"

"I didn't know. I didn't want to know."

"But you know now? What's changed?"

Joe looked at her helplessly.

"Oh, right. Stephen." Marion hung her head in her hands. "And I told you to invite him and his wife over for dinner. Ha. No wonder you didn't. Lord, you've played me for a fool."

"I'm the fool," Joe choked out. "I bent over backward trying to find any other explanation. The more I lied, the more I hurt everyone I cared about, especially you. Don't look at me like that, Marion. I still love you, I've always loved you. I just can't love you like you deserve. I can't be the husband I promised I'd be."

Oh lord, he was weeping like a baby now. He didn't fight it. He let it come until snot was running down his lip and his sleeves were soaked. Marion wasn't doing much better, but she at least had a handkerchief. Joe couldn't bring himself to move.

Eventually, Marion blew her nose and sniffed. Her posture straightened. Joe looked up at her from where he'd hung his own head in his hands. It was the best he could manage at the moment.

"Well, we obviously can't tell the lawyers any of this," she said.

"What?"

"We'll have to get our story straight." She wiped her face with her handkerchief again, forcing her expression to calm. She glanced at his sopping confusion and raised an eyebrow. She looked like her mother noticing the antimacassar askew. "We obviously can't tell the court that you're a homosexual. They'll never let you see the children again."

Joe's throat made a horrible keening sound. He knew that. It didn't make it any easier to hear.

"So we have to explain your adultery another way," Marion spelled out to him while he cried into his arms. "I can't sue for divorce unless you're violent or cheating, and you are cheating, so I deserve one."

"Yes. Whatever you want. You can have everything." Joe felt worthless. The fact that he also felt relieved only made him feel even more worthless.

He heard the chair legs scrape over the floor. He looked up, eyes tired and swollen and blurry. Marion was looking down at him, arms crossed, eyes red and puffy.

"I'm not going to take you for all you're worth," Marion said. "But you owe me, Joe. In building your little make-believe life, you've ruined mine."

God. She was right. She was completely right. He'd gotten so good at lying, he'd even believed himself. And he'd ruined not just her life, but his own. If he'd been even remotely as self-aware as Stephen, he might have gone to the right person the morning after that graduation party. He'd made such a mess of everything. He didn't deserve either of them.

✦

Marion left. Gone to the grocery store to keep the wheels turning on the fool charade of their lives. Joe had to go to work and do the same. When Joe finally peeled himself up off the table, it was past ten o'clock. He gave himself a shave, but his eyes were still puffy. It hardly mattered. He got in the car and went to work.

The numbers lined up for him for the rest of the morning. It was a good distraction from what he needed to do next. Before lunch, Joe stood and pushed his chair in at his desk. He walked to Mr. Leonard's office and knocked on the door.

"Come in," Mr. Leonard said. He was on the phone when Joe entered. Mr. Leonard nodded for him to take a seat. Joe sat in the vinyl-seated metal chair and waited as Mr. Leonard wrapped up his phone conversation.

After Mr. Leonard set the receiver in the cradle, he looked up at Joe. "Well, Milner, you look worse for wear."

"I'm getting a divorce," Joe blurted. It felt good.

It did not seem to feel good for Mr. Leonard.

"You are not."

"I am, sir. You were right. The only way is through, and this is the only way through."

Mr. Leonard was usually very in control. His smiles, his frowns—he was always careful to deliver the right proportion. Which made it very strange indeed when he lost control now.

"Milner, you will ruin yourself," he burst out, his hands bracing on the edge of his desk as he started to stand, then stopped. His jowls quivered. "You will ruin your chances for comptroller and my bid for city council along with it!"

It was strange. This was going about as bad as Joe could have imagined it going. But it wasn't hard for Joe to think of a reply. It came quite easily, in fact. "I know, sir. That's why I'm telling you now. So you can arrange for my replacement and keep things flowing smoothly."

"Replacement?!" Mr. Leonard was red in the face now. "You're quitting?"

"What? No, sir, I'm not quitting. Though, if you wanted to fire me, I would understand."

"I can't fire you," Mr. Leonard spat. "As much as I would like to right now for making such a damn fool decision. You've made yourself irreplaceable."

Joe frowned. "I can train someone else in."

"Criminy, Joe, what is wrong with you? What man volunteers to train his replacement to be promoted in his place?"

"I guess I do, sir." Joe's heart was slamming against his ribs, but the words kept coming, so he let them. "I don't particularly want a promotion. I'm not well-suited to the skills needed to be an elected official. If I could go on doing the job I do now, I'd be satisfied, but I don't want to compromise your ambitions with a scandal."

Mr. Leonard stared at him for a long moment. Joe wondered if it had ever occurred to him before, that a man could not want advancement. At length, Mr. Leonard's chin started to work.

"And you're resolved to divorce your wife?"

Joe bit the inside of his cheek and nodded. "And she's pretty resolved to divorce me, I think."

"Milner!" Mr. Leonard ran an exasperated hand over his face. "I told you yesterday to fix this and you've gone and ruined us all!"

"You should find someone better suited to campaigning," Joe jumped in before Leonard could spiral further. "Someone who can door-knock and make speeches that make folks feel good about how the city is spending their money. I'll stay on in whatever capacity I'm able to make that true."

"And you're happy to let some other fellow leapfrog over you and be your boss?"

"Yes, sir." He found that he meant it.

Mr. Leonard leaned back in his chair. He sighed as he rubbed his temples with the fingers of one hand. "I can't say I'm not disappointed."

Of all the things Mr. Leonard had said so far, that one smarted the most.

"I'm not, sir," Joe said to his lap. "I'm not. I don't want to campaign and be in the public eye. I can't ever think of the right things to say. I like accounting and I like the job I do now."

"You'd be the man behind the curtain, with some other fellow as your mouthpiece."

That was sort of the truth of it now, but Joe couldn't exactly say that to his face. Mr. Leonard had been an attentive mentor, but Joe had exceeded his skill at least five years ago. Leonard rounded too much to be able to move money the way Joe could. "Some men would rather not be perceived."

Mr. Leonard seemed skeptical of that notion. "Very well. I'll see what I can do. In the meantime, make sure you keep proceedings as quiet as possible. I don't want any more surprise appearances from your spurned wife. No public fights, no brazen wining and dining of your mistress, none of that nonsense! You don't want to be perceived? Then make sure you aren't."

"Yes sir," Joe said with a nod. He stood and hesitated. "Thank you, sir."

"Don't thank me yet," Mr. Leonard said with an exasperated wave of his hand.

Joe turned and walked out. His shoulders felt immeasurably lighter. He hadn't realized how very much he'd dreaded a campaign for comptroller. He'd thought he owed it to Mr. Leonard to try. But he hadn't. He didn't owe Mr. Leonard anything. In fact, perhaps Mr. Leonard had pushed the idea because *he* thought he owed Joe something after so many years of hard work. Maybe he wouldn't have to quit his job after all.

✦

Chapter 20

Wednesday was Saint Patrick's Day, so naturally Kreuger's was bursting at the seams. Mae West got there ridiculously early, though, so the boys had managed to hold on to their usual booth. Stephen arrived after work and scooted onto the end of the booth. Dickie and Walter were there, along with Marge and Violet, and Mae of course. He was greeted with a bubbly green beer.

"A toast!" Walter called, raising his glass. "To Stephen's third day at his new job. May he have a fourth!"

"Thanks," Stephen said after the bubbles stopped tickling his nose. "So far, so good."

"You sound thrilled," Dickie observed archly. "Not going how you expected?"

"No, it's not that—"

"—Wait, let me guess. Are you running into your esteemed coworker, Mr. Milner, too often?"

Stephen glared at him. "No. I haven't seen him since my first day, actually." His chin was still tingling with the ghostly scrape of Joe's stubble. Unsettling as it was, he hoped it never went away.

Mae leaned forward. "So you saw *him* on your first day, but you didn't come to celebrate with *us*? Some friend."

Walter rolled his eyes. "He's not obligated to come to the bar every single day, Mae."

"But it was his first day! I was going to buy a bottle of champagne."

"I don't think any of us actually want to drink the poor excuse for champagne Mrs. Kreuger has behind that bar," Dickie said.

"Now we'll never know," Mae sighed.

"Joe probably bought him better champagne anyway," Marge shrugged.

Dickie's eyebrows arched. He swung round to look Stephen squarely in the eye. "Is *that* where you were? Drinking champagne with your little soulmate? I thought you said you didn't want him?"

Mae gave a scandalized gasp.

Stephen made a point to be very interested in his beer. "Say, how do you suppose they get it so green?"

"It's food coloring, Vin," Walter said dismissively. "I think you'd better answer Dickie's question."

Stephen winced. "Nooooooo."

"Was that supposed to be a word? Or the sound a cat makes?" Dickie wasn't going to let it go. In fact, Stephen's absolutely miserable attempt to change the subject just made him sink his claws in. Now everyone around the table was looking at him expectantly.

Stephen's upper lip curled up as he tried to find a sympathetic face.

"Oh my god, Vin, what did you *do?*" Marge exclaimed.

"Nothing! I didn't do anything. I … I talked with him and …"

"And!?" Mae was half standing on the booth.

Stephen's cheeks flushed hot. He couldn't stop himself from grinning. "And he kissed me…"

Mae screamed. "AH! Yes! I knew it! I KNEW IT!"

"I don't know that celebrating is in order," Walter said

in a tempering tone. "It was just a few weeks ago that we were helping Stephen drown his sorrows. What changed, Vin?"

"What are we screaming about?"

Frank Atlas had arrived. Stephen looked up and then did a double take at the fellow he had brought with him. It was remarkable how Frank could pass off an arm around another fellow's shoulder as a friendly masculine gesture.

"Who's this?" Stephen asked as Walter and Dickie scooted in to make room.

Frank gave a feral grin. "Oh, this is my pal, Jeremiah. Jerry, say hello to the boys."

"Hiya," Jeremiah said, with a friendly smile. "Happy St. Paddy's, eh boys?"

Jerry looked like a magazine clipping from a catalog for Mormon door-knockers. Stephen wouldn't have blinked an eye if the fellow had asked him whether he had accepted Jesus as his lord and savior. The man was blonde, square-jawed, dashing enough to be in the movies, and broad enough that he and Frank Atlas' shoulders were jockeying for the same space. A tender morsel, to be sure.

"Yes, happy St. Patrick's," Dickie drawled. His arch brows had entirely transferred their attention to the extremely good-looking newcomer.

See, it was always a pain when someone brought a new person to the group. No one ever knew how glib they could be, or whether the fellow was one of the boys or not. Stephen had no right to be annoyed, after forcing them all to socialize with Joe for months knowing full well they'd have to pretend.

But Stephen was extremely annoyed.

He didn't exactly want to give the sordid details to everyone about what had happened on Monday, but now that they knew he'd kissed Joe, he desperately wanted to know what they thought. He hardly knew what to think himself. He'd been wafting through his mother's boardinghouse for two days barely able to scrape two thoughts together without thinking about that kiss. When he wasn't mooning, he was agonizing over a thousand possible ways this could all go sideways. His heart was entirely in Joe's hands, and he'd made a point to say he wasn't going to involve himself until Joe had everything arranged, so he couldn't even see him. It was *torture*. He needed to know whether this was the beginning of his happily ever after, or if he'd just made an enormous mistake.

And now that *Jerry* was here, he wasn't going to find out.

"Jerry's my pal from the gym," Frank grinned. "He's a bible salesman—"

Mae West squawked a hysterical laugh. He coughed and forced his face into a strange imitation of grace and poise. "Excuse me. How fascinating."

"Yeah, any of you boys interested in a shiny new copy of the King James?" Jerry said with a slick smile. Good god, that could mean anything. He could be a shyster with a penchant for hanky-panky at the gym, or he could genuinely be a bible salesman and Frank was embarking on his greatest conquest yet.

Dickie was looking at Frank with his face frozen in a pertly polite expression. "Frank, how many have you purchased?"

Frank laughed. "Oh, four or five by now."

Stephen's money was on the shyster.

The bible salesman didn't seem to have any problem drinking green beer. So, not a Mormon. Another round was ordered and they learned that apparently, bible sales were way up after the war.

"Yeah, bible sales and the birth rate," Frank laughed, taking a swig from his pint glass.

"Too bad that's not true of new housing builds," Jerry intoned. "I have some friends—they got two kids, nice married couple, you see—they can't find any place to live."

"Yeah, it's near impossible to even find an apartment," Dickie drawled. "I have to room with this lummox." He gestured at Walter with his cigarette and watched Jerry very carefully.

Jerry didn't blink an eye. "Really? My friends are living in a tin can up in Roseville."

"Ha, tin can," Marge barked.

"No, I mean it. Quonset huts. They manufactured them for the war as temporary shelters, but now they're selling them to families to meet the demand. We're in a full housing crisis, gentlemen." Jerry cleared his throat and belatedly nodded to Marge and Violet, adding, "Ladies."

"Oh, yeah, it's a nightmare out there," Frank said. "I knew a guy, he went to twenty different places trying to get a room—just a room, mind, not even an apartment—and he got turned down for all of them. Now he's got to live with his mother."

Stephen frowned. He should never have told Frank that. And it was only eight different places, but still.

"That happens more often than you'd think," Jerry said. "Single men, these days, are better off just accepting they gotta keep living at home until they're ready to marry. There's not enough houses for families, much less bachelor pads."

Stephen peered at Jerry. This felt like coded language.

"Ha!" Frank hooted. "How's a fella to sow his wild oats if he's living with Ma and Pa?"

"Exactly," Jerry said. "It's a cutthroat world out there. That's why I've been taking an interest in real estate."

Ah. There it was. A table full of fairy bachelors in a housing crisis, and a shyster bible salesman turned real estate agent eager to to build his clientele. Stephen stood up.

"I'm going to go get a drink."

"There's more green beer!" Mae offered.

"Nah, I need a real drink."

Mae peered into his half-full pint glass. Stephen shouldered his way through the crowd to the bar. It took a few minutes to even attract the attention of Mrs. Kreuger.

"What'll you have?"

"Whiskey sour, please," Stephen replied and laid his coins down on the wet bar.

"Make that two!"

Stephen looked at the person hanging over his shoulder.

"What, you don't want to hear Jerry's earnest real estate pitch?" he asked Mae.

"Ha, hell no. I got a sweet basement rental on Dayton's Bluff. Very private. Dickey can give me as much shit as he likes. I know I got it made."

"How much you wanna bet that fella'd blow us all under the table if it got him a property under contract?"

"I would not take that bet. I'm a lady."

"And not a damn fool either."

Mrs. Kreuger gave them a narrow look as she set their drinks on the bar in front of them. "Two whiskey sours." Her look was sour enough to make Stephen resolve never to make dirty jokes in this bar again.

"So … tell me about Joe," Mae picked up his drink and gave it an eager gulp.

Stephen felt his cheeks flush. If he'd been a more serious

man, he'd have kept everything in strictest confidence. But he wasn't. He needed to know Mae's take. "He's good. Very good."

Mae squealed. "Tell me everything!"

"Nothing happened."

"Nothing but a *kiss!*"

Stephen looked around at the crowded bar and pulled Mae toward the back, by the jukebox. "Yes," he hissed. "Nothing but a kiss."

"But what about his wife?"

Stephen pulled in a big breath. He pulled Mae close by his shoulder and whispered in his ear. "They're getting divorced."

Mae was the best person to tell secrets to. He gave the most salacious reactions. "*What!?* Oh, Vinny, that's so *romantic!*"

"I'm not sure I'd say that divorce is romantic."

"No!" Mae modulated his own volume. "The fact that he's *leaving his wife for you!*"

"He's not. He's not leaving her for me. He's doing it for himself."

"Sure, sure, sure. Was it the first time?"

"Hm?"

"Kissing him?"

Stephen bit his lip and nodded.

"Was he a good kisser?"

Stephen tipped his head back and let the jukebox take his weight. "*Very* good."

"Oh thank god. If the two of you had spent all that time mooning over each other and found out you weren't compatible, you know, *physically*, that would have been so sad."

Stephen frowned. He hadn't thought of that before. Pretty much every guy he'd ever hooked up with had been physically attractive to him on some level. It was the emotional level that he always had trouble with.

"Has that ever happened to you?" he asked Mae.

"What? Oh, bad chemistry?" Mae put the lip of his glass to his mouth and sipped thoughtfully. "Yeah, a few times."

"What happened?"

"Oh, you know," Mae flapped his hand. "I'd meet a guy and we'd talk it up for a while. This is at the bars, not in the men's room, mind. Anyway, we'd hit it off in conversation, but get to the second location, you know, and things would just fizzle out."

Stephen winced.

Mae shrugged. "Oh, easy come, easy go. Or not easy come, as the case may be. Anyway. Sometimes it's not meant to be."

"Why do you think that happened? I mean, he obviously knew you were, you know..."

"A man? Yes, he certainly did. I don't know. Once the fellow was just too drunk. That happens sometimes. Another time, the guy was just out of a long-term relationship. He was all bent out of shape about it. He was trying to rebound, you know, but he just couldn't manage it. Wasn't ready, poor dear."

Stephen frowned. "And he just wasn't into it?"

"Oh no," Mae said gravely. "He was *very* into it. He was just too sad. Felt too guilty, maybe. Just couldn't get it up."

Stephen took a long swig from his whiskey glass. It was just one of Mae's hook-ups. It wasn't as though it were a rule. Besides, Joe was going to be scarce the next few months while he got the divorce. Stephen wasn't sure exactly what that entailed, but it seemed intensive enough that it would take a good amount of time. By the time he and Stephen reunited, he'd be ready to move on. Surely.

"Hey, speak of the devil!" Mae squealed.

Stephen's head snapped up. He was shorter than Mae by a few inches and the crowd was thick. He craned up on his tiptoes to see.

And there he was. Tall, droopy-eyed, talking to Red at the front of the bar. With—

"HOLY SHIT, Mae, that's my boss!" Stephen ducked down and pretended he was very interested in the jukebox.

"The crooked city clerk?" Mae sounded like he was enjoying this too much. "What are they doing here? Why are they together?"

"I have no earthly clue. As far as I know, they're not friends."

"Well, we *have* to go say hello and find out!"

"You know damn well I can't do that—*Mae!*"

Mae had him by the elbow and was dragging him through the crowd toward the front of the bar.

"S'cuse me, pardon us, we'll be out of your way in just a moment."

Stephen was sweating bullets and probably looked like he was on an execution lineup as Mae landed him right in front of Joe and Lawrence Peltier. One glance at Joe told him this was indeed going to be awkward, as Joe gave him a very apologetic expression. Peltier hadn't noticed him yet, though, because he was too busy glad-handing Red.

"Harold, how've you been?" Peltier boomed. "I haven't seen you in an age. When Milner here told me you've been haunting this bar, I knew I had to come by and say hello."

Red's lip was curled up a bit as he glanced from Peltier to Joe, then to Stephen and Mae. His brow went up as he turned back to Peltier. "Yes, it's been too long."

Peltier had followed Red's gaze and homed in on Stephen. "And Vincelli too!" He reached out and crushed Stephen's hand in his. "Wow, it's a regular old reunion, ain't it? This your usual watering hole, Vincelli?"

This felt like a loaded question. "Sometimes."

"Nice," Peltier replied. "Got that hole-in-the-wall charm to it, don't it. You know Harold, here?"

Stephen glanced at Red, whose mouth frowned at the name. "Yeah, we're acquainted."

"Me and ol' Red here used to spend every Christmas together," Peltier said. "Till his cousin divorced me, that is. Anyway, that's exactly why we're here to celebrate."

"Christmas?" Mae ventured. "I thought it was St. Patrick's Day?"

"No, no," Peltier waved him off, like he was used to complete strangers joining his conversation, and put an arm around Joe. "Divorce! My pal Milner here is rejoining the bachelor ranks, and we gotta raise a glass."

Stephen delivered an alarmed expression to Joe, to which he replied with a helpless shrug. He could hear Mae beginning to giggle next to him.

"A round of champagne, bartender," Peltier bellowed to Mr. Kreuger.

Mae was full-out laughing now.

"Hey now!" Peltier gave Mae a chiding look, his arm still yanking Joe around. "It ain't funny. Divorce is a serious matter. But it's also a cause for celebration. See, when you get divorced, like me and Milner, people go round treating you with kid gloves, like you're broken somehow. But I tell you, I've been through it with Esther, and I am here to report that divorce was the best thing that ever happened to me. To her too, since she's on the arm of some corporate big shot now. Sometimes divorce is the *best* next step. So we're gonna raise a glass and celebrate, alright, Milner? No more of those sad, puppy dog eyes. Tonight, you start the rest of your life!"

Stephen was trying to piece it all together. Joe must have sought Mr. Peltier out for advice or something and got roped in. They'd learned how easily Peltier did that all too well a few weeks ago, after all. Did he need an out?

Red was pressed into service passing the glasses of champagne from the bar. Apparently, Kreuger's didn't have champagne flutes so it was served in lowball glasses. There were six glasses, so Stephen and Mae each got one too, as well as some red-haired guy along the bar, who was now apparently also a part of this.

"To bitter endings!" Peltier called, "And sweet beginnings." He winked at Joe and finally dropped his arm so he could step forward and ensure he clinked every glass with his own.

Stephen reached to clink his glass with Joe's, then stepped forward to huddle up with him.

"You okay?" he asked. "You need an escape route?"

"No, I already called Marion and told her what I was doing," Joe said, looking over at Peltier. The fellow at the bar was very grateful for the free drink and Stephen's boss was eating it up.

"And…" Stephen licked his lips. "What are you doing?"

Joe glanced at him. "Having a drink with the city clerk for St. Paddy's."

"And she's alright with that?"

"Yup," Joe replied. He winced. "Though less so once she finds out you're here too."

Stephen froze. "Why would that be?"

Joe wrinkled his nose and looked into his lowball of

bad champagne. "Because I told her everything."

"Everything?" Stephen choked out.

"Well, not everything, per se." Joe's shoulders were up by his ears, and he was looking everywhere but at Stephen. "But … she knows it's you."

It's me. Oh, Jesus. "We can't talk about this here," Stephen said. The din of the room covered their conversation well, but there were people on all sides of them, and the front of the bar was usually a lot more blue-collar straight types than the back was.

"It's okay," Joe said, finally looking Stephen in the eye. "It is. I went to Peltier's office after I got done today because I figured he'd know a discreet lawyer who can get this done for us quickly."

For us. Christ, Stephen was losing his goddamn mind. It was landing heavy in his gut, all these phrases. This was actually happening. He'd actually broken up a marriage.

Stephen took a big swig from one of the glasses in his hands. The bubbles seared his nostrils and he almost spit it out. "Holy *shit*, that is bad champagne." He looked up at Joe. "You know, maybe it's best if I just go back to the booth and you can stay an honest man."

Joe stared at him for a moment. His lips were parted. And wet. (Probably with bad champagne, but still.) And Stephen's chin tingled again, and he couldn't think of anything for a moment except the memory of that truly excellent kiss.

"Yeah, maybe," Joe said low. He looked at Peltier, then back at Stephen. His expression was so pitiful, if he were an actual dog, Stephen would adopt him on the spot. He clearly didn't want to let Stephen go.

Stephen gave a half smile and a nod, then forced himself to melt back into the crowd and go back to the booth.

He sat down heavily on the vinyl seat.

"What, are you double-fisting now?" Walter asked.

Dickie laughed.

"I could use a double-fisting," Frank said, waggling his eyebrows.

The green beer certainly had been flowing back here. Marge and Violet were no longer in evidence, which made sense considering the whole bar was getting pretty rowdy now. Marge hated large crowds; doubly when they were mostly men.

"I don't know about that," Jerry said, in that same confounding tone that made it unclear whether he didn't know about fisting or about whether Frank could take two, "but I do know of an excellent duplex over on Maryland Avenue that's sure to be a great investment."

"A duplex," Dickie purred. "What is that, some sort of gymnastics trick?"

"I don't know if I can do this," Stephen blurted. Loudly.

"That's okay," Jerry said. "I know a guy who can do financing. Mortgages are easier than ever to get these days, especially if you've served."

"No! Not your damn real estate venture. I mean Joe. I mean everything!" Stephen looked up desperately at Walter, the only sane one left. "I'm a homewrecker," he whimpered.

Walter regarded him with some concern. He glanced up at Jerry, who was absolutely the fucking worst, and at Dickie, who was unabashedly flirting with him. He looked back at Stephen rather helplessly.

"Right." Stephen gritted. He saw how it was. Walter *would* get up and find someplace private to counsel Stephen, but Dickie was flirting with another guy and it wasn't clear whether that guy was actually going to make a move or not, and Walter didn't want to leave him alone just in case. Couldn't he see that Stephen was facing something way more important?

"Where's Mae?" Walter asked. Coward.

"Up there," Stephen bit out, tossing a hand in the direction of the front. "With Red and Joe and *my boss.*"

"What the hell?" Walter's eyes boggled.

"Darling, don't swear," Dickie said absently, smacking him on the chest with his wrist without looking away from Jerry.

"I know," Stephen hissed, gripping the table as he leaned forward. "I guess my boss is also divorced, so Joe thought it was a great idea to ask him for advice, and now they're here toasting to 'bitter endings and sweet beginnings.'"

"What?" Walter grimaced. "That doesn't sound like Joe."

"No, it doesn't. He looks like a deer in the headlights. My boss is a piece of work."

"He did hire you."

"Shut up." Stephen leaned forward across the table. Walter mirrored him. Stephen cupped his hand over his mouth and whispered loudly, "He told his wife about me."

Walter's mouth dropped open.

"I know!" It was vindicating to see someone else react with the appropriate horror.

"He shouldn't have done that," Walter hissed, leaning in again. He grabbed Stephen by the shoulder and whispered in his ear, "He's going to get torched in court if she brings that up. Stephen—he could go to jail. *You* could go to jail!"

"But we didn't even do anything!"

"Yeah, but she doesn't know that—"

"—I damn well *hope* she knows that."

Walter was looking at Stephen with genuine horror. He let it sink in.

"Holy shit, Walter, what do I do?"

"You gotta talk to him," Walter said. "You gotta talk to him now. He can't use you as a pawn for legal separation—"

"—He isn't using me—"

"Maybe not on purpose—"

"Dammit, Walter! You're supposed to be the calm one!"

Stephen sprang to his feet.

"What's wrong with him?" Jerry asked sideways to Frank.

"I dunno," Frank shrugged. "He's always like that."

"Shut *up*, Frank!" Stephen waded back into the crowd toward the front.

"Hey Vinny, can Dickie have your drink?" Frank called.

The sound of liquid sprayed over the table. "Oh my *god*, what the hell is that swill?"

Stephen looked over his shoulder and was satisfied to see Dickie had just spit a whole mouthful of bad champagne in Jerry's face.

"Mrs. Kreuger's champagne!" he answered and trundled into the fray.

Chapter 21

Joe was buzzing, but not from bad champagne. The room was so crowded, and loud, and hot. Peltier was holding court now with Mae and a few regulars happy to hang on his every word for free drinks. Red had up and left, and Joe was wondering whether he'd better do the same. But his leg was jangling with the knowledge that Stephen was still somewhere in the room.

He shouldn't have come. He shouldn't be here. The look on Stephen's face had told him as much. He was playing fast and loose with Marion's trust, and he needed her to get through all the next necessary steps. He was resolved to be honest with her now. But he was also aware of this niggling thought in the back of his mind. That he and Marion were through. Paperwork or no, they'd dissolved their relationship. She'd made that abundantly clear when they'd talked last night. While he owed her his honesty and his loyalty, he no longer owed her his fidelity.

All the more reason he should leave now. But all the unpleasant things about the crowded room were also the exact opposite of what he'd find at his cold, sterile, alienating house. Besides, a wild holiday celebration in a dive bar was exactly how he'd found Stephen again to begin with. The room held endless potential. Anything could happen at a party like this. If you played your cards right.

A hand seized around Joe's wrist. His heart lurched as he looked into Stephen's face.

"I need to talk to you," Stephen said. Well, called was more like it. It was so loud, any normal volume would be lost in the din.

"Okay," Joe called back.

And just like that, he was being pulled through the crowd by his hand, weaving between bodies, his heart magnetized like Stephen was true north. Joe reminded himself that he wasn't necessarily sober—Peltier had had a handle of whiskey in his desk and he'd poured Joe a glass to kick off the evening—but that didn't do much to tidy his increasingly errant thoughts.

"Is that *Joe?*"

Joe looked over at the booth with a puzzled expression as Stephen dragged him past. He'd expected it to be their destination.

"Joe, meet my pal, Jerry," Frank called. "He's a bible salesman!"

The man in question waved. "I'm also getting into real estate! I hear you'll be looking soon?"

"Stephen," Joe intoned. "Why is that guy's shirt wet?"

"Oh my god, don't ask about Jerry," Stephen said in an exasperated tone as he pulled Joe into the dark hallway that led to the restrooms.

"Whoa, where you guys going?" he heard Frank call after them, followed by a piercing wolf whistle.

"Stephen, where *are* we going?" Joe asked as Stephen jiggled the door handle to the men's restroom and found it open.

"Don't panic, I just want a damn private place to talk," Stephen said. He was pissed off. Joe could tell by the weight of his brow and the set of his shoulders.

The restroom was a single stall—just a sink and a toilet and a urinal. Stephen led Joe in by the wrist. Joe leaned up against the pedestal sink as Stephen doubled back and locked the door. The room smelled like Clorox and toilet water.

Joe glanced from Stephen to the locked door handle and back. "What did you want to talk about?"

Stephen's expression slid a bit as he collapsed back onto the door.

"What are we doing?" he said listlessly.

Joe felt the air leave his chest. "What do you mean?"

"This," Stephen said, gesturing between the two of them.

"I'm confused." Joe didn't want to guess. He was terrible at guessing what people wanted. And right now he was guessing Stephen was about to dump him.

Stephen sighed. "You … you told your wife about me?"

"Yes."

"Why? What did you tell her?"

Joe was grateful for the support of the sink. "I told her that you were my … the other person. The person I'd, um, fallen in love with. That I'm a—"

"—What? A fairy? A queer?" The slurs dropped out of Stephen's mouth like toads.

"A homosexual."

"Dear god, Joe. Why would you tell her that?"

"Why *wouldn't* I tell her that? It's true!"

"Is it?" Stephen's Adam's apple bobbed in his neck.

Now Joe was pissed too. "Yes. Of course it is. I kissed you. I'm—I'm head over heels in love with you. If there was any other possible explanation, believe you me, I would have found it."

Stephen grimaced and shrugged, his eyes darting away. "There's a lot of guys who've done a lot more than you and would never in a million years admit they're bent."

"Well, I'm not all the other guys you've slept with." It was harsh, but Joe felt harsh. This was one hell of a time for Stephen to get cold feet.

"No, you're not," Stephen admitted. His mouth was all pinched. "You're just the first one to leave me."

Joe gave a frustrated groan. "I'm sorry. I was eighteen and stupid and—god, if you knew all the time I've spent regretting that over the last few months—the last few *years*—"

"But what if it's all a mistake? What if we've built up all these castles in the sky and we're disappointed? What if—"

"What if the Soviet Union drops a nuclear bomb tomorrow and we're all dead anyway? Who *cares* what if?" Joe suspected he knew where this was coming from. "Stephen—even if we end up better off friends than lovers, I'd still want this divorce."

Stephen's arms were crossed. "What if she turns around and ruins us? What if she goes off and tells the whole court we're queers? We could be arrested, Joe. Ever think about that?"

Joe recoiled. "No, I … I admit I haven't. But Marion would never do that. She wants to avoid scandal a fair bit more than I do. She hates being gossiped about."

"Well, how am I supposed to know that, Joe?" Stephen pressed his hands to his chest. "All I hear is that you told her about me, and then you bring my boss to my bar, and *fuck*, Joe, how am I supposed to trust you?"

"What?"

"Privacy isn't just a preference, it's an *imperative*. I thought you understood that." Stephen shoved his hands into his hair. A few curls escaped his pomade and fell over his brow. It was so unfair he could look so handsome while also breaking Joe's heart.

"I won't keep lying, Stephen." His voice was cracking but he could hardly care. "I can't."

"Well, if we're going to be together, you're gonna have to. Not because I'm making you, but because we have no other choice! You don't know what it's like, to hide in plain sight. You've never had to change the pronouns of your partner just to talk about your weekend at the watercooler. You've never had to make excuses to your relatives who want to know why you haven't met a nice girl yet. And you've certainly never had to police your mannerisms to avoid notice by the police. *Joe.* Everywhere I go that's not here, I'm half a lie."

Joe gripped the edge of the sink. The sound of his breath racing in and out of his nose echoed off the tiled walls. "You're right. I've never had to do those things. But that doesn't mean I don't feel like a lie."

Stephen drew in a shuddering breath. "It's—it's—okay. Sorry. I—I spent too much time alone with my thoughts this weekend," Stephen said, rubbing at his forehead. "It's a different sort of lie than the one you've been living. A lie by omission. It's … it's the kind of lie that allows you to tell the truth. To yourself."

Joe swallowed hard. "I need that," he whispered. "I don't need everyone in the world to know my business. But I *need* to be honest with myself."

"I want that for you too," Stephen said, more gently. "But I also need to be safe. I need us both to be safe."

Joe gave a stilted nod. "I … I know you don't want to be stuck in the middle of this. I'm so sorry about how this has all played out."

Stephen sighed. "Don't apologize for that. Maybe it's

delusional for me to try and stay out of it." He stepped forward and pried Joe's fingers off the edge of the sink to hold in his hands. "I'm not very good at minding my own business."

"This is your business. I just made it your business. Also, I really didn't mean to bring Peltier here," Joe added. "He just—you know how he is."

Stephen gave an aggravated nod. "I told him the truth, anyway, so it's not like he'll be surprised." He looked down at their shoes, pointed toe to toe. "Did he have any good advice?"

"Boy howdy, did he. He gave me his lawyer's home phone number and the name of three judges he knows won't ask too many questions. Marion and I talked about it last night. We're going to share the same lawyer. She's going to file on a charge of adultery, and I'm going to enter a guilty plea. I'm going to give her everything she wants, and she's not going to make a fuss. It's better that way. For her, for the children, for you and I."

Stephen's head dropped onto Joe's shoulder and he let out a small, sad sound.

"Stephen?" Joe grabbed his shoulders. "What is it?"

Stephen looked up at him and did the most unexpected thing. He laughed.

"What?" Joe repeated, mystified.

"It's just that …" Stephen laughed again. "Wow, that made me feel a whole lot better. Knowing that. God."

"Good."

Stephen winced. "I just spent the last fifteen minutes in hysterics, is all. This is … This is all very new."

"Completely uncharted territory," Joe agreed. He slid his hands out of Stephen's and over his shoulders. "I'm out of my depth."

Stephen chewed on his lip for a moment as he leaned

into Joe's embrace like it was the most natural thing in the world. And it had been, at one point. When they were young and reckless and thick as thieves. What a relief that it could be like that again. "You know ... I know I said that I didn't want to get involved, but I'm not sure that's actually a great idea," Stephen said, glancing up at Joe carefully. "I don't think I have the constitution to be calm, cool, and collected while you take care of everything yourself behind closed doors."

"Don't you trust me to follow through?"

"I do," Stephen said automatically. Then with more intention, he repeated, "I do. Jeez, I didn't think I would, but I actually do."

"Huh, real nice," Joe scoffed.

Stephen grinned up at him, entirely unapologetic, dimples gleaming. "No, I just mean that I can't stand being kept in the dark. We're all tangled up together now."

Joe gave him a wry smile. "Turns out you like to be in control."

Stephen levelled him with a dark look that made Joe's toes curl. "You don't know how true that is."

The door handle to the bathroom jiggled and then there was a knock at the door. Stephen was still looking at him like that, and Joe was breathless for an entirely different reason than he'd been a few minutes ago.

"Just one minute," Stephen called out without breaking eye contact.

"You've been in there for five. Whatcha up to in there?"

Stephen's expression flattened, but he didn't look away from Joe. "Frank, is that you? Just go use the ladies room. I'm busy."

"I bet you are."

"What're you busy with?" Joe whispered.

"I dunno," Stephen replied. "Depends on you."

Joe knew an invitation when he heard one. He leaned down and pulled Stephen in by his shoulders. He pressed his mouth tight over Stephen's. He was certain that Stephen hadn't kissed his neck all those years ago. He'd remember. Stephen's kiss was singular, his lips slick and pliant, his breath and tongue intruding in ways that made Joe's knees weak. Their chins scraped roughly together. He again was reminded of his gratitude for the sink supporting his weight.

Stephen pressed his body against Joe's. He must have felt how excited Joe'd become, because he put his hands on Joe's waist and sort of arched into him. Joe gasped into his mouth. It … it excited him further.

The doorknob rattled again.

"Okay, wrap it up," Frank called again. "There's a line forming."

Joe scarcely registered the words and chased after Stephen's mouth a bit when he pulled away.

"Keep your pants on," Stephen called toward the door. Joe's mouth ended up pressing against his cheekbone. Stephen turned back to Joe and regarded him with an arched brow. "You too."

Joe backed up then. His mouth made this sort of gasp–gulp sound without his permission. What if he didn't want to keep his pants on? What if he wanted to … to take his pants off?

Good god. Joe was going to be a total novice and make a massive fool of himself when this finally happened. Speaking of looking foolish…

"How are we going to leave separately? It's a one stall bathroom," Joe gasped.

Stephen grimaced. "I mean, unless you want to just

stay in here while Frank takes a leak, then I'd suggest just squaring up and pretending like it's not happening."

"Will that work?"

"I mean, as long as one of the people in line isn't Mr. Kreuger, it should be fine." Stephen was crossing to the door.

Joe followed him. "If you say so." He thought this seemed a little counterintuitive after that whole big speech about privacy and safety. He also sort of didn't want to leave, because of the aforementioned arousal. Both not wanting to be interrupted, and not wanting anyone to notice. He surreptitiously adjusted himself.

Stephen opened the door to the dim hallway and strode out, his face stony. Joe followed him, hoping that no one would notice how flushed he was or how stooped his posture was.

Frank was leaning on the opposite wall with his arms crossed and a feral grin on his face. The blonde guy with the wet shirt was next to him. Joe flushed more, which probably helped the problem downstairs. Frank laughed.

"What were they both doing in there?" Joe heard the blonde guy ask as he walked away down the hall.

"Same thing we're about to do," Frank replied.

"Cleaning their shirts? I can't imagine that's likely—"

"Something like that."

Joe wrinkled his nose as he followed Stephen back to the booth. If only.

✦

Chapter 22

Stephen walked toward the booth, his lips and chin tingling, wondering whether he was being outrageously reckless placing his heart in the hands of Joe Milner. But then he saw who was sitting at the booth. At the last second, he turned all the way around and almost crashed into Joe.

"Jeez, Stephen, what are you doing?"

"Abort mission," Stephen hissed.

"Why?" Joe craned over his shoulder. "It's just those other regulars. What were their names …" He snapped his fingers. "Carol and … John?"

"Jack," Stephen said witheringly.

"Right. The Two Blind Mice, was it?"

Stephen gritted his teeth. "Yup."

Joe looked down at him. His usual wide-eyed wonder narrowed. "Oh. I get it now."

"Yeah."

"And you were the third mouse once?"

Stephen winced. "Sure was."

Joe shook his head, but the corner of his mouth twitched up. "God. No wonder you swore off married men."

"Stephen, there you are!" Dickie called. His voice was tight.

Stephen turned around and plastered a grin on his face. "Here I am!"

"Come over here," Dickie said with hard, urgent eyes. "Come say 'hi' to Carol and Jack."

Stephen gave Dickie a very hard look and walked over. "Hi Carol. Hi Jack."

"Hi, Stephen," Carol said with that one brow perpetually raised. "Long time, no see. Who's your friend?"

Stephen glanced over his shoulder and started. Joe was looming right behind him. "Oh. This is Joe."

"Hi," Joe said politely, reaching around Stephen to shake Jack's outstretched hand. "We met a few weeks ago, actually."

"Oh, yes of course," Carol said with a knowing smile like Patricia Neal. "Nice to see you two kids again."

Her eyes flicked up and down over Stephen and then Joe. Stephen wished he could crawl into a sewer grate. After all the twists and turns of this night, his nerves couldn't take much more.

"Again?" Dickie's brows flew up, and Stephen could have sworn his pupils turned into slits like a cat. Stephen tried to give him a subtle shake of his head.

"Oh, don't be so jejune," Carol drawled at Dickie, exhaling cigarette smoke as she spoke. Heavens, were they about to see two piss elegants face-off head-to-head? "We just met Joe once." She turned to Joe. "It was such a shame we couldn't get to know you better."

"Well, it's never too late," Dickie said, exhaling cigarette smoke of his own. Jack perked up a bit, his eyes glancing furtively up at Joe, then at Stephen. God, that desperate little sissy.

"Awe, look! The Two Blind Mice are 'ere." Mae West had returned. He was drunk as a skunk. "Which one of us're you gonna pick off tonight, Carol?"

Carol gave him a stern look.

Mae giggled. "Thank you, mistress. May I have another?"

"Where'd that fellow, Jerry, go?" Jack said suddenly, his deep voice cutting through Mae's squeals.

"What, are you also suddenly interested in real estate?" Walter said with a sour glance at Dickie.

"You'll have to get through Frank first," Dickie said archly.

"Frank'll be through in…" Stephen looked down at his wristwatch, "…ah, probably five minutes."

"Five minutes?" Carol's lip curled up.

Stephen nodded seriously. "If that."

She frowned. "Hm. Jack darling, maybe we should get going."

Jack's shoulders visibly drooped.

"No, you can't leave without a treat for poor Jack," Mae crooned, draping himself over the side of the booth Jack was seated at. He looked up at Carol. "I know I look fragile, but I can actually be very tough. They don't call me Mae West for nothin'."

Carol didn't look impressed.

Stephen felt more than heard Joe whisper in his ear. "What is happening?"

Though there wasn't a zero amount of amusement in Joe's voice, Stephen felt it best if they cut their losses. He took a step back, putting his arm out to herd Joe back with him, then ran into a very solid presence. He looked up into the wild eyes of Jerry, fresh out from the bathroom.

"Oh, 'scuse me," Jerry said absently, clearly flustered.

"Ah, there he is," Carol called clearly, standing from her place at the end of the booth. "Say, we never got your card."

"What?"

"Your business card," Carol reminded him. "We're interested in taking on a rental property, remember?"

"Oh, yes, of course." Jerry fumbled in his pocket. His belt was still undone. Even now, Stephen still couldn't tell if Jerry was playing it up or genuinely a sheep in the lion's den.

"Gee, are you feeling alright?" Carol asked as he handed her his card. She put a hand on his forehead. "Do you need a ride, sweetheart?"

Jerry's eyebrow twitched up with what Stephen thought was likely interest. Jack, folded up in the booth and half bedecked with Mae West, widened his eyes hopefully.

"Oh, come on, Carol!" Mae yelped.

"Yeah, actually," Jerry said, to the shock of them all. Even Carol. He gave a little half-cocked smile. "A ride would be great."

"Yes," Carol crooned, straightening the collar of Jerry's damp shirt. "You look fit to be tied."

Stephen snorted.

Walter rolled his eyes. "Oh, for heaven's sake."

"Come on, Jack," Carol snapped. She actually physically snapped her fingers. Jack scrambled to his feet, towering over her. "Go get the car. Let's get poor Jeremiah home."

Stephen had his hand over his mouth to hide a hysterical laugh. He couldn't help it. He couldn't even begin to imagine what Joe was thinking.

Frank Atlas chose that moment to reappear from the bathroom. "Hey Jerry, where do you think you're going?" His face was wet, like he'd just splashed it in the sink.

"Oh, sorry, Frank," Jerry simpered. "I'm not feeling well. Jack and Carol are going to give me a ride."

Frank's shoulders squared, and he set the meanest look Stephen had ever seen him make on Carol. "What the *hell?*"

One glance at the knees of Frank's trousers completed the story for Stephen. He'd been hung out to dry.

"What, you wanna come too, Frank?" Carol drawled.

Now Joe snorted. Stephen could *not*. He ended up hanging off Joe's sleeve and hiding his giggles in his shoulder.

"*Yeah!*" Frank shot back indignantly.

Carol considered him with an arched brow. "Hm." She tapped her finger to her lips. "I suppose you could make yourself useful."

"What the *hell*, Carol?" Mae screeched. His face was red. "You'll take home a bible salesman and a meathead, but you won't give me the barest second glance? I'VE SUCKED EVERY COCK IN THIS PLACE!"

The timing was unfortunate. Just as Mae got going, there was a natural lull in the din of the place. Mae's voice was loud normally, but when he shouted, he could command a room. It made his point as far as Carol was concerned, but it also got the attention of everyone else in the house. Including Mrs. Kreuger.

The bar was silent. Mrs. Kreuger arched her back, her eyes narrowed like a hawk, and she stalked out from behind the bar. Jack had already obediently gone, but Carol hustled Jerry out, Frank trailing furiously behind her. Mrs. Kreuger came up to Mae and put her finger right under his nose.

"Tch tch," she snapped. "Such language."

Mae was drunk, but even he had the self-awareness to grimace sheepishly. The bar stirred back to life as conversations resumed.

Mrs. Kreuger turned to Stephen and crossed her arms.

"Get your friend home."

Stephen opened his mouth. "Wha—me?"

Mrs. Kreuger didn't stop to see that she was obeyed. Walter crawled out of the booth followed by Dickie.

"I guess you have your marching orders," Walter said and poured Mae toward Stephen.

"What? Why me?" Stephen yelped as Mae draped himself over his shoulders as if in a swoon.

Dickie pursed his lips and exchanged a look with Walter. "Your boyfriend has a car."

"And also Mrs. Kreuger told you to do it," Walter added.

Stephen looked up at Joe, properly for the first time since this entire farce had begun. And Joe, bless his wonderful heart, was smiling genially.

"No worries," Joe said. "We'll get you home, Mae."

Mae gave a soft, tragic sigh, so Stephen knew he hadn't actually fainted. Joe came round and they slung Mae over their shoulders and sidled through the crowd to the front door.

"God, I hope Peltier left before that episode," Stephen grunted as they reached the front.

"He did," Mae bleated. His head was still hanging and his eyes were still closed.

"Well, good," Stephen said, not sure how to address him when, for all intents and purposes, he was unconscious.

"He screwed off to the St. Paul Hotel," Mae added dreamily. "Which is nice because now Red is back."

Red indeed was back, perched on his usual barstool at the front of the bar. Stephen glanced over at Mae again, but his eyes were still closed.

"Hi Red," Mae called. He flapped his hand on Stephen's shoulder.

Red stood up and intercepted them. "You feeling okay, Mae?"

"I'm just suffering from abject humiliation," Mae said, flinging his head back miserably. "I'll be fine."

"Poor thing," Red said, patting Mae's cheek. "These strapping boys'll take care of you."

Mae really was drunk, because his chin trembled and he cried, "I know, I have such good friends!"

"Awe, Mae," Joe said. Stephen suspected he might actually be touched.

"Well, for better or worse," Red said to Joe, "you're part of the lodge now."

Stephen couldn't imagine a less desirable club to be in than this shit show of sloppy cruisers and queens, but Joe was genuinely grinning.

"Thanks, Red," he said.

They manhandled Mae out the door and into the unseasonably warm night. It was still above freezing even this late at night.

"We're due for a snowstorm when this warm snap ends," Joe observed. It was such a normal thing to say after all that. Stephen just wanted to squeeze him.

Mae managed to walk for himself after being half-carried for a block. He seemed like he needed to know he was solid and real. Stephen could relate.

"What made you go after Carol like that?" Stephen couldn't help but ask. "I didn't know you had any interest in being a third blind mouse."

"I don't," Mae moaned. "I hate Carol. I don't know, I was drunk and I wanted to score."

"There were plenty of other choices in that place. It's St. Paddy's. It's like Winter Carnival for the Irish."

"There was a pretty cute redhead up front drinking that cheap champagne with us. But he was straight." Mae sighed. "You're going to think I'm stupid, but I thought it would be easy pickings. Jack's like a little wind-up toy."

"Yeah, but Carol's a stone-cold bitch," Stephen reminded him.

"I just got too drunk too fast," Mae groaned. "I lose all my charms when I get sloppy."

Stephen just gave him a pat on the back rather than argue. They all knew that was true—of them all, really.

Joe's Ford Anglia was parked in its usual spot on 4th Street. They deposited Mae in the back seat, then Stephen climbed into the passenger side door. Joe turned the engine, put on his glasses, and released the parking break.

"How do we get to your place, Mae?" he asked.

"East on 7th," Mae said wistfully. He'd draped himself across the back seat like it was a fainting couch.

Joe's car was facing west, so he went around the block before heading north on Wabasha Street. The heat kicked in by the time he turned east on 7th Street. It was a quiet drive. The roads were a little treacherous with St. Paddy's revelers, but despite what Stephen had said, it wasn't anything compared to the Winter Carnival. Besides, it was late. All the more reputable bars were closing. It was just dives like Kreuger's and the Coney and the Gopher bar left.

Streetlights and neon flickered on the lenses of Joe's glasses as he drove. Stephen couldn't help but look. His long, round face, his narrow nose in profile curving down into his curly Kewpie lips. Stephen thought about the kiss in the bathroom. He thought about the lookout above the State Capitol and the other places around town he knew to have secluded scenic overlooks. St. Paul was a city of seven hills. There were a lot of them around.

✳

Joe waited until Mae got inside the door to his little basement apartment in Dayton's Bluff before he pulled away, signaling to turn left down Greenbier Street.

"Where are you going?" Stephen asked.

"Just gonna go around the block to turn around," Joe murmured. It was quiet in the car, streetlights flicking by. There was a quiet sort of peace, driving when the city was asleep. "I'll give you a ride."

Stephen snorted. Joe supposed with the events of the evening, that wasn't uncalled for.

Joe shook his head, even as he felt his cheeks warm. "I didn't mean it like that. I'll drive you home."

Snow crunched under the tires, the hum of the engine a comforting lull.

"I wish you wouldn't," Stephen whispered.

Joe was stopping at an intersection. He turned and tried to decode Stephen's expression. He was mostly lit by the streetlight behind him, his patrician profile cast in shadow.

Joe licked his lips. His mouth was dry. "What do you wish I would do instead?"

Stephen's cheeks dimpled into a dark smile. "Pull up into the park."

Joe wasn't particularly familiar with this neighborhood, but there was a park limning the edge of Dayton's Bluff. Joe drove a block and turned off into the deserted parking lot, his palms suddenly sweaty on the steering wheel.

He kicked down the parking break and killed the engine. Stephen's hand came down on his thigh.

Oh. Yes.

Joe turned toward him. It was pitch dark in the park, but he found Stephen's lips like they were magnetized.

Joe had spent so much time thinking about Stephen's mouth. How his lips plumped around a cigarette or how they curled back when he smiled. He was smiling now. Joe could feel the curve of his lips, the jut of his chin sharp against his own. The dimples would be there too, winking in the dark. Joe put his hands on Stephen's cheeks.

"Are you fingering my dimples?" Stephen whispered.

"No…" Joe lied.

"Here. Put your hands here." Stephen pulled his hands down by his wrists. Joe shifted, folding one knee up on the bench seat to face him better. Stephen surged forward and straddled his knee. He pushed Joe's hands over the back pockets of his wool trousers. It was an intimate place to touch, one that both intimidated and excited Joe. He used his leverage to pull Stephen closer, and Stephen arched into his chest.

"Ohh," Joe said. His cheeks flushed. He sounded so wanton to his own ears. Stephen gingerly plucked the glasses off his face and set them on the dash.

Then, Stephen slid down against him, chest to chest, groin to groin, pressure in *all* the right places. Joe tried to close his mouth over the next unbidden sound he made, but Stephen nipped his lower lip and said, "Don't. I want to hear you."

The sound Joe's throat returned for that was the most embarrassing of all. Stephen swallowed it up and made one of his own as they kissed.

"I …" Joe gasped. God, he had to get this out. He didn't want Stephen to expect too much. "I don't know the rules to this."

Stephen smiled into his mouth again. "I do. There's

only one. Feel good."

Well, that was easy. *Everything* Stephen did felt good. Probably because it was Stephen who did it. The press of his fingers over Joe's chest, the firm pressure of his groin against Joe's. The slick slide of his lips, his bold tongue tasting Joe's lips and teeth and tongue.

Another desperate little sound came out of Joe's mouth. He suddenly realized that his usual bedroom concerns were all turned on their head, because it was becoming evident that he might make a mess of himself before anything had really even happened yet. He gripped Stephen's hips and tried to hold him back a moment, just to regain a semblance of control.

"Everything okay?" Stephen murmured, pulling his kisses back too. His fingers gave an affectionate tug on Joe's collar. Even that stupid, innocuous gesture made Joe's breath stutter.

"Yeah," Joe breathed. "Feels good."

"Then you're following all the rules." Stephen's chin scraped down Joe's neck. He pressed kisses into his throat.

"Maybe too good," Joe gasped. God, he hoped Stephen would understand what he was trying to say without making him have to *say* it.

"Ah," Stephen said. "No such thing."

Joe caught him by the shoulders before he could dive back into driving Joe crazy. "I wanna make you feel good too. I don't wanna feel like this alone."

The stillness of the night made Stephen's inhale so loud, so close. "Trust me," he said low. "You're not alone."

More stupid, strangled sounds. Joe felt like a mess. His skin was thrumming. His blood was roaring in his ears. His muscles were stretched taut like a drum. He reached restively down and adjusted himself between his legs, trying to relieve some of the pressure.

"Here," Stephen said. His hand closed around Joe's wrist and guided his hand between Stephen's legs. "See?"

Joe shivered. Stephen was firm under his palm. He could feel the length of him, through the soft wool. Stephen's nose nuzzled into the place where Joe's neck met his shoulder. The decadent sound he made as Joe gently squeezed him felt hot-wired straight down Joe's spine and into his own groin. Joe wanted to feel him—all of him—and it needed to happen right *now*.

He reached fumblingly for Stephen's belt.

After a few seconds of struggling, Stephen nudged his hand away and said, "Here. It's faster if we do our own."

He was right. It was much faster.

Joe felt like a lout pulling his trousers open and pushing the elastic of his shorts down. Just his privates were sticking out like a rude lightning rod. He was grateful for the shadows that softened the whole affair. But then Stephen slid forward, his hard length hot against Joe's. Joe yelped and seized Stephen around the shoulders and just panted into his ear. The firm slide of velvety skin on the most sensitive part of him. *God.* And just the thought, just knowing they were doing it together, knowing it was Stephen, wound Joe tighter than a top.

"Yeah," Stephen ground out into his ear. "Joe."

Joe shuddered as Stephen's hand came round them both. His hips jolted up without any thought, sliding against Stephen's firm grip that held him down, held him in, kept him from flying to pieces all over the vinyl upholstery. He turned his head, pressed kisses into Stephen's neck and cheek, over his jaw and throat. He whimpered Stephen's name over and over again. Saying his name made it feel real, not like a memory from long ago that would disappear after he finished. Reminded him that even in the dark, it was just them. Easy. Like they'd never been apart.

Stephen began to tremble. Joe could taste the sweat on his skin, the flavor of his shiver. His arm came up around Joe's shoulder and held on tight. Joe didn't have to imagine what Stephen was feeling. Didn't have to wonder whether he was doing it right. He knew what Stephen felt, because he felt just the same. Trembling, mounting sensation compounding until it felt like he was detonating in slow motion.

The climax was easy too. Just the logical conclusion of everything else they had done up to this point. His chin forward, Joe gritted out an angry, harsh sound as his entire body stopped being component parts for a moment and just melded in one synchronous burst of pleasure.

Stephen made a sound too. He was kissing Joe, deep and urgent, riding his lap until the sensation of them both together in Stephen's hand started to feel too intense on Joe's sensitized skin. Joe didn't have to bear it for more than a moment, though. Stephen was spilling into his hand, hot and urgent. Joe swallowed all of Stephen's sounds, the steering wheel digging into his shoulder blade as Stephen pushed him back. God, what a mess, what a perfect, beautiful, wonderful mess.

Stephen released his vise-grip then. But he didn't stop rocking against Joe, sliding against him and his soft belly, kissing him breathless and tender and relentless. Joe realized he was laid back on the bench seat now, his head cranked up against the driver's side door. He barely cared. He wedged his elbows underneath him so he could get enough leverage to keep kissing Stephen back, returning every lick, bite, and taste.

Stephen made a deep, contented sound and let his whole weight down over Joe like the most delectable blanket. He never stopped kissing him. Joe lifted one hand because he couldn't stand not touching Stephen for another moment. He pushed his hand into Stephen's thick, dark hair, breathed in the smell of his pomade, and wished this would never end. He'd been worried about this. That he'd be terrible, that he'd be scared or disgusted or too tentative for Stephen's liking. He hadn't reckoned on Stephen's sure, gentle direction, or how excited it would make him. Relief washed over him so hard he almost melted into the seat.

"You're perfect."

The words were muffled, because Stephen had spoken them into Joe's mouth.

Joe tipped his chin away so he could look Stephen in the eye. "I love you."

He couldn't see Stephen's reaction in the dark, but he could feel it in the kiss he gave him.

✦

Chapter 23

Stephen took the stairs down two at a time as the telephone called shrill from the parlor the following Saturday.

"Stephen, can you get that?" his mother called from the kitchen. The other three boarders were laborers who worked weekends and would be home any minute expecting a rib-sticking meal.

"On it," Stephen replied as he swung himself into the parlor and picked up the receiver. "Vincelli Boardinghouse."

"Stephen?"

"Joe?" Stephen's eyebrows flashed. "How did you get my number?"

"What do you mean? You gave it to me."

"When?"

"Let's see … 1945?"

Stephen blinked. "B-but you haven't called here in years. You're telling me you still have the number memorized after all that time?"

"Will you find it very pathetic if I say yes?"

"No!" Stephen flopped into the chair next to the receiver. He glanced up at the kitchen, then lowered his voice. "Very romantic, maybe. But not pathetic."

"Good thing you never moved out."

"Ha ha, very funny." Stephen slouched down in the

chair and put his knees up like he had when he was in high school, as if his shins could afford him the actual privacy he desired. "To what do I owe this call?"

"Right. I'm actually calling for your mother."

"Whyyy?"

Joe gave a sigh that crackled in the phone speaker. "Well, I'm looking to move out sooner rather than later."

Stephen sat up. His heart slammed in his chest. "Why? Was Marion upset because you were out late on Wednesday?"

"That probably didn't help." Joe paused. Stephen filled the silences with delicious memories from the Ford Anglia. "But no. I just need the space. Marion needs it too. I was going to stay there until I found an apartment, but there's nothing available."

Stephen sucked his teeth. "Turns out Jerry was right about the housing shortage."

Joe snorted. "Maybe I should give him a call."

Stephen sat up straight. "Don't you dare. That guy's a *harlot*."

"Why? Because he went home with the Two Blind Mice?"

"No!" Stephen lowered his voice. "Because he was back cruising at Kreuger's *last night*. Frank was incensed."

"Are you sure he was cruising? Maybe he was just looking for more real estate clients?"

Stephen could hear Joe's smile in his voice, but he was having too much fun being contrary. "You, my dear, are very naive."

"That's what you love about me."

Stephen snickered and curled the phone cord affectionately in his fingers. "True. Wait—why do you want to talk to my mother?"

"I thought she might have a room I could let for a little

while."

"I'm sorry, what? And you weren't going to ask me first?"

"Why?"

"Are you messing with me on purpose?"

"No?" He could hear Joe smiling again. How annoying.

"Are you thinking this is some sort of grand romantic gesture? To ask my mother to move into her house so we can sleep in adjacent rooms and torture ourselves?"

"I was sort of hoping she didn't have any rooms available, and I'd just have to swallow my pride and room with you for a little while."

Stephen's mouth dropped open. "Are your children home?"

"No—they're with Marion at her mother's because apparently the very sight of me is too awful to bear."

"Joe," Stephen frowned. "Hell."

"It's nothing I don't deserve."

"Don't say that." Stephen gave a sigh. "Ugh, now you made it all sad. I can't even make a dirty joke when you set me up so perfectly with that 'swallow' comment."

"Stephen!"

"As it happens," Stephen said, twirling the cord around his finger, "there is a vacancy. Jenson's moving to Chicago."

"Stephen, that's great—"

"—But his room is downstairs, and mine is in the attic."

"Oh. But still, it'll be a lot closer—"

"I'm still not completely over the idea of you just sharing with me. Fellows are doing a lot of that these days, with so few vacancies."

"It would be odd to share if there's a vacancy. Wouldn't it?"

Stephen slouched into the chair again with a pout. "Yes. Probably."

"And I'd rather not wait until it fills."

"It won't take long. But you're right. Hold on, I'll get her."

Stephen balanced the receiver on the arm of the chair and dashed to the kitchen before he could think of a reason why this was a terrible idea. "Ma, can you take a call?"

Mrs. Vincelli turned around and wiped her hands on her apron. "What? Who is it?"

"You remember my friend Joe? From high school?"

"Oh, yes, Joe! He's always so nice when he calls. *He's* the kind of fellow you should be spending time with, Stephen, not that arrogant fellow you introduced me to at the department store—"

"Dickie," Stephen filled in. God, that had been embarrassing. He'd meant to pretend like he didn't know Dickie, but his mother had swept in and made full introductions and he hadn't heard the end of it since.

"Yes, you shouldn't waste your time with people who put on airs. Joe is a fine fellow, and he doesn't strut or squawk over himself. *That's* the kind of man you need as a friend, Stephen. Wait—didn't he get married?"

Stephen winced. His mother was Catholic. Maybe he should have waited to think of a reason why this would be a bad idea. "Well, actually..."

"Oh no," Mrs. Vincelli said with a tone of sympathy. "Is she divorcing him?"

Stephen gave a grimace as an answer.

"That's so sad," Mrs. Vincelli said, with a notable lack of censure. "You know, your Aunt Bertie got divorced. Did you know that?"

"What? Really?"

"Yes. Her husband was an awful piece of work. Your Joe didn't become an awful piece of work, did he?"

The way she said *your Joe*, so casually, like it was nothing at all to worry about, made him reckless. "No, of course not! He's *wonderful*."

"Well, she's a fool then," Mrs. Vincelli concluded, shoving a spoon into the saucepan and giving it a stir. "Mr. Jenson is leaving for Chicago next month. He could take that room."

"Next month?" Stephen hadn't heard that. "Is he waiting that long?"

Mrs. Vincelli raised an eyebrow at him. "Well, most fellows don't move to a new city without a job or a place to live."

"Right." Stephen dithered for a moment, even though he knew Joe was still waiting on the phone and this conversation had already taken too long. "I think Joe was looking for a place a little sooner."

Mrs. Vincelli rolled her eyes. "Well, if it's so urgent, why don't you just share your room with him?"

Stephen's heart skipped a beat.

"I dunno…" he forced himself to say.

"Oh, don't be so selfish, Stephen. You've got the whole attic to yourself."

"Of course." Stephen made a show of shaking his head. "You're right. It's more important to help out a friend."

"That's the boy I raised." Mrs. Vincelli put a hand on her hip and gave him a fond look. "Well, what are you waiting for? Ain't he still on the line?"

"Oh!" Stephen jumped. "Right."

He skidded out the kitchen door. He couldn't believe his luck.

Chapter 24

That Sunday, the warm weather finally broke and a drizzly sleet gilded the city in ice. Joe left the car at the house, because Marion needed it more than he did to transport the children, and took the bus downtown with his two neatly packed suitcases.

He'd told Chuck and Linda that he was going on a trip. It was what Marion suggested. He'd agreed, because he couldn't face telling them the truth. He'd already been such a distant father to them, watching them grow from behind the bars of the cage he'd built himself. If he could manage to find a place to live, where they could visit and have their own room and everything, he'd feel like he was on firmer footing. He wasn't sure how that would involve Stephen, or how he'd negotiate keeping all the people he loved safe in a shared household, but he could hardly find a place to let at all. He had time to figure all that out.

At the Union Depot station, he caught a second bus back west to the Levee. He could have walked, but the weather and his suitcases made the bus a more appealing option.

He almost slipped on the ice twice making his way down Loretta Street to the Vincelli Boardinghouse. Even his hat was starting to crust with ice by the time he got to the front door and rang the bell.

The door cracked open. Stephen appeared, all gleaming dark hair and winking dimples. The prism of ice Joe had become melted a little.

"You're here," Stephen said.

"Hello," Joe replied.

Stephen's smile settled a little. "Come inside. It's awful out there."

Joe stepped inside. Warm air scented with spiced meat buffeted his wind-chilled face. He set his suitcases down and shrugged out of his ice-crackled coat. Stephen took it from him and hung it on the hall tree. It looked a lot like the one Marion had in their front hall. Joe's heart clenched—the first thing it had done except keep him alive since he'd left his house. Marion's house.

"Do you think we're rushing into things?" Joe blurted. Stephen froze for a moment that felt like a lifetime.

"What do you mean?" Stephen replied, turning back to face him. His expression was pinched. "We've waited eight years."

Joe rubbed his forehead. "Sorry. I'm being stupid."

Stephen peered at him for a long moment. "You okay, Joe?"

"Yup, I'm fine."

"It's okay if you're not."

"I said I'm fine."

"Okay." Stephen looked at him a moment longer before stooping to pick up one of Joe's suitcases. "Let me show you upstairs."

Joe picked up the other suitcase and followed Stephen to the staircase. It was done in a craftsmen style too, with a simple square newel post.

"Stephen!" came a muffled call from the back of the house.

Stephen paused on the first step. "Yeah, Ma?"

"Is that your friend?"

"Yeah, he's here. I'm just helping him carry his luggage upstairs."

"Good boy. Dinner's in five minutes!"

"Okay," Stephen called, ducking his chin down with a wince. "Sorry," he muttered in a lower voice. "She's not the most gracious hostess."

Joe's cheek cracked a bit. "That's okay. I'm just glad she's letting me stay."

Stephen smiled back, just one dimple, and nodded. "Me too."

They climbed up the stairs, up to a landing, then switching back up more stairs before emptying out onto the second floor. Stephen opened the first door on the right and revealed another staircase. It was dark. Stephen flipped an old knob-and-tube light switch and they headed up. These steps were worn and unfinished. Joe had to duck after the landing to clear the sloping roof of the house. The stairs deposited them in an open room with gabled eaves. The ceiling was low—Joe had to stand in the exact center of the room if he didn't want to stoop.

There were windows on each end of the room. The gables of the house ran perpendicular. There was an iron bed in one of the gables with a tidy quilt pulled tight over it. There was a dresser and a bookshelf, a colorful rag rug on the floor. A cozy little hideaway. Stephen crossed to the bed and switched on the bedside lamp.

"Well, make yourself at home," Stephen said, his smile tilted at a sheepish angle. He set the suitcase on the bed. Their bed.

Joe swallowed. He set the other suitcase on the floor.

"We don't have to share," Stephen added, filling the silence Joe knew was probably making him uncomfortable. "I could make up a cot or—"

"That's not necessary," Joe said. He wanted to share, but he couldn't manage to say it aloud. He couldn't manage to say much of anything aloud. He wanted to share, was eager for it even, but he felt so damn selfish for being here in the first place. He refused to let himself think about it. If he started, he'd never stop.

Stephen walked up to him, slowly, like he was afraid he'd spook or something. He stood in front of Joe and looked at their feet, pointing at one another for a moment. He looked up at Joe, then reached out and took his hand in his own.

"Are you … having second thoughts?" Stephen was looking down at their hands together, then glanced up like he was scared of what he'd see on Joe's face.

Joe blinked hard. "And third and fourth and fifth."

Stephen looked very serious for a moment. His hand was trembling. "Shit."

Joe squeezed his hand tight. He pulled on it a little. That was all it took for Stephen to step in for him to wrap his arms around. "But not about you," Joe whispered. "Never have to think twice about you."

He could feel the tension drop out of Stephen's shoulders beneath his hands. Stephen's fists clutched the sides of Joe's jacket.

"Stephen! Dinner!"

Stephen stepped back and wiped his eyes with a weak laugh. "Better get down there."

Joe nodded. Stephen slipped by him to start down the stairs. Joe grabbed his sleeve.

"Stephen."

"Yeah?" He looked up from a step down, yellow light casting planes of shadow across his face, limning his beloved forehead, large nose, his dimpled chin.

"Thanks," Joe said. It was so desperately inadequate.

Stephen gave a shrug. "Anything for you, Joe."

✳

After dinner, Joe joined Stephen and one of the other boarders to watch "Toast of the Town" with Mrs. Vincelli. Eddie Fisher performed, and the Kean sisters' impressions were a riot. It was nice to not have to think about anything for an hour, to just be entertained in company who seemed to care little for the fact that there was a new fellow among their number. When Ed Sullivan bid farewell, Mrs. Vincelli switched the television off and shooed them all off to their rooms as she wheeled the television back into the closet.

Joe climbed the two flights of stairs again with Stephen. He was surprised that Mrs. Vincelli had hardly made a fuss over him, or the fact that he had to share with Stephen. She'd just heaped food on his plate, gave him only one or two pitying glances, and treated him as if his presence were perfectly ordinary. Joe had to wonder how much she knew.

This time when they got to the second staircase, Stephen held the door for Joe, then shut it behind them. Joe wondered what Stephen expected of him, or what he expected from Stephen. He hardly knew. He'd been determined while packing his bags last night, but woke in a fog by morning. He'd wafted through the whole quiet proceedings, kissing the children goodbye before leaving for his "business trip." He hated the lying, but … he and Marion wanted to protect them from everything just a little bit longer. He had no earthly idea how they would react. Perhaps the most frightening prospect was if they didn't miss him at all.

"Penny for your thoughts?" Stephen asked as he pulled his dresser drawer open. Joe realized he'd just been standing there in the center of the room staring down the bed at his suitcase.

"Wishing I wasn't having any," Joe replied.

Stephen sighed. "Joe, are you okay?"

Joe looked at him.

"God, what am I saying, of course you're not okay." Stephen stepped closer to him.

"I didn't realize," Joe found himself whispering, "how much this would cost."

The words dropped out of his mouth like a load of bricks.

"I mean, I think the rent is pretty affordable," Stephen shrugged with a weak little smirk.

Joe laughed helplessly and dropped his head onto Stephen's shoulder.

"Sorry—I couldn't help myself. Too much Kean sisters will do that to you." Stephen rubbed his hands up and down Joe's back. "Do you want to talk?"

"I'd rather do literally anything else."

"It's been a hard day," Stephen replied. "Let's just go to sleep. Tomorrow will be better."

Joe didn't have anything left in him to argue. He went through the motions of taking a pair of pajamas out of his suitcase while pointedly not looking at Stephen, who was pulling his sweater off and his shirt along with it. Even through the cloud of the worst day in Joe's poor, pathetic life, he could still feel his blood hum as he tried to not look at the expanse of skin strapped over shifting shoulder blades a few feet away from him.

It wasn't just that it was bare skin. It was *Stephen's* bare skin. Stephen, who was going to be shoulder to shoulder with him in that cozy bed, who hadn't even kissed him since he'd arrived. Whom he had turned to to catch him instead of standing on his own two feet. Even as much as it hurt to leave that house and the kids and Marion—who he didn't detest, who he admired more than he was ashamed of himself (which was a fair heap just now)—even now, the thing Joe felt the most guilty about was how goddamn relieved he was to be here.

Stephen shrugged his pajama shirt on and tucked his chin down to do up the buttons. A lock of dark hair flopped over his forehead. Yes. Joe was relieved. Relieved, and unbearably fond of the way this mundane little task made Stephen so soft and endearing. A level of intimacy both familiar and foreign all at once.

Stephen glanced up at him. "You're staring."

"Sorry." Joe didn't stop.

"Should I even bother?"

"Hm?"

"With the pajamas?"

No. Give it up as a bad job. Joe shrugged and looked down into his suitcase. He could feel Stephen's eyes on him. He wished he'd make it easy for them again, like he had in the Ford Anglia.

"I'm going to go down and brush my teeth," Stephen said at length. "Give you some privacy."

Joe's eyes followed him as he started down the stairs. *No. Stay. Don't leave me alone.* "Okay."

Stephen disappeared.

Joe's hands pulled out his own pajamas, loosened his tie and unbuttoned his shirt. Looked around for a place to hang his suit, then felt absurd and out of place. He packed his suit neatly into the suitcase instead, pulled the paja-mas on and everything, independent of Joe's thoughts, which were all tangled up in guilt and relief and Stephen,

Stephen, Stephen.

Thoughts of Stephen felt the best. Right and good. Guiltless, or at least guiltless in comparison with how those thoughts had felt before Joe had faced up and told himself the truth.

Joe stowed his suitcase away to the left of Stephen's dresser. He touched the bottle of cologne on top, the comb and the little canvas shaving kit. He felt like an intruder, yet also privileged to be welcomed into this snug little room. He'd never been in it before. Joe had barely gotten a glimpse of the first floor when Stephen had let him come here in high school. It must have cost Stephen a lot to let Joe stay here now.

When Stephen reappeared at the top of the stairs, Joe turned toward him like it was the only thing he was capable of. It probably was. His body was always aware of where Stephen was now, the hair on the back of his neck rising like antennae picking up a radio signal.

"There's always a bit of a line this time of night," Stephen said. His words trailed off as Joe closed the space between them. He pressed his palm against Stephen's prickly cheek, and ducked his head down to press his mouth to Stephen's.

There. A proper kiss. It had felt strange between them when he first arrived, but it was only because he hadn't been able to do this.

Stephen melted against him. He gripped Joe's pajama shirt, pulling Joe down to his level. He didn't deepen the kiss, or make it anything else. He just kissed Joe back with his whole body. Something fragile and tender and heartfelt, softened by the yellow lamplight.

"There," Joe said when they finally, reluctantly parted. "That's better."

*

Stephen didn't sleep well. He was used to sprawling across the mattress and now there was a firm, bony body in his way. But after Joe broke the ice with that *kiss*, Stephen stopped trying not to touch him. Joe had been so skittish. Stephen had feared a touch might spook him so bad he'd run off. His fears had been entirely baseless.

They held hands when they fell asleep. Later in the night, they slept back to back. Later still, Stephen gave up the ghost and wrapped himself around Joe, even though Joe was taller and he ended up with his chin on Joe's spine. Sleeping with another person would take some getting used to, but Stephen was up for the challenge.

When Stephen woke in the morning, diffuse light was beginning to filter through the curtains. He was lying on his back with Joe curled around his shoulder, Joe's nose nudging against his earlobe. He was tired, but he was happy. Stephen took stock of everything around him. The humble comfort of his room, usually such a fortress of solitude, filled with the soft, steady rhythm of Joe's breathing. The arch of his nose, the way his eyelashes dusted his cheeks, the tousle of his hair over his forehead. Stephen had never done this before. Spent the night with a man, woken up in the morning entangled with him. He'd certainly never brought anyone here. Stephen's fingers played over Joe's hand splayed on his stomach. His knuckles had light, almost invisible hairs. They looked especially good without a wedding ring on them.

Stephen was terrible to enjoy this. He'd opened up too much. It was only a matter of time before the other shoe dropped and he was alone again. Except he couldn't even convince himself that that was true. This was Joe.

Joe made a sleepy sound. Stephen turned his head, chin connecting with Joe's forehead. Joe corrected his course, tipping his face up toward Stephen's. It would be rude not to kiss him now.

Sour morning breath and sharp stubble couldn't make a dent in the thrill of waking up with Joe Milner in his bed.

Stephen rolled toward Joe, a hand on the back of his neck. Their legs tangled under Stephen's sheets. Joe was pliant, opening his mouth as Stephen pushed himself up, half on top of him. Stephen was maybe only half-awake, half-thinking, because he pressed Joe's shoulder down into the bed and stuck his tongue down his throat. Joe made a whimper of a sound and gripped him by the sides of his pajama shirt. Stephen wondered if it was too much, too fast, but then Joe's hands were fumbling under his shirt and pushing up over Stephen's bare chest.

Stephen pulled back, sitting up over Joe and yanking the shirt off.

"Christ," Joe murmured. He barely looked half-awake himself, his eyes heavy and languid. "You got hairy."

Stephen didn't think to feel self-conscious, because Joe was pushing his fingers into the hair on his chest as he said it.

"Good morning to you too," Stephen said. His voice was gravelly and low. He leaned down and gave Joe another deep, eager kiss. He put his hands to work on the buttons of Joe's pajamas.

Joe's hands snaked round his shoulders and down his biceps. He kissed back with gusto. It was such a relief after his tepid arrival last night. Stephen had half thought Joe would back off the whole thing. It would be understandable, after all. Leaving his family and his comfortable life behind, to shack up with another fellow in the attic of that fellow's mother's house. God—he couldn't think about that right now. It was a boner-killer, and Joe's shirt was undone now.

Stephen ran his hands down Joe's bare chest as he drank him in. The last time he'd seen Joe's chest was when they went swimming in White Bear Lake the summer before senior year. He'd filled out since then. He wasn't muscular or anything, not with the kind of work he did. But he just looked solid in a way he hadn't in their youth. He was mostly smooth, with only a little patch of hair at his sternum. Stephen kissed him there, then peppered sloppy kisses at random across the expanse until Joe was panting.

"What time is it?" Joe gasped. His hands were back on Stephen's shoulders, pulling him in even as he voiced something like hesitation.

"Seven?" Stephen guessed, based on the light, then kissed Joe's clavicle.

"No one's coming up to do a wake-up call?"

Stephen scoffed. "*God* no." He hadn't even thought about being interrupted. He'd never brought anyone here because he was so ashamed of the ramshackle neighborhood and the boarders and living with his mother. But it was actually a very private space, up here in the attic. He sat up to assess Joe's expression. "We're perfectly safe."

Joe's eyes and mouth softened at that news. Stephen couldn't help but grin, then bent to lick one of Joe's flat, pink nipples.

"Christ!"

"Don't want to be too loud, of course," Stephen added, then did the other one.

Joe yelped, but quieter this time. "God, I can't tell if that tickles or feels good."

Stephen added a hint of teeth to the mix. Joe *moaned*.

His fingers shoved into Stephen's hair and gripped. His hips pressed up into Stephen's belly, and Stephen was struck with a fit of inspiration. Pushing up on his elbows, Stephen scooted himself down the bed and pulled the waistband of Joe's pajamas and underwear down.

"Stephen?" Joe managed with a choked sound. Stephen looked up at him and deliberately mouthed over the plump head of Joe's cock before he had a chance to think twice about it. Joe was up on his elbows now, looking down his chest at Stephen, his mouth wet and gasping and astonished. God, he felt incredible. The weight of him on Stephen's tongue was *everything*. Maybe it was overeager of him, maybe too much too fast, but Stephen swallowed his length down as far as he could in one go, his eyes blinking shut at the sheer intimacy and audacity of it.

Joe made a strangled noise. Stephen glanced up to see him with his knuckles in his teeth.

How encouraging. Stephen bobbed up and down, holding Joe's eyes as he did it. Watched as Joe's eyelids fluttered and his mouth went slack. Watched him unravel with every stroke of Stephen's tongue. God, he loved this. Taking a man apart with his mouth, doing the thing so many were too chickenshit to do. There was nothing demeaning about going down on a guy. It was power itself, to be able to strip a man back till he was nothing but wanting.

Joe wasn't just mindless wanting, though. When Stephen looked up at him, mid-bob, his eyes weren't gripped shut in the throes of passion. They were on Stephen, watching him, with an expression so tender Stephen couldn't think of any other word to describe it. And he faltered for a moment, forgetting his practiced rhythm, shivering. Stephen knew what he was about; he knew how to suck cock. But he'd never done it before with someone who *loved* him. Was he making it cheap? Performing a sex act with flawless execution, but no depth of feeling? Dear god, how did one *make love?*

He'd paused too long now. Joe let out a shuddering breath.

"I've been thinking about your lips for months now," Joe whispered.

Stephen blinked in surprise. He was afraid to say any of the things that sprang to mind. He didn't want to make this raunchy.

"I couldn't remember if you'd kissed me at the graduation party. On the neck. And I couldn't stop thinking about it."

"I didn't," Stephen admitted. "I was too afraid."

"I know," Joe breathed. "Because when you kissed me in the car, I knew I would have remembered how that felt."

Stephen just stared at him, aware that he was hovering over Joe's spit-wet erection, but unable to stop the way he flickered insubstantially remembering that fear. He'd pulled Joe off so furtively that night eight years ago. Hands shaking but determined, the heat of Joe's velvety skin searing his palm. Watched every expression cross his face carefully, so he could remember it forever. Even in the midst of it, he'd sensed that he'd flown too close to the sun. That Joe wouldn't be able to look him in the eye afterwards.

"I'm sorry I was such a coward," Joe said with a crack.

"Don't," Stephen replied. "We're here now."

"I'm not afraid anymore," Joe continued, his hand carding gently in Stephen's hair. "God, Stephen. I want you so much. I've never felt like this before."

Stephen let Joe's words fill him until there wasn't

a shadowed corner left in him for his fear to lurk. He cracked a smile, watched Joe's limpid eyes dart to his mouth and his cheek. Oh, to his dimples. God. "I love you, Joe." He didn't wait for a response. He simply dipped his head and showed Joe how much. Joe's reedy gasp was more than enough to reassure him that sex with feelings was still sex. Just better.

When Stephen tasted that Joe was close, he pulled back, circling Joe's cock with his fingers while he teased the tip. Joe *writhed*. He was desperate now, gripping Stephen's hair with both fists and thrusting helplessly up at him. Stephen let him squirm a moment or two more, watching the flush that was spreading across Joe's chest. His nipples were tight pinpricks now. God, the look of him made Stephen positively feral. He gave just the head another firm suck. Joe sobbed, louder than he probably should have. Stephen probably should have cared more about that. Instead, he plunged back down Joe's length. His fingers pressed into Joe's hips and his breath labored through his nose as he looked up and held Joe's eyes. Every twitch, every gasp, that ardent gaze—they were all to Stephen's credit. If Joe kept looking at him like that, it was only a matter of time before Stephen fortified fully. He didn't need the whole world to see him. Just Joe.

Joe's voice cracked and heaved and his singular taste burst onto Stephen's tongue. Stephen didn't even have to think about it and swallowed with something akin to reverence, which might have been embarrassing if he'd been with anyone else. But he wasn't. He was with Joe. In his bed. For the foreseeable future. He made to sit up, but Joe pulled him down against him, chest to chest.

The heat against his skin, the heave of their chests against one another—god, it was everything. Two living things, with two beating hearts, loving one another.

What could be more real, more solid, more *inherent* than that?

"Is this how we wake up every morning?" Joe asked breathlessly.

Stephen laughed. "It could be."

"Seems ambitious."

Stephen wanted to kiss him, but he wasn't sure Joe would want to taste himself, so he settled for a tender kiss to his cheek instead. Joe stroked his hair. God, Stephen was almost embarrassed by how much he loved that.

"Do we just get up and get ready for work now?" Joe asked.

"I suppose that's the idea," Stephen replied, trying not to make his persistent boner Joe's problem by shifting his hips.

"Seems kind of cruel," Joe said. God, the gravel and the softness at the same time, the low timbre and the tentative unspoken question together. Stephen wanted to lick it out of Joe's mouth. Joe's hand was on the small of Stephen's back, and he pressed there, pushing Stephen's groin down against his.

"I mean, there is still time…" Stephen murmured as he kissed the spot just below Joe's earlobe.

"What do you want me to do?"

Stephen's mouth went a little dry as he considered all the options. But they had time. They had maybe even the rest of their lives spooling out before them. "Your hand. While you kiss me."

Joe turned his head and caught Stephen's mouth with his own. Joe's hands were pushing Stephen's drawstring pajamas down to his knees, long fingers wrapping around his needy length. Stephen hovered over Joe to give him full access. Let his feelings mingle with sensation until he felt like he viscerally understood what it meant to make love.

It didn't take long. Joe's gentle kisses and rough tugs were just the flavor Stephen was developing a very singular taste for. After, he sat up to admire the mess he'd made of Joe with a ravenous grin.

"A man could get used to this," Stephen said.

Joe gave the most hound dog of smiles. "I hope you will."

"*We* will," Stephen corrected, and kissed him.

*

EPILOGUE

A year and three months later…
Excelsior, MN

The property was palatial. The modern building sprawled on the embankment of Lake Minnetonka, lawns yawning under the cover of old-growth oaks and maples. Everything was crisp orange brick and wavy glass blocks. There was a gentle gable over the expansive living room Joe now stood in, a massive picture window of the lakeshore at one end. Men in their best suits mingled as everyone waited for the event to begin. Joe wasn't exactly sure which of them the house belonged to, but whoever it was, he must have had an enormous amount of money.

Stephen appeared at Joe's elbow, slightly breathless, with two crystal champagne flutes in hand. "Walter and Dickie are here."

"Thanks," Joe said, taking one of the glasses. "Where are they?"

"In the kitchen that looks like it's got its own zip code," Stephen replied. "They've got a tower of champagne, like in the movies. You've got to see it."

"Seems like a lot of stops to pull out for a fake wedding," Joe observed as Stephen led him toward the yawning cased doorway that opened onto the kitchen.

"Mr. Moneybags is richer than God," Stephen replied.

"I think his great grandfather was James J. Hill or something."

"What's his real name?"

"Honey, we don't deal in real names here."

Now that Stephen mentioned it, Joe didn't know any of their friends' surnames, and in the case of Mae West, his first name neither. At least not that he could remember.

Some of the men they passed on the way to the kitchen had dressed unconventionally for the occasion. There was a fellow wearing full tails, a cravat, and silk top hat, leaning on a cane. Another had an enormous feathered hat and ostentatious clip-on earrings, though he wore a slightly shabby tartan suit. In the large space-age enameled kitchen, there was a fellow in a gown, which made Joe do a double take.

"Is that the bride?" Joe asked low, trying not to point.

Stephen gave the fellow a glance. "No—I think he's just in the spirit of the thing. Maybe he does some female impersonating on the nightclub scene or something."

"Ah," Joe said. He was trying to mirror Stephen's casual disinterest in the whole affair, as though it were both expected and a bit embarrassing, like a strange family reunion. But to be honest, Joe thought it was kicky as hell and couldn't stop grinning.

The female impersonator was standing in front of the champagne tower and gave a regal nod to Joe as they passed, false eyelashes fluttering. His makeup was both immaculate and garish, like a caricature of Jean Harlowe.

"Is that a wig?" Joe whispered in Stephen's ear.

"Yes, of course it is. Stop staring," Stephen hissed back. "Now here's something really impressive."

"You in a suit that fits you?"

Dickie and Walter walked up, each with their own glass of champagne. There was indeed a tower on the table behind them, stacked four layers high. Joe supposed it was impressive, though it probably would have been more so before everyone had picked it over.

"Ha ha," Stephen said sourly. He straightened his jacket, even though the tailoring was immaculate. He'd splurged on it after they'd put their down payment on the little house near the airport.

"Cream. How daring."

"It's after Labor Day," Stephen sniffed.

"You look very nice, Dickie," Joe said placatingly.

"Thank you," Dickie replied, putting the tips of his fingers to the pearl necklace tucked around his collar. "I wasn't sure I liked it with the navy blue, but Walter insisted."

"Well, I bought it for you, and you hardly ever get a chance to wear it…" Walter said, but trailed off. He seemed uncomfortable. Joe couldn't understand why. But then of course he did. It was such a normal thing for a man to do for his partner—buy jewelry—but a fellow wearing a string of pearls wasn't particularly the thing, well, anywhere really.

Except, perhaps, at a drag wedding.

"Of course you should wear it," Joe said firmly. "If not here, then where?"

"You're in the spirit," Dickie observed, placing a cigarette between his lips and giving Joe the up and down with his arched eyebrows. Stephen said there was no way he didn't manicure the hell out of those things, and Joe was inclined to agree. "What is that, a pink pocket square?"

"I thought it added a little pizzazz," Joe said, tucking his chin to confirm it was still visible.

"Very charming. Darling," Dickie drawled, tugging on Walter's collar. "Give me a light, would you?"

Walter dug in his pocket. Stephen pulled his cigarettes from his breast pocket and offered one to Joe. They all leaned in as Walter lit their cigarettes along with his own.

"Anyone else here yet?" Stephen asked in a puff of smoke.

"I should think half the queers in five counties are here," Dickie drawled.

"I haven't seen anyone else yet," Walter replied. "But I think Frank is coming. And obviously Mae's here somewhere."

"There's a fair number of fellows from the Viking Room around," Dickie sniffed. "But the St. Paul side of the family isn't particularly well represented."

Joe looked around the room. There were more people than he'd expected, once Stephen had explained to him what it was. Over a few shoulders, he saw a familiar face.

"Oh, hey look, it's Jerry," Joe grinned.

Stephen craned his neck to see. "I wonder how he got an invitation."

"Probably in a bathroom stall somewhere," Walter glowered. Dickie made a very exaggerated expression of disinterest.

"Don't be rude," Stephen said. "That guy bent over backward to find us a house we can afford."

"He's been bending over all around town," Walter said with a disgruntled puff to his cigarette. "Where did he come from anyway?"

"Frank's gym, remember?" Dickie said. "Be civil, he's spotted us."

"He's from Kansas City, actually," Joe said. "Moved up last year to try the real estate market. Apparently, the Twin Cities are up and coming."

"According to who? *Farmer's Almanac*?" Dickie muttered as Jerry approached their circle. "Hello, Jeremiah. Didn't expect to see you here."

"Me neither," Jerry said with a grin. He was decked out in a black cutaway tuxedo. "Ended up with a last-minute invitation."

"Hmph," Walter said.

Dickie pinched him and smiled. He really was a very handsome man, with a smile like a Hollywood starlet. He just hardly ever used it. "Are you with the bride or the groom?"

"Hm? Oh, the groom, I suppose," Jerry smiled and stuffed his hands in his pockets in the 'aw-shucks' posture Joe had come to associate with him. "I like your necklace."

Dickie actually flushed, his hand coming to his throat again. "Oh. Thank you."

"Looks a lot nicer than the pearl necklaces I usually give fellows," Jerry winked.

Dickie's face went full red. So did Walter's, for that matter. When Joe looked over at Stephen, he was helplessly snickering into Joe's shoulder. This happened from time to time at Kreuger's too. Someone would crack some obscure innuendo and everyone would laugh or secretly snicker and Joe would be left to decode it for himself. It was pretty frustrating.

"What kind of necklace is that?" Joe ventured, with full understanding he was about to be called Sleeping Beauty for the rest of the night again.

Dickie snorted. Walter shook his head and took a deep drag on his cigarette.

Jerry grinned. "Ah, you know. Homemade, as it were."

Stephen pulled on Joe's arm. "Let it go," he giggled. "I'll tell you later."

"Or show him?" Jerry laughed.

Joe frowned. He had an inkling now.

"Shut up, Jerry," Stephen said. "Look, Frank's here."

Joe looked out into the living room, where Stephen indicated. Frank Atlas was wading through the crowd. He spotted their group and headed in their direction. He had on a bow tie that looked like it might snap at any moment around his thick neck.

"Hey, boys," Frank said as he approached. "Oh, look. Champagne!"

Frank's suit didn't fit him well. It was so tight in the shoulders, Frank could barely reach up to grab a flute from the top level of the tower. Joe couldn't help but notice that Jerry had slipped away.

"So, when's this thing getting started?" Frank asked. "I thought I was late."

"Soon," Dickie said absently, looking around the room.

Frank turned to Joe and proffered his easy, boyish grin. "So I hear congratulations are in order."

Joe squirmed a little. Stephen squeezed his arm. "Yes, the hearings are all done and the papers are signed. I'm a free man now."

Stephen smirked. "Well, not *that* free."

"What better time to toast to a divorce than at a wedding?" Frank grinned and raised his champagne glass.

Joe laughed awkwardly as the rest of the fellows clinked glasses and drank. It was nice to celebrate the relief that came with it, even though it had taken much, much longer and much more money than he'd ever imagined. In fact, it had taken them a whole year to save up a down payment on Stephen's salary while he squared away Marion's alimony and child support. But finally, they had a little bungalow with three bedrooms where they could host Charlie and Linda every other weekend. It wasn't *Father Knows Best* by any means. Stephen and Linda got on like a house on fire, but Charlie… well, Charlie would come around.

After a few minutes, the party began to filter downstairs. The house was built on a bluff overlooking Lake Minnetonka. While it appeared to be one story approaching from the street, there was a lower level built into the hill facing the lake. The orange brick wall continued along the bottom of the staircase, where a large room with wooden beams stretched out, paved in glittering terrazzo. Chairs had been set up on both sides of a white aisle. At the head of the aisle, a buxom blonde in a pink chintz dress directed guests to their seats.

"Mae, wow, I hardly recognized you!" Joe exclaimed as they approached.

Mae had dark false eyelashes on and fluttered them prettily. "I'll take that as a compliment. Thanks ever so."

Truly, the bust on that gown had to have been a feat of engineering. They were enormous, poking out like two torpedoes in the demurely draped chintz.

"Watch out, Mae. You're gonna take someone out with those," Stephen laughed.

"I don't know whatever you can mean," Mae said. His voice was affected, high and breathy. His lipstick was lined well outside his actual lips, making his mouth look round and pouty. "Now, are you here for the bride or groom?"

Stephen shrugged with a wolfish grin. "We're with you, doll." Oh, he sounded so good when he put on that low voice.

Mae giggled too. "Let's have you on the groom's side." He ducked in conspiratorially, but his bombshell meanor stayed ironclad. "It's looking a little sparse there."

Stephen flashed his dimples and Joe followed him down the aisle. It was strange, this farce of a wedding. Joe liked it, but in a way that felt naughty, like one liked alcohol or stolen kisses in the dark. Even with only a little champagne flowing, he could feel the impish energy of it all, delivered with a wink and a nod.

He took a seat next to Stephen in the fifth row. The room was truly enormous, not as cavernous as the living room upstairs, but just as large, with more windows overlooking a pool and the lake beyond. A little arbor had been set up at the head of the room and there, in full priest robes and a garish bishop's hat, was a fairly short, round fellow with eyeliner and lipstick. Joe hadn't been raised Catholic—he'd actually come up in the anti-clerical Sokol tradition—but even he squirmed a little bit at the profanity of it.

"Who's the groom?" Joe whispered to Stephen as Dickie, Walter, and Frank filed in beside them. "Is it Mr. Moneybags?"

"No…" Stephen elbowed Dickie. "Who's the groom?"

"I dunno, I…"

The groom had been facing away from them, but he turned just then and Joe caught his profile.

"Holy shit, is it Jerry?" Stephen squealed.

"What?" Frank turned.

"It *is!*" Dickie exclaimed in a hush whisper. "Groom's side *indeed.*"

"Where's Mr. Moneybags, then?" Joe hissed. He had an insatiable curiosity about the man who would stage this whole production without involving himself.

"There," Dickie said, pointing very surreptitiously toward the rear of the room. While Mae had secured the invitations for the group, Dickie was also acquainted with the hosts. "He's schmoozing with those older fellows near the window."

It was clear then who the fellow was. He was rotund, with a thick, clotted mouth and so old he had age spots on his temples visible from across the room. His white hair was thin, forming a Caesar's wreath around the back of his head. Yet, his suit was impeccably tailored, his waistcoat expensive-looking silk, and his shoes shining in the slanting afternoon sun.

"Looks the part," Walter commented.

"I'd *have* to have a lot of money if I looked like that," Frank added.

"Don't worry, Frank, you'll never look like that," Dickie said offhandedly.

"So let me get this straight," Joe said to Stephen and whomever among their group who could overhear it, "Mr. Moneybags is fronting the costs of the wedding, but Jerry is marrying the bride? But isn't the bride actually *with* Mr. Moneybags?"

Dickie arched a manicured brow. "Moneybags is the Daddy."

"He's giving away the bride?" Joe clarified.

"Yes," Dickie replied. "But, you know, not forever."

"What?"

"Oh lord, you darling boy," Dickie sighed, then smacked Walter in the chest. "Walter, explain."

"I can't explain!" Walter exclaimed.

Frank leaned in. "Some fellows like to watch their ripe, young things with other ripe, young things. You dig?"

The frontier of what was possible never ceased to amaze Joe, but for whatever reason, these notions made him markedly less uncomfortable than the times he and Marion tried in vain to raise the mood. Before, scandalized himself with the mere thought of sugge

Marion face away from him during the hypothetical act. Yet he himself had taken such a position with Stephen now, and deeply enjoyed it besides. There was something primal about it which lit him up from head to toe. He wasn't so experienced that the thought of it didn't make him flush, but he felt worldly now, in a way he hadn't before.

It was the effortlessness, the indulgence, of his friends' behavior—the naughtiness of it—that thrilled him, even if it wasn't something he ready to try. In a way that the notion of a man giving his partner away to another handsome man tickled his curiosity, instead of his mortification. He was enjoying this farce more and more.

"I wouldn't exactly call Frannie ripe," Dickie drawled, his fingers playing with his necklace again as he looked over his shoulder. The guests were all seated now. A fellow in a tailcoat seated himself at the piano on the wall opposite the arbor and began to play.

"Tell me that's not 'Let's Misbehave,'" Stephen chirped, his grin stretching from ear to ear.

"Oh, it is," Dickie replied with a sneer. "How on the nose."

What a tune to walk down the aisle to. Joe grinned along with the rest of them as Mae, relieved of his duties with the guests all seated, scurried through a door under the stairs, bosom bouncing.

"How does he do it?" Joe whispered to Stephen.

"Hm?"

"Mae with the, you know, bosom."

"Oh!" Stephen paused to think. "I'm not sure. Something in balloons, maybe?"

"Pudding," Dickie said resolutely.

"In balloons?"

"Definitely. And a great big brassiere." Dickie cast

them a worldly look. "How else could he get them to bounce like that?"

"That's a lot of pudding," Joe muttered.

The piano crescendoed, then slowed the ragtime beat to a more stately march, though still moving through Cole Porter's melody. The crowd turned around as one.

Out from the door under the stairs marched a slender bridesmaid clutching the arm of a dapper gentleman in a tuxedo. After a few measures, a second couple began to promenade after the first.

"Wow," Joe murmured. They'd really pulled out all the stops with matching gowns and everything. The bridesmaids were even wearing pumps, walking in them like it was second nature.

Then Mae came out, clutching the arm of his tuxedoed escort. He was taller than the young fellow whose arm he hung off, but heavens, one hardly noticed with the way he strutted down that aisle. He managed to step slowly, matching pump to pump for each beat, while also switching his hips and shimmying his ample bosom. All the while, his carefully painted face feigned the kind of wide-eyed sanctity one might expect from a whore in church. Laughs erupted from both sides of the aisle. But it wasn't embarrassing. If anything, it fueled Mae's audacious promenade, so that by the time he got to their row, he was winking and exchanging flirtatious pouts with half the guests in the room. Wolf whistles were ringing out now, as well as a few yelps that felt more appropriate to a football game than a wedding. Stephen was watching Mae through his fingers, grinning helplessly in spite of himself.

"He did say he was going to steal the show," Stephen said as an aside to Joe. "Boy, is he going hard for it."

Mae lined up with the other two bridesmaids and

gave a big shimmy. The false bosom swayed wildly. The crowd erupted in a laugh and it took Joe a moment to notice the bride had already appeared. She was already halfway down the aisle when the crowd finally hushed and the pianist pumped out "Here Comes the Bride."

The bride had a dark chestnut wig cascading in waves halfway down her back and a white veil over her face, marching at a stately pace on the arm of Mr. Moneybags himself, his broad belly swagged with a golden pocket-watch chain. The person portraying the bride moved elegantly, slender and poised like a ballerina. It was impressive but less entertaining than Mae's performance. The bride wore a gown of white lace from throat to foot, a train cascading behind. Joe reeled again at the money that must have been spent.

Mr. Moneybags approached the arbor and faced the bride. He reached up and pushed the veil back from her face. Joe supposed Dickie was right—the bride's face wasn't the most youthful. But her red-painted lips smiled demurely as Mr. Moneybags gave her a thick-lipped kiss on the cheek, then handed her off to Jerry, who cut the most dashing, fresh-faced, eager groom Joe could have ever imagined.

The officiant had a low, sonorous voice that rang off the terrazzo floor and ricocheted off the beamed ceiling. Joe wasn't sure what he'd expected. Salacious innuendos or wild homilies to vice? But the ceremony was tremendously traditional. In fact, Joe was quite sure he'd heard much the same at his own wedding eight years ago. After a while, Joe tuned out the familiar diatribe. His eyes began to wander across the guests. He wondered if he'd recognize anyone here from other walks of life. City Hall, or the Sokol Hall, perhaps. High school. But he didn't. It was almost disappointing, really. It would have been a relief, in a way, to know that this singular group of men, who shared a private secret no one could publicly name, was everywhere. That no matter where he went, there were others like him whom he could look to, nod quietly, silently see and be seen. Despite not recognizing anyone in the crowd, he still felt a semblance of that. He reached over and squeezed Stephen's hand.

"Does the whole 'love, honor, and obey' line make you sentimental?" Stephen quipped quietly in his ear.

"No," Joe replied under his breath. "I'm just taking full advantage of my liberty where and while I can."

Stephen dimpled and pressed his shoulder against Joe's.

"Lord. For a performance, they sure heaped on a lot of vows," Joe commented at length.

Frank leaned over Stephen. "The more vows, the more fun it is to break them," he said with a wink.

Joe frowned.

"Shut up, Frank," Stephen said with an elbow to his ribs.

The officiant finally collected all the vows. "Do you, Jeremiah, take Frannie as your lawful wedded wife, to have and to hold, through sickness and in health, as long as you both shall live?"

"I do," Jerry said in his most sincere voice. He looked up from the bride and delivered his wholesome grin to half the crowd.

"And do you, Frannie, take Jeremiah as your lawful wedded husband, to have and to hold, through sickness and in health, as long as you both shall live?"

Frannie looked at Jerry for a long moment, then flicked his big, blue eyes down at Mr. Moneybags in the front row.

"Frannie, honey, it's alright to say yes on your wedding day," Mae burst out. The crowd, perhaps sick to death of this dirge, gave a great guffaw. Frannie looked back at Mae over his shoulder with an accusing glare, then turned back to Jerry.

"I do," he said, his voice also affected higher.

"Then, by the power vested in me by the great state of Minnesota, I declare you husband and wife," the officiant cried. "You may kiss the bride!"

The crowd stood and cheered like a fraternity at a homecoming game as Jerry reached for Frannie's face and kissed him. They whooped and hollered when he swept the bride by her waist and dipped her low for extra effect. The piano struck up the wedding march once more as Frannie recovered his feet and was led breathless back down the aisle on Jerry's arm.

"How the hell did Jerry end up as the groom?" Dickie wondered aloud as the wedding party passed by. "My *god*, that boy gets around."

"Don't sound so jealous, Dickie," Stephen teased. Walter shot him a contemptuous look as Frank laughed.

"Trust me, you're not missing that much," Frank said.

"Why, is that what Carol and Jack told you?" Dickie sniped.

Frank ignored him and turned, holding his hands out like a fellow might measure a fish he'd caught. Except, of course, significantly less than the size a man would tend to brag about.

Dickie slapped his hands. "That's nonsense. Shut up, Frank."

"It's not!" Frank shot back. "Trust me. I keep track of these things."

"Oh yeah, you keep a ruler in your back pocket?"

"In my throat, maybe—"

"—Okay, come on, you guys," Stephen interrupted. The guests were beginning to file out of their seats.

The guests filtered out onto the patio, fanning out around the glistening pool.

"You think people will swim?" Joe asked, eyeing the pool uncertainly.

Stephen grimaced. "If they do, that might be our cue to leave."

"Why?"

Stephen shrugged. "If I wanted to expose you to that kind of display, I'd just bring you to a bathhouse."

Joe took that in for a moment. Nudity, it most certainly implied. He imagined a scene of naked men lounging insouciantly in and out of the water. "Sounds terrible."

"That was very convincing," Stephen replied, eyeing him from under an amused brow. He turned and straightened Joe's tie. "Oh, my Sleeping Beauty."

"Ha ha." He was trying for sarcastic, but Stephen leaned in and pressed a kiss to his cheek, and Joe ended up grinning. It was so nice—so, so nice—to be able to be together. It was for that reason alone that he hoped this wedding never ended.

✦

"Oh, yoo hoo!"

Stephen turned from kissing Joe's cheek like a kid caught with his hand in the cookie jar and saw Mae West wiggle toward them with a handful of champagne flutes between his fingers. Miraculously, he was able to distribute one for each of the six of them.

"So what's your angle?" Stephen asked with a sip. "You changing your name from Mae to Marilyn?"

"Oh, you're so kicky, Vinny," Mae giggled breathlessly, refusing to give an inch on his act. He'd clearly had his hair freshly bleached for the occasion. "I just love that you've all come to celebrate with us. Wasn't it a gorgeous ceremony?"

"Just like every other wedding I've ever been to," Frank grinned. "'Cept for the bride's got a cock."

Dickie slapped his arm. "Just because there's no cops around doesn't mean you can talk like that."

"Yeah!" Mae pouted. "There are ladies present!"

"Sorry, Miss," Frank said, then reached out and gave one of Mae's fake tits a honk. "Didn't see you there."

Mae squealed and smacked his cheek. "You big lug! How dare you!" he cried breathlessly, then flopped forward so that Frank ended up catching him in his arms. "Get your hands off me, you great gorilla!"

Frank was laughing so hard he almost dropped Mae. He reached around and gave him a goose on the rear as well. "Don't be so eager."

"'Scuse me, miss. This guy bothering you?" Jerry's good-ol'-boy routine popped into their circle.

"Oh!" Mae gasped, straightening and popping his enormous chest toward Jerry. "Mr. Jerry. I don't think I've had the chance to congratulate you and Frannie yet!"

"No, I suppose you haven't," Jerry grinned. His eyes kept flicking down to Mae's outrageous bosom.

"Is he doing that one actress?" Joe asked, leaning in to Stephen's ear.

"Oh, yeah, that one actress," Stephen replied flatly. "You nailed it."

"Mae, are you doing that actress from 'Gentlemen Prefer Blondes'?" Joe asked, circumnavigating Stephen.

Mae's eyes twinkled but still, he didn't break. "I can't know what you mean! Between dining with barons and box tickets to the opera, I find I haven't the time for moving pictures."

Frank laughed. "Don't say that, you little liar. You and I saw that movie at least six times together."

"Well, a toast to Jerry," Dickie cut in, raising his glass. "To your unexpected nuptials."

Jerry grinned. "Wait. I haven't got any champagne."

"Don't worry, Daddy," Mae cooed to him. "You can share mine."

Stephen had not pegged Jerry for a fellow interested in female impersonators, but if there was anything Stephen had come to rely on Jerry for, it was surprises. Jerry had his arm around Mae's waist now and a feral grin on his face as he plucked the proffered flute from Mae's fingertips.

"To matrimony," Dickie declared. They all clinked their glasses together. Stephen drank deep while glancing at Joe. He'd been unsure all afternoon whether Joe was enjoying the farce or covering a measure of discomfort with it all, given he had just ended a real marriage.

Joe's expression was affable and vague.

Stephen frowned. He shouldn't have brought him here.

Jerry grabbed Mae by the chin and pressed his mouth to his cheek. Mae squealed and champagne dribbled down his chin. "Mr. Jerry! What will your bride say?" Then Mae grabbed Jerry by the collar and kissed him, right in front of everyone.

Stephen found himself startled. He'd never seen a man kiss another man in public like this. Well, not public. But even at Dickie's dinner parties, where they could dance and joke in private, he'd never seen any of his friends kiss on the mouth.

"Mae!" Dickie cried, similarly scandalized. How odd, the way they flouted propriety in so many ways, yet toed it so obediently. This level of freedom felt danger

Stephen looked out to the trees surrounding the property, to the lake. Were there neighbors near enough to observe?

Jerry was laughing and Mae was ignoring everyone else to lower his lashes at Jerry as they parted. There was lipstick smeared on Jerry's chin.

"Matthew! What are you doing?"

Stephen turned and saw the bride stalking toward them, flanked by the other two bridesmaids. Mae physically flinched at the name. A cloud passed over his painted face, but then it solidified into something more sinister.

"Francis, honey," Mae simpered, more in character than ever despite the pointed use of Frannie's full name. "Are you quite alright?"

"No," Frannie snapped. He was tall and slender and carried himself with a level of sophistication even Dickie was too big-boned to achieve. "Jerry, you're needed inside."

"Oh, sure," Jerry grinned, dropping his hand from Mae's waist. The lipstick smear on his cheek bastardized his wide-eyed farm boy routine. He shrugged and let Frannie lead him away. One of the bridesmaids snatched the handkerchief out of Jerry's breast pocket and flapped it at his face as they walked toward the house. Stephen could hear Frannie loudly lamenting how provincial St. Paul was.

"Mae!" Dickie hissed once the wedding party was out of earshot. *"What do you think you're doing?"*

"What?" Mae with wide-eyed innocence.

Frank doubled over laughing. "I didn't think this was *that* kind of party!"

"What kind of party is that?" Mae wondered. "I thought it was tradition to kiss the newlyweds."

"Maybe the bride?" Joe pondered.

Mae shrugged. "Frannie has made it pretty clear this week that she has no tolerance for anything disrupting her special day. And I was able to pull in a few favors to get Jerry to fill in at the last minute—"

"A few *favors?*" Frank asked. "What favors does Jerry owe *you?*"

Mae shrugged with an impish smile. "A lady never kisses and tells."

"You don't have to when you do it in front of everyone!" Dickie exclaimed. "What on earth were you thinking, Mae?"

Mae pouted at Dickie. "This house is on two acres. Other than Frannie being a top-grade bitch, what have we got to worry about?"

"Wait, I need to catch up," Stephen said. "Are you and Jerry…" He didn't even know how to finish that sentence. 'Dating' implied a level of romance that he knew Mae wasn't interested in. Probably Jerry too, for that matter. Entering into a sinister alliance was more like it.

Mae didn't need him to finish his sentence. He just shrugged and grinned.

"You little devil. What are you planning?"

"To have fun," Mae replied with a smirk and a little shimmy. "How often do we get an opportunity to enjoy ourselves like this?"

Stephen flicked a gaze up at Joe. Mae had a point there. Stephen had kissed Joe on the cheek earlier. It had set his heart thrumming. His eyes swiveled back to Mae slowly. Dickie and Walter were exchanging unsteady glances as well.

"Don't look at me like that, Vincent," Mae pouted. "I'm a lady tonight."

"That you are, Mae," Frank said. "Sounds like they've

got music inside. Care to dance?"

"Ah, I'd love to!" Mae gushed and let Frank pull him toward the house.

Stephen exchanged a look with Dickie. They all danced at Dickie's dinner parties from time to time. But that felt different. That was a record player in someone's living room. There was always the excuse that they didn't have enough ladies to go around. He turned around and looked up at Joe.

"I'd love a dance," Stephen said.

"That would be wonderful."

The music was coming from the piano player on the upstairs baby grand (two pianos in one house—how absurd). A fellow was standing nearby and singing in grand, swooping notes like Sammy Davis Jr. He was doing an overly sentimental Eddie Fisher waltz. Stephen led Joe onto the dance floor and pulled him close, a hand on his waist.

"Who's leading?" Joe asked in a wavering voice.

Stephen shrugged. "You can if you want."

"I think I'd prefer if you did," Joe replied. Stephen smiled. Joe had a way of seeing deep inside Stephen, finding the things even Stephen didn't care to admit to himself that he wanted, and handing them to Stephen as a matter of course. He'd never felt more solid than he did with Joe in his arms.

So many of their fellow guests were enjoying the opportunity to dance close to one another. Some had clear comfort embracing cheek to cheek, while others danced stiffly, as if they were still getting used to the idea that no one was watching them. The bride was there with Jerry too, striking a perfect ballroom waltz pose while Jerry shuffled through the steps and cruised the crowd with his eyes.

"You alright?" Stephen whispered into Joe's ear as they turned slowly on the dance floor.

"Never better," Joe replied. "I'm dancing with you, aren't I?"

Stephen enjoyed how that warmed his chest. For as hard as Joe was on himself, he certainly was free with his praise for others. Especially Stephen. "I … didn't really think about how glib this party would be in the face of everything that's happened."

"Oh, you mean finalizing the divorce?"

Stephen winced. "Yeah… I suppose an irreverent drag wedding is perhaps not the nicest way to polish off a legal separation."

Joe shrugged. "It's okay. I'm not offended or anything." They swayed together for a few moments. "I'm just really enjoying being here together."

Stephen curled his fingers into Joe's suit jacket. Despite leading, his height perfectly positioned him to rest his cheek on Joe's shoulder. Across the room, he spotted Dickie and Walter in the corner of the room, near a fern. Walter was leaning in, saying something as Dickie fiddled with his necklace. Then, Dickie turned and kissed him. Not in a salacious way, like Mae and Jerry had. In a slow, reverent way. In a loving way. Stephen had never seen them do that before.

"Are you alright?" Joe murmured in his ear.

Stephen shook himself a bit. "Yeah. Of course."

"You seemed far away there, for a moment."

Dammit, Joe. Even after all those years apart, he still read Stephen like a goddamn book. Stephen looked up at him. He glanced around the room full of people, just living and loving and not being embarrassed or ashamed. For years, Stephen had floated through life feeling half there, like a shadow of a real man. He was so used to hiding, he hardly knew what to do when he didn't have to. What was he holding back for?

Stephen dropped Joe's hand and cupped his cheek. "I love you. I love being here with you."

Then Stephen kissed him. On the mouth. In the middle of a room full of people. And it wasn't tawdry, or embarrassing, or cheap. It was perfect.

Mrs. Milner Gets a Kitchen

Chapter 1

Wednesday, November 16, 1955
Saint Paul, Minnesota

Marion Milner lifted a dark eyebrow as she peered sidelong out the window of her heavy front door. Mrs. Dvorak was hovering on her front porch across the street holding a paper plate laden with cookies and Marion prayed that those morsels were not for her. No tray of cookies was worth the price of Mrs. Dvorak's simpering brand of passive-aggressive interrogation and besides, Marion's kids got enough sweets as it was without errant plates of cookies showing up in their kitchen.

The kitchen. That was why Marion lurked in the entry, impatiently watching the corner of the frosty street. The General Electric salesman was due at any moment and she could hardly wait. Finally, all those nosy women at Sokol would have something to whisper about other than Joe leaving. Rather than being the poor, unfortunate divorcee, Marion could elevate her reputation to the aloof, elegant housewife with a fully modern, fitted, *electric* kitchen. All she would have to do was sit back, read a magazine, drink a cocktail, and then she'd be swanning through potlucks with a rotisserie chicken automatically cooked to perfection through the miracle of modern living. She'd be the envy of the entire neighborhood.

Just then, the gleaming, white truck appeared through the snow flurries, with General Electric emblazoned in crisp letters along the side. Marion grinned to see Mrs. Dvorak's mouth flap in the wind as the truck pulled to a stop in front of Marion's house. On cue, Marion swept the door open, the cold metal weather stripping giving a crack, and stood confidently in the entry in spite of the chill. She wore her rust-colored rayon dress—not so fancy as to look like she was trying too hard, but nice enough for an independent woman of means to welcome the sale of a significant home upgrade. Thanks to the settlement, she wouldn't even need to worry about convincing a bank to give her a loan. She could pay for the whole thing out of pocket without even needing to wait for Joe's next alimony check. She supposed there were silver linings to one's husband being so wracked with guilt for leaving her. It made him very generous with his pocketbook.

Two men climbed out of the truck. One was tall, his dark hair slick with pomade, a fine wool coat over his navy blue suit. If the first man appeared to be auditioning for the General Electric spring catalog, the second man, who drove the truck, appeared to be shooting for John Deere. He had a red check flannel coat over brown overalls, a flat cap with fold-down ear warmers, and a knit scarf slung over one shoulder. The salesman and the contractor. Marion slotted them neatly into the roles their uniforms denoted and felt her heart flutter as she opened the storm door for them.

"Welcome, gentlemen," she called as they made their way carefully up the icy front walk and mounted the stoop steps.

"Mrs. Milner, I presume?" the salesman said, shining a

row of straight, white teeth at her. He was tall and sharp and dashing. Magazine ready. Nothing like Joe's quiet, bespectacled lankiness. This man stood straight like he had nothing to hide.

"That's right," Marion replied and allowed herself to enjoy the fellow's attention, even if he was only there to make a sale. "Please, come in out of the cold."

She ushered the salesman and his shorter contractor into the entry. Before she shut the door, Marion met Mrs. Dvorak's dumbfounded gaze across the street with a gracious smile. It was deeply satisfying.

When she turned back to the crowded entry, the two men were stomping their feet on the rug and shrugging off their coats. Milly, the family's dopey elderly cocker spaniel, snuffled around their ankles, and the contractor bent to give her a scratch behind her floppy ears. Marion imagined the swelling violins of the dramatic, daytime infomercials about electric kitchen appliances as she slipped past them, gathering their coats to hang on the hat tree. "Thank you so much for coming out in such chilly weather."

"Oh, it's our pleasure," the salesman replied with another toothy smile. He had a narrow, Clark Gable mustache. "After all, there's no such thing as bad weather—"

"—Just bad clothes," Marion finished for him with a knowing nod. "Can I get you any coffee?"

"No, that's alright," the salesman said, just as the contractor, pulling his cap off to reveal a shock of red hair, replied in a surprisingly deep voice, "Yes, thanks."

The salesman, whose hair was a much more dignified shade of brown under the fedora he'd hung on the hat tree, glanced at his companion. "Well, I suppose if you're serving…"

Marion glanced between the two of them, then smiled.

"Of course. Make yourselves comfortable, and I'll be right back."

She swept through the sitting and dining rooms and into her miserably outdated kitchen with Milly at her heels. It hadn't been updated since 1928. She knew this because Joe's grandmother had been the one to do it. Marion filled the coffee pot with water from the hulking enameled sink under the window and set it to heat on the free-standing gas stove at the far end of the small room.

She chided herself; she should have started heating water before they arrived. This was going to take too long. While she waited for water to boil, she snatched out a serving tray from the hoosier cabinet opposite and arranged coffee cups on saucers, along with the sugar bowl. As she filled a pitcher with cream, she wondered if these fellows were going to insist on speaking with her husband before beginning work. Christmas was only a month and some change away, and she wanted her kitchen finished before the Sokol Ladies Auxiliary Christmas party in mid-December.

When the coffee was ready, Marion swept out with her tray to the sitting room where the salesman and the contractor perched together on her sofa. The salesman's legs were so long, he looked a bit like a spider on her little settee. Marion gave a coquettish smile as she set the tray on the coffee table. She bent and carefully poured out three cups before she sat down in the armchair across from the settee. Milly settled carefully at her feet with a wary woof, though Marion was certain if the contractor offered the dog any further attention, she would readily abandon her master for the fleeting pleasure of getting a good scratch under her chin.

"Lovely home you have here, Mrs. Milner," the salesman said, his eyes casting appreciatively over the woodwork. "It's a wonderful Craftsman. Duplex?"

"Yes," Marion replied, crossing her ankles daintily. "It was built in 1915 and has a kitchen to match."

"Oh my, it's a good thing you called us!" the salesman laughed. "I'm Gerald Stinson, by the way, and this is Mr. Harry O'Conner, our contractor for West Side installs."

"Nice to meet you, ma'am," Mr. O'Conner said, tipping his ginger head respectfully before he reached for a coffee cup. He was short, maybe only a few inches taller than Marion's five and a half feet, and square in all the ways that Mr. Stinson was long. He didn't add anything to his cup before he took a sip.

"Have you had a chance to look through the catalog we sent you?" Mr. Stinson asked as he spooned sugar into his cup.

Marion grinned, her heart leaping at the chance to answer a set of questions she knew all her answers to. "Oh, yes." She pulled the catalog out from her dress pocket. "I'm interested in a total remodel."

She spread the catalog out next to the coffee tray and pointed out the spread she had been admiring for the last two weeks. "I want everything fitted, with built-in cabinets and sink. I would love a double wall oven, and the electric stove. I saw one of your commercials where the refrigerator's shelves swing out and can be adjusted, so everything can fit without too much trouble. And I want to make sure it's got frost protection on it."

Mr. Stinson raised his eyebrows at Mr. O'Conner with a playful grin. "My, I'm not sure I even need to be here. Mrs. Milner, you'd have me out of a job."

Marion tucked her chin to hide a sheepish smile. She thought to say something modest, but what came out was, "Nonsense. Without you, how would I see a sample of the teal finish?"

✦

Harry hated going on sales calls. Hated it with every fiber of his being. It wasn't just because Gerald was an ass who always made him drop the financial bricks on the customers (he could say that because they'd been friends since grade school). He just wasn't very good with these housewives. They always seemed worried he was going to get engine grease on their upholstery or something, which was ridiculous because he was a carpenter, not a mechanic, but that didn't seem to make a difference to the neurotic ladies up on Crocus Hill.

There was something different about Mrs. Milner, though. Probably because she was the first customer they'd had who lived at the bottom of the hill, in the Little Bohemia area of the West 7th neighborhood. Most of these folks were laborers or clerks; they couldn't afford the Kitchen of the Future G-E was hawking. And even if they could, their older houses didn't have the electrical capacity to support them. (Harry hoped Gerald would make sure to touch on the electrical sooner rather than later.)

Gerald was laughing again and drew samples out of his briefcase for Mrs. Milner to consider.

"Now," he said as Mrs. Milner flipped through them, "the matching steel cabinets can be an investment, and somewhat difficult to install in these older houses. Do you have lathe and plaster?"

"Oh, yes," Mrs. Milner replied dismissively as she chewed on her lower lip. She'd put on lipstick for this occasion. Harry wasn't sure who she meant to impress—maybe it was the appliance suite itself—but, well, she did look rather impressive. She was all mahogany hair with a square face slashed with thick, arched brows and dark, full-lashed eyes. She had to be Bohemian—most of the people in this neighborhood were—but she couldn't be first-generation by any means. She had no accent and seemed to be putting on a sort of air that he usually associated with actresses in the movies. It was obviously an affectation, but, well, it was also working for her. Harry felt a little bit stupid every time he looked at her. Which was extremely rude and unprofessional, for multiple reasons.

"Sometimes," Harry said, clearing his throat roughly, "the lathe and plaster can't support the steel cabinets with the same integrity as—"

"—I thought the steel was lighter than wood cabinets," Mrs. Milner interrupted. "That's what the catalog says."

"No, you're right, of course," Gerald chuckled amiably. He was very good at affecting amiability, which was why he was the salesman and Harry was not. "You've done your homework."

"It's not a matter of wood or metal," Harry cut in. "It's that a lot of the houses in this neighborhood cut their plaster with other materials to cut costs when they were built, so their plaster just crumbles whenever I drill into it."

Mrs. Milner raised that arched slice of eyebrow at him and blinked. "Have you done many kitchen installs in this neighborhood?"

Harry shifted uncomfortably. "No, but I did a fair amount of handyman work around here before the—before I did kitchens."

"Oh good," Mrs. Milner replied, "because I have my heart set on being the envy of the neighborhood."

Gerald glanced between the two of them before he

exclaimed, "I have no doubt that you will! We scarcely ever make sales calls down the hill."

Harry bit the inside of his cheek to keep himself from bringing up the electricity as Gerald leaned over the catalog, discussing oven models and features. Mrs. Milner's fingers curled around the edge of the coffee table as she leaned in and Harry noticed, very much in spite of himself, that she wasn't wearing a wedding ring. He frowned and took another sip of coffee. That was utterly irrelevant information. The cocker spaniel nosed his other hand just then, so he settled into petting the dog while he waited for Gerald to wrap up his sales pitch.

After about fifteen minutes of discussing which features would be most advantageous to Mrs. Milner's workflow, Harry couldn't take it anymore and suggested they take a look at the room before they started talking specifics. All the conceptualizing was moot to him if he didn't know what kind of space he was working with.

Mrs. Milner led them through the dining room and into a cramped, unfitted kitchen with a free-standing stove and icebox taking up most of the space on either end.

"Oh, Mrs. Milner," Gerald said in his most sympathetic tone. "This is worse than you made it out to be."

Harry tried very hard not to roll his eyes. If he had a nickel for every time Gerald gave out that tired line…

Mrs. Milner looked at Gerald sidelong. "What part of 'utter disaster' did you think I was exaggerating?"

Harry snorted and then tried to cover it up by coughing. Mrs. Milner tipped her pointed chin at him and smirked.

Gerald and the lady of the house went to stand in the center of the room and talked at great length about minimizing steps and stooping and triangular floor plans while Harry took the liberty of measuring out the room.

"For greatest efficiency, you'd have to have your refrigerator against this wall," Gerald said emphatically. "Right now, with it across the room, you are walking actual *miles* more than you need to just traveling back and forth across the room all day."

Mrs. Milner tipped her head and gave a slow smile. "No wonder I wear out all my shoes."

Harry couldn't help himself. He grunted.

Gerald grimaced. "Uh oh, that's never a good sound."

"No, I can't imagine it is." Mrs. Milner straightened. "Is there something very wrong, Mr. O'Conner?"

Now Harry felt stupid. "No, ma'am," he said. "It's just the model of refrigerator you're talking about is too deep to fit on this wall." He pointed his tape measure against the wall in question, on the far side of the radiator. "If you put it where he says, you'll cut off traffic to the stair door."

"How deep?"

Harry touched his tape measure to the wall and stepped back to indicate the depth of the model in question. "If you got your double ovens perpendicular, you ain't gonna be able to pass through."

"I see." Mrs. Milner pursed her lips and stood for a moment with her arms crossed over her chest. Her dress must have had a crinoline beneath it, because it perfectly accentuated the supple hourglass of her figure. Which Harry certainly wasn't admiring. How could he be? He was too busy raining on her parade.

"Well, you could just knock out the wall and bump out into the dining room a bit," Gerald suggested helpfully.

Mrs. Milner frowned, her lips pursed into an endearing little frown. "Wouldn't that take quite a lot longer?"

Harry set his jaw and focused his eyes on the wall in

question (and resolutely away from the mouth of their latest client). "Yes. I don't think I'd be able to get the job done by Christmas if we rebuilt the wall. And of course, it would be more expensive."

Mrs. Milner flapped her hand dismissively at him like she was some Summit Avenue princess, and Harry felt like he had to check again to make sure he was indeed at a house on the bottom of the hill.

"The price isn't an object. It's just—I'm hosting a party on December 17th and I need the work to be done by then.

✳

Marion served lemon bars when they sat at the dining table after Mr. O'Conner had taken every possible measurement known to man inside her cramped kitchen. She'd almost cracked a line about how he'd be measuring her next, but it was clear after fifteen minutes of him being much too serious for his years that he was the kind of man who would not appreciate the joke.

"Well, Mrs. Milner, I think I have a really good idea of what you're looking for," Mr. Stinson said with an easy smile. She only felt a little sorry for herself when she'd noticed his wedding ring. (It wasn't like it would change anything anyway, but it was nice to dream.) "Will your husband be home soon? Or is there a number I can reach him at?"

Marion's stomach dropped out from under her, even though she knew to expect this. She tipped her chin up more defiantly than she felt. "I don't have a husband."

Mr. Stinson was taken aback. "Oh, I—I'm terribly sorry, but ... ah, what?"

"I said I don't have a husband," she repeated through a tight jaw. "I will be taking care of this expense on my own."

"Uh…" Mr. Stinson snapped open his briefcase and started rustling through his papers. Avoiding her eye contact. "I'm not sure we can get financing for a … well, do you work? Sorry, I just thought, since you're *Mrs. Milner—*"

"No," Marion interrupted crisply. "I don't work. I am newly divorced and I have come into some money. Financing won't be necessary."

Mr. Stinson forgot all his manners and stared at her. To his credit, Mr. O'Conner was very focused on his lemon bar instead of studying her like she was some sort of carnival sideshow. Milly, unaware of the awkwardness of the situation, whined at his feet, begging for a morsel.

"I will pay in cash," Marion clarified.

"Are you sure you can afford it?" Mr. Stinson blurted out. He looked horrified at himself for saying it, but he also didn't hurry to smooth it over.

Marion glowered. "Yes, given my calculations from your promotional materials. Provide me with your estimate, Mr. Stinson, and I can confirm."

Mr. Stinson, inexplicably still flustered, rustled through his papers some more. "I, um, certainly. Give me a few moments and I can draw that up for you."

Mr. O'Conner, who was holding half a lemon bar between his teeth, scratched some numbers on the back of an envelope with a carpenter pencil he drew from his breast pocket and slid it around Mr. Stinson. Marion picked up the paper. Oh hell, that was *a lot* of money. Even so—it wasn't beyond her means. And she had her renters upstairs and Joe's alimony besides. She did her very best to conceal her response, straightening her shoulders with great dignity as she said, "Yes. That will do."

Mr. Stinson regarded her for a long moment. His mouth flapped for a moment like a beached codfish before he said, "Very well, let's get down to brass tacks, then."

⁎

Harry and Gerald made their way down the icy walk toward the truck.

"What did you write on that envelope?" Gerald asked as he climbed into the passenger seat and pulled a pack of cigarettes from his breast pocket.

"Twice as much as you would have," Harry replied, turning the key in the ignition, and releasing the parking brake.

"What!? And she didn't even bat an eye. Astonishing."

"Guess she's loaded," Harry shrugged as he pushed the clutch and shifted into first gear.

"I wonder what the hell her ex-husband did?" Gerald mused. "Because if she's newly divorced and rolling in it, you can bet he did something pretty rotten."

Harry pressed his lips into a grim line and turned left on St. Clair Avenue. He couldn't imagine the kind of man who could be married to a woman as pretty and decisive as Mrs. Milner and spurn her so horribly that she'd get enough in the settlement for a whole new kitchen. But then again, what did he know? Given how things had gone with Alice, he was a pretty poor judge of character.

⁎

Mrs. Milner Gets a Kitchen is available in a free eBook to newsletter subscribers at www.janehadleywrites.com.

FOOTNOTES

Kreuger's bar is based on a real place. In 2013, when Minnesota governor Mark Dayton signed marriage equality into law in our state, there was a huge party in St. Paul on the EcoLab plaza. It was held there because the EcoLab building was constructed on the former site of the little nondescript bar with the flickering Liquor sign called Kirmser's. The bar had been a nondescript gathering place for working-class LGBTQ+ people in the 1950s. How do we know this?

Because of *The Evening Crowd at Kirmser's,* a memoir by Ricardo J. Brown. His unflinching portrait of the post-WWII working-class queer community in St. Paul is a priceless piece of queer history. I inhaled the slim volume in one feral afternoon. All of the boys at Kreuger's owe their inspiration to people Brown knew: Betty Boop, the Flaming Youth, Lulu, Lucky, the Three Kind Mice, and all the others. I wonder if they ever knew about Brown's characterization of them, or how much they would mean to local queer history. This book is an homage to Brown's memoir and a salute to the queer ancestors.

Post-WWII Minnesota did indeed have a housing crisis, which led to many young, single people living with their parents. Many of the people featured in Brown's memoir lived with their families (probably more than I had in my book). Stephen's character was drawn from Brown's narrative voice. Brown's writing style itself was truly an inspiration (though I'll be honest, I will probably not be using the term 'cornhole' again…).

A few other locations that are also pointed out in Brown's book, and were in historical fact part of St. Paul's queer landscape, include the Coney Island bar, the Hennepin Baths (which also had a mention in *Oh! You Pretty Things*), the Bremer Arcade, and the restrooms in the basement of Dayton's department store. I'm also indebted to the research of Stewart Van Cleve, author of *Land of 10,000 Loves: A History of Queer Minnesota* and the work of many at the Minnesota Historical Society and the Twin Cities Pride organization who built the interactive Twin Cities Pride History Tour and the Greater Minnesota Two-Spirit & LGBTQIA+ History Map. These are invaluable resources that recognize queer people have always been here in the Upper Midwest and share their stories. Check them out online!

One of the things I was surprised to learn was how very difficult it was to get a divorce in 1954. I had written more than half of the book already, and published *Mrs. Milner Gets a Kitchen*, before I found out that in order for Joe and Marion to get divorced, they had to *prove* adultery, abuse, or abandonment. This sent me into a panic, because Joe's affair with Stephen could not be presented as evidence under any circumstances. The law was clear at that time. Sodomy was a criminal offense. Brown tells one story of a man he knew who served a year in jail after being caught *in flagrante* in a car during Winter Carnival. I took a little creative license rather than dig deep enough to figure out whether Joe's paramour would be required to present evidence in the case. As a result, I cannot confirm how accurately divorce is portrayed in this time period.

Details about the city government are all grounded in newspapers from the time. The city hall described here is still in use, an extraordinary standout of art deco architecture funded in the 1920s and built in the 1930s, which means that they got all sorts of luxury building materials for enormously cheap. As far as I can tell, pretty much everyone who worked there was indeed named Joseph.

The Upper Levee was an Italian neighborhood on the river flats. Local restaurants Mancini's and Cosetta's were both founded by families from the Levee. Brown's family also came from the Levee. It was demolished as part of urban renewal shortly after this book was set. It's now a dog park and a collection of new apartment buildings which narrowly avoided being underwater last time the Mississippi flooded (some lessons are never learned).

Mickey's Diner continues to operate. They were open continuously since 1939, and closed for the first time for the COVID-19 pandemic in 2020. It reopened again in 2024, and we were all seriously concerned that the seasoning on the griddle had been compromised by the Health Department inspection. It is no longer open 24/7, which I learned the hard way late one night not so long ago. On a cold night, the Mickey's Diner windows fog up with condensation and it's a wonderful landmark I have an enormous amount of nostalgia for. Best hangover breakfast, hands down.

The Winter Carnival is an unhinged winter tradition in St. Paul that goes back to 1886. It revolves around the legend of King Boreas and the Four Winds, who are unseated by the Vulcans, the harbingers of spring. It's usually held in late January, when the Minnesota weather is the absolute worst. The 1950s was a heyday of the Winter Carnival, reaching something like a state fair level of engagement. The event is well documented and provided plenty of fodder for my story. Ricardo J. Brown also attested that Winter Carnival was one of the best nights to cruise at Kirmser's, because the event brought people in from all over the state, some of whom looked for queer company at the places scrawled on bathroom walls at the bus station. I can promise you this isn't the last time Winter Carnival will appear in one of my books.

If you get anything out of reading this book, I hope it's that *The Evening Crowd at Kirmser's* deserves to be bumped up to the next book on your TBR.

If you haven't yet, I invite you to read *Mrs. Milner Gets a Kitchen*, where Marion gets her happy ending. It's free to newsletter subscribers on my website: http://www.janehadleywrites.com.

Acknowledgements

I have loved every minute of writing this book. I should probably first and foremost thank my children for putting up with my inability to focus on them when I fell deep into this world. The day I read *The Evening Crowd at Kirmser's*, they were admittedly looking for my attention and they did not get it. I hope that their boredom will blossom into imaginations as deep and wild and exciting as my own.

The well of gratitude is deep for my co-conspirators who cheered this book along, helped me iron out details, and listened to me agonize (as ever) about how much I hate writing epilogues. Thank you Louise Mayberry and Alivia Fleur for reading, giving incredibly helpful feedback, and sharing your experience and guidance with me so freely. Thank you Corinne for noticing the tiny offhand mention of Stephen in *Mrs. Milner Gets a Kitchen,* assuring me that at least one person was excited to read about her philandering absentee ex, and very generously teaching me about the world of insanely arbitrary compound words in your copy edit. I'm so honored to count you all among my friends.

To my friends in the Not Quite Write to Market Discord group, thank you as ever for providing community and support in this lonely endeavor of writing. I'm so grateful to have a landing space where everyone is honest, vulnerable, and willing to share their knowledge and expertise. Your support has meant more than ever this year. In the ever-wise words of Paul Wellstone, "We all do better when we all do better."

To Sean, sorry for reminding you of that time you got blitzed in my basement and had to swear off gin and tonics forevermore. Your feedback and support made this a better book. Thanks for being my oldest friend and for educating me about bathhouses over your lunch break.

To all of our friends who used to haunt Bin with us—I thought so much about our escapades around downtown St. Paul in the 2010s when writing these banty bar scenes. While none of these characters are based on you (please hold your libel suits at bay), our drunken shenanigans were nonetheless an inspiration.

And finally, as ever, to Kyle, the love of my life and my best friend, who taught me everything I know about happy endings.

ALSO BY JANE HADLEY

<u>Mrs. Milner Gets A Kitchen</u>
St. Paul, Minnesota. 1955.
A divorced mother contracts the installation of a new electric kitchen and falls for her contractor under the nose of their conformist 1950s immigrant community.
Sequel to <u>Mr. Milner Gets Divorced.</u> Out now.

✦

<u>Secret Soldier Series</u>
Fort Snelling, Minnesota. 1861.
A woman dresses as a man to enlist in the Union Army only to fall in infuriating infatuation with her strapping bunkmate.
<u>A Fine Looking Soldier: Volume 1</u>
<u>A Right Honorable Soldier: Volume 2</u>
<u>The Venus of Lebanon, or the Ruin of Elias Hower: A Salacious Short Story</u>
Out now.

✦

<u>Oh! You Pretty Things</u>
Minneapolis, Minnesota. 1970.
A closeted genderfluid university student joins a pro-to-glam rock band and gets drawn into a messy love triangle that pushes him to find and claim his own queer identity.
Out now.

✦

<u>A Rogue's Gallery</u>
St. Paul, Minnesota. 1929.
An aimless flapper contrives a fake relationship with the queen of the St. Paul gangsters to shake off a persistent ex-boyfriend, only to find herself longing to convince her that it could be real.
Coming 2026.

✦

For more information and updates, head to
<u>www.janehadleywrites.com</u>